I0736636

CURSE OF THE FAE

THE COMPLETE WINTER'S THORN COLLECTION

MILA YOUNG

CONTENTS

TO CATCH A FAE

TO SEDUCE A FAE

TO TAME A FAE

TO CLAIM A FAE

WINTER'S THORN SERIES

To Catch A Fae
To Seduce A Fae
To Tame A Fae
To Claim A Fae

TO CATCH A FAE

WINTER'S THORN, BOOK 1

TO CATCH A FAE

Long ago, darkness and light came together and created beauty... a beauty that will destroy this world.

The dream comes again, always the same dark twisted woods; a place I knew too well, a place I've traveled hundreds of times before.

But it's just a dream my foster mom insists, then why is *he* in my head all the time. He who has no name, who refuses to give me his name.

Little wolf, he calls me, telling me secrets, listening to me, and makes me blush with the dirty things he says. Until the day everything changes.

I'm not ready for a world that shouldn't exist. To meet three stunning hot men with powers I can't fathom, each more dangerous than the next. One dominant and terrifying. One cruel with his words. And one who unmistakably stole my heart and insists I'm his.

I'm in danger they say, but is their protection enough to keep me safe, to help me find a happily ever after before it's too late? To awaken me to the truth of who I really am.

FAE LEGENDS

Long ago, darkness and light came together and created beauty... a beauty that will destroy this world.

PROLOGUE

There was nothing right about the woods today.

I slipped backward a few steps, my heart thumping loudly as a figure watched me from behind a gnarled tree.

Shadows swallowed his presence, holding no shape and fading against the spreading darkness, but I felt his eyes—always on me. And the unease made me sick to my stomach.

Warped branches spiked into the stormy clouds, swinging back and forth in the wind like claws reaching out for me. Terror roared inside me, yelling at me to run, and my flesh pricked with electricity.

He'd kill me if I stayed. I knew it, felt it in my bones.

I swung away and darted down the strip of naked land, summoning the energy to push myself faster than before. His breath grazed my neck, his footsteps thumping the ground.

Panic tore through me at the idea that this time he'd catch me.

Thorny bushes and broken trees filled the land. Flashes of freedom lay behind the forsaken forest, snippets of a grand kingdom that reflected the golden rays of the sun. The kingdom stood so far away, reachable only by stairs made of twisted stone, and by crossing an arched bridge that spanned two mountains. I'd never get there in time. I might as well be trying to reach the moon.

The breaking of leaves and twigs came at me, and I jerked around, fear coiling over me like a heavy winter coat, smothering me.

Utter blackness closed in, the wind shrieking in my ears.

A cry fell past my lips. My palms tingled with power, its scorching pain spreading over me.

He slammed into me.

I screamed, my feet tangling beneath me. Pivoting back around, I jutted my hands out, embracing the power, and shoved it into the shadow.

Then I fell. My world became a pit of blackness, taking me, dragging me under.

And I let myself go. Like I always did.

CHAPTER

ONE

"Are you awake, Guen?" Debbie's voice broke through the silence, startling me back to the present. Reminding me that I sat in her office... Not that I hadn't known that, but sometimes I forgot things.

My foster mom nudged me in the arm, then shifted in her seat, huffing. "She's always daydreaming, this one. I swear she lives in her head more than the real world."

I slouched in my seat, meeting Ms. Williams' deep brown eyes. She sat across her desk from us, and she looked young except for the threads of white amid the brown curls. I'd guess she was in her mid-forties.

She studied me, probably making mental notes about how I'd changed since our last catch up. Her work desk was impeccable, like the rest of her sterile office, and she had her name and title on a plaque sitting on the edge of her desk.

Debbie Williams, M.D.

Clinical Psychiatrist

Like anyone coming here could forget they were seeing a psychiatrist who specialized in mental disorders.

"How have you been sleeping?" she asked.

"Not well." Never well. The dreams always came and when I woke, I'd be exhausted.

"Have you tried the new medication I prescribed?"

9

I nodded, as did my foster mom, who pushed the loose strands of chestnut hair out of her face. She made sure I took the meds. They knocked me out, but the dreams still came, no matter what I did.

Schizophrenia. I'd read the word in the doctor's notes a few weeks ago when she hadn't been looking. Even if she hadn't given me a diagnosis, at least now I had a name to what was wrong with me. I'd read up on it, tried to self-diagnose myself on Google, and found four types of Schizophrenia. I wasn't sure I fit a specific disorder; it was more like I had some symptoms of each of them.

But maybe Ms. Williams suspected something else was wrong, which was why she hadn't given me a final prognosis. Could there be something worse than Schizophrenia?

My stomach churned when I thought about it, and for some reason, the room was too bright today, despite the lights being off. The sun's reflection on the white walls stung my eyes.

Ms. Williams stood from her chair, straightened her A-line blue skirt, and crossed the room to lower the blinds, stealing some of the glare. I liked her, even if she watched my every move, my every reaction, and made an analysis of my behavior. I'd been seeing therapists like her for as long as I'd been in foster homes... my whole life.

"Are you still having unusual dreams?" she asked.

I nodded, lowering my gaze, remembering the shadow who always came for me. "Sometimes. But I'm feeling better."

I raised my head as she jotted something in her notebook. I just forgot things sometimes, dreamed of a kingdom that didn't exist, and felt like I didn't belong... in my skin. No, in this *world*.

I glanced at the clock on the wall. Half an hour was almost up.

"Well, we might end our session there." Debbie handed my foster mom a new script. "Jen, if you have a moment?"

Up on my feet, I collected the bag from under my seat and headed to the door. "Thank you," I threw over my shoulder as I reached for the handle, hating these sessions that made me question everything about myself. The two of them often had a private talk. What secrets did they hold about me that I should know? But I'd learned long ago that reacting angrily only got me more medication prescribed because I was unstable. Crazy. Unreliable.

You're so much more than insane, little wolf. The low rumble of his voice wrapped around my mind, deep and smooth, reverberating through my bones. He who had no name, who refused to give me his name, who was always in my head. Something I never told a single soul; otherwise, I'd end up in an asylum.

"Wow, you're full of compliments today," I mumbled under my breath.

Outside, I marched through the waiting room, leaving my foster mom behind. Head low and pulling the jacket tighter around myself, I crossed the room, not wanting to exchange glances. We all lived with darkness in our heads, and I didn't want to see their insanity etched on their faces.

"Dad can't be bothered to come here and said I could collect the prescription on his behalf. I have a signed note," a guy growled at the nurse over the counter.

I glanced his way. His brow furrowed, ice-blue irises crowned by the longest eyelashes met mine. Short, black hair sat spiked on his head. I recognized him. He made every girl at school swoon with that sneer. His mouth twitched before he jerked his attention back to the nurse who lectured him, and I shoved through the front door and stepped outside, where I could breathe easier.

Seemed the most popular guy in school and me had something in common after all. Something crazy.

I rubbed my hands for warmth, staring out at the parking area for a bit before heading to the small convenience store nearby. There, I grabbed an energy drink from the fridge and scooped money out from my pocket before placing it in the hand of the old man at the counter.

"There you are," Jen bellowed from the door of the store, dressed in her tailored pants and white blouse that pulled taut across the buttons. She'd been on a diet forever and recently lost some weight, and she looked good. "Told you to always wait for me near the car. Between you and Oliver, you both drive me insane."

With the can in hand, I followed her out. "Just needed a pick-me-up before class. And Oliver is a pain in the ass to everyone." My foster brother was the devil incarnate.

She huffed. "He's only nine; he'll grow out of that stage. And I hate when you drink that stuff. It's not good for you."

"It keeps me awake." I pulled back the metal ring and the drink hissed. "So, what'd the shrink say after I left?"

"I like Debbie better than the last one. And she's just worried about you not getting enough sleep."

Swallowing the mouthful of cherry-flavored goodness, I waited for Jen to find her keys in her bag. A quick glance at my reflection in the car window showed my blonde hair fluttering in the breeze, light eyebrows I hated, and the blue eyes that did nothing to take away from the whole pale as snow look. I'd been contemplating dying my brows, a do-it-myself-job, but didn't want them looking like dark caterpillars across my brow.

Jen finally yanked open the passenger's door of her silver sedan.

"You gonna tell me what she said." I got inside, and she climbed into the driver's seat.

"What do you want me to say, Guen? She costs an arm and a leg, so she's got to know what she's doing." Jen looked over at me, her perfectly manicured eyebrows rising. She jammed the key into the ignition.

Pinning the can between my thighs, I strapped myself in. "The government pays for it," I reminded her over the groan of the engine. But she still complained about the cost at every fortnightly session like she somehow missed out on taking the cash herself.

She edged out of the parking and soon enough merged into the slow-moving morning traffic.

"So, you going to tell me?" I took several more mouthfuls.

"What difference will it make? You take your meds and you'll be fine." The corner of her eye twitched.

"I can tell when you're lying."

"Stop staring at me. Have you got your books for school?"

"Yes, I have them. Please, Jen, what did Debbie say to you for real?"

"I told you not to call me that."

I sighed heavily and shoved myself back into the seat, staring at the oversized buildings we passed, the storefronts, people darting amid the crawling traffic to cross the road.

"She said she worried you might be dangerous."

I stiffened.

Dangerous? I'd never harm anyone. Never had.

"Why did she think that?" Unease crawled over my chest. A small part of me died inside when I accidentally stepped on an ant. How could I be dangerous?

Her lips pursed when she looked over to me. "Because you don't need anyone and insist on being alone."

The words swam in my mind like flies on roadkill. So being a loner made me dangerous?

"Have you tried making friends?" she asked, like she hadn't seen me mingle with students at the last three schools I'd moved to because she kept relocating us to be near her newest boyfriend.

"I have a friend at Brax High."

"Don't say Antonio, or I'll—"

"Yes, Antonio is my friend."

Jen's grip tightened on the steering wheel. "And a bad influence. I told you I saw him once buying drugs at the corner store. Don't get involved with trouble."

I heaved and pressed my spine into the seat. "He's a nice guy, and he talks to me while others glare."

"Aren't there girls at your school you get along with?"

I gritted my jaw. "They hate me, so no, I don't get along with them."

I twisted away to stare at easing traffic we now passed. Other families laughing, talking about normal things, like what was on television that night.

"Maybe if you had more friends, you wouldn't always get in trouble."

When she kept going on, I leaned down and dug my hand into my backpack, finding my earphones. I stuffed them into my ears and jammed the connector into the base of the phone before blaring my music.

Let them hate you. His voice broke through the music. *As long as they fear you, little wolf, you will be fine.*

CHAPTER

TWO

"See you later." I slammed the door to Jen's car and turned toward the school as she drove away. Brax High was a long brick building with steps out the front, rusting racks, and, at the moment, locked front doors because class had already started.

Gray clouds spread over the sky while the wind howled, heralding an encroaching storm. A bitter cold crept over my skin despite my long-sleeved school shirt, and I rubbed the shivers out of my arms. My blue school pleated skirt danced over my thighs, doing nothing to keep the cold at bay.

I prefer it when it's just the two of us.

"It's always just the two of us." Which was sort of sad.

No, no, no. He laughed, the sound devious and, in a weird way, sexy.

I shouldn't think that about the voice in my head, but then again, I was talking to myself. If I was crazy, I might as well enjoy it, right?

When it's just us two, you respond, and I can make you feel things. Make you forget everything else.

"While that sounds tempting, I have school now," I mumbled. "Go back to wherever you came from."

Ouch. You want to know where I came from?

"Not this again. You came from the shadows, from the darkest of night, blah blah."

No response? Good.

With my bag in hand, I hurried up the front steps of the school and paused in front of the double doors before pressing the buzzer to be let in. I pulled the doctor's note out of my pocket. A whirring sound drew my attention to the camera overhead turning to check who was at the front door.

I can break you, he whispered.

I lowered my head from the camera to respond. "You can't break what's already broken."

I wasn't talking about your mind.

His words startled me. If he was just in my mind, how could he physically hurt me?

In the most delicious way, he said in a voice that could easily lead to sin.

Heat rose through me a bit too quickly.

The front door opened, and I flinched. Principal Johnson stood before me frowning, dressed in his tailored brown pants and matching vest over a black buttoned-up shirt. His gaze fell to my outstretched note and he clicked his tongue.

Without a word, he accepted the offering and scanned the note before waving me inside. "Classes just started. You shouldn't have missed much." His tone was harsh today. Someone had pissed him off.

"Thanks." I nudged the bag strap over my shoulder and swung down the quiet hallway fiercely lit by a line of fluorescent lights overhead, which cast the lockers in a yellowing hue.

I pushed open the door to history class, the hinges squealing like a banshee, and I stepped inside with every eye on me. Wonderful.

"Quickly, take a seat," Ms. Brown ordered in her black dress and heavy kohl eyeliner, making her look racoon-ish. "Who can tell me," she said, barely missing a beat, "why the church was upset with Galileo Galilei?"

Head low, I dragged my feet down the side aisle of seats, targeting the empty one at the back, watching every step I took on the linoleum floor.

"He was called a heretic by the Catholic Church," someone called out. "He believed that the Earth revolved around the sun."

"Yes, and what were the church's values that came under threat with Galilei's theory?"

Someone kicked me in the back of a knee, and in a heartbeat, my legs buckled and gave out from under me.

I yelped as my feet teetered, losing their balance, my heartbeat pounding in my ears. I hit the ground with a thud, my knees and elbows taking the brunt. "Son of a..." I groaned.

An explosion of laughter flooded the room, students clapping.

I froze, my face burning up. Fury charged through my veins.

"Everyone sit down now!" Ms. Brown shouted.

Shoving myself off the floor, I glanced back as half the school stared at the loser—me—but my eyes locked on Sabrina. The beauty of the school with perfectly shiny hair, perfectly flawless skin, perfectly arched eyebrows. Five-foot seven, willowy, with blonde curls falling to her waist, I loathed her more in that moment than I thought possible.

I glanced down at my five-foot-three frame, not exactly thin, breasts too small, hips too big.

And I knew she tripped me… it was always her.

Anger glinted in her cruel, cold eyes, and all I could think was if she was going to take me down, I'd fight and drag her into hell with me.

I'd caught her smoking in the girls' bathroom a few weeks ago. She'd gotten busted, and ever since, I'd apparently been the one who must have ratted her out, but it wasn't me.

"Sit down this instant!" the teacher barked, but no one listened.

Students chatted and chortled at me.

Up on my feet, I bent over and swiped my bag off the floor, then swung it up and wide in the blink of an eye, side-swiping Sabrina across the face with it, wiping the grin right off her face.

She screamed, blood splattering across her lip where the zipper tore at her mouth.

I swallowed hard and rushed to my seat, not feeling guilty one ounce.

"She attacked me!" Sabrina cried, blood dripping down her chin.

"Enough," said Ms. Brown. "What I saw was you tripping Guen. Now hurry to the nurse's office and get that cut looked at, then go to the principal's office."

Sabrina's lips twitched. "But she just struck me. I'm bleeding."

A smile tingled at the edges of my mouth, but I lowered my head instead and slouched in my seat.

"Leave now!" Ms. Brown said, unmoved by Sabrina's pity-seeking.

I'd always liked Ms. Brown. She asked me how my day was while most teachers pretended I didn't exist.

Sabrina snatched her books and bag. "Why is a freak like her allowed in our class? I heard she takes medication so she doesn't lose control and kill us all. Look what she did to me! Wait until my parents find out about this."

You should have pulled her tongue out for that.

I cringed on the inside, but I wasn't a fool. Everyone at school gossiped about me.

Laughter streamed through my head, the sound strangely soothing. *Let them fear you. It's better to be a wolf than the lamb.*

I kept silent, said nothing until the door slammed shut, and then raised my eyes. Sabrina's friend glared my way. In hindsight, maybe I shouldn't have hit Sabrina.

You should have hit her harder.

"All right, back to Galileo." The teacher clapped her hands to draw everyone's attention from me and to the front of the class.

I opened my textbook and drowned myself in words that blurred in my vision, letting the lesson swallow all my worries and dread over the can of worms I'd just ripped open. With pencil in hand, I sketched a tree in the corner of the page, limbs twisted and long, and I drew more of them to pass the time.

At lunch, I grabbed a quick sandwich, my head blurred with fog. I pinched the bridge of my nose to ease the pain behind my eyes, then shoved my backpack into my locker. Students crammed the hallway, their voices loud, blending into a cacophony of chaos. I pushed off the locker and went against the grain as everyone made their way to the cafeteria. Today I couldn't do crowds.

The way out stood just ahead, and I rushed past the swinging doors, gasping for air.

"Freak!" Someone nudged past, their shoulder knocking into mine.

Sabrina's friend glowered, hatred twisting her features. Black hair cut to a perfect bob-style without a strand out of place, she looked pale... too pale. Her school shirt tied across her stomach, showing flesh. All part of whatever look she was going for this week. The sad thing was that I didn't even know her name... didn't care to learn it either.

Hands deep in the pockets of my school jacket, I marched away from the main building and headed round the back to the outdoor basketball courts.

With concrete and metal everywhere, this school was older than my previous couple of schools, but they all merged into one in my mind. We'd moved here for Luke, Jen's newest boyfriend she'd met on Tinder. So far, they'd been dating for several months and had had no major arguments. Maybe I'd stay at Brax High longer than a year. That'd be a world record for me.

Dried grass crunched under my sneakers, and I hoped he waited for me, so I fluffed up my hair. The breeze picked up, and my school skirt fluttered over my thighs as I glanced out to the empty courts.

"Flashing your cute blue underwear?" a guy murmured.

Antonio! I felt his gaze on me before I turned around, and my heartbeat went into a frenzy.

He leaned against the rear of the school building. My pulse stopped in my veins at seeing him. Honey-blonde hair draped over his ears, complementing his tanned skin. He loved surfing, he'd told me, and when summer came back around, I planned to go watch him in action. Where he wore no shirt. Maybe I'd ask him to teach me how to surf.

With a wink that nearly melted me into a puddle, he took a drag from the joint pressed between his thumb and index finger, his cheeks growing gaunt as he inhaled.

From my first day when I'd met those brilliant blue eyes in the hallway, I'd lost myself to him. And like then, as he looked at me now, his eyes seemed to smile with a devilish glint in them.

He blew out lazy smoke rings that floated onto the air, stolen by the breeze, but not before the faint hints of pine mixed with a skunky smell filled my nostrils.

"Wanna taste?" He stuck the joint out for me.

I shook my head and moved to shelter beside the building, out of the wind. "My head's already feeling foggy."

"Might help with that." His voice was genuine and so dreamy.

So I reached over, our fingers grazing when I plucked the joint. My skin tingled from where we touched and my heart sprinted.

One inhale, and smoke rushed down my throat. My lungs seized, and I hacked a cough, cloudy smoke pouring from my mouth and nose.

Taking the joint back, he laughed. "Takes a bit of getting used to."

Catching my breath, I coughed again, my throat raw and chafed. Heat curled up my neck and cheeks as I choked. He'd know I had never smoked weed before.

Have another, he murmured in my head. *It'll calm you.*

"Think I've had my fill."

"How'd the session go this morning?" Antonio took another drag.

The meeting crossed my mind, along with the shrink's worry. "She thinks I'm dangerous," I blurted out, hating that I'd said that out loud. But Antonio was the only person I said such things to, even if I worried one day he'd stare at me like I was too weird.

"Dangerous to whom?" That smile returned, the one that calmed me, that promised me all the things I'd been dreaming about with Antonio.

"Exactly! If you have no friends, then it's loser city."

"Hey, you have me." He pointed to his chest while still gripping the joint, his brows pulling together in a cute way. "Don't listen to them. All docs are the same. Need to make things up so they can justify having a job, to get money. Bet she offered you another script for meds?"

I chuckled and nodded.

He leaned back against the wall, his body slouched and still so freaking hot. His black pants hung low on his hips, the school shirt untucked, his collar sitting crooked. "God, I feel so high. This stuff's good. Been thinking of getting a tat."

"Oh yeah? What of?"

He shrugged. "Still thinking about it. But thinking of getting it here." He pushed the sleeve of his shirt up, and I traced over the line of his bicep, the muscle, the tanned skin. My fingers tingled.

A torn-up school poster with the words *Lighting It Up* tumbled past us and into the parking lot.

"Hey, so the school dance is coming up," I murmured. "You gonna go?"

He shrugged. "Haven't even thought about it. When is it?"

"Two weeks from Saturday." My stomach tingled with the notion of asking Antonio to go with me. I *should* ask him.

No, you shouldn't.

The question lingered in my mind, and I trembled with nerves at the idea of asking him. He was my only friend at school, so I didn't want things to be strange between us if he said *no*. He wouldn't say *no*, would he? Then again, I'd seen the way he looked at me, like I was more than his friend.

Don't!

He took his final drag before pinching the smoke between his fingers and tucking the end into his pocket.

"Not sure if I'll go," he admitted. "But it could be a blast."

An explosion of joy burst through my chest at his *maybe* response. I sure as shit wasn't going alone if he said *no*. When I spent time with Antonio, he just got me. He spoke to me like I wasn't a freak, and somehow, I thought better of myself.

He doesn't know you like I know you. He can't...do things I can do to you.

I blew *him* off, tuning out my crazy mind.

Antonio was crazy hot, and if he went, maybe he'd say *yes* to going with me. He might even kiss me.

A rolling growl swept over my mind.

I really needed a mute button on *him*. I leaned back against the wall.

"So, I was thinking." My face burned up, my palms sweating, and I wiped them down my black pleated skirt.

Antonio was busy staring out toward the basketball courts. "Think I can shoot perfect hoops if I played today?"

"Probably." I found my voice. "Anyway, I was gonna—"

The school bell rang like a church bell, deafening and persistent. I flinched, and Antonio shoved to his feet.

"Gotta go. I have P.E. Might see if Mr. Humphrey will let us play basketball." He threw one of his perfect smiles my way and took off. "Catch you later."

And just like that, I was alone.

"Yep, sure." I pushed off the wall. "Next time," I mumbled to myself.

You are meant for so much more than this.

"Shut up. I'm sick of you renting space in my head." I headed back toward the lockers to grab my books.

Before my ass hit the chair in algebra class, my name was called out.

"Guen, the principal's office," Mr. Carpenter called out across the class, eliciting *ooh*s and *ahh*s from everyone.

Just great.

THREE

I sucked in a ragged breath as a chill worked its way along my spine. I'd busted ass to get my homework done on time and stayed up late studying to show Principal Johnson I could keep up with everyone else. To avoid ending up in his office regularly... And here I was again. I hated Sabrina.

You need to make her pay. Make her bleed.

I struggled to swallow past the boulder in my throat, shutting *him* out because I couldn't deal with this. Not now... Not when on my last visit to the principal's office, he threatened me with expulsion. Jen would go mental if that happened.

"Sit," he ordered, and I slid into the chair across the desk from him. He wore his tie printed with the Star Trek emblem again. He loved old geeky shows and if I ever got around to watching some, I might find myself with an upper hand for whenever I was called to his office.

His office reeked of sandalwood, his desk crammed with piles of folders and papers, two coffee cups, paperweights, a calculator, and pens. The miniature water fountain sitting on top of the filing cabinet emitted a faint trickle of water.

"Do you know why you're here?" he started, like he always did, his brown eyes fixed on me, his black short hair messed up like he'd been outside in the wind.

Panicked thoughts shoved through my mind that I'd be thrown out for hitting Sabrina.

Rain hit against the windowpane. *Tap. Tap. Tap.* Trees thrashed about in the front yard of the school.

I turned my attention to Principle Johnson and nodded. "I know it was wrong. It's just that they keep pushing and pushing me. I wanted it to stop."

His bushy brows pulled together in a confused frown. He plucked up a remote control from under the mess on his desk and turned to the TV on a stand in the corner. "Let's watch."

My heartbeat slammed in my chest, and I inched closer to the edge of the seat.

The TV screen flicked on, blurry at first, then it snapped to the image of the sidewall of the school, the CCTV scanning the grounds. God, he saw me taking a drag from Antonio's joint? I should have known, should have checked for cameras. But Antonio had been smoking there for so long, never getting caught.

But that wasn't it. Dread punched me in the gut because I knew what I was looking at even before I stepped into view of the camera.

I couldn't breathe, couldn't move.

Standing in front of the wall, I pulled out two spray paint cans, one in each hand, and went to work on the brick wall. Something I'd done last month, weeks ago on a shithole of a day when my concentration had been shot, when everyone had seemed too loud, when I'd gotten shoved into the girls' bathroom and locked in there for three hours until someone had heard me screaming.

We'll get revenge on Sabrina, make her beg for mercy.

I ran a shaky hand down my face, mumbling, "Shut up."

Principal Johnson glanced my way with a raised brow, and I stiffened, refocused on the TV. On the screen, my attention was a million miles away, my eyes glazed over. Was that how I looked when I painted?

"I've seen enough," I murmured, lowering my gaze to my hands in my lap, well aware I couldn't deny my actions this time.

"I'll concede that the image you drew was spectacular," he started, drawing me to look at him, with hope in my chest. He handed me a photograph of the mural I'd spray-painted.

The path in the dark, twisted woods, the grand kingdom that reflected the golden rays in the far distance, the bridge arched between two mountains. And the shadow in the forest, lingering, always watching.

"But you vandalized school property." The principal's voice climbed. "And this isn't the first time. I can't overlook this anymore."

In the grip of silent panic, my mind lit up, my breaths coming too fast. My whole body felt like it had seized up. I didn't want to start another school when I had Antonio here, and I couldn't deal with Jen's fury.

"Please, sir. I'll do clean up duty for a year. I've really been trying." I wanted to crawl up inside myself and hide.

My little wolf, don't beg. I'll teach you to make them all fall to their knees at your feet.

"Have you?" Principal Johnson retorted. His annoyance was like fire on my flesh. "You got into a fight in history today, and from the moment you stepped into my office, I could smell what you've been smoking."

The room suddenly felt too small, too tight, the air heavy and wavering. He watched me, studied me just like the shrink had that morning.

I can tell you what to say to this man, what will make him keep you at this school.

My mouth couldn't open or respond, not while Principal Johnson glared at me.

I pushed my sleeves up nervously, my mind spiraling out of control.

Tell him Antonio made you smoke, convinced you it'd help, threatened if you didn't. That you'd listened to him for weeks, believing him, and his smoke made you paint on the wall.

My attention lifted to meet the principal's eyes, to see the disappointment on his hard weathered face, but I couldn't blame this on Antonio. Couldn't drag him into my shit, and he'd hate me if got him into trouble. I wouldn't do it. He deserved better.

"Please," I begged. "One more chance. I promise to change."

He shook his head. "Your foster mom is coming to collect you. A few days at home might do you well until I make a decision."

His words sunk through me like a boulder dragging me into the deepest pits of the ocean. I barely took a breath and slouched in my seat, trying to sort out my excuses to Jen. I wanted to fight and scream that he couldn't do this.

Trying my best to hide my fright, I said, "Okay. I hope you can give me one last chance."

Weak, so weak.

And I hated the voice in my head right then, loathed *him*.

Better to hate and not lose that fighting spirit.

"Go wait outside my office."

I jolted to my feet, bag in hand, and marched out, letting the door shut behind me. Slumped in a seat across from the front office desk, I closed my eyes and let a wave of dread wash over me, my body frozen. What I needed was a better-paying job than my weekend gig at the local cinema. Then I could save enough money to go off on my own, to not rely on anyone else. I knew it was crazy, but I'd had enough of constantly being reprimanded for shit.

Someone touched my arm. Startled, I looked up to find Jen there, her name badge over the pocket on her shirt from her job as a social worker. Her eyes glinted something dark, her mouth twisted. But she kept her composure, her voice sharp. "Just going to talk to your principal. I won't be long."

My knees bounced as I sat there, waiting as the receptionist offered me a curt smile, but she knew I was in shit. The whole school would find out soon enough.

Jen returned minutes later, her handbag clutched tightly under her arm. "Let's go," she barked.

The bell rang as we stepped outside into the hallway. Students emerged from classrooms, heading down the hall to another.

Jen marched ahead of me down the hall toward the exit when I glanced up, seeing Antonio. My heart clenched, my eyes flicking from Jen, who was waiting at the door to get buzzed out, and back to him, wanting to tell him why I wouldn't be at school for a while. The guy didn't do texting, so I didn't want him to think I'd vanished.

I stepped closer toward him while Jen checked her phone. "Hey—" But my words dissolved when Sabrina emerged from around the corner, my pulse on fire over the fact that I'd been thrown out of school, but she remained.

"Sabrina," Antonio called out, and my stomach tightened. I'd never seen them talk before.

When she turned to face him, something gleamed in her eyes, her mouth pouty, her chest sticking out a bit too much.

The only similarity was our blonde hair, but mine sat straight to my shoulders, straggly, and nothing like hers. Nothing of me was like her. How could I compare to her?

Just seeing her stare at Antonio, share breathing space with him, left me shaking.

"Hey, what's going on?" she teased, smirking too widely. God, she was flirting with him.

I steeled myself for his response, holding my breath, hoping this was nothing more than him telling her she dropped something, or that someone was looking for her.

He ran a hand through his hair. "Heard the school dance is in two weeks. Wanna go?"

Her face lit up triumphantly while a sickening rage tore across my stomach. It came through me like a hurricane, ripping me to shreds. I'd thought he... I choked on my breaths. I'd thought he liked *me*.

I just stared at them, my body numb, my heart on fire. I stumbled forward, part of me insisting I tell him how I feel. Maybe he'd never realized how much I wanted him.

"You coming?" Jen's voice made me flinch. Her hand was on my elbow and she wrenched me away, but on the inside I died. And I just stared at them still chatting, claws digging into my heart.

I staggered alongside Jen while an inferno swallowed me. He chose that bitch over me? When I saw her smile, the way she flicked her hair over her shoulder, I saw nothing but hate. Look at her. Those designer sneakers, the new phone, the expensive cordless headphones. She had it all, so why take Antonio from me?

Staring at him, all I felt now was the stab of a blade to my heart, pressing deeper, cutting me in two.

The rest of the world around me grew hazy. Tears blurred the darkness coming for me. Maybe she'd turn him down. Maybe then he'd choose me.

People lie, his actions don't. Told you, you don't need him.

Everything spun, my life, the school, the sky... me.

"Hey, you okay?" Jen asked, her fingers pressed into my arm.

My knees gave out, and suddenly I was shaking violently, my vision fuzzy. The last words someone screamed were, "She's having a fit!"

***

Someone poked my arm, over and over, and I grumbled under my breath, torn from my dream. The one that always came for me, the twisted forest, the fear, the promise of freedom if I escaped.

When I opened my eyes, Oliver's face was hovering over mine, smirking. I jumped in my skin at how close he stood. Those brown eyes, his nose smothered in freckles.

"What the hell are you doing?" I shoved my nine-year-old foster brother aside.

My gaze swept the pristine white walls, the window showing me only an overcast sky and rain hitting the glass. I inhaled the clinical smell of the hospital I lay in. The last thing I remembered was passing out at school.

"What am I doing here?"

I'll always be here for you. His voice softened my mind, caressed me into a lull, and the temptation to finally give in to him edged so close today.

Are you ready to fall?

"You're in so much shit." Oliver laughed the words, breaking me out of my haze.

"What?" The blue curtain lay half-closed around my bed, so I couldn't see the doorway. But voices I didn't recognize whispered from other beds behind the curtain. Other patients.

"Where's Jen?"

Just as I asked, she appeared from around the blue curtain with a tight smile. "How are you feeling?" She sat on the bed next to me, taking my hand in hers, and now terror choked through me.

"W-What's going on?" I stammered.

She glanced at me with compassion, with worry. She patted my hand. "The doctors think you may have had an epileptic fit, so they're running some tests. They say you might be able to go home tomorrow."

Epilepsy? I had enough crap to deal with. I didn't need this... didn't want it. Adrenaline pumped through me so fast, I tasted bile at the back of my throat like I might spew.

"It's not confirmed that's what happened. Personally, I think it was stress from everything that happened today." Her voice lowered. "Why did you let Antonio convince you to smoke weed? I bet that caused all of this."

Had it? Maybe... I had no clue. So much had happened too fast. "I'm sorry," was all I said.

Her phone rang, and she jostled to her feet before running out of the room.

Incessantly smirking Oliver sat in the visitor chair, watching me.

"Why aren't you in school?" I snapped.

He rolled his eyes. "Finished a couple of hours ago. God, you're stupid."

I shook my head, not having time for him.

"Mom's so pissed at you," he began. "You did drugs, she said. And she's had enough."

My stomach clenched at how out of control everything had gotten so fast.

"She said they're searching for a new foster family for you," he muttered.

I twisted my head in his direction, and he burst out laughing. "Oh my God, you should see your face."

Prick. There were times I hated my foster brother, like right now... that little shit lied through his teeth, yet his words scraped the insides of my head.

And now I couldn't escape the idea he'd planted in my head. Was Jen looking to find me a new foster home?

The dream came again, always the same, a place I knew too well, a place I'd walked hundreds of times before. And the more times I visited, the more I couldn't help but feel this was where I belonged... in my head, not outside. Not standing here in front of the mirror wondering what to do for the day, not to mention my life. Not stuck in the real world with everything that entailed. Foster care, school sucking, and the part-time job that came with a few perks like free movies.

I dragged the orange tee over my head and down my stomach. The logo, *Cinemaximum*, ran across my chest. Then I combed my hair into a high ponytail and reached for the orange elastic band. Shadows still collected under my eyes, and I leaned closer to the mirror in my bedroom, pressing to find they weren't puffy anymore. My blue eyes looked pale like ice, too similar to my pale skin and white-blonde hair. I ruffled my bangs, looking half-decent, even if I resembled a bit of a ghost.

Wait till you show them the real you.

"I'd prefer that never happened," I murmured. "Not the girl who speaks to herself and has weird-ass dreams. Better they see the normal girl I am on the outside."

Normal is so overrated.

"Says the devil on my shoulder."

You haven't even seen my bad side.

I stilled, sometimes taken aback by the things that came from my head, things that seemed too real.

I'd definitely been cooped up at home too long for the past week, mostly in bed or on the couch watching reruns of *The Chilling Adventures of Sabrina*. It reminded me of Antonio asking Sabrina to the dance, and the scene replayed in my mind over and over. I shouldn't have tortured myself, but I couldn't stop. Maybe believing Antonio saw me as anything other than a friend had all been in my mind.

I'd spoken to my boss at the cinema the other day about going back to work this weekend since I'd missed last weekend's shifts. I hadn't experienced another fit for a week now despite the docs saying I could be suffering from epilepsy and they needed to carry out more tests. With all that shit on my mind, I had to get out and Saturdays were the busiest day at the movie theater.

If you head back to bed instead, I could make you forget.

"Whoa, where did that come from?"

Guess I'm in a playful kind of mood.

"Think I've fallen far enough by even talking to you."

Little wolf, you don't know the meaning of falling... not yet anyway. Like they say, the deeper you dig, the deeper you fall.

"Who said that?"

Someone.

"Ha. You just made that up."

Pretty poetic, hey?

"Actually, it's not bad. I'll give you that."

He laughed heavy and dark, coming from somewhere deep, eliciting a smile from me. *So, we're going back to bed to snuggle?*

"Very funny. I have work." I stepped into my black sneakers, noticing my bed lay undone, the blanket heaped in a mess. Then there was the worn easel near the window, along with dozens of my rough paintings in a messy pile on the floor, face down, knowing Jen would insist I clean up my room.

I can tease you endlessly and I do it very well.

"Well, showoff, I'm going to work, so feel free to take a cold shower."

Shooting sounds from *Fortnite* blared through the house. Oliver would spend the day gaming.

"What's for breakfast?" I asked as I entered the open living and kitchen area, where the sun drenched the space. He sat on the L-shaped couch, controller in hand, glued to the big screen. I turned to the side table against the wall. I stuck my hand into the bowl where we kept all keys, and every other knickknack like tiny screws, coins, hairbands, and miniature toy cars.

"I can whip up some waffles," Jen responded from the kitchen.

"Sounds good. Have you seen my car keys?" I scooped out the mess, searching for them.

I glanced over my shoulder to Jen, who poured premade batter onto the waffle maker, seeming to have not heard me.

"Oliver, turn that thing down," I yelled, but he simply stuck out his tongue and increased the volume on his game.

Luke, Jen's boyfriend, strolled into the room in his striped pajama pants and black tee. He was tall and thin, wore his brown shaggy hair loose, reminding me of a sheep, and he smiled all the time. Everything about him was kind and happiness. He was my favorite of all of Jen's past boyfriends, so I hoped it worked out for them.

"I need my car," I shouted over the gunfire.

"That old rustbucket was way past its retirement date," Luke murmured as he passed me, his bare feet tapping the floorboards on his way into the kitchen. "Still, Collin's Car Yard gave us a good payout for it."

His words slammed in my head, and I jerked around. "Excuse me! Jen, what did you do? Did you freaking sell my car?"

She huffed and tossed her deadly stare at Luke.

His eyes widened and his cheeks blanched. "Didn't you already tell her?"

"No! I was waiting for the right time."

"*Right time*," I blurted out. I marched into the kitchen, keeping the island between us so I didn't throttle her. "Like the morning I was meant to go back to work. Why did you sell my car?" My voice climbed.

"Oliver!" Jen screamed and finally, he turned down the volume.

I shook from anger that she'd done that behind my back, hadn't even consulted me, had made the call on my behalf.

"Guen." She pulled down the waffle maker lid before turning to me, resting a hip into the counter like we were talking about the weather. "When I bought you that car, I didn't know it had so many problems. It's leaking oil among other things, and it'd cost too much to fix. Plus, the doctor recommended you don't drive in case you experience another seizure."

"You didn't have to sell my car! Or at least you could have spoken to me about it first."

Luke nodded, looking over at Jen. "She has a point."

"Oh, shut up, and you can finish the waffles now." She closed the distance between us, but I recoiled, unable to be in her company a second more. My life was spiraling out of control as it was. I couldn't cope with this on top of everything.

"Go get my car back!" I shouted.

"Sweetie, this is for the best. And we could use that money we got from the car yard."

"No, it's what's best for you, not for me. I can't believe you." I jerked around, grabbed my house keys and bag from the table, and rushed outside.

"Guen, your waffles," Luke called out as I slammed the door.

My back slumped against the door, tears flowing from my eyes. Everything in my mind was on fire, my body burning, but I wiped my cheeks dry. I hated how out of control I felt, how pissed I was at Jen for taking something I'd had for myself, for stealing the last thread of independence I'd held on to.

You will always have me.

"That doesn't make me feel better." I pushed off the door, wiping away the escaping tears, and swung down the sidewalk, past rundown townhouses, abandoned homes swallowed by weeds, and kids playing on the side of the road, drawing pictures on the asphalt. But I made up my mind right then that I'd find a way to claw myself back up, maybe save enough to get my car back, or another.

I pushed the earbuds into my ears, then let myself drown in the heavy beat, hurrying to work on foot.

She'd sold my car! I couldn't believe it...

Ten blocks away, I breathed heavily, and Southbridge city surrounded me, oversized and bright from the morning sun. My vision shimmered at the edges, and I couldn't tell if I was breathing right. I needed to get out and get more exercise.

People rushed in and out of stores and diners. Cars honked and filled the road. Everything blurred into one image and a sinking feeling of despair crashed through me, suddenly not recognizing the area, not knowing which direction to go.

I strolled near an alley and looked down a bright passage where the air quivered.

My vision cleared, the path darkening before my eyes, opening up to the twisted woods. Wind tore at the branches, shaking them viciously. Glimpses of the castle lay far in the distance, the bridge swaying, and the skies an ominous gray-black. Thunder roared, shaking the ground under my feet.

I stumbled backward, my heart racing.

"Watch out!" Someone shoved me in the back, and I swung around, my head whirring.

"Sorry," I muttered to the man in a business suit who marched down the sidewalk. Turning back to the alley, I saw only a dumpster and a pile of boxes. No sign of the kingdom I swore had been there seconds earlier, the same image as my mural on the school wall, on anything I sketched.

I rubbed my eyes and stared up at the Main Street sign.

Fear coiled around me too tightly, scraping my insides because, I didn't want to admit—*couldn't* admit—but maybe Debbie and Jen were right. Maybe I was losing grip on reality.

I ran the rest of the way to work. Didn't stop until I burst through the front doors of the movie theater, heaving for breath, shivers coating me. What was going on with me?

Instead of letting myself freak out, letting the panic rolling through me turn into an avalanche, I hurried into the back office to start my shift. A distraction was exactly what I needed.

"Never seen the cinema so packed," Lee, a woman only a few years older than me, said. She always wore her hair pulled into a ponytail and heavy Kohl eyeliner, bringing out her hazel eyes. "So glad you came in today." Her smile held promise and belief I wasn't a lost cause, and I liked her for not judging me, for not knowing anything about the real me.

We all carry a shadow with us, even her.

I glanced around the foyer to see several faces from school. My chest tightened at seeing them, but this was work, and I'd just put a smile on my face and ignore their stares.

Lee turned to the popcorn machine, refilling it while I approached a waiting customer, more pouring through the doors.

This menial task is below you, my little wolf.

I ignored the voice in my head and smiled at the customer as I handed her movie tickets.

I will teach you to be great, to take your place amongst the feared, and I'll show you pleasures you've never experienced.

"I'll be with you in a second," I said to the next customer with a smile, crouching down behind the counter and pretending to grab something from the drawer as I whispered, "Will you shut up and get out of my head?"

I only see the truth and you're refusing to open your eyes that you are so much greater than this, to make others who hurt you bleed, to remind them who lives amongst them.

"You're making me crazy."

I never said I was a good person. I heard the devious smirk in his voice, almost pictured his smile stretching from ear to ear.

Except this was all in my mind, in my twisted, broken mind.

"What do you want from me?" I mumbled.

"Guen, you all right?" Lee asked, and I freaked out.

I grabbed a handful of promotional flyers and jolted to my feet, forcing a smile. "Yep, just topping these up."

"Ah, good idea, but let's do that during downtime."

"Of course." I turned to find the customer frowning, so I stabbed his order in the register screen.

I want you to be mine. To tremble under my touch, to scream my name. To love my bad behavior.

I clenched my jaw, ignoring the words that made so little sense, the terror that somehow I could speak to myself this way, the fear that a part of me inside liked it more than I wanted to admit.

When the crowd finally dissolved, I turned to my boss. "I'll be back. Just need a quick bathroom break."

She nodded, and I locked my register before rushing to the empty toilets. There I threw myself against the sink and splashed cold water over my face with shaky hands.

"What's going on with me?" I asked out loud.

I lifted my head and stared into the mirror, at the dread etched on my face, the paleness of my lips.

"Please just stop. Stop saying shit about hurting people. That's not me. Just leave me alone."

Silence followed, and I embraced the peace, the absolute stillness. Wiping my face with a paper towel, I turned to the door.

I may be a monster, but you're naive.

CHAPTER

FIVE

"Luke's daughter, Evelyn, is going to live with us for a short while. She'll take the spare room in the basement," Jen exclaimed as she pushed the bowl of mashed potatoes into my hands at the dinner table. She shared a hurried glance with Evelyn, who sat across from me.

Evelyn was the kind of girl I'd love to hate with her flawless red curls, the perfect bone structure, skin as smooth as silk. She was thin, and just overall radiated beauty.

"Why?" Oliver blurted out, his mouth full of potatoes, and I couldn't hide my smile to know he wasn't a little jerk to just me.

"My ex-wife is going through a rough patch," Luke explained, watching Evelyn with so much admiration it made me long to have a father who loved me that much.

If my parents hadn't abandoned me in the woods when I'd been only a few months old, would they look at me with that kind of love? Evelyn had someone who adored her, always would. Jen cared a lot in her own way, but it wasn't the same.

"I'd love to have her with us permanently," Luke added. "You know, Oliver, Evelyn works at the fair by the beach and runs the Ferris wheel. She might be able to give you a free ride if we all go down there one night."

"Yeah, I can do that," Evelyn mumbled, her voice strained.

How did one get a job to manage a Ferris wheel? What qualifications were needed to push a button?

But Evelyn wasn't smiling, rather, her brow furrowed into a dozen lines. "Mom's an alcoholic, Dad, just say it as it is. She passed out, then ended up in the hospital. That's what happened." Her voice cracked and she lowered her head, staring at the pork chop on her plate.

At first, she looked like the type of person who'd steal guys from other girls… but seeing the hurt on her face, the tears bubbling in her eyes when she thought no one was looking, my heart sank. She wasn't like Sabrina, not at all.

Life tossed shit her way as much as it did me, so I understood and sympathized with her.

"Evelyn's the same year as you," Jen continued. "You can go to school together tomorrow."

I cut her a hard stare. Was the woman going senile? "Did you forget I got suspended?"

Evelyn's eyes were on me. Maybe she saw another person in distress, someone who didn't have their crap together.

Maybe she's judging you?

"Guen." Jen finally looked my way, her mouth pulled into a tight smile like she was about to deliver good news. "Forgot to tell you, Principal Johnson rang up late Friday to say he's giving you one more chance, and you better not step a foot wrong this time or I'm sending you to a nunnery, I swear to God."

So many thoughts twisted in my mind, crushing my brain. "Why are you just telling me this now?"

"It slipped my mind." She shrugged and glanced over to Evelyn, then back to me. Was she trying to impress the new girl?

Everything was getting to me, and fire soared through my chest.

"Are you kidding me? First my car, now this. It's like I don't exist in this house." I shoved away from the table and marched out and straight to my room.

"You're on dishwasher duty tonight," Jen yelled out before I slammed the door shut.

A tiny bit over the top, but I like it. Show them who's boss.

I rubbed my eyes, exhausted from everything. Going back to school meant seeing Antonio, knowing he wanted Sabrina over me, and it tore me apart. Plus, I hated catching the school bus since Sabrina caught the same bus. But now I had no car. I wanted to scream.

I threw myself onto my bed and let myself drown. I didn't know how much time passed, but when the house finally fell silent, I returned to the kitchen to find everyone had gone to bed, the light still on and a pile of dishes waiting for me in the sink. *Gah.* So I got to washing them before Jen gave my room to Evelyn and made me sleep in the basement.

Ferris wheel? Is that some kind of weapon or sex toy?

I almost choked on my breath, the slimy plate slipping from my hands, but I caught it before it smashed to the floor.

"What are you talking about? It's just a ride at fairs," I whispered, looking toward the hallway momentarily.

There was no response for a while, so I went about washing the dishes, the only sound the clink of plates.

These rides are sold at fairs? Where do the rides take you?

I prodded my chin, thinking. "It takes you high up into the sky to see an amazing view, then back down. It's a huge circular ride made of metal and seats."

Do you like these rides?

I shrugged and pinched my lips. "Yeah, they're not bad. A Ferris wheel is where lots of couples go to kiss."

Is that what you wanted to do with Antonio?

My muscles tensed and a plate slid out of my hand and into the water. "Why are you bringing up that shit? If I were up there with him now, I'd shove him off the ride."

He laughed so beautifully evilly, I couldn't help but laugh with him. Glancing over, I expected someone to come and check on me, but no one did.

"Why do you think he doesn't like me?" I mumbled as I scrubbed the pot with mashed potato residue.

The question isn't why he doesn't like you, but why do you want him to?

"You're deep sometimes."

It's my curse. I am the prince of darkness, after all.

"Is that right, Your Highness?" I teased. "And why would someone so regal waste his time chatting with someone as mundane and broken as me?"

Because inside, you're a monster just like me. I'm here waiting for you to join me, to fall so deep, you'll finally find yourself.

"Yeah, you gotta know that sounds a helluva lot creepy."

I really shouldn't have been encouraging this or finding myself enjoying it to the point where talking to myself and responding was normal... exciting.

You can't run from your shadow.

"So is that who you are?" I wiped my hands on the kitchen towel and headed to bed, switching off all the lights on the way. "Who are you exactly? Someone I made up to keep me company? To deal with the crazy dreams and visions I have?"

Doesn't matter who I am. Who are you?

My brain cogs weren't working fast enough to make sense of his question because I had this feeling the answer was so much deeper.

"All right. How about you tell me who I am?"

Long ago, darkness and light came together and created beauty... a beauty that will destroy this world.

"Whoa, okay, wasn't expecting that. Where did you steal that from? The Bible?" Though I'd never read the Bible.

I stripped and climbed into my pajamas before getting into bed. I drew the blankets up to my chin and leaned over to switch the bedside lamp off.

You've been forgotten, little wolf. But I know exactly who you are. I just need to find you.

"Right! And you only speak in riddles when I ask you to elaborate? Whatever. I'm going to sleep."

The silvery moonlight from the large window fell over my bedroom, illuminating all the shadowy corners. That had been the exact reason I'd selected this room. I wasn't the biggest fan of the dark.

I turned over and shut my eyes.

***

I startled awake, coated in sweat, darkness clearing from the edges of my eyes. The shadow in the twisted woods always came for me—always. Night still cloaked the room. The clock on the bedside table showed 5:01 a.m. I fell back in bed, breathing heavily, still feeling like I remained in my dream.

I'll breathe so much easier when I feel your heartbeat, your weight against me.

Clearing my throat, I opened my eyes. "Very poetic for so early in the morning," I croaked.

Our conversations mean so much more than you'll ever know.

In all honesty, I didn't know how to feel, how to respond to the voice in my head saying that.

I thought about you while you slept, he teased, his voice sultry.

"Oh yeah?"

I crave to run my fingers over your body. Tell me... He breathed heavily. *Tell me how it feels?*

My eyes flipped wide open. I hadn't been expecting that in the slightest. "No! And if you're in my mind, you know."

I knew my little wolf was devious.

My cheeks shouldn't have heated up, but already a trickle of flames zipped through me, diving so deep, I tightened my thighs at the sensation.

"Stop talking crap." I pushed the blankets off me and climbed out of bed, the floorboards cold under my feet.

These desires have delightful ends. Something about his voice left me trembling with an overpowering sensation that engulfed me fast and had my heart pounding so loud that I stumbled on my feet, barely able to catch my breath.

Let me show you.

"No! Just no." The notion terrified me that somehow I'd enjoy it so much, I'd lose myself even more than I already had.

I flicked on the lights and glanced over to my easel, deciding that painting was the perfect distraction from my mind seducing me. God, I was going insane.

With a fresh canvas set up, I prepped the paints and brushes before starting. I drew a long stroke, then another and more, the twisted tree coming to life. *He* no longer spoke and I let myself go.

"Guen, are you ready?" Jen called out from the hallway.

I snapped out of my concentration to find daylight flooded the room, and the clock flashed eight o'clock. "Oh, shit." Where had the time gone?

Setting the dirty brush in the water jar on the floor, I ran to the bathroom to get ready.

Once dressed, I took my meds and tossed my backpack over my shoulder.

Jen handed me a brown paper bag. "Waffles and sandwich. Now go. Luke's giving you both a lift this morning."

"Thanks." Rushed, I grasped the breakfast and headed outside to find Evelyn sitting in the front seat of the small hatchback. Fine by me. I jumped into the back, glad I wasn't catching the bus today.

Students crowded the school hall this morning, a few sending cutting stares my way, surprised I'd returned, no doubt. With Evelyn in the main office getting signed in, I stuffed my earbuds into my ears and shoved my way down the hall.

Before long, someone grabbed my arm, and I spun around to come face to face with Antonio.

My heart fluttered, my stomach dropping through me. I wasn't ready for this, couldn't find my words.

"I was calling out to you," he murmured.

I pulled out my earbuds, looking around for any sign of Sabrina and finding none. "What's up?"

"Heard you got kicked out. Great to see you're back." He had no right to smile that gorgeous grin and lure me into believing he liked me. I knew the truth now… It wasn't me he craved, but Sabrina. I was the freak girl he hung with, whom he probably laughed at behind my back about how I was more broken than him. Standing in front of him hurt, burned like acid in my throat.

All I could picture was him laughing with Sabrina.

"Yeah, thanks. I gotta go to class." I hurried away.

"Guen, you okay?" he called out, but I didn't turn around, didn't dare look back, or I'd crumble and give into him. I pushed the earbuds back in and hit max on the volume to tune out everything, even *him*.

Most of the classes passed in a blur, where I focused on lessons and nothing else. At lunch, I grabbed my meal and sat in the farthest corner, expecting to dine alone, but someone set their sandwich and juice near mine and sat.

Evelyn was grinning. "People are weird at this school."

"How so?" I took a bite of my waffles, staring at how viciously she ripped open her lunch, then tucked the red locks behind her ear.

"Like these girls were all chummy with me in biology, even shared their chocolate with me, then in the hallway, they tripped me and laughed."

"Rule number one: This school is infested by bitches. Rule number two: The guys here are the lowest scum on earth. Rule number three: Remember the first two rules."

She laughed and bit into her sandwich. A shadow fell over us.

"Hi, Evelyn."

I glanced up to see Noah with his black, spiked hair and those blue, dreamy eyes every girl in school swooned over. Did he remember me from the psychiatrist's waiting room? Probably not, considering his gaze wasn't on me.

"Hi," she responded, but she said nothing more and ate her meal.

"So, you want to go to the school dance with me this weekend?" The words just poured so easily off his tongue, as they had from Antonio's. In the background, half a dozen girls watched Noah, hypnotized by him. Were their hearts shattering to see him talk to the new red-haired beauty at school?

"Thanks," Evelyn responded. "But gonna say *no*. I'm probably just gonna go with Guen and have a girls' night out." She glanced over, smirking.

I liked Evelyn right then more than I'd thought possible. I grinned wildly, especially when Noah's mouth dropped open in shock. Without another word, he licked his lips, stuffed his hands into his pockets, and headed out of the cafeteria. I had nothing against the guy, but a sense of satisfaction filled me.

"He's not my type," she said. "He's been following me around all morning, talking non-stop about himself, how all the girls at school want him, but he only has eyes for me." She fake-gagged. "Who says that?"

"A desperate loser." I chuckled.

"Can you believe he tried to bribe me by saying his dad owned the biggest car yard in town, and he'd get me an amazing deal if I wanted a car?"

I half-snorted, but then reality punched me in the throat.

Wait! Collin's Car Yard. Noah's surname was Collin.

His dad had bought my car! The craziest idea crossed my mind, banging inside my head like a drum.

I shoved up out of my seat. "I'll be back."

Then I ran out of the cafeteria.

CHAPTER

SIX

"Get in," Noah ordered from the driver's seat of his red sports car parked under a broken streetlight.

I scanned the dark street I'd just run down, the wind shaking the trees along the sidewalk. No sign of Jen. I prayed she hadn't heard me crawl out the bedroom window and followed me. I dove into Noah's car, heaving for breath, and strapped myself in.

"You ready to do this?" he asked, his voice calm, his mouth curling into a smirk.

I nodded and turned his way. "God, you must really hate your dad! You don't look nervous at all." I was sweating like a beast.

He snorted a laugh. "My dad is a dick on a good day, and he deserves so much worse than losing one car."

His words surprised me, but like *he* said, everyone had shadows.

Good girl.

I shifted in my seat, staring out at the road. "You got all the papers signed and — ?"

"Relax, you're making me jumpy. Got it all sorted. No one will bust you for stealing a car. I've got it signed back to you." He revved up the car, the motor purring, slamming the glass-knob gearshift into position, then he hit the gas, sending me back into the seat, and my stomach lurched to my throat. We raced down the quiet road. It was close to midnight.

"Bet your girlfriends love it when you woo them in this car?"

41

"Yeah, I guess." He glanced at me, the shadows dancing across his expression, his gaze all over me. "You spoke to her?"

"Yes, Evelyn will go to the dance with you. A deal's a deal."

Don't make deals, little wolf.

But I'd made up my mind. I'd tell Jen I used my savings to get my car back.

"So where am I picking up my car from?"

"The Car Yard."

My insides tightened. "You said you had it all ready." My voice strained and my knees bounced. "Don't tell me we have to break it out of the yard? Hasn't your dad got security cameras?"

"Just be cool. I said I got this, didn't I?" He shook his head and took the next turn a bit too fast, his back wheels skidding.

I grasped the door handle, convinced I'd made a terrible mistake thinking I could trust him. I didn't need Jen finding out since I wouldn't put it past her to actually send me to a nunnery.

Leave now then.

I raised a brow at his stupid suggestion. At the speed Noah was driving, I'd die if I tried to do a sudden roll out of the car.

Soon houses were replaced by the industrial district, and Noah pulled over in the shadows, far from the nearest streetlamp.

I squinted my eyes, staring into the dark. "Where are we?"

He fiddled with something in the middle console, his movements producing the jangle of keys, and excitement rose through me. I'd get my car back, gain some control of my life. Evelyn was easy to convince as long as I hung around with them during the night. I happily obliged.

You're not thinking straight, little wolf.

I reached for the door, whispering under my breath, "You're wrong."

"You're real cute, you know."

Frozen in my seat, I twisted my head around, convinced I'd misheard. "Don't say shit like that. I don't need your flattery or whatever you're doing."

"Who have you been listening to that you can't take a compliment?"

"Okay, this isn't a conversation I expected to have with you—ever." Heat rushed up my neck and over my cheeks. "You've never really spoken to me before, so, well, you get the gist."

He shifted in his seat to face me, his hand in his dark hair, raking it back. "That was my mistake." He paused. "You look cute in that sweater, by the way."

I looked down at the black outfit I'd pulled out of my closet for one purpose: looking like a ninja to sneak out of the house.

"Why are you doing this?" I asked.

"Doing what?" He smiled so perfectly, his full lips delicious. There was something alluring, almost taboo, about him. Something I hadn't noticed before, but with the way he looked at me, my stomach unleashed butterflies.

"Being nice to me," I explained.

Little wolf, he growled a warning.

"Because you deserve it."

Noah reached over and his fingers pushed a few strands of hair off my face, his touch delicate... oh-so delicate. My heart's tempo rose and rose, and when I met his ice-blue eyes, I let myself believe his words. Let his hand cradle the side of my face. And for those few moments, it was Antonio I shared the car with, who touched me, who leaned closer. I needed him against me. To make me feel like it was me he chose. Me he wanted.

No, little wolf.

Lips clamped down on my mouth so fast, so chaotic—it all happened too quickly. His tongue drove against my lips, hands raking over my shoulders, down my arms, pulling at the fabric of my sweater.

Heavy breaths beat against me, and I could barely fill my lungs as he pressed closer, his arms pinning me to my seat.

Run!

A horrible feeling surged through my belly, and panic came with it, thick and fast. I shoved my hands into his chest, but he was a brick wall, unmovable.

His tongue licked at my neck, fingers curled in my hair. Something behind his eyes shifted, darkened with power. His hands grew forceful, more demanding.

The air was like molasses, heavy to breathe, and dread strangled me at the thought that he wanted more than a kiss, so much more.

"Stop, Noah, please!" I pushed against him.

Tell him... Tell him you want him to take you to a different place. To the back-seat. His voice grew, furious. *Then run.*

My fear spiked as Noah's hand swooped under my shirt, finding flesh. He moaned, and my heart thundered with terror. I thrashed against him. "Get off me!"

"Quiet down," he growled.

Tell him!

Noah kissed me again, harder this time, his hand pushing under the band of my jeans and underwear, his fingers gliding over the small bundle of hair and deeper.

I cried out. My body writhed, shoving against him, adrenaline beating into my veins. His mouth pressed fiercely on mine, and he half-climbed over the middle console like a monster mounting me.

Heavy, raging breaths swept over my mind like a thundering storm about to erupt. *Do it! he* bellowed. *Now!*

"B-Backs-seat." I reached for the handle, scrambling, straining to push the door open. My fingers curled over the metal, and I yanked, but it didn't budge. The bastard had locked us in.

"L-Let's go in the backseat."

Noah snarled against my mouth, his hand ripping at the buttons of my jeans. "I'm fine here."

"Don't!" I drove my fists into him, my world darkening the more I slammed my balled hands at his head, his shoulders. His teeth ripped at my lip with fierceness, blood coating my tongue, while his hand jerked at my underwear, the rip of fabric piercing the night.

"Be a good girl and shut the hell up."

Numbness took over me. My brain couldn't focus as I searched for a way out.

But the darkness feathered at the edges of my teary eyes while Noah's disgusting mouth pinned against mine, his grubby hands all over me.

The sports car gave a shudder under me, and Noah didn't notice that or the sudden creak.

He'll pay, little wolf. He'll pay with his life for ever touching you.

An invisible grip fastened around my neck, and I shuddered when another wave came at me, faster than the first, my world blurring, bile hitting the back of my throat.

In a heartbeat, my body burst into a fit on the front seat, fear sliding into my heart.

The car shook violently, the windows quivering. Metal groaned, sounding like a great beast roaring. Suddenly, the car hood flipped upward, the metal buckling right before my eyes.

Noah flew back into his seat, his eyes wide with fear, staring out the front window. "What the hell?"

In a blinding flash, everything was ripped out from under me, and I fell into a pit of darkness, the world stolen from me. My screams pounded in my head. I jerked my arms out, grabbing for something, for anything.

I tumbled so fast, seeing nothing.

With a thump, I hit something bouncy and soft that caught my fall as a cry slipped from my lips. I swept my gaze around me to the large window, the chest of drawers, the mirror, the easel. And beneath me was my bed... I was back in my room, clutching the glass gearshift from Noah's sports car.

"W-What's g-going on?" I tossed the gear stick to the end of the bed as if it were some vile part of him.

Confusion pummeled into me, and I couldn't make sense of anything. My flesh crawled, my mind drowned over what had happened with Noah, how I'd gotten back here in an instant. How had the metal of his hood twisted on its own?

I kept glancing around the room, blinking hard, expecting this to be a vision, a dream—anything but reality. Expecting myself to wake up to clear the blurriness in my head because these things didn't happen in real life. They couldn't.

I hiccupped a breath and scrambled under my blankets, wanting to hide from the world, convinced this was somehow a horrible dream. As I curled in on myself, the tears refused to stop, and I couldn't stop the dirty feeling slithering over my flesh. I shut my eyes, praying I'd just fall asleep and never wake up again.

And I'll be here to catch you, little wolf.

"Are you awake yet?!"

Jen's voice shook me awake, my eyes wide open. Sweat dripped down my back as threads of the twisted woods lingered like cobwebs, pulling me back into my dream.

I stared up at the white ceiling, my insides not feeling right, somehow tangled like part of me remained in the dream. The part that couldn't quite remember what day it was, what I'd done last. An in-between world where I floated freely.

Stormy clouds cast shadows through the window, reflecting the trees outside like broken and gnarled branches. Something about them looked familiar, and not because I'd seen them in my dreams or in my room before. Similar shadows I'd seen elsewhere, all warped and bent and tapping on my window, while I remained cradled and bundled in my blankets. I remembered a dim room that smelled of the sweetest clementine and someone's panicked whispers in my ears.

Not much of my early years stuck in my head, but this rushed forward, sitting on my mind like a rock, like it wanted me to remember.

"Are you getting up anytime soon?" Jen yelled from outside my room, shattering my concentration.

With a groan, I pushed myself upright before she barged in, but my attention fell on the glass gearshift at the end of my bed.

All the events of last night steamrolled through me, ripping the peace from my mind. Bile surged into the back of my throat.

Noah.

Forcing his hand down my pants.

Me falling out of his car and landing on my bed.

I wanted to crawl out of my skin and float away. Nothing made sense but the sickness sliding through my gut that Noah had forced himself onto me.

His tongue will be a trophy on my wall.

"Then make it happen already! Do something worthwhile! Be a hero... Something. *Anything!*" I growled under my breath, shaking over the fact of what Noah had done to me, that he'd deceived me into lowering my guard. Did he even have my car, or had that been a lie too?

I'm no hero.

"Then what are you?" I blurted out.

I'm the wolf who will take revenge. The monster behind you who bathes in your misery. The only one who will put you back together.

"Stop talking in riddles," I cried, fresh tears burning my eyes as I stormed out of my room, crossed the hall, and flung open the bathroom door before shutting myself in.

"You keep telling me you're here for me. That if I fall, you'll catch me." I trembled, my spine pressed against the tiled wall as I slid to my ass. "I'm ready now. Take me from this place. I've fallen far enough." Tears marked tracks down my cheeks, and I hugged my knees, torn by the hurt and disgust I felt inside.

Oh, little wolf... His voice cracked, then faded.

"Yeah, that's what I thought."

You have no idea how far I'll go for you.

I drowned in my sorrow and wanted nothing more than to be left alone. To be invisible. To forget all the memories, all the bad, all the hate. I recalled a memory that stuck with me from another foster home. An older girl had once told me that if I wanted to be forgotten, I had to ignore myself, a comment that took me years to fully understand, hating her all the while over the fact that she'd say that to me. But she knew better than me. To survive, I had to ignore my feelings, no matter how much they shredded and scarred me. No one saw my insides and all that ugliness but me.

Maybe all these occurrences were only in my head, and Jen needed to know, to help me. I considered what the shrink had written in her notebook. *Schizophrenia.* Was this what it felt like?

A bang came at the door, and I jumped in my skin. "Don't think you're getting out of school today," Jen bellowed.

I wiped my eyes and climbed to my feet. "Give me five and I'll be ready." Shoving all the pain and agony aside, I got into the shower and embraced the emptiness.

I could do this, and so I did.

The day flew by.

Hours.

Classes.

I kept to myself, didn't say a word, and skipped lunch to avoid talking to anyone... mostly Noah and Antonio and Sabrina.

When the last bell of the day rang, I joined the masses in the hall and let them carry me out. Someone grasped my arm and wrenched me out of the sea with such strength, I tripped over my feet. Lifting my head, my gaze met Noah's.

"Get away from me." I burned on the inside at seeing him, hatred bubbling like acid in my gut that he thought he had he any right to touch me again.

His mouth warped, making me sick, ready to vomit at what his lips had done to me last night.

His whispered words spat in my face. "What did you do to my car, freak? You went psycho and my car is all twisted and a complete wreck. I don't know how you did it, but you owe me for that car. You're not running away this time, you bitch." Hatred enveloped his expression, darkening his eyes. "And I want my gearshift back."

But all I saw was red. I didn't remember moving, but my fist swung and smashed him on the jaw so hard, my knuckles screamed with agony. I hit him again and again, seeing nothing but sheer rage. "You fucking asshole!"

He never struck back, but cowered, covering his face, recoiling. His gaze swung to the gathering crowd and back to me.

Adrenaline pushed and pushed me, my fists striking him until he turned and ran, shoving students aside like a piece of shit.

Heaving for breath, I didn't look up, ignoring the voices, the words I loathed. *Weirdo. Sick. Mental problems. Unstable.*

My breaths rushed in and out of my lungs, my adrenaline rampant. I grabbed the bag I'd dropped and ran down the corridor, past everyone, out of the school, and all the way home.

Emptiness gathered in my chest, and fear swept through me. How could I ever face anyone at school again?

I gasped for air, wiping away the constant tears. My legs cramped, but I didn't care or stop until I reached home. I slouched against the door and flicked on the camera on my phone to check my face. The tears had dried, but redness rimmed my eyes. Blonde hair sat flat against my head like I hadn't washed it. I stared at my knuckles, the skin bruised and scored when I extended my fingers completely.

So proud of you, little wolf.

"He deserved so much worse."

And it will happen.

I reached for the door handle, toying with the idea of telling Jen everything, getting it off my chest, having her help me decipher what had happened last night.

She won't understand. None of them will. They'll give you meds that will take you from me.

I nodded, but what if something was seriously wrong with me? Maybe Noah was right and I had run home last night, but my mind had blocked it out? Then how had I ended up with his gearshift?

They don't want you like I do.

My mouth opened with a response, but I stopped short. I'd been shoved from family to family my whole life because no one wanted me... Did *he* have a point?

I shoved open the door, dumped my bag near the shoe rack, and headed down the hall to my room. Without thought, I automatically picked up my paints and brushes with a new canvas I stored in the back of my closet.

Here I lost myself, forgot everything, and didn't have to be anyone but myself. My thoughts swirled with my dilemma. Tell Jen or keep pretending I was fine?

I couldn't tell how much time had passed before I took a bathroom break, but when I returned, Jen stood in front of my canvas tapping a fingertip on her chin like a critic.

My stomach dropped. "What are you doing in here?" I rushed toward her.

"Guen, you drew this? It's unbelievable." She stretched a hand toward the painting. "Especially—"

"Don't touch it. Don't look at it." I stepped between her and the image, something I'd never shown a soul. The snarled woods was my place, something only I knew about, not Jen or the shrink or anyone.

Except me.

She stared at the canvas. "That is incredible. How did you come up with something so beautiful?"

I'd never tell, ever. The place was my kingdom, the one in my head, the one no one could rip away and destroy.

Jen stepped back, and I hurried to grab one of my shirts from the floor and draped it over the painting.

"They're all of the same forest and castle. You've painted the image over and over. Where did the idea come from?"

I turned and Jen was bent at the waist, flicking through my other paintings propped up against the wall. They were all two-foot square canvases because they were the cheapest sizes at the local discount store.

"Just leave them alone." I grabbed the bundle and moved them away from her reach.

"Sweetie, you're being rude. You're so talented. Don't hide them."

I shook my head. I didn't want anyone to see them because once they did, they'd find a way to rip that place away from me. To somehow turn the one thing I enjoyed into an explanation for my sickness. Or some other shit excuse to turn it into something ugly.

"Just leave them alone," I said. "They're not for anyone but me."

She nodded, her mouth pulling downward at the corners. "Okay, okay. Just open the window in here. It's stuffy."

When she left, I set the paintings back down against the wall and collapsed onto my bed, shaking, feeling like someone had just ransacked my room. This was why I made it clear that no one was allowed in my room.

Little wolf—

"Not now. Please, just leave me alone." I turned onto my side and stared at the bruise forming over my knuckles, wanting only quiet.

Two more days passed. School. Home. Sleep. A simple routine, but it worked and I was left alone. As I stepped out from the school entrance on a sunny day, I rushed down the front steps and swung left, like I did every day to catch the bus home.

"Guen," a woman called me, and I turned around to find Jen poking her head out the driver's window of her car, waving at me to join her.

Hell yeah, I'd accept a lift home. I ran toward her, darting around students. In my rush, I bumped into Antonio, who grabbed my wrist in my attempt to flee.

"Hey. Haven't seen much of you," he murmured in that smooth, velvet voice.

But all I could focus on was his hand on me, my chest beaming with excitement... except when I looked at him, I only saw Sabrina. And on cue, the devil bitch sidled up to him. She must have felt her horns burning. Her eyes fell heavy on me as she curled an arm around his, possessively claiming her territory.

"Hey, babe. What are you doing?" she purred with the voice of a back-stabbing cow, while her eyes narrowed, hurling hatred my way.

I ripped my hand free from his grip.

Kick him in the balls.

I ought to, but instead I didn't waste my breath on him before running to the car, hating how hot my neck and face burned from his presence. Hating that seeing him with her still sliced my insides. They deserved each other.

In the car, I buckled in and stared straight ahead, too shaken to look elsewhere.

Jen, to my surprise, didn't ask a question, but she would have seen me talking to Antonio, seen him with Sabrina. She just pulled away from the curb and drove away. Once we passed the swarming traffic around the school, I eased into my seat.

"Thanks for the lift," I said, looking over at Jen, who offered me a huge smile. I shouldn't have been suspicious, but my *shits-about-to-hit-the-fan* radar was blaring in my head. "What's the special occasion?"

"I wanted to show you something. And I need you to have an open mind."

I shifted in my seat, and there it came. "What did you do?" Part of me didn't want to know, but I wasn't getting a choice in the matter.

"I'm so proud of you, Guen, and I want you to see how incredible you are. The last couple of weeks, a lot has happened, and you handled it better than I thought. With everything from the sale of your car to that jerk Antonio having another girlfriend, you now need some good news."

I swallowed hard. If only she knew half of the shit I'd been going through.

"I've got a small surprise for you."

In general, I didn't do surprises well, but I nodded and smiled back. "Can't wait."

Twenty minutes later, we parked along the main road in the heart of our small city and climbed out. I scanned the surrounding stores. A pizzeria, café, clothing store. If this was the surprise, I'd take it.

But when Jen curled around the front of the car, she strolled past all three establishments, so I guessed we weren't going into any of them.

I rushed after her. "Where are we going?"

"You'll see." In a heartbeat, she grasped my hand in hers and whirled me in through an open door into a huge white room. The walls were covered in paintings, and my stomach dropped at the idea that she intended on taking me on some kind of art gallery tour.

A dome-shaped haystack sculpture made of thousands upon thousands of sharp sewing needles sat in the middle of the room. An old-fashioned spinning wheel sat on top, also made of silver. The sun pouring in from the floor-to-ceiling windows glinted off the structure like a star, and all I could picture was someone tripping and falling into the contraption. Death by a million pins.

Jen dragged me to the rear of the room, and dread rose through me like a storm.

On the back wall of the room hung my painting with a tiny plaque underneath with my name.

Guen's Fantasy

"What do you think?" Jen prodded my arm, but numbness spread through me. My private piece was tacked to a wall for all to gawk and critique. I felt sick to my stomach.

"You had no right," I muttered, keeping my voice low so the other couple in the room didn't hear us.

"Guen, honey. The moment I showed the artist running this exhibition your piece, she loved it and insisted she add it to her gallery. She had no hesitation and her only condition was that she could meet the artist. You have a real talent here. This could take you so far and be your thing."

"My thing?" I didn't even know what that meant, but I figured it had something to do with finding my path in life, to ensure I didn't end up a homeless loser.

"You should have—"

"Hello," a woman's faint voice came from behind us.

We both turned to face the most beautiful woman I'd ever laid eyes on. Tall, almost glowing with the sun at her back, porcelain skin seeming to glisten, and hair black as the night. The skirt of her golden dress billowed around her knees from the breeze rushing through the open door. Her pale gray eyes scanned me from head to toe, her smile widening as if she approved of what she saw. "Guen?"

"This is Guen," Jen responded for me, practically gushing. "She's talented, isn't she?"

"Absolutely." The tall, angelic woman took my hand in hers, her skin silky soft like she soaked her hands in a tub of moisturizer every night.

"My name is Áine."

"That's a beautiful name," I said.

"It's an Irish name, meaning 'radiance.'" Her smile beamed, perfectly matching her name.

"Are you Irish?"

She half-laughed. "No, dear." Then she turned me around to face my painting. "Your mom wasn't sure what you wanted to call this piece, so I'll have it amended right away. What do you call it?"

My head was spinning to think straight. "I-I'd never given it any thought."

"Don't think too hard," said Áine, all sweetness. "What's the first thing that came to mind when you painted this image?"

"You can do this, sweetie," Jen added.

I shrugged. "I don't know. Maybe *Twisted Dreams*." The moment the words left my mouth, I wanted them back. I'd said too much, not wanting Jen to know this came from my dreams, but already I felt her stare on me, the wheel behind her eyes ticking away.

"That's perfect," Áine said before yelling over her shoulder. "Jean-Claude, a new tag for this piece, please. *Twisted Dreams*."

I cringed on the inside.

Áine returned to my side in moments, her arm threaded through mine, pressing close, and all I could smell was her strong floral perfume with hints of citrus. Maybe she was French or from some other European country where being touchy-feely with strangers was the norm.

"I'd love to hear about your inspiration for this piece," she said.

Jen interrupted. "Oh, she's a closed book and won't tell anyone." I appreciated her saving me.

"Nonsense, every artist has a muse." Holding on to my arm, she swept me around the gallery. "All these works of art came from somewhere deep and personal to the artist, so where is yours from?"

Something about her pushiness was rubbing at my nerves. "What does it matter?" I glanced over my shoulder to find Jen chatting with a tall, man with gelled hair and black eyeliner busy replacing the tag under my painting.

Áine's grip on me tightened, and she was stronger than I'd expected. When I looked up at her, a glint of silver crossed her gray eyes, her beauty darkening, and for those few seconds, the room seemed to freeze over. Even my breath misted in front of my face.

"Let me tell you something." Her words sliced the air like a blade, her fingernails digging into my wrist. A greedy hunger tightened her features, her expression changing to someone who'd just found a dragon's treasure.

"Ow, you're hurting me." I pulled against her, her nails cutting into my flesh, her nose wrinkling, and she almost looked like a different person. "Let me go."

With the speed of a striking viper, her breath was on my ear. "Guendolyn, we finally found you."

CHAPTER

EIGHT

"**G**uen!" Jen called from across the gallery.

I jerked around, blinking fast to clear the fuzziness in my vision. Why in the world did it feel like I'd been run over by a truck?

Jen rushed forward, fear tightening her expression. Once at my side, she grasped my hand. "Are you going to be sick? What happened to your hand?" Her panicked voice was strained.

When I looked down at the inside of my wrist, blood bubbled and rolled over the sides of my arm from three small cuts the size of fingernails. Red dots hit the perfect white floor, like blood drops in snow. My heart was racing as I tried to make sense of what Áine had just done... had said.

Jen pulled a tissue from her handbag and pressed it to my wounds. "How did you cut yourself?"

Glancing over my shoulder, I found that Áine was nowhere to be seen. Had she run out of the store? "Where is she?"

"Focus," Jen insisted.

My head felt like someone had blown a puff of smoke right inside my skull. "Her fingernails," I murmured. "They were so sharp. Her face—"

"She did this to you?" Jen hissed, drawing the attention of the couple nearby in the main exhibition.

But I couldn't think straight and just nodded.

Guendolyn, we finally found you, she'd whispered.

55

The voice in my head had said something similar. *I just need to find you.*

They couldn't be related... no. How could it be? He was in my mind, my delusional mind, part of suffering schizophrenia... I guessed.

I read somewhere that coincidences meant you were on the right path. Except nothing felt right here, and only heaviness worried through my gut.

"Sweetie." Jen's tender voice lulled me out of my thoughts. "Stay here for a second. Don't touch anything."

As if I would. My sights swung to an enormous structure made of actual pins still attached to their metal heads. I stepped closer to the wall, terrified I'd have a fit and fall straight onto that thing.

Jen stormed to the back of the gallery, her arms swinging by her side, and shoved Jean-Claude aside. She pulled my painting off the wall, then tucked it under her arm and marched right back to me before taking my hand and hauling me out of the establishment.

She turned back for a brief moment. "Don't buy anything from here. Áine is an abuser. She attacked my girl and made her bleed."

Without a further word, she guided me to her sedan. I adored Jen more at that moment than I'd ever thought possible. Despite all the shit I'd caused, she only wanted the best for me. She believed in me after all of my crazy drama.

Once we climbed into the car, she reached over and checked my cuts, wiping the blood clean with the stained tissue. "I'm so sorry. I never should have brought your painting here. I should have listened to you."

"You didn't know she was crazy and would attack me."

Her lips pinched, and her brow furrowed. "I'm supposed to protect you, do my best for you, and I should have known better." She met my drowning eyes. "Did she hurt you anywhere else? What did she say to you?"

"Not much, just gibberish about paintings."

"Tomorrow I'll put a complaint in with her landlord to ensure she loses her rental privileges at the gallery."

"How do you know she doesn't own it?"

Jen started the engine and merged into the traffic. "I know the person who owns the whole complex. He's a cousin of a friend at work." Her hands strangled the steering wheel. She shook her head, and every now and then, she glanced over with a sympathetic smile.

I kept repeating the incident over and over in my head, unsure what had happened, but I was left with more questions than answers. Why did Áine behave so weirdly... So aggressively?

What if she knew more about me than I did? My past was a black hole.

No biological parents, no history—nothing but a single name. Was it even mine?

"Is Guen my real name?"

Jen studied me with a raised brow. "What do you mean?"

I shrugged. "They said I was found in the woods as a baby abandoned with nothing but a ribbon tied to my ankle with my name on it. So could Guen be short for something else?"

Her lips pinched to the side, thinking about my question for a long time. "Let me check the archives at work tomorrow, okay?" She patted my thigh.

"Thank you for everything. I know I don't say it often, but I appreciate it."

Her smile was so much more than words could express, and despite the outcome to the whole gallery shitstorm, I wouldn't change a thing, as it had made me realize something. Made me see that Jen was so much more than a foster mom. She was my guardian angel. My fairy godmother, if such things existed.

I wiped away the blood on my arm and stared at the half-moon-shaped wounds, blood already clotting at the edges. Áine had been so angry, so adamant to tell me she'd found me. None of it made sense, but maybe she was just another person whose head wasn't screwed on right.

"How does pizza sound for dinner?" Jen suggested.

"Luigi's? Pepperoni?"

"You bet."

"Perfect." I lounged in my seat, holding the tissue tightly to my cuts, and figured a night of stuffing my face with pizza to forget everything was exactly what the doctor ordered.

***

There was something unusual about the woods today.

Twisted branches stood still—too still, the breeze absent—and shadows crowded the woods like never before. They darkened the place I knew too well, stealing the breath out of the forest.

A chill slithered down my spine, and I turned toward the castle, the kingdom that promised freedom beyond the dark forest of teeth and thorns. A place to escape if I reached its sanctuary in time.

I swung away from the gloom swallowing the forest, like I always did, my sights set on the place just out of reach, the place I felt I belonged.

A hum of whispers rose around me.

Not one person, but so many watched me today, their eyes heavy on my back. My skin crawled from the sharpness cutting into my forearm. I looked down and the blood ran free from the three wounds. The drops hit the dirt. Where once broken things grew, my blood turned anything it touched black.

My heart raced too fast, strangling me, and I ran to the only place I felt safe. The kingdom.

Movement darted through the woods alongside me, suddenly sliding across my passage.

I stopped dead in my tracks, my breaths ragged and harsh.

They'd catch me today—I sensed it deep in my bones. They had my scent now, the delicate spice of my blood on their tongues. Today was the end.

A figure emerged from within the darkness. A masculine man, tall and powerful. He stood in the distance. Dressed in a military-style coat that reached his knees, with silver buttons and a high collar, he was spectacular.

He carried power... Oh, so much of it dominated the land... and me. Dark leather pants hugged strong legs and a shirt the color of midnight, in what looked like silk or some kind of fabric that I'd never seen before. It looked wicked expensive. Pricier than anything I could ever dream about buying, that was certain. The shirt sat open around his throat.

This man couldn't be more than a few years older than me, but he carried enough confidence for both of us. Long hair fell to his shoulders, black as the night, skin lightly tanned like he barely spent time in the sun.

Sweat drenched my skin, and I glanced around for an escape, but thorny bushes and trees blocked my way. Except I knew this path; I'd traveled it hundreds of times before. I shouldn't have been afraid. This was my place... even if today the shadow that always just watched me emerged from his hiding spot.

"Who are you?" I called out, finding my bravery.

"Doesn't matter who I am. Who are you?" his masculine, seductive voice replied.

My mouth clamped shut in a heartbeat when my mind fixated directly on who stood in the distance, and I recognized him at once.

Him. He. The man with no name. The voice who made me laugh and fear him, who left me trembling. Who promised me things.

He stepped into the dim light, a breeze blowing around us now, rousing the trees from their sleep, greeting us with rustling songs.

I couldn't help myself, and my gaze roamed over his face, finding the most beautiful eyes I'd ever seen. Bright like fire dancing on water if such a thing were possible, but on him, they burned, crowned by dark eyebrows. Curiosity had me staring at the sharpness of his cheekbones, the rugged defined jaw, full lips with a slight curve in them, like he might break into a smile. What did he find so amusing?

He strolled closer, moving with the grace of a man used to being in the public eye—shoulders broad, chin raised, but those eyes... intense and powerful and dangerous. He saw everything, missing nothing, so why was he staring at *me* like that?

I stiffened. It didn't matter how drop-dead gorgeous he was; something about his presence left me uncomfortable. He moved closer, towering over me, and my feet shuffled backward.

Threads of fear coiled around my chest in his presence.

He smiled. Should I smile back or run?

At my hesitation, he raised an eyebrow, the corners of his mouth quirking. "Hello, little wolf."

The cogs in my brain still grinded to catch up, clouded further by the smoothness of his voice, the heat he ignited within me. "Sorry, what?"

His laugh boomed, just like the times I'd listen to him in my head. This was my dream... I knew, always knew, but this time was different. He was different and shouldn't have been here.

"What are you doing?" I asked, utterly mesmerized that my mind had conjured such a handsome man to go with that delicious voice.

"I told you I'd finally find you."

Heat crawled up my neck. "And *I* told *you* how creepy stalkerish that sounds."

His mouth pulled into the deadliest of smiles that left my knees shaking. When he looked at me with that grin, his gaze dipped over my face, boobs, legs. I felt utterly vulnerable, and extremely turned on. Except all of this was in my head, in my dream, right?

Yet part of me had this urge to run up to him and hug him like we were long-lost friends or something, but if I did that, I would be insane. Besides, he didn't seem the hugging kind, no matter how much I'd love to be in his arms. Point proven, I'd just gotten horny over the imaginary guy in my head.

So, I swallowed back the confusion and ignored the fire sparking in my gut. "Seeing as you've finally stopped hiding, want to show me around? Like maybe how to get to that kingdom over there?" I nudged my chin toward the palace in the distance. "And who the hell are you really? Do you have a name, or should I call you my shadow?"

A smirk slid over his gorgeous mouth, but he shook it off as quickly as it came, his gaze never leaving mine. "You still have a sword for a tongue, I see."

"And you still talk in riddles. What's new?"

"I have so many secrets to tell you," he began. "Things you've seen a thousand times, but never like this."

"What sort of secrets?"

"The kind that will show you the truth about your past."

"My past? Like my parents?"

Branches and leaves snapped in the woods around us. I turned when his hand grasped over my bloody wrist and hauled me against him so fast, my feet stumbled, and I slammed into a wall of muscles. My hand was trapped between our bodies, and panic had me clenching his shirt desperately. His woodsy masculine scent teased me and the earlier fire burned all the way through me.

"This place is no longer safe for you," he growled, then lifted my hand to his mouth and flicked a tongue over my wound.

"Eww, did you just taste my blood?" I tugged my arm from him, but he wasn't releasing me.

"It'll heal quicker."

My blood ran cold when the crunching of foliage came again. I jerked around, scanning the woods. Movement came from within the folds of darkness.

"Who's out there?"

"Monsters?"

I looked up at him, his eyes darkening. "You once told me you were the monster."

"How do you think one destroys them? By becoming one."

His words swirled in my head as fear clung to my ribs, and I pushed myself away from him, but he held on tightly and spun around, then started walking away, hauling me behind him. My feet stumbled over the ground to keep up. I didn't relent and kept tugging against his grip, still half-baffled how broken my mind was to make up this shit. How I actually felt his grip on my skin. Dreams weren't this tactile.

My heart hammered in my chest, my skin pricked with shivers. "Let me go! I mean it."

"You need to leave," he chided, his words raw and savage, his grip so tight, he'd stopped the blood circulation to my hand. "Play nice."

"You aren't the voice from my head," I spat. "You can't be because he'd never hurt me. He promised to save me and to make those who hurt me pay." My voice quivered.

"And I said I was no hero. May the gods have mercy on those who wronged you because I won't." He paused and turned me so I was forced to face him. Shadows crawled under his eyes, and his smile terrified me.

"You're just words." I jerked from his hold, but it was useless. Disbelief raked through me over the fact that he'd changed so quickly.

"Those hiding in the dark will rip you apart, suck the marrow from your bones, wear your skin as decoration, but... my little wolf, most of all, you *should* be scared of the deadliest monster of them all. Me," he hissed. "You have no idea how far I'll go."

I swallowed the shudder consuming me, and he just sneered at the hitch of my breath.

I hated his words, his twisted face, him. My throat constricted. "You're a cold-hearted liar."

I hadn't realized until now that the man inside my head was the actual devil, and he glared at me with lustful hunger in his eyes.

He *tsked*, and deadly power rippled off him.

"Who are you?" I cried with terror in my voice as shock warped my insides.

"You'll find out soon enough." He shoved his hands into my shoulders, sending me reeling backward, my body going slack. A sob escaped from deep in my lungs. A spark flashed across my vision and my world faded fast.

Darkness took me, and even though I knew he'd still be there in my head, waiting for me, I screamed.

"Guendolyn," I whispered, but she didn't stir. Shivers crawled down my back, but there was no time to waste.

This was a terrible idea, a shitty idea, yet here I stood in her bedroom, night draping over her but hiding nothing.

Somehow Guendolyn had opened the gateway to her whereabouts in the human realm, and about damn time, except her aura now revealed her to every damned soul-sucking deviant in the Wandering Realm.

Shadows already stretched and shifted across the land outside her window. I prowled across her chamber. Clothes and books lay on the floor, paintings and an easel near the window. I stepped past a book with the cover of a skinny, short-haired man in tight pants, his skin covered in markings, his ears pierced. Was this what females liked in this realm?

Looking around, I'd seen brothels cleaner than this.

Guendolyn laid in bed, the blanket pushed down to her waist, her top scrunched halfway up her stomach, exposing soft milky skin, and my fingers curled to reach down and run my hands over her, to taste her with my teeth.

If I were true to the Shadow Court, I'd walk away and let the wolves take her because the truth of who she was could destroy everything... including me. I should have done it long ago because looking down at her now, the tightness in my chest grew. I couldn't leave her, not like this.

Her heavy breaths filled the night, but her eyes flitted behind their lids.

62

She was beautiful, a lot more so than I'd expected, even in the human rags she wore. A bit thin for my tastes, but her breasts were full. White-blonde hair draped over her pillow, and a light trail of freckles dotted her petite nose. When I'd first laid eyes on her in the woods, this damn iced heart of mine had thumped in my chest.

She shifted in bed and a moan escaped her red lips.

Captivating.

Intoxicating.

I had to have her.

Faint vibrations in the floorboards and walls alerted me. The wolves were almost here. Outside, the trees shook violently. The woman in front of me held the key to changing everything in the Wandering Realm.

But I was getting ahead of myself, dreaming of a darker world, a place now possible, but first Guendolyn needed to survive. Ice moved through me at the thought of her harmed.

And I'd take her away, protect her the only way I knew how.

The need to protect her roared through me with intensity. I bent over, sliding my arms under her back and knees, and pulled her against me, reveling in the soft curve of her breast pressed to my chest. She was light and so warm. Heat sparked across my skin. Her vanilla, sweet scent found me and my balls tightened. Those lips, so rosy, so lush. I wanted to taste them, mark them, feel her writhing beneath me.

My pulse pounding, I craved a taste of her.

Her eyes fluttered open... bright as the bluest ocean. Gorgeous. But there was fear behind them.

Innocent and so fragile.

Fear widened them, blanching her cheeks. She was even more beautiful when frightened.

"Sleep, little wolf," I cooed, power flooding me, floating on my breath, flickering and sparking over her face.

"Y-You," she mumbled.

She shouldn't have been able to resist me, but her eyes twitched, her body convulsing. She shook her head, fighting the enchantment sweeping over her. My voice carried power over those who didn't know better, who didn't recognize the strength of my words.

An explosion of growls came from outside, and I shot a glance to the darkness.

"Sleep." Panic strained my voice, my head spinning. *Your life will never be what it once was.*

Her eyes finally slid shut, and she fell limp in my arms.

Shadows strained in the corners of the room, and from them came the sound of something being dragged across the floor. A low guttural growl, a threat.

Fear choked me, not for my safety, but for my little wolf. How in the seven hells had they found her so fast?

I spun away, feeling their heavy presence, and my muscles tensed. "Open," I growled.

Thump. Thump. Footfalls hit the wooden floor, racing up behind me.

My hackles rose, desperation bursting through me.

The air in front of me shimmered. Not waiting for a second longer, I threw myself through the opening gap of the veil between our worlds, Guendolyn tight in my arms. "Close!" I barked.

Claws dug into the flesh of my back, slicing skin.

Arching, I grunted. I stumbled on my feet, swallowed by darkness, my back burning like flames.

I spun around, terror blinding my thoughts. The portal was gone. A severed clawed arm squirmed on the forest ground, blood soiling the dirt. "Lucky that's all you lost, you bastard."

Howls pierced the night, and sweat clung to my skin. *Fuck!*

I turned and ran through the woods, holding her tightly against me and praying I wasn't making the worst mistake of my life.

"Where is she?" Ahren's stiff words hung in the air between us, his shoulders growing rigid.

"She's safe here and nothing you need to worry about," I insisted as I shoved off the couch, my muscles tense from listening to my brother's ranting. I didn't for a moment think he'd let this go—I expected him not to—but hearing the disapproval in his voice was starting to wear on me.

A cold breeze swept into the room through the open window, carrying the chill of the encroaching winter.

Ahren pushed strands of his long hair out of his face, hair as white as snow, eyes ice blue. They matched the rest of the family's, well, except for me and Grandfather, the demented king. Many believed green eyes were signs of harnessing the power of second sight. The elders said spending too much time in others' minds drove him insane and killed him in the end. But I knew the truth. Grandfather's downfall had been because he'd entered my father's mind when he shouldn't have.

Deimos, my youngest brother, lounged on the sofa, smirking, watching us for pure entertainment. He still wore his leather hunting pants, mud splattered over them. Red blood streaked his neck and spotted his white hair that was pulled into a ponytail. He'd been hunting for fairies again, those blood-sucking vermin that had wiped out a nearby village loyal to our Court, leaving only decapitated bodies. They fed on brains and eyes. Filthy things.

"Don't feed me lies," Ahren barked, his face stern, the same look as Mother's when she was furious. Same high cheekbones and pale blue eyes. "And you know it's not her safety I'm worried about. You risked too much by going into the human realm. If Father finds out…" Disappointment crossed his face as he paced across the room, his heavy, black robe dragging behind him over the black stone floor. I looked away, tired of his theatrics.

I shook those memories away and marched to the window. "I don't expect anything less from you, brother."

The Shadow Court spread out below, palaces after palaces of royals and aristocrats. Each building shone black beneath the midday sun with trims of varied colors around the roofs and windows. Down in the valley, the rest of the fae lived in small cottages. The higher anyone lived on the mountain, the more important their positioning. But I grew tired of the games, the backstabbing, the killings within the Shadow Court. Not to mention the endless battles with Ash Court. The Wandering Realms had been at war for as long as I'd been alive—twenty-five fae years.

Ahren's heavy breathing filled the room, and it irked me that he always had to oppose anything I suggested.

"You're not king yet," I announced. "You hold no power over me. And hell, you snort like a boar when you're pissed."

Deadly silence carved the space between us. Ahren's face twisted, his wry expression promising retribution. "Your childish remarks are not becoming of a prince."

"Fuck you. Is that preferable?"

"It might be entertaining to have a toy around the house," Deimos said, interrupting, his voice holding nothing but menace.

I turned on him, swallowing my anger. "Brother, you've killed every toy you were ever given. She isn't yours."

"And she's not yours, either," Ahren bit out, his mouth curling into a sneer.

My stomach warped in on itself, but fire soared through me. "I found her. She's mine," I snarled as a gust of icy air rushed into the room, pushing against my back, nudging me to step forward. I'd spent too long in her head to give her up so easily now.

"So, then, what's *your* plan?" Deimos reclined, one leg crossed over a knee, his arms stretched out on either side of the back of the couch.

"My plan is to save the girl. You know the stories of her past as well as I do. I finally tracked her down, so I took her before the wolves from Ash Court got a chance to slice her throat."

"Why? Her treachery isn't our business, and if that is her destiny—"

"Destiny," I bellowed. "Treachery? Have you forgotten what family you serve? That girl is the key to putting right what was wronged so long ago."

Ahren scoffed, forcing a laugh. "You're *not* my brother." He swung to Deimos. "Have you seen Luther? Because whoever this imposter is could never be my brother if he speaks of peace with the enemy Court."

I closed the distance to Ahren in two strides and grabbed him by the throat, my voice a growl. "You're going to be king one day. Do you intend to rule blindly or find a way to take control of both Courts under your command before every last standing fae is killed in battle? Otherwise, you may as well abdicate from the Shadow Court now."

Hate lashed his blue eyes. "Now, that's the Luther I know." With a hard shove against my hand, breaking my hold, he dragged me into a hug and pounded my shoulder with a flat hand. "We use the truth of who she really is to align the power to our side. Of course that might mean she must marry into our family so we can retain our power."

All I felt was anger boiling my blood, fury climbing over my body. Maybe I'd made a mistake telling them, but they'd have found out soon enough. We shared this palace... A location guarded and protected, enchantment instilled in the walls to make them impenetrable. This was the safest location for her, so I had to make them understand.

Ahren laughed, and a growl rolled through my chest, knowing exactly where he was going with his comment. When he said *marry into our family*, he meant *marry him*. I shoved against him, my vision blurred from the fury burning me. "She's not yours to take."

"Brother, since when are you averse to sharing?" Ahren's jaw clenched. "I haven't seen you this riled up since Father confiscated your pet eagle when you were six."

I arched a brow. "Confiscated doesn't come close to describe what he did."

"Told you not to go into Uncle's head," Deimos reminded me.

"Yeah, but we found out where he butchered that maiden girl," Ahren said.

"And yet I lost my pet." Because using my power of second sight on fae gave me away in a heartbeat, and Father forbade the use of such power in his kingdom.

"What's really going on, Luther?" Ahren asked, his voice softened for a change. "This isn't like you."

"They were going to kill her," I murmured, unwilling to share with them how I thought about her every day, how I longed to hear her voice in my mind, how I'd let myself fall so far that I'd risked everything to bring her to safety. "She holds power even if she doesn't know it yet."

"And yet you'll bring every wolf to our door because she might be special? She's been a rumor, a myth for so long... How can you be sure she is the one anyway?"

"You've both got it wrong." Deimos leaned forward on the couch, his arms pressed against his thighs. "If this girl is the rightful heir, if the stories are all correct, she's cursed. You both know the legend. If this is her, there's a reason she was sent away. Her return would cause both our enemies and even those in our family to wage war against us."

Ahren paused to consider the words, his posture still, a thumb running over the tips of his fingers as it always did when he was in deep thought.

"She won't be going near the Ash Court if I have anything to do with it."

Deimos and Ahren both stared at me with disbelief in their eyes. "Is that so?" Ahren said. "So you propose we keep her locked up forever? How will that benefit us?"

Deimos's mouth opened with a response, but the creak of the floorboards stole his words.

We stilled and swung our attention to the main door sitting slightly open.

A shadow slid behind the other side of the door, listening to us.

ELEVEN

Something nudged my ribs.

I rolled over. "Stop it. I'll get up soon."

Another poke, and I grumbled. Swear to god, I just needed a few more minutes. Eyes opened, I croaked, "Jen, if—"

But it was a cat with eyes the color of topaz crystals staring at me. Another head bump from the black feline before she spun on her feet and leapt off the bed with a thump. "Hey, what was that about?" But when I looked around, my heart raced. Wait, this wasn't my room.

Black velvet curtains framed the windows in generous folds while lace curtains billowed in the refreshing breeze. This room was elaborate from the black granite walls to the carved mahogany headboard to the golden chair near the door with black cushioning, the arms chiseled to resemble bear paws.

Meow.

I leaned over the side of the bed, peering down at the little panther. "Where am I?"

She turned away, her head and tail high, and slinked across the room before hopping up on the chair. After turning in two circles, she curled up on the seat.

Right. Pushing my legs out of bed, I still wore my blue pajamas, the ones with the cute smiling moons. Dorky, but no one saw me in them.

At the window, I shoved the curtain aside to a brilliant azure sky, free of clouds. A dark forest spread out as far as the eye could see, while mountains crowded in the distance like an army ready to strike.

Nothing seemed familiar, no sign of the castle or bridge. One minute I'd faced the man from my dreams—I rolled my eyes at how ridiculous I'd just sounded, even if he was the hottest man I'd ever seen—and the next, I'd woken up here. The rich room, the woods outside, me not at home. Yep, this was definitely a fantasy world inside my head.

I padded across the cold floorboards, unease curling in my gut. A quick scratch of the cat's head, and I stepped through the gap of the open door.

I encountered more elaborate furniture, where the black theme continued in a lounge room of sorts. I could get used to reclining in a pristine cushioned sofa with untouched silky cushions, overlooking the view. A huge stone fireplace swallowed the side wall. A thud came from behind me, and the small panther trailed at my feet.

"Decided to check up on me, I see?" I paused for her to catch up, then scratched behind her ears. She rubbed herself against my leg and led the way into a corridor with a garnet rug running the length of the hallway.

I should have been scared, but something about this place left me feeling calm. More than anything, I wanted to find out where I was because in the back of my mind, I suspected this might be the palace from my dreams. An explosion of warmth spread through my chest as I rushed along, staring at the dark walls, my bare feet tapping the cold stone floor. I ran a hand over black-and-white vases decorated in swirls and patterns that made no sense to me. Statues of lions and bears in attacking positions filled every nook. Walls barren of paintings and photos indicated a home devoid of memories.

Glass spheres hung from the ceilings on a chain, flames flickering inside them. They were mesmerizing and I had no clue how they burned.

Hiss...

I recoiled around so fast, my head spun. The little cat, her fur spiked, her tail bristled, stood on the tips of her paws inches from my leg. *Hssss.*

"What is it?" Dread skated down my spine. The whole sixth sense animals had played on my mind. What in the world did the cat see? I retreated farther along the hall until my back hit something... or someone.

My heart in my throat, a small cry fell from my lips, and I jerked around to find an ornate vase wobbling back and forth.

My fear spiked, strangling my heart. My arms jutting outward, I steadied the damn thing that stood taller than me.

"Sweet freaking Jesus." I didn't need the vase smashing. Sure, it was a dream and all... I thought. But this place just felt real somehow. My dreams usually made my head feel fuzzy, but not now; this felt like a crisp new day. Regardless, I'd seen enough movies to know that making noise brought out the bad guys.

Hiss.

Behind me I found a dog sitting in the middle of the corridor, a cross between a German Shepherd and a Doberman, easily reaching my waist. Fluffy and golden in color, he stared at me with the biggest puppy eyes that melted me.

"Hey, where did you come from?" I asked in a singsong voice.

Little Panther backed away. I glanced around, and only the door I'd emerged from stood there. Moving closer to the dog, I reached out a hand. "Where were you hiding?"

A spark of electricity raced down my arms, and the air around the animal shimmered. Then his fur faded into thin air, vanishing, leaving behind a brown pelt, ears narrowing, stretching to sharp points, a long, thin tail whipping behind him with a barbed club on the end.

My mouth dropped open.

I couldn't breathe, couldn't comprehend what I'd just seen. My feet slipped backward. I had to leave. My heart thumped while somewhere behind me the cat hissed again. She knew better than me. This wasn't a cute dog, but a freaking hellhound.

His ears flattened, two rows of teeth bared.

A whimper fell from my lips.

Don't run from dogs, they say. They smell fear, they say.

To hell with sayings. I was about to die, so I catapulted myself away from the beast, a scream shoving forward. Heavy footfalls pounded the rug behind me. Heavy breaths, a snarl that promised my death.

My feet slammed the ground and a scream tore free past my throat. This felt too real to be a dream... God, I was going to die here and never wake up again. I'd heard that somewhere. Die in a dream and you're a goner.

Hissing buzzed right past my ear, and a black blur zipped in front of me. Panther had grown black bat wings, and she rushed ahead, beating them furiously.

Wait! Cat wings?

Nothing made sense right now, nothing but running for my life, knowing somehow that if the hound caught me, I'd be dog food.

Deep guttural threats thundered closer, and my skin rippled.

Panicked, I darted around the curve of the hallway, desperately searching for a way to escape.

Several doors lay ahead, and every muscle in my body clenched.

A sudden tug on the fabric of my pajama pants pulled them down.

I cried out, grappling to keep my pants on. "I swear to god if you eat me, I'll haunt you for eternity."

Panther hissed at the goddamn dog, and I grabbed the closest weapon: a golden statue of a rodent that weighed a ton, even though only the size of my head. I hurled it at the mutt.

Black eyes pierced my soul. He leapt out of the way inches from the statue slamming into his head and growled. The rodent hit the ground and cracked in two halves.

I threw myself at the nearest door, my hand scrambling with the handle, and fell through. The bat-cat swooshed inside just before I slammed it shut.

One hand tugging up my pants, the other shoved to the door, my heart pounding.

Thump.

The door shook, its hinges groaning. I flinched but stayed there, plastering a shoulder against the door, holding it, terrified the hound would chew his way in here. What dogs had two rows of teeth anyway?

Shaking like a leaf, I reached down to the back of my pants, finding a gaping hole. That shithead could have ripped my leg off. I could barely make sense of what that dog was, let alone what was going on in this weird building.

Meow.

Bat-cat fluttered to the ground, her little black wings folding and tucking against her body, blending into her fur.

"What exactly are you?" I crouched low and scratched her head, then slid my hand down her back as she arched, my fingers reaching over to her side, the thin bones of her wings sitting under her fur perfectly snug. They were real, all right. She curled against my hand, purring, and strolled deeper into a large room.

Several black couches sat in a U-shape, facing statues of beautiful women dressed in warrior Xena-like skirts, holding shields across their chests, carved into the sides and mantel of the fireplace.

Tapestries of lions and wolves caught in battle covered one wall, while an enormous butterfly display case hung from another. Wings of all colors...

silver, mauves, coral, apple green, and so many more sat pinned to the white board. Butterflies? Couldn't be. They were twenty times larger with a slightly transparent hue. Each was pinned to the board, on display. What flying insect carried such huge and beautiful wings?

A thump crashed into the door, the dog scratching to get in.

Adrenaline pulsed through my veins. With hurried steps, I rushed across the windowless room to another set of dark doors, far from the hellhound. The handle was icy to the touch, and I pushed it open, heading out just as the mutt growled furiously. Shutting the door to the room quickly, I retreated.

Except I hadn't stepped into a room, but some kind of indoor bridge. Wooden planks ran across the floor and an arched ceiling, tiled in the color of pearls overhead. Beautiful. But when I glanced to the waterfall cascading down a rockface to my right, my mouth fell open. I rushed over, and I hit a glass wall enclosing the beauty.

Sunlight poured in over the edge of the cliff. Was there a way out of this place? I'd never climb that sheer rockface safely, but maybe I'd find a way behind this glass.

Below, there was only darkness from my vantage point. Panther strolled past me, rubbing herself along the wall where glass globes sat on small pillars. Real fire flames flicked inside them.

Where was I?

I moved with fast steps along the wooden bridge that curved around the waterfall only to come upon another set of doors, one slightly ajar.

Faint voices floated from inside, and my stomach clenched. Definitely male. Quick steps took me closer, and I pressed an ear to the wood listening, while Panther looked up at me.

I pressed a finger to my mouth, praying she kept quiet.

"She won't be going anywhere near the Ash Court if I have anything to do with it," a masculine voice insisted, and I recognized him at once. The voice from my head, the man from the twisted woods who scared the hell out of me. And now I couldn't breathe and it felt like someone was choking me.

"Right?" another male responded, his voice deeper, more authoritative. "So you propose we keep her locked up forever? How will that benefit us?"

Were they talking about me? What in the world was Ash Court?

Panther shifted to head into the room, and I lunged after her, snatching her into my arms. The floorboards groaned under my step.

I clutched Bat-cat to my chest, not moving an inch. No one said a word from inside for a long moment.

"I know it's you, Guendolyn," *he* called out.

Hell!

TWELVE

Shoulders back, I sucked in a breath and pushed into the room, my chin high. The first rule of intimidation was looking confident, even if I was crapping myself on the inside. And what was the worst that could happen? I'd wake up from this insane dream?

Panther purred in my arms as I stalked into the room.

I raised my head to find three men looking my way. My feet stopped working, as did my heart, because these guys... Sweet Jesus!

They were handsome... impossibly handsome. Pale skin. Red lips. Eyes full of sin.

I was helpless... and standing here in my pajamas left my cheeks burning up. But with their presence came a desire swirling inside me when I should have spun on my heels and marched the hell out of there, remembering the sexy man's words back in the twisted woods.

My attention lingered on him with his midnight hair draped over his shoulders. His presence left me covered in shivers.

When he smiled, his amber eyes lit up. He had something about him that made me swoon on my feet, left me staring, trying to work out what made him so perfect.

These three were unlike anyone I'd seen before. The tall guy stared at me with a crooked grin like I wasn't exactly what he'd expected. Long, white hair draped over his shoulders, adding a strange allure to him I couldn't quite work out.

The stranger on the couch wore his white hair loosely pulled into a ponytail. His shirt sat gaping open at the throat, splattered with a spray of blood. I should be afraid, well aware of how cruel guys could be.

"W-Where a-am I?" My voice shook in front of them. I wasn't the best around guys, even in my dreams apparently. Sucking at this was my specialty.

"You're home, little wolf. Well, not quite, but close enough." He bit his lower lip like he was nervous, and my heart clenched.

He strolled toward me in a deep green sleeveless robe over a shirt, tied together with a thick leather band around his waist, and dark pants. Already a smile played on his face, and he reminded me of Robin Hood. When he stretched his hand out to scratch the cat's head, my gaze raked over his strong forearms, corded muscles that could overpower me. Everything about him was dangerous... Yet all I could think about were the things we'd said to each other while he'd been a mere voice in my head. All the promises he made.

"You'll like it here."

His voice... melted me. It was the one attribute that belonged to the guy who comforted me after Noah had tried to rape me, who'd been there when I'd felt so alone in the world. But something about this dark-haired stranger stirred anxiety within me, a thick knot forming in my throat.

Panther leapt out of my arms, her wings extending in an instant, and she jumped onto his shoulder, sitting there like a parrot. With a shake, her wings tucked away and she rubbed her head against his.

"I see you've met Viper."

"Never seen a flying cat before, but cute name." Viper was the type of name I'd expect a guy to call his cat. "Sure beats Cujo in the hallway." I snorted a laugh and regretted it at once, my cheeks burning up. *Great job, Guen.*

"Cujo?" He arched a brow.

"The hell dog in that movie who attacks everyone?"

"Think she must be talking about Sir Wolf-A-Lot," the guy on the couch murmured. His voice was so deep, it cut through my heart.

"Fancy name for a hellhound who almost ate my pants," I blurted out, garnering no reaction aside from a cheeky grin from Amber Eyes scratching the cat on his shoulder.

Silence.

I felt their gazes on me, hungry eyes sliding over my moon pajamas, covering me in electric tingles. The tall guy was beyond good-looking and why was he wearing a cape? Everything about these three told me to run, but instead, my mind danced with other possibilities. Insane things like flirting and finding out who they were because anything was possible in a dream.

"So," I said, slicing through the awkwardness in the room, my voice deciding at that moment to break. "Is someone going to tell me what's going on? How I got here?"

Hunger burned in the tall one's eyes, blue as ice, and I lowered my gaze from his. I ought to be wary of him, I felt it in my bones.

"Yes, Luther," the stranger on the couch with the cutest, most devilish grin teased. "You going to tell her? Today might turn more amusing than I thought."

Luther? I stared at the man in front of me, the voice who I'd been talking to for years. Every day I'd expect to hear his voice, even if he annoyed me. I'd gotten used to having him there for me. But standing in front of him now, I kept losing my thoughts.

I rolled this name over in my mind, liking how it sounded. Luther. Dark and sexy. "Why didn't you tell me your name before when—?"

His hand took mine, his touch warm but firm, and he dragged me in a rushed walk across the room. Viper flew off in the opposite direction, while I stumbled after the man.

"Come, you must be starved."

We moved at a fast pace to another door at the other end of the room, the two others watching us with curiosity.

"I'm not hungry," I began, preferring to chat about who everyone was, but the moment Luther pulled open the enormous mahogany door, the waft of cake had my stomach rumbling. "Well, maybe a bite. I'm curious to see how food tastes here."

He looked down at me strangely. "You're suspicious?"

"Should I be?"

He guided me to a round table with seating for at least ten people. Designs of animals were carved into the molding of the high ceiling, vases flowing with white and yellow flowers filled the shelves, and statues of more animals adorned the corners.

"Fancy dining room," I said. "We usually just eat on the couch while watching TV."

"Take a seat." He shut the door behind us, closing the others out, and a chill hit my middle. Why was he shutting us in here alone?

He strolled across the room to a small side door, vanishing inside. I toyed with the idea of heading back the way I came. I wasn't sure who to trust here.

I looked out past the floor-to-ceiling windows to the ocean of trees, to the snowcapped mountains, the sun sitting high, meaning it had to be around noon.

The view was extraordinary and made the perfect postcard shot. Where was my phone when I needed it?

Footfalls sounded as Luther marched back into the room, carrying a bowl. He placed it in front of me on the table. "The kitchen is preparing more food for you."

Stew sat in the bowl with large pieces of carrots and potatoes and meat, the aroma overwhelming and delicious. Taking the spoon, I flopped in the seat and dug right in when an older man in black clothes and a white apron rushed out to bring me a plate of freshly cut bread and butter. His face remained stern, and I caught him sneaking a look up at me... curious to see who I was.

I smiled, but he lowered his gaze and marched back to the kitchen. Okay, strange.

I had no idea how hungry I was, but I grabbed a piece of bread, smeared it with butter, and ate like I'd been starved for days.

Luther sat one chair away, reclining. I pushed the bread plate to him and he helped himself.

"This is good, especially for a dream. I mean, technically, I can eat what I want without getting fat, right?" I pushed another spoonful into my mouth.

"You think this is a dream?"

I raised my gaze to him. "This is all in my head. Just like you."

"You think I'm just in your head?" He took a bite of the bread in his hand.

His question threw me. "When you say it like that, I don't know."

The servant returned with a silver dish piled high with slices of steaming roast, surrounded by vegetables, as well as a plate of various cheeses and fruit.

Everything smelled divine. "Thank you," I called out as the man rushed away.

"Eat up," Luther murmured, watching me with curiosity in his gaze.

"This is a lot." But I didn't stop and filled my plate. "So let's say this isn't a dream as you say. Why did you bring me here? What do you want?"

He just sat there, watching me eat. His lips twitched each time I opened mine to take another bite. He was enjoying himself, enjoying just staring.

"Enjoying the show?" I asked.

"It's a fascinating one."

Everything he said was deliberate and intended to affect me. Just like the things he'd say in my mind. Before, his voice had been enough to leave me breathless, but now merely looking at his full lips undid me, the intensity of his eyes. I kept having thoughts I shouldn't have. Like how his lips might feel against mine, if someone like me even interested a man like him.

"Is it good?" he asked, continuing to stare at me.

"Delicious."

Sitting in such close proximity, all I could do was admire him, those perfect angles, the square jawline... Flawless.

"Why didn't you tell me your name whenever we spoke?"

"Names come with power and you never know who's listening," he said bluntly.

"Listening to our thoughts?" I huffed and dug back into my food. "As if."

His eyebrows arched, but he just ate his sliced bread, amusement behind his irises.

We'd spoken every day for years, his presence my only companion. He was the only one there for me when shit had gone sideways. It was always me who'd opened up, never him, but he'd listened... had always listened.

So how well did he know me? Because he wasn't what I'd expected.

"Am I what you expected?" I felt stupid asking the question and lowered my attention to the food. "That's dumb. Forget it."

"Not at all. You are... like a storm that's burst into my home and nothing will ever be the same again."

I stared at him, lowering the bread from my mouth. "Wow, really? I'm that bad?"

"Why do you consider that bad?" His lips tensed, but he remained reclined in his seat, studying me.

I rolled my eyes. "Forgot. You answer everything with a riddle."

"They're not riddles. You're not listening."

With more food in my mouth, I answered, "Because I'm naive."

His lips curled into a smirk, and that right there was exactly how I'd pictured him every time he'd made such comments to me. He'd always clearly been dripping in arrogance, but I'd never expected to react to him so insatiably. To see chemistry behind his eyes, an invitation to get closer. My heart beat harder.

"Who are you really, Luther?" I bit into a piece of roast when the servant returned with gold decorated glasses filled with something reddish and a plate of purple cake.

I smiled at the older man, who nodded and left with haste. Chasing the food down with grape juice, I kept looking up at Luther, who watched every move I made, never missing a beat, not even when I picked a crumb off my pajama top. He looked at me as if he knew my desires, my wishes, my fears, leaving me trembling. When he was in my head, was it only my words he sensed, or everything?

"In the Wandering Realms, I'm the prince of darkness, a lord, a master." He spoke so smoothly, but beneath his words stirred power. "My older brother is the heir to the throne, while my younger brother and I will remain princes by his side."

"Throne? Who is your dad if he's king? What country are we in?" I wasn't sure my mind was this elaborate to make up such stuff.

"You still seem to think this is a dream."

I offered him a crooked smirk. "Well, isn't it?"

"You'd wager your life on that?" His mouth tightened. He climbed to his feet, but I stood with him, my pulse racing.

"Don't go. Tell me more. What is the Ash Court?" He'd make me wait when I had so many questions.

His eyes narrowed, his breathing quickened. "Spying is an offense punishable by death in the Shadow Court."

I studied his beautiful face, waiting for him to break into a smile, to laugh, something to indicate he was joking. Except his gaze darkened.

"How much did you hear?" he demanded to know.

"J-Just that part," I croaked, clearing my throat. We both stood there, not a word spoken. My mouth was parched and I wracked my brain for something to say. What didn't he want me to have heard? That they were going to keep me locked up forever?

"Come," he said. "You'll wash and then I'll properly introduce you to my brothers."

"I'm perfectly fine." But my words went unheard as he stormed toward the kitchen like a charging bull.

"Hey, I said *no*," I called out, standing my ground.

He halted and looked at me over his shoulder, his brows pulling together. "You seem to have forgotten your place."

My jaw clamped together. He was a man used to getting his way, to others doing as he ordered. I knew this... had heard it in his voice so many times, but I kept my head raised, not hiding my defiance.

"I don't belong to you."

He licked his lips and the fire in his eyes ignited. "You were always mine, little wolf. You just never knew it."

CHAPTER

THIRTEEN

"Don't touch me," I yelled, batting away the servants' hands.

Two women, older than me, tugged and pulled at my pajama pants and top. It was bad enough they'd dragged me through the kitchen, down a hallway, and into another room, but now I had to take a bath? They each wore a floor length black medieval-style dress with short, flared sleeves, and an elastic waist.

And Luther leaned a shoulder against the doorway, smirking, enjoying himself. Was he going to watch as they stripped me?

"I'm not going in there. My pajamas are staying on." I stumbled from their reach and eyed the freestanding metal tub with golden clawed feet, filled with water. At home, I'd jump at the chance, as we only had a shower, but I didn't do communal baths. I wanted to be sick.

"Mistress, you need a wash and to wear proper clothes. Not those..." The redhead flapped her hand toward my pajamas, scrunching up her nose. "Those are not fit for the princes' eyes. They'll be burned."

"No!" I squeaked. "They're from Jen. Don't you dare." I wrapped my arms around my middle, recoiling. Jen had gifted these to me on my last birthday, insisting I'd look cute in smiling moon PJs. I'd disagreed but had never had the heart to tell her, yet I wore them regardless.

The brunette with bouncy curls lunged from my left, and I darted in the opposite direction, swerving around a chair, my sight on the doorway. I'd bowl right through Luther if he didn't get out of the way.

82

I threw myself past him, but his hand lashed out across my stomach, and roughly swooped me off the ground, cradling me like I was a child in his strong arms.

I lost my breath from the sudden impact, being so close to him, from the solid hardness of his muscles, but it didn't stop me from driving a fist against his chest. "Put me down. I'm serious."

Not a word. He carried me across the room and dunked me straight into the tub, clothes and all. Lukewarm water swallowed me. I splashed and sat upright, water sloshing everywhere. I wiped my eyes, fury bubbling in my veins.

"Who do you think you are?" I yelled.

Luther stared down at me, his gaze laser-beaming to my chest. My nipples pushed against the wet pajama top, and my arms twitched to cover myself.

"This is my home and that means following my rules." He ripped his attention from me and marched out of the room, his boots hitting the tiled floor before shutting the door behind him with an echoing thunk.

"Asshole." My fingers gripped the edge of the metal tub.

The maids were on me in a second, both pulling the wet sleeves of my top, dragging the rest up and over my head.

"Hey! Don't take my pajamas."

One lathered my hair roughly, taking out her revenge on me refusing her orders. Water sloshed over my face, getting into my nose and mouth.

"You're either a very brave or stupid girl," the red-haired woman murmured.

"How do you figure?" I winced at their roughness, searching for my top outside the tub.

"You raised a hand to the prince. That's instant death." Shadows danced over her face from the sphere lights, but fear pulled at her expression.

"Is there anything you can do here that won't lead to *instant death*?"

The brunette grinned, her eyes laughing at my comment.

The red-haired woman heaved at my pants. "Take them off," she barked, fierceness behind her gaze, her hands already pulling on the fabric. I shuffled out of them, sliding them down my hips, and yanked them off me. I sat in the water naked and curled my knees to my chest, feeling vulnerable, ashamed. She stared at my bare body with a smug grin. My hips were too big, my chest not big enough, and I had no waist. I pushed their hands off me. "Let me wash myself. I can do this.

Just don't destroy my clothes," I pleaded, not meeting their judging eyes.

"Fine," the redhead huffed. "I'll get them washed." With a flick of the soap into the tub, she hurried out of the room, her steps heavy despite a slight limp. When the door shut, I raised my gaze to the brunette.

"She has a snake's tongue but is harmless. She can't let the princes down. None of us can." The rest of her words went unsaid...

The maid sat on the edge of the tub folding several towels, and in a way, she reminded me of Jen. There was an easiness about her, a caring nature, even if she wasn't the most tactful person in the world.

"So, he's really a prince? Or..."

"Absolutely, mistress."

"You don't need to call me that. Makes it sound like I'm having an affair." I found the soap in the water, rolling it over and over in my hands, suds building and spreading over my hands. "And his brothers, one is to be the king?"

She nodded. "Be wary of him most of all."

Dread cut across my gut. The heir's icy eyes had carried a savage hunger and my instincts screamed to not trust him.

Her cheeks paled, and she gasped with panic. "Forgive me. I never should have said that." Her attention sailed to the door and back, panic buckling her posture, her hands gripping the towel. What had the princes done to scare her so much?

I reached over, laying a wet hand on hers. "It's okay. I won't say anything. Promise." In truth, the more time I spent in this world, the more I questioned if this was a dream. And with that came a fear that squeezed the life out of me. Such places didn't exist, but I'd seen the kingdom my whole life through my dreams. Even once in an alley. It looked as real as the buildings back home. I wasn't sure of much lately, even my own identity.

"Do you know who I am?" I murmured, drawing back into the water, lathering myself.

She stared at me with her brows pulling together. "Should I? You're just another woman the princes bring to their palace. It isn't our place to question such things."

I splashed the soap from my arms, unsure what to make of her response. So they brought others here regularly... I wasn't a fool, knowing what she implied, but her words left me torn, my insides cold that Luther had had others here just like me.

The red-haired lady stepped back into the room, distracting me. Deep violet fabric draped over her arm, satin and spiderweb-like. Her bulging eyes locked on me. "You're not ready yet?" she snapped.

"Give her a few moments, Lys. She's just a child." She spoke almost like she pitied me, as if she knew my fate. I wasn't being sacrificed... was I?

I ran the soap over my legs before the woman with red hair and redder eyes manhandled me again. Out of the tub, I dried myself as they watched me, and then they drowned me with the dress.

My arms shoved in the air, the towel tumbled down from around my body. The women poked and pulled, shuffling the outfit down over my head and dragging it down my body. Soft satin brushed over my skin, tight across my chest, the skirt made of several layers that fell to my feet. Long sleeves sat off the shoulder, lacy and loose down to my knuckles.

Taking in a deep breath came with effort. "I think it's too small. I need the next size up."

I ran a hand over my chest, squished into the dress, the tops of my breasts sticking out like perfect half-balls. On the bright side, this made it look like I had bigger breasts than I did, and that was a bonus in my books any day. I shifted the material around my waist, but the red-haired woman slapped my hand.

"Do you wish to ruin the gown?"

"It's too tight. I need to breathe." The deep violet gown shimmered like a night's sky. For the first time, I had a thin waist. Maybe sacrificing breathing was worth it to look like Barbie.

"Sit," the bossy woman ordered, and I did as she instructed, the taut material digging into me, making bending close to impossible. They combed my hair while I grimaced and gritted my teeth, convinced I'd have no hair left after they were finished. The brunette stood in front of me and placed a golden band around my head, settling it high on my brow. I reached up, fingers fumbling over the thin band made of lots of small joined stars.

She then pinched my cheeks hard.

"Ouch." I flinched away. "What're you doing?" My face still stung from her attack. "Why would you do that?"

"To bring color to your face, girl." She rolled her eyes like this was common practice.

"That's why blush was invented." Damn, my cheeks hurt like hell.

The red-haired woman kneeled in front of me and pushed my feet into pointy, black flat shoes that hugged a bit too tightly around my toes. She shook her head. "You say strange things. Now up. We need to go." On her feet, she grasped my hand and hauled me out into the hall, dragging me with haste.

Dark stone walls, fire spheres, and rugs. No paintings to decorate the hall. Even the statues were absent in this part of the mansion.

With each step, the fabric of the skirt split from ankle to mid-thigh across each leg, revealing too much leg.

"Wait. I'm not ready," I insisted, pulling against her, straining to make out in the dark where she dragged me.

"You're more than ready," she murmured while wrenching me by her death-grip. We passed so many doors in this palace, I couldn't remember how to get back to the bedroom if I tried.

I stumbled after her in our mad rush, where there wasn't even a mirror to view how I looked, but there was a bigger problem.

"Stop. I'm not ready," I said.

We paused in front of a door and the woman faced me, a sneer twisting her lips. "You won't last, none of them do, so just follow the rules and get this over with. Never say *no* to the princes. Never talk back. Never insult them."

I stilled, my mind reeling from her instructions. "I can't say *no* to anything?"

"No one says *no* to them. Do you understand?" Her voice grew stern.

The idea of them having such control of me was terrifying.

She glared at me before pushing the door open. I blinked into the brightly lit room.

"Smile and do as they say," she whispered, shoving a hand into my back.

I stumbled into the room on wobbly legs. She slammed the door, closing me in there alone. I rushed to grab the handle, trying it, but it was locked.

"Yeah, thanks for that," I mumbled.

A light breeze brushed through my wet hair, down my arms, and flut-tering through the layers of fabric from my skirt, the touch like tender fingers running over my legs.

I glanced around the narrow room with a long, wooden table and a dozen chairs made of deep cherry wood.

A battle scene between bears was carved in the mantel over the fire-place. Flames crackled and spat embers, casting long shadows over the rug woven with intricate patterns. Tapestries hung off the rest of the walls, each depicting landscapes. Men on horses hunting in the woods. Castles glimmering beneath the moonlight. I stepped in front of one image... a bridge suspended between two mountains. Just like the one from my dreams. I'd always thought the kingdom had to have been a special place. Why else would one have to climb a mountain and cross such a long bridge to reach it?

Across the room, double doors suddenly opened, sunlight pouring into the room. I flinched, my heart slamming into my ribcage.

Luther stood there, his expression full of surprise. Intrigue. A smile crept on his face, and the air in the room thickened.

Heat seared my cheeks. Any intention I had of demanding the truth and forcing the point until the princes relented dwindled.

Luther's gaze sharpened on me with that raw hunger I'd seen his brothers wear earlier. His stare was the kind I'd expect from a predator stalking me.

He rocked on his feet toward me, tall and so handsome. For those few moments, as he closed the distance between us, he'd captivated me. The power he carried. The breadth of his shoulders. The intensity of his stare, his gaze roaming over my body, his lips curling into a devilish grin.

Something about him drew me toward him like we were bound by an invisible string, drawing us closer and closer together.

"You look spectacular." Leaning in, a brush of his breath over my cheek left me quivering.

He smelled masculine and of musk, and my heart thumped so hard, its thunder beat in my ears.

"The fabric of your dress is feather-light, following every delicious curve. Looking like this..." He shuddered, his hands on my arms tightening, but he never finished his sentence. He was holding back, but why?

"What's wrong?" I whispered.

His eyes narrowed with intensity, as if whatever was on his mind was overwhelming, consuming. "What do you want to hear? That I can't get you out of my thoughts? How I want you pinned to the wall, beneath me?"

Fear should have pulsed through me, and I ought to have been scared, but arousal settled through me instead. With those few words, a tickle stroked my inner thighs, and I pictured myself beneath him, begging him to show me how to forget the world. I yearned to touch him, to see him fully. I'd never felt this way before, not to this intensity. I'd never had a guy speak to me in a way that left me too paralyzed to respond.

"You're not ready for me. I see that now." He gripped my hand and drew me toward the balcony, our connection electrifying, leaving me breathless, unable to think about anything except his fingers on me.

But his words hurt. He thought I wasn't ready to be with him? That I was too young, too naive, too... too what?

Except I was letting him get to me, allowing him to play with my mind.

Swallowing hard, I followed him onto the balcony, a red-tiled oversized ledge with a black metal fence around us, formed into roses and thorny stems.

An ocean of green and blues and whites burst across the forest landscape beyond. "Wow, it's incredible from up here."

"Best view in the kingdom."

I glanced over to him, my heart still racing, my body tingling all over.

"Come. Take a seat."

Behind him, his two brothers reclined in grand golden chairs. Mesmerizing eyes. Lips parted. The whitest hair that seemed to gleam in the sunlight.

A rush of air and something nudged my hip. I turned to find no one, but when I glanced down, the blackest irises met mine. Pointy ears, short brown fur, and his pointy tail stilled. The hellhound!

My stomach dropped like a brick sinking to the bottom of the ocean. Instinct flexed through me. I flinched against Luther, my hands grappling for him, my fists holding on to his shirt while I shoved myself behind him. Not my finest moment, but I didn't need that beast ripping me apart.

The two princes laughed. Yep, they'd watch me get eaten without breaking a sweat to help, and I hated them for enjoying this moment.

"He won't hurt you," Luther insisted. I didn't believe him.

"Sir Wolf-A-Lot wouldn't hurt a fairy," Luther cooed and reached over, scratching the mutt's head.

"Is that meant to make me feel better?" I murmured, then remembered the maid's warning about dealing with the princes. But I didn't care, not when my heart pounded so hard, it might break through my ribcage.

The mischievous prince with his hair pulled in a ponytail reclined back more in his throne-like seat, watching me.

"It's true," he said. "That's why he's our pet dog now. He runs away from things he ought to hunt. Luther came up with the childish name, but now the animal won't answer to anything else. It's like he enjoys mocking us each time we call him."

The dog stared at me intently and not with loving eyes. Yep, he saw me as a meal.

Luther's hand was on mine. "You're safe. I give you my word."

I loathed that they saw me helpless, scared.

"Sit," the tallest prince commanded in a low tone, gesturing to the small stool in front of them.

I raised a brow, but with a push at my back from Luther, I moved to my designated seating, gritting my jaw.

In my perfect gown, I hunched low on the small wooden chair with only three legs, my knees tight and raised from the low seat. Gripping the fabric of my gown, I kept shifting around, annoyed I didn't get a fancy chair. Knowing my luck, this thing would break under me, and I'd flash them all gloriously.

Sir Wolf-A-Lot padded toward me and sat less than a foot from me, staring at me as if he might lunge at any moment and bite my head off. My hands shook while I clenched the fabric tighter.

Ignoring the sweat rolling down my back and the mutt who probably smelled my fear and was licking his lips, I stared up at the three princes on their regal seats.

"Why don't I get a proper chair?" I blurted out, not wanting to be at the same head height as Cujo.

"Why do you think?" Luther asked in a serious voice.

"So you can feel superior." I smirked at him.

The prince with a ponytail laughed. "She has a spine. Let's keep her."

Luther wore a grim expression. "I'll get her a different chair." He huffed and got to his feet, leaving the balcony.

I turned away, staring out at the landscape, still clueless as to where I was, and I hugged myself over the fact that I had to deal with this stupidity, these games. A test of obedience? Trying to see if I'd sit there like an idiot or stand up for myself?

Moments later, he returned with a chair and I slid into it once he set it down, crossing my legs and facing the three of them. Now I felt less of a peasant and more like someone at an interview.

"Guendolyn, let me introduce you to my two brothers," Luther began, and my mind pulsed at the name he'd called me like he knew more about me than I did.

He glanced over to the tallest man. "Ahren Lorcayn, the eldest and heir to the Shadow Court. Next to him is Deimos Lorcayn, my younger brother and third prince of the throne."

They all stared at me as if waiting for me to introduce myself. "I'm Guen."

"It's Guendolyn," Luther corrected with a smirk, to which I furrowed my brow.

"It's Guen." My voice rose more than I'd anticipated, rousing Cujo into a low, gravelly growl.

"Never talk back," the maid had said.

"Guendolyn," Luther warned.

"The thing is..." Ahren leaned forward, his ice blue eyes invading my space, spearing through me. "Everyone knows who you are here, that your name is Guendolyn, what you represent... Everyone except you."

My defiance crushed down around me. To have him speak as if he knew me, of things they kept from me, left me feeling hollow, like someone had stolen everything I owned while I wasn't looking.

"I know of your dreams of our land. How it possesses you to paint what you see," Ahren declared.

"What do you know?" I whispered, terrified of what secrets had been kept from me.

"That you have fae blood in your veins, that Guendolyn is a name that has passed over the lips of most in the kingdom, that you're the lost girl taken from our world."

I blinked a few times at Ahren, waiting for my brain to catch up, for the wheels to make sense of what I'd heard. Breaths came too fast while the three of them watched me like somehow Ahren's words were real. Fae? Really? Taken from their world?

Yep, I'd finally broken down. My brain had snapped, and I'd watched way too many fantasy movies.

A nervous laugh fell from my lips. "Well, if I were a fae, I'd have found my wings long ago, my ears would be pointy, I'd... I don't know, what else do fae do?"

There was no crack in their stiff demeanors, and it felt surreal to speak so seriously about such things with three men who belonged on the covers of magazines, who left me swooning.

"Only fairies have wings." Deimos scoffed like I ought to have known that tidbit. "And you don't want to go anywhere near them. Now, as for pointy ears"—he shrugged—"some fae have them; others don't. It's more of a family line attribute."

My mouth gaped open, unsure how to take his response. Luther had implied earlier that this wasn't a dream, but if he'd spoken the truth, then what? I'd somehow come into a fantasy land of fae and fairies and kings?

Sir Wolf-A-Lot licked himself loudly. Oh, right, and freaking shape-shifting hellhounds.

The servant from earlier came in carrying a silver platter and handed Ahren a drink in a jewel-studded crystal goblet, then the other two princes, then me. I accepted and drank two mouthfuls, quenching my dried throat. "So, I'm a lost person from this world, you say." I pressed the goblet to my lips, finishing the refreshing minty iced tea. The man refilled my drink from a golden pitcher.

"Something like that," Luther added.

I shifted in my seat. They might have been the most beautiful men in the world, but they lied through their teeth and kept secrets. It lay behind their gazes, their clipped responses.

"If I'm from this place, where are my parents?" I asked.

Something shifted behind Ahren's eyes but vanished as quickly as it had come. "There's no news on your parents. We've searched." The corner of his eye twitched.

Liar. Big, fat liar.

My breath came too fast, and I couldn't hold back the words. "If you don't intend to tell me the truth, don't mock me with lies," I retorted. "Speak honestly."

Never insult them.

Ahren bristled, his nostrils flaring as he glared at me with narrowing eyes. "Do not challenge me," he roared, his hands gripping the arms of his chair. "On your knees."

Fear strangled me, and I looked to Luther for help, but he sat back with a curious expression, goddamn enjoying himself.

I shouldn't have said anything when I had absolutely nothing nice to say, but the response flew out. "Like I told your brother, I'm not yours to control. You hide so much behind that smile, but like someone once told me, we all have shadows. I'd rather we speak the truth."

Never say no to the princes.

Ahren shot to his feet, his expression twisted and warped, darkening, but his gaze never left me. He marched closer, and panic soared through me. I jolted to my feet, but he moved too fast. His hand shot out and seized me by the throat, squeezing.

I grasped for his hand, pulling at the fingers that blocked my breathing. And terror... real terror locked around me like a straitjacket. This was real and this madman would kill me. Tears sprung to my eyes.

"Little girl, you keep pushing me," he spat. "Next time, you'll learn how to fly off my balcony."

FOURTEEN

A scream tore from somewhere in the distance behind the walls of the bedroom.

I shuddered. The terrible sound came every now and then for the last hour, drowning me in images of the princes torturing someone... picturing how it could be me next.

I paced from the locked door to the lush bed I'd woken in that morning. The servants had locked me in here at Ahren's furious command, terror etched on their faces for their own safety. Except I'd been warned, and I hadn't listened. Stupid.

Didn't make me hate him less. I hated all of them, and more than anything, I prayed I'd wake up from this horrible dream. I'd had enough of this pretend world.

Except the worrying ache in my stomach told me otherwise. I shook my head, refusing to believe this was real. It couldn't be...

Images of Noah hurting me in his car burned across my mind, pushing and pushing. He'd thought he could take what he wanted from me.

Fingers pulling at my sweater.

Lips clamped on my mouth.

Stop, Noah!

But he never did... Never listened to me.

I hugged myself, trying to shake away the memories.

Memories that were scars on my mind, deep and painful, hateful things that reminded me how alone I felt in this world.

I'd begged Luther to take me from that life... just as he'd promised he would, but if this was the world he'd brought me to, was it any better?

For so long, I'd dreamed of a fantasy world and wondered what lay behind my dreams...needing an escape. But now, all I thought of was home. To hear Jen bossing me around, Oliver saying crappy stuff, and Luke being the voice of reason over dinner. I didn't miss school, especially not after my last encounter with Noah. Those jerks never let anything slide. My mind started to spiral down into that darkness, but I shoved it aside, marching back toward the tiny window.

I didn't miss Antonio and sure as hell never wanted to see Sabrina again.

I'd only been here a day, but it felt like a week.

I was the girl who wanted to fit in. To be normal. To be accepted.

I was the girl needing to understand who I was. Where I'd come from.

I was the girl dying to find my real parents.

The broken girl.

Ahren said they'd searched for my parents. I didn't believe him, but he'd revealed that indeed, I belonged here.

Hours passed.

Tired of pacing, I slept most of the day, and someone must have come into the room to leave my smiley moon pajamas, freshly washed and laid on my bed.

The sun had long ago dipped behind the mountains, and a single fiery globe flickered in the corner of the room, suspended from the ceiling, tossing shadows about. I padded toward the window, where the breeze rushed in, sending the lace curtain into a flurry and chilling my skin.

Outside, the drop from my window was a fifty feet drop into woodland, and my stomach lurched. I'd never get out. Forest spread outward on either side of the black stone building, revealing nothing else. Even if I tied all the bedsheets together, I'd never make it all the way down. An urgency pulsed through me that I'd die if I remained imprisoned in this room.

Are you hurt? Luther's voice startled me. I turned toward the room, expecting to find him there, my gut tight with anticipation... betraying me when I found myself alone and his voice lingering in my head.

Are you mad?

I instinctively touched my neck where his brother had choked me. "A bit."

A bit hurt or a bit mad?

"Both."

My brother has a temper, but he'd never endanger your life.

"Could have fooled me. He threatened to throw me over the balcony." My voice climbed, my breaths racing more than they should have.

You were very confrontational...

I bristled, my mouth gaping open at his comment, but I shut it back up because it wasn't like he was standing in the room with me. "Are you kidding me?"

This isn't like your realm, little wolf. Speaking out of place can get you killed here. There was almost a thread of concern behind his voice, like he feared the trouble I'd get into by not thinking things through.

"Well, I'm sick and tired of the secrets. Why won't you tell me who I am and where my parents are?"

Silence fell. At least he had the decency not to lie to me like Ahren, but was ignoring me any better?

There are two sides to every story.

"I get the feeling I'll be the sucker in both stories."

Why would you think that?

I shrugged to myself and flopped onto the hard mattress. "Because with my track record, things never go well."

I have a surprise for you.

"Yeah, what's that?"

You shall see soon.

"Like *tonight* soon?"

He laughed, the sound honeyed, breaking through my defenses, reminding me of the times we'd talk for hours about nothing and everything.

You miss me already?

Mischief curled over his words, and unlike previous times we'd talk, now I pictured the devilish grin, the amber eyes lighting up, the full lips I wanted to taste. Heat swept over me so fast, I collapsed onto my back, hugging a pillow.

I was a walking contradiction, but Luther had been part of me for so long. Without him... I wasn't sure what was left. Loneliness?

"I said nothing about missing you. I was just curious about this surprise."

Promise it will be worth your while.

"I'll hold you to that."

Silence.

"Why am I locked in my room?" And why hadn't he come to talk to me in person instead of speaking through my mind? The words played on my mind, but I couldn't say them out loud, still torn between being pissed at him and wondering if this was a dream. Or was I simply having the biggest infatuation with a made-up guy in my head? The latter worried me... *terrified* me. To add to that, he had two douche brothers I wanted to punch in the face and kiss at the same time. I was completely and utterly broken.

For your safety, in case anyone outside the palace finds out you're here.

Almost too afraid to ask, the words came in a whisper. "Who wants to hurt me?"

It's complicated. I'll tell you soon, I promise. You need to trust me.

Trust was the kind of word that grew thorns and drew blood when you least expected it.

"It's funny, you know," I began. "Talking to you like this feels like just us in the world, and I can say anything. Hell, you've seen me at my worst."

But?

"But... When I see you in person?" I grimaced to find the right way to say this; some part of me worried I was headed down a dangerous road. Did I really know him despite talking to him for years, sharing all my fears and worries with him? "It doesn't feel like you," I breathed.

You think I'm a different person?

"No, not like that." I rolled over on my stomach, swinging my feet up and down on the bed. "More like I struggle to find my words. You..." Intimidated me. Looked so freaking hot that if I'd worn panties, they would have melted right off me. I'd fantasized about feeling his hands and lips on me.

He said nothing and my heart stopped.

"Can you hear my thoughts when I don't speak them?" I had a heady feeling at what he secretly knew about my innermost desires.

Would you like me to?

"Hell no!" My cheeks were on fire. "I don't even know how this is happening."

It's a bond I created. I can't tap into your thoughts unless you open a link and let me in.

"Yeah, it's better we keep it this way." My mouth felt dry and I licked my lips, convinced I'd die if he heard all my thoughts.

But I can feel bits of your emotions when we're connected. Like right now, I'm burning hot... I know you desire me, that you—

"Stop. Don't." Oh, my god, I wanted to fall into a pit and vanish.

Keeping my words in check I could do, but my emotions... they were uncontrollable beasts.

I meant what I said earlier today.

His voice slid over my skin like tender fingers, and I didn't need to ask—I knew exactly what moment he spoke of. His words rolled over my mind: *"I want you pinned to the wall, your legs open."*

Those words tortured me, leaving me consumed by so many thoughts. I never expected to feel such things, never expected him to react the same way to me.

Until now... until Luther breathed hope into me.

Or was it another cruel joke? I got the impression these three brothers loved to play games.

Did I embarrass you?

"No." I forced a laugh that had me cringing at how fake I sounded, but his question left me feeling more exposed than when he'd whispered those words. He saw right through me, all pretense aside, so how could I be anything but myself with someone who sensed every emotion I had?

I will let you sleep, little wolf.

"Goodnight."

I curled up in bed, clutching my pillow, and hated the tingles in my stomach, for believing Luther wouldn't harm me. I closed my eyes. *Please let me wake up at home. Please.*

***

"Guen!" Jen yelled from across the living room. "What were you thinking?"

I just stood there, back at home, staring at her, at Oliver playing a game on the TV, Luke cooking in the kitchen. And I knew this wasn't real. I always knew when I dreamed... I was there, but not really.

"Are you even listening?" she ranted, rage warping her features.

"What?" I mumbled, running a hand through my hair. My fingers caught on the metal headband and I pulled it off my brow. Why was I still wearing this? I ran a thumb over the golden link of stars.

"We have to pay for all damages to Noah's car!"

Her words grabbed my attention and I jerked my head up. "I didn't damage his damn car."

She stormed across the room and yanked open a drawer in the kitchen, pulling out something, but I didn't feel right, like I was the intruder in this home... in this life. Like this whole time I'd been an imposter pretending to fit but never could, no matter how hard I tried.

"Then why was this under your bed?" She gripped the glass-looking gearstick from Noah's car.

My heart squeezed. "Were you searching my room?"

"It's not your room anymore," she snapped, her voice shaky. "You're moving to the basement. Evelyn will stay in your room now. And you will pay back every cent to Noah's dad with the money you earn from your part-time job."

"No, that'll take me forever. I did nothing to his car." Even in my dream, the guy was a douche.

"Guen." She kept shaking her head, her disapproval cutting through me.

Fury curled my hands into fists, the golden stars of the headband digging into my palms, breaking skin. I'd had enough of everyone blaming me, thinking I did everything wrong. The constant accusations stung, fueling the flames inside me.

Stop.

Breathe.

But my brain refused to pause.

"You wanna know the truth?" I shouted, my words quivering. "I tried to get my car back because Noah said he'd help, but instead he tried to rape me." Words and tears poured from me, the world shattering around me.

I blinked back the tears, but already the darkness came for me, and while I couldn't hear Jen's words, her terrified face cut into my heart. But I knew that had been a dream with Jen, it felt fuzzy in my head like the twisted woods dreams I'd had in the past. And in a heartbeat, my world fell into darkness.

***

My eyes flipped open to the perfect white ceiling, to elaborate moldings in the corners. I didn't move, didn't breathe, didn't do a damn thing.

I'd woken up back in the fae world, and my insides sank.

But my head remained at home... focused on the pain I'd seen in Jen's eyes. The sharpness in my chest deepened, and tears drenched my cheeks.

I shouldn't have told her. And I wouldn't tell her when I finally returned home from this place. I'd rather she believed I'd crashed the car than see the anguish on her face at knowing what Noah had done. She shouldn't hurt for me—I didn't want her to. I lifted my hand to find no cuts in my palm, and on the bedside table, sat the golden headband. Just a dream. A freaking stupid dream.

When I finally pushed my legs out of bed, a piece of paper tumbled out with me.

I snatched it off the floor and unfolded it, moving over to the window for better light.

Leave this place. Run before it's too late for you.

I stilled on the words before turning the note over, finding no other message. The longer I stared at the warning, the more chills crept down my spine.

Footfalls sounded in the other room, and I shuddered, my hands fumbling just as the wind snatched the paper from my hand. I reached for it, but it was gone, floating outside.

I trembled, unsure what to make of the message. Where would I run anyway? Were the woods safer than this palace?

Turning to the door, I pulled on the handle and it opened.

"Hello?" I peered into the adjacent room, only to find a dress draped off the back of the couch. A platter of food sat on the small table near the couch. Porridge and honey, bread, jams, and fruit. My mouth salivated.

I collected the burgundy-colored dress and headed back into my bedroom to change before they forced me into a bath again. A fitted bodice, with wrist-to-shoulder lace-up sleeves, and a straight skirt down to my ankles. Back in the bedroom, I stripped and slipped the dress over my head and down my body. It was a looser fit than the last gown, with only a single layer of material. There was no sign of underwear, and I sighed. But I did find black slip-on shoes near the door.

Footsteps sounded in the other room, and I rushed there, expecting Luther.

The brunette maid was setting a teapot and cup on the table. Viper bound into the room, too, heading for the windows and staring out at the falcons flying past.

"Morning, mistre—my lady." Her eyes lit up when she found me dressed. "That color suits your blonde hair. Come eat and I'll style it for you."

I wanted to ask her about the note, if she'd put it there, but the red-haired lady waltzed in as if on a mission. Her lips in a grim line, she marched into my room, presumably to tidy up. Had she left the message?

"What's your name?" I asked, feeling bad for never asking before now.

"Dana, my lady. Livy also helps me, even if she's grumpy often." The smile on her face told me the women were close.

"You can call me 'Guen.' So, what's on the agenda today?" I flopped onto the couch, my stomach growling for food, and I picked up the bowl of porridge and the spoon.

"Agenda?" she asked.

"What am I meant to do today?" I scooped a spoonful into my mouth, the creamy cinnamon-and-apple porridge melting on my tongue. It was to die for.

"The princes have left the court for a few days. Until then, we're instructed to keep you in your chamber."

I dropped my spoon into the porridge glob. "For a few days? I wanted to explore the palace." Find out more about my past, my parents—somehow come to terms with the fact that this could be real.

"Out of the question." Dana shuffled to stand behind the couch and collected my hair roughly into her hands before pulling it off my face. "We will bring you entertainment to keep you busy. This morning, you will learn the art of needlepoint and later the skill of using a harp."

I rolled my eyes and remembered Luther's words about someone wanting to hurt me if they discovered my whereabouts. Then why was someone warning me to leave the palace?

My feet tumbled across the forest floor, foliage crunching and getting caught on the hem of my dress.

"I missed you all day," Luther murmured, his voice silky and tempting.

In the dark of the night, I could barely discern his black clothes and hair while his amber eyes held a glint to them.

"Hey, wait up," I called out as he walked backward, smiling wickedly, his hand stretched out to me.

"Hurry, little wolf."

I stretched out an arm, my fingers grasping on to his. He held on and drew me closer.

"You need to move faster. No one can know we're out here," he whispered with a forbidden tone that drove me insane. This felt like we'd run away from our chaperones to steal a first kiss. If only.

I glanced over my shoulder at the lights of the palace through the trees: the enormity of the place, the fiery torches outlining the servants' door to the building we'd snuck out from.

"Why didn't you reach out through my thoughts while you were gone?" I pressed close to him as we stepped over a fallen log, his hand interlaced with mine. "I endured three utterly boredom-inducing-harp-and-needle-point-days. God, I was at the point where I would either poke my eyes out with the pins or strangle myself on the harp strings."

He laughed. "We traveled with Father. Others in close vicinity can sometimes sense it when I use my power, and I couldn't risk it."

"Risk them finding me?" I tensed at being kept in the dark with what was going on.

He nodded. "Father's forbidden me from using my ability."

"So you're the rebel of the family," I teased.

He brought my hand up to his lips, kissing my knuckles quickly as we walked. "If you only knew, little wolf."

So many questions whirled on my mind, and I was left conflicted about my feelings for Luther. About being stuck in this world... or "realm" as he and his brothers called it. And with each passing day, the truth grew inside me that maybe this was where I belonged. That this was a real place and I'd got myself stuck here.

That only opened up new questions, like why had my parents abandoned me in the woods near a hospital? What was wrong with me? Was I really a fae? I had no idea what being fae really meant, but it might have explained the dreams, the episodes I had felt since arriving here... the reason I'd fallen out of Noah's car and right into my bed.

"Are you ready for your surprise?" he teased.

"What is it?" I squeaked.

Something looked different about him tonight. He smiled too much, his touch warmed my body, and why was he so excited? I longed to sit with him and just talk about us, learn more about him, but when he'd burst into my room excited, insisting we had to leave right away, his exhilaration was a fever enveloping me. Talking could wait, I'd guessed.

"You'll see," he said, his grin captivating, and we ran on through the woods. With him, I didn't feel scared. Maybe I should have, but not tonight.

When he finally came to a stop, we stood in front of a square wooden platform with a railing on three sides. It was big enough for two or three people inside.

"What is that?" I breathed heavily, while he barely broke a sweat.

He stepped inside and guided me to follow him. "Welcome to my Ferris wheel."

I eyed him suspiciously, but on the inside, I squirmed with joy that not only had he remembered what we'd talked about, but he'd made one? I looked nothing like the ones back home, since this was made of a simple platform that I assumed planned to take us upward. But he'd never seen one and based his creation on my description, so I was excited to see what he made. My stomach somersaulted at the notion that he made this for me.

"I'm at a loss for words." I stepped onto the platform. This was nothing like a Ferris wheel back home, but I was willing to try out his version.

"That'll be a first." His hand found my lower back, drawing me closer, and I sagged against him. "Now hold on."

He was so close now, I felt the hard muscles of his chest, smelled his breath. Honey and blueberries and all masculine. He tugged hard on a rope with one hand, and in a heartbeat, our platform lurched and catapulted upward. A whirring sound buzzed like rope running over a metal wheel.

My stomach pitched. I shuddered, clutching on to him, my hands bunching up his shirt, while I plastered myself to him.

He laughed as the wind brushed against us, his large hand holding me in place, his other gripping the wooden railing. We could be soaring through the skies with how fast we traveled, sliding up alongside lofty pine trees, their scent wafting on the breeze.

"Do you like my Ferris wheel?" he asked, his voice buffeted against the rush of air.

I held on to him for dear life, the heat of his body pouring over me. "It's fantastic."

Wind fluttered through my hair, pushing it into my face when we finally jerked to a stop.

I glanced around at the tops of pines spreading out in every direction. The waning moon hung high like a Viking horn, throwing silvery hues over the forest. "Wow, people would pay a fortune for this view."

"Turn around."

Grabbing on to the railing, I shifted on the spot, the platform giving a slight wobble, and my heart thumped.

But I forgot everything once I lifted my gaze. I was captivated.

A majestic castle stood atop the nearby mountain, as if conjured out of a fairy tale, and I gasped out loud, inciting an amused laugh from Luther.

"Holy crap on a stick, it's a real-life castle," I murmured. Steadfast stone walls, towers, moonlight shining on its proud turrets, dark windows like slits in the thick walls, flags fluttering in the breeze. Globe lights everywhere brought the spectacular fortress to life. Trees clustered close to the walls looked like an army ready to defend.

I glanced at the palace we'd come from, farther on my right. I'd thought that was the most elaborate thing I'd ever see, but I'd been so wrong. "That castle is insane."

"It's where my parents live." Luther leaned in behind me, his solid chest against my back, his arms grasping the railings on either side of me, and I lost all ability to think. Gone were the questions I'd promised myself to ask him.

All that remained was the heat pouring from his body, his quickened breaths grazing over my hair, and I knew what was coming, I craved it, *needed* it since the first time he'd entered my head and scared me half to death. But this was deeper. We were so much more than burning up with desire. After tonight, he'd hold more than just me as hostage. My heart would shatter. He'd have my heart, too. I wasn't foolish enough to forget the truth that even if I was from this world, he was a prince. Me... who knew? Except this moment had been in the making for years and I wouldn't ruin it. Couldn't.

"It's peaceful up here, away from everything and everyone," he whispered in my ear, sending sharp shudders of pleasure down my spine. His hand slid to my jaw, his fingers tender and so warm. He tilted my head back and looked down at me, the moonlight brightening his face.

How had I never noticed that the color of his eyes with the outer ring of the iris a strong amber? I studied his defined cheekbones, his square jaw, his full lips that seemed slightly crooked from my angle.

"I have a gift for you," he said.

"Really?" I pressed my back to his chest and he wrapped his arms around my shoulders, holding me tightly.

"Remember when I promised you revenge for what Noah did to you?"

Worry dragged over my mind on what a gift and getting revenge had in common. "What did you do?"

"Not enough, but from this realm, it was the closest thing to making him regret touching you."

I blinked hard and twisted around in his arms to face him. "I'm scared to ask."

The corners of his mouth twitched, like he was holding back a grin. "I arranged a small glamor over his dreams. Whenever he sleeps, he dreams of being savagely murdered, experiencing every ache, every fear, every moment like it was real. Each night, a different girl whom he's hurt will visit him." His wicked smile split his lips. "It will slowly drive him insane."

Staring at him, I wasn't sure how to feel. I didn't hate the idea because that jerk-head deserved so much freaking worse, but it also showed me Luther reveled in his cruelty.

"You don't like it?" Worry pinched the bridge of his nose. "I could arrange for something worse."

"No. Actually, it's rather creative and clever."

"Exactly." The moonlight hit the side of his face. My back to the railing, I glanced up, and his hand cupped the side of my face.

"You deserve so much more than the life you've led. All those who hurt you had no clue who you were."

"Wish *I* knew who I was."

Slow and sweet, his thumb dragged over my lower lip. "You will as soon as my brothers and I work out a solution."

"Solution?" He made it sound like I was a problem.

He pressed the edge of his nail down on my lip, eliciting a sharp pain, but I didn't wince. Not when I struggled to tame my wandering emotions and the heat flaring between my legs.

I parted my lips, slipping my tongue out, flicking the tip of his thumb. The amber rim of his eyes lit up like fire, and I indulged him, leaning closer, sliding him into my mouth, inch by inch. Lips clamped over him, I closed my eyes and tasted his saltiness and traced my tongue over his thumb, enjoying the way his breath hitched.

"Look at me." His voice was raspy and fierce.

My eyelids flipped open and stared into his intoxicating eyes.

Arousal curled behind his intense gaze, and I clenched my thighs. I adored that look, the idea that I held control over him.

Electricity sizzled over my flesh, and he pulled his thumb out of my mouth with a faint popping sound.

He leaned closer, burying his face in my hair, inhaling me. "Mine," he murmured.

His lips closed against mine, and lust flooded me. A desperate ache blazed through me, my brain firing off sparks. I opened my mouth and moaned as he slid his tongue inside, battling with mine.

I drove my hands into his long hair, tugging on the roots, breathing heavily.

His grip on my hips tightened.

I ran my hands down his strong shoulders, over the hard planes of his chest and stomach. My fingers slid under his shirt, finding fiery skin. He hissed a breath at my touch, pulling me against him roughly, kissing me with such savagery, I lost myself to him. It scared me how much I let myself go, how much I craved him.

I wanted him. Needed him. Plain and simple, I had to have this gorgeous man.

His kisses drifted over my cheek, across my brow, and to my ear, leaving me trembling. "There are so many secrets I plan to share with you, my little wolf. Secrets that will make you the most powerful fae in Wandering Realm."

I froze and looked up at him. Gone was the deadly edge of arousal he'd brought me to, replaced with curiosity. There was so much I didn't understand. "What are you talking about?"

His hands snaked down my back, curving over my ass, infusing me with heat, his gaze narrowing on me. "Why do you think everyone in the Realm knows you?"

"Maybe because—"

A piercing hoot sounded from somewhere down in the woods, and my heart shuddered.

Luther jerked away from me and glanced down over the railing. His face paled two shades when he met my gaze, and my breaths stopped for a moment.

"We need to go. Now!" he hissed.

He reached out with his hand to the rope, golden sparks erupting from his touch. The platform beneath us lurched and we dropped. My stomach hit the back of my throat, arms frantically grabbing for the railing, wind throwing my hair everywhere.

Luther's arms grasped around my waist, holding me tight. "I've got you. Once we land, we run. Whatever you do, don't look back, don't let go of my hand. Understand?"

I nodded, my heartbeat galloping. "You're scaring me."

"Good, then you'll follow my instructions." His words deepened.

Darkness reared up around us as we dove into the woods, fear churning in my veins.

I jostled on my feet as the platform hit the ground. Luther snatched my arm and lunged into the forest, dragging me after him, and we ran. He moved with such swiftness. I felt like I flew through the air, my legs barely keeping up.

Panic lashed over my chest, squeezing my lungs. I pushed myself to keep up. Goosebumps shivered up the back of my legs like someone watched us. Ducking under branches, we never stopped, but kept moving. Adrenaline drove me faster and faster. Fear shoved against me like the cold wind.

Whatever you do, don't look back.

Desperation begged me to glance into the woods, see what scared Luther so much, what terrified someone who looked like he could wrestle a bear. But I never did... I couldn't bring myself to see the monsters hunting us down.

Darkness closed in, and only the fiery lights of the manor in the distance called to us.

Branches snapped behind us, and a guttural growl shot through the night.

Goosebumps raked over my flesh as Luther's grip tightened, drawing me forward quicker. My foot caught on a tree root, and I fell forward. My heart dropped.

I gasped out loud, reaching for Luther, the floor rushing up to me.

Luther pivoted, swinging his free arm and swooped it under my arm, steadying me. I stumbled to find my footing, and instinct had me turning around. I shouldn't have.

A hulking shadow on two legs charged forward from deeper in the woods, breaking branches, feet pounding the ground. White glinted in his eyes, a savageness in his curled posture. This wasn't a beast, but a lunatic chasing us.

A scream rushed past my lips.

With a grunt, Luther wrenched me after him. "Run, little wolf, run," he yelled.

The wind blasted into us, and we moved with speed.

We rushed out of the woods and darted to the shadowy edges of the mansion.

I glanced back as Luther fumbled to open the side door, the servants' entrance he'd told me.

The man chasing us emerged from the woods, eyes shining in the moonlight. Clothes ripped and ragged, he heaved for breath, his chest rising and falling, mouth gaping open with a terrifying growl no human should make. He burst after us, and I retreated just as Luther seized my arm and dragged me inside. He slammed the door shut and locked it with several bolts.

Night smothered the empty kitchen. No one else was around.

"Quick, you need to get back to your room. You'll be safe there." He grabbed my hand and we ran through the dark kitchen as something slammed into the door behind us.

I could barely catch my breath, and it had little to do with the endless running. But everything to do with whatever lingered outside.

CHAPTER

SIXTEEN

"Luther!" I mumbled, panic turning into something else... something with sharp teeth and aching pain. "Don't go." The darkness of my bedroom pressed around me, choking the breath out of my lungs.

He shook his head, dread darkening eyes that earlier had held intense desire. His hand slipped from mine, the cold already enveloping me, and he hurried to the doorway.

I staggered after him, fear burrowing through me. What was he running from? "Who was that in the woods? Why were they coming for us?"

"You're safe here. No matter what, never leave this room with anyone but me or the maids. Understand?"

"You're scaring me." Shivers crept down my spine, as I was unsure I could stop anyone if they found me. Where could I hide in here? And what had he meant back in the woods about me being the most powerful fae? The whole being-a-fae thing still hadn't gelled.

The familiar sound of claws tapping the floorboards came from the hallway and Sir Wolf-A-Lot wandered into the room, right past me without a glance.

"I have to go." Luther retreated, his gaze over his shoulder, his brow furrowed. "I have to go."

"Don't leave Cujo in here with me!" I gasped, watching the furry little beast walk around like he owned the place.

Luther shut the door and left nothing behind but his faded steps.

The mutt leapt onto the couch and lay on his belly, making himself comfortable, like he somehow knew his tasked mission was to defend me. While I worried I'd wake up with him chewing on my leg, part of me liked having company. Someone other than just my thoughts.

Flames crackled and spat in the fireplace, tossing light across the living room.

I stood there for a few moments, drowning in too many emotions. The consuming heat Luther stirred in me, the dread that someone wanted to hurt me, the need to go home.

I pictured Jen panicking that I'd been gone for a few days, reporting me as a missing person, and guilt pressed down on my chest.

Only the crackling logs and the dog licking himself permeated the dimly lit room. I paced to the window and stared down at the forest drenched in night and the light of the silvery moon and tried to find the location Luther had taken me to in the woods. But my search proved fruitless, as it was too dark.

I smiled at how far from the real thing his Ferris wheel had been, but I'd adored it to bits. I still burned on the inside for him, still ached to kiss him all night, still wished he'd slept in here with me.

My heart pounded, and the taste of Luther lingered on my tongue, flowing into me. I inhaled his scent. Honeyed, masculine, and something dark. They poured through me, almost like he'd tried to leave his mark on me so I'd never forget him. But that was insane, right?

"Looks like it's just the two of us." I swiveled toward my companion for the night, but he already had his chin resting on his outstretched paws, his eyes closed.

I dragged myself into the other room and pulled out the chamber pot from under my bed, hating that this was my toilet. Then I'd go to sleep and maybe, just maybe, I'd wake up back home.

***

Something feathery brushed over my face. I shook my head, my nose itchy, and opened my sleepy eyes. At first glance, I could have sworn I was hugging a massive fur blanket, but when the reek of dog hit me, I startled and scrambled out of bed, my heart slamming into my ribcage.

Cujo remained on the mattress where I'd been snuggling him seconds earlier, and he strained to look over his shoulder at me with that look in his eyes, like sleep still clung to his brain.

I glared at him.

He made a whiny sound and flopped his head back on my pillow. "Wow, you're a bed hog, and for your information, if we're gonna share, stay on your side of the bed." He lay right down the middle.

The floorboard creaked in the next room, and my ears pricked. Cujo scrambled to his feet, kicking my pillow aside, and lunged out of bed before running into the living room.

"It's just me, Sir Wolf-A-Lot," Dana responded, and I dragged myself toward her to find she was placing my breakfast on the small table.

"Morning, my lady."

"Hey." I rubbed my eyes, yawning, still smelling like wet-dog Cujo. "Any chance of having a bath?" As much as I disliked taking a bath with maids watching me, I needed a wash badly.

She glanced at me, smirking. "Of course. I knew you'd enjoy them."

I liked her. She always greeted me with a smile and made me feel comfortable.

Dana bowed her head, a smile pulling on the corners of her mouth. "Enjoy your meal and I'll come back to collect you shortly." She spun on her heels, holding on to the white apron over her navy blue dress as she rushed toward the door.

"Dana, have you seen Luther this morning?" I called out.

She shook her head and turned around. "Not yet. But could I be so bold as to speak my mind?"

"Of course. What is it?"

"My father, Goddess bless his soul, once told me that sometimes it is difficult to break one's path to embrace a new future. But to survive among monsters, one must adapt any way possible."

I stared at her, trying to wrap my brain around what she'd said, convinced most in this world spoke in riddles.

She wiped her hand on her apron, her mouth pinching. "You look confused, my lady."

"Just a weensy bit."

"I know this place must seem strange to you, but this is a deadly realm for someone so unfamiliar with the dangers. Just be cautious, but be quick to accept this realm as your own before it's too late."

"Too late?" As my own? This wasn't my home.

She bowed her head. "I've said too much and I'm out of line. I just don't want to see you..." She cleared her throat. "Hurt."

"Thank you."

Dana hurried out of the room, and now I was a thousand times more confused.

And I wanted to speak with Luther desperately. He'd left me with so many questions last night. Not to mention the memory of the most divine French kiss in the world. Some guys knew how to kiss, others were like dribbling fountains and sucked. Luther had left me breathless, like I couldn't live without kissing him again.

When I turned around, Cujo had his front paws up on the table, lapping up my porridge.

Gah.

***

Deimos circled me in slow, soundless steps. He was tall, six-two maybe. Gorgeous from the depths of his green crystal eyes to the rugged expression on his face. He'd let out his hair tonight, white strands cascading over broad shoulders and down his back, almost glinting with a bluish tinge in the flames of the fireplace. Predatory eyes swept over me, corded muscles moving under his skin. I shouldn't have felt a thing for him but hatred, not the shortening of my breath, and definitely not the bursting desire inside me to have this powerful guy stare at me like I was his meal.

Dangerous.

Vicious.

Gorgeous.

I watched him, my breaths quickening. His hand was on my chin when he stopped in front of me. Like Luther, his touch warmed me in a heartbeat, and he forced my head up to face him.

"I expected more," he growled.

"More?" I strained my eyes to look over to the dinner table set up with plates of stew, roast pheasant, baked vegetables, and a number of other things I didn't recognize. "I'm sure the cook can whip up more food if it's not enough."

His eyes narrowed, and I offered him my cheekiest grin. The guy had cornered me the moment I entered the dining room. After a day on my own in my quarters, I'd hoped to finally find Luther, but instead it was Deimos who'd waited for me.

His hand slid over my cheek, his fingers combing through my hair, dropping to my shoulders. Greedy fingertips explored my neck, leaving a trail of shivers in their wake.

"More beauty, more elegance, more everything," he said softly.

I stiffened and flinched from his hold, but his hands were fast; they grabbed my arms and drew me against him. "I didn't say you could leave."

"You aren't too great yourself," I muttered, completely and utterly lying. He was perfection, indulgence, temptation standing before me.

"Watch that mouth of yours," he threatened with a smirk, enjoying his power play.

I swallowed hard and reminded myself whom I was dealing with... a prince used to getting his way. But gorgeous hunk or not, it wasn't okay for him to step into my personal space. I pulled back, but he stepped forward with me, my back pressed to the wall, his face in mine. He was so close I inhaled his scent... masculine and woodsy and the sweetest citrus combined in one. Something stirred in my gut, and my gaze fell to his mouthwatering lips, which sat in a crooked grimace.

"Luther will break you easily, then he'll get a replacement." He spoke so calmly, like he might be ordering a latte—which he'd never probably tasted in his life—but I didn't believe his threat. Not after the night I'd had with Luther. He wouldn't.

"I know what you're doing," I quipped, glaring at him.

He pushed closer and brushed his lips over mine, my whole body bursting with adrenaline. "Is that what you expected?"

I clenched my jaw, my skin burning over the fact that he dared—

"You'll be fun to keep. Might even take my turn breaking you."

"Is that your idea of sweeping a girl off her feet?"

His laughter sounded divine, which was wrong because he wasn't allowed to sound like the best thing I'd heard my entire life.

"I prefer girls with more, not less."

A shiver shook me, and I pushed my fists against his chest, but he stood there, trapping me, unmoving. His fingers slid into my hair, twining the strands.

"Maybe you should have put your hair up tonight," he said. "Would have looked prettier."

"Is that all you do—insult? Well, it's not working on me, so move out of my way."

His hand grasped my hair, and I winced. "You're adorable when you're angry. Think we'll have a lot of fun together."

"I'm not yours and I sure as hell ain't staying in this insane place." Despite my words, my body hummed from his closeness. My body betrayed me when it came to this jerk, my lips still tingling from his kiss.

His breath washed on my face, and as much as I wanted to say it reeked, I loved the way he smelled. Damn him... I hated him.

"You're not Luther's, either, and where will you go? It's no easy feat moving between realms without magic. You're stuck in our realm now."

"I'll find a way back."

He pressed his mouth to my ear. "So human of you."

I stiffened. "What's that supposed to mean?"

His green eyes flashed to mine, desire deepening within them. He lips met mine too fast for me to react, and he nipped my lower lip, his teeth nicking flesh.

"Ouch." I shoved my hands into his chest, but he didn't move. He just stood there as hard as a boulder, licking the trickle of blood on his mouth.

I touched mine and my fingers came back bloody. "What are you doing?"

Fingers slipped over my shoulder, drowning me, clouding my thoughts, leaving me leaning into him while trying to recover any control of my wavering emotions.

He pressed his face to my neck, inhaling, tasting, and I shuddered under him, the softness leaving me shivering with a new kind of arousal. I should have stopped him, should have shoved him away, but I couldn't. Something brushed over my mind, feather soft and blurring my thoughts for a moment, before it pulled away.

Teeth were on my neck, a sharp prick fast and electrifying.

Mist blurred my mind, everything erased except Deimos and me. Focusing on steadying my breathing did nothing to calm my thundering heart. Arousal trembled down my spine, invisible fingers sliding over my back and lower still.

A sudden roar tore through the room, ripping me out of my lulled state.

"What the fuck are you doing?" Luther growled.

Deimos stumbled away from me, his laughter hypnotic. He wiped his bloody mouth with the back of his hand, his eyes devouring me, calling to me like nothing I'd ever felt.

"She's exquisite, brother. So much more than we could have anticipated. You were right to collect her for us."

"She isn't yours to touch or mark. Fuck, Deimos!"

The wall held me up as the fog in my head faded, my thoughts clearing, and there was a pinching ache at my neck. I clasped the wound where he'd bitten me.

"Bastard," I mumbled. Whatever he'd done had served as some sort of magnet, luring me to him.

The tension in the room exploded. Luther heaved like a beast, his arms trembling, and when Deimos's eyes fell on me, they felt like marks on my body.

"Why?" Deimos asked with a raised brow. "You think I don't know you already marked her too? I tasted it in her blood. Anyway, we both know Ahren will claim her in the end."

Luther moved in a flash and bulldozed into his brother, both of them slamming into the side of the table before tumbling to the ground with several chairs and the platter of roast veggies.

I flinched, trying to clear my thoughts.

Potatoes and carrots rolled around on the ground with the two brothers punching and kicking each other, their growls escalating.

A kitchen servant appeared at the commotion but froze in fright in the doorway, his eyes enlarging at the sight before he swiftly retreated.

My stomach dropped at their battle. They were the worst kind of animals. Fighting over me... over marking me. What about what I wanted? Deimos's words lingered in my mind about Luther getting another girl after breaking me... was it a lie or me being too blindsided by their attention to see the truth?

I trembled.

Fear radiated through me and nothing would have prepared me for this. I inhaled sharply and burst into a run past the brawl and out into the hall. I didn't stop, never looked back, until I reached my bedroom and shut myself in there. My back to the door, I hugged myself and slid to my ass. "What the hell just happened?"

My hand shook as I pressed it to my neck, which stung, and I sucked on the cut across my lower lip.

How could I stay here with three princes who were more dangerous than I'd first thought? One dominant and terrifying. One cruel with his words. And one who'd unmistakably stolen my heart.

SEVENTEEN

"Wake up!" A female's voice grazed over my ear, her hand on my shoulder, shaking me.

It took me a few seconds for my thoughts to slide back into place. The palace, the princes, Luther... "Dana?" I groggily asked, rubbing my eyes.

Someone was standing over me in bed, the dark stealing her features, leaving the hair on my nape bristling.

"Get up, Guendolyn. Fast!" Terror pulsed behind her words.

"Wait, you're not Dana." Or Livy. Panic slammed into my chest like I'd been hit by a wrecking ball, tearing the sleep from my head.

"Who are you?" Had Luther left the door unlocked?

She straightened her posture, revealing a lithe body, standing tall, six-foot or six-foot-one. A flash of silver glinted in her eyes, and something familiar came to me, but I just couldn't place who I was staring at.

With the click of her fingers, a flame ignited within a small globe sitting in the palm of her hand. Light burst outward, brightening her face, and I pushed myself upright in bed, squinting for a better look.

Gray eyes. Porcelain skin that glistened. Her hair blended into the night, and long, elf-like ears poked out from her hair.

"Pointy ears are more of a family attribute," Deimos had said.

"You're in danger, Guendolyn. We need to go, now."

"Wait, Aine?" It was the gallery owner who'd dug her nails into my arm, drawing blood, who'd vanished… She'd called me Guendolyn back at the gallery but hadn't had long ears then. "What are you doing here?" But even as the words left my lips, I knew the answer. Knew that she'd somehow come from this realm. The whole time, she had to have known more about me. My head spun.

I shuffled backward across the bed, farther from her reach, kicking the blankets aside as I got out of bed.

"You knew, didn't you? When you saw my painting, you knew that I came from here?" The words felt clunky and odd on my tongue because now I was admitting I'd been born in the Wandering Realm. Since arriving, I hadn't experienced a single psychotic episode. Maybe it had all been in my head, but my emotions and thoughts just felt too real.

Áine nodded and sighed. "I've been searching for you, and you couldn't have ended up in a worse location." She rounded the bed, and I backed away. "These are your enemies," she explained.

"Okay, you found me. Can you take me back home?" I swallowed hard. Maybe this was my chance to finally return.

She shook her head, and my hope shattered.

"I'm here to take you to your mother. Your real mother."

I stiffened and looked at her, trying to detect the lie on her face. "You know my mom?"

She nodded, her hair bouncing over her shoulders as she stepped closer. "Why do you think I had to meet you after viewing your painting?" She reached for my arm, and I pulled away.

My mouth was dry, and I couldn't move. Couldn't think straight. Everything from the past week was muddled inside my head, and all the conversations I'd had with Luther over the years were crowded over me.

"You dug your nails into my arm, breaking skin, and then vanished."

Her overexaggerated exhale sliced through the air. "I have so much to teach you about this realm. Unless you're gifted with the power of the tongue, like some fae, the only way to travel between realms is magic and blood. But I don't have time to explain the details… not yet."

I was shaking my head, trying to process everything, but it all kept coming back to my mom and how long I'd waited for such a moment. "But Luther—"

"Do you even know who the three princes really are?" She towered over me, the globe flame in her hand beaming under her chin, tossing shadows upward, disfiguring her face. For those few seconds, she looked different. Wider eyes, a longer nose, pinched lips.

My stomach clenched, and my back hit the cold wall.

"They're monsters who'll break you until there's nothing left. Thank the moon I found you before it's too late." Her hand reached for mine, her fingers coiling around my wrist. "They aren't even the real heirs to this court." Her words flew out fast and clipped.

"What do you mean?"

"When the King of Shadow Court remarried, his new queen brought with her three sons, who became the next in line since she was barren after having them with her first husband. But I can explain those things once we're safe. Someone wants to hurt you, they're coming for you, and I'm here to help."

"I want to speak with Luther first."

A whimpering sound came from somewhere in the hall, and she glanced over her shoulder, tugging me closer. "You'll have time, but first, come and see your mother. Find out the truth of what happened, how you ended up being the lost girl in the Wandering Realm."

For so long, I'd fantasized about the day Mom would finally come for me and explain how someone had stolen me. Or a dozen other scenarios I'd made up. Anything but Mom abandoning me. She'd never do that.

But now I felt torn in half, remembering Luther's warning, while a savage desperation ripped through me that I might finally find my mom, discover who I was... How I might no longer be the girl who had a mental disorder. I'd been searching for this my whole life, wanting... *needing* a way out.

A feather-soft touch brushed over my thoughts, stealing the anxiety, and I lowered my shoulders, the decision suddenly clearer.

When I looked up at Áine, her eyes seemed to glow, then she smiled. "Shall we go? We won't be long." She pushed the light into my hand, the globe fleshy in my hand, yet a tiny flame flickered and danced inside, curving and turning upright as I rolled the ball in my hand.

She drew me across the room, and I hurried with rushed footsteps behind her, excitement building in my chest that I'd see Mom, finally be able to ask her why I'd ended up abandoned in the woods.

"Your mother is so excited to meet you."

I nodded, my throat thickening, while I trembled with fear that I'd find out she'd decided to get rid of me because I hadn't been what she'd expected. Because something was wrong with me.

Out in the dark hallway, Áine drew me to the left. I glanced back down the corridor smothered in night, where something thick and dark lay on the floor near a bear statue. I lifted my hand with the globe, the light stretching outward, finding someone lying on the ground face down, red hair sprawled across the rug. Blood smeared the floor and the bear's leg.

Goosebumps raked over my flesh, and I rocked on my heels, pulling against Áine. "Livy?"

"She's the enemy," Áine growled in my ear. "She would have led those who wanted to harm you to your door."

"So you killed her?" Ice wrapped around my heart so hard, it almost stopped beating.

"We need to go before they come." She wrenched my hand, and I tripped over my feet, but I fought against her grip, only then noticing that part of the wall had opened up to a secret passage.

My pulse raced because nothing felt right. I should have followed my gut instinct. "Stop. I'm not going anywhere with you."

Áine spun toward me with such speed, I barely caught my breath. Her hand pressed to my brow, and the smell of bitter lavender flooded my senses.

"Sleep."

I shoved her hand away, and that feathery touch skimmed over my mind again, blurring thoughts, stealing them from me. My eyelids heavy, they fell, and darkness took me so fast, my world vanished.

EIGHTEEN

I jostled about in a cold seat, my nose frozen, and forced my eyes open as fresh air rushed into my lungs.

My vision sharpened to reveal a small carriage around me, walls covered in lush, black fabric, silver studs peppering the frame of the windows and door. Áine sat across from me, one leg crossed over the other, studying me with a raised brow.

"Did you sleep well?" she asked, sounding calm, as if she hadn't just kidnapped me.

I frowned, gritting my teeth. "Of course I didn't." I looked outside the window to discover we were rushing through the forest with extraordinary speed. What was pulling this carriage, dragons?

"Where are we going? Take me back to the palace—now." I trembled so hard but refused to let her see. She didn't seem to be the kind of person who was swayed easily by emotions. And I didn't trust her at all, though my mind swung back and forth between attempting to escape and finding out if she actually knew my mom.

"Too late. We've already been traveling for most of the night." She shrugged, and heaviness dropped through me at the revelation that we were so far from the palace.

She was wrapped in a white coat with fur along the lapels, gloved hands in her lap. Dark hair pulled off her face, and she seemed so at ease, while pins and needles raced up my arm from lying on it. "I used winter cherry," she explained, like I should know what that meant. "And a little lavender powder to help you calm down. Seems it put you to sleep." She smirked, knowing that was exactly what would happen.

Wind whistled through the gaps in the carriage door, the draft reaching me with its icy fingers. I shivered and rubbed my hands together, finding myself wearing a long, black coat. I tugged it open to find I still wore my smiling moon pajamas underneath. Well, why the hell not meet everyone in my pajamas? Then I spotted the black boots on my feet and wriggled my toes inside them. Pretty decent fit, considering they weren't mine.

"We'll dress you accordingly before your greeting with your mother."

"Why would it matter what I wore?" Nothing about this felt right, and being forced to go with Áine raised the hairs on the back of my neck. I insanely wanted to see my mom, but there was still so much I didn't understand about the games these fae played. Especially this fae.

"You still don't believe me?"

"Not after you killed Livy!" I snapped. Images of her dead body in the hallway clawed over my thoughts. "Why not tie her up or something? Her family is going to be devastated."

"She has no family. None of the servants do. It's part of working as a servant. No connections to the outside world."

Even though she'd been grumpy most of the time, Dana and I would still miss her and mourn. Poor Livy!

The carriage wheels hit something hard, and I was thrown back into the seat. Áine lurched forward, her arms jutting outward, her hands plastered to the windows of the small carriage on either side to catch herself.

"I don't show sympathy to my enemies." She straightened herself in her seat, pushing hair out of her face. "The royals in the Shadow Court are as cold as our winters. They've spilled enough blood in my kingdom to know they are the real monsters in this realm."

She sounded so bitter, but hatred did that to someone if they held on to it long enough.

The carriage jostled about and we swayed left and right, starting to feel sick, but I'd missed dinner after Luther and Deimos had broken into a brawl, so I wouldn't be vomiting anything up. I raised my hand to the side of my neck, a small scab already healed over where he'd torn skin, my spot still sore. I didn't understand his flirty aggression, or why my knees weakened in his presence. Did he have some kind of power over me?

Áine watched me, and I pulled the collar of my coat tighter, glancing outside as we rushed through the woods. My head felt queasy. What if she was right about my real mom? Would I stay here or return to Luther's palace? I couldn't wait for him to wake up already and find me missing so he could reach out to my thoughts.

"Why are we going so damn fast?" Dread curled in my throat that we were so far from the kingdom, I'd never find my way back.

"Bloodcursed," Áine stated, and I stared at her blankly.

"Am I supposed to know what that is?" I scrubbed a hand down my face, frustrated to hell and back over being taken like this. No one would know what had happened to me, and would I even see Luther again? My life was sailing away, and I was losing control of everything.

"Cursed race of blood suckers. When they haven't eaten in a while, the blood frenzy hits, and they attack anything that moves."

"And you think they're out there now?" My voice almost squeaked as I searched the woods outside, squinting for any sign of movement. Fear tangled within me, tightening my chest.

"Perhaps. Hard to tell, but if we move fast, we might not catch their attention." Her smooth tone suggested we were talking about the weather, not beasts that could kill us.

I couldn't stop staring at the forest now. My knees bounced. "So what do they look like? Rabid wolves? Bears?"

"Fae."

I lurched forward from the bumpy road and thrust out my hands, clasping the sides of the carriage to stop myself from falling face-first into Áine. "They're fae?" I gasped.

"Once upon a time they were, until the curse infected them and changed them. Now they're sensitive to light, they hunt for blood, and they grow in numbers each time they kill."

My stomach roiled. I thought back to Luther when he'd taken me up in his Ferris wheel, the sound he'd heard. Had that been a bloodcursed? "So they're like vampires?"

"If that's what you want to call them."

My back pressed to the wooden seat, I couldn't stop staring outside, imagining fae with red eyes and huge fangs. The fae already had the whole pale-thing going for them. "Can we go any faster?"

Áine gave a soft laugh.

"Tell me about my mom," I said. Anything to distract me from the monsters living in these woods. "Is Dad with her as well?"

She paused for a moment. "It's complicated with your parents. Your mother is beautiful, with the most magical smile. Her kindness is unlike anyone else's in the realm. She gains the eye of any man she favors, like you, I'm sure."

Her comment threw me off, but I just sighed and glanced away, still heartbroken over Livy, scared of these bloodcursed, terrified of where exactly she was taking me. I didn't know what to make of Áine and I couldn't decide if I could trust her motives.

I shivered again, and we fell silent. All I could think about was Jen, and how she'd not always been the perfect mom, but she'd looked out for me. What was she doing now? Crying after finding me missing? It hurt to think of her in distress, and I couldn't reach out to tell her I was alive.

I didn't remember how much time passed, but in the distance, the golden-blue glow of the rising sun had already emerged, and my back pressed into the back of my seat as we climbed the mountain. Better than Áine, who pressed a hand to the wall to keep herself from sliding forward.

A sudden thump slammed against the metal roof of the carriage, sending us into a small wobble.

I slunk low in my seat and glanced up, curling in on myself, then shot a stare at Áine.

Her lips thinned and fear slashed across her gaze. "Hellish bastards."

"Please tell me it's not the bloodcursed."

She bent forward in her seat and reached a hand under her seat. "Would that make you feel better?"

"Yes!" My heart was beating so hard, I swore it would explode.

She pulled out a long dagger, the silvery hue from the moon glinting against the steel.

Áine grasped the hilt with two hands, waiting.

I shuddered, hugging myself.

Áine smiled, enjoying this, while my breaths raced, heavy and raspy.

"So a sword kills them? Guessing it's to their heart?"

"Just the heart? They can die just as easily as you and I, but their real danger comes when they hunt in numbers. They're fast and unstoppable. Luckily, they're not always coordinated."

"Great." Now all I could picture were the zombie movies I'd watched, and how the worst looking zombies were running at you. They freaked me out the most.

Áine sat back in her seat. "Not long now." Just as she spoke, something slammed against the window and clung there like a spider, sending the carriage into a sway from side to side.

I flinched backward, ice punching through me. "Holy sweet Jesus, we're going to die."

Torn clothes hung off the creature, cuts and wounds slashing over his arms and neck, his skin pale and filthy. Eyes black as midnight sunk into his hollow face, and fangs pressed over his lower lip. The bloodsucker hissed, his hand ripping at the door.

Áine jostled with the dagger. She kicked open the door and shoved her blade right through the monster's throat.

His eyes bulged out before he tumbled backward.

A flurry of freezing winds rushed into the carriage, ripping at my hair and clothes.

I cowered in the corner as Áine lunged forward to shut the door, leaving the cold outside. She wiped the blood from the dagger on the sides of her pants and sat back down, holding the weapon.

"See, you never should have taken me from the palace," I said. "At least I was safe there."

"I highly doubt that." Her smugness irritated me.

Dread pounded through my mind at the thought of how I'd survive this. "The horses and driver!" I blurted out. "They could be attacked."

A blur zipped past my window, and I jumped in my seat.

"Calm down. There were none. This is an enchanted carriage that knows where it needs to take us and won't stop for anyone. I just need to keep pushing these filthy things away until we arrive."

"I am not calming down with those things out there. I'm going to die out here, aren't I? Then I'll come back as one of those soulless things, and the first thing I'm doing is coming for you."

She raised a thin eyebrow, then dropped her gaze to the sword in her hand and back at me. But I wasn't scared of that when monsters outside wanted to drink my freaking blood.

Thoughts collided into me, raging inside my skull. Something else blurred past outside, and I shuddered. "I hate this place. Everything wants to kill me, and why the hell does everything want blood? The zombies in the forest, the freaking prince, and next—"

"You let them taste your blood?"

I shut up and said nothing.

"Tell me the truth!" Her face hardened, her eyes filled with horror. Was that look of disgust over the fact that I'd let the princes get close to me, or something worse?

"Why are you asking me that?"

"Stupid, stupid girl." She shook her head. "An ancient one is going to have to cleanse you. Maybe it's not too late to get it out of your system completely."

"Get what out?" She was scaring me.

She leaned over and snatched my arm, drawing me closer.

"Once a fae takes your blood, you belong to them. It's like what you humans call marriage."

I jolted backward, laughing hysterically even if I found nothing funny. Nothing in the slightest. "That's ridiculous."

"If we don't remove the mark quick enough, you'll forever be bound to serve them until they decide to release you. Which is never. Those bastards would kill you before letting *you* go," she spat, the cords in her neck flexing. "They'll hunt you down, and that mark they placed on you makes you a beacon to them."

Air rushed from my lungs, and all I could picture was Luther when he licked my bloodied wrist in my dream. Deimos biting my lip and neck, tasting my blood. *Motherf—*

Something slammed into the carriage so hard, it rocked sideways and flipped us up on two wheels.

I screamed, sliding down the seat, slamming into the wall. Áine groaned across from me, pushing herself toward the uplifted side of the carriage.

"Shit!" I was going to die out here—I knew it, knew it!

Everything happened so fast. We traveled for a split second on two side wheels, and I held my breath, gripping hold of the seat. Then the whole thing flopped onto its side. I jostled and smacked my head on the ceiling, stars dancing in my vision, my arms and legs flailing about, tangling with Áine, her feet at my head.

She wrestled with the dagger in her hand, the weapon swinging toward me from the momentum.

My life flashed before my eyes.

Death was coming swiftly.

I'd never see my family, Luther, or anyone again. The monsters would drink my blood and I'd come back as one of them.

God no!

The tip of Áine's blade stopped inches from my face. I lay on my back, my legs in the air, practically upside down. Sweat drenched me. Breaths raced. I'd almost died. Almost died. Almost freaking died.

Áine stood over me gripping the dagger, frozen for a few seconds, all the blood drained from her face, before she rapidly drew the weapon back.

"You could have killed me!" I shouted.

Áine grumbled, her lip split and blood dripping over her chin, while my head felt like it'd cracked in two. I rubbed the back of my skull, my fingers coming back spotted with blood. *Crap.* Did I need stitches?

A savage growl roared outside, and I trembled, staring up at the door sitting above us. We were like sardines, waiting for those things to come in and tear us out. I scrambled to get up.

Áine reached down, grabbed my coat by the shoulder, and dragged me to my feet with ease. "I'll hold them off, and you run. Run like you've never run before and go through the golden gates at the top of the hill. The palace is protected. The bloodcursed can't cross. Don't look back, no matter what. Understand?"

I nodded but couldn't move, terrified to go out there.

"Can't we wait here until sunlight?" I hugged myself tightly, my back pressed to the wall.

She shoved open the door and waited for a moment, watching the forest. "The scent of our blood will draw them to us in no time. They'll tear apart this carriage to reach us."

She slid her dagger out past the door and set it on top of the carriage. One foot propped up on the seat, she heaved herself out. Kneeling, she scanned the area rapidly and stuck her arm back inside.

"Take my hand," she whispered. "We move fast."

I grabbed her arm, followed her lead, and pushed off the seat inside. She dragged me out toward her, and my stomach pressed against the door frame. Legs kicking, I wriggled myself out.

Áine swept her gaze over the landscape. The fiery sky over the horizon lit up the tops of the trees, but within the woods, it was so dark, I could barely see a thing.

One hand on the dagger, the other on mine, Áine drew me to the edge. Before I got a chance to catch my breath, she tugged me forward and we jumped off the carriage.

My stomach lurched and we landed with a thud on the hard soil.

My heart pounded against the inside of my ribs, my gaze swinging left and right.

"The sun's almost here, so they'll be retreating. Now go."

"Maybe we risk waiting in the carriage?" My words raced.

She glared and shoved me by my shoulder toward the path that climbed at least a hundred feet to the top of the hill. Lofty, enormous pines crowded either side. Night still clung to the path, and dread froze me on the spot. I had no weapon, nothing.

"Run!" Áine shoved a hand against my back and pushed.

I burst forward in an instant, racing up the hill, my boots punching the ground.

I couldn't help it—I looked back, just for a split second.

Áine ran up behind me, sword in hand, her gaze sweeping the grounds, protecting me.

I had no idea who this woman was... a guard of my real mom? She resembled nothing of the gallery owner back home.

Twigs and foliage snapped in the woods on either side of me, and a scream pulsed in my throat.

From the shadows on my right, a figure darted toward us. Skin pale and blotchy with blood. Clothes hanging off his lithe frame.

"Run!" Áine screamed, and I drove myself up the hillside as she'd instructed, never stopping.

Growls and the horrific slurping sound of body parts being ripped apart erupted behind me. Terror smothered me. The crest of the hill came into view. I pushed one leg after another when another bloodcursed emerged from my left so fast, I didn't react quick enough.

He crashed into me, throwing me off my feet.

I screamed, kicking, punching.

Teeth gnashed so close to my face, he smelled like rotten garbage. I shoved my fists into his neck, yelling, my muscles straining to keep him from my face. His eyes black as hell, his fangs extended, his lips peeled and cracked.

Something slammed into the vampire and suddenly they rolled off me with such speed, I didn't see what happened. I shoved myself off the ground.

Then I sprinted up the hill.

A cacophony of snarls burst around me. I hesitated for a split second to glance back, to see a black wolf with enormous fangs facing off three vampires where a second ago, Áine had been. I knew somehow it was her... had to be. I turned to run, but the image of Livy's corpse lashed my thoughts. I wasn't like Áine. I couldn't run if there was a chance she might die.

"Fuck," I mumbled, spinning, racing back toward her, scooping a branch off the ground as a weapon.

Strong arms swooped around my waist, my back pressed to a rock-hard body. The branch I'd held fell to the ground from the impact. I screamed and bucked against my attacker.

"Quiet, little wolf." The hushed words grazed over my ear.

I startled and turned my head to find Luther behind me. Blood streaked his cheek, another gash over his shirt, the material torn. No gaping wound that I could see.

"Oh my god, where'd you come from?" I turned and hugged him, never wanting to leave his side. "Why didn't you reach out to me in my thoughts?"

He didn't answer at first, just snatched my hand and charged with me up the hill. "I couldn't reach you no matter what I did, but I could sense you, so I rushed to track you down."

Dread burned up my spine that Áine's sleeping powder had been responsible in blocking out Luther from my mind. Over my shoulder, she lunged at two bloodcursed, the third fallen to her feet. Even if she had killed Livy, she tried to protect me. I couldn't just leave her. "We need to help her!"

His hand tightened around mine. "She's an assassin and can look after herself," he hissed while running, tugging me alongside him.

Assassin? My head hurt to keep up with everything going on. If she intended to kill me, why protect me from the bloodcursed?

Luther charged with lightning speed, and my feet tripped over one another to keep up with him. As we crested the top of the mountain, an enormous castle rose into view. The same kingdom from my dreams. A strange déjà vu hit me like I'd been here before…

I shook with disbelief as the castle gleaming over the horizon. Five broad towers with pointed roofs dominated the heavens, all connected by fortress-strong walls made of white stone. Ornate windows peppered the upper walls far from the ground.

"The castle…" I began, but Luther wrenched me away from it and to the right. I stumbled after him, unable to stop staring at the enormous arched gates forged of gold sitting splayed open just feet from us. Fifteen-feet high, made of golden, twisted rods, the tips curled into spear heads. They led to a passage made of flat gold stones and the castle from my dreams. Stone walls spread out from either side of the gate, enclosing the castle.

I slammed into Luther, who'd stopped running. Peering past him, half a dozen bloodcursed had tipped another carriage. It must have been his.

My brain short-circuited. I couldn't deal with this. I whimpered, pulling back, ripping my hand from Luther.

Several guards lay dead on the ground in pools of blood, and others were being devoured by the monsters. Throats ripped open, chest cavities slashed.

Bile hit my mouth and I tore my gaze away, terrified, my feet already retreating, a branch snapping under my foot.

A bloodcursed with the whitest eyes jerked his head up toward me, unleashing an ungodly screech. I winced and covered my ears.

The other creatures' heads popped up as well. My heart pounded and if there was ever a time I'd suffer a stroke, this was it.

The white-eyed bloodcursed hissed and nearly levitated off the ground as it leapt toward us.

Luther moved like the wind. Grasping two blades from his belt and in a blink, he crisscrossed his arms, then slashed them apart at the attacking monster. Its head lopped right off and hit the ground before the body followed like a sack of potatoes. Blood gushed over the ground, squirting disgustingly.

Footfalls pounded the ground behind us.

I turned around. A dozen or so bloodcursed rushed forward, like starved beasts, mouths gaping, eyes ravaged.

I seized Luther's arm and hauled him with me. Fear clawed at my chest, and my sights fixed on the gate.

"They won't follow us in there, Luther. We need to go!"

He jerked backward with me, his gaze leaping to the gate, to me, and the oncoming monsters. Dread stole all the life from his face.

"No, I'll fight to save you. You can't go in there or you might as well be dead."

"Are you insane? There are too many. Luther, no," I pleaded, tears already sliding out. I held on to him like a lifeline. "You're not doing this. You're not, you're not." My pleas were a broken record, but I died on the inside.

At least a dozen bloodcursed raced toward us, the gate but ten feet away from us. Luther nudged me to stand behind him with an elbow. "Stay close, little wolf." But his words trembled, and it scared me to hear so much fear in his voice.

"You won't beat them." I ripped my hand from him and ran toward the gate, panic gripping me so tight, I thought of nothing but the need to escape.

"Guendolyn, no!"

Inches from the gate, he snatched the back of my coat, dragging me against him, his lips on my ear. "You're cursed!" he yelled. "Always have been. You cross that threshold into Ash Court and you'll fall into an endless sleep and the blood of fae will spill for eternity."

I couldn't breathe; his words barely made sense. "Wait, what? Why am I cursed?"

A sudden hiss scraped my ear, and Luther's hand flew to the monster at my side, jamming a blade into its eye. The horrible squidgy sound it made disgusted me.

Grubby hands grabbed for me, ripping hair, tearing at my clothes. "Luther!" I screeched.

He punched one and sliced his blade at the onslaught, but it was useless. We stood no chance. Couldn't he see this?

Every muscle clenched. I'd never been this close to the door to escape.

I wrenched free from their grip, seeing nothing but more monsters pouring out of the woods. I reached out after Luther, fisted the back of his shirt, and hauled him backward with me.

"Guendolyn!" he cried. There was such darkness in his voice, such desperation and fear.

His foot hit mine and he tripped. Momentum sent us reeling through the open gateway, both of us hitting the ground in a heap.

I scrambled backward, but the bloodcursed threw themselves toward us. They hit an invisible barrier that sparked with energy, zapping the creatures until they collapsed to the ground.

A heavy sense of drowning seemed to swallow me from the inside. Something felt wrong. Like I didn't quite fit together, my body twisted.

Luther scrambled over to me, cradling me in his arms, tears on his cheeks. "What did you do, little wolf? I'm not ready to lose you. I just found you."

"I don't understand." I held on to him, clutching his collar, but my insides were twisting and knotting. Shadows feathered my vision. My arms weakened.

"Don't let me go," I cried, and Luther held me tightly to his chest. His shaking was a blade to my heart.

My hands trembled, the sensation spreading over me so fast, I started falling into a familiar darkness.

"I'll find you again," Luther promised. "I'll tear down the world to find you."

And in a heartbeat, I was gone.

EPILOGUE

There was nothing right about me today.

I didn't know who the person staring back at me from the mirror was.

Eyes of every shade of the sky. Cheeks rosy like I'd been running. White, shining hair. And lips red as blood.

I wanted to scream, laugh—feel something. Except I couldn't remember my name, the black coat I wore wasn't right, and I didn't even know this room.

Not the bed with a smiling moon comforter, or the stack of school-books, or the easel sitting near the window. Sunlight poured inside, and the room seemed nice, I guessed.

But it wasn't me.

The mirror shimmered and I rubbed my eyes, but the closer I looked, the more my features changed. My hair extended to my waist, my nose was stronger, my lips paler, my cheekbones sharpening. Within seconds, the image faded away and the most beautiful man I'd seen in my life smiled back at me from the mirror, like he knew something I didn't. His eyes were crystal blue, and everything about him was perfection, intoxication, danger. I couldn't look away if I tried.

"Who are you?" I asked, and he just kept smiling.

The mirror's surface suddenly started to ripple.

Without warning, he pushed out of the mirror, first his arms, then the top half of him following rapidly.

My breaths raced, turning ragged and harsh. "Get away." I recoiled, but hands clasped the side of my face, holding me. His mouth captured mine, kissing me so brutally, so forceful, I winced, driving my fists into his shoulders.

Our tongues fought hungrily. Persistently, he pushed and pushed, sending wild shivers down my spine, awakening sensations that felt so familiar, so devilishly tempting.

My heart raced, and my toes curled against the floorboards, leaving me breathless. That fire raced through my veins, my flesh electric, flooding me with memories.

Palaces.

Fae.

Three princes.

Guendolyn... That was me!

And everything came back with the force of a storm. Everything I'd gone through hammered into me.

A rush of euphoric rapture engulfed me. I inhaled his musky and citrus smell like it was our first time, his scent imprinting on my mind like a photograph. Relief beat into me, and I desperately pressed myself toward him, needing him like I needed oxygen. I kissed him back, kissed him deeper, my fingers spearing through his hair. I thought I'd lost him.

My hands at once fell through him, and I stumbled forward, fear ripped in my heart.

"Luther!"

His breath ghosted over my face, and I reached for him, my fingers and head bumping into the hard surface of the mirror as he faded away. I gripped the edges tightly, my hands sore, burning, anything to hold on to him.

"Luther, no!" I cried. My voice broke. I thumped my fists into the mirror. "Take me with you. Don't leave me." Whimpers beat out of me, dragging me deeper.

He never came... Never returned.

I was alone.

Startled and teary-eyed.

Guen.

Guendolyn.

The lost girl from the Wandering Realm.

The girl misplaced in a world I didn't belong in.

I knew that now.

I wasn't asleep, and this wasn't a dream. Two worlds existed, and for years I lived in one, but dreamed in another. Until recently when I went into the realm with Luther. He woke me up from the curse, but left me behind.

I lifted my fingers and probed my lips, staring into the mirror. An ache flared from the pulsing, soft, reddened flesh, and I winced. As I stared, the redness darkened to a bruise from his fierce kiss.

The voice in my head, the prince who'd stolen my heart, had reached through the void to claim my lips with his hunger. A hunger I felt in the depths of my soul now shredded me into a thousand pieces.

My heart tumbled and ached.

This was no dream.

This was a nightmare.

"Luther!" I pounded my fists into the mirror once more, tears drenching my cheeks as my world crumbled. I smashed and smashed until the glass shattered under my fist, splintering outward like hundreds of tiny daggers. I suffocated on the pain, blood staining the mirror, but there was nothing left. Nothing left.

I fell to the ground, the sharp ache in my chest breaking me, and cried for the prince I lost.

TO SEDUCE A FAE

WINTER'S THORN, BOOK 2

TO SEDUCE A FAE

Three dangerous fae, two worlds at war, only one savior who can change their fate...

I left my foster home and all the baggage of my old life behind for a new start at university, hoping that things would finally change for the better. That the terrifying nightmares, disturbing visions, and strange voices would stop. That I'd get to be normal.

But it wasn't meant to be.

Three of the most dangerously stunning fae warriors suddenly crash into my life and change my fate forever. According to them, I'm their savior.

These smoldering princes insist I belong with them, *to them*, in the Wandering Realm, a place where love is lost, where war brews like poison, and where the once-powerful royals are hunted and slaughtered by the thousands.

This is the world they want me to save. But among these monsters, there can be no salvation. Even the three fae princes sworn to protect me are keeping dangerous secrets. Ones that if I don't unravel soon just might be the death of me...

FAE LEGENDS

You're cursed. Always have been. You cross that threshold into Ash Court, and you'll fall into an endless sleep during which the blood of fae will spill for eternity.

CHAPTER
ONE

GUEN

2 Years Later

"He's definitely watching your ass," Nickie whispers in my ear, glancing over her shoulder at the line of guys by the bar. "I bet he ends up being your date."

I exhale loudly. "Why did I let you talk me into a blind date? I suck at talking to strangers. My tongue does that thing where it swells to twice its size and I drool."

"Flimflam. You just need to find the right guy. There are guys who love droolers." She pokes her tongue out at me.

What sucks the most is that I think she's right. About finding the right guy part, not the drool-loving thing. Find the perfect match, and everything will come together, right? Except I'm not sure I believe in the whole fairy-tale ending, the prince coming for me, and me discovering I'm perfect just as I am. Maybe some people are just not meant to find their mates or live happily ever after.

Someone clears her voice from somewhere behind me. I turn to the organizer. She's in a short skirt and tank top, standing near the doorway to this small private room next to the bar. "Ladies, please take your seats.

We'll begin in one minute." Her voice is stern, and I can tell this isn't her first rodeo.

Nickie nudges me in the back toward one of ten two-seater tables set up around the room. "It's show time."

"By the way, you sound like a granny saying *flimflam*. Just letting you know as a friend." I smirk at her and poke my tongue out this time. I love my best friend, even when she's being super pushy. Except, she's radiating excitement from getting me on this blind date, and as much as I hate to admit it, the energy is contagious. What if I meet a decent guy? What if I find myself easily tossing out smiles that demand attention? I've watched guys fall prey to Nickie's flirting, so tonight might be a good time to try it out myself.

"I'm on a no-swearing diet," she admits, which is news to me since she was swearing like a sailor this morning. She pulls down on her tight red skirt that inches up her thighs, though she can wear a hessian sack and she'll still attract attention. She has a blue band around her wrist just like I do... this bar allows those under twenty-one to enter as long as we wear bright bands so no alcohol is sold to us.

Nickie has that girl-next-door beauty where she barely wears makeup, and yet, has unblemished skin, lips that are naturally pouty, and stunning red curls I might kill for. Me... I have to work to look half as good as her, but what I adore about her is that when we're together, she's down-to-earth and she doesn't judge me.

"Plus, Jack loves when I talk like this in the bedroom." She winks.

"Ew, I don't want to know. But for real, what the hell am I meant to say to my date? Talk about the weather? Ask what he does for a job? God, I'm already bored." And I'm talking too much, a sure sign of nerves, not to mention my hands are sweaty. I can't shake anyone's hand now. I rub them down my black dress. It's simple with spaghetti straps, and the best part, the shape gives me a cinched-in waist. Brings out my slightly curvy bust and hips that hide in most clothes.

"You look hot in that dress by the way, the black really makes your pale skin pop. Like one of those porcelain dolls."

"Is that a compliment?"

She scrunches her face and shakes her head at me. "Of course it is. Have you not seen the latest in fashion? Tans are no longer in style." Her eyes dart around the room. "Now, when the lucky man arrives, just chat to him normally like you're at college."

"I can't even do that." I start to walk away because this isn't going to work, and I made a mistake agreeing to this in the first place.

Nickie tugs my arm and pivots me back to my seat, to the table with a big number seven painted on a piece of paper.

That's what I've been reduced to. Specimen seven for a random guy to come and try out, as if this were an ice cream sampling booth.

"It's just a blind date, and it's being done as a group so everyone feels more comfortable, so you don't need to be nervous. Sugar knows, with all those strange dreams about kingdoms and princes you keep having, you need to get laid by a real guy."

"I do get action!" I whisper a bit too loudly, gaining the attention of a cute redhead girl two tables away, who winks at me. But Nickie's words hurt because I confided in her about the dreams that have been plaguing me my whole life. Dreams that I swore were real two years ago... Dreams I can barely remember anymore.

"I've seen all my potential dates somewhere at the bar, and none—"

"Gah! Just sit your ass down and stop overthinking this." Nickie flips open her tiny silver purse and pulls out a small piece of folded paper. "I made you something to help if you get stuck, because I knew you'd freak out." She leans in close and presses the note into my hand. "I pray your date is that fine glass of whiskey in the pin-striped suit. Did you see the size of his feet? Always look at a man's feet for everything you need to know. His shoes tell you how wealthy he is, how much he takes care of those close to him by the state of his shoes, and how loud he'll make you scream in the bedroom."

"If this goes wrong, I'm blaming you."

"Have fun," she murmurs before strolling across the room toward the door that leads into the main bar area, while the desperate and lonely remain gathered in this room. Balloons decorate the corners, obscuring lights covered in a red fabric, tainting everything in a reddish hue.

I feel stupid and uncomfortable and—

"Let's begin." The organizer draws the glass door shut to our room, closing out the chatter from the bar, and all I see is Nickie pressing her face to the glass, pulling a face at me.

I flip her the finger, and she laughs before vanishing into the crowd in the other room.

And this is why no one ought to ever let their friends set them up on blind dates, or any dates for that matter. Though I'd be lying if I said I'm not a tiny bit excited to see whom I've been paired up with out of pure scientific curiosity, of course.

The man who joins my table offers me a gentle smile. He's tanned with beautifully inviting green eyes and short-cropped hair. He's cute, not panty-dropping hot, but easy on the eyes. Probably a couple of years older than me. Twenty-one or twenty-two.

"I'm Holt. Great to meet you." His expression is neutral. He looks at me and sticks his hand out as if this were a business transaction, and maybe that's how some see the whole blind-date gig. Punch your details into a machine, and then it matches you to the most compatible person. And apparently, Holt is the one for me based on whatever Nickie added into my profile.

"Hi, I'm Guen." I shake his hand, and he sits down quickly, his hand on his lap, and I don't miss the quick swipe of his palm over his jeans.

Why did I shake his hand?

My heart is beating a million miles an hour, and heat is crawling up my neck.

"You look a bit different to the profile photo you sent in," he says right off the bat, so that's not a good sign. "Didn't realize your hair was so blonde. Is it dyed? Not that it's bad, I just wasn't expecting it."

I stiffen. Who in the world raised him? Wild dogs? I'm trying my hardest to give Holt the benefit of the doubt, but the shit dropping from his mouth has me clenching my teeth. "Actually, funny story, my roomie submitted the photo on my behalf, and well, I had just gotten out of the shower. So, I wasn't wearing makeup, and I only had a towel wrapped around me before she snapped the pic. Crazy friends, right?" I reach for my complimentary glass of cool water and gulp down a large mouthful.

"I prefer the natural look on women. Fewer clothes, less makeup, hair down and not dyed. Why mess with what God gave us, right?" He juts out his chin and chest with smugness, and I hold back an eye roll.

"This *is* my natural hair color!" I'm gobsmacked and push back the blonde hair I spent all night trying to add small curls to. My hair has a terrible time holding curls.

He stills, then eyes me like I might be the monster from his dreams, and already alarm bells are going off in my head. There is no way in the world Holt can be my perfect match.

In reality, I thought I had met my real match two years ago in another place, another world...

Luther.

One of three princes from Shadow Court in Wandering Realm in another world to ours.

But with so much time passing, I've forgotten many things, including why I thought he was the one for me. I'm starting to question if it wasn't all in my mind as the clinical psychiatrist my doctor ordered me to see insists. It's the only reason I agreed to this blind date. As a way to move on with my life and forget the imaginary man in my heart. The man who promised to come back for me, which he didn't. Which further confirms my theory that fairy tales don't exist.

Holt fills my glass with the jug of water from the table, giving me a wonky smirk. "I didn't mean to offend you; sometimes I have a way of saying the wrong thing."

"It's okay." I nervously drink more of my water, already out of ideas for a conversation.

I remember Nickie's note and fumble with opening it in my lap.

"So, what do you like to do in your spare time?" Holt asks, not sounding nervous, while I'm drowning in sweat.

"Paint landscapes when I can." Landscapes of the world that used to come to me in my dreams of castles, and a deadly forest made of twisted trees and teeth and claws. "But most of the time I'm completing assignments. I'm studying art at the local university. And you?"

"Scaffolding on construction sites is my day job. My newest project is just down the road. Maybe later we can go for a drive, and I'll show you. My last couple of girlfriends live on the way."

I'm at a complete loss for words, unsure what he's implying, and now all I can picture are all his girlfriends tucked in a row for Holt to wave to as we drive past. But I won't be going anywhere with him tonight or ever. Over my dead body. "Oh, that's nice."

He breaks into more chatter about how many girls he's dated this year, because that's fantastic conversation on a first date.

In all honesty, this date is cringe-worthy as hell. Perhaps I should have stuck to my guns and said no to Nickie when she told me she arranged this for me. There ought to be an escape button.

The back of my neck prickles with a warning, like someone is watching me from behind.

I quickly glance around to see everyone is focusing on their date, and I look across to the glass door leading into the main bar. People are everywhere, but no one is staring my way. Still, my skin crawls.

I glance back down at my note from Nickie.

If you're reading this, you've hit the desperate stage.

If you like him, ask him about sports or gaming or (you fill in based on interest) and listen to him.

If he's a creepo, tell him you're into foot fetishes or something gross and plan to move to Japan in a month.

I scrunch up the paper and fidget. *Wow, great advice, Nickie.* Around us, women are giggling, flirting, one couple holding hands. I want to exchange my date. I've never had luck with guys. Back in high school, one guy I crushed on hard saw me as nothing but a friend and ended up dating my arch-nemesis, while another guy I didn't like thought I was good enough for a forced one-night stand. Maybe the universe is trying to tell me something. Though one day, I like to think I'll find someone who doesn't just jerk me around.

"My last girlfriend had a lot of bad experiences with guys mistreating her. As a man, I will admit so many of them suck."

"Yes, we can agree on that. Guys suck." I'll go further and say falling in love is tragic. I've seen Nickie so miserable after her last boyfriend dumped her. They dated for eleven months, and now, I really hope Jack will be different. She once compared finding love to Russian Roulette with the true man of her dreams being the one bullet, and the rest are the empty chambers. I tried explaining to her how her analogy was wrong. Finding the one bullet is the one thing you do not want in Russian Roulette. She brushed me off and insisted it made sense in her mind.

I glance around for the organizer to try to call her over to escape, because Holt is definitely like finding the bullet under my definition.

"Ugh, right?" he says. "Except me. You can ask my exes."

"Will you excuse me for a moment? Just need to use the ladies'." I'm on my feet before he can respond. "Won't be long."

I saunter out of the room, noticing Bigfoot had scored himself a petite little brunette with tight curls who is batting her eyes. Well, at least someone is going to be screaming with pleasure tonight. I push open the door and slip into the other room, where the chatter and music engulfs me, then I rush like a madwoman through the crowd.

My body goes rigid when a guy calls my name behind me. All I can picture is Holt following me. I turn around with a *fuck off* on my lips, except there's only a crowd of partygoers behind me. Weird. I shove myself through the masses until I finally track down Nickie, who's sitting in her boyfriend's lap near a small table, swinging back a drink.

I march up to her and shout over the music, "I can't do this!"

Nickie flinches, spilling some of her orange juice down the front of her chest. "Fuc... Furry fudge, Guen, you scared the hell out of me. What are you doing here?"

I'm shaking my head. "I got the whacko of the bunch, Nickie, and your tips sucked." With a flick of my hand, I toss the scrunched-up paper on the table in front of her. I flop into the empty leather couch nearby and cross my legs. "He was so creepy. Talking about his ex-girlfriends, and he likes girls *au naturel*. He's probably a nudist. Why did you send that photo of me in a towel?"

Her boyfriend, Jack, is kissing her collarbone, licking up the spilled drink. He's handsome with short blond hair, and a perfect match for Nickie. They both have quirky personalities and click.

She's laughing, then refocuses on me. "Just give him a chance. He's nervous. Look how nervous you were."

I dig my claws into the couch. "You'll have to drag me back in there before I return to creeper town."

But she doesn't hear me, as she's kissing Jack, and I just roll my eyes and check out the number of other men in the bar who might have made more suitable dates. Most are drinking while trying to pick up. Maybe Nickie is right, and I was too quick to judge Holt?

My gaze lingers over the crowd to a man with broad shoulders and a smoldering look amid the shadows. The chatter and music are deafening, but in those moments as I lay eyes on this stranger, I hear nothing but the steady rising of my heartbeat. Alongside everyone else, he stands out, like he doesn't belong here. And I can't look away from him, as if I'm lost in a trance. He's powerful, and he radiates a sheer aura of danger, sending my pulse into a frenzy.

I want to look away, do something other than blush like a fool.

He's tall. Six-two, maybe six-three, his shirt hugging those wide shoulders and width. Dark clothes and short black hair blend into the shadows like he's morphed from them. And that face—sharp angles and strong jawline, eyes crystal green, almost glowing amid the darkness surrounding him.

Sweet hell, he's scorching hot, and his presence is arousing something from deep within me, something primal and fiery.

I get to my feet and gravitate to him in a lustful trance I can't seem to shake. Maybe this is my chance to find out who he is. The only other person who has ever made me feel this way was Luther, but that was two years ago, and apparently, in my imagination. Except it had felt so real, especially after he promised to come back for me... but never did.

Someone moves between the hunk and me, our eye contact broken. I'm swooning for this stranger, and when the crowd parts again, he's gone. Scanning the room, I can't see him anywhere.

Nickie says, "Get back in there and get him."

"Yeah, sure," I mumble before strolling across the room, staring where the sex god was seconds earlier.

I'm lost in my thoughts when the organizer from the blind date session suddenly steps in front of me, her expression filled with disappointment.

My stomach drops to my feet, and I wrack my brain for the perfect excuse as to why I can't return, except the opposite slides out. Saying the wrong thing is what I excel at. "Oh, I'm on my way back now." I mentally slap myself for giving in so fast. I've never been good at saying *no* to people. If I ever became a superhero, that will be my kryptonite.

I'm already walking with her and glancing over my shoulder for my mystery man.

"If you don't give people a chance, how will you ever meet your perfect match?" she reprimands me as we step into the dating room, and I lower my gaze cringing further on the inside.

"Sorry," I repeat, staring into her kind hazel eyes, deciding then I'll be honest with Holt and end this now.

"It's not too late," she says with hope in her voice, and I quickly turn around to take my seat to find it's not Holt sitting across from me.

"It's you." The words slip from my lips.

I twist in the seat when my skirt catches on the edge of the wooden chair, and I hear the first rip.

Sweet Jesus, no!

"Is everything all right?" his deep, raspy male voice asks... the complete opposite of Holt's.

He's the same man I spied back in the bar with those bejeweled green eyes that shone so brightly, they might be polished emeralds.

Up close, he's so much more handsome and divine, and did I mention *large*, like he might have eaten Holt to take his place? Short chestnut hair, longer at the top, a strong jawline and nose, full lips. But his eyes keep calling to me, like somehow they belong on a different face. I have no idea why I think that, but I'm lost for words.

That smoldering look of his assesses me as I'm scanning him, my mind racing ahead to figure out what to say. I feel the rising panic inside me, my face burning at being so close to him and likely making a fool of myself. He looks like he can pick and choose his girls, and doesn't need to work too hard for their attention.

"I may have sat at the wrong table." I go to leave as I feel my skin surging with embarrassment, but the rip in my skirt grows longer, and I'm about to scream, picturing myself with a huge hole over my ass.

"No, it's the right table. You're seven. The previous boy had to leave urgently."

Fisting the fabric of my skirt caught somehow on this hellish chair, I look up to the sex god staring at me, waiting for my response.

"Seven, yep, that must be me." I tug on the fabric to free myself, but it's jammed in there like Satan himself has sewn it to the chair to make me suffer.

"Oh, I'm Guen," I say, flushing so hard, I'm burning up. I take my glass and drink it down in one go.

"Dei—Demi," he says, seeming to struggle to remember his name.

I arch an eyebrow. "Demi? Really?" His lie makes me tug harder on my skirt in an effort to get out of here while smiling at the man my ovaries are preparing to marry. Then a louder rip sounds. I half-fall out of my seat, the chair coming with me.

My heart soars to my throat, and I'm picturing myself on the ground and my skirt up to my waist.

Strong hands catch me, and Demi is at my side incredibly fast, lifting me back upright. My heart is racing so hard now. If I was blushing before, now I'm a supernova, diving back into Earth's atmosphere at five hundred degrees.

He's kneeling near my seat, finding the cause of my small mishap.

"You seem to have your gown caught."

Gown? I shake my head and glance around to find others looking at me, and I'm mortified. "It's nothing, seriously. Don't worry," I insist, placing my hand over the gaping hole revealing my thigh to just below the line of my thong.

But he's fiddling with something under my chair, and having him kneeling, reaching me at head height, my whole body is tingling.

His fingers gently graze the side of my thigh. Just a simple touch, but it's enough to leave me losing my breath and get my nipples tightening. I imagine his hands all over my body, his mouth dragging over my skin, his head between my thighs.

What is wrong with me?

He takes hold of the fabric to release me from my torture, causing electrifying shivers to race through my body. My mind is speeding with wild thoughts of me leaning over and tasting this stranger's lips. But my head is waltzing with the commotion and embarrassment.

The couple close by keep watching us, and I just smile and give them a small wave, then drop my hand, feeling dumb.

"It's stuck in there hard," Demi says.

Oh, god!

He wrenches the caught-up fabric so suddenly, my whole body shuddering from the move. A horrendous rip screeches, and I'm about to die.

I look down to see him holding half my skirt in his hand, and the rest partially covering my thong.

Kill me now.

I stare at him hard, and if I had the power, I'd shoot laser beams from my eyes. "Are you kidding me?"

His mouth curls into a smile. "That wasn't meant to happen."

"Really? *You think*? Oh my god," I mumble, reaching over to find half of my ass exposed, and this is my worst nightmare come to life. Finding myself naked in public. Maybe I'll wake up and find that this is another of my insane dreams. Please let it be that.

"God won't help you, but I will." Demi is unbuttoning his shirt, revealing a strong, broad chest with not much hair, but so many muscles.

My mouth drops open as I take in the sight of a half-naked, muscular built man with a mouth poised in a smirk. He knew exactly the effect he has on me. Panty-melting gorgeous... hell yes.

"What are you doing?" My eyes are twice their size. I reach out to pull his shirt back on before everyone sees and assumes we're about to do something, considering I'm missing most of my skirt. Thank god it's dimly lit in here.

"As much as I'd like to take this moment to admire your naked rear, I insist you take my shirt." He shakes the shirt off his log-sized arms and hands it over.

I waste no time to slide it over my arms, his manly scent invading my senses. Oh, why does he need to smell so divine? This is completely unfair. The black shirt swims over me, and as I finally stand, the fabric falls to my knees. No ass cheeks in sight.

"Thank you." I look over to Demi, who's on his feet, topless and the most incredible thing I've ever seen. Planes of muscles and ripped abs all taper into the perfect V, where his black tailored pants hang low on his hips. My fingers tingle with the temptation to reach over and see exactly how hard those muscles are. In all honesty, my head is still spinning at how fast everything went down, and I offer him a piece of advice as I'm still fuming. "Next time, use your real name on a date, and try not to rip a girl's skirt off her body."

"I just saved you." He stares at me with amusement in his eyes.

I raise a brow. "*Saved* in the very loosest sense."

"Think I'll call this my very lucky day," he muses with a twitch of his lips.

I want to punch him in the arm, though by the size of him, I doubt he'd feel it.

"It's not often I get to help a maiden who flashes me her beautiful round rear." He eyes me, lips curling upward.

"Round?" I was wrong about him being oblivious—he knew exactly what he was doing with my skirt. "Yeah, it was your lucky day," I say. "Hope you got an eyeful, because it'll be the last time you see any of my *rear*." Why is he talking so strange anyway?

Someone nearby gasps, and the redhead girl sitting near us has her mouth hanging open, drawing everyone's attention to us, stealing envious glances.

"Put it away," a guy hisses, and the organizer is rushing over, her eyes flickering between me and the gorgeous, partially naked guy.

"Is everything all right?" She gasps, her eyes lingering on Demi's bare chest.

My mouth opens with an explanation, but Demi butts in. "We've had a splendid night, and now I'm taking the lovely lady to her friends. Farewell." His hand is on my back, and he's ushering me to the door.

My head is all over the place, while my body is trembling with tingles from his large palm against my back, from each inhale of his sexiness smothering me.

True to his word, he guides me through the crowd, who cheer us on as if we've just had sex in the bathroom. The night is going from terrible to horrendous.

Before we reach Nickie, Demi's hands slide to my hips, his bare chest pressed against my back, warmth spreading over me like an inferno. We pause near a quiet spot along the wall. His breath is on my neck as he inhales deeply.

"Did you just smell me?" I murmur, but despite wanting to shove him off me, I find myself clenching my thighs from the sparks erupting deep in my stomach. Something about the darkness of the bar, the thumping music, and his closer proximity has me trembling with lust, blurring my thoughts.

His teeth are on my neck, dragging over my flesh, and there's something almost deliciously familiar about the way he does that.

"Don't stop." My whisper slips past my lips.

Hard breaths are on my neck, and a moan slips past my lips as a pressure is mounting inside me.

"What's your real name?" I manage to speak the words, unsure where they're coming from. I'm trying to swim my way out of the fog swallowing my ability to think.

He exhales loudly, filled with arousal and frustration. Then he breaks our connection in an instant and steps back from me. "I'll be seeing you around, Guendolyn." His words fade.

Everything inside me stills at hearing him call me by my real name.

The last person to call me that was... "Luther?"

I whip around to find him gone. With it comes the void in my heart that I thought I'd buried after two years, gaping awake like a giant black hole.

TWO

DEIMOS

Guendolyn is as tempting and dangerous as the Seven Hells of Wandering Realm.

Following her energy to this tavern, I tracked her to that glass room and can't tear my gaze from her.

Captivating.

Alluring.

Sinful.

One look at her, and the world dissolves around me.

Her black dress falls mid-thigh, showing off toned legs, the bodice tight, maybe too tight as it pushes up her breasts, showing them off. Stunning, but I'm not impressed by the asshole in front of her leering. So when she excuses herself, I summon him to me with a little of the influencing magic the gods blessed me with, and I boot him out the door. Then I take his seat to talk to Guendolyn and discover how much she remembers about her past. I was warned that her memories would most likely be wiped of the events.

But I fail in my mission miserably tonight and gain no answers, what with her skirt incident, the image of her ass on my mind, and my thoughts not on returning home with her. That's not easy on any man. My stepfather, the King of Shadow Court, would lecture us that a man should never let his dick lead him. I was too young to understand how hypocritical those words were coming from him. Until I grew up to discover I lived in a kingdom of lies.

I shake those thoughts away and keep my attention on beautiful Guendolyn to make the best of the situation.

With what she is, I shouldn't be staring at her this way, thinking about the things I want to do to her, but I am.

Images flash of those legs around my hips, her head back and moaning as I drive into her.

I take in a sharp breath to steady myself. She's changed in the two years since we last met, her figure curvier, her beauty as brilliant as the rising sun. The girl who came to the realm then seemed younger, wary, still beautiful, but not like this. Not like this woman, whom I can't stop staring at. There's something about her beyond her hair falling perfectly over her bare shoulders, those hypnotizing blue eyes, and how much I want to rip those clothes off her body.

I can't stop remembering our first encounter alone two years ago in the Wandering Realm... our dance of words, her resisting me. One quick nip of her neck, and her blood flowed onto my tongue. Guendolyn now doesn't remember the night, but her taste has stayed with me. Indescribable sweetness like nectar and unlike any female fae I've tasted.

There's a power I sense beneath the surface in her presence. It's dark and deadly.

As Ahren, my eldest brother, once put it, *"Everyone knows who she is, that her name is Guendolyn, and what she represents... Everyone except her."* That's why I'm here to collect her. To take her back to the Wandering Realm and help us end the curse she unknowingly started two years ago.

Now, I watch her from within the shadows. My shirt covers enough of her, but it isn't like I can forget the creamy curves of her ass and what lies underneath the rest of her dress. Those long legs stretch out from the shirt, and in black heels, she fills me with filthy thoughts. She strips me of my focus and mission. Gods, she has the full package, and coupled with her blushing, my dick punches again in my pants, against the zipper.

She stole my second eldest brother's attention, but I barely knew the girl two years ago... Now I see what Luther means by his soul shattering for her.

Hell, she's gorgeous.

Everything about her calls to me. She's perfection. And maybe Luther isn't wrong in insisting we come to collect her and use her power to save our Kingdom. Sure, his intentions are to claim her for himself, but now... I exhale deeply. Now, I need to remember my mission and nothing else.

I track her movements from the glass room where she's gone to search for me, and her action ignites a spark of fascination within me. Confusion stains her expression, and she is off again, searching for her friend and passing two men, who eye her head to toe and look at her as a girl they plan to fuck and be rid of. She shouldn't be in a place like this.

I don't like it.

I should have stayed with her, but in her presence my head blurs, and remaining close to her tonight will end with me hilt-deep in that tiny thing. A shiver shudders over me at the thought, and I groan as a pulse rages in my cock.

Focus evades me, but I need it to help her open the gateway between our worlds so we can return home, before the curse spreads into Shadow Court and kills everyone. The trick is going to be getting her to tap into her powers.

She doesn't know that yet, but I'm an expert at getting people to do what I want.

For tonight, she's my concern, and that means ensuring no one touches her.

CHAPTER

THREE

GUEN

By the time I'm in bed, I'm exhausted. Nickie and her boyfriend are already in her bedroom, and the thump of her headboard hitting the wall is an irritating rhythm. I reach over and grab my earphones, then push them into my ears before selecting a playlist—any playlist—just to shut them out. A pop song begins, and I crawl under the blanket with only the silvery hue of the moon from the huge bay window drenching the bedroom. Yet all I can think about are those green eyes.

I shouldn't drool over the first cute man to cross my path. I shouldn't daydream about him endlessly. I shouldn't picture him naked. But it's all happening. His words ring in my ears, while my skin tingles with the memory of his hands at my waist, his broad chest pressed flat against my back.

I'll see you around, Guendolyn.

Who in the world is he? He looks nothing like Luther or his brothers from my dreams, yet he knows my real name. Nickie swore on her life she had nothing to do with setting me up with him, so I'm at a loss.

It took my shrink two years to finally convince me the dreams *were* all in my head. Most of the memories from those hallucinations, as my doctor calls them, have faded now. They left after I no longer heard Luther's voice inside my head... words that are like a memory I can't quite grasp. Now all I'm left with are recollections of three princes, longing emotions, and an extravagant kingdom.

154

Maybe it's for the best... except after tonight, old anxiety threads through my veins.

I roll over in bed and hug the blanket tight against me, then close my eyes, urging sleep to sweep me away.

Still, all I see are green eyes as he kneels before me, staring at me with a look of utter lust.

His hands touch my knees and push them wider apart.

Of course, I resist, but he's too strong to fight, and when his touch slides along the inside of my thighs, I tremble, unable to make a sound. I'm terrified he'll uncover my shameful secret.

The tips of his fingers are gentle, so tender and electrifying against my skin. He grazes me ever so lightly over my bikini line. Nothing stops him. He edges closer to my heat, where he'll discover how wet I am for him.

I draw in a sharp breath, unable to move, waiting for his fingers to slide into me. But he never does, not even when I'm pulsing with desire. My nipples tighten, rubbing against the fabric of my dress.

"Please," I beg, my body thrumming with arousal.

He laughs, making a sound that covers me in shivers, and when he slides two digits under the elastic of my underwear, I melt under his touch. My legs widen for him, and he swallows me with his gaze.

"You've wanted me from the moment you saw me, haven't you?"

I want to respond, but I can't, not while his touch is sliding up and down over my slickness, then circling over my clit. I'm muffling the sounds of my moans, and an orgasm rips through me fast like an earthquake, shaking me at the core. My muscles tense as I quake with pleasure. My eyes shut, and all I can think of is him.

Sprawled across my bed, I'm smiling insanely. Drawing the blanket over my chest, I take a deep inhale and count slowly to ten to calm my raging heart. It's been a long time since any man has had such an effect on me, and no man has ever had me climaxing by thought alone.

And still, I have no clue who he is, or even his name.

LUTHER SCRAMBLES OVER TO ME, *cradling me in his embrace, tears on his cheeks. "What did you do, little wolf? I'm not ready to lose you. I just found you."*

"I don't understand." I hold on to him, clutching his collar, but my insides twist and knot. Shadows feather my vision. My arms weaken.

"Don't let me go," I cry, and Luther holds me tight to his chest. His shaking is a blade to my heart.

My hands tremble, the sensation spreading over me so fast, I start falling into a familiar darkness.

"I'll find you again," Luther promises. "I'll tear down the world to find you."

And in a heartbeat, I'm gone.

～

Have you heard from the mysterious hunk?

I stare at Nickie's message on my phone and consider the orgasm I had last night from thinking of him, so yeah, I remember him well. My recent dream with Luther also pushes to the forefront of my mind. It's been two years since I last dreamt of him, and the memory leaves a deep ache in my heart I can't explain. I can't seem to recall what came before that part of the dream, or after—just the heartache that sits on my chest, like I've lost something so precious to me that I might die if I don't find it again.

I blink hard to push those thoughts away, then I look down at Nickie's message. Right. She's waiting for a response.

You know I didn't give him my number. I go to slide the phone into my back pocket, then remember I'm at work and wearing my black skirt— knee-length, skintight, which makes walking close to impossible and offers no pockets.

Painting has been my passion since forever, plus I needed a part-time job, so when my foster mom sent me a job application for the local gallery in Hyde Park, not too far from my university, I applied and got it. I manage the front desk for most of the hours I spend here. I'll admit, answering calls isn't fun, but Johanz, the owner, has been kind, and he put one of my paintings up in the lobby for show. That brings a smile to my face every time I glance to it hanging over the waiting room couch.

Thorny bushes and broken trees fill the landscape. Snippets of a glorious kingdom that reflect the golden rays of the sun can be seen in the distance, reached only by stairs made of twisted stone, accessible by crossing an arched bridge that spans two mountains.

I meander over to the reception desk and flop into my leather chair when my phone beeps with a message.

Your Cinderella man may turn up and surprise you yet. He has a shirt to claim back, remember?

At the mention of his shirt, I catch a light whiff of that delicious manly, outdoorsy scent, as though he's right next to me. Heat ripples down to the deepest pits of my stomach, as it had last night. Except, I'm only deluding myself if I let myself crave this stranger, and tonight I decide I'll throw his shirt in the wash to rid my room of the smell.

I reply to Nickie, *If only fairy tales were real.*

The office door to my right opens with a swishing sound.

Panic throws me into motion, and I toss my phone under the unopened letters on the desk. With a smile, I raise my head to see Johanz emerging. He's a tall man who wears a navy, pin stripped Armani suit like a second skin. Johanz is a handsome man, a lot more on the thin size for my liking, and he wears his black hair slicked back with a dash of blue color that glints in the sunlight. Though made of money, he didn't grow up rich. He once confessed that he came from a poor family, which is why, in my opinion, he's so humble.

"Guen, I'm out for a couple of hours. You're okay on your own, right? There are no showings today." He smiles, and all I see are those glorious pearly white teeth, the tanned lines bracketing his mouth.

"Of course, Mr. Landstone. I've got this covered."

He nods, pushes past the glass door, and makes his way to a black Mercedes parked right in front. One day, this will be me... owning a gallery, selling my own masterpieces, and driving the flashiest car around.

I reach for my phone, when the door suddenly jingles open.

"You forgot something?" I ask, tilting my head up, except it's not my boss but a man in jeans, sneakers, and a long-sleeved tee. Not the usual clientele, since the cheapest piece on sale is just over a thousand dollars.

The man with dark hair and a large, crooked nose shuts the door, then strolls past the reception area and through the arched passage into the gallery without a glance my way. We're open to the public, of course, but in all honesty, those who visit usually have a huge bank account. It isn't uncommon for people to wander in off the street, but most of the time, they leave very quickly once they see the price tags. The guard who normally sits at a little podium just inside the gallery is at lunch, and it doesn't occur to me until now that I should have locked the door until he returned, so I'm not alone.

Except, I'm sure this is just another wanderer about to walk out.

"Hello, how are you today?" I make my way toward the main showroom and find the man with short, messy hair staring at a painting of a train speeding through an old village on a rainy day. "That's an Ellaine Gray piece. She's a local artist here in town." I've always loved the rawness of this piece. "See how the juxtaposition of the industrial train against the wooden huts of the small town reflects the progression of civilization and lets go of the past? I mean to me. Everyone sees different things in paintings." Which is why I love them so much.

When he doesn't say anything but continues to stare, I figure I was wrong about him and maybe he is a buyer. I try to shake off the eerie feeling he gives off and treat him like any other customer. "What do you like about the painting?"

"Do you know this location?" He points to the image, and I'm shaking my head, even if he isn't looking my way.

"Sorry, I don't, but the artist will be coming into the gallery next week, and I can ask her."

He nods and looks around at the other pieces, and there's an unsettling strangeness about him I can't quite put my finger on.

The door behind me opens as a second man with a thick neck, tanned skin, and short, blond hair enters. He reminds me of a bodybuilder. He's also dressed in casual attire.

"Hello," I offer, like I do to everyone who arrives at the gallery.

He nods at me and makes his way over to the other man. He leans in close, exchanging heated whispers before they both look over at me.

The hairs on my neck rise, and I feel sick on the inside. I'm alone in the gallery, and concern has me glancing outside to see if Ted, our guard, has returned. I should call him to return. I swallow hard, and my feet slip backward as I turn toward my desk. My phone and bag are there, and I have pepper spray in the inside pocket.

"Um, excuse me, ma'am," one of the men asks, his voice raspy, like he's chain-smoked his entire life. Except the reek that normally comes with smokers doesn't linger in the air from his arrival. "Do you have any paintings with dragons?"

His question stops me in my tracks, and I turn to face him. He seems genuinely curious. I'm not sure how to respond at first, when the sign outside the building clearly states contemporary art.

"Unfortunately, no, but you'll find a gallery several blocks away specializing in fantasy, so they may have something you're looking for.

"What about that one?" His friend points into the reception, and I turn to see he's referring to my painting.

"Oh, there are no dragons in that image."

They both meander toward my piece, the blond guy striding so close to me, his arm brushes over mine.

I flinch backward from his unwanted touch, but he keeps walking to the painting as if bumping into me is meaningless. The nerve of that prick.

I rub my arm where he touched me. The skin is icy cold beneath my fingers. It's nothing, I'm sure, and I rub my arm to bring warmth to my flesh.

Both of them now stand in front of my work, staring at it, and I'd be lying if I didn't admit there's a moment of pride to have someone paying attention to my creation for a change. Even if it is two men who leave me uncomfortable. I move closer to my painting but keep a nice distance between us.

Blondie's nose flares at the image, and a tinge of sharpness pierces my chest at the thought that he might be mocking my piece, stealing my earlier joy.

"I'd recommend going to the other gallery for what you're looking for." My words come out harsher than I anticipate, but I don't care and march over to my desk, but footfalls follow me. Shivers zip up the back of my legs, and I move faster.

"That's your painting, isn't it?" one of them asks, and I'm too panicked to discern who's speaking.

I turn to face them and find they're both standing less than a foot away, towering over me, somehow looking taller than they were moments earlier. Something glints in their dark eyes, something almost fiery and red.

I stumble back, my hand reaching for anything on the table to use as a weapon. Pen. Stapler. Where in the world is my bag? All rational thoughts dissolve, and I struggle to unstick my feet from the floor. My heart is thundering harder when Blondie steps forward.

"You need to leave," I demand as my fingers graze the metal envelope opener on my desk, and I clutch it hard in my grasp. It's sharp enough to pierce flesh and do some real damage if they step any closer.

There's no surprise or shock crossing their faces. Blondie rolls his eyes, then checks his watch, as though he has another appointment with someone else to creep out.

"Is it time?" the dark-haired man with a crooked nose asks, and his friend's lips twist into uncertainty.

"Should have happened by now. I touched her, so it should have triggered the portal."

I grab my phone from under the envelopes on the desk and dial 911. "One tap and the cops will be here in a flash. Understand? Now get the fuck out of the gallery!" I have no idea what they're talking about, but they're freaking me out.

A heavy silence thickens the air between us, and I'm shaking.

The front door opens, and I'm about to cry with happiness when Ted, our guard, walks in, all broad shoulders and furious. He's in his black uniform and the best sight in the world. His gaze meets mine, and I try I give him my best panicked look before eyeing the two men near my desk.

"Can I help you two?" he growls, stepping closer, rather intimidating with his height.

The two pricks retreat, with Blondie taking the lead. "Not at all. We were just leaving."

"That's a very smart idea!" he booms.

They stroll out of the gallery, as if Ted doesn't look like a bear about to rip them apart. The bastards aren't afraid of him, and that realization punches me in the gut.

"You okay, Guen?" he asks me, his voice is gentle.

I'm nodding before he finishes talking. "Just freaked out."

"I'm going to check the back entry and lane. Stay here." He storms into the gallery to reach the rear door.

I'm frozen with shock, my brain screaming. I run for the door, slam it shut, and lock it with shaky hands just until Ted returns. Retreating, I keep scanning the sidewalk outside through the glass door and windows, expecting them to come back. The white walls of the gallery feel like they're closing in around me, and I'm choking for breath. Biting down on my lower lip brings a sharp sting. It tells me this just happened. It's real.

All I want is to go home and hide in my room. I start searching for my handbag near the desk to find it's fallen behind the chair.

A sudden pounding sound comes from the window behind me, and I flinch so hard, a small scream streams past my lips. I grab my pepper spray and swing around, ready to spray the hell out of the person's face if they break into the gallery.

Johanz frowns at me from outside of the gallery window, and it takes me a few moments to unstick my feet from behind the reception desk. I exhale with relief and hurry over to the door. My hands are still shaky as I unlock the bolt and let my boss inside.

"I'm so sorry I locked the door. These strange men came in and... Did you forget something?" My breaths came in shallow puffs, my mind whirring with memories of the incident.

"Just breathe, Guen," he says, worry threading his words, his gaze sweeping the gallery behind me. "Did they hurt you?" He's rubbing my back, and his eyes show the same genuine concern my foster mother had every time she took me to see the shrink. She never gave up on me when everything seemed to be against me. Not even when the doctor suggested that I might be suffering from schizophrenia.

"I'll bring you some water," my boss insists. "Lucky I came back. I just forgot my wallet."

"These men were standing really close, saying weird things." I feel stupid in this moment as I hear my words and what I'm freaking out about. But it's the eerie feeling that leaves my skin crawling.

"You did the right thing by locking the door."

I sit at my desk and feel like there was more I could have done. My boss quickly crosses the room and collects a bottle of water from his office before returning. After several mouthfuls of the cool water, I feel somewhat calmer.

Ted returns from the back room, his cheeks flushed, as though he's been running. My gaze falls to his hands, half-expecting to see blood on them from a fight, but aside from the rapid rise and fall of his chest, he's fine. "They're nowhere in sight."

"Come," my boss says to me. "I'm going to drive you home, and you can tell me what happened. Then you're taking some time off, all right?"

I'm shaking my head, my stomach suddenly hurting over the idea that he might not see me as fit enough to keep running the front of the gallery. "I'm fine, really." I tilt my head up and clear my throat, not wanting him to think that I'll freak out when any strange men enter the gallery. I love this job, and he pays so well. "I need the—"

He raises his chin, persistent enough to get his way, stealing my words. "I'm not taking no for an answer, and you'll be paid normally on those days off, I promise."

I nod and am already grabbing my bag and phone, struggling on the inside to accept that this is nothing more than a bit of time off. "Thank you."

"I'm sorry I left you alone. I should have made sure Ted was here. This is my fault."

My throat tightens at the heartfelt worry in his voice. "It's not your fault there are shitheads in this world."

He turns away, not seeming to listen, and walks toward the door. I grab my coat off the back of my seat and chase after him, braving the cold weather.

"Shit, Guen, you need to keep a baseball bat under your work desk," Nickie says while fluffing up her red curls in my bathroom mirror. "But on the bright side, you have some paid time off."

"Yeah, that's the part that worries me. The gallery has a huge showing this weekend. I might call Johanz in a couple of days and reassure him I'm doing fine." I lean a shoulder against the doorway to my bathroom, my gaze slipping to my friend applying ruby lipstick. "Do you think I overreacted in front of my boss?" She's wearing a body hugging dress in a metallic silver. She glints every time the light hits the fabric. It's hugs her from the bust to her butt, and the rest is flesh. On her, that dress makes her look like a goddess. On me, I'd be an embarrassment.

She whips around to face me, her eyes widening. "Why would you say that? Those two douches saw you alone and thought it was an opportunity. Sick fucks. Don't apologize for your reaction. Your boss should have ensured the guard was there." She lowers her lipstick to the counter and strides over to me, dragging me into her arms until I can't breathe. Despite her strength, her touch is warm, and she smells like a meadow of flowers. Kind of overpowering and sweet. I like it. "I'm always here for you, babe."

"Thanks. That means everything." When I can't take enough air into my lungs, I wriggle free from her anaconda-like grip. "Maybe I should stay home tonight? What if those jerks show up?"

"Babe, I bet they were just some dicks on the street and saw you alone in the gallery and thought you might be easy. Don't let them get into your head. But if you're really not up to it, we can hang out here and celebrate my birthday." She smiles widely, and I know she genuinely means it. Except, she's been talking about going to this club for her twenty-first for six months. The place is impossible to get into as it is.

Maybe she's right. I shouldn't let those asses get into my head. "Nah, let's go out. Some fun will help me forget the shitty day."

"Yes!" She jumps on the spot, then studies me up and down, her lips pinching tight. "So, you wearing that tonight?"

I stiffen and glance down at my blue skinny jeans that took me a legit fifteen minutes to climb into, so no way in hell are they coming off. I've also got on black combat boots and a button-up transparent black shirt with a black bra underneath. "I'm going for the casual, I-don't-give-a-fuck-but-you-can't-glance-away look."

She makes that humming sound like she always does when she doesn't agree.

"You'll need the jaws of life to pry me out of these jeans, so they're staying," I say.

"At least put some heels on. I'm going to get you mine."

"No, it's—" I reach out to stop her, but she darts out of the bathroom too fast. There's no stopping her. I step closer to the mirror and run my finger under my eyes where the makeup is slightly smudging. The woman staring back at me looks so much more confident than how I feel inside. Blonde hair cascading over my shoulders gleams from the glitter I sprayed it with, the same rainbow of color lashing over my eyelids. Kohl makeup lines my eyes, which look particularly blue tonight. Though, underneath, unease bubbles in my chest. There's a fog in my head, like I'm only half-living in this world. That sense of forgetting something is always with me... always has been, for as long as I can remember.

"Here you go." Nickie returns and places a pair of shiny black heels near my feet.

"You had to get the tallest ones, didn't you?"

She smirks with an evil glint in her tawny eyes, and I can tell she's loving this. She's been trying to dress me up in her clothes ever since we moved in together two years ago. "You look so sexy with heels, girl. Put them on, and let's get going," she orders with a laugh.

By the time I'm geared up in shiny black stilettos with open toes and straps around my ankles, we're rushing outside where an Uber awaits.

The city blurs past in bright lights and cars, and after a flash of the tickets Nickie bought months ago, we're in the club before I know it.

Strobe lights throb across the room, people crowd together on the circular dance floor, and the floorboards thump beneath my shoes from the thundering music. The whole place is a heartbeat coming through the speakers.

"This place is insane," I shout at Nickie, just to be heard over the noise.

"And it's just getting started. Wait until the dancers in the cages come out." She snatches my wrist with an excited giggle, and we force our way closer to the bar, then she lets go of me. I'm caught up in the enormous pedestal in the middle of the dance floor with people up there dancing for everyone. A loud cheer explodes around us, and I lift my head to the four large bird-style cages lowering from the ceiling. They pause halfway down and inside each is a woman in a bright pink sparkling bikini, pole dancing with the bars.

People shove past us to join the crowd, and I've never seen a place this crazy. I love how my pulse dances in my veins. Everything about this club is made to invigorate you as soon as you walk inside.

Nickie slides a glass of something green into my hand, and it smells like Midori. "That was fast service," I say before I drink it easily, it being so sweet. Exactly what I need to forget the day and have a wild night.

"A guy at the bar bought them for us. How generous, right?" She's sipping hers, staring out into the crowd.

I blink hard. "Wait, you accepted a stranger's drink? He could have spiked it." Oh geez, I just drank mine as though it were candy water. If I make myself vomit, will I stave off any drugs in my system?

My chest tightens as I turn my head toward the bar. So many people are huddling close to the counter. "Where is he?" I ask.

"It's okay, babe," she reassures me by nudging her arm up against mine. "I accepted it from the bartender directly, and the guy just paid. He insisted it was for both of us. He was a freaking hot beast."

"Really? Hot beast, you say?" I glance around.

As we finish our drinks, a tall man in his mid-twenties with short, sandy hair and tanned skin approaches Nickie. He's in a shiny blue shirt and black pants, hair parted down the middle. Not handsome in my books. Even with them standing so close, I can't hear the whispers over the noise in this place. Is he the hot beast? He's too much on the skinny side for my liking.

Next thing, Nickie grabs my arm and draws me toward the dance floor. Launching forward, I stumble on my heels, convinced I just murdered half a dozen toes on the way. I quickly slip my and Nickie's empty plastic cups onto a nearby table we pass.

Bodies sway around us. To be surrounded by so many people all dancing is electrifying, and I'm loving every moment of this. Somehow, we end up in the middle near the pedestal. I can't recall how long we've been dancing when someone catches my eye from across the masses. Familiar dark hair and a crooked nose. Next to him is Blondie, the other stalker from the gallery.

Air chokes out of my lungs, and I feel as though I'm suddenly drowning.

My feet are sliding backward. No, this can't be happening. That can't be them.

Panic lashes over my chest.

Run.

That's all I'm thinking.

Nickie. I find her in the crowd to my right. "Nickie," I call out over the music, but it's impossible to hear anything in here. I push myself through the masses to reach her, when a new song comes on and the whole crowd goes insane with excitement. Screaming and shoving as more people enter the dance floor.

Nudged and elbowed, I stumble about and lose sight of Nickie. The stalkers are gone too.

I press myself in the same direction Nickie was moments earlier as I scramble to pull my phone out from my back pocket. Bumping into others doesn't stop me.

"Watch it, bitch," someone snarls, and another person shoves me in the back.

My heart is pelting against my chest with the need to escape.

The phone is trembling in my hand as I frantically hit Nickie's number. Pressing it to my ear, I shove past the masses and glance around, unable to see the stalkers.

My chest constricts desperately with fear. All I want to do is scream for help, but I can barely hear my own thoughts.

"Hello," Nickie answers, her voice barely reaching me.

"Where the hell are you?" I stare out over the crowds, shouting at her so she hears me.

"If I haven't answered, it means I'm out having fun. Leave a message."

"Fuck," I mutter under my breath as I hang up and jam my cell into my back pocket.

At the edge of the floor is a huge guy in a black T-shirt. Out of instinct, I gravitate toward him. "Excuse me, are you a bouncer here?" I ask, but he doesn't seem to hear me and pushes right past me.

Rude much?

I retreat and move past him.

There are people everywhere, and my heart is hammering hard. I don't know where to look. Everyone is exploding with applause from the tune. I don't know the song, don't care. People are pushing past me, and I want to hide somewhere. My stomach in my throat—I should have stayed home, should have followed my instinct.

Someone grabs my arm, and I swing around, my skin pricking with dread.

Blondie's wry grin greets me. He says something, but I can't hear him.

I don't think but fight back, kicking him and trying to wrench my arm from his, but it's useless and he just laughs at me. With one swift pull, I'm stumbling on my feet after him toward the rear dark corner of the club.

"Help me," I choke out as I reach for people. I grab their shirts, their arms, bags, anything, but they all shake me off, don't even bother to look at someone kidnapping me right in front of them.

Dread is choking me when the other one shows up. Dark hair. Crooked nose.

"Leave me alone!" I shout, but it's too loud in here.

They leer at me, and I feel violated before they even hurt me. Blackness pulses through every inch of me, emptying me of any possible hope.

Blondie grabs my arms and slams my back to a wall, my skull hitting it hard. Stars explode behind my eyes, pain jolting over my head.

My blood runs cold as he pushes up against me, his face in mine, and all I can smell is putrid decay. A chill creeps up my spine.

I don't know these men, but I despise them. I hate the terror throbbing inside my chest. Hate how petrified I feel with every breath that I take. I want them to scream with pain.

I stare in the face of my nightmare and battle against him, punching and shouting at him. He moves so fast, I don't see the hand coming until it grips my neck, lifting me off the floor, and I'm on tippy-toes as he pins me to the wall.

The sounds around me seem to fade, the nightclub receding into the distance.

"Your fate is death, Guendolyn," he snarls. Big brown eyes and bushy eyebrows are all I can see.

I don't know how he knows my real name, but I loathe the sound of it on his lips. Loathe how he stares at me like I'm dirt.

His fingers squeeze harder, and I'm suffocating, my lungs strangling themselves for air. My heart punches into my chest, faster and faster, until darkness feathers the corners of my eyes.

Suddenly, he's flying backward, ripped from me.

My knees buckle, and I drop to the floor as the air buffets against me. I drag breaths into my starved lungs, trying my best to see through the tears and dimness of the club.

A large figure emerges out of the shadows and approaches me. But I'm too far gone.

Darkness swoops in and steals me from the terror.

FIVE

GUEN

I open my eyes to a white ceiling and circular chandelier, dripping in crystals. It doesn't look familiar. This isn't the club or my apartment, and a sliver of fear creeps through me as I try to recall how I got here. *Buzz...buzz...buzz.* My pocket is vibrating.

I push myself up from a black leather couch and grab my phone from my back pocket. Fog blurs my mind. I'm waiting for my brain cogs to restart. To remember where I am. There have been many times when I've woken up and couldn't remember my own bedroom, as if I didn't belong there, as if it weren't my room. It used to scare me to hell to feel so lost, to feel like my life was a maze I couldn't escape from. I wondered if one day I'd wake up and not remember who I was at all. I shake those thoughts aside, focusing on the now, on the thoughts pushing forward.

A luxurious open room surrounds me. White walls, paintings of beautiful landscapes and women in golden frames. An unlit fireplace sits in front of me, and a large dining area to my right has an enormous television on the wall. There's a hallway that leads to more rooms. I twist my head to see floor-to-ceiling windows behind me. I'm on my feet and staring outside at the bright lights at night time.

I swallow hard and turn back around fast. Someone brought me to a hotel. The club incident grows crystal clear. I slump my back against the window, heaving for breath.

Thoughts blur in my panicked mind, but I don't want to be one of those women who crumble and scream. I need to think this through and get the hell out of here. I start crossing the room to the door.

So many things aren't making sense, such as why I'm in such a fancy hotel. If those stalkers kidnapped me, why here and not a dingy basement? Someone would have seen me carried up here unconscious. Maybe it's not them who brought me here?

My phone trills again, and I look down at the ID splashing over the screen. *Nickie.* I answer the phone.

"Holy shit, where are you? I've been calling for hours. You had me freaking out. Where are you?" Her panic is contagious, and now I'm pacing faster toward the door.

"I-I don't know where I am." Dread climbs through me, heavy shattering dread that tells me I've been kidnapped. What other explanation is there? "I'm in a hotel room, maybe the penthouse, somewhere in the heart of the city."

"Fuck, why didn't you tell me you were leaving? We had a pact."

"Nickie, I've been kidnapped. Call the freaking cops."

"Son of a bitch. Run. Get out of there. No, wait. First, tell me where you are."

I'm frantic, my gaze swinging left and right, and I spot a phone near a hotel notepad. I launch for it just as the front door clicks and swings open.

My heart freezes in my chest, and I try to change direction to hide. But I'm too slow, and already, a man is striding inside.

I turn to run away, but when I catch a glimpse of his face, I'm utterly shocked. My feet tangle in the lush white rug under me, and I fall before I can stop myself.

Thump. I hit the rug with my hip, and I'm scrambling back to my feet as I mouth, "Demi?"

He stares at me as if confused, then realization washes over his face as he clearly remembers his made-up name. Dickhead.

"What the hell is going on?" I bark.

His eyes sweep over me appreciatively, and then he smirks.

"Guen, what's happening?" Nickie is yelling from the phone in my grip.

Demi shuts the door and stands there, huge and sexy as hell, wearing black jeans and a matching tee. He's carrying a plastic bag with three large cola bottles. Serial killers wear black, right, but what's with the soda? He steps past the fireplace and sets down the plastic bag.

I break out in a cold sweat and feel myself falling apart into hundreds of pieces as I consider the idea that this man has been stalking me for god-knows-how-long. And now he's got me where he wants me. Serial killers do that. Follow their prey, keep a wall of pinned photographs of their victim until they make their move. And his plan must include a penthouse for some reason I don't understand.

"I'm not going to hurt you, Guendolyn. I'm here to protect you." He walks closer. "Now, give me your phone."

"H-Help me?" I stammer. My breath catches in my lungs.

I run for the door, grasping the handle and rattling it, but it's not opening.

"Locked," he says.

With the phone to my ear, I'm breathing heavy now, and spy the notepad with the hotel name again.

A shadow falls over me.

He snatches my phone from my hand.

I lunge after him, but he drops the phone to the floorboards and stomps his heel onto it, smashing it.

I scream and punch him in the arm. "Why did you do that? I'm still paying it off."

He walks away nonchalantly and picks up his bag of soda before placing them on the table. I fall to my knees.

The front panel of my phone is completely shattered, his heel having crushed the entire life out of it. Nothing is salvageable. When I hit the power button, nothing happens. *Sonofabitch.*

"Fuck you! You're buying me a replacement," I growl, though on the inside I'm shaking. If he meant me no harm, why lock me in here and smash my phone?

He's at the table, opening one of the soda bottles. He then proceeds to gulp down most of it in one go. Is that part of my torture? Make me listen to him burp endlessly?

As if on cue, he unleashes a belch that rivals Godzilla's roar.

"That's disgusting, and why are you guzzling that shit?" I yell.

"We don't have such sweet, fizzy water at home." He reaches for the second bottle.

"That stuff will kill you," I remark.

He halts with the bottle pressing to his lips, then lowers it. "It's poisonous?"

"In a way. If you drink a lot of it."

He honestly looks confused and blinks hard as he studies the bottle.

"Then why do you people drink this?" He sets it down and wipes his mouth with the back of his hand.

I raise a brow as I climb to my feet. "*Us people*? Whatever! Let me out of here before I scream for the whole hotel to hear."

"Not happening, so get comfortable. I have a lot to tell you." He grabs the hotel food menu and tosses it to me. It hits me in the stomach and falls to the floor. "Order us a feast. I'm starved."

For a moment, I think he's going to stand over me to make sure I order him food, but he meanders over to the fireplace. While tempted to hurl the menu at the back of his head, I play along.

"Sure thing, asshole."

His lips break into a smile when he looks at me over his shoulder. His teeth are perfect. Everything about him is perfect. And if he can afford a penthouse, why kidnap me? Sweet talk me, and I'd probably come with him here on my own. Something isn't making sense about this whole scene. I can't help but feel as though I'm being pranked.

I pick up the phone on the small table near the window and hit the front desk button.

"Hello, how may I assist you?" a female asks.

"Yes, call the police. I've been kidnapped. He's locked me in the penthouse." My words are rushed, and I steal a glance at the dick who's lighting up the fireplace, chuckling to himself.

"Ma'am, I assure you that you are in safe hands. Mr. Lorcayn is highly regarded here, and he has informed us that you might call us. Guendolyn, if I may call you that, you are one lucky woman. I will arrange to send up champagne and strawberries for your honeymoon."

"No, wait... What?"

She hangs up, and I'm gritting my teeth.

I slam the phone down, and questions are reeling over my mind. Listening to my inner conscience, I pick up the receiver and dial 911.

The phone line goes dead in an instant, and I look up to see the asshole standing at the other end of the couch, the cut phone line in one hand and a *blade* gripped in the other.

Fear spreads its vicious wings, and the food I ate earlier in the day lurches in my stomach. Except I won't be a victim or show him I'm scared. I swallow the trepidation buckling through me and lift my chin.

"So is Lorcayn even your surname, or is that another lie?"

He doesn't respond right away, but I hear the sharp intake of breath.

"Would have preferred if you'd ordered us food." He tucks his blade back into his boot and flops down into the single-seater couch.

"I don't want food. Who are you? Are you following me? And how do you and those creepy asses from the club know my real name? And why am I here?" Half a dozen more questions pepper my mind, but with the amused way he's staring at me, I'll be lucky if he answers one.

My life has sucked enough as it is. Growing up with hallucinations, dreams that felt real, voices of a prince in my mind, and now this. I'm already broken. After this shit, I'll need therapy for life.

Feigning courage, I fold my arms over my chest and press my hip against the side of the sofa. All I can see are those green eyes. He stares at me as if I ought to apologize for something. It might have to do with how my body reacts around him, how I'm picturing his hands on me and him naked. Thoughts that don't belong in my mind, since I'm his captive.

We stare each other down. I pray Nickie is smart enough to call the cops, and that the cavalry arrives soon.

Eyes the color of a stormy ocean, green with tinges of blue and gunmetal gray study me. He lounges in the seat, and the corded muscles in his neck twitch. His T-shirt sits a little too tight on him in the most delicious way. I can't tear my gaze from his full and expressive lips. The sincerity in his dark gaze confuses me.

"Are you just going to stare at me, or tell me what's going on?" I chastise, intending to keep him talking until help arrives.

His face is solemn as he speaks. "Deimos Lorcayn is my real name. I came to collect you to help save my family, except it seems first you need *my* help. And that might be partly my fault."

All I can remember is his name.

"Deimos?" I repeat. "Why does that sound familiar?"

"Because we've met when my brother, Luther, brought you into Wandering Realm two years ago." He blinks with those thick eyelashes most girls would kill for.

Disbelief crashes over me, and the more I stare at this man, the more I don't remember seeing him before. "Luther had two rude brothers, but... Wait. How do you...? If you know..." I'm rubbing my eyes, my brain stretched taut with confusion.

Something is very wrong here.

My dreams aren't real. My shrink said so.

Two years of no dreams.

Two years of no Luther in my head.

Two years of no memories.

"Please don't tell me you've been stalking me and found out about my past from the shrink's files? Seriously, that would freak me out beyond belief."

"Shrink? And I'm not rude. Just honest." A glimmer of amusement flashes in his eyes.

"You *are* rude," I correct him as he tries to get under my skin. "Why didn't you use your real name the other night if you're telling the truth?"

"I had to be sure it was you, and when I was... well..." He licks his lips. "There were distractions that caught me off guard. Like when you had your skirt ripped off you."

He seems to catch his breath.

"*You* ripped it off me, remember?" I snap, and at the memory, my cheeks flush.

He responds with a grin that tells me he regrets nothing.

"I don't believe you, by the way," I retort.

"Are you calling me a liar?"

"If the shoe fits."

His gaze lingers over me.

Something about the way he looks at me triggers a longing that sings in my heart, a feeling that haunts me, and yet, I have no recollection why.

"Guendolyn, you don't belong here. I've come to take you home, before it's too late. And maybe your memories about what happened two years ago will come back once we leave this place and enter our realm."

It takes a moment for his words to sink in. *Home.* I've never felt quite at home anywhere, but to think my home is in a different world feels odd. Two years ago, I believed in the other realm, the kingdoms, and the fae who lived there. A child's fantasy, my psychiatrist insisted. Now my brain fights against his words and their implication. Two years it took to finally feel semi-normal. Now my brain resists the possibility that I might have been right all along. This can't be.

"What happened to me?" The words fall from my lips.

There's sympathy in his eyes at my question, but I brace myself for the answer, to hear the truth I've missed my whole life. Is it that bad that he hesitates?

I blink slowly, trying to calm my accelerating heartbeat.

"It's complicated," he insists. "Half of what I've heard are from legends."

"Legends?" Okay, so the vagueness is a sure sign of him fabricating his stories. I won't deny a sting of hurt jabs me in the heart because for a few seconds there, I believed that maybe this might be real.

I glance over to my phone, smashed to smithereens on the ground, then back to Deimos. Seeing this man sit back and relaxed has me uneasy. This isn't how kidnappers are supposed to behave. Well, based on the knowledge I have from books and movies.

Bang. Bang. Bang.

I flinch and jerk my attention to the door.

A muscle twitches in Deimos' jaw.

Sweat beads my palms, and I'm backing up. The cavalry has arrived.

In the same heartbeat, the door bursts off its hinges. Blown apart, shards of wood fly in every direction.

A shuddering scream rips from my lips. I drop to the ground. Arms over my head, I crouch near the couch for protection.

My heart's pounding.

The police aren't messing around.

An explosion of sounds detonates around the room. Growls and shouts. I glance up just as the small couch is tossed across the room. It crashes into the table, breaking its fall. Bottles of cola explode like they'd been shaken. Fireworks of foamed soft drink pepper the air.

A flinch of terror pricks through me. I peek out from behind the couch, my stomach balled up tight.

Deimos hurls a fist into a man's face, sending him flying into the wall with unimaginable strength. The blond man doesn't even groan and peels himself out of the hole in the wall. He growls, his eyes as red as blood, and I know him.

Oh, fuck. He's the stalker from the gallery, from the nightclub. I'm too shaken to think straight or work out why he keeps following me. But it's clear he isn't working with Deimos.

His mouth stretches into a grin. Sharp fangs slip out, pressed over his lower lip. He throws himself at Deimos, both of them hitting the ground in a swarm of violent hits and punches.

It's too fast... too fucking much. Maybe I'm not seeing clearly, because this isn't right.

My gaze swings to the smashed door lying open, and I shove up off the floor and run. The fight rebounds behind me while the faint wail of a siren echoes in the distance.

"Guendolyn!" Deimos roars from somewhere behind me.

I don't look back as I bolt out of there.

Instinct drives me out into the small corridor leading to an elevator.

Footfalls pound the floor behind me.

I'm freaking out, my hand reaching for the elevator button.

A swoosh of air collides into my back, sending me reeling over my tripping feet.

Fierce hands snatch my hair and wrench me backward. My legs buckle under me. I'm screaming. My arms fumble out for anything to grab on to. A bowl of apples sits on a small table against the wall. My fingers grip the edges and I seize it. I swing the bowl and whack it against the stalker's head.

Crack!

He releases me, and I stumble away. I'm trembling, my whole body racked with terror. I press my spine against the metal elevator doors, and my hand frantically slaps the button. *Come on. Come on. Come on. Open already.*

I stare straight ahead at the hulking man with a crooked nose. Something's wrong with him. His back is curled forward, eyes a smear of red and black. Fangs slip out from under curling lips. He moves with shoulders curving forward, a snarl rolling through his heaving chest. He closes in.

This can't be real. It can't be real.

Through pasty lips he hisses, "Fucking abomination. Enough games. We will take you back tonight to face your judgement."

"Whoa, that's a bit much." I have no idea what he's talking about, but I can't stop shaking.

Deimos is flung out of the hotel door and smashes into a mirror hanging on the wall in the hallway. Shards of glass shatter over him. Hundreds of pieces fall down over his head. I jump in my skin at the sight of him slumping to the ground with a loud grunt.

But the monster in front of me flies at me.

I scream just as the elevator door dings and opens with a *whooshing* sound.

He slams into me.

We tumble inside, my head cracking against the floor. Pain spears over my skull. In the tussle, the fight for my life, darkness surrounds me from all sides, swallowing me.

Claws and teeth scrape my flesh. His body shoves onto mine, his weight like a mountain. Breath that reeks washes over me.

My panic flares. I buck against him, hands and legs shoving everything I have to get him off me. My breaths come raspy and hard. I lash out, scratching his face. But terror is beating into my body.

Waves of a chilling cold crash through me, faster and faster. The world around me blurs, in and out.

My whole body is convulsing. No, no, no. I haven't been sick like this for the past two years. Fear shackles my chest. I can't breathe, can barely move. A bitter scent of electricity floods the air.

I know what's coming. Death is coming for me. The word reverberates through my mind. *Death*.

The elevator shakes ferociously. A terrifying sound of metal buckling roars like a dragon.

With those dead fucking eyes piercing into me, darkness calls to me.

The world recedes in a flash... gone is the elevator. Trees and night engulf us. A bitter cold sweeps past, ripping its fangs into my flesh.

I scream and the strange world is ripped away. A fraction later, we're back in the elevator.

The fucker on top of me freezes, his eyes wild. "There you are... There you fucking are! I knew you would open up the portal for us. Now do it again!" he bellows. "The King of Ash Court has called for you."

His mouth gapes open, his fangs exposed.

Cries fall from my lips, and I only see the end coming.

CHAPTER

SIX

DEIMOS

I hit the floor like a sack, pebbled glass raining on my head and shoulders. Sharp edges cut into flesh. But I don't care. I don't give a fuck about me. I'm on my feet in a heartbeat, when the hairs on my body rise.

Magic.

It pricks over my skin, lapping at my insides like a cruel sea. Sharp and jagged, it spills into my chest and curls around my heart. Dark magic, the same kind that ripped the Wandering Realm in two.

Power ripples from within the elevator... I'm drawn to it. Guendolyn and that Bloodcursed vanish from existence before my eyes, then flash right back.

She opened the portal. She fucking opened it, but can't hold it long. Never mind. That time is all we need to enter our realm.

The sonofabitch throws himself on top of her, and my muscles tense, my nostrils flare.

I shove forward as dust falls from the shaking ceiling and walls. The elevator doors are closing, and fear squeezes my heart. I throw myself between them just as they jam against my shoulders, then bounce back open.

Adrenaline pulses through my veins with a thunderous beat.

She's screaming, and her gaze finds me from beneath the blood-sucker, cutting me like glass.

I snatch the back of his shirt and wrench him off her, then hurl him out of the elevator. But in the next second, the Bloodcursed lunges at me out of nowhere.

His fist connects with the side of my face. I reel backward as he launches at me. My back smacks into the elevator wall, and my head explodes with pain.

Fuck!

I throat-punch him, but the bastard barely reels.

Guendolyn huddles in the corner, hugging her knees, mumbling things I don't understand.

The damn Bloodcursed comes at me, all claws and teeth. I duck his attack in the small confines of the elevator, then pivot. I fist his hair and the back of his top, then toss him out as hard as I did his friend. He flies across the hall and crashes into the other fucker as he tries to get to his feet.

Stay down!

The doors of the elevator shut with a ding, and we're lurching. I turn to Guendolyn and reach for her arm. "Get up." I yank her to her feet. My heart is thundering. "Open the portal now!"

She's shoving a hand into my chest, wriggling out of my grasp. "Get the hell away from me!"

"I'm not going to hurt you, but you need to open the gateway before they return. They'll never stop coming for you, do you understand?" I growl.

But she's shaking her head, looking lost. Her eyes are huge. She's terrified. "What's going on?"

"You vanished a few moments ago with a Bloodcursed, then reappeared. Whatever you did then, do it again."

She hugs herself as she pushes herself into the corner like she might vanish. "I don't know how I did that."

My thoughts are too scattered, and I don't have time to train her to use her power in the little time we have and while she's scared.

The elevator dings, and I jerk around. My hand instinctively grabs hers, and I drag her behind me when I see the foyer of the hotel is clear of those blood-suckers. There's only one person at the counter and two staff. I wave at them while Guendolyn calls out for help.

All fae carry a power unique to them. My brother Luther has second-sight and can enter someone's mind, even if it's forbidden in our kingdom. Me, I have the power of persuasion via the sound of my voice. It's not foolproof, nor does it always work, but it got me a free hotel room and kept them from believing her when she called reception. She's very predictable.

The two women behind the counter smile at me, their eyes lustful like so many females in this world.

I rush outside with Guendolyn in tow.

She cries out, and we're drawing more attention.

My muscles tense. I can't persuade whole crowds.

"Let me go!" She batters her fist into my arm, and I have half a mind to toss her over my shoulder and run. Except they don't do such things here, Luther told me. Along with giving me lectures on everything human he could think of. I have the knowledge, I know many things, but experiencing this world is a very different thing.

"Quiet!" I bare my fangs out of pure frustration. "Believe me, I'm helping you."

Her cries cease, but now she's thrashing and kicking me in the leg. And I'm staring back toward the foyer through the glass doors, expecting those two Bloodcursed to spill out after us. Thankfully, they're nowhere in sight. Though I don't trust that to remain the same for long.

To my right, I spot the young valet man I spoke to when I first checked into the hotel. The tall and lanky guy is in an ill-fitted blue suit with his hair combed off his face.

"Hello, sir." His gaze falls to a wild Guendolyn. I draw her against my side tightly, my arm clasping against her side, pinning her arms down, and I pretend to push hair out of her face as I cover her mouth.

"Is she all right?" he asks, his brow quizzical.

"Yes, of course," I growl. "She hasn't had her beauty rest, so she gets grumpy. Now bring me your fastest carriage. Hurry."

"Carriage? You mean car? Can I see your ticket, please?"

I exhale loudly. Remaining calm is getting harder to do with Guendolyn thrashing and trying to bite my hand. I glare into the man's eyes. "Go get me the fastest car you have—now!" The brush of magic floats on my breath, and the young man stiffens suddenly.

"Right away, sir." He runs down the driveway.

Please let something go my way for a change.

Just go to Earth, Luther said. *It'll be easy. Find Guendolyn, and she'll open the portal for you.*

I'm seething because everything's gone wrong. Hell, two Bloodcursed snuck through the portal when I crossed over a few days ago, and now I can't use magic to return, and Guendolyn has no clue who she is or how to open a portal.

Looking down, I pull my hand from her mouth. She's gasping for air.

"Are you trying to kill me? What the hell is wrong with you?" Her words are venomous, and despite the shitty night, all I can stare at are those full lips and how cute she looks when angry.

I glance into the hotel foyer. Clear for now.

A roaring sound comes from behind, and I snap around with Guendolyn, still holding her tight against me.

Red is all I see. Glinting and shining in the lights. A car glides up in front of us, and the driver's door pulls open in an upward motion, reminding me of a butterfly's wing.

The valet climbs out of the car and runs over to me, leaving the motor running.

"Here, sir. You are ready to go."

"What is this?" I gape at the car with a golden bull symbol on the front grill. "Why is it so low to the ground? I wanted the fastest car, and one I can fit into."

"This is the fastest, sir." He simply stares at me, his eyes glazed over.

I roll my eyes. "Help me get her into the car."

He rushes to open the door.

"No you don't," I cry. That vixen slips from my grasp, and I lunge after her. Grabbing her around the waist, I lift her off her feet, even if she's screaming and kicking, then I shove her awkwardly into the passenger seat and quickly shut the door.

She's fiddling with the door but seems unable to open it. "Good. Stay in there."

I dart around the car when I spot the Bloodcursed tearing across the foyer. My stomach drops. I dive into the driver's seat and drag the door down.

"You're going to get arrested and shoved into prison for life. A pretty guy like you will be hot property in there." She's shouting at me, but I have no idea what she's talking about. I'm trying to remember all of Luther's instructions for driving a car.

Why does this one have so many gadgets?

I shove the gear into first, one foot pressing down on the clutch, something I remember from Luther. I push down on the handbrake in the middle of the console. Except it isn't going down, and I'm thumping my palm down on it. *Come on, you bastard, go down.*

"Geez!"

Then I see that the end of the handbrake is tipped with a button. How in the Seven Hells did I not see that? I click it and shove the whole thing down.

We're moving as I maneuver the dual pedals. The whole car jerks, the engine squealing. Fuck, what I wouldn't give for a horse and carriage right now.

Bang.

The door shakes and Guendolyn screams, deafening me.

I twist my head to see a Bloodcursed has thrown himself at her window and is clawing at it in an attempt to get inside.

"Go! Hit the gas!" she yells.

I punch a button and blades wipe across the windshield. Another button and a clicking sound echoes around us.

"The gas, the gas, the long pedal on the right."

I slam my foot down on the thing, and we lurch forward. The tires screech around the next bend I take a bit too fast.

We take off like thirty galloping horses are pulling us. I'm thrown back in my seat. The motor is roaring, and that bastard flies off the car. This vehicle has speed.

"Where are we going?" she asks while staring behind us, back at the hotel.

"No idea, just getting as far from them as possible."

"Good, then tell me what's going on."

The car is making a groaning sound. "What now?"

"Change the gears," she instructs.

"Right." Luther told me about this part, but it slipped my mind.

I push the gearstick, and a horrid clunky sound comes from the motor.

"You're killing it," she hisses. "Do you even know how to drive a sports car?"

"Yes, of course I do." I'm lying. I've never driven anything like this. But I'm smart, and I catch on quickly. I shove the gear into place, which refuses to budge at first. I release the accelerator and hit the other pedal. This time, the gear shifts. And we're running smoothly again.

"Where to start?" I say as I curve onto a highway where there are hardly any cars, and that's good. No traffic.

There's a silence between us.

"Okay, where to start?" I repeat. "Those two coming after you are Bloodcursed. It's a long story, but in short, they're cursed fae who have been outcast from the kingdom and have an addiction to blood. Thing is that two years ago, they were as wild as animals, unable to think beyond the lust for blood. But now they're unlike the creatures back home. They're intelligent, so I don't know what's going on. But I do know they're tracking you down by your scent."

She just stares at me, and I can't work out if that's a sign things are sinking into her mind.

"My what?"

I cut a quick glance at the disbelief washing over her face. Her mouth purses. I expected more of a protest or something, but she doesn't say anything else. So I continue.

"It's a thing fae emit because of the magic we use. It makes us easy targets, which is why we use cloaking potions. Sometimes, it's just a touch that's needed to trigger the scent."

I wait for her to speak, but when she says nothing, I continue. "You are highly sought after back in Wandering Realm, and it's about time you returned home so we can keep you safe."

"Why?"

That one word seems to apply to everything, and I know she means it that way.

"Because you're a fae like me. Because of the blood in your veins, and your magic. Because if they kill you, the curse can never be incinerated."

She fumbles with her hands in her lap. "So you're telling me I was born in this realm because I'm a fae, and somehow ended up living here with humans, and now you want me to go back there where there are freak vampires on the loose? Oh, and I can do magic? As in Harry Potter magic?"

I look at her, my eyes narrowing, unsure what she just asked me. "Not too sure what vampires or Harry Potter are, but yes." I give her a smile, but she doesn't seem to notice as she stares out at the straight road. The city and its neon lights fade behind us.

I feel her eyes on me, studying me, trying to make sense of everything. This would have been so much easier if she had her memories, if Luther had made it through the portal with me.

"Are you saying I'm a fairy?" She chokes on a fake laugh.

"Fairies are blood-sucking vermin. They feed on brains and eyes, so no, you're not a fairy."

She swallows hard, studying me like I might be lying.

Back in the Wandering Realm, my two brothers and I were ambushed in the forest while we used a potion to open the portal between our world and

Earth. The Bloodcursed have risen against us in the thousands, killed so many, and spread their virus. I made it through to this realm, and when I looked back, an onslaught of Bloodcursed rushed for my brothers. Then the portal shut. I pray my two brothers survived. We risked everything to find Guendolyn, because the only person who can stop the curse on our land is the person who unleashed it. Her.

Coming to this world is our only chance of survival... Guendolyn is our last hope. She's so much more than she realizes.

I steal a glance at her in the passenger seat, and frustration twitches in the corners of her eyes. Feet tucked up on her seat, knees to her chest, she leans against the door to be as far from me as possible. She's small, and still, the power in her veins can undo so much right...and so much wrong too. It comes with cruel memories of the cost we all paid two years ago. An ache settles beneath my ribs. An ache that cuts so deep at the losses in our families, the death, and the curse unleashed on the Wandering Realm.

"There's so much more to tell you, but not tonight. Try to get some rest."

She doesn't respond. Just stares out into the night.

There's a reason I never planned to wed. Life, and mostly watching everyone else's mistakes, has taught me to avoid attachments or anything long-term. Because nothing is permanent. Such things make you weak... something my stepfather, King of the Shadow Court, would tell me constantly. Might explain why he rarely spent time with us; then again, our real father walked out on us to marry a fae princess young enough to be his daughter. That kind of shit makes you question the value of marriage.

CHAPTER

SEVEN

GUEN

The wind rushes in through the open window of the Lamborghini, swirling in my hair, buffeting against my face. Night smothers everything in sight. Not that I can see much from the freeway. We've been driving for hours without a break, and I'm still processing everything Deimos told me... Deimos Lorcayn to be specific. My mind is still blurry from two years ago, but what I do recall is he's the youngest of three princes to the Shadow Court. Luther is the middle son, and Ahren is the eldest and heir to the throne.

No matter how much I wrack my brain, the other details don't come to me. I grit my teeth, frustrated with the memories I know are there. I can feel them, but just can't grasp them. The man driving this car looks nothing like the prince I met two years ago. Anxiety pours through me at the realization that I can't remember everything, and how it could all be such a blur.

I turn in my seat and hit the button for the window to close, shutting out the ferocious wind. All I can smell is fine leather and his ridiculously sexy scent. Woodsy, earthy, and laced with a hint of a crisp meadow.

"Feeling better?" he asks, his voice almost unbearably tender.

I meet his gaze, determined to show him I'm grasping on to some semblance of sanity. I have no clue where we are and have no phone or wallet. Though if there's a silver lining, it's that I'm far from those two stalkers. Or whatever they were. I shiver, still feeling their claws raking

184

down the elevator walls and the evil in their eyes that wasn't human. I push the bad thoughts aside and turn my attention to Deimos.

"Why don't I recognize you if we've met before?"

"Glamor," he answers, like that tells me everything I need to know. "An ability all fae have to modify their appearances."

My mind buzzes with half a dozen more questions, his intoxicating scent making me woozy, but they evaporate in an instant.

Before my eyes, Deimos is changing. His dark hair fades until it turns as white as snow and extends, growing past his shoulders. Cheekbones sharpen, his jawline becomes stronger and more pronounced. Shoulders expand, as does his chest, now making him look huge in this sports car.

I'm frozen, my mouth hanging open.

His spectacular eyes, greener than I could have ever imagined, drill into me as my brain scrambles for an explanation. Except as he looks at me with a crooked smartass grin, I recognize him. I've definitely seen his face before, that much is clear. But all the other memories of our interactions and what he did—they aren't in my head. My hand instinctively goes to the side of my neck, a tenderness stirring there.

Goosebumps ripple down my arms and warmth seems to engulf me, swallowing every inch of me in its wake. I can't look away from that gorgeous face as he rakes a hand through his hair.

God, if I thought he was spectacular before, now... now he is every woman's wet dream. I suddenly feel intimidated in his presence, like there is no way someone like him can see me as anything but plain.

He keeps glancing at me and back to the road, waiting for my reaction, for me to say something. "Do you like?"

I've forgotten how to breathe.

"Deimos!" My heart stutters. "I do remember you." Well, his face is familiar, which is a start to maybe more memories coming back to me. But now I know for certain that we met before... and just like that, Luther comes to mind. So either I've completely lost my mind and am hallucinating everything, or the fragments of memory I recall are real.

My world is spinning. I want to ask him questions... things that seem to be on the tip of my mind, but I can't grasp them. I blink hard, wracking my brain, chasing those thoughts. Except they evade me.

His thick eyebrows arch slightly. "We've already established that you remember me."

I punch in him the arm. Not that he'd feel it with all those muscles. I'm not someone to react in such a way or throw tantrums, but with his smugness and him only telling me this just now... What can I say? Something inside me lashed out.

"*Hey*." He groans.

"Why didn't you show me the real you earlier?"

"My appearance isn't exactly made for blending in amid humans."

I tell myself not to react, even if his smile makes me want to punch him in the face. Except, now I'm more confused than ever. The more I stare at the white-haired fae swerving the Lamborghini all over the empty road, the more I can't deny the truth. It's staring me in the face.

He's a fae.

He's come from another realm.

He's come to take me with him.

Monsters are freaking real!

"If I'm a fae, where are my wings, and my ears would be pointy, right?"

"You asked almost this exact question two years ago." He speaks with absolute conviction, and I can't help but believe him.

"Only fairies have wings, not fae. And pointy ears are a feature some family lines have and others don't."

We keep driving. His big hands grip the steering wheel as he concentrates on keeping us in one lane. I drop my gaze to my hands and try to think everything through. How my parents abandoned me at a refuge when I was only a few months old with nothing but a ribbon tied to my ankle with my name on it. *Guen.*

It lends itself to me coming from this realm—their realm—but it's the whole fae-and-fantasy part that baffles me. Yet, I've seen things with my own eyes. Those stalkers had fangs. Deimos transforming in the car. And I know that back in the elevator I slipped into another world. I felt it in my bones. Something I'd done before... well, the shrink made me believe I'd dreamed it. But what if she was wrong about everything?

That reality is like a kick to the teeth. Bile rises to my throat. I open the window again for fresh air and stop myself from spewing all over this expensive car.

"Once we get some rest, I need you to remember how to use your magic to open the portal."

In truth, he might as well be asking me to lasso the moon. I swallow down the fuzziness in my head.

"Sleep will be good," I mumble. Anything to make it stop feeling like I'm sinking in a vortex.

I don't know how long we've been driving, but I drift to sleep, and it's the crunch of gravel under our tires sounds that wakes me.

There's a huge neon *Motel* sign in front of us. The bright blue light whips over Deimos' exhausted face.

He brings the car around the back of the long one-story building, slowing down.

"Where are we?" I shuffle upright.

He starts to talk but we're interrupted by the horrendous crunching sounds from the car as he tries to change gears. I'm cringing on the inside. We are bunny hopping down the driveway. I'm jostling and jumbling about. Then the car just dies.

"This spot will do," he announces.

I look out to see we are parked right in the middle of the parking area. "Yep, sure. Perfect." My voice is filled with edginess. Outside are forests and endless darkness behind the motel. "We're in the middle of nowhere."

"Exactly. It'll take those Bloodcursed longer to track you down. We sleep for a few hours, eat, then we leave before dawn."

"So do you have a destination in mind?"

"Nope. We keep driving until you work out how to tap into your power and get us home."

"This *is* my home," I explain quickly, gaining myself a side glance as if he's surprised by my comment.

"Not your true home."

A headache crawls up the back of my neck. My bladder is full, and I'm suddenly bursting to find a toilet. Once he switches off the engine, I reach for the door, but he grabs my wrist and forces me to face him.

"Don't think about running, understand? You do, and I'll tie you to me." There's a darkness to his eyes, and I don't for a second doubt he wouldn't enjoy binding us.

Heavy shadows dance over his face, and in the back of my mind, I remind myself that Nickie will call the cops when she doesn't find me at the hotel. They'll have a nationwide manhunt and are bound to track us down. Until my thoughts come back to me to be sure this isn't part of some strange... whatever it is, I need to remain cautious.

"I got it." I rip my hand free from his grip and climb out. The wind is cold tonight and just staring out into the pitch black of the woodland beyond the parking area leaves me trembling.

"Let's go," he says, his body shimmering back to his glamored self. He waits for me, and I join him, and when I stare up at him, I can't help but feel like he's the guy who kidnapped me, and in his blond form, he's the man who is brimming with mysteries I'm dying to discover.

Together we head to the front of the motel.

He's the lesser of the two evils, right? He hasn't tried to kill me.

As we draw closer, I note only a single light shines from a glass door with the word *reception* printed on the window.

Inside, it smells of smoke and the front desk is unattended. I can make out a shape through the doorway leading to the back room. A short man pops out, a cup to his lips and his eyes widening at the sight of Deimos. He's burly and powerful and intimidating, even dressed in casual jeans and shirt.

Spurting coffee everywhere, he places his cup on the counter in a hurry. "So sorry. Didn't hear you come in." He's plucking a tissue from the box on the counter and wipes his mouth and chin, staring up at Deimos.

I smirk to myself. Yep, when the police plaster details about Deimos on the television, Mr.—I glance around to see the man's name on the business cards in a small Perspex holder—Mr. Peppers will remember this moment.

"We'd like your finest room," Deimos starts, and already I see Mr. Peppers' expression shifts. From one of shock at seeing such a huge, glorious man who belongs on the front of a magazine to one of spellbinding charm. Deimos is entrancing the poor man somehow, just as he did that valet guy back at the hotel. "My wife and I will be staying here for one night. No disturbances. And we need food. Bring me one of everything you make."

"Motels don't do room service," I explain.

Except, Mr. Peppers just nods blindly. "There's a small town not far and they deliver food. I'll arrange it right away."

I roll my eyes at how much he's trying to impress Deimos. "And wife? Who do—?" I begin, but his hand lashes out and grasps the back of my neck, then wrenches me against him. Bastard shoves my face into his side, and all I can inhale is that hunky masculine scent with a hint of perspiration that makes me melt on the inside. I hate him for smelling so divine, how my gut explodes with butterflies at being so close to him. I shove my hands against his side, to rip myself away from him. I kick his leg, and he finally releases me.

I gasp for air and glare at him with the dirtiest stare I can manage. "Stop freaking doing that."

Mr. Peppers hands Deimos a key. "Number thirteen."

"Let's go." He growls, an edge of impatience in his tone. He grabs my arm again before whisking me out of the reception. I toss a look over my shoulder to see Mr. Peppers not paying attention, completely oblivious to what just happened.

"You hypnotized him, didn't you? Are you doing to that to me too?"

"Trust me, if I could, I would. It'd definitely be easier." He offers me a mocking grin, and I glare at him in response. His eyes darken, a serious expression washing over his face, and I can tell he means every word. Bastard.

All the rooms we pass have no lights on, like the motel is completely barren of guests. Then again, why would anyone stay out here?

We stop in front of a door. His vise grip on my elbow releases. I stare at the bronze number thirteen on the door. I'm pretty sure that's an omen of bad luck to come. Why doesn't that surprise me? Behind me, the night has claimed everything. Even the freeway out front is silent and barren of cars or street lights.

I step back from him, but he lashes out an arm and seizes me by the back of my top before shoving me inside.

He kicks the door shut, and my pulse skyrockets, then he switches on the light, illuminating the wonderland of brown dullness. Wooden walls and ceiling, faded carpet and bedspread, even the paintings.... You guessed it. Brown.

"Wow, they spent a lot of money on the decorating here." My shoes are sticking to the carpet, and I'm gagging at staying here.

Deimos locks the door.

I traipse across the room and push open the bathroom. Shower, bathtub, and toilet. I turn to face him toeing off his boots. At his own demise because no one ought to walk on this carpet barefooted ever. "You're sleeping on the..." I glance at the tiny two-seater couch that would have his legs hanging over the edge. "On the sofa."

Unconcerned, he blinks and shakes his head. "Not happening. We're both sharing the bed so I can keep an eye on you all night." He speaks without a hint of emotion, like this is an everyday occurrence, but I see his roaming gaze over my body as much as he pretends he isn't feeling the inferno between us.

His delusional assumption surprises me. As if he can watch me all night. The car keys are in his pocket, and I can stay up all night without a problem. Nighttime is when I do my best homework for college. I'm a pro at this.

He's studying me, leering at me with distrust, and I just grin. "I spread out when I sleep, so if I kick you a dozen times, don't be surprised. You're safer on the couch."

Not a single reaction, and he's reading me. Keep it cool. He can't read my mind... or can he? I stare back just as intently. *I want to lick him all over.*

Wait, why did I think that? Heat swims over me at the thought of him naked, me in charge of such a man, and discovering how big he really is. I shove the images out of my head. They can't belong to me, except my gaze has dipped to his groin and now my cheeks are ablaze.

Calm down.

He's still watching me, but he's not reacting to my thoughts, so I'm taking that as confirmation that he can't read my mind. There's a fierce fire in his eyes as a slow grin pulls on his lips, and his expression is confusing me.

My breaths are racing now. God, maybe he did hear my thoughts? "So... what's your superpower as a fae?" I burst out laughing, and if anyone ever sounded like a hyena, I just pulled it off royally.

His eyes narrow. "Power of voice. Have you not noticed this?" he muses.

"Right, right. Yes, with Mr. Peppers and the valet guy. And that's it, right?"

That sexy grin of his widens. "You fear I can do more to you?" He pauses, looking me up and down, his breaths quickening. "That I can hear your thoughts?"

I swallow past the boulder in my throat. "What? Why would you ask that? Crazy. But you can't because no one can do that, right?" God, why am I babbling? He has to guess about now that it's exactly what I was worried about and knows why my face is on fire now.

He closes the distance between us, never taking his gaze from my lips. Reaching across, his large hand cradles the side of my head, a thumb brushing across my cheek.

My breath hitches at his touch, like it has since the first time I met him. And us being this close isn't helping my raging heartbeat or focus.

Eyes of shattering green meet mine as a tremble of fear and arousal ripples through me. It's wrong of me, but my thoughts burst out of control as my pulse roars to life. All I can picture is me biting his lip, licking them, climbing this mountain of a man. To have him reach for that throbbing pulse between my thighs.

"I can't read minds," he says, blazing right through my fantasy. "But my brother Luther has that ability."

I exhale loudly with relief and lock that piece of information in the vault in my mind for later, trying to shove back the lust that's heating me as if I were standing in front of a fire. "Okay, gonna freshen up. Don't steal my bed." I make my way quickly into the bathroom and shut the door behind me. I release a long exhale, finally able to breathe with ease.

What is wrong with me? I'm out of control around him.

Frantically, I search the room for anything I can use for a weapon. Something to knock him out. Then I'll leave, because what will he do to me when I can't open the damn portal he keeps talking about? I don't even know what happened back in the elevator.

I splash cold water over my face and across the back of my neck. Looking back at me from the mirror that's chipped at the corners is a girl with bloodshot eyes and red cheeks. I honestly can't remember the last time I looked so tired and hyped up on adrenaline at the same time. When I think of Deimos, my stomach flutters like I'm back in high school. Yet he annoys the hell out of me.

Gripping the counter with both hands, I look closer at myself. "What are you?" I don't know how long I stare, expecting my brain to finally crack open and spill the answers, but they never come. So I pop open the button of my jeans and go to the toilet.

I have the plan already in my mind. Pretend to sleep, and a couple of hours after he's in deep REM sleep, I slide out, grab the keys, and I'm gone.

Once finished, I heave my jeans back up my thighs, and there begins my battle with my jeans. Hopping up and down, tugging them up and over my butt. Why did I wear these again? Right, because these bad boys defy the law of physics as to how they even fit me. But they do, and they give me the best toned looking legs and curvy ass. Sure, they're two sizes too small, but it works. I suck in my gut, holding my breath, and force the button closer to the hole, getting it halfway in.

Bang. Bang. Bang.

I flinch from the knocking at the door, and my jeans spring open.

Gah! "What?"

"Food's here."

"Okay, thanks." Not that I can fit anything into my stomach while wearing these pants. Ten minutes later of jiggling, I'm zipped up. Okay, no going to the toilet the rest of the night.

Out in the room, Deimos is sitting at the round table, with so much food in front of him, I'm convinced he can feed everyone in this motel. How much power does Deimos have over people?

"Wow, you're hungry."

He's taking a slice of a pepperoni pizza into his mouth and waves me over, then points to the seat across from him. The waft of food calls me, and I'm sitting at the table with a slice in my hand before I know it.

"If you and your brother have an ability, and I'm a fae, what is mine?"

"Only you will know yours. It's something you're born with."

"Well, that's a bit hard since I had no clue what I was until today."

"You knew two years ago," he corrects me as he keeps eating. How can someone be so sexy, even as they stuff their face? Yet, I just want to shove his face into the food for being so arrogant.

"Right." I take another bite of pizza and eye the small bowl of mac and cheese before I claim it as my own. He reaches for it at the same time, his hand on mine. Those tingles come back, the ones that engulf me each time he touches me.

I snatch the bowl from his grasp. "Mine," I say. No one comes between me and mac and cheese. It's my staple, my go-to dish, my everything when I need comfort food. And probably why I don't fit easily in these jeans.

With a shrug, he pulls back his arm and keeps eating while watching me spoon the baked noodles into my mouth. His mouth opens slightly when I part mine.

I swear, seeing him drool over me eating has my body reacting so fast. His gaze isn't on the bowl in my hand, but on my lips.

"Would you like a taste?" What the fuck am I doing? Flirting with him? My head isn't screwed on right.

He reaches over and takes my mac and cheese without hesitation. "Hmm, this is so good." It's gone in seconds.

"Yep, it was good." My stomach growls for more while my chest clenches at the thought that it was the food he drooled over and nothing more. "Anyway, tell me more about your realm, more about what's going on there."

"There are two realms," he begins. "Shadow Court and Ash Court. Dire enemies for as long as I remember. A curse was unleashed on our world, and now everything is in chaos. The Seelie fae, those from my kingdom, are being hunted."

"Curse? Like those Bloodcursed?"

"No, this is different." He lowers his head and keeps eating, having fallen quiet.

"How is it different?" I ask.

"This isn't the time to talk about such things." He shuts me down with those few words, and the air thickens between us. I don't understand what's going on, or why he's reacting this way. But I get up, having had enough of the food.

"I'm going to lie down."

"Good idea."

A twinge of fear unfurls in my chest. He's hiding so much from me, and it scares me, since there is so much that still doesn't make sense. I pull off my heels, surprised I haven't snapped these stilettoes in all my running around. Nickie will murder me if I do. I rip off the top blanket from the bed and toss it to the ground. Still clothed, I crawl under the bedsheet and shuffle to lie on my side in the middle of the bed. Now I wait.

The bed bows under me at my back.

My eyes snap open to darkness, and Deimos is climbing into bed with me.

I must have fallen asleep. I wriggle to turn around to claim more of the bed and push him out.

A large hand loops around my waist and hauls me toward him so fast that I don't have a chance to react. My back crashes against his chest, and all my thoughts fade at having him pressed up against me so close that I can feel every inch of him. Even the soft bulge nestled against my ass. I squirm to get away, but only manage to rub myself against him, as his grip isn't letting up.

"You enjoying yourself?" he purrs.

I feel a faint twitch from the growing hardness pressing against my ass. "Oh, that better not be what I think it is."

"You keep rubbing yourself against me, and it'll be a much bigger problem for you."

I grit my teeth and push away from him, but in truth, I'm burning up. I'd never felt such intensity for a man before. Shivers travel over my skin. My dating record is non-existent to compare this to, though if I'd had some serious boyfriend material, I somehow doubt they'd compare to Deimos.

"You're not going anywhere," he whispers in my ear, and his leg clamps over the top of mine. Which is so wrong because, like a flick of a flame, my desire surges like a volcano and it's unstoppable.

"Hope you're comfortable because I'm not."

"This is the most comfortable I've been in years." His sarcastic breath tickles my ear.

The pleasure building in me is blazing over me.

"Liar," I say, lying still on my side, knowing moving is futile against this mountain of a man. I can't move. Can't think. Only listen to my heart pounding in my ears while my nipples tighten.

"Do you know what they do to those who call a prince a liar?"

His deep voice grazes over my nerve endings, and a shudder travels down my spine. Not from fear, but from the proximity of him against me. From the slight twitch of his fingers as his palm splays out over my stomach.

"They kill them," I mutter, focusing on his touch, on how I'm certain he's slowly inching his hand up my stomach.

He doesn't respond, but breathes heavily, and I laugh. "Did I steal your thunder?" I ask.

"There are far worse things than death, Guendolyn."

Those words affect me—they haunt me—because his tone tells me he's experienced such punishment firsthand. "Who would threaten a prince?" I say, glancing back over my shoulder at him. The shadows steal his expression, except for those green eyes that seem to glint in the night.

"The king," he confesses.

His father? I want to ask more questions, but I turn back around and lie there. He has an asshole father... I can only guess mine is similar, since he gave me up. Still, to hear the hurt in his voice, to know he struggled, touches me. I can relate so fucking hard.

"I ought to tie you up," he mumbles so close to me, his breath is on my neck.

"Yeah, bet you'd like that." I squirm against him.

"I might," he teases, his hand adjusting to hold me against him. In a swift move, he rolls me up and onto him.

I'm frozen, lying on my back on top of him. All I can picture is him losing control and claiming me. Taking what he desires. My body aches, and I'm shuddering with lust. I picture him ripping off my clothes and dipping down between my thighs. My pelvis curls upward from the thought alone. Each rapid breath sears my lungs. My heart is beating so fast.

My core clenches, and I'm slick with desire from the anticipation when he suddenly rolls me back down on my side. His arm is now tucked under my neck. "That's better."

I'm as still as the night, and my cheeks are on fire from expecting something...else? I feel like a fool. I want to disappear. Thank the universe he can't see my blushing face.

"If you say so." I try to pretend my pulse isn't out of control, that I feel nothing for him.

His skin is hot against my cheek, and that doesn't help me in the slightest. He feels ridiculously amazing.

He falls silent, and it isn't long before his breaths deepen with the sound of him falling asleep. Well, it kinda hurts that here I am all revved up from his touch, and he just crashes.

I lie here and bide my time and wait. In my mind, I'm already picturing how fast I'll drive out of here. I need to be as far from Deimos as possible before something terrible happens... like throwing myself at him.

"I prefer girls with more, not less."

A shiver shakes me, and I push my fists against Deimos' chest, but he stands there, trapping me, unmoving. His fingers slide into my hair, twining the strands.

"Maybe you should have put your hair up tonight. Would have looked prettier."

"Is that all you do, insult people? Well, it's not working on me, so move out of my way." I clench my jaw. He thinks it's okay to speak to me that way?

His hand grasps my hair, and I wince. "You're adorable when you're angry. I think we'll have a lot of fun together. Don't you agree, my kitten?"

"I'm not yours, and I am damn sure I am not staying in this insane palace with you and your brothers." Despite my words, my body hums from his closeness. My body betrays me when it comes to this jerk, my lips still tingle from his earlier kiss.

His breath washes on my face, and as much as I want to say it reeks, I love the way he smells. Woodsy, earthy, sexy. "I hate you."

He grins. Seemingly, my words turn him on. "You're not Luther's, either, and where will you go? It's no easy feat moving between realms without magic. You're stuck in our Wandering Realm now."

"I'll find a way back." I jut my jaw out.

He presses his mouth to my ear. "So human of you."

I stiffen. "What's that supposed to mean?"

196

His green eyes flash to mine, desire deepening within them. His lips meet mine too fast for me to react, and he nips my lower lip, his teeth nicking flesh.

"Ouch." I shove my hands into his chest, but he doesn't move, just stands there hard as a boulder, licking the trickle of blood on his mouth.

I touch my lips and my fingers come back bloody. "What did you do?"

Fingers slip over my shoulder, his touch drowning me, clouding my thoughts, leaving me leaning into him while trying to recover any control of my wavering emotions.

He presses his face to my neck, inhaling, tasting. I shudder under him, the softness leaving me shivering with a new kind of arousal. I should stop him, should drive him away, but I can't. Something brushes over my mind, feather-soft, before it pulls away.

Teeth are on my neck, a sharp prick fast and electrifying.

Mist blurs my mind. Everything erases except Deimos and me. Focusing on steadying my breathing does nothing to calm my thundering heart. Arousal trembles down my spine, invisible fingers sliding over my back and lower still.

A shadow tears through the room, ripping me out of my lulled state.

"What the fuck are you doing?" Luther growls.

Deimos breaks from me. His laughter is hypnotic. He wipes his bloody mouth with the back of his hand, his eyes devouring me, calling to me like nothing I've ever felt.

"She's exquisite, brother. So much more than we could have anticipated. You were right to collect her for us."

"She isn't yours to touch or mark. Fuck, Deimos!" Luther hisses.

～

I WAKE WITH A SUDDEN JOLT, my eyes springing open. Sweat collects over my nape as I push myself up in bed. Reality and dreams blur in and out. I sit there, the vision tilting my world upside down because I remember that moment in the kingdom. It comes back to me crisp and clear. It's only a pocket of time, and what comes before and after remains clouded by shadows.

I fist the bed sheet draped over my lap, starting to recall more of Deimos from when we first met. His cruel words. His devious flirting. And that ass *bit* me.

The space next to me on the bed is empty. I frown in confusion and swing my attention to the open bathroom door.

As if on cue, the devil steps into view, wearing only black pants that hang low on his hips. With him standing there almost naked, my resolve to escape dissolves into a puddle in his presence. That isn't fair.

The way he looks isn't fair. Not those strong lines of muscles, his biceps, the ripped abs that have me staring far too long. My body hums, and I seem to have forgotten what I was thinking moments earlier. I can't tear my gaze from his strong, hard form, from the sprinkling of light hair trailing below his navel and vanishing beneath his pants.

"How did you sleep?" He leans a shoulder in the doorway, and I'm starting to breathe harder.

"All right," I squeak before clearing my throat, cursing myself for falling asleep when I had plans to get up and leave. I can't seem to control myself around him apparently—well, not when he looks like perfection. And after last night's vision, I'm not so quick to escape Deimos. If we've met before, then what secrets is he withholding from me? Why can't I remember my memories? He knows so much more than he's letting on, and I intend to find out.

My throat dries as he strolls into the room, a twisted smile curling into a smirk. He's studying me and can see exactly the effect he has on me because I suck at poker. My emotions are scribbled all over my face, and like a damn fool, I'm drooling over him.

I shake those thoughts away. "I had a dream last night," I begin.

"You can tell me about your fantasy dream later." He dismisses me with a wave of his hand.

"*Excuse me*? It was not a *fantasy* dream. It was a dream featuring you being a jerk."

He ignores the comment. He seems distracted and says, "We need to leave. Put your shoes on."

I drag my gaze from him and climb out of bed before finding my stilettos and staring at them. How I'd love flats right now. My feet throb with pain just looking at these shoes. I place them on the bed for now, and my stomach rumbles with hunger. Then I make my way to the bathroom.

A shuddering shriek comes from somewhere outside, piercing and skin-crawling. I flinch, and my head jerks back at Deimos. He's at the window, pushing the curtains aside and peering outside, where the rising sun streaks the sky in reds and oranges.

"What is it?" Is it one of those things?

"Get ready quick," he commands, his words deepening with fear. "I'll be back fast."

"No, don't leave," I cry out, but he's already pulling the door locked behind him.

Fear drums in my chest, quickly turning into a storm. I've always tried to be strong, to be cautious, but to do whatever the fuck it takes to get through life. My foster mom always said I had a strong sense of self-preservation, and I agree. But the feeling of being hunted is a blade in my gut that keeps twisting and twisting. And at this moment, I feel powerless.

I rush into the bathroom, and by the time I'm finished and zipping up my jeans with shaky fingers, my panic is full-blown. I press my back to the wall near the bed and stare at the window. I try to slow my breaths, to not make a single sound.

Deimos hasn't come back. There's no sign of the car keys… Of course, they'd be in his pocket. So I can't steal his car. What the hell am I supposed to do?

I'm breathing fast, picturing Deimos lying somewhere dying, while those stalkers are coming for me.

The faint creak of the balcony comes from outside. My equilibrium is jarred at the sound, and I stumble on my feet. I won't fall apart with fear. I won't.

Scanning the room for a weapon, the only cutlery I find with the leftovers from last night is a disposable plastic fork. I grab it anyway and lightly push aside the curtains to look out the window. All I see is the freeway. Not a car in sight. What am I meant to do? Sit here and wait for those creeps to find me? If anything, I can let Mr. Peppers know in reception something is going on, and to call the cops. After my dream, I know I've seen Deimos before; I remember us having that conversation. And he saved me from those creeps, so I want to believe he's telling me the truth.

A quick look at those stilettos. I can't bear to wear them just yet and endure their excruciating torture.

Barefooted, I creep to the door, and my hand is shaking furiously as I grab the handle. In slow motion, I pull it open and my gaze darts left and right.

All clear.

Cowering in the doorway, I struggle between staying and going. Deimos said to wait, but he's been gone for too long. Maybe I'll find him outside somewhere.

Clutching the fork in my hand, I slink left and make my way outside. *Please don't let me bump into those stalkers, please.* The silence is almost deafening.

At the front of the motel, there's not a soul in sight. The reception door swings open and shut in the breeze. I rush inside, but there's no one there.

"Hello?" I whisper.

No one responds or emerges through the closed back door. I approach and hold my breath as I push down on the handle, figuring I'll plead ignorance if Mr. Peppers gets mad. Except it's locked, and I exhale heavily. My nerves are on edge and sweat beads down my neck. I give a light knock and grit my teeth, waiting while staring out the door. *Come on, come on.*

Any hope I held on to earlier is snuffed in seconds. I scan the reception desk for a phone, but there's nothing. No computer, either. A glint draws my attention to a silver letter opener. I dump the fork and snatch the dull blade off the desktop.

On the balls of my feet, I push back outside, and unease crawls through my gut. Trees flanking the motel sway in the wind, and a bird crows somewhere in the distance. The morning sky has turned orange, staining the heavens.

I lift my gaze to the freeway along the front of the motel. No car has passed since I came out here. There are no houses out here, nothing but this lonely motel and trees in every direction.

I hate the apocalyptic feel to this place, how Deimos just *vanished*, and where the hell is Mr. Peppers? Danger ripples over my skin, and I have to find Deimos and get out of here with him.

Before I can think it through, I'm following the driveway to the rear of the building.

The Lamborghini is still here, so there's that, I guess. He hasn't taken off without me.

I wish I knew what the fuck was going on.

There's a strange energy in the air today, and I turn to head back to the room, when a thunderous scream bellows. The sound invades my thoughts from the woods behind the motel.

I freeze, the gravel cold on my bare feet. Leaves rustle, and shadows dance from the forest in front of me. My heart drums quickly. All I can think of is of Deimos in danger.

Fury and terror surge to the surface, sending a line of ice down my spine. I pull away but stop and look down at the silver weapon clutched in my hand, at the white of my knuckles. But Deimos might need my help.

I suck in a shaky breath and push one leg in front of the other, then another until I reach the edge of the woodland. All I want is to turn and run back to the room, but then what? Wait and when Deimos doesn't return, go back out to search for him again? I might be too late to help him then... I'm not sure how me with a letter opener can make a difference, but I have to try.

Farther in the woods, the earth is sharper under my feet, and I cringe with pain from every step.

Up ahead, movement stirs. Definitely a person, maybe two or three. My heart stutters, and terror cuts through me like a blade. Their voices murmur somewhere ahead, angry voices, and I squint for a better look, refusing to move.

Is Deimos with them? I swallow hard and take a step forward. *Please don't let me be making the worst decision of my life.*

With careful steps to avoid making a sound, I move closer, my ears pricking.

Tucking myself behind a huge gnarled-looking tree, my spine presses into the trunk. My breaths are racing. Why did I think this was a good idea? I should have banged on Mr. Pepper's door, or broken it down, found a phone, and called the cops.

In the span of a breath, a guttural snarl, one flooded with engorged pain, roars through the woods. A whimper presses on my throat, but I swallow it back.

I glance out from my hiding spot.

The two goddamn stalkers are there, and my heart slams against my ribcage at the realization that they followed me all the way out here.

They're tracking you down by your scent. Deimos' words swirl in my mind. He was telling the truth.

Deimos stumbles on his feet in front of them, cuts grazing his arms and chest. Fury lashes over his face. Blood seeps into his clothes, while another wound bleeds from under an eye.

Incisions lace his neck, crimson dripping down into his jacket. He's a complete mess, losing so much blood. He's going to get killed.

I'm trembling at seeing him this way, my heart shuddering at his state.

He isn't backing down but stands firm, hands fisted, eyes narrowing. He's going to fight to the end, but he sees his death. It's right there in his haunted gaze.

Both Bloodcursed lunge at him, their feet pounding the ground in their rush, kicking up detritus.

Deimos is thrown off his feet, his head hitting the ground with a sickening thud. I cringe as he grunts in pain. The monsters throw themselves on top of him, laying punch after punch into his face and chest. They're going to murder him, and tremors are racking my body.

Muscles tight, I lurch forward, my grip tightening on the letter opener.

The stalker with almost black eyes snarls, his head tilted back.

From my angle, his extending fangs are in full view.

I want to yell, to tell them to fuck off, anything but approach them.

Except anger rises to the surface within me, bubbles like an explosion about to detonate. I'm running toward them before I can think this through. Letter opener raised in my fist, I'm on him in seconds.

He turns toward me as I attack. Dark eyes with a glint of red blink in my direction. The momentum has me spearing the weapon toward him. His dark eyes widen, and he starts to retreat, but he's too slow.

Silver glints in the sunlight as I plunge the weapon into his back. Ripping into shirt and flesh, the dull blade drives right into his back like butter.

He roars, arching backward. Black wisps float from his wound. His back is reacting to the silver, seeming to smoke. I scramble backward, but he howls and stumbles about, grasping for the letter holder shoved deep into his flesh. His arms swing wildly, and one clips me in the head with a backhand.

I'm thrown off my feet and hit the ground hard, my vision wavering.

There's a shuffle as Deimos shoves off the forest floor, a scuffle breaking out as the other stalker jolts in my direction.

I try to push myself upright, but the creep is too fast and throws himself against me. We hit the ground, me beneath him.

Fangs.

That's all I see.

Long, pointy incisors dripping with saliva. He hisses in my face.

I throw my fists into his jaw, scratch and tug on his hair, but he doesn't stop.

The beast's mouth gapes wide, his strong fingers pressing my chin up, exposing my neck.

I scream and thrash against him. I can't breathe.

"You should have died long ago, bitch."

Death. That's what I picture coming for me. I hate how pathetic I sound, how tears are already blurring my vision, how all I can think about at this moment is my foster family and Nickie, and how much they'll cry at my burial. Stupid, painful thoughts crowd me.

His hand dips between us, and he's tugging at my jeans.

I hate him, loathe this piece of shit. I mean so little to him that he'd rape and kill me at the same time.

I rake my nails down the side of his face.

His lips jerk to my neck, teeth scraping my skin.

I'm paralyzed.

In a fraction of a second, he flies off me and hits a tree before collapsing to the ground like a sack.

Deimos stands in front of me, bloody and my fucking hero. "Don't move." He growls and snatches a thick branch off the ground, its end naturally pointy.

He lunges at the stalker and seizes him by the throat. With his other hand, he thrusts the stake into his gut ferociously and pins him to the tree. Releasing the monster's neck, he grabs hold of the branch and drives it deeper still. I can't even imagine the kind of strength he needs for that.

Arms quivering, he steps back.

The beast is crying out with pain, blood pouring from his wound. It's gruesome and cruel, and the creature is still squirming, but they were going to kill us both.

Deimos hunts down the black eyed creep who's staggering farther away, still trying to remove the silver embedded in his back. It isn't long before Deimos has both monsters staked to different trees. Blood spills over the leaves like bright red paint. It doesn't look real.

But I can't look away, wanting these stalkers to suffer for what they almost took from us. Our lives.

I'm shaking so hard, and stars are still dancing in my vision. Rage still mingles with terror.

They almost killed us.

Deimos storms over to me, takes me by the elbow, and marches us out of the woods in long strides. My bare feet are screaming with pain each time I step on something sharp.

I fight against him, and I know he's pissed. He drags me all the way to the Lamborghini, then hauls me against him. Chest to chest.

Out of instinct, my hand juts up between us and splays across his chest. He's on fire, my hand searing from our connection.

I shake so hard, my hands curling into balls. "They could have killed you."

"I told you to stay in the room," he reprimands me.

"Right. And if I had obeyed your stupid command, you'd be dead. Then what?"

"You coming out here could have gotten you killed," he roars, his cheeks flushing with anger. Fingers squeeze my arms tight as he holds me so close, so damn hard. "I want to spank your ass for pulling that shit out there."

We stare each other down, and that burning fire in my chest explodes. All I see are those full lips, the look in his eyes drowning in need. "Let me go!" I yell.

Instead, he angles closer, and my body responds instantly. Our mouths clash, and our kiss is primal and chaotic. Teeth and lips and hands everywhere. I rake through his hair, fisting it, wrenching him closer. I bite down on his lip, and sweet, metallic blood lingers on my tongue. My hands seize his collar, and I'm hauling him against me. I've been dreaming of kissing him since seeing him in the bar, and now this is actually happening.

I may hate him so much, but I want him even more.

Strong hands grasp my hips, and he has me in his arms and off my feet so fast, it takes me off guard. I clasp my legs around his hips, and he pins me to the side of the car, kissing me with the hunger of a wolf.

The bulge in his pants is rock-hard, and he's working it between my thighs, grinding into me. Liquid fire melts me from the friction, and I am lost to the feel of him.

He groans deeply as his hand is on my breast, his fingers pinching a nipple.

I gasp at his touch, and I'm soaking wet instantly.

I'm drowning under him, unsure of who I am right then, but I clearly feel like a woman ready to die if she can't have him. I forget all about the stalkers, fae, and my lost memories.

"I want you," I breathe into his mouth, and I hear the growl in his chest, the animalistic desire that slams into me too.

He claws at my shirt, dragging it off my shoulder as he finds my lips again. I'm breathing frantically. "You want me to fill you?"

I nod, my breaths coming so fast now, I can't trust my voice.

His tongue plunges into my mouth as his hand slides under my shirt.

I still with the touch.

He rips the fabric of my bra, and his fingers clasp on to my pebbled nipple, squeezing it. A moan spills from my lips as he tugs at my flesh while grinding into me.

God, I'm going to explode.

He pushes and pushes me, devouring me.

"You're mine," he commands.

With those words, I burn alight. I lose all control, and I'm shuddering against him. Nearby, there's a groan of warping metal, but I'm too lost to work out what that is. I release a whimpering moan and convulse with euphoria pulsing in my body. The orgasm comes so fast, so damn harsh, that the world blinks in and out. The climax tears through my body, my core clenching.

Deimos bites down into my shoulder, breaking the skin.

I cry out with painful pleasure.

The parking lot around us suddenly ripples and is stolen away from around us, the Lamborghini with its doors buckled startles me because that was the sound I heard. It then vanishes in a flash.

Darkness smothers us, closing in in a snap.

A vicious wind slaps against us as a howl in the distance rends the air.

We blast apart, breathless, and we both stumble in dimly lit woodland. But when I turn to look behind me, I rock on my feet with shock.

Gone is the motel and daylight.

An enormous castle wall sits behind us. Fading night smothers the land, and overhead, two full moons descend from the heavens.

I want to run, to flee, and it takes all my willpower to not scream.

Confusion pummels into me, a feeling of dread crashing over me. "What did you do?" My voice shakes.

"This is all you, my kitten."

"What the hell?!" I wrap my arms around myself, trembling. All I can do is stare with wide eyes at the stone castle towering over us. A goddamn castle with arched windows up above, turrets, and crenellations. No doors anywhere.

"Where are we?" I mutter, but in the back of my mind, the words *Wandering Realm* stream over my thoughts.

I know where I am from the snippets of memory I have, from what Deimos has told me... and goosebumps sprout over my flesh.

Knowing and believing are two very different things, though. But I can't deny what my eyes are seeing right now.

"Fuck," Deimos growls, his human guise gone. He's standing here beside me in all his fae glory. Long, white hair beating in the wind against his back, his striking green eyes narrowing as a sneer develops on his face. "Of all places, you have to bring us here."

I stiffen. "Is this your realm?"

The dense woodland nearby shudders in the wind, and I jump in my skin, half-expecting something to leap out at us. My blonde hair tumbles over my shoulders and in my face from the blustering air. My heart is racing so fast, and my brain is trying to catch up but failing miserably.

My skin prickles and tingles as a surge of heat thrums through me in undulating waves. The sensation comes and goes, feeling like static, the hairs on my arms standing on end.

Cold air whooshes past and does little to cool me down.

The realm from my dreams, the palace where the princes are from... This is where we are. And still, the hole in my memories stretches into a black abyss.

"We need to leave now." He snatches my hand, and we're running. "We're in the fucking Ash Court." A snarl rumbles in his chest—he's furious —and he grumbles things I don't hear under his breath.

He pounds the ground with each step, and I'm practically flying behind him because of how fast he's hauling me. His grip pinches my arm so hard, I wince.

"You're hurting me." I pull against him, but he's dragging me behind him until we're under the shadow of an enormous oak. Its shiny, bronze leaves glint in the moonlight.

We stop, and I'm gasping for air.

"Listen to me," he whispers in a rushed voice. "This is the Ash Court, home of the Unseelie fae. They find us on their land, they'll kill us in the most painful way possible. Do you want to die today?"

His dark words leave me shaking, and I see the fear in his wide eyes, his dilated pupils taking in our surroundings constantly. And all I can think of is what the Bloodcursed had said to me back in the elevator: *The King of Ash Court has called for you.*

I'm breathing hard, and my words won't come, so I shake my head. To hear the fear in Deimos' voice doesn't make me more inclined to meet this king.

"Good. Then we run as fast as we can, and no matter what happens, you don't stop. If I fall behind, you don't stop. If I die, you don't stop. You run until you reach the fence and you climb over it. Then head north. Do you hear me?" His hands are on my arms, fingers curling tight into flesh. He's terrified. I haven't seen him like this before, not even when facing those two stalkers.

"You're scaring me." Sweat is pouring down my back now, and for the life of me, I have no clue which way is north.

"You should be scared. The Unseelie are ruthless and malicious—they are the darkest of the fae. We are their enemy."

There are two realms. Shadow Court and Ash Court. Dire enemies for as long as I can remember.

I don't even know these fae, but he classifies them as my enemy. "Aren't you all just fae?" The words dribble from my lips as tension flares over me.

"There are two sides to one coin." He glances over his shoulder.

Terror drags through my chest like barbed wire. I don't know this place, but someone wants to kill me.

"I'm not afraid." I lie terribly, but I want to convince him so he doesn't see me as helpless.

Breaths are coming fast, and I keep staring at the castle behind us. At the shadow the lofty castle casts. I suck back the tears, hating the fact that I'm so scared, that I can't control my emotions. I don't want Deimos to see me crying and freaking out. Even if my pulse is raging like a wild river in my veins.

"Let's go," he orders.

I barely flinch at his command, but on the inside, I'm shuddering.

He starts to move out, his hand tight over mine, fear flooding his gaze.

We're running across a field, my bare feet hitting the grass and soft soil. The more distance we put between us and the castle, the heavier the woodland grows.

I promised myself I'd try to be normal and stay in the real world. I'd not lose control of my emotions again.

Then came Deimos, and today sucks beyond words. Not even foster care, where other kids beat me, stole my stuff, and cut my hair while I slept, scared me this much. In my chest, my heart is rupturing, and it has everything to do with that grating feeling in my chest. The one that tells me this isn't in my imagination but real.

That I am a fae.

That this is where I belong.

Déjà vu hits me like I've been here before.

I have no clue what's really going on, but I'm running for my life. I still don't know why me coming back here will in any way save two realms at war. That has nothing to do with me.

Shadows shift around us, but I don't look. I can't, not without letting fear steal the sliver of control I'm grasping on to.

Adrenaline floods my veins, and each breath runs ragged through my lungs.

Deimos kept talking about a portal, and I never understood. I don't know how, but we came through it while I experienced the best kiss of my life. Go figure.

In the distance, mountains rise around us, the peaks white with snow.

"This way." Deimos swings me into a sharp left toward the woods.

I look quickly behind me to the castle, to the shadows sweeping over the land like figures following us. A flickering light illuminates from one of the arched windows.

I burst into the woods in a heartbeat, my bare feet tripping over dead branches and foliage. My soles are screaming with agony from the sharp things I keep stepping on, but Deimos won't let me stop. He's moving so fast, I might be flying soon behind him.

We rush out of the woods and into a small clearing. Feet away stands a fifteen-foot stone wall that spreads out from either side.

"Stand on my shoulders." Deimos already crouches low. "Hurry."

I'm breathing so hard now, and I have no time to overthink this. A cold wind hits my back as I quickly climb up, my hands flat on the icy stone wall for balance.

Deimos shifts, standing up slowly, his hands tight on my ankles.

I stumble for balance, lurching sideways. My stomach hits the back of my throat, but I dig my fingers into the grooves of the stones and hold myself in place.

My hands reach up for the top of the wall, fingers gripping the small edge protruding out. My heart is galloping at a thousand miles an hour. I cling to the wall like a monkey, sweat bathing me despite the cold.

"Quickly, climb over and jump."

I push myself up, but my arms tremble. I don't have the strength to pull myself up from this angle. "I can't," I breathe.

Next thing I know, Deimos grasps my ankles hard and shoves me upward.

The food in my gut swirls, and I'm grappling to push myself up. I swing a leg over and stare down on the other side. Dried, brown grass that leads down a slope to a river down below. Beyond that lies a ragged, shaggy forest that gives me the shivers. The land on this side doesn't have glinting leaves or perfect lawn, and instead, resembles a haunted woodland.

"Jump over," Deimos reprimands.

"What about you?" I look over at his side, but he's already scaling up the wall with perfect ease. I hold on to the top for dear life and stare out over the treetops to the castle. It gleams almost golden beneath the dual moons' hue. It's spectacular, and that earlier buzz over my skin intensifies.

Deimos snatches the back of my shirt and drags me up on my feet like I'm a feral cat he found on the street. Pressing me up against him, he jumps down with me in tow.

I want to scream, but I swallow back the panic.

We hit the ground hard, and I fall to my knees, a grunting sound spilling past my lips.

"Let's move." He grabs my arm, and then he's whisking me down the hill.

I want to stop and catch my breath, to ease the ache in my thighs, to stop my racing heart before it explodes in my chest.

We finally pause, and I slump against a tree while pain seizes my body. I can barely feel my legs except for the throbbing pulse, the sting of strained muscles. Breathing steadily is impossible. "Where are we going?"

"Shh," he throws my way, his brow furrowing. "Not a sound."

So many questions pound through my mind, like why the two courts hate each other. But more than anything, I wish I had my phone to Google fae and understand exactly what *Seelie* and *Unseelie* mean. There's a reason behind every dispute, every war. Throw in power and all chaos will break out, so do these fae battle because of politics, for power over the land?

Deimos is as silent as the night, not heaving for breath like me, as he surveys the dark woods around us. He's been protecting me from the beginning, and even now, I trust him to do the same. Though what worries me is where we're going, and what that will mean for me. Instinct tells me I'm not going home anytime soon.

Deimos jerks toward me instantly, his face blanching. Dread hits me square in the chest... I know that look. It means something terrible is going to happen.

I begin to pull back, but he's grabbing my arm and shoving me behind the tree.

Air swooshes against my back, tossing hair over my face.

And in an instant, Deimos is ripped away from me, gone from sight.

I stumble from the motion, and I'm clamping a hand over my mouth to keep from screaming.

Sweat prickles my nape. I spin on my heels, my back jammed up against the tree. I have no idea what to expect, but the terror throbbing in my veins is spreading.

I can't see Deimos.

And holding it together is impossible.

A scream rushes out past my lips.

The darkness shifts, and a shadow lunges at me.

My knees buckle out from under me as my life flashes before my eyes.

CHAPTER

TEN

GUEN

A figure rushes at me from within the shadowy woods, and I freeze in terror.

Adrenaline beats inside me, fueling my instinct.

I need to move, to fucking escape.

I swivel around on my heels and run. As quick as they can, my feet pound the forest floor. Air swooshes in and out of my lungs frantically. Branches swipe at my hair and face, but I don't stop. I don't care.

Panic grips me, numbing my brain. It's the stalkers. They tracked me down.

A large hand snatches the back of my top and wrenches me backward.

I'm screaming as my back hits the ground.

A man is staring down at me, offering me his hand. Dark hair peppered with silver is cut short and parted down the side. He has a white, short beard, and there's a softness in his eyes that confuses me.

I roll in the opposite direction and scramble to my feet, backing away.

"Who are you?" I snap. "Are you one of them? A Bloodcursed?"

The man with a healed scar running down the side of his face laughs at me, and I instantly hate him. He's wearing a black leather doublet, laced up at the front to his throat. A thick belt circles his waist where a blade sits in its sheath on either side of his hips. There's a menacing look to him... a warrior who has me swallowing hard.

"You're not from around here, are you?" he asks, his voice raspy, his gaze dipping to my chest and lower, then to my bare feet. My toes curl, grass and dirt squished between them.

He steps closer to where the moonlight slices across his face, revealing an older man, maybe in his fifties or sixties. Pointy ears catch my attention. They aren't super long... but they're fae ears. Deimos' words come to me about some family lines having long ears.

I blink hard.

"Master of Game, Gabel Wulfe." He reaches for me. "Come. We need to get out of the woods."

"Don't touch me," I snap, flinching away from the man, breathing heavily. "Where's Deimos?" The dark woods reveal nothing, and all I feel are the waves of fear rolling down my body.

A shadow stirs to my right, in the direction opposite of where I came from.

The bushes shake ferociously, and I'm struggling to breathe.

Gabel doesn't bat an eye, and I squirm under his stare. "What court are you from, lovely lady?"

Leaves and branches from the shrubs are swooshing about, and my heart is about to burst out of my chest. "Deimos, that better be you!"

A groan from the darkness trembles on the wind.

My mind drowns in images of a beast about to attack us. I recoil when someone explodes out of the shadows so fast, they're a blur. They lunge at Gabel. Both of them crash and hit the ground with expelled breaths. All growls and fists, they roll about in the dark.

I suck in ragged and harsh breaths, shaking all over. I reach down and grab the first thing my hand finds. A rock. The need to run presses on my mind, but my feet aren't moving.

In the tangle of limbs and snarls, white hair catches in the moon's hue.

"Deimos?" I bellow, my voice suddenly rising. My hand constricts around the stone.

Gabel is laughing hoarsely as he shoves Deimos off him with such ease. Deimos grumbles and climbs to his feet. Without a glance my way, he stalks over to the old man and drags him to his feet by an arm.

"You know each other?" I blurt out, barely restraining myself from tossing the rock at them for scaring the hell out of me.

I want nothing more than to tell everyone to go screw themselves. I'm tired of jumping at every sound, of being so afraid. I've forgotten how to react like a normal person.

Deimos turns to me as he brushes off dirt and leaves from his clothes.

"Huh? Did you say something?" He has a tiny twig and more dead foliage tangled in his hair.

I pinch the bridge of my nose, ready to scream at him.

As if sensing my frustration, he says, "Gabel is an old family friend. He taught me good ambush moves when I was younger, like that stunt he just pulled. Plus, he used to take me out to hunt game a few times when he wasn't hunting with the king."

"Son, I don't think everyone at Shadow Court would agree I was a family friend." He claps a hand to Deimos' back.

I drop the rock from my grasp. My gaze moves from one man to another until they both turn to me. No matter how hard I stare at Gabel, I don't recognize him.

"Gabel, this is Gue-Gainy. An acquaintance of Luther's. She's not from these parts, so expect strange questions." He laughs, and I grit my teeth. He is the worst at making up names. Looking down at the rock by my feet, the earlier idea pulses through my head.

Fine, I don't mind if Deimos doesn't want this man to know where I'm from, but don't make me out to be an idiot.

"A pleasure to meet you." Gabel stretches out his hand toward me, and I accept it reluctantly. He draws my knuckles to his mouth for a small peck before releasing me. I didn't expect that. I didn't expect many of the things I've experienced these past few days. But a kiss from a stranger surprises me.

"Any acquaintance of the princes of Shadow Court is a friend of mine," he admits, though there is tightness around his eyes, frustration flashing over his face.

"While night is still upon us, we need to leave this place," he says.

There's something unsettling about the way he talks about the night. The cold wind sends a chill up my spine, and I'm ready to move quickly out of here.

Gabel turns around, surveying the woods, and the sword strapped to him catches my attention. It sits in a leather sheath sitting diagonally across his back.

Deimos is quiet, and I wonder if he's really a friend of Gabel.

"Are you out game hunting?" Deimos finally asks Gabel as he steps closer to me in an almost protective manner. I'm still seething over the fact that he scared me, but I can feel the heat radiating from his body and am glad to have him near me.

Deimos cuts me a quick glance with a look in his eyes that confirms my fears. An ominous feeling prickles along my skin. I don't know if I should be afraid of the woods or this armed stranger.

Gabel is combing a hand through his hair, still messed up from their earlier battle, weariness drawing at his features. He glances over his shoulder. "I have personal matters to take care of with your father, the king," he whispers.

"He's not my father." Deimos spits the words. "I hated when you said that years ago, and I detest it even more now."

"Being married to your mother makes him your father in the eyes of the court."

Deimos lowers his head momentarily, mumbling darkly to himself before addressing Gabel.

"Are you here under orders of Queen Sarey? Or are you changing allegiances from Ash Court and coming back to ours?" The hatred in Deimos' voice startles me, and I may not know what's going on, but what I do know tells me there are two opposing kingdoms, and the words *Ash Court* trigger alarm bells in my head.

Those from my kingdom are being hunted.

"Son, you know why I had to leave Shadow Court all those years ago."

"We would have protected you." Deimos' voice climbs, his body leaning forward, like the past with Gabel is a wound still not healed. The wind picks up, tossing his white hair like a banner over his shoulders.

"Prince Deimos, you think me a fool? Do you honestly think that you and your brothers could have saved me from your mother's wrath? She convinced King Tibout to slaughter so many loyal to the previous queen. I had no choice but to leave."

"Why Ash Court of all places? There are two other courts farther east."

Gabel doesn't respond right away, but darkness gathers under his eyes. "Survival." He keeps his chin high, and deep inside, I feel he's telling the truth. "I hoped to do more good from within the enemy's walls."

A distant wolf's howl distracts me, and I bite my lower lip, feeling vulnerable standing out here. I pray there aren't monstrous wolves out here. Werewolves? *They aren't real, right?*

"Is that the reason for your trip to my court?" Deimos asks, his posture stiff, and he somehow looks different from the man whom I first met at the bar. Back then, he carried incredible sexiness that called to me. Now... he still affects me like no other, but there's also an air of authority about him.

Gabel gives a sharp nod, but offers no insight into the message he's delivering. "We must leave this place. We're too close to Ash Court."

"We're headed in the same direction. Join us," Deimos adds, and his hand is already on my elbow. His invite isn't a friendly one—I can hear it in his voice—but one filled with hope that he might pry some of the information out of the man who defected to the enemy's court.

"Stay close," Deimos whispers, and he draws me into a quick walk. The soil is cold and hard on my bare feet. What I wouldn't give for sneakers right now.

There's no pause, and with Gabel taking the lead, we're moving with speed. Deimos holds me against him, making the walk easier as he takes a lot of my weight.

"When do we go back home to my world?" I whisper.

He hushes me and shakes his head before lifting his gaze to Gabel ahead of us and back at me.

Sure, later when Gabel isn't around. It's always later, and by then I might be eaten by wolves out here.

I DON'T REMEMBER how long we've been traveling, but I'm out of breath and my feet are killing me. I'm also pretty sure I've stepped on every sharp object in this forest.

Groaning, I draw Deimos' attention. "Is something wrong?" he asks.

"I'm tired."

He lifts his head. "Gabel, let's take a break. Food would be good."

The man nods and veers left, where the land slopes downward. At the base, we come across a ragged stone mountain, and we follow a path. I don't remember where we are, but the hardness of the ground is excruciating. I'm about to wrench free from Deimos, when Gabel waves us closer. He vanishes into a cave.

Yes, thank you!

Inside, the air smells musty, and I can't see a thing.

Gabel rushes in and out of the cave, bringing sticks with him. Within moments, there's a frantic scrape of wood. It isn't long before a flicker of fire flashes from the middle of the cavern. Gabel is kneeling in front of a pile of sticks piled up right into the shape of a teepee.

Deimos gathers large rocks from around the cave and creates a circle around the wood.

I stand there, completely clueless about how to start a campfire without matches. The only camping trip I've ever been on was with school, but everything was set up for us.

My eyes flicker over to Deimos, who leaves the cave and comes back with more wood piled into his arms.

"I'll let you finish," Gabel instructs. "I'm going hunting for food."

"Thanks," Deimos says, like there wasn't a bucketload of tension earlier between them.

I don't feel comfortable in the slightest with Gabel conveniently heading out to hunt. I press my tongue to my teeth, praying that Deimos knows what he's doing.

Deimos

I sit next to Guendolyn, stretching out my long legs toward the fire. The crackle and snap fills the silence. She watches the cave's entrance like a hawk.

"You are safe," I say.

"What if Gabel returns to Ash Court and brings back an army? Aren't you worried?" She swivels on the ground and stretches out her bent legs.

My attention falls to her bare feet, the dirt covering them, the rawness of her soles. Something hurts deep in my chest at the fact that I didn't notice she's been barefoot until now.

"First, the court is too far for him to go there and return before we leave this cave. Second, why didn't you tell me you aren't wearing shoes?" I reach forward, grab both her ankles, and swivel her around by her legs to face me. Placing her feet in my lap, I hold on to her as she fights me to pull away.

"What does it matter? I'll be fine." She pushes against my arms, and I eye her sharply.

"It's the least I can do after making you suffer."

She's shaking her head and huffs. I adore how cute she looks when she's angry at me, her nose scrunching, her breaths loud, her lips pinching to the side of her mouth.

"Fine, but just be careful with your big hands."

I smile to myself at her intended insult and turn my attention to her small feet. A large leaf is stuck to the base of one foot, and I peel it off, followed by every loose piece of debris attached to her. With both hands, I rub my thumbs in small circles over her soles. She has scratches all over them. She's lucky they aren't cut up and bloody.

Out of the corner of my eye, I catch the pleased smirk she tries to hide by looking away.

There's only silence between us, the fire keeping us warm, and all I can think about is the strange attraction I feel for her. How wrong it is knowing Luther adores her. How I selfishly don't want to return her to my brother's arms.

"Why am I here?" she asks, breaking me from my thoughts. "I know you said something about helping the realms and a curse, but why me?"

I brush more of the grit off the tips of her toes, scrubbing with a thumb where the dirt stains her skin. "Because you were taken from here as a baby and left on Earth with human parents."

She stiffens, her eyes widening, and whispers fall from her sweet lips. "My parents aren't human, are they?"

I meet her gaze and keep massaging in the tender spot in the arch of her foot. "No."

"So you know who they are?" Her voice is hopeful, and she's staring at me with that look that breaks me because I have to lie. I don't want to, but telling her the truth puts her in harm's way. It's better for now that she doesn't know.

I shake my head and decide to change the topic, as I can tell she'll keep asking questions. "My brothers and I believe you have a power that can end a lot of bloodshed in our court."

She blinks, studying me, and I can see the wheels behind her eyes spinning. "Is that why my mother abandoned me? Because of my power?" Her brow furrows, and she looks at me with panic in her eyes. "I don't even know what my power is, but it must be horrible for her to dump me in another world and never come to find me again." The heartbreak in her voice is gut-wrenching.

I tighten my hold on her feet in my lap. "Nothing about you is horrible." I fight the truth wanting to come out, words I can't tell her without hurting her worse. At least not yet, not until she's safe and understands how all of our survival depends on her. This is not the kind of information I intend to scare her with tonight.

She sits with her hands wrapped around her middle, her brow furrowed, her eyes half-hooded.

There's an innocence to her she tries to hide, and no matter how hard she fights her destiny, she can't push away what is meant to be. Not when so many other lives are at stake. Like the rest of us, she didn't pick this life, but as my grandmother once said to me, *"Living with fear is a life wasted, so do everything like it's your last day alive. Live."*

I lower my gaze and run my fingertips over the length of Guendolyn's toes and back up to her ankles. Her skin shivers under my touch, her breath quickening, and I swallow hard. Her reaction to me has me twisted in knots. I can't seem to get her kiss out of my head. Her intoxicating desire is like a storm. It sweeps in and tears anything in its path apart. In this case, me.

Everything about her calls to me. I want her all to myself ridiculously bad, but there are dozens of reasons I can't get involved with a woman like her. A dozen reasons that don't align with her destiny. This is the moment I should vow to never kiss her again, to never think about her in any way but being a savior to our kingdom.

The words don't come, and tearing my gaze away from this girl is impossible. I want her beneath me, ruddy cheeks, crying out my name, splayed open. For me to show her the darkest sins that will have her begging for more.

I always thought it fickle to see Luther pine over Guendolyn since losing her two years ago, but now I understand. Not that I'm in love... hell, that's not for me. I've seen what broken marriages do to families, and I don't want any of that. Shattered hearts, endless tears, rejection... That knife is still embedded in my chest.

My real father comes from House Larmathier, one of the oldest families in the Wandering Realm. He went out hunting one day and never returned. He's a gutless weasel, living in a court in the east, married to a princess half his age. Mother tried to have him assassinated—as one does—but the assassin ended up dead. I know Mother will never give up until he's buried. I've given up caring.

"Is it common for fae children to be abandoned on Earth?" she asks as she looks at me with desperation in her eyes, wanting me to tell her this is commonplace, that she's not alone.

I don't want to lie to her, though.

"It's an old practice from the ancient traditions that isn't seen too much these days. Fae would replace human babies with their own as a way to infiltrate the Earth Realm, to uncover what magic that world held. But once they discovered it didn't offer much in the way of enchantment, they stopped doing it."

"What happened to those children?"

I swallow hard but answer her question. "A guard would bring them home, where they were interrogated on everything they discovered. Not many survived. Those were barbaric times that have been outlawed. My stepfather has made going into your realm illegal and punishable by death."

Her head tilts up. "But you risked coming for me?"

"Because we need your help. And he doesn't know I went there—and he won't until we are certain you're safe."

Her breaths quicken, and I see the shiver in her trembling body. "That's why you didn't want Gabel knowing who I am," she whispers as she takes a quick look to the cave's opening.

"If anyone finds out who you are, they'll hurt you to gain power in this world."

"But you got to me first. Took me before anyone else could." Her blue eyes darken, and her voice fills with venom.

"No, that's not—"

She looks away just as Gabel returns, holding two rabbits he already skinned and gutted.

Guendolyn quickly draws her feet from my lap and tucks them under her. I want to pull her aside, tell her she's wrong to think we're the enemy. I want to rip away the pain etching her face. She looks away and wipes at her eyes. Watching her is a punch to my gut.

"I brought food," Gabel says as he sets about skewering the meat.

I toe my boots off and remove my socks, before laying them near the fire to warm up. "Gainy, I'd offer you my shoes, but you'll trip in them. Take my socks at least."

She stares at me, still mad, but doesn't touch the socks, so I leave them there for now. I know she'll take them.

With my boots back on, I take one of the skewered rabbits and hold it over the flame as it starts cooking.

No one talks, and I let my mind wander anywhere but here. To the river behind our castle that no one else visits. Where I can swim for hours and be left alone to sleep under the sun, to hunt, to escape the chaos of the kingdom. That was before everything went to hell after the curse spread. Now, the Bloodcursed are rampant around Shadow Court, breaching the walls to get inside. One bite and the virus takes the victim. We're under attack, and those easy times feel like a world away.

"Back in the woods," Gabel begins, turning the almost cooked rabbit, "I swore you were going to tell me this lovely lady was Guendolyn." Gabel laughs, and I join him, chuckling louder.

"I heard she's long dead," I offer, hearing the sudden hitch in Guendolyn's breathing. "Gainy here is just a girl Luther met at a tavern east of our border and has been obsessed with. A common barmaid, but if she makes my brother happy for a night or two, who I am to question his carnal needs?"

Guendolyn starts choking, and I reach over to pat her back hard. She whacks my hand away, and her stare can peel the skin right off my body. She's on her feet. "I'm going outside for fresh air," she growls.

"Just outside the cave where I can see you," I command.

She glares down at me, and I pray she doesn't say something stupid. I meet her gaze, imploring her to keep her anger in check.

Gabel turns to grab more wood for the fire just as Guendolyn kicks me right in the ribs. I groan from the sharp pain, gritting my jaw. *Damn.*

I watch her march out, and all I can stare at is that tight ass and think how much I want to spank it. She stands just outside. I see only part of her from where I'm sitting, and it takes everything I have to not follow her out there. She glances over her shoulder at me and flips me the middle finger. Wonder what that means?

Fuck, she drives me insane with desire.

Suddenly, she storms back in, snatches my socks from near the fire, and saunters back out with her head high.

"Feisty," Gabel says. "She must be from very far east, as she wears strange clothes and doesn't show respect to princes and nobles alike."

"You know Luther. He likes his girls wild and fiery." I reach over for more cooked meat, and my side flares with pain from her kick. I rip into the charred rabbit.

The small issue of her not remembering her past is something we'll work with once we get her safely to our kingdom.

I get up and go outside to where she's standing with her back to the rock, hands folded over her chest. "Come have something to eat," I say to her. "We have a long way to travel."

ELEVEN

GUEN

We stride through the dark woods, Gabel on my right and Deimos on my left. Night cloaks the forest in every direction, with only the two moons overhead lighting the way.

Deimos' socks slide over my feet, but they offer a layer of protection from the forest floor, so I suck it up and keep tugging them up my legs.

It's hard to decide if I want to kiss him or punch him most of the time. He's hiding so much from me, and I can't help but feel as though I'm walking into a trap. They want me to somehow help with their realm problems, but I have no clue how to begin, or if they even have the right person. What will happen to me if I can't perform whatever miracle they're expecting?

I keep catching Gabel stealing glances my way, and fear burrows deep in my gut. The kind that tells me he didn't buy Deimos' lies. But I don't know who to trust. These two fae don't trust each other. So where does that leave me?

"Gainy, what village are you from again?" he asks, and there it is, the web unraveling at my feet. I hold back a grimace, my mind scrambling for what to say.

"Wavertorn," Deimos responds on my behalf.

"It's a wonderful place," I add quickly. "My family and friends are there. I grew up right by the water."

"Water? Isn't Waverton located near the desert?"

My throat dries like the desert, and a flash of confusion washes over his face. "Near the oasis, of course." I need to stop pretending like I know anything about this world. Under his gaze, I'm squirming, so I change tactics.

"What exactly is a Game Keeper?"

Gabel's face cracks into a smile, and he lets out a heavy laugh. "I guess this must all be very new to you, having come from such a small town." His words scare me... He knows I'm not from Waverton. I can hear it in his voice.

But I keep it cool. Breathe normally while my head is screaming to stop talking.

"My role in the kingdom is to take the king or queen out on hunts for game."

"Is that all? Sounds like a fun job." Sweat trickles down my back, and I glance over to Deimos for assistance, but he offers nothing.

"It may seem that way on the outside, but there's so much more to the role." He leans closer. "When we hunt, it's usually just me and the king with only a few guards traveling for long periods of time. I use that time to everyone's advantage."

My eyes widen. "You have him all to yourself, to find out things, to whisper in his ear."

He nods with a curt smile. This man is dangerous, because I suspect he's holding so much knowledge and influence. That's why Deimos told me to be cautious, to hide my real identity.

"That's a matter of perspective," Deimos adds. "What one man imparts to the king or queen can be very intentionally skewed in his favor."

"Absolutely," Gabel responds. "But I have always been a man of honor, if you recall from when you first arrived at Shadow Court with your brothers. It was me who influenced the king to give you three your own palace, away from the court drama, away from the hatred your mother, the new queen, brought to the kingdom. Royalty should be servants of the people, not focusing on petty court politics. You three are the future of Shadow Court."

"And you were the one who convinced the king to make us work the land, ploughing soil. I remember hating you so much for that." His features contort toward Gabel, still not over the incident apparently.

"Aww, come on, Deimos, you know the benefit of royalty working with the land, not owning it. It was something the previous queen had believed in strongly. Something you admitted you saw the benefit in when you were younger."

"Working on farms sounds like a good idea." I add my two cents, though no one seems to be paying attention. Both of them are caught in their own mini battle of words. At least it takes the attention off me.

Deimos grumbles under his breath before responding. "Every action has a consequence. Wasn't it an ambush of villagers who attacked and killed the previous queen as she worked in the field? Angry, hungry fae, who didn't have enough food for their families so the queen could sell our crops to another kingdom at triple gold crowns?"

Gabel's lips draw down. "She did it to pay off the debt of this kingdom, so you're right. Everything comes with balance. What happened to her was devastating. But you want to know the truth," Gabel says, turning to me.

I jerk my chin at him and nod.

"I consider myself a fae searching for the truth and bringing it to the common folk. They have a right to know what is happening in their king-dom. Always be alert, because nothing is what it seems in any court."

"You tell the truth, even to the detriment of the court, right, Gabel? When—" Deimos pauses as soon as a guttural roar sounds from the woods ahead of us.

I ease back, not wanting to find out what made that sound. "Maybe we should choose another path."

Deimos grabs my arm and hauls me to his side, clutching me tightly. I feel the fear rippling over his body, and that scares me more.

My muscles tense with the urge to run, except I have nowhere to go.

"They're coming from two sides." Gabel twists around to look behind us at the trees and bushes. He draws the sword from the sheath on his back with such grace, I can't stop staring. Nothing compares to the reddish gold of the metal; it looks as if it's made of gold and blood. It has a rounded tip and resembles a long, thin leaf more than the swords I've seen in movies.

"Deimos," Gabel calls as he hands him the sword, then pulls out the two blades from his belt. Silver glints in the moonlight, the tips seriously sharp.

I want something to defend myself too.

My gaze is swinging back and forth at the shadows everywhere, and I can't distinguish shapes from the night. Glancing at my feet, I find there are rocks and twigs all over the place. I quickly grab a thicker branch.

Deimos watches me, and he nods approvingly, but he's scared. It's in his eyes, in the tightening brackets around his mouth. "Whatever you do, don't let them bite you. Stay behind me as much as you can, understand? And remember what I said before about going north should anything happen."

I nod, unable to find my voice. My heart is beating so hard, I can't concentrate. I nibble at my lip, my hand squeezing the life out of the stick.

Wielding his sword, Deimos steps forward. I hate to admit it in this moment, but this fae is so attractive, especially while holding a sword. The muscles in his arms flex, his chest sticks out, and I'm lost in the sight. That whole protective vibe radiates off him. I'm melting on the inside. It annoys me that he affects me so much, yet I don't look away.

The snap of a twig comes from somewhere in the woods around us.

I freeze, lifting my weapon.

Two figures burst out of the woods with such speed, I stumble backward. Their skin is pale and blotchy, blood dripping from their mouths. Clothes hang off lithe frames. Their ribcages are so pronounced, I want to gag. It pains me to see how scrawny and starved they look.

Deimos lunges toward them in a heartbeat, moving so gracefully and swiftly, I'm left stunned.

Holding the sword with two hands, Deimos slashes it through the air ferociously. The weapon cuts right through the first creature's neck, the head sliced right off. Blood gushes out from the wound as the body drops to its knees and flops forward with a thump.

I scream, unable to hold it back. I can't take my eyes off the head rolling away into the treeline.

Bile hits the back of my throat.

More Bloodcursed pour out of the woods.

I forget everything but fear. Gabel moves with speed, hacking his blades across the beasts coming for him. He throws himself into a roll and leaps onto the creature's back before slitting its throat. The skin where his blade touches the Bloodcursed sizzles on contact. Just as the letter holder did when it broke through the skin of the stalker back home.

These monsters drop to the ground, the burning flesh eating away over their bodies.

Sickness surges through me.

I can't do this. The stick is trembling in my hand, while Deimos spins away from an attack, his sword swinging wide, and catches two of the attackers across the chest. They stumble backward but don't fall, and come at him again.

One of them bypasses him and scrambles in my direction with savagery in his eyes. Instinct takes me over while my brain remains mush. I don't want to die here. So I swing the branch at his head, sending him into a sideway stumble. Then I whack the end of the stick at his chest as he unleashes a savage screech. Lips peel back to stained teeth and breath that could call death itself from Hell.

As if on cue, Deimos whips around, his blade slicing through the Bloodcursed's neck.

"Ouch." I cringe and look away, but bump into someone behind me.

My heart is pumping hard, and I swing around, branch high in my hand.

"It's just me, lovely lady," Gabel says, gasping for air.

I take a breather and stay close to him. Trees around us are rustling in the breeze, and the only sound is that of Deimos groaning as he fights.

Deimos is all power and brawn. He dodges an attack and kicks the assailant away before swinging his sword and chopping off its head. Then with a spin, he regroups with us.

"That wasn't too bad," he brags, his chest huffing and puffing. Blood splatters are across his cheek, and he wipes it with the back of his hand, making it a smudgy mess. He turns to me and cups the side of my face. "Did any of them bite you?"

I drag in a quivering breath and shake my head.

His thumb grazes under my eye, and a hopeful look crosses his gaze. I imagine him leaning in close, tracing his lips across mine. That single thought has my nipples hard. But he breaks away and juts his chin toward Gable. "Time to get out of here fast."

The land is scattered with half a dozen bodies, most missing their heads. I take mental notes that decapitation and silver works against these monsters.

"A handful are easy to kill," Gabel murmurs. "What worries me is how many others are near."

Deimos grabs my hand, his palm swallowing mine, and the three of us are running through the woods. I can't think straight and am barely keeping it together, praying we find somewhere to lie low. I gasp for air. All I can picture in my mind are the heads rolling.

But just as I think we're far away from the attack area, that screeching sound I'm beginning to loathe closes in around us.

I shudder and inch closer to Deimos.

A raging river of Bloodcursed breaks its banks. So many are racing toward us from the woods ahead.

My knees wobble under me.

Twenty, maybe thirty.

All I can see is my death. Slaughtered and bitten, I'll roam this world forever as one of those creatures. I curl my fists, ready to fight, and lift my stick.

Electricity pricks down my arms suddenly. It crawls over me like an army of ants swarming across my body.

Crack.

Crack.

CRACK!

The sound booms and fills the night. Beneath my feet, the ground trembles as though it's coming to life.

I flinch with fear, my adrenaline skyrocketing.

Trees rip back and forth, even though the winds have stilled.

Roots shudder across the ground, breaking free from the confines of the compact dirt.

They grow and stretch before my eyes. Slithering like vipers, they strike the Bloodcursed, curling around limbs, around throats, dragging them backward and into the ground itself.

Claws scratch at the soil, their screams ringing the air with terror.

I'm shaking, startled at what I'm seeing.

Their hollering is terrifying.

The few Bloodcursed who escape the tangled woods scramble toward us with gaping mouths, fangs exposed. Their greedy fingers are stretched out for us. They snarl like rabid dogs.

I recoil, my heart thumping hard against my ribcage. I never signed up for this. I'm just a normal girl... Well, *normal* is subjective and overrated, but before those stalkers arrived in my life, my life wasn't in danger. I blame them for everything. Except in the back of my mind, I know the real danger is the person who ordered them to come after me.

Gabel lunges forward and cuts his way through the masses. His grunting and their screeches pierce my ears. My pulse is jumping with all kinds of emotions. Fear mainly—that overpowers everything else.

I look up at Deimos, close to nudging him to go help him. I absolutely want us to survive the night.

Except his eyes are glowing white, and he's mumbling silent words. The air from his outstretched hand ripples outward like a sonic blast. It travels out toward the woods, to the spot where the Bloodcursed emerged.

Where the tree roots have come to life.

He's doing it. He's making them attack. I have no real idea how, but he's a fae. They have magic, just like he could convince people to do things with his voice alone.

The ground trembles beneath my feet. It's hard to tell if that's from the stampede of Bloodcursed or moving trees.

With Gable fighting frantically, I rush to help him with a fury that borders on insanity.

Swinging my branch, I go wild and whack a Bloodcursed latching on to Gable's arm. I don't stop and slam the stick into the thing's head until Gabel slips free. With a swift turn, he plunges the blade into the side of the creature's neck. Blood splatters, and I stumble out of its reach and watch the creature stumble to the ground, gurgling his last breaths.

The ground is shaking furiously now, a roar belching up from under our feet.

Bloodcursed are wailing, the roots attacking as many as they can. The hairs on my arms stand on end from the magic.

It's chaos.

Panic rattles in my veins, and I gasp for air. Everything is happening too fast, and I don't understand half of it.

The ground at once jolts with ferocity. A gaping hole cracks open, stretching to the length of several small cars. It groans with the might of tearing the world apart.

Soil under my feet softens, and it starts sliding under me in seconds, pulling closer to the fissure's edge.

I scramble backward, leaving behind the socks sucked off my feet. Ten feet away, Gabel slips to the ground with a thud, and he's sliding fast to the deathly edge.

"Gabel!" I throw myself at him and grasp his arm with two hands.

He squirms and groans, his legs dangling off the edge. Pure terror lashes over his face as he thrashes for escape.

Bloodcursed are tumbling in all around us, and Gabel's weight is too strong for me. He's pulling me with him.

The fingers on Gabel's free hand dig into the ground for purchase, but my feet are now caught in the quicksand. I'm slipping forward, lurching backward.

"Deimos!" I bellow just as a horde of more Bloodcursed rush onto the scene. Growls fall from the monsters, lips curling as they expose sharp fangs. Whatever these vampire things are, I want them as far away from me as possible.

The trees are turbulent and unrestrained, their branches and roots striking and whipping the creatures.

The hairs on my nape rise, and I'm pulling at Gabel with all my strength, with everything I have.

"Deimos!" I'm yelling, but it's not his shadow that falls over me. He stands in my peripheral vision, casting his power to hold back the swarm of monsters trying to kill us.

All I can think is that this is the end. This is *my* end.

Strong hands snap around my waist in that instant and rip me away from the chasm.

"Gabel!" I shout as I fight against the creature dragging me away from him. He's sliding fast now, and my stomach plunges.

Another figure rushes forward and yanks Gabel to safety by the back of his doublet. Relief washes over me to have these strangers jump in and help.

I fall to my feet and stumble free from my captor before turning around to find a tall man in a cloak, his hood concealing his face.

"Who are you?" I ask. They're too tall, too broad to be the stalkers from home.

But when a heart-shattering scream cracks the air behind me, I jerk around just as two Bloodcursed crash-tackle Gabel, ripping him out of the other man's arms.

Gabel's feet skid over the rich soil. He's crying out, and I lunge for him, but the momentum tears him down into the chasm with the Bloodcursed, swallowed by the ground in seconds.

"No!" My scream echoes in the night.

Deimos is on his knees, his shoulders curled forward, his head low. He heaves for each breath, and I'm terrified for him. The power he used brought trees to life!

I'm numb all over.

I hurry over to Deimos. He's still fighting for each inhale, his body shuddering. He's so pale, and his lips have bled to white. That magic he used has worn him out. When he opens his eyes, I expect to find them glowing white, but instead, I stare into spectacular green eyes. Bloodshot as though he's been drinking all night, but still stunning. I crouch down next to him.

"Are you okay? What you did out there was insane and amazing. Guess as a fae, anything's possible, right?" My words just pour out of me like the emotions that overwhelm my mind. But talking helps me not think about them, or panic that I just saw someone die. "I'm so sorry about your friend Gabel."

He doesn't say anything.

"Who are those two guys? Should we be trying to escape?"

"They're with us," he murmurs, his voice low and distant.

I want to ask so much more, but I don't. Instead, I sit with him for the longest time.

"I will ensure his heroic battle will be remembered, and that his family is looked after. Are you hurt?" he croaks as he raises his hand to my cheek. I lean against his touch, the warmth electric. I want to cry, that's how I feel after everything that's happened so fast.

"I'm not sure I'm made out for this life-and-death lifestyle." I try to laugh, but it comes out as a clumsy snort, and I don't even care how embarrassing I sound.

"Once we get out of this, I promise to teach you how to fight."

The idea sounds perfect. In truth, this world is my picture of Hell, so if survival means learning to master a weapon as I'd seen Deimos do, then I'm ready. "Deal. I want to wield a sword as well as you."

His smile brings one to my face.

He draws in a long breath and lowers his hand. The tips of his fingers look like they've been plunged into ink. I stiffen and quickly take his hand into mine, studying them.

"What is this?" I run my index finger over the blackness. It feels rough, like a peach's skin.

"Bits of my soul, burned away each time I use magic."

My mouth gapes open, and I lean back, eyeing him warily. "Is that meant to be a joke? Because it's not funny."

Except he's not laughing. There's only the twitch at the corners of his lips. Why does everything in this realm have to be deadly and come with gigantic problems? Deimos was right. *Every action has a consequence.*

"You're going to die?" I gasp.

"Eventually, we all do, but my time might come quicker. I lose years of life with each use of Arcana magic." He must notice my confused expression because he explains more. "Don't worry for me. It's the magic I harness from nature around me. Elemental magic, the oldest of its kind for fae. A power I gained from my father. I've accepted my fate long ago."

My fingers curl around his hand, and I hold on, his warmth seeping up my arm. I want to ask him how many times he's used his magic, how many years he's lost already. But I can't bring myself to do it. I'm too terrified of finding out the truth.

When I stare at him, I notice the sharpness of his cheekbones, the hardness of his jaw, the soft angles of his nose. His breathing has calmed, and he looks at me with those vivid green eyes. He wants to say something. His lips part, but the words never come. His gaze lifts over my shoulder.

Behind me, the two cloaked men are staring in our direction, and I'm not sure what to expect.

"So you definitely know them, right?" I ask Deimos.

They stroll around the gaping hole in the ground, stepping over the bodies and coming toward us. Their swords drip in blood. I'm convinced if they were after me, even Deimos couldn't stop them. I inch closer to him.

They're both large in stature, broad-shouldered and powerful.

Deimos climbs to his feet. "We're safe," he says, even if his voice is stiff, and I'm not sure what to make of it. He takes my hand and helps me up.

My muscles twitch with exhaustion. I look over at the chasm. We lost Gabel, and my chest clenches. I barely knew him, but he fought alongside us, he believed in helping others. I'll never know his true intentions, but he didn't deserve to die. Not like that.

Deimos walks up to the men, and he hugs each one with hard claps on their backs. Their mumbles confirm he knows them very well. One of the strangers hands his blood-stained sword to Deimos, then motions toward me. Deimos and the other man wipe their blood-stained swords on the clothes of the dead. Then they step closer to the gaping crack in the ground and stare down. Are they looking for any sign of Gabel?

The wind comes out of nowhere as I stand, the air swirling around my legs, throwing my hair over my shoulders. There's something about these strangers that holds me captive. The man coming toward me is striding with purpose and so much power.

His cloak billows in the air behind him. It tears open at the front, showing me a glimpse of a military-style jacket, silver buttons and a high collar underneath. Black pants stretch over strong legs.

His hands reach up, and he pushes the hood off his head. My heart beats faster... he's incredible. Stunning. Mesmerizing. Hair dark as midnight tumbles to his shoulders, piercing eyes the color of flames. They flicker as if alight, crowned by the darkest eyebrows.

Rugged jaw, sharp cheekbones, and lips full with an upward curve, reminding me so much of Deimos'.

My breath catches in my lungs. My brain is stuttering, and I bite on the corner of my mouth.

"Luther?"

The way his gorgeous mouth pulls into a grin confirms I'm right. I've seen him in my dreams, his name having never left my thoughts. The strange thing is that I don't recall much about him or our time together or the emotions I know should be there, yet the ache in my chest at seeing him deepens and is close to knocking all the air out of my lungs.

He chuckles and closes the distance between us. Standing right in front of me, he looks down at me, intensity burning in his eyes.

"Do you remember me, little wolf?" he asks.

My body shudders at hearing that deep baritone voice, and I release a harsh chuckle that comes out awkward.

He looks at me with a crocked grin.

But I'm drowning in his scent of freshly cut timber, perspiration, and something like dark cinnamon. It engulfs me and leaves me trembling with a need I don't understand. Fire rages across my chest. There's something about him that sets me alight with desire, something that responds to his presence with a savageness I've only felt with Deimos.

What I feel for Luther is so different. It comes from deep inside me, from a place I didn't know existed until now.

Winds roar around us, my hair lashing across my head.

Luther. The name sweeps over my mind like it has so many times.

"Yes," I breathe, my gaze dropping to his full lips before climbing back to his gaze. "I know you."

He laughs with a sound that breaks me, surprising me by how much it turns me on to just hear that gorgeous sound. "That's a good start."

"But there's more, and I just can't..." I squint, trying to concentrate. My chest tightens, feeling like I should recognize my own yearning ache, but it's buried in my mind and unreachable.

"It's okay," he says. "Part of the curse included wiping your memory. The main thing is you're home."

I feel so many emotions. Excited, confused, unsettled. "This isn't my home, Luther."

That's where you're wrong. I just need to help you remember things.

His voice streams over my mind, insistence clipping his words. I'm blinking hard at him. He's spoken to me in my mind before. Yet my heart is pounding in my chest.

He pauses as if searching for something to say. Staring at me like he knows more about me than I do.

Don't worry, little wolf. I'll show you everything in due course. And I can only read your mind if you let me. He smirks devilishly.

Everything has happened so fast. Stalkers attacking me. Deimos rescuing me. Me arriving in this world. The Bloodcursed. Fae. Gabel. And now Luther reading my mind. It's too much.

The world seems to stand very still.

The tightness around his eyes soften, and despite my crazy emotions, something in my mind tells me to be careful around him.

"Come with me. The woods aren't safe." He takes me by the hand, and we stride toward Deimos.

Confusion blurs my mind, and an ache burrows deep in my chest.

When I look over, Deimos is watching me, his expression hardened.

Foliage pricks the underside of my feet with each step I take, now that I've lost my socks.

"You've met Luther," Deimos mutters, as if he'd prefer to be anywhere but here. "And this is the Prince Ahren."

Ahren pushes the hood off his face, and his presence leaves me gasping. Impossibly gorgeous and full of sin. Pale skin. Red lips. Captivating green eyes just like Deimos', except Ahren's are pale and glistening. With his hair, white as the clouds, reaching halfway down his back, he stands regally. His face is longer than his brothers', lips quirking at the edges, and like the other two, he has those chiseled cheekbones.

Ahren is the heir to the throne... a nugget of knowledge that seems to have stayed with me. And he doesn't appear very happy to see me.

A frustrated sigh slips from his lips. "What is she wearing?"

I narrow my eyes at him. "Really? That's what you take out of this whole scenario? Not that we could have died? And I'm standing right here. If you want to say something to me, talk directly."

Right off the bat, I dislike him. And I suspect I didn't like him the first time I met him, either.

"I see you haven't changed and still don't know how to show respect." His voice drips with disdain.

A harsh laugh bursts from my throat, and I love that I can laugh at anything after everything I've been through. "I never asked to be brought here, but apparently, I'm the only one who can save your ass. So maybe it's *me* who should ask for respect." My words are razor-sharp. On the inside, I'm a hot mess, but I refuse to show him that side of me. I keep my chin high, wanting to get a rise out of him.

His nostrils flare when he glances over to his brothers, expecting them to respond.

Deimos stands there without saying a word, and I can't decipher his expression. Gone is the calmness from earlier... Now he's a storm. Dark and wild. He saved me from death, and now he stays away. His hair flutters in the breeze, blood streaking his cheek, a small dimple in his chin I didn't notice before. This image of him sends a blaze to my heart.

Idiot. Thinking I am anything but a savior to these men will get me killed. And I refuse to have my heart broken at the same time. They're princes, and me... I'm merely a cure to their problems.

"She's been through a lot," Luther says, glancing my way with his heart-stopping smile.

Ahren licks his lips like a wolf, his eyes pulling down a fraction. "We move. If she puts us in any danger, we ditch her. I don't care *who* she is."

Luther stiffens, while Deimos shifts, his jaw tightening.

I eye the prick who frustrates the hell out of me. All that whirls in my mind is trying to come up with a plan to get home. Find out as much as I can from these fae about who I am, and get the hell out of this hellhole.

Ahren turns away from me, and it irks me that he treats me like nothing.

"Why do you hate me?" I blurt out, hating that I sound desperate.

He pauses and glances over his shoulder at me, his brow a furrow of lines. After looking me head to toe, I expect him to respond. No matter what he says, I'd rather know than wonder why he detests me.

Just one crack of an arrogant, I'm-going-to-make-you-pay smile and he walks off. "We leave now."

Lifting my chin, I watch him walk away with Deimos at his side. *Rude bastard.*

Here I am stuck with three brothers. Three princes who might just kill me with insanity.

Deimos is keeping his distance, suddenly pretending I don't exist.

Luther is a mystery I haven't worked out yet, but he radiates danger, and it scares me how easily he slips into my mind.

And Ahren, staring at me like he's conjuring up the best way to kill me.

Well, this is going to be fun.

I'm too frustrated, too worked up, and to be honest... too damn disappointed. There's no one to blame but myself for expecting a curse to be anything but a fucking blade to my heart. But I'll take it over never seeing Guendolyn again.

She's my weakness, always has been since I first discovered her.

For years, I spoke to her by thought alone; with me, she shared her fears, her aspirations, her broken life. I never meant to fall for her... far from it. But she crawled under my skin, and now I fight the urge to continue from where we'd ended.

Where she fell for me, looked at me like only I existed. That's gone, and I bristle at the thought. We're strangers once again, and I'm left with empty memories.

When I look at her rushing alongside me in the forest draped in night, her breaths racing, I want to kiss her. To put my hands on every inch of her body, to strip her, to sink deep into her. But most of all, I want her to remember who I am.

I'm the prince who found a lost girl, a girl who thought herself shattered, a girl who needed finding. And I was that man who found her. *I am* that man.

The mage's spell I bought so long ago was meant to track down my fated mate... all fae have one, and I was tired of waiting to find mine. Turns out my mate happened to be a cursed fae, the girl who'd destroy us all. But she's also the only one who can save us all... at a price. Of course it comes at a fucking price.

She stumbles over a tree root in the night. I grasp her hand to keep her from falling.

"Thanks." She offers me a soft smile, one I remember well. But I just nod, and we keep racing ahead.

Long, blonde hair so pale, it might be almost white glimmers in the moonlight. She hasn't changed much since I last saw her. Milky white skin. Still on the thin side, but that's made up for by her full breasts. Freckles smatter her petite nose. Everything about her draws me to her, from the strength that comes out in awful circumstances, to the blush on her cheeks, and those rosy, lush lips.

Tasting them floods my mind, as does marking them.

Captivating.

My mate.

Mine.

Wait. I stare at her limping. "You're hurt?" I survey her legs in tight pants for wounds but find her feet bare and coated in dirt. "Where are your shoes?"

"Long story." She frowns, her hair fluttering around her face from the cold breeze whooshing past. "Are we at your castle yet? I'd love to sit down."

"We've only been walking for a short while," Ahren mutters.

"She left her shoes back in the Earth Realm," Deimos tosses over his shoulder, and Ahren pauses, turning toward us.

"What's the holdup?" Ahren growls. He's irritating me tonight.

I have no idea how I didn't end up killing him before now.

He's been bitching for the past few days as we waited for Deimos' return, complaining about the spell I bought to open the portal. How much easier it would have been if all three of us had gotten through. Well, shit happens, and magic is unstable in our world right now.

"She'll leave a trail of blood for the Bloodcursed to follow soon enough. These grounds will rip her soles to shreds," I say.

Ahren breathes heavily and pinches the bridge of his nose. "Fine. Give her your shoes then."

I lean down to take mine off without hesitation.

"Take mine." Deimos is already bending down to take his off.

"I can't wear those," she says. "I'll trip all over the place. You're like size 100. But thanks." Her blue eyes glisten as she stares out after Deimos, who turns from her. I remember the way he touched her face, how she clung to him while we fought the Bloodcursed. I'd taught him well... care for her with his life, which seems to have gained him her attention.

"I'd rather go barefoot," she says.

Ahren grumbles. "Are all human females this dramatic?"

She glares at him with death in her stare.

I am toeing off my shoes to at least give her my socks to help with her feet. "Let's just get out of this godforsaken forest."

I take Guendolyn's hand and give her my woolly gray socks. She smiles and pulls them onto her tiny feet. And then we're moving again.

She watches the dense woods we pass through. My ears prick to listen for anyone following us.

Ahren takes the lead, a sword on his back. Deimos falls behind us, and we move with haste.

Bloodcursed are active at night, and normally walking the woods is suicide. With the curse on our land, most of the creatures are now surrounding Shadow Court to break in rather than hunting in the woods. And dread of what's waiting for us prickles through me.

Still, the urgency to get Guendolyn out of harm's way smothers me. We need to move faster to reach home, where a mage waits for her to find a way to reverse the curse.

I fight the urgency to pick her up so we can travel faster, my addiction to her growing darker. And that need to keep her safe roars through me.

I sigh and look at the night sky, stars stolen by the storm clouds rolling overhead.

I want to drag her into my arms. The desire ripples through me, but I have control. Semi-control, sure, but I need to wait for her to remember me. Even if it kills me.

Time passes quickly as we move with silence.

"Can we stop? Please." Guendolyn's voice pours over me, awakening something in me, and I halt, as do my brothers.

She's gasping for air. "Just for a bit to catch my breath."

"We need to keep moving," Ahren hisses, staring out toward the dark horizon.

A gust of wind swooshes past us, the trees rustling, branches groaning. We're sitting targets out here.

Deimos remains behind us. We still have a decent half-day walk ahead of us—at least—but we need to get out of here. "Swindon is not far. We'll go there and get a carriage," I suggest. "Then we'll reach the court faster."

"The outcast town, loyal to no kingdom?" Ahren growls. "The ones likely to kill three princes traipsing through their town?" His tone is venom, but I know my brother. He's being trained for the position of king, trained from the moment we stepped foot into Shadow Court, modeled after our king. Mother's new husband. Doesn't excuse him... I believe a king should be kind and rule with intelligence, not a fist.

Guendolyn's hand in mine quivers, and I glance over. Her face blanches, and I watch her chew on her lower lip nervously.

"We'll disguise ourselves," I offer. "Since when are you averse to concealing your true identity, brother? You used to sneak out of the court every few days to meet—"

"This is different," he growls. "With the curse, everyone is uneasy. We're not welcome here. And you want someone to discover the girl?"

"Guendolyn," she says. "That's my name."

"I know someone at the local tavern who can help us." Deimos' footsteps close in from behind me.

Ahren studies us three with hatred in his eyes... No, not hatred, but frustration. Like the rest of us, he wants to get out of the woods and to safety.

He impatiently turns from us, his hands on his hips, the same way he does back in the court when we're forced to attend endless boring meetings with the council.

A twig snaps.

I stiffen.

A large shadow leaps out of the woods and slams into Ahren, both of them crashing to the ground.

Instinct pounds into me, and I lunge toward them to save my brother.

Growls ring in the air. It's too dark to make out the beast, but I can smell the wet fur stench.

Fucking Leacnan. Part wolf, part scavengers, part blight on our land. They eat what the Bloodcursed leave behind and attack anything that moves when hungry.

I jump into the chaos of limbs, grabbing a blade at my belt. I snatch a handful of thick, coarse fur and wrench the beast free. Damn thing reaches my waist in height and isn't to be messed with.

The Leacnan snaps back around with speed, its long snout in my face, its razor teeth shaped to needle-like points. It drools everywhere.

I'm going to die from the putrid stench alone.

The beast lunges at me, its mouth gaping. My muscles react too slow, and it hits me. We both slam to the ground. I drive my blade right into its gut and twist.

The crying howl shudders in my ears.

Next thing I know, the beast is flung off my body, and I gasp for air. Deimos shoves the thing aside and draws his sword. He silences the creature's cries in seconds. Thank the gods.

Twisting my head, I find Guendolyn watching us with huge eyes. That innocence, that fear, it does something to me. It turns me on insanely. I want to protect her, keep her safe, have her clinging to me. "You all right?"

Shoving myself up and off the ground, I turn to find Deimos pulling Ahren to his feet.

Guendolyn doesn't move. "Sweet Jesus, he's bleeding." I follow her pointed finger to Ahren. He's stumbling on his feet with a hand pressed to his side. Blood runs in rivets between his fingers and down his pants.

"Hell! It bit you?" I stride closer as Deimos helps keep him upright.

"We need to keep moving. I'll be fine by the time we head home," Ahren insists. My brother wouldn't admit he's in pain with his dying breath.

"Are you insane?" I say. "That was a damn Leacnan. It howled loud enough for others to hear it. Putting distance behind us won't matter. They're coming for us now!"

"Swindon it is," Deimos declares. "We need to run if we can." He wraps an arm around my brother's back, taking his weight, and then they're running. Ahren limps, but it doesn't slow him.

Panic claws at my heart, and I rush to Guendolyn. *Little wolf, we need to go.*

She beams at me, her curling posture so vulnerable. There's innocence in her eyes, and I inhale her fear.

The forest is a blur. I wrap my arm around her waist, drawing her closer to take some of her weight so we cover the ground faster.

Howls bay around us.

Fuck!

We run and keep going. No stopping, following the downward slope of the hill. These beasts hunt in packs of twenty or thirty animals. We stand no chance of fighting them off.

Faint lights peer out from between the trees farther ahead.

Footfalls pound the ground somewhere behind us. Branches snap.

Guendolyn is huffing, and she keeps looking back, her nails digging into my palm with fear.

The four of us burst out of the forest as a shudder races over my shoulders. I hate being the prey. I do the hunting, not these damn scavengers.

A worn path takes us to a small gated town, its metal doors shut. Walls made of solid bronze stand at least fifteen feet tall.

Deimos is there first, pounding his fist to be heard through the oversized door.

We catch up to my brothers, and I push Guendolyn behind me. I turn toward the woods, to the shifting shadows amid the trees.

Leacnan.

Yellow eyes glint in the moonlight. At least two dozen stare at us from within the darkness.

My fingers fall to the daggers on my hip, each hand wrapped around leather hilts.

"What the fuck do you want?" a grumpy asshole calls out from a tiny window opening in the metal door.

Guendolyn whimpers and presses up closer to my back. In my head, I've got it all planned. If the beasts attack, I'll do my best to hurl her over the wall, and then fight. It's not much of a plan, but it's all I've got right now.

"Hurry the hell up," I snarl as another howl pierces the night.

Deimos is negotiating something with the gatekeeper. Ahren is slumped against the door, his hand clutched to his bloody side, and I pray there's a healer in this town.

Shadows emerge from the woods ahead. Black as midnight, they slink forward. Only their sharp teeth glow in the moon's hue.

My heart's pounding when the loud clank of a lock rings out, and the door opens.

Relief crashes into me as we all dart inside. Guendolyn's by Deimos' side, and I collect Ahren to move fast.

My skins pricks with terror as we charge forward.

The doors shut with a thud behind us, followed by the assault of growls and snarls on the other side. I look back to the entrance rattling on its hinges. How often did this town get attacked by these creatures?

"Fuck, that was too close." I glance over to Deimos, who's raking a hand through his hair like he always does when something bad is about to happen. The ache in my gut hurts. "What did you offer the guard to get us in here?"

He grimaces, and meets my gaze. Dread curls behind his gaze. "You're not going to like it. But this isn't the place to talk about it. Let's get everyone into the tavern so we can deal with Ahren's bite. We need a room."

He takes the lead with the man who let us in, down a small, dusty path with wooden round buildings on either side of us. There's no one around, not at this hour.

"Let me go in first," Deimos tosses over his shoulder as he heads into a tavern.

I turn to Guendolyn and lift her into my arms, one arm under her back, the other under her knees.

She fights me, shoving her hand against my shoulder. "Put me down."

"Quiet, silly girl." Ahren cringes with pain as he grasps his bleeding bite mark. We're standing to the side of the tavern in the shadows. Still, we're easy targets out here.

I cradle Guendolyn to me. She smells beautiful and intoxicating, like the sweetest berries, but beneath that is her heady scent that breaks me.

My heart beats frantically, and all I can concentrate on are her breasts crushed up against my chest.

"Let's go," Deimos orders as he sticks his head out the door and waves us in. Ahren stumbles in, and I follow.

"I can walk," she murmurs, her body tense in my arms, and I grasp her tighter. I adore how she feels so close to me, how she glares at me.

"I'm well aware," I say. "The problem is this is a male's tavern. The only females permitted are hired by the hour. Any females walking into the place are fair game."

"Are you kidding me? So the loophole is you can carry in your own woman?" She's rolling her eyes. "I didn't realize fae were so sexist."

"Why? Females have their own tavern, which we are not allowed inside without an invite."

Her blue eyes are burning with fury. Under her angry gaze, I want us alone so I can force her onto her knees. To remind her of her place by my side. She fights us at every turn, and I miss that about her tremendously. The intensity in her reaction to me excites me.

"And the women carry the men indoors?" she says with sarcasm.

I chuckle. "I'd like to see them try."

She purses her lips and glances toward the Pig's Wheel sign over the tavern door. "Appropriate name."

"Just lower your head." I march into the tavern, secretly terrified of what mess Deimos has landed us in. He's never been a good negotiator. Ever!

The dimly lit tavern smells of beer and sex. I hold on to Luther's jacket while in his arms, staring out into the large room. Every eye is on me, and my skin crawls. I'm the woman this fae has claimed and plans to bed, according to all the leering men. Right! I'm blazing with rage about that shit. But it's sucked away, like all my emotions, bleeding me dry since I know I have to play along to survive. Outside the gates, vicious wolves await us, and in here are fae who'll murder the princes. I don't even give thought to what they'll do to me. I refuse to have those notions in my head.

Half a dozen men sit at the circular bar on tall stools. Another handful occupy the scattering of tables around the joint. Animal pelts drape from the wooden walls, and an enormous black fireplace roars to life with a large fire in the far corner. It'd be cozy if it didn't smell like a barnyard in here. Shadows dance across the wall behind the bar. There are shelves of bottles filled with booze of varying colors—greens and oranges and blues.

The enticing note of a flute played by a young man next to a window fills the silence. It's like a bird's call, pure and smooth.

It isn't long before everyone returns to chatting and drinking, having enough of gawking at the newcomers, and the raucous chatter drowns out the music.

Near the bar, Deimos is talking to whom I assume is the owner in whispers. He gives the man something with a slide of his hand. The man glances down, and I catch a glint of gold in his open palm. He's a tall man with a handlebar mustache, his ears pointy and long, similar to his nose. He's wearing simple clothes, brown pants and a button-up shirt, but the greedy smile spreading across his lips shows me he's no different from anyone else. Even in this world, anyone can be bought. With an upward nudge of his chin, he guides us toward a door alongside the bar and opens it to step inside.

Deimos takes Ahren's arm and places it around his shoulders as they follow the bartender. A trail of blood drips in their wake. With that much blood loss, how bad is the bite? Sure, the guy is an arrogant ass, but I don't want him to die—or turn into something—if he's been bitten. My stomach knots at the thought.

"Will your brother change into a werewolf?" I look up at Luther, whispering the question. I feel stupid asking, but I'm in a world where tree roots attack blood-sucking fae, so anything might be possible.

"He's not shifting into anything. That's not how bites work."

I'm not sure how *anything works* here.

Luther shuffles us sideways through the doorway. He pulls me even closer to him, our chests sandwiched together. It makes me more aware of just how much bigger and more powerful he is than me.

He kicks the door to the hallway shut behind us, closing out the noises from the main tavern and drenching us in darkness. Light spills out only at the end of the hall from a room Deimos and Ahren vanish into, following the bartender.

Luther pauses, looking down at me. Shadows shift under his golden eyes, seeming to flicker like a flame.

My heart hammers, heat pouring over me. When he looks at me like nothing else in the world exists, the familiar ache in my chest surges forward. The one that insists we have a past. But he's secretive and dominating. He hasn't told me anything about our past.

This fae confuses me—they all do. Maybe I'm missing something and just falling for the charm and trickery of these gorgeous men.

He's still for a moment as though he's stopped breathing. Heat from his body engulfs me. "This world is dangerous to someone like you."

I simply stare at him... someone like me?

"You need to be cautious about attracting the wrong kind of attention, especially from fae men, especially in a place like this," he says as he lowers me to my feet.

Fae men like him?

He combs a hand through his dark hair, the muscles on his forearm flexing. I drown beneath his stare, at his rugged appearance. His long dark hair is windblown and messy, the military-style jacket he wears is gaped open at the base of his throat.

His fingers find my waist, and he grips me hard. "I won't let anything hurt you, but you need to stop fighting me."

I tilt my head and stare at those spectacular eyes. "If by not fighting, you mean be a push over, then that's not going to work."

"So what will work? Letting you get hurt to learn your lesson?" His brows furrow together.

"No, that's not what I mean." I swallow down the lump in my throat. "I'm not used to being carried around so other men don't see me as an easy lay."

He blinks at me, and I'm not sure if he's confused or taking in my words. But that fierce determination on his face remains. He's a prince used to getting his way, and I'm a lost girl in this mad realm who has no idea how anything works. Luther's presence rattles me. My heart says he's mine, but my head insists we can never be together. So letting myself believe anything else is stupid. Still, he distracts me with the way his gaze lingers over my body.

"Whether you like it or not, I will always intervene. You don't know this world like I do."

"I can look after myself. I've been doing so for years, and maybe you can tell me what I'm about to do wrong." I snap. "Instead of just taking charge."

His hand grips my arm, and he leans in closer to me. His intoxicating scent leaves me dizzy with bliss. "I'm not saying this to upset you, but to ensure you don't die."

He stays so close, our brows are almost touching, and I'm drowning in the heat of his body. But I hate when all I can focus on is his chest pressing up against mine. I can't stop the thoughts rushing over my mind. Me pinned to the wall, him ripping the fabric off my body before he takes me. My core clenches with need.

I struggle to breath, struggle against him. But I can't let myself go there.

"You said earlier that the curse wiped my memories. Why me? What happened between us?"

He sighs, the corded muscles in his neck flexing. "There is so much I need to tell you once we reach the kingdom."

I stiffen and step back from his reach. "No, I'm not moving until you tell me something. I'm tired of being kept in the dark. I was dragged here, almost killed. I deserve to know the truth."

Luther swallows hard and seems lost in thought. The corners of his eyes pinch tight.

He's massive, standing tall, and every inch captivating. That chiseled jawline draws my attention to his soft lips. His expression is almost stoic. I want to run my hands through his dark hair, force him to look up and just be honest. But I know us touching will only distract me.

When I meet his gaze, I see he's already staring at me. "You were cursed as a child, Guendolyn."

I blink, staring at him, waiting for more, but that's all he gives me. He watches me, and I have no idea what he's thinking.

He pulls away, but I grab his wrist. "Then what happened? Please, Luther. I have to know."

I reluctantly let go of his arm and study the emotions he fights. Hope flares in my chest that he might finally tell me everything.

"When you returned to the Wandering Realm two years ago, you unleashed the curse that had been laying dormant in you for years." His steps closer, his words low and hushed. "The moment you crossed the threshold into Ash Court on your first visit, the curse activated and you fell into a deep sleep... a spell that wiped your memory. And now the prophecy says the blood of fae, Seelie to be more specific, will spill for eternity."

"I did?"

"Unknowingly, yes." He lowers his head, his voice dark, and places a hand to his chest as if the words pain him. "It's my fault for bringing you here two years ago. But I'll make it right. That's why we brought you back."

"Why was I cursed in the first place?"

The creak of hinges gets me to turn around, my chest clenching from the information I've just learned. A younger woman in a long, blue dress and black apron emerges from a door to our right. She's carrying a bucket of sloshing water, her shoulder strained and sloped from the weight.

Luther pulls away from me.

"Let's join my brothers. We'll discuss this later, in a place where walls don't have ears." He brushes past me and marches up to the younger woman to aid her. He says something, and she giggles, clearly captivated by his charm. She pushes aside the hair fallen over her face and bats her eyes at him.

I'm sucking in sharp breaths. I ignore that tiny tingle in my chest as

Luther carries the bucket into the room, and she trails after him. I'm angry at how my body trembles from his absence.

The shadows in the hallway seem to close in around me, and for the first time in the last few days, I'm partially alone. Running anywhere isn't an option. I'm stuck with these fae. Stuck to returning to their Shadow Court. Stuck until I remember who I am exactly and how to return home. Add to that the need to understand this curse and why Luther would bring me here if he knew I was toxic?

Just thinking like that leaves me with a bad feeling in my gut. Why would anyone make me carry such a curse and then hide me on Earth?

I've always dreamed of discovering the truth of who my real parents are, and why they got rid of me. I know those answers lie here. The sliver of information Luther shared confirms it for me.

The princes know so much more than they're telling me yet. My life is anything but a fairytale.

Coldness from the stone floor seeps into my soaks and sends a chill up my legs. The whispered voices from the room reaches me.

Deimos sticks his head out of the room and looks at me. No words, just a quirked eyebrow.

I sigh and march toward the room, filled with frustration. I glance into another room along the hallway where the woman with the bucket had come from, and candle light reveals another door. The wind nudges it open from the outside and curls inside. It wraps around me with its icy claws. My skin crawls from how cold it's grown outside. I hurry down the hallway.

Inside, a glowing fireplace crackles, throwing light across the bare, white walls. The smell of stuffiness and dust fill my senses as I step inside the large, wooden room.

Ahren lies on one of the two beds on his back, groaning. His jacket and white top lies on the floor near the bed. He's bare-chested, his hands clenching the bedsheets. My stomach hurts at seeing the excruciating pain wash over his face.

All I can do is stare at him, at the perfect angles of his body, the light drizzle of light hair over his muscular chest, his strong jawline, the muscles on his biceps. I shouldn't be going there, but my gaze roams over all of him.

Luther is next to him, aiding the woman in cleaning the bloody mess on Ahren's side. There's so much blood, and I'm fighting the urge to turn away from the open wound. The dark red blood, the torn flesh.

"Clean these." Luther hands me a blood-stained rag.

I stare down at the water swirling with blood in the bucket. Biting down on my tongue, I plunge my hand inside with the rag and squeeze the blood out of it with both hands. Soaking and rinsing until it comes out semi-clean, I wring it and hand it back to Luther.

"He needs the wound sanitized," I say, gaining myself strange looks from everyone. "Alcohol," I explain. "To avoid the wound getting infected."

The bartender nods. "Of course. Boy, you come with me." He gestures to Deimos.

They both hurry out of the room, and when I look back, Ahren raises his gaze to me.

Vulnerability. That's all I see in his eyes. His lips twist with a snarl, then his eyes clamp shut. His body convulses. I wince at his pain. Maybe I'm a fool, but I don't want to see him hurt this way.

Thundering footfalls enter the room, and I look over to Deimos, who rushes in, carrying a clear bottle by its neck. The pale blue contents inside swish around like a wild sea during a storm.

"Good timing," Luther murmurs, meeting Deimos' gaze.

The maid wipes her rag over the bite mark with four distinct puncture wounds.

Deimos goes to his brother and lifts his head off the pillow. "Drink. You'll need this."

Ahren gulps down several mouthfuls before he spills the drink. Alcohol runs down the sides of his mouth and over his chin. He pushes the bottle away and growls. "Just get it fucking over with."

The young maid sweeps the damp cloth across his wound once more. Deimos lowers the bottle and tips the blue liquid over the injury. It splashes and runs into the torn gashes before running over his side and onto the bed.

Ahren hisses, then howls, his body thrashing.

My stomach roils at the sight of his flesh sizzling around the injury.

I turn away for a moment, my chest clenching, unable to look at the agony. My eyes tear up, and I can't cope. I glance around at the worn room, at the sun-tinged curtains, the scratched dresser. There's an adjoining small room that might be some kind of medieval bathroom with only two wooden pails in sight. I study the long, coppery rug running the length of the room, the wooden floorboards—focusing on anything but the screams.

Someone nudges my arm, and I flinch.

I glance back around to face Luther. "You need to hold the bandage down and apply pressure. You think you can do that?"

I'm nodding and already sidling up against him. "Of course." I breathe so hard and place a palm over the layered bandages on Ahren's side. The heat leeches through the white fabric easily and skitters up my arm.

The corded muscles in Ahren's neck twitch, his eyes still shut, pain straining his face.

I press my hand against the bite, holding the bandages in place, and sit on the edge of the bed.

Deimos is helping the young woman pack up, thanking her, and he carries the bucket of dirty water out for her. Luther goes with them, closing the door shut behind them.

My heart is beating. It's just us two, and I look over at Ahren.

Sweat beads his brow, and I look around to find a damp cloth left near his feet. With my free hand, I grab it and wipe it across his forehead. There's something almost normal about him lying here. Almost human. Except he's the heir to the throne of Shadow Court, the information that has always stayed with me about him. Will he make a good king?

"Guendolyn," he whispers, his voice barely audible.

"It's all right," I say. "You're safe."

His eyes slide open to reveal the palest green irises, like a faded green leaf. They're half glazed over. I expect him to wrinkle his nose or glare at me, but he doesn't. He just stares, like he's seeing someone else.

"Did you know you're destined to be the death of us all?" he says softly.

His words leave me gasping. I'm trying to decipher his insult.

"What do you mean?"

His face scrunches up with pain, and I wait a few moments for his breaths to slow as he glances at me again. "Luther was never meant to bring you to our realm. You aren't supposed to be here."

I don't know what to say, and feel the weight of the world on my shoulders.

"You need to make this right," he murmurs with his eyes shut tightly.

But I'm getting tired of these games. "Then tell me what's going on so I can make the right decision." Annoyance roars through me. "Tell me what I need to know." My voice climbs.

He grimaces with pain.

His hand moves down to mine and eases the pressure I'm placing against his wound.

Breathing easier, a curl pulls at his lips.

"Wow, did you just smile?" I say. "Pretty sure the world is going to come to an end now."

"Your sharp tongue will get you in trouble." He opens his eyes.

"Is that what you want? To see me punished for coming to your world?" I position myself near the bed to face him better, my hip against the mattress, my hand still on his bandages.

He shrugs and winces with pain.

"You deserved that," I say, not regretting one word. He's the eldest of the princes, the fae poised to become king one day, but right now, he's pissing me off.

"It's not to insult you that I tell you these things, but for you to be prepared for what you have unleashed." He pauses for a moment, his jaw tight as he battles the agony ripping through him.

"If someone cursed me, be angry at them, not me." Fury races through my mind.

"One day, I intend to kill the fae who spelled you."

I still, taken back by his admittance, and shoot him an incredulous look. "Who was it?" I say through an adrenaline rush. "Do you know why they cursed me?"

His breaths grow shallow, and a shadow slithers in his eyes. "To kill you." He glances at me. "You are from the Unseelie Court, Guendolyn. If you return there, they'll kill you on sight."

Unseelie Court... Deimos' words come to me.

"The Unseelie are ruthless and malicious. They are the darkest of the fae. We are their enemy!"

Am I these princes' enemy?

I glance at Ahren while my mind is spinning out of control. "So that means the Unseelie fae cursed me! Why would they, when the curse affects everyone in the realm, including them?"

"There are four kingdoms in the Wandering Realm, each aligned with different gods, elements, and magic." He goes quiet and still for a moment, then he clears his throat. "The curse was made only to affect Shadow Court, to eradicate us. And for the past two years, we've been at war with an endless ocean of Bloodcursed attacking our kingdom, destroying nearby towns, and leaving everyone running for their lives." He swallows hard, his face growing paler.

"I don't know how to remove this curse, you know that? If I knew, I'd remove it instantly."

"You need help from our mages to undo this catastrophe, so you need to trust us."

The words come blurting out before I can tame them. "I *don't* trust you."

The hurt is clear on his face, but let's be real... Did he really expect anything else? I don't know him, and I've been dragged into this world.

"I don't *know* you," I murmur.

"So what will it take to gain your trust?"

My back straightens at his comment. "Show me how to go home."

"I promise to aid you in your return home. Unharmed." He studies me with narrowing eyes. "Once we remove our curse."

"How long will that take?" I ask with clipped words.

"As long as is needed."

A battle rises within me, and fury burns me from head to toe. He has no intention of rushing to help me. It's only his court he cares about, and me... I'm the key to dealing with his problems, then I'll be disposed of. Maybe killed. I am their enemy, according to Deimos. All Unseelie are.

"I hate you," I mutter. "I thought you said you wanted me to trust you."

"You can't hate someone you don't know. Not yet anyway, but once we reach home, I will show you so much more. I can work with stubbornness." That smirk spreads his lips again, and I want to punch him right in the wound. Even with the bandages over it. Yeah, it makes me a bitch, but I'm fuming at his arrogance.

"Ouch." He tries to shift in bed, his nose wrinkling. "It's burning."

"What are you talking about?" I almost forget about his wound.

He shoves my hand away from his injury. "Your hand is burning me through the bandages."

"What?" I say, trying to replace the bandages. But he's squirming on the bed, trying to slide away from me.

"Your hand feels like it's on fire."

"That's your wound fighting infection. Don't be such a baby. Be still."

Heat flares across my palm, growing hotter by the second.

Ahren howls with agony and jerks away from me on the bed.

The bandages fall to the mattress.

His bite mark is completely healed—no broken skin, just the stain of blood.

I blink hard at the burning hot handprint on his flesh. *My* handprint.

He looks down at his side and back up at me. There's fury in his sharp eyes. "What did you do?"

I have no idea, but I can't keep the grin from stretching my lips.

"*The problem with love is that it makes you weak.*" The king's words drum through my mind. I used to loathe when he'd say that to me, because the bastard married *my* mother. I still hate the asshole king, but I see some truth in his words. Falling for someone steals your focus; it gives your enemies an easy target. It's how his first wife died while pregnant with their firstborn.

The only reason he wed my mother was because of her House Larmathier lineage, as she's a prominent member of one of the oldest and wealthiest families. After the death of his first wife, the king needed money and a wife quickly... before his sister stepped in and took the rulership from him.

Our kingdoms are absolute monarchies. The king and queen hold the power, but there are some restrictions to their authority, such as the fact that they must be married to an appropriate bride or groom of an acceptable heritage, or they'll lose the throne. The king or queen cannot rule alone. And when it comes to the heir to their throne, it's always the firstborn—the oldest. So with the current king having no children of his own from his first wife, Ahren is set to take the throne when the king and queen are no longer fit to serve. Add to that the king had a devastating fall from his horse many years ago, leaving him incapable of bearing any more children. So, he resigned himself to adopting us three as his own and for Ahren to take the throne one day.

Of course it becomes tricky, because not only does Ahren as the heir ascend to the throne, but he must marry immediately to claim that position.

I look down the hallway to the closed room, where Ahren and Guendolyn wait. My little wolf brings chaotic confusion to my life. Seelie and Unseelie fae are forbidden from being together. My chest clenches, and my nerve endings crackle with the apprehension of what is coming. The wreck is about to drag me down to the pits of Seven Hells, and I can't seem to move out of the way of the charging destruction.

The door across the hallway opens, and I push off the wall. Deimos emerges.

I say to him, "We should talk."

He bristles and regards me from behind hooded eyes. "What about?"

"The trip into the Earth Realm—since we haven't had a chance to properly talk."

"You've been sitting out here all this time while I helped them collect more water from the well to ask me about her? Fuck, you're so transparent, brother."

"You misunderstand me," I lie through my teeth, but I'm tired of him giving me shit over Guendolyn. "Earth isn't an easy place to navigate. And you took too long to return."

He runs a hand over his face. "Well, firstly, I wasn't meant to go there alone, or deal with that stubborn girl alone, or have two bloodthirsty Bloodcursed on our asses I had to deal with on my own. But *you're welcome* for the fact that I brought her back to you. I went through hell," Deimos growls.

"Don't be such a wuss."

He stiffens at my response. There's a darkness in his eyes, an unrelenting anger.

At this rate, the two of us will end up in a brawl over pure stubbornness. I reach over and place my hand on his shoulder, squeezing lightly on the thin, human shirt he wears. "Lighten up. Since when are you so serious and can't take a joke?"

He shakes me off him and rakes a hand through his hair. It takes him a few moments, and he glances back at me with a grin. There he is, the brother I grew up with and went through so much shit together.

"Thank you for bringing her safely here."

He half-smiles, but his brow is furrowed.

"What's going on with you?" I ask.

For a moment, Deimos stands frozen, his eyes locking on the wall behind me. "I might have fucked up."

Deimos never admits to a mistake—ever! Those words sit on my chest like a mountain. "What did you do?"

His lips thin with obvious pain. His gaze shifts to mine. "I need a stiff drink." He turns for the door leading to the tavern, but I lash out and grab his arm.

"Talk to me now. What happened?" My mind is racing with scenarios... something to do with Guendolyn and him together.

His hesitation is killing me, and my fingers grip him harder. My muscles are tense as hell.

"I may have offered this backwater town, Swindon, our kingdom's allegiance." He rips free from my hold and trudges up and down the hall.

"Why the fuck would you do that? Didn't you use your persuasive voice?"

"You think I didn't fucking try. It doesn't always work when I'm stressed."

I march after him and snatch his elbow before dragging him into the tavern. "I need that damn drink now."

I shove open the door from the hallway and into the tavern. Half the drunks have left the place, so it's a lot quieter. There's a soft melody in the air performed by a single flute.

"Two glasses of Noxious," I toss over my shoulder at the bartender as I drag Deimos to the farthest corner of the room, where we can be alone and near the fire to shake away these chills.

"Sit," I order my younger brother. "So then, that's how you got us past those gates. Offered him our allegiance?" My knees are bouncing under the table. "Couldn't you offer him something else, like your firstborn?" Clearly, my sarcasm isn't working, but this shit could get him killed. King Tibout may be our stepfather, but he'll take any excuse to eradicate us. "If the king finds out, he'll either kill you or imprison you for life. No one is allowed to decide whom we assign allegiance to."

"You think I don't know that?" he barks just as the bartender delivers two glasses brimming with a coppery-colored drink. Noxious is made from a poisonous plant and fermented for weeks until it's safe to consume. The stuff comes with a slight tingle, and is known for fast intoxication if you drink too much. But it's fucking strong, and I need that shit now.

Once the bartender leaves us, Deimos swigs downs half his drink. His nose scrunches and he shudders, then he drinks the rest. "We were at the gate. The Leacnan were almost on us. You were yelling. Guendolyn was whimpering. And Ahren looked ready to die. And that bastard asked for our allegiance at a time I couldn't say *no*."

Deimos swallows hard and waves at the bartender, then points to his empty glass to order another round of drinks. "I tore the sigil pin of our court from Ahren's coat outside the gate. I gave it to the man as confirmation to let us in."

"You know what this means?" My breaths came sharp and fast, my jaw clenched tight.

"Hell, yes. They can call for our commitment to aid them anytime they need it, but they in turn don't need to hold any allegiance to us. Gods, I'm so fucked."

"This was exactly how House Gailet went down, you know. Forced to hold up such a pact, and they were ambushed and killed. And now, we're obligated to protect these townsfolk who'd stab us in the back the moment they get a chance." Unease settles under my ribcage with that feeling of being cornered. This affects all of us, and it irks me that we ended up in this shitty situation.

I glance around the room of drunks. Most are probably mercenaries.

"You're not making me feel any better!"

I'm nodding as I finish my drink, swirling bitter and sweet citrus aftertaste lingering at the back of my throat. Our second round of drinks arrive.

"So what do we do?" Deimos asks, his face panic-stricken. "After I helped the maid with the water bucket, I went to speak with the guard just now about taking the pin back and offering a large sum of gold in exchange. He laughed in my face and said he's already given the pin to the Lord of Swindon. I would have killed him right there if he still had the pin. Fucking swine."

"Shit! All right. First, we don't breathe a word of this to Ahren." I lean closer and scan the room to ensure he hasn't snuck up on us. "You know how he is when he gets stressed. Acts like a prick and can't keep his mouth shut. Second, what else does this horrible deal get us? A carriage back home?"

"I'll get on that," he says, reaching for another glass of Noxious.

"And third, we're going to have to come up with a plan to deal with the king when this lord turns up on our doorstep."

"This is going to go bad—I can feel it." Deimos finishes his drink in one long gulp. He's going to feel this in the morning if he doesn't stop.

"The king doesn't know that you brought Guendolyn back two years ago and she unleashed the curse. He sure as hell doesn't know we went back to bring her back again now. This is just us. If we want to survive, no one can find out."

My head is already swaying and maybe drinking these so quickly on an empty stomach wasn't such a great idea.

"We stick together. Get Guendolyn home safe, then we speak with my mage to help fix her connection to the curse," I say. "We pray the lord in this town doesn't come knocking at our court anytime soon."

Deimos is on his feet, and I get up to join him, the room tilting slightly. We both head across the room, and I feel like I'm floating. The rush to my head is fast. "That drink is stronger than I remember," I say.

"Ahren is going to be so pissed to see us stumbling about."

"Hush." I shove my hand over his mouth, feeling so drunk now, I can barely stand on my own feet.

He shoves my hand away and laughs. It's contagious, and I'm howling in laughter. We're in so much shit, and I can't stop chuckling.

I glance over to the bartender, who watches us. I dig my hand into my pocket and pull out five gold crowns which more than covers our drinks. I hand them over, and he stares at them with huge eyes. In truth, this town owes us so much more than a room for one night and a handful of drinks for our kingdom's allegiance, but I won't make this man pay for the decisions others make.

Side by side, Deimos and I are leaning close and staggering down the hallway. I thump open the door abruptly with a palm.

Guendolyn and Ahren are facing off from across the bed. They both jerk to stare at us. Deimos bangs the door shut and turns around before face-planting to the ground. Two seconds later, he's snoring like a bear.

"What the fuck?" Ahren growls.

But my attention falls to the pulsing red handprint on my brother's side. "Hey, your bite mark is gone." I hiccup, and my laughter bursts past my lips as my head spins.

"Apparently, Guendolyn is a healer," Ahren snarls. "Have you two been drinking?"

I glance over at her, and my heart beats so hard, that's all I can hear. "You're so beautiful." I'm drawn to her, like always since we first met. Stepping over my brother is a mistake. The toe of my boot catches on him, and I fall forward too. My head hits the floorboards, and all I can think about is Guendolyn. Guendolyn and sleep.

Guen

"Wʜᴀᴛ ᴊᴜsᴛ ʜᴀᴘᴘᴇɴᴇᴅ?" I murmur as I stare down at the two princes lying on the floor, fast asleep.

"Damn idiots went and got drunk."

"That fast?" They were only gone fifteen minutes, if that.

"They can't hold their liquor," Ahren snarls, stomping across the room and locking the door.

I watch the fluid movement of the muscles flexing across his back, the strength of his shoulders, the tightness of those black pants over his ass. When he walks, it's more like prowling, his body radiating power. And I can't help but shiver at his primal presence.

The closer I stare at him, the more I notice the healed whip marks criss-crossing his back. I cringe, and my heart squeezes. Someone hurt him that much?

He turns toward me, and I drop my gaze to his brothers. I chew on my cheek, unable to unsee the wounds.

When I glance back up, Ahren is studying my handprint, trying to rub it off with his thumb.

"Is that going to scar?" I ask as I crouch near Luther and push the hair off his face. He's fast asleep and will probably feel like shit tomorrow. Serves him right for drinking while leaving me alone here with his grumpy brother.

"It should vanish once my wound completely heals. Your print is like a magic bandage. Though I've seen some healing marks remain for years."

"A girl's handprint on your body might be hard to explain on your wedding night if that remains." I half-laugh to myself at the image.

"She would know it's a healing mark," he answers stiffly, my sarcasm completely wasted on him.

"That was a joke," I say as I stand, but he's looking at me, confused. I'm too tired to explain my lame jest. "So what do we do now?"

"Get some sleep, and in the morning we head home." He walks over to his bed with a slight limp, telling me he's still in pain.

"What about them?" I point to his brothers.

"They're sleeping. They can stay there for all I care. That's what they get for getting drunk."

"You're harsh." I move to the other bed and grab one of the two pillows, then snatch one from Ahren's bed and head toward the princes on the floor.

"A soft heart will get you killed in the Wandering Realm," he explains as I lift Deimos' head and stuff a pillow under it. I do the same with Luther before I return to my bed. It's located parallel to Ahren's, and I'd rather it were in a different room. He's shaking his blood-stained sheets before climbing in on the clean side. My handprint on his side seems to have paled slightly.

"Guess you need to have a heart in the first place," I retort as I take Luther's woolly socks off my feet before getting under the sheets of my bed fully clothed. How I'd love to peel off these tight jeans, but that isn't happening anytime soon while in the company of these three fae.

"One day I will be king, and to show such disrespect can get you strung up by your ankles in the field of death."

"I don't care if you're a god. You're still an arrogant jerk." I groan. He annoys me to no end, and after everything that happened today, I'm ready to sleep and forget it all.

I turn my back to Ahren as he blows out the candle on the bedside table between us. He grumbles, and his bed groans as he shuffles about, trying to get comfortable. I've never done anything to hurt this fae. I even freaking healed him... god knows how I did that, but I don't understand how antagonistic he is toward me.

Once he settles, only the flicker of the low fire in the hearth remains, throwing shadows over the wall. There's something soothing about the sound of a crackling fire. Well, except for the light snores from the two princes sleeping on the ground.

"Guendolyn," Ahren says, his voice soft and seemingly calm.

"Yeah?"

"Thank you."

I don't expect such words from Mr. *I Live in an Ivory Tower and Will Kill You Anytime I Feel Insulted*. "You're welcome," I breathe, peering up at the ceiling covered in swirling shadows. I assume he's thanking me for healing him. And with that, all I can think about are the marks on his back. Is that why he's such a prickly ass?

"How did you get those wounds on your back?" I ask.

He doesn't respond right away, and I assume he won't. It isn't my place to pry, but curiosity always gets the better of me.

He heaves a breath, and the bed creaks under him as he shuffles around to face me. "My real father would use a whip on me as a child whenever I disobeyed him." His voice is very matter-of-fact, like he's practiced for so long to disassociate any emotions from the beatings he got.

I surrender to the pity that scoops out my insides, and now I can't help but feel horrible for snapping at him. I roll onto my side and face him. Shadows dance over his strong face.

"He sounds like a fucking dickhead," I say.

"That fae had a dark side, and when he looked at you with evil in his eyes, you knew what was coming. But when he started paying attention to my younger brothers, I stepped in and attacked him. He broke my ribs and arm, and it took me weeks to mend, even with a healer's help. Nothing Mother did stopped him."

"So sorry you had to go through that." I don't know what to say to someone who's experienced such abuse. It hurts to hear his story, and it reminds me how lucky I was with my foster mother, who loved me from the moment I moved in with her family.

"It was long ago and a reminder of the kind of king I will not become one day. Anyway, good night, Guendolyn."

Only the brother's soft snores filled the void between us.

"Just one more question, please," I say. "Why do you dislike me?"

"I don't dislike you," he responds quickly, his tone snappy. "Quite the opposite. I just worry about my brothers." He doesn't say anything else and rolls onto his back before he shuts his eyes.

Quite the opposite... Does that mean he likes me? But he thinks I'll hurt his brothers.

The thought swirls on my mind.

I don't know what to make of that, so I pull the bedsheet to my chin and shut my eyes. Sleep rushes forward quicker than I expect.

THE TOPS of the trees seem to glint against the moonlight. Standing up here on the platform amid the trees, it feels like I can touch the stars

"Look at me." Luther's voice is raspy and fierce.

I turn and train my gaze on his heart-stopping countenance.

Arousal curls behind his intense eyes, and I clench my thighs with the building heat. I adore that look on his face, the idea that I hold such control over him.

Electricity sizzles over my flesh.

He leans closer, burying his face in my hair, inhaling me. "Mine," he mutters.

He closes his lips to mine, and lust floods me. A desperate ache blazes through me, my brain firing off sparks. I open my mouth and moan as he slides his tongue inside, battling with mine.

I rake my hands into his long hair, tugging it.

His grip tightens, and I let out a gasp of excitement.

I run my hands down his strong shoulders, over the hard planes of his chest and stomach. My fingers slide under his shirt, finding fiery skin. He hisses a breath at my touch, drawing me tighter against him, kissing me with savagery. It scares me how much I let myself go, how much I desire him.

I want him. Need him. Plain and simple, I have to have this gorgeous man.

His kisses drift over my cheek, across my brow, and to my ear. "There are so many secrets I plan to share with you, my little wolf. Secrets that will make you the most powerful fae in the Wandering Realm."

I freeze and look up at him. Gone is the deadly edge of arousal he brought me to. "What are you talking about?"

His hands snake down my back, curving over my ass. His gaze narrows on me. "Why do you think everyone in the realm knows you?"

"Maybe because—"

A piercing hoot sounds from somewhere down in the woods. I flinch in response, and my heart shudders.

Luther jerks away from me and glances down over the railing. His face pales two shades when he looks back up at me. "We need to go. Now!"

The smell of eggs cooking rouses me from sleep, but my mind still floats on the dream of Luther. A perfectly arousing dream that has me longing for his lips and touch, but at the back of my mind, I feel the urgency from the dream too. The need to run from something bad. I sigh at not remembering what that was... It's another piece of the puzzle that is my memory. I recall the moment, but not what came before or after. Just the emotions of how much I longed for him. If that is even just a sliver of what we had together, I'm starting to understand his reaction last night over me not remembering him.

My stomach rumbles loudly with hunger, and I hear the clink of cutlery against plates as I push myself upright. I lift my head, my eyes opening to find the three princes around the small table in the room, having breakfast and drinking what smells like coffee.

"You better not be eating my portion," I croak. My mouth feels like I've swallowed a porcupine.

"Morning," Luther says. "There's plenty for you."

Deimos shuffles over and squeezes the fourth chair between him and Luther.

Like a zombie, I lurch toward the smell of food and flop down on the chair. I grab a slice of bread and smear it with butter and marmalade. It takes like heaven on my tongue, and I soften in my chair as I devour it. The last thing I ate was a bit of rabbit and I wasn't a fan.

Luther is filling my plate with eggs and slices of fried meat.

I glance from one prince to the next, each one dressed up in the same clothes as yesterday, but their faces are fresh, their hair perfect, while I feel like a monster who's just dragged herself out of a swamp.

"Why didn't you all wake me up if you were up so early?" I ask.

I pat down my wayward blonde strands from what I assume is horrible bed hair.

"You looked so cute sleeping," Ahren says before drinking coffee from an earth-colored ceramic mug like he hadn't just publicly called me *cute*. All I can think is back to our conversation from last night, his worry that I'll somehow hurt his brothers. I want to laugh because I am the furthest thing from a girl who plays guys. I don't have guys fawning over me—all this attention is new to me.

Halfway through the food on my plate, I look over to Deimos. "How was the floor?" I mock, grinning at Luther.

"Best sleep I've had in years," Deimos retorts, that sly smirk curling his lips as he stands to leave the table. He walks over to the dresser and picks up a pile of clothes and shoes. "I managed to find you something clean to wear. Hopefully, they will fit."

I swallow the food in my mouth and swivel on my seat. "Wow. Thank you. Where did you get them from?"

"The guard to this town owes me," he says quietly.

I'm on my feet at once. "Where's the bathroom?"

Ahren and Deimos stare at me, confused. "The what?" Ahren asks.

"The privy," Luther answers, and I've never heard the toilet called that before.

"We'll leave you here to change, then I'll show you the privy...bathroom once you're ready." Deimos is already crossing the room, and his brothers follow him. Without waiting for me to respond, they're out in the hallway and close the door, leaving me alone.

I drag my jeans off with a bit of work from my clammy body. It feels refreshing to have my legs free. I peel off my shirt and grab the dress from Deimos. It's the color of garnet stone. I drag it down and over my head, threading my arms into the short sleeves. The fabric is on the thicker side, like a plush velvet, and it cascades down to my ankles in soft waves. Around the black corset, I tug at the laces to tie it up without constricting my lungs. I look down at myself, at the square neckline sitting low over my chest. My breasts are pushed up significantly in this outfit. I tuck down the corners of my black bra peeking out, then reach for the black boots and step into them. Perfect fit. Deimos did well.

Tucking my clothes on my bed, they are filthy and the hems of my jeans torn. I move to the door and open it to find the princes suddenly fall silent from their conversation.

Three sets of eyes on me.

"Damn," Luther says. "You look gorgeous."

Ahren and Deimos don't say anything, but I'm not blind to the appreciation on their faces. It leaves me bushing. I'm not normally a dress-wearing kind of girl so their admiration gives me a huge confidence boost.

"Let's go," Deimos says.

With my head low, I pass the two princes and follow Deimos to the far end of the hallway.

I look back over my shoulder to see Ahren step into the room and Luther staring out after me. It's too dark to see his expression from his angle, but my butterflies are swarming in my gut.

Deimos stops in front of a door and guides me through another corridor to a door that opens up to the outside.

A freezing breeze washes over my face, and I hug myself. The sun is out, the sky is blue, but it's icy cold. Still, somehow, today feels like a new start. Farther away, horses are bound amid towering dark-bark trees.

Deimos doesn't wait for me but is marching ahead along a path in the woods to a wooden outhouse. I sigh loudly, my skin already creeping at the whole notion of going in there.

"Hey, wait up," I call out as I hurry to keep up with the prince. "What's going on?" I ask him. "Why are you so standoffish?"

He looks at me. His lips quirk as if surprised by my question, but I'm not blind to his behavior. Instead, he opens the door to the outhouse and says, "Hurry up. We need to leave soon. I've put a fresh bucket of water in there for you."

I stare up at him, words bubbling in my mind, but the impatience in his gaze tells me he's not going to tell me anything. So I march inside, then draw the door shut behind me.

Light drenches the room from a tiny window high up on the wall. A small bench to my right has a bucket of water, and I peer inside. It looks crystal clear but I'm not touching it.

"Guendolyn," Deimos calls from outside, his voice rushing. "I'll be back in two quick moments. I've spotted the lord of this town. I have to speak to him. I won't be long."

"Okay, sure." Whatever.

His footsteps fade.

Against the back wall is an enclosed bench with an oval lid over what I suspect is the toilet hole. Nearby is a small pile of thinly trimmed leaves. Wow, I can't believe I'm about to do this. I swallow hard and hurry and get this over with. To my surprise, it doesn't stink that bad, and I take my time. Turns out the leaves weren't too different to toilet paper and just as malleable. By the time I finish and wash my hands, I head outside and breathe easy. The cool breeze swirling over my skin and around my legs is incredible.

Glancing around, I see no sign of Deimos. Figuring he's still talking to the lord of this town, I head back down the worn path amid the scattering of pine trees. The air smells fresh today, while the temperature has dropped to freezing.

The crackle of dried leaves comes from my right, and I look over, expecting Deimos. Instead, it's a brute of a man in black breeches with buttons running down the side of his pants. His white shirt has ruffled long sleeves, and that scraggly beard and wild golden wiry hair tells me looking after his appearance isn't a priority.

"Are you lost?" he asks, his gaze leering over my body, pausing on my chest.

I frown and turn away. "No, I'm not lost." I march forward, but he grabs my wrist and wrenches me back. His grip pinches so hard, it hurts. I swing around with my fist and slam it into his fat head.

He doesn't shift or even react, just smiles, revealing missing teeth. The ones that are still there are stained yellow.

A shiver slithers up my spine.

"Ew, get off me." I kick him in the shin.

"Ow, you fucking cunt." He hauls me against him, one hand grabbing my breast.

I drive my fist into his chest and scream, my pulse on fire over the fact that this dick thinks it's all right to hurt me.

A large hand snaps around the man's wrist, another to his throat, and wrenches him away from me.

I'm left stumbling from the momentum.

"The lady said *no*," Deimos snarls and shoves a fist into the man's face, sending him reeling back. The prince's muscles clench as he marches after the pig of a man.

"I-I d-didn't know she was with you," he stammers.

Deimos doesn't pause and pummels fist after fist into the asshole. The prince moves fast and snatches his wrist, then snaps the forearm over his knee.

Ouch. I cringe, gobsmacked at what I've just seen.

Cries of pain pierce the air, stealing the earlier feeling of a gorgeous morning. But I can't look away. I want that man to suffer for what he intended to do to me.

The man falls to his knees, cradling his arm bent the wrong way.

I rub my sore wrist, my heart beating loudly in my ears.

Deimos is rubbing the blood on his hands down his pants and marches back to me with determination.

And all I can think about is how much I adore him for what he just did, how incredibly handsome he looks being all protective. Something inside me warms up at the thought. And that's when I realize why it bugs me so much that he's ignoring me. I'm falling for him too damn fast.

Luther

"We need to leave," Ahren orders, standing from the table. "We have a fair distance to cover before we reach home."

I don't want to think about what's waiting for us, so I nod. We step out into the hallway and make our way toward the bar. The place is barren, except for the bartender, who's washing glasses in the sink.

"Luther, go get the other two. I'll find the horses Deimos arranged for us and pay for our stay."

I'm ready to leave this town, though part of me toys with the idea of paying the lord here a visit... Would it make a difference? What Deimos offered the man is equivalent to finding a dragon's treasure. He's just gained immunity from our attack and protection from anyone. But in truth, how can I blame Deimos? I would have done the same thing in his position. Life-or-death situation, right? I just doubt our king will be so quick to agree. But we'll have to tell Ahren once we arrive home. He has to know, no matter how pissed he'll be.

The rules state that an allegiance offered by any immediate royal family members must be honored. Hence why the king forbade any of us bestowing such gifts.

Outside, the wind is crisp and cold. A few people are about town, including a farmer walking two cows down the middle of the town. Three of his boys, around ten or eleven years old, are dragging a stack of hay behind them by a rope. The children are tiny and thin, their ears pointy and eyes huge when they glance over at me. I dig my hand into my pocket and take out three gold crowns, then approach them.

"Something for your hard work. Put it in your pocket and don't look at it until you arrive home." I place one in each of their tiny, dirty hands.

I turn away from them just as Deimos' voice rings out from around the building, so I walk in that direction.

A small child cheers with excitement in the background, and I smile to myself.

I step around the corner of the tavern to see my brother and Guendolyn.

"Did he hurt you?" Deimos growls, grasping Guendolyn by the arms.

I pause and watch, my pulse suddenly racing. I shouldn't be seeing this moment, but I can't get myself to move. Farther to the left is a sniffling man on his knees, crying like a baby. That bastard must have laid a hand on Guendolyn, and my rage roars. I'm going to rip his spine out.

She's shaking her head at Deimos.

My brother drags her into his arms, a hand on the rear of her head, another on her back.

The inferno in my chest is burning. She's melting against his chest, and to see her affection toward him has my lungs closing up. I can't breathe.

"Good," he says. "Or I would have gutted that son of a bitch. Maybe I still will for daring to touch you." He holds her tight, and she embraces him. Those small arms wrap around his body.

She looks up at him the way she used to look at me... I recoil back around the corner and press my spine against the wooden building. A blaze lashes across my chest. My hands clench when they shouldn't, because I share everything with my brothers. The problem is that I've lost what I had, and that coils tight in my chest.

I shove off the wall just as Ahren emerges from the tavern.

"Have you found them?" he asks, then his eyes widen as he glances over my shoulder. Footsteps close in, and I don't have to look back to know it's them. If I look at Deimos now, I'll end up slamming him up against the wall. I shouldn't be jealous, but it bleeds through me like poison. I just need time to think this through.

The first time Guendolyn arrived in Wandering Realm, I caught Deimos biting her. The bastard marked her. I knew then he'd been drawn to her, despite his denial. And I should have known the taste of her blood would affect him too. As it did me.

"There you are," Ahren says. "Deimos, they insist on giving us just one horse, something to do with whatever you negotiated with them."

"Fucking bastards," he snarls, and marches past me and back into the tavern, with Ahren on his heels.

"Horses," Guendolyn says. "I'm not sure how I feel about that. I've only ridden them once in school. I thought we were getting a carriage?"

My breaths are racing. *Calm down.*

"You alright, Luther?" she asks as she steps in front of me, that gorgeous face staring up at me. Blue eyes more spectacular than the sky search my face for a reaction, for anything. That deep scarlet dress follows the curves of her tiny waist, drawing attention to the tops of her gorgeous breasts. She looks every bit fae in that gown with her long, blonde hair dancing in the wind, her pale skin, and those mesmerizing eyes.

"I'm fine." Venom drips from my words, and I hate that I struggle to control my emotions around her. That she makes me feel vulnerable.

She blinks, taking a moment to process my words. "You seem upset." With the inflection in her voice, it seems as though she's surprised.

I swallow past the thickness in my throat, wanting to roar.

She narrows her eyes at me, and I'm reduced to her giving me pity.

Except, Guendolyn is the key to our survival, to all of the fae in Shadow Court, so letting emotions test my limit will turn everything into a mess. As infuriating as the situation is, as tempting as my little wolf is, I need to get my head straight. Focus on our mission. And stop letting my cock make my decisions. I refuse to let her see how deeply she impacts me, how much I desire her, how I will never give her up until she remembers us.

"Nothing to worry about," I say, and the scuffing of shoes on the dirty path draws attention from a few passersby along the road running down the middle of the town.

Flames lick at my heart. Like Mother says, I'm weak because I think with my heart, not my head. That is my weakness, that is who I've become.

"Okay, but if there was something, you'd tell me?"

I nod and smile, my gaze falling to her ruby lips. She looks innocent in every way, but I know what lays inside her is anything but innocent.

Images of Guendolyn in my arms, naked and calling my name, plague me. Her breaths pick up, the swell of her breasts rises and falls quicker. My cock twitches at the sight. I raise my gaze once again to those full lips. How

I'd love to nibble on them as I fuck her and bring her to the edge of climax, before slowing and building her up again and again.

"We're ready," Ahren states, ripping me from my beautiful vision.

Guendolyn doesn't stop staring at me... I feel her eyes on me. What is she thinking? That I'm hiding a secret from her?

"Horses are waiting for us at the front gates." Deimos takes the lead, and we cross the town in no time. I ignore the stares from the locals following our every move.

Outside the town, the guard with a shaved head and round face from last night is smirking at us. My hands twitch with the urge to rip that smile off his face. He took advantage of us during a moment of weakness. Instead of helping us, he filled his pockets.

"Guendolyn rides with me," Ahren announces as he moves to stand near the biggest of the three horses. His is a monstrous black stallion digging at the dirt with his front hoof.

Everyone is staring at Ahren, his decision out of place for him, but I'd rather she goes with him right now.

Guendolyn is hugging herself, her teeth chattering. The weather has turned fast, and winter isn't far. I wouldn't be surprised if it started snowing in a day or two.

While they saddle up, I swing back to the guard and snatch the fabric of his shirt, tightening it at his throat. "Listen here, you fucking idiot." I sneer in his face. "Be very careful about coming to claim your stolen allegiance. I will not forget how you only helped us once you were paid a heavy price."

I shove him backward, and he stumbles. His eyes narrow with hate. I expect him to respond, to say something, but he just stares at me with fury in his eyes. Grasping the reins of my chestnut horse, I lift my foot to the stirrup and swing up and onto her back.

Deimos takes the lead. Guendolyn sits on a double saddle behind Ahren, her arms looped around his waist, clearly terrified. And me... I will trail behind. A nudge of my heels into the horse, and we are on the move.

What I need is to forget everything and focus on what is waiting for us once we reach home. That is going to be the most dangerous part of our journey. Yet all I can picture is Guendolyn in my arms.

CHAPTER

SEVENTEEN

GUEN

The ride through the forest is quiet, leaving me lost in my thoughts and growing uncertainty. I hold on to Ahren's waist, fisting his jacket so I don't slide off the enormous horse. No matter how much I try not to bump my breasts against his back from each jostle, I fail miserably. So fuck it. I give up and just attach myself to him. There's something extremely intimate about sitting behind someone while riding a horse. Legs straddling their backside, being plastered to their back. Yep, I'm starting to wonder if the reason he insisted I ride with him is because he wants me all to himself. He did say last night he didn't hate me.

The clopping of hooves beating the ground keeps us company, along with occasional snorting and tail swishing. A chill settles in my bones, and my teeth gnash as I jolt and jerk on the horse's back. Ahren's body is warm, so I hold on to keep the cold at bay.

The forest blurs around us, greens and bronzes and purples, the trees so colorful, they're mesmerizing. It reminds me of the park near home during fall. Would Nickie be freaking out right now? Have the cops put out a missing persons search for me? There's zero I can do about that when the priority is surviving here first, then finding a way home.

I glance back to Luther, who rides farther behind us. Even from this distance, I see him brooding. It's hard enough remembering my own memories, let alone dealing with the prince's drama.

"How much longer to go?" I call out to Ahren. It's past noon, and we've been traveling since early morning.

Ahren's hand reaches back and finds my thigh as he glances over his shoulder. A sizzle of warmth races up my leg and into the pit of my gut. My heart is immediately racing. All it would take is for him to stop and drag me over his lap, then I'd be at his mercy. It's ridiculous how quickly my body lights up to these three fae. Those thoughts confuse me. He's been a jerk since I met him, yet having his hand on me like this stirs something inside me.

"Not long." His hand lingers on my thigh, and suddenly, I'm struggling to breathe. All I think about is his touch, the way his thumb curls in on the inside of my knee. Yesterday, we were ready to kill each other, and today... today, he's sending out mixed messages that toy with my emotions.

Except we aren't from the same world, and I don't see how anything can work between me or any of the princes for the simple fact that they *are* princes. Me... I'm a woman who doesn't even know what she wants out of life, or who her real parents are. Well, according to the princes, they're in this realm... in Ash Court. Oh, and I'd be killed on sight if I went there. My head is still reeling and hasn't pieced all that together yet.

We soon crest a hill, and I tighten my grip on Ahren, his hand drawing away from my leg. We come to a stop on the peak of the hill. All of us stare out across to the huge castle sitting on another mountain. My mouth drops open.

It's magnificent, standing tall and proud atop the mountain. It's a picturesque fairy tale view, and I desperately wish I had my phone with me. Which I would, if Deimos hadn't destroyed it.

Steadfast stone walls glint in the sunlight. Turrets, cone shapes project into the sky above the towers, flags fluttering in the breeze. Trees greedily crowd around the castle.

"Wow!"

"Looks impressive, doesn't it?" Ahren says with pride in his voice. "Now look lower into the valley, into the woods leading up to our home."

My gaze sweeps from the spectacular wonderland, and it takes a few moments to make sense of the valley below. There's so much movement down there, as if a river has broken its banks, but when I squint for a better look, I see them and gasp.

Hundreds upon hundreds of people are shoving and fighting and clambering over one another to reach the castle. The trees shake viciously all around the mountain; glimpses of bodies climbing between the branches reveals the swarm.

My mouth goes dry. "They're all Bloodcursed, aren't they? Oh shit, with that many, how are we going to get past them?"

"Let's get moving." Ahren nudges his horse to canter along the apex of the hill we're traveling. "Our kingdom is protected by mages who have erected a magic shield. We've been facing this onslaught for the past two years."

"You've been living with those things on your doorsteps for that long?" The curse... I remember them explaining to me the blight I apparently unleashed, and this is the impact?

"The Bloodcursed are hexed. They throw themselves to their deaths every day to enter our kingdom," Luther explains. "We have villages filled with fae living in the kingdom, families and children and animals, and then the castle. There are so many lives at risk of being killed if the Bloodcursed breach the magic."

Panic is clawing up my spine and over my head. I can't even fathom what it would be like to live with that on your doorstep for two years.

We travel swiftly without a word. My heart is drumming, and I hold on to Ahren tighter. Our travels take a while as we seem to be going around the mountain.

When we finally come to a stop, I'm scanning the woods, half-expecting the creatures to burst out of the shadows.

"Let me help you down," Luther says to me, and I turn my head to find him standing near our horse. Worry pinches his face, and that only scares me further.

"Yes, please."

He reaches up with strong hands around my waist and drags me off the horse, which is probably the worst way in the world to dismount from a horse. Especially in a skirt. Somehow, I managed not to flash the world but end up stumbling into Luther. My chest presses against him as I try to catch my balance. His hands steady me, and I'm embarrassed at how clumsy I am.

"I've got you." His hands don't leave my hips, and he looks at me like he might kiss me.

My heart is pounding so loud, all the princes have to hear it.

Ahren clears his throat, and I quickly pull out of Luther's arms. "Thank you," I say.

"Of course." He then turns away from me abruptly and proceeds to pull the saddle and straps off his horse, as does Deimos. Ahren climbs down from his steed and pulls out the sword from a scabbard attached to the animal's side. Then he unleashes the horse.

"What's going on?" I ask, staring at the forest around us, feeling like it's closing in on me.

"We're on foot from here, and these horses have earned their freedom," Deimos explains, his voice taut. Everyone is tense, and I'm trembling. How have they been living like this for two years, too terrified to leave or return to their home?

The fae shoo their horses away, guiding them in the direction opposite of the castle. And something warm stirs inside me that even during such horrifying times, these princes care about those horses.

Something light falls onto my nose, feather soft and cold. Then another and more. I glance all around me and stick my hand out.

"It's snowing!" I gasp, not expecting such a change of weather.

"Winter is running early," Luther says, staring up at the billowing clouds overhead. White snowflakes land on his face, and I can't stop looking at how handsome he is. How much I want to remember if we had kissed when we met two years ago. How he tasted. God, did we have sex? The thought ought to shock me, but instead, my core quivers with anticipation.

"Luther, you're with Guendolyn. Deimos, you and I take the lead," Ahren orders as he draws out a knife from his belt. His abrupt voice draws me back to reality.

Luther settles in closer beside me and slips a dagger into my hand. The leather on the hilt is soft and comfortable to hold. "Don't hesitate to use that. Hopefully, you won't need it."

"I hope so." I remember Deimos' offer to help me learn to wield a sword, and maybe it's something I'm going to insist on if I'm going to be stuck here.

Ahren and Deimos are whispering quietly about the best direction to take, pointing to different parts of the woods.

"Do you think we'll be alright?" I ask Luther in a low voice.

He steps closer and towers over me.

I swallow hard, staring into his spectacular eyes, the color of golden flames. "If I die today," I say, "please let my family know so they don't keep worrying about me being missing somewhere."

His hand takes mine, our fingers interlacing. "The only way you will die is if all three of us are killed first. And if that happens, gods help Shadow Court."

"Okay." My voice squeaks. Talk about scaring the hell out of me, but whatever.

He leans closer, and his breath brushes my ear. "How can I let you die when I still haven't collected my kiss?"

A heady feeling overcomes me as I study his sexy expression. His exhale is like a feather on my neck.

"I haven't agreed to such a thing," I tease.

"It's the protocol when meeting a new prince," he counters, still so close, all I can smell is that sexy cedarwood, musky scent that drives me wild.

"Well, I'm afraid I'm going to have to decline the offer."

"There you go again, opposing a prince." The faintest smirk touches his mouth, and now all I can picture are his lips on mine. Hell, I will more than enjoy it, as I remember the way Deimos kissed me. Intoxicating. And with that intoxication comes a scorching heat that refuses to leave me. I clench my thighs at the lingering pleasure.

Luther straightens himself and places a hand on my back, putting pressure on it to nudge me forward.

The more time I spend with the princes, the more I realize I'm losing control around them.

"It's time," Ahren announces.

I look over to him, his long lashes obscuring his eyes as he looks down at the weapon he tightens in his grip.

Deimos has already started marching ahead, so we follow.

The path darkens the farther we travel into the woods, the slope ascending with each step. In this forest, there are hundreds of Bloodcursed. That's all I need to remember to keep my head screwed on. Sweat rolls down my back from fear alone, and I'm walking faster now. Luther remains at my back.

Ahren's white hair flutters over his shoulders like a cape, the long sword strapped diagonally across his back. I remember the way he and Luther swooped in without hesitation to fight the Bloodcursed in the woods last night. They're strong, but their inability to stop and think things through might make them dangerous. Still, if I have to trust anyone in this damned world, it will be them.

My breaths are rasping from the steepness of the slope; my thighs sting not only from this climb, but from the horse ride. Everything hurts.

When we reach the edge of the woods, we pause. I lean against a tree to catch my breath. I need to begin going to the gym. I'm huffing while the three princes haven't broken a sweat. The snow is now falling quicker and heavier, tainting everything in the forest with its white touch.

They peer out to a small clearing ahead of us, where a blanket of white gives the place a fairy tale look. Except it's deceiving... monsters live out here. Eyes will find us, then those freaks will attack. I try to ignore my panic, but it's gathering speed like an avalanche.

Across the field lies more forest, but behind the trees, a towering rugged stone wall merges into the mountain.

"Are you ready?" Ahren asks me.

"Not really."

"You have no choice," he answers, which of course I know. "Behind those trees lies an enchanted tunnel. We just need to reach that, and once we're in, we're safe."

"You make it sound easy, though I feel a *but* coming on." I wipe the sweat from my brow with the back of my hand.

He looks at me with that confused expression, and I just shake my head. "We run for our lives, then we enter the magical tunnel."

"Yes, and you must watch out for the fairies that live on those trees."

I still, a chill settling into my bones. "And there's the *but*," I mumble to myself. "Okay, so how do we deal with the fairies?"

"Don't stop," Luther says. "But don't hurt one, as that angers them all."

"Got it. Escape from the bloodthirsty creatures, be nice to the nasty fairies, and stay alive." I'm being sarcastic, yet all three are nodding.

Ahren lifts his knife. "As a precaution, we should do a blood bond so you can open the tunnel, just in case we don't make it."

I glance out past him. It doesn't look that far. "Pretty sure we can run that quickly."

Ahren slashes the meaty part of his palm with a short slice. Blood bubbles across his hand.

"Whoa, we're doing this now?" I back away, but I bump into Luther, who steadies me with his hands on my hips.

"It won't hurt you," Luther says, while Deimos looks away, his expression darkening. "He's simply offering to transfer some of his magic so you can open the tunnel."

"Will I change?"

Deimos growls. "We're wasting time."

"Let me do it for you," Luther says.

The pressure is coiling tight inside me, and I like the idea of being able to rush into the tunnel in case I'm trapped. But I hate the idea of a blood bond when I have no clue what it means or what impact it will have on me.

"Quickly," Ahren rushes me.

Luther takes my hand and turns it palm side up. In his other hand, he grips a dagger.

I look away, cringing before the tip even touches me. "Just hurry up."

The slice comes fast and sharp, followed by a deep bite. "Done."

I look back around just as Ahren takes my hand into his, both our wounds pressed together, blood merging.

"Blood for blood, I transfer the magic of Tathrey to you for the length of one day."

"Tathrey? What—?" An electric charge jolts through me, and I rock backward, but Ahren holds me locked to him. Power sizzles over my flesh like hundreds of ants swarming over my skin. The sensation vanishes as quickly as it arrives.

"Done." Ahren draws his hand back.

I glance down at my bloody hand, noting the cut was barely a nick. Yet it thumps like it has its own heartbeat. I shake my hand and can't help but feel that something more than just this Tathrey power has passed into me.

Terror clings on to me but I can't keep cowering in fear. I am done with hiding and being weak. I am now left with no option but to stand and fight.

"Let's go," Deimos mutters as he gestures toward the clearing with his chin. Luther pushes me to stand in front, and in a heartbeat, we're running.

My stomach lurches to my throat. My feet pound the ground. Fifty yards to cross.

Shadows fall over us, blotting out the sky.

I make the mistake of looking up.

Bloodcursed are falling down toward us. They're throwing themselves off the cliff's edge all the way around. Some from dizzying heights.

Fear drags through me like barbed wire.

I sprint faster as the creatures hit the ground around us with a thud. The splattering sound sickens me. Bones crack, but still, they climb back up, arms dangling by their sides, necks twisted and broken. They still fucking climb to their feet.

One hits the snow covered grass right in front of me. I trip over the body and tumble forward, head over heels. I scramble to my feet, shaking frantically. When I turn, I find the princes slicing the Bloodcursed, who don't seem to die easily.

The ground shudders under my feet as though a stampede approaches.

"Run! Go to the tunnel!" Deimos yells.

I spin around just as an ocean of Bloodcursed emerge from the trees either side of us, running like ravenous demons toward us. All I see are those hellish dark eyes and gaping mouths.

I sprint like I never have before. Like a madwoman.

Death. It's all I see.

I don't look back. I can't.

Terror is latched around my chest, and I'm traveling on adrenaline. I don't feel my body, but my head is shouting at me to never stop.

Growls and screeches ring through the air.

Get to the tunnel.

I can't stop myself and look back. Deimos is the closest to me, battling three monsters coming my way. The others are under siege. And swarms more are almost upon us.

"Run!" I yell to them. They can't kill them all.

"Go!" Deimos growls while swinging his blade across a Bloodcursed's throat.

I pivot on my heels and dart toward the trees. In seconds, I burst through them. Branches lash out, tearing at my face and arms, pulling my hair.

I don't stop as I tear through the woods.

Heavy footfalls fall behind me, and I glance back quick.

Three Bloodcursed are charging after me. I'm shaking, and I want to cry. My knuckles are white around the blade I was given. But I can't fight three of them. I just can't.

Something swooshes right over my head, yanking a hair strand. But I'm barely feeling it when I'm sprinting for my life.

Another swoosh, but I keep going.

The woods are thicker, darker here, the snow only trickling in through the gaps in the canopy, and I can't see any mountains or tunnel. God, please don't let me have steered in the wrong direction.

There's more buzzing over my head and around me. They're the biggest bugs in the world, and I bat them away. But when I catch the iridescent glint of wings, I pay closer attention.

Tiny round faces, big black eyes, and wide mouths. Their bodies are covered in what looks like pale blue and green scales from their necks to their toes. Thin arms and legs remind me of insects. Wings shaped like those of butterflies, translucent in every color.

Fairies.

They are beautiful.

Don't hurt them.

Unless the Bloodcursed behind me does the job first.

I'm pounding the ground, running through the swarm that seems to be growing thicker. They keep fluttering around my arm; I feel tiny nips on my clenched, bleeding fist.

Great, they want blood too. Everything in this world only drinks blood.

I look back and the monsters are closing in.

The cry in my lungs spills past my lips.

Fairies are everywhere, and all I see are rainbows of colors from their fluttering wings. They swarm my arm, taking small nips of my skin, pulling at my fingers to open my fist.

Something crashes into my back.

I scream and fall face-first to the ground, dropping my knife. Not waiting a second more, I scramble to my hands and knees.

Fairies are all over me, fighting and hissing for the blood on my hand. I can't see my arms through the explosion of beating wings. I feel their tiny feet, their tongues licking.

I try to shake them off, but it's impossible.

I scramble away from the charging Bloodcursed, getting to my feet, my screams echoing into the air. The echoes are like tiny screams all around me, which I soon realize are the fairies mimicking me.

The bastard throws himself on top of me. I'm thrown sideways and hit the ground with my back. He's right there, on top of me. I thrash and beat into him with everything I have. Fairies are everywhere, around my arms, between us, in his face.

The other Bloodcursed rush for me, one snatching my wrist. He wrenches me out from that first creature, then drops to his knees.

Lips curl back over fangs sharpened and dripping with saliva. I shove my fist into his face and scramble up to my feet, but the third Bloodcursed lunges. It pins me to a tree, my mouth gaping open.

A fairy with the bluest wings slashes tiny claws over his eye. He flinches, and I rip myself out from under him.

Then I run, fairies coming with me, tugging at my hand, devouring the blood dripping from my wound.

A huge shadow darkens the woods to my left. The mountain. I veer in that direction.

Heavy footfalls shove against the wall, foliage snapping and breaking.

Over my shoulder, the trio charges after me. Behind them, there are more shadows closing in.

My teeth are chattering nonstop, and my whole body is wracking with sobs. Terror consumes every inch of me, but I sprint and keep pushing. I'm not ready to die, not ready. My foot hooks into a tree root, and I stumble forward before landing on my knees.

I swivel back around on my feet, my call for help coming out strained. Fear surges through me like a storm, feeling unstoppable.

The ground quivers, and the branches shake furiously, dropping all their leaves, which drift around us like snow.

A charge of energy jolts through me suddenly, and I stumble into the boughs of a tree.

The fairies around me all rush with me, mimicking my chaotic running.

They ascend around me like a swarm. Sparks of blue lines of light crackle around their wings. I shove myself up from the tree and swipe a branch off the ground to face the Bloodcursed coming for me.

Fairies dip and rise with me, copying me.

The monsters dive at me with their greedy claws and fangs to rip me to shreds. Muscles flexed, I flinch at the oncoming attack.

In a flash, the fairies flock toward the creatures. Every single one of them attacks to the point where I can't see anything but those fluttering wings. I stagger away from them.

The sight is beautiful. Morbidly beautiful.

Sucking and flesh ripping echo through the woods.

Barely seconds pass when the fairies flutter away, bits of blood and body crumbs falling to the wayside. When they finally disperse, all that remains are bones, three skulls, hair, and a pile of clothes. Some fairies are still feasting, sucking the marrow in the broken bones.

It should sicken me, but it doesn't.

I lift my gaze. Deimos is standing several feet away. Blood splashes his cheek and arms, his clothes a red mess. He looks like he's returned from a massacre. Except his eyes are enormous like orbs, drowning in fear as he stares at the remains. He glances up at me with a look that somehow implies I did this.

Did I?

"Let's go," I call out, finally getting my legs to budge. He sidesteps around the remains before taking my hand. Farther behind him, Luther and Ahren are charging toward us at full-tilt. A mass of attackers race after them. *Fuck!*

Deimos and I are running, abruptly emerging from the trees in front of a stone wall. I was so close.

"Open it." He draws out his sword and rushes back to help his brothers.

I'm shaking so hard. I stare at the entrance wall and something translucent shimmers over the front entrance. The magical protection.

What am I meant to do? I'm practically hyperventilating, and my world is spinning.

I rush up to the shield. "Open. Let me in. Open fucking sesame." Nothing. I'm rubbing my eyes when a spark from my hand draws my attention to the cut on my palm. Most of the blood is gone and my wound is completely healed over. Tiny sparks are dancing over my fingertips, just as I'd seen them do on the fairies' wings.

"Open it! Use your hands," Luther yells, all three of them charging my way like raging bulls.

I lash out and jam my palms up against the magic. Sparks erupt around my fingers and with a pop, the shimmering vanishes.

Luther runs past, seizing my arm, and drags me into the cave. His brothers are right behind us, and the wall zaps back in place just as fast as it had disappeared.

A horde of Bloodcursed crash into the invisible barrier, thrown back, as if touching a live wire.

I tremble and recoil. "There are so many. What if they break through?"

"They haven't yet," Ahren says. "We need to go."

And we do. With my hand in Luther's, we rush into the dark cave. In the distance, a single light shines, like a beacon of salvation. But I'm not sure I trust anything in this world to not want to kill me.

CHAPTER

EIGHTEEN

GUEN

"W here are we?" I ask. Around us are black stone walls, torches sitting in metal brackets, and statues of lions and bears on either side of the hallway. It adds to the whole gothic, Dracula vibe.

Glass spheres hang from the ceilings on chains, flames flickering inside them.

Ahren takes the lead and pushes open a door to his left. Light streams out, chasing the dark away. I squint at first after having spent the last hour climbing steps to reach the princes' palace. The castle is located even farther up the mountains, and I'm stumbling forward on wobbly legs, still dazed. So I couldn't be happier we're stopping.

My mind still hums with the memories of the Bloodcursed and fairies.

Death had been calling me down in the forest... but destiny had other intentions.

Now I follow the three princes into an elaborate bedroom that drowns in luxury and decadence. The walls have black velvet fabric draped from them. There's a king-sized bed with an upholstered headboard. Midnight silk sheets with puffy pillows look so tempting when I'm barely standing. A dressing table and foot bench are carved ornately, while a candle chandelier drips in crystals and gold. More crystals of every color hang off the ropes tying the curtains to the side of the numerous arched windows with dim sunlight coming in. Outside, the snow is falling, and if I hadn't just run for my life from monsters, I might have enjoyed the beautiful scenery.

"Holy shit," I murmur. "It looks intense in here."

"A shame you don't like it." Ahren mocks me with his grin. "Because it's *your* room."

My mouth drops open, and I quickly close it, trying to silence my hyped-up heart. "You'll be happy to know I *love* intense." Still, this room is insane. I keep staring at the bed and make my way there. I fall face-first onto it, arms stretched out. I inhale vanilla and rose, and the mattress softens beneath me.

"After today," I say as I roll on my back and stare up at the ceiling dotted with tiny diamond reflections of the light, "I might sleep for a week."

"Some house rules first," Ahren says.

I groan as I push myself to sit up.

Deimos is staring out the window, reminding me of our time in the motel when he looked outside for the Bloodcursed. That feels like a lifetime ago. Luther, on the other hand, walks out of the room, and I'm curious to know where he's going.

"You can't leave your room," Ahren starts.

"Wait, what? You did all that heroic shit out there to just keep me locked up here like Rapunzel?"

A confused look flashes over his face again, and I'm guessing it relates to who Rapunzel is. But he keeps going.

"Second, the only people who will know you're here are us three, Luther's mage, and a small handful of our staff. Under no circumstances can the king find out about you."

I arch a brow. "Why?"

"Some very powerful fae want you dead," he growls, and within seconds, the frustration on his face vanishes, as though he hadn't meant to morph back into angry-Ahren.

"Three—"

"How many more rules are there? I'm hungry and exhausted."

Luther returns to the room with a man and a woman following him. The older lady wears a floor-length burgundy dress and white apron, her black hair pulled back into a bun. She keeps her head down, not even looking our way. The thin man with short trimmed hair is in simple black pants and a burgundy button-up shirt. They both seem to be in their mid or late thirties and follow Luther into another room from the bedroom. I try to look inside that room, but I can't see much from my angle, except the corner of a window.

"Three," Ahren continues, "you will share this room with one of us at all times."

I roll my eyes at him and sigh. "So now I have to share my prison with a prince? I thought you said—"

"Lower your voice. These are not matters to debate here. Our priority is to keep you safe."

So many questions whip through my head, but what *is* clear is that I am a secret. And I know it relates to the curse, to me coming from Ash Court, and a dozen other things I still have to learn about. So now he wants me to hide myself from the kingdom.

Ahren crosses the room and sits on the bed next to me. There's compassion in his eyes, and something else... something *darker* when he looks at me. How does he really see me? Only as a solution to their problems? My stomach hurts at that notion. For once, I want to have meaning in life.

"For all of our survival, including yours, we need to be careful. You need to trust us."

"I have questions," I say.

"And we'll answer them. But not before some rest and an enormous feast."

"Fuck, I could eat an entire boar right now," Deimos grumbles from near the window.

Luther emerges from the other room, as do the two helpers, who rush back into the hallway. "They're preparing a bath for you," he says to me.

I straighten and smile. "Sounds perfect." I look over to Ahren, and eye him with a teasing gaze. "Will you three be staying for that too?"

He doesn't flinch or react. "Would you like us to?" Hell, he's completely serious, and I'm blushing instantly.

But I push aside the images of me naked in a tub with him out of my mind. Instead, I tap my chin. "Hmm. Let me think about it." I laugh and fall back onto the bed, loving the idea of being off my feet.

"There's a fourth rule."

Of course there is. I might end up missing the forest quicker than I thought. "Give it to me."

"You'll need to come up with a new name."

I scrunch up my face and sit up on my elbows, staring at him. "Part of no one finding out who I am?"

"Exactly. So think of a name, or I'll come up with one for you."

I arch a brow. "No thanks. I can just imagine what name you'll come up with. Something royal and pompous and embarrassing."

The man and woman who came with Luther earlier now rush back into the room, each carrying two wooden pails of water. "Should we go help them?" I get to my feet just as another man steps into the open doorway to the bedroom. The man stands tall and proud. Short, white hair, a thin, long nose, longer ears, and a scar curling up his neck from under the collar of his military-style jacket. Two rows of golden buttons run from his waist to his shoulders. He looks to be in his forties and glances at me from the corner of his eyes quickly.

"Pardon, Your Royal Highness." He bows his head. "Your father has requested your immediate presence in the throne room."

"Thank you, Mael," Ahren responds, his voice hard. "Tell the king we will be there shortly."

Sighing deeply, the man doesn't move, but his frustration is clear on his face. "Excuse my language, Your Royal Highness. His exact words were, 'Haul Ahren's ass up here now, or your head will roll.'"

"*Fuck*," Ahren roars as he jumps up from the bed. "Okay, Luther, you're with me. He's going to ask where we've been, so come up with something by the time we reach the castle."

Ahren looks to me. "Deimos will take care of you until we return." He turns and marches out of the room. Luther exchanges a worried look with Deimos, who gives a tight shake of his head from whatever unspoken message they exchanged. Then Luther heads out after Ahren.

"Looks like it's just us two," I say.

Deimos hasn't moved from his spot near the window, and I somehow suspect he's not going to make his presence known.

I SLIDE down into the hot water of an oversized crystal tub, made from a large clear stone carved out in the middle to a smooth finish. The round shape can easily fit two or three people inside. I've never seen anything like it and don't want to know how they got this huge crystal up here. Reclining back against the smooth stone and breathing easily, I love how incredible the heat feels against my skin. How my cut and scratched-up feet throb with delight. I glance out the window where the clouds now conceal the sun. The snow falls heavily with the backdrop of the forest and mountains. It's beautiful. Spectacular.

The door leading into the adjoining bedroom suddenly flings open. I lurch forward, splashing water everywhere as I go to cover myself.

"Sorry, my lady, it's just me." The female helper in the burgundy dress walks inside with a tray that she places on the table next to the tub, her head low to avoid looking at me. There's a cup of something steaming and a bowl of fruit. She also hands me a bar of soap from inside her pocket.

"Thank you so much."

"You're welcome." She bows, taking a quick look at me through her lashes, and quickly leaves the room, but she forgets to close the door.

"Can you shut the door please?"

Her footfalls fade, and she's gone. Great. I can see the top part of my bed from here, and there's no sign of Deimos.

"Are you all right in there?" he asks, his footfalls closing in.

"Hope you don't think you're coming in here," I say sternly.

He laughs, the sound delicious and playful, but he never answers me.

Arms clasped over my chest, I wait for him to enter the bathroom, but he never comes. The silence stretches, and I finally recline back into the tub. Lathering my hands with the soap, I run it over my arms and neck and face, then my hair.

"It feels amazing to have a bath," I call out. "Back home, we only had a shower, and it's nice, but this feels like I have my own personal massage spa. If I had a tub like this at home, I'd use it every day."

"Would you like me to come in there and massage you? Will that help?"

"Ha, you're so funny."

He chuckles, and there's something comforting about the sound.

"So, do you think there are fae out there who really want to kill me?" I ask, unable to stop thinking about Ahren's words.

"I want to say *no* so you don't get frightened..." He doesn't say anything else, and I guess I have my answer.

I lie back and submerge myself under the water to my chin, trying to push everything out of my mind.

"What happened in the forest with the fairies?" he asks. "I've never seen them attack one group of people but not others standing nearby. They're predatory, and once they smell blood, they go into a frenzy."

I lift my hand up, water trickling out of my palm. The knife wound from where Ahren and I did our blood bond is completely healed up. I run a finger over the fleshy part—smooth without a scratch. I remember that the blue lines of energy from the fairies' wings were on my hands as well, though I didn't understand what they were at the time.

"They saved me from the Bloodcursed. As I ran, they kept licking the blood on my hand. When I was being attacked, they mimicked my movements, then they went crazy on those creatures. Is that normal behavior?"

No response.

"So it's that bad?" I say, my voice barely a whisper while my chest constricts.

"I used to hunt fairies. They'd attack whole villages and feast on dozens of fae, leaving little of them. But I've never seen them behave the way they did in the woods."

Fear slips into my mind. "Maybe they just didn't like my blood." My attempt at laughing comes out strained. Or maybe it's related to the blood bond I had with Ahren. Did they sense his royal blood? Is that even a thing?

"Or they liked it a bit too much and were protecting you for a bigger feast," he suggests.

"Shut up. Stop trying to scare me," I snap, and grumble under my breath that I let him get to me.

He bursts out laughing, and I hurl out my soap, hoping to hit the wall to scare him, but instead it flings through the doorway and slides right under the bed. *Oh, crap.*

"I expect you to bend over and go collect that bar of soap," he mutters.

"And I expect you to jump out of the window, but none of those things are going to happen now, are they?"

He chuckles, and I groan under my breath.

So many thoughts refuse to leave me alone, from what Luther and Ahren have told me, to what I've experienced. I assumed coming to the kingdom, I'd be safe. So why am I being kept hidden in this room? "Hey, Deimos?"

"Yes, Guendolyn?"

"Why do I have to hide from the king?"

His sigh reaches me. "Many know about the girl from our world who was prophesied to unleash a curse that would destroy Shadow Court. And considering the war we've been fighting the past two years, the king has already expressed how he'd like to murder you for bringing this curse to his kingdom."

"But you know that—"

"That someone had cursed you and you were the carrier. But anger can twist people's minds. So we need to keep you safe until we find a way to undo the curse."

I don't know what to say. Someone used me as a pawn, and now I'm mixed up in this mess.

By the time my fingers resemble prunes, I'm out of the bath, dried with a thin towel-like fabric, and slipped on a dress the woman left for me. A pale blue gown with long sleeves. The dress fits loosely until I notice laces in the bodice that wrap around my chest and waist, and I start pulling them tight. The fabric is silky soft and smooth, and falls in waves to my feet. I comb my fingers through my knotted hair and push it off my face as I walk into the bedroom.

Deimos is sitting with his back to the wall right near the door to the bathroom, his arms draped over his knees. He looks up at me with a devious smirk. The door to the hallway from the bedroom is shut.

"How was the bath?" he asks.

"Incredible. That's the way to relax."

He climbs to his feet, standing tall. "Did you know that fae find mates for life?"

"So no dating then?" I study him and the glint in his eyes. "Where did that question come from?"

He runs a hand over his gorgeous mouth, pulling at those full lips I can't stop staring at. "Just thinking about when I first saw you in your realm, and how humans attempt to find their life partners."

"To be honest, I don't know if people really have a true life partner." Explains why the divorce rates are through the roof. "Does anyone anywhere really know if we do?"

He takes my hand and places my palm over his heart. "Fae feel it in here. It's electric and instantaneous and punches you in the chest."

My heart starts racing. All I feel right now are strong muscles. "So it's not based on family status and money?"

"Some marry for those things. Others for companionship. And the lucky ones find their fated mates."

"Have you found yours yet?" I feel stupid asking, because I sound like I'm prompting him to pick me, and I want to retract my comment. I look away, but he steps closer and tilts my head up by my chin.

"I'm looking at her right now," he responds with a glorious smile. This gorgeous man who makes my breath stop can't be serious.

"You don't need to say that."

But he's leaning in already, and his mouth touches mine. My body reacts immediately, softening against his, arousal surging through me in the span of a single breath.

His thumb brushes across my jawline and down to my neck. He kisses me softly, our tongues sliding together, exploring each other. Deimos fills me with desire and an explosion of need. Everything about him is heaven.

And the pulsing thump between my thighs reveals the thought that I have any sort of control to be a lie.

Our kiss grows impatient. I'm drowning under him, and I slide my hands to the back of his neck, lifting myself to my toes to reach him. Just like during our last kiss, my heart is roaring in my chest, and the arousal is liquid heat between my legs. He has this way of captivating me. Is that what being his mate means?

I break from him to catch my breath, our foreheads touching. His touch is cool against me as I'm burning up.

"I've been waiting to kiss you again for days," he murmurs. "You don't understand how special you are, how beautiful."

"Maybe we shouldn't do this," I whisper, still holding on to the front of his shirt.

"Why not?"

"How can I be your mate? That doesn't make sense. I'm nobody, and you're a prince. You live here, and I'll end up going home to Earth."

"Finding your mate isn't about logic. It's primal and raw and instinctual. I want to show you that you are mine. That you will beg for me, and I'll give you everything."

I try to speak, but his hand is on the back of my neck and draws me closer. Our mouths clash, and I'm falling for him. I couldn't stop myself if I tried. But that's the problem. I don't want to try. His hands pull the fabric away from my shoulders, his mouth finding the soft skin.

He's so built, his chiseled muscles rippling under my touch.

Moans spill from my lips.

Kissing me again, he walks me back with urgency until my heels hit the wall. He smells divine, intoxicating. His hands tug up on my dress and with his hands on my thighs, he hauls me up to be eye level with him. I wrap my legs around his waist. I love this side of him. The dominance. The hunger.

I'm turned on as hell. Every inch of me hums with pleasure, and the inferno between my legs is so wet. I adore the Deimos who is straight to the point when it comes to taking what he wants. I've craved him from the first time I laid eyes on him.

His body presses into me, the bulge in his pants grinding at the apex between my thighs.

A moan wells in the back of my throat when his hand lowers. The backs of his knuckles skim the tight peak of my breast, and I arch in response. His hand dips farther between us and slips under my skirt, his fingers quickly finding my clit. I gasp. He flicks my nub over and over.

"Please, Deimos," I beg, my heart pounding in my chest. I've only been with one other man before, and he didn't compare in the slightest.

"I've been waiting so long to touch you like this. To taste you. To fuck you. So are you ready to fall?"

I can barely think straight as his fingers slide over my heat. One pushes into me, and my moans morph to cries. I buck against him, my body burning up. His tongue plunges into my mouth as he fingers me.

He dips his head to my neck, nuzzling me. "You smell incredible."

I groan, aching for more. So much more.

Something shifts in the atmosphere around us. My skin pricks, but all I can feel is the power from Deimos, his intoxication fogging my brain. I brace myself, holding on to his shoulders, crying out with pleasure.

Fire slams into me, the kind that rips right through me. It explodes within me, and I scream from the building intensity. The force causes me to shudder, and I tremble in his arms.

Scorching hot energy flares, and suddenly, electricity is flooding the room, thickening as I inhale it.

Deimos lets out an animalistic growl and buries his face into my neck, his teeth dragging across my skin. His fingers rub over my pussy so fast, I can't see straight.

The wall feels like it's trembling behind me. I must be imagining it because I'm drowning in waves of ecstasy, erasing everything else.

Deimos is all that matters. He pushes two fingers into me, stretching me, and I scream with pleasure, letting myself go. An orgasm shudders through me.

And in that exact moment, the whole room shakes violently. Energy radiates from my chest, and bursts out. Spilling down my arms, pulsing through me.

Blue shards of electricity shoot out from my hands and criss-cross through the room.

Was I hallucinating?

Ahren

THE SIGHT of the throne is imposing, but it doesn't compare to who sits in it. A ruthless king without sympathy. Speaking out of place can get you killed here. The great hall is long. Marble and gold statues of maidens in flowing gowns and wings line each wall. Columns flank the passage running down the middle. No matter where you stand, the point of focus of the room is the same—the throne.

Black as the night, it sits high up on a platform thirteen steps high as a good omen. The chair is large with a high back, jagged across the top with bear claws at the ends of the armrests. Behind the throne stands an enormous round window, light pouring inside. From our angle, all we see are clouds. Dragons once roamed the Wandering Realm, and the window was created for the beasts to fly in view in the background as guards to the king.

Now, the king, my stepfather, sits in the chair, the one next to him empty. Where is Mother?

Luther marches alongside me, his strong shoulders straight and confident. He knows... never show weakness in the court. We've always faced Father together. I bring the voice of reason, he brings the knowledge, and Deimos is the dreamer and fighter. He loathes court drama and always says the wrong thing. So it's better he's not involved.

"My king," I say, fisting a hand to my heart two times as I lower myself to one knee. Luther does the same.

"Get the fuck up. It's just us," he roars.

As I stand, I lift my gaze to see the king trudging down the steps, his bulky form taking up a good width of the stairs. The golden crown sits on his head, his wild hair seemingly tangled in it like it has become a part of him. He's dressed in a black coat buttoned to his chest. He's trimmed his long, white beard, and his hair is cut short like Mother has always asked of him. Seems she finally has him listening to her.

"I've been hearing rumors," he bellows, stepping closer to us, disdain in his gaze. "Rumors that my three sons have left the kingdom without my permission."

I swallow hard but don't flinch.

"Rumors are like a bad wine, Father. They always leave you disappointed," I say. "If you have need of us, come directly to our palace."

He huffs and scratches his neck as he always does when he considers traveling the hundreds of steps between the castle and our palace. He never does, which I'm grateful for.

Luther says, "We heard of breaches down with the villages in the kingdom, so we personally went to inspect them and assure our people they're safe."

"Inside and *outside* the kingdom?" he snaps back.

"Both," Luther answers.

The king's eyes narrow with a disgruntled look. Feeding him a partial truth covers our asses should anyone have seen us reenter the kingdom. *Thank you, Luther.*

"Is this true, Ahren?" He pauses in front of me, those dark eyes rounding, our words taking him by surprise.

"Yes."

He studies us with doubt and disbelief. "Seeing as how you're still breathing, I assume you addressed any breaches?" He half-snorts a laugh derisively.

"Just a little magic, no harm done," I say. "And the families feel safer."

Shadow Court is filled with traitors. I've learned this from the moment we entered this kingdom. So beyond my brothers and a few close staff, I trust very few. Including my mother. I love her dearly, but she's like the sun. Glorious and all providing, but they both burn you should you get too close.

"Is Mother not at court today?" I ask, just as a crackling energy shivers up my arms, lifting the hairs across my nape.

The air thickens, and I stiffen. Magic, I feel it in the air, stinging my nostrils with each inhale

The king stiffens. He feels it too.

"Ahren!" Luther cries out just as a spark of blue electricity dances right in front of the throne.

"Guards!" the king yells. "Breach!"

Shadows unfold out of nothing before our eyes, and they spread outward. The mass grows into an oval shape, blackness peering back at us from inside.

My heart is beating too fast, and I reach for the blades at my hips, stepping in front of the king.

In seconds, an ear-piercing bell shatters the silence.

Footfalls hit the marble behind me as the guards approach, except my gaze is locked on the shimmering shadow. Luther is by my side, sword in hand.

The dancing blue lightning quivers around the black hole, holding it open.

Magic.

Out of the black lunges a thin figure, head tilting back and unleashing a terrifying screech. Then another creature emerges and half a dozen more.

My palm pricks, and I glance down to the healing cut on my palm from my blood bond with Guendolyn. A pale blue spark jumps over the closed wound... identical to the one around the portal.

Panicked thoughts tumble over my mind. "Fuck!" I have no such magic... this is Guendolyn's. Gasping for air, I look up at the portal and the same power dancing around its edges.

"Bloodcursed have breached the castle," the king yells.

More creatures pour out of the passage like a river, and death flashes in my eyes.

Death for all of us.

TO TAME A FAE

WINTER'S THORN, BOOK 3

TO TAME A FAE

FAE LEGENDS

There's a legend that says when fated souls meet, the Universe will move the stars themselves to ensure their love endures.

CHAPTER
ONE

DEIMOS

y lips whisper over the tender curve of Guendolyn's neck, and I kiss down to her collarbone. She pushes my head down to her full breasts. Her nipples easily respond, pressing erect against the fabric of her blue dress. I cup one in my mouth with the cloth between us.

Her breaths rush as she moans, and her arms wrap around my shoulders, fingers digging into flesh. I have her pinned to the wall, those delicious legs around my hips, and her blue dress pushed up to her waist. My fingers stroke those beautifully swollen lips between her thighs. She's so fucking wet. So stunning and exactly where I want her to be.

I lift my head and capture her lips again. Her scent paralyzes me, the taste of her mouth rousing an intense raw hunger within me. She kisses me with a brutal desire, and I dart my tongue inside. My cock punches in my pants as I return the chaotic kiss. My finger swirls around her bud, then flicks her clit.

I need so much more of her. I need it all, over and over.

She hisses out a breath against my mouth. At the same time, her hand dips down between us, and she strokes my erection through my pants, moving up and down. The friction drives me absolutely insane. I push my cock against her hand, letting her feel how hard I am, how fucking much I want her right here, right now.

I press one finger into her, then two. She tilts her head back as whimpers fall from her lips. She makes me feel filthy with desire. I'm so horny, I can barely hold myself back.

"Gods, you feel incredible," I growl.

She belongs to me, and I belong to her.

This is how it should always be.

Me and her.

Kissing.

Fucking.

Every-fucking-where.

My heart hammers in my chest at how drawn I am to her. The sensation snaps through me. Truly snaps at the realization that she affects me so strongly.

My balls pull up so tight, they ache for release. It's a fucking beautiful ache that robs me of all reason. I lick her neck, and memories of finding her on Earth come to mind. This lost girl who needs to be reminded of who she is. Our times together never leave me and heighten with each lick. Us escaping through the Wandering Realm woods, barely escaping the Blood-cursed to enter the kingdom. Her still not remembering her last visit to our kingdom. My brother, Luther, insisting that she's his. Thoughts fly through my mind of how close we came to losing Guendolyn. My brain won't shut the hell up.

"Deimos." She purrs my name and I lift my head. She looks at me with those intoxicating ocean blue eyes. Her white-blonde hair sits messily and is still slightly damp from her earlier bath. But those eyes stay with me... They were the first things I noticed about her when I met her two years ago on her first visit to the Wandering Realm. Back then, she had no idea who she was dealing with when she met us or the trouble she had been brought into. That craving I felt for her back then never dissipated. It waited for the moment we reunited. For when I made it through the portal to collect her from the human world and brought her back to the Wandering Realm, where she belongs. She may not accept it yet, but she will soon see this is her home.

She softens under me. This is how I've pictured her. Spread and wet and calling for me. I nibble on her lower lip, gently tugging on it with my teeth. I finger her harder and faster.

Her eyes glaze over, her body trembling with pleasure. I could get used to having her by my side every day.

An ache builds deep within me to the point that it almost hurts. I don't know where it's coming from, but I push it aside along with the thoughts. What I want is right before me. I desperately need her.

Pleasure consumes me as energy flares down my arms. All I feel is the sensation drumming through me, the arousal curling around me.

Guendolyn's body shudders as I continue fingering her. She groans louder, and my world spins. I'm drowning in her presence, in the lust tightening my cock. The entire room seems to be shaking, though I'm certain it's all in my head.

She is so ready for me.

I'm on the verge of losing control and being a savage animal with her. Of ripping off her dress and going all wild with her. I want to hear her scream as I fuck her raw.

My skin ripples with a sudden energy that races down my arms like tiny bites. Energy that feels like mine except I haven't called to my power. Before I can pull back and make sense of it, a huge, metal bell peals in the distance. The sound rolls through the whole kingdom like thunder, signaling a breach in our kingdom.

God damn the Seven Hells of the Wandering Realm.

The bells keep ringing.

FUCK! I pause and take a deep breath. Anxiety suddenly rips through my chest at the idea of things going to shit at the worst possible time.

Guendolyn freezes against me.

I jackhammer my head up abruptly, and with one fluid movement, pull my fingers out of her sweet core. Gathering her into my arms, I lower her to her feet.

The ringing continues, hammering in my head. Each dong vibrates through me. Someone has broken into the kingdom. It has to be the Bloodcursed.

"Shit!" I hiss between clenched teeth and storm over to the door. My heart is pounding a mile a minute.

"What's happening?"

I hear the fear in her soft voice as she follows me. I bite back the need to take her into my arms, to tell her all will be right. We just arrived at the mansion today, and we told Guendolyn we ought to keep her a secret from the king until we work out how she can use her power to eradicate the curse placed on our kingdom. Except that plan's a fucking waste if the kingdom falls in the next few hours. Tension flares between my shoulder blades.

"The kingdom's under attack," I explain. "Those bells you hear signal a breach." I abruptly open the door as I talk.

Maids are running down the hallway in a panic. My mind activates survival mode, adrenaline pulsing through my veins. The last time those bells rang was two years ago when Guendolyn unknowingly unleashed the curse on our kingdom. When she was ripped from our world and thrown back onto the planet she'd been raised on. When those blood-sucking Bloodcursed poured into our home. We spent weeks eradicating them and lost so many lives. This can't be happening again. Not with Guendolyn here as well and in danger.

"Is it the Bloodcursed?" she asks.

I face her. "Stay here. I'll go find out what's going on and come back."

"Maybe I can—"

"No, you're staying here." I kiss her quickly on the mouth, then whip outside the room, shutting the door behind me.

I don't have time to argue with her, and I can't put her in harm's way.

Heavy footfalls accompanied by voices echo down the hall, and I sprint toward them. My gaze skims over every shadow for any sign of chaos.

Around the corner, Mael, Ahren's advisor, is standing tall with his back to me. He bellows at the helpers, "Everyone, listen up! Leave everything behind and go to the underground cells now." He turns to his right and sighs at a maid who seems shell-shocked. "Dana, are you listening?" He snaps his fingers as she gathers her long skirt in her hands and darts through the door that leads to the stairs.

There are underground cells for everyone to hide in during emergencies, and Mael is right about everyone getting to safety fast.

As if sensing my presence, he pivots around. His brown eyes are wild with terror, his face blanched. His short, white hair appears messy, as though he's run his hand through it half a dozen times.

"It's the Bloodcursed," he says between panting breaths. "There are so many of them."

"Where did they enter from?" I demand to know.

"The throne room."

His response has my mouth dropping open. "What?"

"Your Highness, you need to evacuate before it's too late," he pleads.

My insides freeze. Luther and Ahren were in the throne room with our stepfather. But how did the Bloodcursed breach the throne room? It's located in the most central spot in the palace. Someone would have noticed them if they broke through a wall or our magical barriers. The notion horrifies me.

Mael watches me, waiting.

"Go with the rest," I command. "Keep them safe."

"But what—"

"I'm fine," I reply when soft footfalls approach from behind. I know it's her before I turn around. She doesn't listen to me, so it doesn't surprise me that she refuses to stay in the room. Did she leave the room the instant I did?

I turn to Guendolyn. She's staring at the door the staff left through moments earlier, but her eyes widen as soon as she realizes I've noticed her.

"Gue-Gainy, good timing," I chide.

She arches a brow in reply. She hates the fake name I gave her, but now isn't the time to have Mael ask questions. Everyone knows the name Guendolyn in this kingdom, and I have no time for questions.

"Mael will take you to safety until I come to collect you."

The captivating blue of her eyes belies her fiery demeanor. Her lips twitch, and her nose wrinkles, drawing my attention to the light fanning of freckles over her pale nose. "I need to come with you to the throne room."

How long was she listening to our conversation?

Her stubbornness infuriates me. I glare at her as she stands before me with her hands behind her back like she's testing me. We don't have time to argue.

"Your Highness?" Mael asks me.

"This isn't negotiable." I raise my voice at Guendolyn, looming over her. My heart would shatter if anything happened to her. Doesn't she see this? I don't take my gaze off her, saying over my shoulder to Mael, "Take her with you—by force, if needed."

"Deimos, please, no. You don't understand," she insists.

"I do understand. You are safer underground until I get a handle on the situation." I grimace.

"No, you don't," she snaps back as she rushes past me, her shoulder knocking into my arm on purpose. She stops near the wall behind a marble statue of an eagle, so I'm guessing she wants to talk to me in private.

I march up to her. "What's going on? We don't have—"

She places her hands out in front of me, out of sight of Mael. Blue threads of energy dance around them.

My breathing steadies as I study her hands. "Your magic—" I whisper, but she cuts me off.

"It's the same feeling I had each time I opened up the portal between our worlds." Her words send a shiver down my spine at the realization of what she's saying.

I tilt my head forward and whisper, "Your magic caused the breach?"

She shrugs, that paleness returning to her cheeks. "I think so." She chews on her lower lip nervously.

Hell! Guendolyn's magic has been all over the place, so it's very likely she opened a portal from outside the kingdom to the throne room. The blood drains from my face.

"And the energy isn't going away like last time." She glances down at her hands. "I think the portal is still open." She holds her arms across her stomach to hide the magic lingering on her hands.

Nerves in my temple twitch like a tiny heartbeat. I rub my jawline, the roughness of growth grating against my touch. If what she says is true, she'll be the only person capable of closing the portal.

"Have you tried closing it?"

"Yes. That was the first thing I did, but something's wrong. Usually, it closes itself, but why is the magic still on my hands? I think I need to be near the portal to see if that makes a difference."

I sift through my thoughts.

My decision made, I turn to face Mael. "Change of plans. She's with me. You make sure everyone else gets to safety."

Mael studies me, languishing there like he's about to protest. He has always been a kind fae, and he moved to this kingdom with us when Mother married the king of the Shadow Court. He's always looked out for us. Mael is close to fifty in fae years and more of a father to us than our real father, so I trust he won't speak of this if he saw or overheard anything.

He doesn't argue. He simply bows his head and rushes through the open door to safety.

I snatch Guendolyn's hand, a prickling sensation flaring up my arms from her magic, and drag her into a run with me down the long corridor. We bound down the stairs before I realize I'm not carrying any weapons on me. "Fuck, fuck, fuck."

The dark stone hallway we pass through is silent. We employ a skeleton staff to keep the drama and gossip of the kingdom out of our lives as much as possible, but now I feel the bareness of the place.

We pass statues of bears and wolves, and I hate those damn things. Our stepfather insists on them to ensure our mansion shows some semblance of royalty. How the hell statues represent royalty is beyond me.

I swing left down a long hallway and stop outside my chamber. "Give me a moment." Pushing open the oversized black door, I'm greeted by bright sunlight pouring into the room. I loathe curtains that steal the natural light, so I had them ripped off my windows long ago. I march across the room toward a long, wooden box that sits a few feet away from the stone fireplace. Rapidly, I pull it open and reach down to collect a sword. The leather feels soft and perfectly fitted to my grip.

Guendolyn stands in the doorway studying my room, her gaze lingering on the enormous bed. What's my little kitten thinking? What it will be like to sleep in my bed while in my arms? I intend to bring her back sometime and introduce her properly to where I plan to have her spend time with me. But now, we need to hurry. I march toward her and take her hand.

"We need to run," I say.

She doesn't protest, and an expression of determination crosses her exquisitely beautiful face. Together, we take off down the hall and follow the main vein of the mansion, which takes us to the grand bridge that crosses between our mansion and the palace.

"What if the king sees me?" Guendolyn asks, her words breathy.

I meet her gaze. "Right now, that's the least of our worries. If we don't stop the Bloodcursed, there'll be no kingdom left."

Looking back, part of me knew that being intimate with Guendolyn might activate her power. Or maybe I hoped it wouldn't happen. I should have known better.

CHAPTER

TWO

GUENDOLYN

My heart lurches in my throat.

The sight in front of us crashes through me like a tidal wave. It hits me over and over and still my brain refuses to accept the chaos spreading before us. Bloodcursed fill a spectacular hallway made of marble with gold trimmings along the crown molding, and guards are battling them in a vicious fight.

The soldiers wear metal helmets and armored chest plates. They brandish swords and slice at the infected fae. These creatures have lost their souls and now crave blood and flesh to feed. One bite is all it takes to become one. Their skin is pale and blotchy with blood. Clothes hang off their lithe frames, but they move fast—terrifyingly so—and the sure-fire way to stop them is to cut off their head.

Savagery pours from the monsters' gazes, while my hands prick with the magic that released them. The same magic I inhale. It smells like a dying fire, but underlying the magic is the stench of blood choking the air.

"Where's the throne room?" I ask Deimos in the corridor we're hiding in, my voice barely a whisper to avoid drawing any of these things' attention to us. My gaze sweeps over the battle, the hairs on my arms lifting.

"It's just beyond this hallway," he responds.

Sounds of metal hitting bone flood the room. In the distance, a Bloodcursed overcomes a guard. He falls, his sword clanking to the marble floor, then two fellow guards jump to his rescue.

Deimos charges forward from our hiding place at a creature rushing in our direction. I flinch at how quick the Bloodcursed moves, how I never saw it coming at us.

Sword pulled back over his shoulder, Deimos swings the blade out, cutting through the air ferociously. The sharp edge bites right into the Bloodcursed's neck, slicing all the way through. The slurping sound of a blade cutting through flesh leaves me grimacing. The creature's knees buckle, and it drops down, landing feet from Deimos with a dull thunk.

My heart is racing, and all I can think about is how incredible Deimos looks fighting without fear. All those muscles. Long, white hair swinging across his back with each movement. His broad shoulders and chest.

Another scrambling fiend rushes for Deimos.

He pivots and kicks a deadly blow to the creature's gut. It stumbles back, slamming into the wall, but Deimos doesn't waste a second. He leaps after it and drives his sword through the monster's head, then back out with a disgusting wet sound.

I scan the room for the other princes and find Ahren, the eldest, at the rear of the room in combat. He's powerful and swings his sword with tremendous strength. He's captivating to watch, but I don't have time to stare at him and get lost in the things I want to do with him.

Closer to my left, two Bloodcursed charge a soldier. They jump on his back, and he flails, crying out in terror. The sight leaves me shuddering.

Deimos' brother Luther emerges with speed from behind a marble column like a knight, wielding short swords, one in each hand. Two swipes, and the creatures' heads roll off their shoulders. Their bodies follow seconds later, dropping to the floor like sacks.

The whole scene horrifies me. Bloodcursed outnumber the soldiers.

Luther tucks one weapon into the sheath on his belt. He reaches down with his free hand and fists the back of the fallen guard's jacket before dragging him to his feet. Fright startles the man's face, which is splattered with blood, but he doesn't seem bitten. Luther pats his shoulder and swings back toward the fight, just as he catches me peering out from behind the corner. He does a double take, and his eyes widen with shock. They glint with the color of flames.

Then he mouths my name, his brow furrowing. But I can't hear his voice over the commotion and thuds of battle. Dark hair sits messily around his face and flutters over his shoulders as he flies across the room toward me. He's still wearing his military-style jacket with silver buttons running down the middle and a high-collar top underneath.

"What are you doing here?" he growls as his hand closes around my arm and pushes me backward.

"Don't." I knock his hand aside and lift my palms to show him the thin threads of magic lingering over them. "I think I accidentally opened a portal in the castle, and that's how the Bloodcursed came in." My words rush out in one breath. "I don't know how as it's never happened like this before."

I tilt my head back, taking in his strong jawline, his full lips turned downward, his sharp cheekbones. And those intense eyes that seem to pierce right through my soul. Luther is a fae who leaves me weak, and his presence squeezes my heart. I used to wake up with fragments of dreams about him and his name on my lips. Even if our past remains hidden from me, I feel the ache in my chest that he means so much more to me than I remember. But now, he looks at me with a terrifying realization as my words sink in. I don't want to be someone he loathes or fears. The thought is a blade to my heart.

"What did you do, little wolf?"

My breath catches in my throat. "I'm sorry." The words slip past my mouth. "I didn't mean for it to happen. But I can fix this." I pray I can. I have to, because I can't destroy their kingdom on my first day in the palace.

My hands prick with lingering magic while my heart beats frantically as I wait for Luther's fury to pour out. I can't blame him, because I caused this. I should have been more cautious, should have remembered that last time I kissed Deimos, we teleported from Earth to this realm.

"Then we need to get you to the throne room," he instructs, believing me instantly, while doubt curls in my chest. What if I can't get rid of the portal? What if... I suck in a shuddering breath and shake myself. I can't overthink this. It has to work.

"Deimos," he calls out over his shoulder impatiently. Tension and fear cloud Luther's eyes when he glances to address me. "We get you into the throne room, you do your magic, and I'll take you back to the mansion. If the gods are blessing us, our stepfather won't find out about you. I don't want to deal with his shit on top of everything else."

I don't want to face the king, either. Please let this work smoothly. I don't ask for much, Universe, but just this once, back me up.

My entire body goes rigid as I keep thinking about wanting to tell Luther what's on my mind. How I'm scared that I won't be able to close the portal. I want to have him tell me I'm being foolish and embrace me.

Except this isn't the time for weakness. Everyone is standing tall and fighting for all our lives, so weakness has no place here. I can't lose my shit, so instead, I find my bravery and throttle it.

Deimos darts toward us, heaving for breath. He holds his blade by his side, the steel coated in red. Splatters of blood dot his shirt and a few blotches mark his neck. He stands next to his brother. Both are similar in size, but they're like night and day. Deimos has pale skin and white hair, while Luther has fiery pupils and hair the color of ravens feathers.

In the short time I've known Deimos, he's captured my heart, and I feel closer to him. Even if my heart aches for Luther, there's so much I still don't understand about our past...which isn't helped by my vanishing memories ever since I unknowingly unleashed a curse on the Wandering Realm. A curse that makes Shadow Court the target for every Bloodcursed in the entire damn realm. And now, I've brought these monsters into the castle... into the throne room, of all places.

God, if the king finds out, he'll have me killed.

"I'll carve a path while you stay behind her and keep her safe," Luther orders Deimos. "With so many soldiers here, we may be able to avoid an ambush by these fucking Bloodcursed."

Deimos' free hand settles on my lower back. "I'll keep you safe the whole while. Don't stop following Luther. Hopefully, we can do this fast."

"I'm ready," I admit, even if uncertainty clings to my ribs.

We swing toward the main hall, and the Bloodcursed are close. Guards fight as more creatures keep pouring in. How long before the monsters overpower the army and win?

"Now!" Luther snaps as he surges forward into the grand hallway, swinging his sword at a fiend's head. He's carving a path for us through the mass battle and makes it look effortless as he destroys the enemy.

I breathe hard and rush out after him, sensing Deimos at my back.

Creatures are too close for my liking as the tangle of battles rage around us. I step over a decapitated head and rush to keep up with Luther. My feet slide out from under me across the blood. Deimos catches my fall, his strong hands on my back, then pushes me back upright. My insides clench, but I won't stop because I have to end this.

A Bloodcursed springs toward me. I raise my fists.

Luther sidesteps toward it, driving an elbow into its face. One swift turn followed by Luther's extending arm, and his blade bites into the tenderness of the fiend's neck.

I look away at once to avoid the spray of blood.

Don't scream. Just keep running. Keep running.

The deafening clink of armor and growls flood the hall. Nothing about this place is normal, and I'm starting to suspect I'll never experience normality again.

I push back the terror clawing at my flesh, and somehow, manage to race forward and remain coherent through all of this. Everything about this attack screams at me to run and hide, but I don't dare. I can't.

Devastation surrounds us, but I never stop following Luther.

A hand snatches my arm, icy cold fingers digging into my skin.

I flinch and spin around, coming face to face with a monster. Sunken eyes, the life stolen from them, worn lips thinning over rotten teeth.

Deimos hauls me against him and away from the Bloodcursed. I slam into Deimos' body behind me, and he's like a wall of strength and protection. With one hand clasped over my chest, the other drives his sword through the predator's gut, sliding in as easy as knife in butter.

Luther is already on his heels, bringing his sword to the fiend's neck.

My stomach plunges at the sight, but there's no time to dwell on it. We're already racing forward, shoving past others.

To stop means death.

We know this too well.

Another creature grabs my arm and yanks me toward it. A scream strangles my throat before Luther swings around and drives a fist into its face, then kicks the thing into a mass of Bloodcursed bodies.

When we reach the other side of the enormous hall, we don't pause. We follow Luther as he races down a corridor, and we stop in front of a grand room. Double doors as dark as night stand wide open, one hanging off its hinges.

The war continues around us, but inside the throne room, it's so much worse.

It's a ruined mess. Golden statues of women with wings are pushed over and broken near the side walls. Bloodcursed bodies layer the floor, and there's too much gore and body parts to assemble the pieces. A few soldiers are lying among them, and my heart bleeds. Others are fighting.

Seeing the chaos makes me sick, and bile hits the back of my throat.

The room is enormous, and toward the back is a set of platform steps. Two black thrones stand on top. Behind them is an oversized round window, light pouring over the massacre.

More Bloodcursed are stumbling out of the portal that sits in front of the thrones. There's a large black hole, the edges sparking with blue energy. The same power that curls around my hands.

"It's too dangerous to go in there," Luther says as he twists around. "You need to close the portal from here.

"Deep breath," Deimos murmurs in my ear. "You can do this."

I suck in several harsh breaths and try to ground myself. In my mind, I reach out to the magic.

Energy dances along my skin as the power intensifies. It thrashes through me, lashing out like a whip, and spears outward. It ripples the air, barely seen, but I recognize the energy. My chest is burning with fury at myself at the sight of the injured guards, at the destruction I've caused. Scorching energy erupts in violent sparks from my body.

But nothing is happening. It's like I have the key in my hand, but it's not fitting into the lock.

Panic flares over my mind.

"What are you waiting for?" Luther growls. "It needs to close now."

Before I respond, he's thrown himself at the assault surging in our direction.

I try my hardest to think this through, to figure out how to close that portal. Everything always comes back to the same thing.

I glance over to Deimos. "You need to kiss me like I mean the world to you."

His eyebrow arches. "I always kiss you like that."

Snatching the fabric of his shirt across his chest, I draw him toward me as I push myself onto my toes. Our mouths clash like they're engaging in a great war of their own, lips crushing, tongues tangling. Except I don't feel the surge of energy. We break apart, both exchanging glances, our breaths shaky.

"I don't know what's going on," I insist.

He sweeps his gaze over the hallways and throne room, where dozens of guards are slowly losing to the onslaught of Bloodcursed. "We don't have much time. You have to close it now."

Rippling power is everywhere. I feel it in the air, clawing at us, seeping into my very essence. Why the hell can't I summon my power to shut that fucking portal?

I feel the whole room closing in around me. I choke on the stench of blood and death while everything starts to blur together.

Soldiers battling Bloodcursed. More creatures pouring in from the open portal. My princes fighting. But I can't get a handle on my power. Goddamnit, I only just discovered I carried such an ability, so I don't have any clue how to wield it. But I have no choice now.

People are dying because of me.

Panic curls in my chest with each raspy breath I suck in. I have to calm myself if I intend to figure this out. But how the hell am I meant to uncover anything about the power in my veins at this moment?

Sighing deeply, I realize I need to rethink this.

"Guendolyn, hurry," Deimos urges me from behind, his back against mine as I face the open doors leading into the throne room. He uses his body to shield me from the creatures, and I adore every single inch of him.

I search my thoughts, going over every incident where my power flared up.

Kissing Deimos.

Battling the Bloodcursed back on Earth.

All moments of high stress. High anxiety. Intense emotion.

Death surrounds me, so I don't think it can get crazier than this. Except there's a small difference. Back then, my focus was wholly on the attack and the kiss, while now my brain is scattered with the battle, the fear of not controlling my magic, the fear of letting the king see me. My thoughts fray at the edges.

Deimos tenses against me.

I swallow a shudder and dig my heels in, ready to make this work.

Concentrate.

I shut my eyes, and the portal in the throne room flutters in my mind. I grasp on to the thread, and there's a sudden shift in the air that ripples down my arms. The thin blue lines snap wildly around my fingers like a live wire flickering and whipping about. It's responding to the change in the atmosphere, just like the threads of magic I've seen around the fairies' wings. They crackled and popped as those little critters swarmed me outside the kingdom's entrance. Did they carry a similar power?

Deimos bumps into me. My eyes flutter open, and I slam into the open door. I jerk around, my pulse racing.

Two Bloodcursed attack him, and he jumps at them in response, his sword swinging.

I grasp onto the entrance to the throne room and stare at the black portal, at the creatures coming through.

That's all I imagine now, and I picture it closed, calling the power to me, drawing it into me. I shove all other thoughts aside.

A surge of energy sweeps through me, bitterly cold. It punches me in the gut, biting into my skin, leaving a bitter, metallic taste in my mouth. I look down, and the blue lines are dancing over my body. My heart soars with the possibility that I can do this, my adrenaline racing.

Fae howl and roar with rage around me.

The hairs on my head shift, and the air around me once again seems to change. It carries a chill.

I imagine it coming from me, rushing across the throne room and crashing into the portal, lacerating the connection, shutting out the creatures.

Pain lashes my chest, the moment drawn out as I stare at the portal, wishing it out of existence.

Sweat drips down my spine, and a nerve pulses in my neck. Energy suddenly snaps outward from my body, leaving me stumbling on my feet.

In the blink of an eye, the portal pops out of existence. Just like that, it's gone. No more Bloodcursed coming through.

"Deimos!" I cry out. "I did it!"

The rush of power surges through me once again, stronger than before, as if retaliating against me. It shakes me to the core as terror cleaves through me.

In the middle of the throne room a darkness descends, shaping into a solid form. A long oval shape...just like... My stomach drops through me as I watch another portal coming to life before my eyes.

I want to scream and cry as the earlier spark of hope inside me shatters like glass.

A heart-wrenching screech snatches my attention. I spin on my heels and look out into the hallway behind me, where everyone fights. Where no one knows how close I came to stopping this. Sorrow clings to my ribs, swallowing me.

Until my gaze sweeps over to Deimos.

A Bloodcursed savagely bites into his shoulder, and he collapses to his knees.

I scream and stumble forward. My world dies as I watch him fighting the beast that overpowers him. My movements seem to decelerate, my every step agonizingly sluggish, like I'll never reach him.

He looks at me, his green eyes meeting mine, burning with terror.

Blood pours from the wound, then another creature lunges for him.

Blinding rage bursts inside me, dark and violent. "Get away from him!" I scream. I want to die right this moment.

I charge through the masses, pushing past them with unimaginable strength. A terrifying ache splinters my heart in half.

With fury, I grasp the back of one of the monster's torn coat, fisting the fabric, and haul him off Deimos with all my strength. I'm shaking uncontrollably, and all I can picture is ripping his head off with my bare hands.

"Sonofabitch!" I bellow as Ahren spears the second Bloodcursed in the head with his sword. I lift my gaze toward him. But the first creature turns on me in an instant. It snatches my neck, bony fingers digging into my skin with a vise-like grip. It sneers, blood dripping from its mouth...Deimos' blood.

My hands fly at the creature's face instinctively, pushing my palms against its forehead to keep the gaping mouth as far from me as possible.

I can't breathe, and I swing wildly at him with my free hand as I stumble backward.

My back slams into a wall in the hallway. Then it all happens too fast.

The creature suddenly pushes past my hand and bites my forearm. The momentum sends me flinching backward, and my head cracks into the wall. My vision reels from the blow, throwing the room into a spin.

Sharp teeth sink deeper into my arm, tearing. I feel every lick of its tongue, every rip of skin. Tears rush from my eyes.

Unbearable pain shoots up my arm, feeling like blades ripping over my skin.

I'm choking but don't stop slamming my fist into its head, over and over. The fuckwit is still latched to my arm, making slurping sounds that sicken me. The edges of my vision feather with darkness. I picture my death, being left in this realm to wander as aimlessly as one of them. A Bloodcursed.

I don't want to die.

I hit the monster with the last of my strength, then something buzzes past my ear. Seconds later, a small bird flutters above the Bloodcursed.

No... not a bird, but a fairy. The same type I'd encountered outside the kingdom's entrance.

A tiny face, big black eyes, and a wide mouth filled with serrated, pointy teeth. Translucent wings reflecting a rainbow of colors rapidly beating. Greenish scales covering a humanoid body. She's small, maybe the size of my outstretched hand.

She watches me. Then something brushes past my arm, and dozens of fairies rise up around me. They dive at the Bloodcursed, ripping at its flesh. Vicious little things, they leave nothing untouched.

Wings slap me in the face, and I pull sideways, fighting to rip my arm free.

They wrench the fiend backward, away from me. I stumble and use the wall to catch myself when I break free. I desperately gasp for air again, filling my lungs.

A cloud of fairies bombards the Bloodcursed, who bats its arms at them, but it's too late. It vanishes behind a wall of whipping wings, unleashing a screeching sound.

My heart is hammering frantically. I clasp my bloody arm and cradle it against my stomach. It stings so badly, I want to collapse and just bawl my eyes out. I stare at my injury, and all I see is blood and deep red flesh.

How long before Deimos and I become one of them?

The room around me morphs into pandemonium.

Energy jolts through me, rattling me as though the earlier power has again awakened inside me. All I feel is the devastating ache from the bite.

Fairies swoosh through the palace, attacking every single Bloodcursed.

Madly, I push myself off the wall in the hallway and whip around to look into the throne room. Fairies are flying out of the second portal, not

Bloodcursed. Somehow, I've called them, opening a doorway to these little beings who saved my life once before. I welcome them to do what I can't.

They ravage the Bloodcursed, not touching any other fae. They make fast work of the creatures, ripping into and devouring them. All that remains are bones, hair, and clothes.

"Deimos," I cry, my cheeks drenched as I try to peer through the chaos in the hall behind me to find him.

Those green eyes are all that remain in my mind... The devastation in his eyes when he knew it was too late for him.

I hiccup a cry, hurrying forward as half a dozen fairies zip around me.

Translucent wings flap wildly. They congregate over my wound, and I feel their tiny tongues licking me, tasting me. No teeth. They don't intend to harm me, I know it... They're feeding on me, and I can only assume it's my payment for their help. Just as they did down in the woods when they saved my ass the first time.

They saved me, so I have no intention of pushing them away.

I shove forward through the chaos regardless.

"Deimos!" I yell out. "Ahren!" All I see is the flutter of fairies flying all over the place and Bloodcursed falling everywhere.

A tiny squeal that pierces my ears has me cringing.

I twist my head in the direction of the sound to see a soldier grasping a fairy by a vibrant blue wing. The other wing is bent backward, broken. The fae raises his blade with his other hand.

Instinct takes over, and I rush to him, screaming, "Stop!" I remember Deimos calling them "blood-sucking vermin." Except to me, they're my saviors.

The soldier doesn't hear me, and I practically bowl him over. He teeters on his feet, his eyes wide with shock, and drops the injured fairy. I hastily snatch her out of the air. I have no idea of the gender, but she seems like a female to me. They all do.

"What the fuck?" he growls.

"They're saving us," I bark back. "Look around you. Do you want them all to turn on you?"

He blinks hard and looks around as if seeing the reality of the situation for the first time.

I gather the little fairy closer and hold her with one hand to my chest, her good wing tucked against her body, the other sticking out at a strange angle.

"Sorry, little one. I'll help you. I promise," I coo, but first I must reach

Deimos before we both turn into monsters. I want to tell him how sorry I am. The thought leaves me dizzy, but I swallow down past the fear.

The tiny fairy glances up and shakes her head before pressing her cheek to my chest. I hear the soft whimpers of her pain.

I whirl around to find Deimos leaning against Ahren, who has an arm around his brother, holding him up. Deimos clutches the side of his bloody shoulder, moaning.

Color has drained from his face, and he looks sick. Gravely sick. The infection is moving fast through his body, yet I feel none of the infection in my body yet.

He meets my gaze through the bloodbath surrounding us and gives me a half-grin. Despite everything, he still smiles. This is why I fell for him so fast, why my heart bleeds at seeing him hurt.

"Deimos." I shudder and rush up to him, stepping over bodies as the flutter of fairies starts to slowly dissipate. I look behind me and into the throne room, where many are flying back through the portal. They've left only dead Bloodcursed in their wake.

"Guendolyn, what did you do?" Ahren growls, his gaze lowering to the fairy in my hand when I face him.

My bitten arm dangles by my side, the pain excruciating, but no one seems to notice.

"I'm fine," Deimos lies terribly, drawing my attention to the terror that swims in his eyes. I hear the fear in his voice.

"Deimos, stop pretending." My voice breaks.

"I've never been a good actor." He half-snorts into a laugh.

"No, you haven't," Ahren snaps. "And you sure as fuck aren't going to die today."

Blood oozes from between Deimos' fingers, dripping onto his dark shirt, seeping into the fabric.

Ahren maneuvers them through the masses. The Bloodcursed are all dead, and fairies are zipping out of the room quickly.

"Guendolyn, stay close," Ahren orders. He's barely looking at me, his eyes all over the room. "We need to get him to the healers."

I move alongside them, sidestepping the dead. The soldiers stand around bewildered. But I glance back at the fairy portal, needing to close it.

The fairy in my hand chirps like a small bird. I look down, and she raises her hand and puts it to her mouth, then dips the fingers forward. She blows a breath, and out comes a blue fog, similar in color to the magic threads.

She chirps again and points to the throne room.

I don't waste a moment and turn around, facing the open doorway to the throne room, staring at the gaping black portal. The last few fairies vanish inside. With my good hand, I tuck the fairy inside the top of my dress, then place a palm to my mouth.

Lowering my fingers forward, I focus on the image of the portal shutting. Then I blow out a breath.

A surge of energy rises through my stomach, up to my throat, and rushes out. A pale blue fog spears from my mouth and rushes through the air, darting around bodies, over heads, until it reaches the portal. It smothers the opening, and the black passage dissolves, crumbling into thin air.

Several guards explode into cheers.

I look down to my new friend. "Thank you." She's exactly what I need... someone to help me understand my power. And I need to work out how my ability is related to these fairies.

"Hurry up," Ahren growls. He doesn't say my name, but I know he's talking to me.

With a hand clasped over the fairy, I twist around and hurry after the princes.

Deimos' face is a gray color now. "Hold on," I say, my shattered heart breaking into even more pieces.

He blinks before looking up at the ceiling. A tear pools at the corner of his eye.

"Deimos, fuck." I'm trembling. "I need you. You can't..."

Two soldiers push past me and shove me aside. I stumble on my feet, holding on to the fairy so as to not lose her.

"Don't fall behind," Ahren calls out. "I need you to stay with me to heal him."

My head still spins, and his words jumble in my mind. How can I heal him when I've been bitten too?

I move to catch up to Ahren and Deimos, who've vanished down a corridor, the shadows stealing them from view.

My throat tightens, and I choke on my breaths. Agony tears at my insides as all kinds of images of our time together slam into my head. Ones that make me feel like the worst person in the world, because I caused this. I hurt him. Deimos was bitten by a Bloodcursed. For those few moments, I struggle to move. Maybe I deserved to be bitten... It's payment for what I unleashed here today.

I search the room for Luther.

Slipping past a group of guards, I glance over my shoulder instinctively, as if sensing someone watching me. I suspect it's Luther.

My gaze collides with a well-rounded man who stands tall, his chin raised, eyes narrowing on me. He's dressed in a black coat buttoned to his chest and has a short, white beard. My sights land on the golden crown sitting on his head.

All the blood drains from my body.

Fuck!

CHAPTER

FOUR

LUTHER

My muscles feel heavy and sore from fighting.

Sucking in a sharp breath, I lift my gaze to the hallway littered with Bloodcursed. The soldiers are aiding injured fae, and their voices blend together into a humming sound in my ears, just like the buzzing of the fairies who came to our rescue.

For the life of me, I can't work out how fairies got into the palace as well.

One moment we're battling for our life, and the next, those little vermin are rushing in and attacking the Bloodcursed. I guess I can't exactly hate them now, seeing as they assisted us. But so much doesn't make sense. How did they get in here? Why did they only target the Bloodcursed? Don't get me wrong, I'm not complaining, but things aren't adding up. There's a reason for everything.

Tucking my swords into the sheaths on my belt, I groan from the ache in my arms as I walk through the aftermath. Cutting off heads is fucking hard work.

Everyone is running all over the place to provide help and start the cleanup. I catch sight of two of our mages walking into the throne room, scanning the massacre. Their black robe-skirts drag over the dead bodies as they step over them, the metal chains they wear around their waists rattling with each movement. A tiny fairy skull the size of my fist hangs from their necks and sits halfway down their bare chests. Their white hair is kept short and is woven with feathers, their cheeks imprinted with various magical symbols—markings inked on their faces on their first day as mages. Not many of their kind are born. They carry the power of multiple abilities, stronger than most fae, and most end up working under the king's command for life.

Which begs the question: Did they open the second portal and bring in the fairies? It was a risky move that paid off, if that is the case. Except I've never known them to have such a power.

My stepfather marches into the throne room toward the mages, and I turn away before he sets his sights on me. The king is the kind of fae who believes a busy man is a happy man. In truth, he uses that line to order people around to do his shit. And considering the mess in his throne room right now, he'll be a raging bull.

I have no doubt he'll come and interrogate us about what we saw. He'll turn this kingdom upside down to uncover how the Bloodcursed entered.

There is no way I can let him get his hands on Guendolyn. He's already promised to kill the girl who cursed Shadow Court. Coupled with that, if he finds out she accidentally let those fucking bloodsuckers in, she'll stand no chance.

What I need is to uncover how the hell she did it and ensure it never happens again.

Soldiers grunt around me as they start to haul Bloodcursed outside for burning. I sidestep a guard and end up stepping right into Guendolyn's path.

Her eyes widen with a beaming smile. "Luther!" She blows her hair out of her eyes and stares up at me as if she's been lost.

My attention zeroes in on the fairy half-sticking out of her top in her cleavage.

"What the hell—?"

"Don't. Not here." She quickly glances behind her at the throne room, then hurries toward the corridor where I found her earlier. I track after her and ensure no one follows us.

Once we reach the shadows and are clearly out of earshot of the others, I grab her arm and force her to stop and talk to me. She winces and flinches from my touch.

I look down at her arm. There's blood everywhere. The flesh on her forearm is torn and dripping with blood.

I can't think straight for those few moments, but reality punches me in the chest. "Fuck, Guendolyn. Don't tell me that's a Bloodcursed bite."

"Luther," she begins, her voice trembling.

So much pain crowds behind her eyes. I should have done more to keep her protected. I believed each Bloodcursed I slaughtered made her safer, but I was wrong.

I let her down just as I did my real father, who reminded me daily I was worthless in his eyes. In the years since he left my mother, I've wondered how things might have been different if I'd been the son he wanted.

I didn't get a chance to fix that shitshow, but with Guendolyn, maybe all hope isn't lost.

"Fuck!" I roar as my heart jolts in my chest. I pace back and forth in the corridor and run a hand over my face. Ice rushes down my spine and penetrates my bones.

"Don't freak out," she pleads.

"How else am I meant to react?" I snap. The girl I found years ago on Earth, a lost fae from our world, who I believe can save our realm and who stole my heart, is now going to die from a fucking Bloodcursed. I want to drive my fist through the wall over and over.

I pause in front of her. "I can't lose you." I taste the words in my mouth as they roll past my lips.

"Luther," she whispers while I'm breaking apart on the inside.

I cup her face with my hands and draw her mouth to mine, kissing her desperately, memorizing everything about her as she kisses me back. I want nothing more than to claim her, to conquer her until she is mine forever. I want to really taste her, to finally sink between her gorgeous thighs, to release every piece of built-up emotion that has slowly driven me crazy over the past two years.

She pulls away from me, staring into my eyes as if she might remember more about our past. I grasp on to that hope, but when she doesn't say anything, I know it's just my tortured mind craving her.

"How did you open the portal, little wolf?" I ask to break the silence. "And why the hell are you holding a fairy? They're vicious." I look down at the critter, who watches me with its huge black eyes, its lips peeling back off the row of sharp teeth. It knows I'm talking about it.

The thing hisses at me while Guendolyn steps back and shifts her hand to hold it closer to her chest. It looks up at her with admiration swirling in those dark eyes. How in the Seven Hells did she tame such a creature?

"Dammit, Luther, listen to me," she scolds. Her anger seems to outweigh her distress. "I was bitten, but I'm not feeling any symptoms yet. The real problem is Deimos was bitten too, and he's slipping fast. I don't know where Ahren took him, but I need to see him." Her words dance with shakiness as heartbreak slides over her face and fresh tears track down her cheeks. I'm not blind to the fact she has strong feelings for Deimos, and I swallow past the hurt. Right now, that's not as important as my brother's impending transformation, the news a punch to my chest.

"Deimos got bitten as well?" An invisible hand seems to wrench into my gut and rip out my insides. I choke on air, struggling to get it into my lungs.

How did they both get bitten? We just arrived back at the kingdom today, and all hell's broken loose already.

"I don't know where Ahren took him," she cries. "Where would he go?"

In my periphery, soldiers linger at the end of the corridor, collecting bodies. With my stepfather and the mages nearby, we need to get a move on. There's so much at stake.

"This way," I command, wanting to take her hand, but I realize with her holding that fairy and her other arm mangled, it's not going to happen.

"Do you have a cure for a Bloodcursed's infection?" she implores as we storm down the corridors of the palace as far from the throne room as possible. She gives me a ghost of a smile, filled with hope.

"No, but we have healers who might be able to help," I lie, the words sour on my tongue. Many fae have turned into Bloodcursed from bites in the last two years, and our healers have been helpless to save them. But I can't terrify Guendolyn any more than she already is. I let out a hard breath and let the lie linger between us in a silent moment.

We rush past marble walls that are elaborately decorated with gold trimmings. Tapestries. Paintings. Vases. Candle chandeliers. Midnight blue rugs run the length of every hallway in this place. No soldiers or guards anywhere, which is a good thing right now.

Instead of worrying about losing Guendolyn and my brother to this curse, I focus on moving as fast as possible and ensuring no one sees her leaving the palace.

When we reach the rear exit, I push open the metal-studded door that connects the palace to our mansion. The wind is ferocious outside, the sun blinding.

I shove my shoulder into the door and hold it open for Guendolyn. She spills outside onto the stone bridge that spans the one-hundred-foot distance.

She's clutching on to her fairy and glances around at the enormous castle we just emerged from. Our mansion in the distance is made of steadfast stone walls that glint in the sunlight. On either side of us is a slope from the hill the castle is built upon. Hundreds of homes flood the landscape within the kingdom walls.

Black and red roofs gleam beneath the sun with trims of varied colors around the windows. Down there, the rest of the fae live in cottages. The homes built higher up on the mountain and closer to the palace belong to the more affluent families.

I turn to Guendolyn, who looks so lost, her cheeks scarlet. Her blonde hair flutters over her face, but she just doesn't seem to care. Her irresistible blue eyes seem cold today.

Panicked voices from the fae down below tell me word has spread about the Bloodcursed breaching the palace.

Guendolyn whirls on her heels and runs onward toward our mansion, and I run after her.

I try to tell myself she and my brother will be fine, except I've seen the effects a bite has. Terror crawls up the back of my neck and the world spins with me. The thoughts won't leave me alone, flashing images of them both turning. Being faced with the decision to end their suffering or imprison them for life until a cure is discovered terrifies me.

Those thoughts are poison to my soul.

When she reaches the door, she cuts me a quick look for help as she can't open the door with her injury while holding the fairy. I dash over and tear open the door for her. Once we're both inside, I take the lead and head directly to Deimos' chamber.

From a distance, I see that his door lays open and hear voices stream from inside.

My heart clenches, and I can't get there quick enough. Suddenly, I'm running.

Don't let him be turned into a Bloodcursed. Gods, please.

I burst into the room. Ahren twists toward me, his face grim and pale with a look that carries a dark burden.

I lose all semblance of composure and march up to the bed, where four healers hover around my brother. Maids are rushing out of the room.

"Get the fuck out of my way," I bellow to the healers, who just stand there. They're useless, and I shove myself past them.

Deimos lies on his back in bed, his eyes shut, his shoulder bandaged. He isn't moving, but I notice the rise and fall of his chest.

A golden transparent haze encases my brother.

"What is this?" I choke out.

"A temporary device to keep him alive until a cure is created," a deep voice speaks, belonging to the dark figure who emerges from the shadows across the bed from me.

Jasion Crow. Another mage from the palace, except he works closely with Ahren. He stands tall, his shoulders broad, dressed just like the other mages with a skull hanging down the middle of his bare chest. He's powerful, terrifyingly so, but he remains under the king's command. No matter what he says about doing his own thing, I highly doubt he truly does. He'd do the king's bidding without question.

"How long does he have?" I ask Jasion, and he doesn't blink or show any form of emotion. Not much scares this mage. He isn't too much older than Ahren, yet he and my brother bonded after we first arrived at the palace. Both were young and new in the kingdom, both in roles where a lot was expected of them. They formed a friendship as they went through training together. Many, including Ahren, say Jasion should be positioned as head mage. The king doesn't seem to agree.

"A week or two," Jasion answers.

My blood ices in my veins. "How the fuck are we meant to find a cure in that short of time?"

"You need to give me a day or two, Your Highness," he says.

"I'll run more tests to see how fast his blood is changing to give you a better indication. But you know the truth about this toxin." His hooded eyes intensify, and I know exactly what he's talking about. We've tested so many Bloodcursed, their blood, different spells...everything one can think of, we've tried. But nothing helped because it came down to one thing. The only way to break a curse is to use magic from the creator.

I growl in response and turn toward Ahren, but it's Guendolyn my eyes settle on.

She stands there with red eyes. Fresh tears keep falling down her cheeks as she glances at Deimos, and she's still clutching onto that damn fairy.

My heart rips in half, grieving for my brother, terrified for Guendolyn, and confused by so many things I don't understand.

I move closer and cradle her in my arms without squashing the fairy. Guendolyn softens against me. In my mind, I picture her lying next to Deimos, both of them taken by the infection. Breath catches in my throat.

"How are you feeling?" I whisper.

She doesn't respond, but her breaths turn to sobs.

I lift my attention to Ahren.

Fury burns behind his gaze. "What the hell happened back there?" he growls.

I lean in closer and whisper, "Somehow she opened the portal in the palace while she was in the mansion."

My brother turns to everyone else in the room. "Everyone, leave now. Out!"

The maids scurry out while Jasion strolls past us. His pale gray eyes fix on Guendolyn, showing too much interest for my liking. Nothing good comes from piquing a mage's curiosity.

With the click of the door, Guendolyn pulls away from me.

"What is that?" Ahren snaps, staring at the fairy in her clutches as if seeing it for the first time.

"They helped us defeat the Bloodcursed," she answers with confidence. "And this little one hurt her wing, so I promised to help her."

"Promised whom? The vermin who attack fae?" Ahren asks.

"We have a bigger problem," I say, interrupting. "Guendolyn's been bitten too."

Ahren's face pales, his gaze scanning her body and landing on her arm. Blood is dripping onto the floorboards.

"Gods no. We need Jasion back."

"No," she says. "Please just wait a moment. I need to catch my breath since so much has happened so fast. Yes, I got bitten, but I'm not feeling sick yet. I saw how quickly the infection took Deimos, but all I feel is the freaking pain shooting up my arm." She lifts her arm and whimpers. "Please help me with the bleeding and pain first, because it doesn't sound like your healers have any real solution."

I pivot on my heels and dart into the bathroom, where the maids left buckets with hot water and material for cleaning wounds. I collect what I need and am back by her side in moments.

Ahren has her sitting on the couch, and next to her is the fairy looking pretty miserable as well. One of her wings sits twisted and broken.

I kneel in front of Guendolyn and lay her arm on her thigh with the wound facing upward. Dunking one of the rags into the water, I wring it out and dab her messed-up wound.

She winces, but I press on and wipe the injury, needing it clean before I bind it.

"Talk to me," Ahren begins, drawing her attention from what I'm doing. "What happened today?"

She licks her dry lips and keeps glancing over to Deimos and back at us. "When you left to visit the king, Deimos and I started talking." She swallows loudly, struggling to find her words.

"And then?" Ahren encourages her to speak.

"Then I kissed him. He kissed me." Her cheeks blush furiously, but she never looks away, knowing how I feel about her.

My thoughts are stuck on the word *kissed*. It shouldn't bother me. I've seen the way Deimos and Guendolyn are both drawn to each other. We three have shared girls before. I won't deny jealousy roars through me, igniting my insides like an inferno. I still haven't had a chance to spend time with Guendolyn. To help her remember our past. I taste her deeply on my lips and want more.

"The whole room started shaking," she continues. "I felt the magic in the air. Last time Deimos and I kissed, we were transported from Earth to this realm. So I think this time, it opened the portal. I'm so sorry. I don't even know how I did it or why it was different from the last time."

I lower my head and keep cleaning her wound, finding it's a lot more superficial than it first seemed. I start bandaging it and will have to disinfect it later, but I need to stop the bleeding first.

"The kingdom is encased in magic to keep the Bloodcursed out, so maybe it's distorting your portal ability," Ahren suggests, which makes sense.

"And I think when I tried to close the portal, I somehow opened a second doorway for the fairies." She looks down to her new friend and smiles.

I take a seat next to Guendolyn.

"And how are you controlling the fairies?" Ahren's thinking it all through, trying to piece everything together and make sense of her power. How to keep it from happening again. It's what Ahren is good at.

"I don't know," she admits. "They just seem to like me."

The fairies don't like anyone unless they're tearing into them and sucking the marrow out of their bones.

Silence falls heavily across the room, and everything seems to shut down inside me. Everything but the instinct to fight.

Every time I look over to Deimos, a sledgehammer smashes into my chest. How the fuck did we end up here?

"All right, so we know the following," Ahren begins, counting on his fingers. "Guendolyn can't control her power, and it's triggered by kissing, perhaps?"

"Well, not completely true," I interject sheepishly. "I kissed her earlier in the corridor, and there was no transportation between realms."

Ahren's brow arches, studying me. I can't work out the look in his eyes.

"Does that mean the power responds differently to certain people, or is it just a state of stress? Jasion told me his power can fluctuate depending on what emotions he feels on any given day."

"I've never heard of that before." The times I've worked with the king's mages, they share information easily, so to never have heard this is a surprise.

"We need to account for what we're dealing with. We know that fairies seem to respond well to you, Guendolyn, and they help you, so there's something there."

She nods.

"And for some reason, you're not reacting to a Bloodcursed's infectious bite."

"We don't know that yet," she murmurs.

"True, but we'll know by the end of the day, as I've never seen an infection take long to spread." His brows pinches with the look he always gets when he doesn't believe what he's hearing.

"You missed the most critical part," I announce, lifting my chin toward Ahren. "Deimos has limited time left in that magic haze before the toxins transform him and we lose our brother for good."

Ahren stands before Luther and me with the light from the window casting a glow around him. His long, white hair is pulled into an alluring man bun at the back of his head, a few strands hanging messily around his face. Those pale green eyes look right through me. Ahren is spectacular. Tall and broad-shouldered, he stands with confidence. I can easily see him sitting on a throne, leading this realm. He has a way of reminding you he's the heir and will never take no for an answer.

In truth, all three of the princes leave me swooning. But that doesn't make them any less frustrating or dangerous.

Everything has become more complicated since arriving in this kingdom. Things were messy enough as it is... I'm a fae from the Unseelie Court, the princes' mortal enemy, apparently. My parents are in that court, but no one can tell me anything more except I might get killed by the Unseelie if they find me.

My head hurts just trying to make sense of it all. Now, Deimos has been bitten, and I can somehow command fairies. If things weren't crazy before, they sure are now.

"Guendolyn," Ahren whispers, and I can tell by his tone he wants something of me. "When we stopped in that backwater town, you healed my bite mark. Do you remember?"

How can I forget? Those wolves almost killed us, but I know exactly where Ahren is going with his question.

"I don't know how I did that, but I'll try on Deimos. I'd do anything to help him." I stare down at the fairy, who's sitting with one blue wing wrapped around her and the other kinked outward. I have to help her as well somehow. I get to my feet and take quick steps to Deimos, remembering how Ahren's bite mark vanished when I touched it, leaving behind my handprint on his skin. I hope he's right, as I can't stop worrying it won't work in this case.

The transparent haze over Deimos glints like golden jewels beneath the sunlight pouring in from the windows.

"Can I touch it?" I glance over my shoulder at Ahren, who steps alongside me.

"The magic holding him won't affect you." He studies me as if I'm about to perform some kind of awe-inspiring trick.

There's no doubt the whole situation is a shitstorm waiting to happen. Luther stands by the window, not saying a word, and I can feel the tension rolling off him in waves. I don't blame him. This is a fucked-up position to end up in.

Facing Deimos, I try to push aside my fear, and with a deep breath, I lower my open palm to his bandaged shoulder. The magic feels cold against my skin. With my eyes shut, I imagine my energy pouring through me and into Deimos.

I seize my power.

The floor shakes beneath my feet, and I snap open my eyes to find the walls trembling. Wobbling backward from the movement, I lash out a hand toward Ahren to steady myself.

He snatches my wrist and wrenches me against him as the walls quiver and groan.

In moments, the shuddering settles. Everyone freezes, and no one says a word as we wait.

"Was that you?" Luther stares right at me.

"I'm sure that was her power," Ahren responds on my behalf.

Quickly pulling free from Ahren, I rush back to Deimos' side to inspect his shoulder. Please, please be healed. I pull at the bandages eagerly, my heart banging.

The white fabric peels away from his flesh, bringing with it blood and the sight of the open wound. So much blood pools up around the bite mark.

I cringe and want to scream. Hastily, I reapply the bandage tightly to stop the bleeding, then look toward Ahren and shake my head.

"I felt the power, but it didn't work," I murmur.

Luther sighs. "The only thing to counteract their magic will be a cure from the creator," Luther explains.

I jerk my head toward him. "Then why am I still not feeling the symptoms of my bite?"

"I can speculate," Luther says, his voice matter-of-fact, as if he's been pondering this already. "You have Unseelie blood in your veins, and the curse on our court is from Ash Court, where the Unseelie live. I'd say that makes you immune, and the spell targets Seelie bloodlines only."

There's a coldness in the way he delivers those words, like he almost resents me for being Unseelie. I didn't even know fae existed before these princes brought me here, let alone that there are two factions.

"I'm going to collect Jasion," Ahren grunts while crossing the room for the door, his footfalls thumping the wooden floorboards.

"Shouldn't we wait until I show symptoms?" I say, seeing the worry on Ahren's face, his impatience.

Each time I glance over to Deimos in the bed, I want to cry. We've been running non-stop since he first took me from the nightclub back on Earth. Somehow, during all the complications and fighting for our lives, I found myself drawn to him. I believed with time I'd discover what my emotions for him really mean, if the tenderness he showed me is real, and now I don't know if I'll get the chance to uncover the truth.

"Jasion might know more about Unseelie magic and perhaps even something about fairies so we can work out why you can control them," Ahren explains. He doesn't wait for a response, just marches out of the room like he can't stand still doing nothing while his brother lies unconscious.

Luther crashes on the lounge, on the opposite end of the little blue-winged fairy. He leans forward, his forearms on his thighs as he stares out the windows at the spectacular view of the mountains.

He's devastatingly handsome, and I feel so many mixed emotions for him, things I don't understand. Confusion seems to now cross his face. Since meeting him, he's been patient with me when it comes to remembering our past together, but I can see the pain behind his eyes when he looks at me. Now, he's miles away.

I'm still jittery from the day's events, and my insides are frayed.

"I think what you said before about why I'm not feeling the infection might be right," I say to eliminate the silence.

Luther meets my gaze. "I already know what Jasion will say. He's said it before. We need to find a cure from the creator in Ash Court, and that's not going to fucking happen."

The corded muscles in his neck pulse, and I feel the pressure on my shoulders, weighing me down. What he's saying between the lines is that Deimos is fucked. What I hate more than the guilt flaring through me is seeing it across Luther's face.

"You know, I didn't do this on purpose," I reply.

"Never said you did." He lifts his chin and lets out a breath. "I'm not blaming you, little wolf. I'm trying to work out how to save my brother."

I give myself a shake to dislodge the sadness in my thoughts and walk across to Luther. Sitting next to him, I reach over and place my hand on his to let him know he's not alone in this. Grief has a way of bringing out the worst and best in people, my foster mom used to tell me.

I don't know what to say, but when Luther twists his head my way, all I see are those vibrant dark eyes with a golden rim around the edges. They almost seem to glow when the sunlight hits them.

He clears his throat. "When I was fourteen, I fell off a horse. My foot got stuck in the stirrup and I was dragged by the startled animal. I was going to die, and I knew in my heart that this was how everyone would remember me—as the prince who couldn't ride a horse. Except I didn't realize that Deimos was galloping alongside us, determined to stop my steed. He managed to leap onto my horse's back and calm him down. I remember him jumping down and staring at me as I lay there beaten and bleeding. The first thing he said to me was, 'This proves I'm the better rider.'" Luther chuckles softly to himself at the memory. "He's always been competitive, but he's never let me down. So I can't lose him or let him be known as 'the prince taken by the Bloodcursed.'"

My heart nearly spills out of my chest at the realization of how much he's hurting.

He studies my hand in his lap before glancing back at me. "I haven't the headspace to show you the kingdom and help you remember our past as I promised. At least, not until I know my brother is safe."

I swallow the unease forming in my throat. "I wouldn't expect you to, not with this going on." My voice comes out ragged, making me sound like I lied. I smile at him to show him I understand, not revealing the disappointment in my gut. That makes me sound selfish, but I'm trapped in this realm away from family and friends, and there's danger at every corner. And I want Deimos to heal with every ounce of my being, but I'm supposedly from this realm, and this place would feel a little more home-like if I remembered what happened before.

"So what happened to you after the horse incident?" I ask to pull myself out of my sinking thoughts.

"We never told a soul. We explained the cuts and bruises by telling our mother that Deimos fought a boar that tried to attack me."

"You two are super close, right?"

He nods.

"What about Ahren?"

Luther shrugs. "Unfortunately, as the eldest, he was forced to take responsibilities from a young age and didn't spend as much time with us while growing up. While Deimos and I rode horses, he was forced to work with tutors on the etiquette of being a king."

"That's kind of sad for him," I say. "He lost his childhood."

"You may think it's sad, but he's been dreaming of being king ever since he could speak. So his king lessons were a dream come true for him, a promise of what will come."

Thinking back to my conversation with Ahren in Swindon, I know his real father had beat him senseless. Of course, he'll aspire to be as different from him as possible.

"I have a younger foster brother, and he's a little snot on good days."

Luther's brows pull together in confusion.

"He's just annoying and likes to irritate me," I explain.

The hinges to the door give a small groan, and we both turn around. Ahren marches inside the bedroom with no sign of the mage on his heels.

"Change of mind?" Luther asks.

"Jasion is occupied and will join us later."

"So what does Jasion do in the kingdom?" I ask.

"He's a mage and has a stronger affinity to the magic all fae possess," Ahren explains. "Usually, they carry control over four or five abilities. As soon as they show such signs at a young age, they are taken to temples for training, and most end up working for one of the four kingdoms in Wandering Realm as protectors and advisors."

"And to carry out the king's dirty work. Everyone knows they practice with dark magic," Luther announces automatically.

"Jasion is not like the rest of them," Ahren snaps.

Luther shakes his head. "I get that he's your friend, but if the king gave him an order, Jasion would carry it out like all mages, no matter the consequences. That's the part that I have problems with."

Ahren's jawline clenches, but he just shakes his head and moves toward Deimos as if they've had this argument too many times before. I don't know what to make of the mages, as this is all new to me, so I say nothing and sit next to the fairy before collecting her into my hands. She lifts her head and gives a small yawn, her mouth filled with dozens of tiny sharp teeth. She shifts in my hands and winces, glancing at her injured wing.

I place my palm over her wing, not touching it, and concentrate on driving what energy I have in me to the wing to help heal her. She has no curse on her that I am aware of, so this might work.

"Put that thing in here," Luther says.

I lift my head as he pulls open a drawer on a mahogany chest located across the room. It's elaborately engraved with spirals and looks like it belongs in an antique store.

"Deimos' clothes will make perfect cushioning for it to sleep," I suggest.

"You're not keeping that thing in this room with Deimos," Ahren growls. "Fairies attack and eat fae, and he's defenseless right now."

Luther clicks his tongue, and rage flares over his face. Before he explodes, I interrupt.

"How about the fairy sleeps in the drawer just while we stay in this room? Then I'll take her with me to wherever I'm staying."

"Sounds perfect to me," Luther responds eagerly.

Ahren watches the way I hold the fairy against my chest, and as if in a gesture of good faith, he nods.

I hastily tuck her in and leave the drawer open. "Sleep, little thing."

She curls in on herself on a blue, soft fabric. Her kind saved us, so I intend to care for her until she's ready to join her family once more.

"I'm going to arrange for food and drinks." Luther heads across the room. "I'm fucking starving."

The tension between him and Ahren fills the room, but I remind myself of what my foster mother said about grief.

Luther heads out of the room, his chin high and held confident as always. Though today, I saw a crack in his tough exterior.

Ahren leans against the windowsill, his hands deep in the pockets of his pants, his legs crossed at the ankles.

"Luther brought you to this realm two years ago," Ahren says, breaking the silence. "He found you through magic and never should have looked for you or carried you back to this realm."

His words don't make me feel wanted in the slightest. I don't know how to respond to that. Typically, I would answer his passive-aggressiveness with my own. Except I can feel Ahren's eyes on me as if expecting nothing less. "I never asked to be brought here."

Ahren's mouth flattens in a thin line. "But he did, and by doing so, he started the tragic events that led to you unleashing the curse on Shadow Court. The reason I'm telling you is so you know that he lives with that guilt every day."

His explanation takes me off guard. Here I thought his intention was to insult me, but all along, he just wanted me to see that Luther is hurting. Maybe he meant to do both. Since meeting Ahren, he's worn a grizzly exterior around me, infuriating me. Though I've seen snippets of what lies beneath that tough mask, so he's not who he pretends to be. He's aggressively caring and always thinking about everyone else. His past is horrifically tragic; his real father whipped Ahren whenever he disobeyed him. The past pain from the scars criss-crossing his back might give him the strength to keep fighting for what he believes is right, but to me, they're bruises on my mind, a reminder that those memories will always be with this strong, confident fae. No one deserves such a terrible upbringing.

"I didn't realize Luther blamed himself," I mutter.

Ahren pushes off the windowsill, his posture stiff. "I wish you knew how much it destroyed him when you disappeared back to Earth for two years."

He saunters over to Deimos and stands over him, watching him silently.

My stomach sinks right through me. Luther's heart lies damaged, and I need to talk to him. Some needy part of me wants to clear the ache from his soul and comfort him. But most of all, I wish the missing memories would just flood back already.

As I sit on the couch, I curl my legs under me. Ahren truly cares for both of his brothers, even if they growl at each other, and that touches me deeply.

A light breeze sweeps into the room and across my back, sending shivers down my spine.

I turn toward the door as a man pushes it open. He's large, intimidating, and scowling. A golden crown sits crooked on his head. He marches inside like a charging bull, and he's coming straight for me.

CHAPTER
SIX

GUENDOLYN

A fierce instinct drives me to stiffen. My head screams to run, but I can't move. What I want to do is disappear into thin air, but instead, I curl in on myself on the couch.

The king swings in my direction, each step striking the floorboards like a drumbeat counting down to my death.

He must remember me from the throne room. Shit! He must have seen me there...but how much did he witness? Me trying to close the portal? The princes protecting me? The fairies?

Ahren darts between me and his stepfather in a heartbeat. "King Tibout." He fists a hand to his heart two times. "We weren't expecting such an honorable visit." His voice sounds as strained as he looks.

"Stop fucking groveling and get out of my way. And I told you to not be so formal when we're not in the throne room."

King Tibout's frustration almost makes me think he wants Ahren to call him "Dad" or something more personable. Maybe the princes need to give their stepfather a chance?

But I somehow doubt the king will be that lenient with me when he realizes I opened a portal to the Bloodcursed in his throne room, and oh yeah, released the curse on his kingdom.

Nudging Ahren out of the way, the barrel of a man looms over me. He's changed his clothes and now wears a silvery blue coat tightly buttoned from his navel to his throat, as well as black pants and black, shiny boots. He stares at me as wildly as his unruly short, white hair.

"Who are you?" he demands, giving nothing away as to what he might have seen me do in the throne room. What exactly drove him to seek me out? Does he recognize every person living in his palace?

I feel overwhelmed and can't find my voice. I've just dealt with Bloodcursed and figuring out how to close portals, now this.

"Do you have a voice or are you mute, girl?" he persists.

"G-Gainy. That's my name," I mumble, hating that the first thing to pop in my head is that stupid name Deimos gave me.

"And where are you from, Gainy?"

I watch the wheels spin behind his eyes as he pieces it all together. A new person in his palace on the same day that Bloodcursed mysteriously break into the throne room. I would come to the same conclusion. But I can't let him know the truth. The frown sliding over his face doesn't belong to an understanding man.

My heart beats frantically, preparing to rip out of my chest and escape.

"I—"

"She's just a healer from the village in the kingdom. Why are you interrogating the poor girl?" Ahren remarks. "I would have thought you'd be more concerned with Deimos being bitten."

The king's head jerks toward the bed, his posture straightening. All the color drains from his face.

"For fuck's sake," Tibout snarls and storms across the room to Deimos' bedside. "Your mother is going to be devastated. Fuck!"

I slump back into the couch and can breathe again.

Ahren gives me a reassuring look and joins his stepfather. They talk to one another trying to figure out how Deimos must have gotten bitten, considering he's an exceptional warrior. I picture the scene in my mind. One Bloodcursed catching him off guard, then another moving fast to take him down. But talking about the past isn't going to fix the problem. All I care about is that they try to help Deimos, who's languishing in front of them.

I roll down the sleeve of my dress over my bandaged arm.

"Update me the moment you hear from Jasion," the king grumbles and sweeps toward me, sending a swarm of shivers up my arms. "I may still have a connection or two in the Ash Court."

Ahren clears his throat and meets the king's stare with one made of sorrow. "I've received grave news about the Master of Game," Ahren responds. "Gabel Wulfe passed in a terrible battle in the woods recently near Ash Court."

The king's features weaken, his grief deepened by the news. "How did I miss the message?"

My heart clenches at the memory of Gabel. He was a fae who believed in being fair and truthful to the people. It hurts to remember his death, which occurred while helping us battle Bloodcursed in the forest.

"Can't say." Ahren shrugs and steps toward the door, guiding the king out. Except the king turns back to me. He doesn't miss a beat, does he? I can't say I'm surprised, but I appreciate Ahren's attempt to get rid of his stepfather.

"You look familiar," the king addresses me. "Have we met before today?"

"You might have seen her down in the city," Ahren answers for me, his voice a lot smoother and convincing now.

"Your Majesty," I say quickly, "Luther encountered me healing my neighbor and asked me to come talk to your healers about a potential position to work here."

They both look at me strangely, and maybe I should have just let Ahren do the talking. But I've found if there's going to be a lie, it's always more convincing when two parties bounce off each other with the lie. Except with the way Ahren studies me, I'm guessing I must have said something out of place.

"Luther is hiring staff for my palace?" the king asks.

Ahren snorts a condescending laugh. "You know the locals; they'll say anything to be hired by the palace. Luther simply asked her to join us so he could ascertain how effective her healing actually is."

The king doesn't seem to buy it as he scrutinizes me with a stern gaze. I wheeze in a breath.

"That's me. I'd do anything to work here." God, I hate how desperate I sound.

With a scratch of his white beard, the king's lips tilt into a frown. "Is part of your healing capacity to consort with fairies and carry them around? You are aware they attack and devour fae?"

Ah, there it is. He'd seen me with the fairy in my grasp, and that bit of knowledge gives me the confidence to speak freely.

"If a person or animal is hurt, I don't discriminate, Your Majesty," I respond. "The fairies were clearly helping us defeat the Bloodcursed, so the least I could do was aid one who had her wing damaged."

"You mustn't be well versed in etiquette around royalty, or my sons have misled you to believe that meeting my gaze so freely is acceptable." There's a tightness in his voice.

Considering I looked him in the eyes before, I'm guessing what he really doesn't like is having anyone correct his assumptions. I swallow roughly, lower my head, and begrudgingly submit. I don't want him pushing for more answers and discovering I caused the breach today. "My apologies, Your Majesty."

Footfalls tapping the floorboards recede toward the door. I lift my gaze and turn as the king tosses over his shoulder, "If I find any more vermin fairies in my kingdom, girl, you will be held personally accountable."

I want to argue back, but I bite my tongue instead.

Luther barges into the room and skids to a halt at seeing his stepfather. Luther's panicked gaze flicks from him to me, then Ahren.

"You two, we need to talk about today," the king snarls at the princes. "Follow me," he orders as he storms out of the room. "We also need to move Deimos to the palace. Your mother will want him close to her."

Luther frantically looks at Ahren, who whispers something to Luther I can't hear, so I can only imagine he's bringing him up to speed on what we told the king. Then both of them head outside the room, shutting the door behind them.

I collapse on the couch and gasp for air. "Fuck!" Will my heart ever beat calmly again?

A knock comes at the door, and I leap onto my feet. What the hell now?

"Come in," I say.

The door swings wide and an older lady with brown, bouncy curls walks in backward. She's wearing a floor-length burgundy dress with a white apron tied around her waist. Wheeling a wooden food trolley covered by white fabric, she drags it across the room and places it next to the couch.

The maid's eyes sweep over to Deimos, and she does a small double tap to her heart, mumbling what I guess is a prayer under her breath.

When she looks at me, her eyes widen, and a smile tugs her lips upward as if she recognizes me. She waits for me to respond, but I don't know her. "My lady, you have returned. It has been years since I have seen you last. The princes wouldn't tell me what became of you, but blessings, you are safe."

One interaction with her, and I already like her. "I don't remember things too well," I admit.

"Oh, my lady, I had no idea. I'm sorry." She bows. "My name is Dana."

"Don't be sorry. It's wonderful to meet you, Dana. Again, apparently." I can't bring myself to tell her my name, as I have no clue what I called myself the last time I was at the mansion.

She quickly turns to the trolley and unwraps her goodies, a ceramic teapot and several stacked cups. Next to it is a large platter filled with what looks like scones and jam, triangle pastries, strips of dried meat, and a bowl of chopped fruit. My stomach responds with a growl. It feels like forever since I last ate.

She sets out the cutlery and napkins along with a gold plate for me.

"Enjoy, my lady." She bows and heads out of the room.

"Thank you," I call out after her. The moment the door clicks shut, I dive into the food and don't even bother with the cutlery. I taste a bit of everything. The triangles are cheese and spinach and taste divine. The beef jerky is a bit too salty for my liking, but the scones just melt on my tongue.

When I think I might burst, I collect the bowl of fruit made up of apples, pears, grapes, and a pink thing that looks like melon, then return to the couch.

Still no show from the princes, so I help myself to the fruit while staring outside at the snowflakes drifting downward.

It isn't long until a thick blanket of white has fallen over the green landscape. With this spectacular view, I can easily forget where I am. I glance over to Deimos, and my heart squeezes. "Please get well."

A sudden rush of cold air surges into the room as the door is shoved open, stealing with it my small reprieve. I twist around in my seat.

Ahren and Luther shut the door and march inside. Before they say a word, they're gorging on the remaining food, using their hands just as I had.

"Is everything all right?" I ask, embracing the fruit bowl in my lap.

"Yes," Luther answers. "Just had to convince our stepfather that I hired you temporarily to be my healer for the agonizing headaches I've been experiencing. I told him you'll be staying in the mansion with us while I require your services."

The way he said that almost made it sound like I'm offering him different services, and I can't stop the smirk from spreading across my lips.

"And we convinced him we knew nothing about the breach," Ahren adds.

Has Jasion come back?

Luther's low voice sweeps over my mind, smooth and dangerously sexy. His ability allows him to speak in people's minds. Though he told me that it's prohibited in the kingdom under the command of the king, he apparently doesn't care.

I meet his gaze and shake my head, even if my insides quiver from the intimacy of having his voice in my head.

He grabs more food and wanders over to Deimos. I don't say anything for a long moment and remember Ahren's words about Luther's pain.

"Are you all right?" Ahren asks, drawing my attention to him.

"I feel wrecked. This has been the most insane day of my life. I can't even remember how many times I almost died."

"Little wolf, I'll take you to your room. Maybe you should have an early night." It's more of a statement than a question.

Exhaustion ripples over me, and while I have no idea what time it is, I'm guessing it's late afternoon. "I'd like that," I answer.

Luther turns and walks right past me before leading me into the hallway.

"Good night," I say to Ahren as I quickly go and collect the blue-winged fairy from her drawer and take her with me. She's half-asleep and hardly notices I'm carrying her again.

Luther doesn't say a word to me as we travel down the corridors. Left and right, we turn so many times, I completely lose track of how to get back to Deimos. Not that he'll be there by tomorrow, as the king will have him moved to the palace. Luther stops near a huge black door and opens it for me.

"This isn't the room you brought me into when I first arrived at the mansion. Why are you changing my bedroom?" Paranoia spikes my question.

"This room is safer. Lock the door from the inside," he tells me as he stands tall near the doorway, making no attempt to lean closer and steal a kiss or remind me of what we once had.

"Sleep well." He reaches over to slide a loose strand of hair out of my eye. For those few moments, I expect more from him. Words that everything will be alright, a hug—damn, anything but this cold demeanor.

Instinctively, I lean against his touch, but he pulls away. I blink at him, my heart skipping a beat.

"See you in the morning, little wolf." He starts walking away, his head bowed forward, and the shadows swallow him. When he vanishes, the hallway stands silent. Too silent for my liking, so I quickly shut the door and lock it. Then with the fairy in hand, I step deeper into the enormous room. Black velvet curtains cover the windows, and the walls are made of dark granite. A huge stone fireplace cracks and spits embers into the metal grill, throwing light over the two long couches facing each other, and a wooden coffee table sits between them.

To my left stands a doorway to another room, and inside I discover a generous bed with a mahogany headboard and dozens of frilled pillows on one end. Near the bed is a chamber pot, and I cringe at the idea of using it, but I'm no longer on Earth. Gotta do like the locals.

"Well, looks like this is our place to share for the night."

The fairy looks at me from half-closed eyes. She looks worn down, and I worry about how much she's sleeping. But what do I know about fairies?

Using the pillows, I make her a little nest in the corner of the room and lay her in the center, where she curls in on herself and is already making tiny snoring sounds. I don't for a second have any concerns that she'll attack me during the night. I trust her, which I know is strange, but I do.

Considering there's nothing else to do in this room, I yawn and climb into bed only to find a deep blue nightgown tucked under a pillow. I get changed, jump into bed, and curl up under the blanket.

I don't want to overthink everything from today.

I need sleep, and I pray tomorrow makes up for today being an asshole of a day.

I WAKE with the driest mouth in the world. I gasp as I try to swallow, but it's impossible.

Golden flames from the fireplace in the other room chase away the shadows in the bedroom.

Getting out of bed, I stretch and somehow feel semi-normal. When I peer past the heavy curtains, night has claimed the landscape but I can't see much else. I look down to my bitten arm and pull back the bandages to find the mark completely healed over. Running my fingers over the skin, there's not a bump or bruise. How in the world did that happen? How did I end up immune to the Bloodcursed's bite?

I pad on bare feet into the main room, still dressed in the nightgown. I remove the bandage from my arm before placing it on a side table. I search the room, but there are no water bottles or glasses or any indication of water. Swinging toward the door, I unlock it and stick my head out. It's dark, and the globes of light dangling from the ceiling illuminate the walls and an array of animal statues. The kitchen is bound to be somewhere

nearby, so I pull the door shut behind me and decide to go left, the direction Luther headed after leaving my room.

I wander through the mansion corridors quickly, trying random doors, but they're all locked. From what I've seen, only the princes live in the main rooms and the helpers stay in their own quarters, probably downstairs.

The next door I try ends up being a small medieval-looking bathroom. There's a long bench against the back wall with a wooden lid located in the middle. I open it and find a hole like outhouses. To my surprise, it doesn't smell, so I shut the door and ease the buildup in my bladder.

Once I'm back out, I continue my search until I bump into Dana around the next corner.

She leaps back, startled by my presence. "My lady, what are you doing out here and in your nightdress?" That part seems to shock her the most.

"I'm thirsty and looking for water."

She tsks and rushes into a room behind her. Inside, the light is bright, and I spot a small kitchen with a counter on one side and a cast-iron stove on the other. Moments later, she re-emerges and hands me a smooth silver goblet filled with water.

"Thanks." I drink the whole thing down in several mouthfuls, and it's the best-tasting water ever. I'm guessing this is what real mountain water should taste like, not the stuff in grocery stores.

She collects the goblet from my hand. "Now quickly return to your chamber. No respectable lady would ever be caught in her nightdress."

Not sure I can ever call myself respectable, but I give her a nod. "Thank you." Then I pivot on my heels and hurry back the way I came.

I don't know how long I've walked around, but I'm certain I've gone in a circle a few times as I eye the same statue of a roaring lion.

Clunk.

I flinch and tear my gaze from the lion and look farther down the hall to where the sound came from. One of the doors sits slightly ajar, and curiosity has me padding towards it on bare feet. Inching closer, I peer through the sliver of a gap into a room not too different from Deimos'. I shift to see more of the room, and Ahren comes into view. He's sitting on the couch in front of a blazing fire, and my mouth drops open at the sight.

He's not wearing a stitch of clothing.

CHAPTER

SEVEN

GUENDOLYN

Ahren is reclined on the couch, his long fingers wrapped around his heavy cock. Head tilted back, eyes shut, he's oblivious to me watching him. The golden hue from the fireplace illuminates his insanely perfect body—his strong chest muscles, his muscular bicep flexing with each stroke. His shaft seems to tremble in his grip, as if he's barely holding back from climaxing. Excitement ripples over my body at having accidentally stumbled over this scene, and I know that I will never forget it.

I see every delicious inch of him, and God, he's hot as hell. Long, powerful legs lead up to tight balls and an almost golden blond thatch of hair at the base of his cock. A drizzle of light hair runs down the middle of his abs. He is completely absorbed, and seeing such a powerful man succumb to this desire undoes me.

I should run away embarrassed and not invade his private moment, but I can't move. I can't look away. How can I when I have a front-row seat to a dirty fantasy that has crossed my mind more than a few times?

My heart is practically in my mouth, and I am utterly fascinated. My mind imagines what it would be like to be with a fae like him, to have him strip me of my clothes. Would he be rough or gentle?

I clench my thighs together, intensifying the ache building inside me, but nothing helps when this is the hottest thing I've ever watched. Gnawing on my lower lip, I'm struggling with the intensity pulsing through me. I reach down and push the bunched-up fabric of my nightdress

342

between my thighs. My fingers press up against my heat, and I imagine him touching me there.

His hot skin against mine, his kisses on me.

My heart pounds in my ears, and I'm breathing rapidly. I'm turned on, and everything is spinning within me.

There are so many things wrong with this situation, yet I can't convince myself to go. Everything about Ahren captivates me. His hand moves faster, and my breaths match his rapid actions.

This is actually happening.

My mind screams to get out of here. To run back to my room and lock myself inside.

I squeeze my thighs even more as I'm imagine him inside me, while my nipples harden and press against the fabric of my nightdress.

What is wrong with me, and why am I enjoying watching this? This isn't me. Except, who am I kidding? I am lapping up the sexy scene in front of me and nothing will make me turn away.

Then he growls, and his chest arches. A small moan presses on the back of my throat, the heat inside me melting into liquid fire. It drips down the inside of my thighs. If I had worn my underwear before I went to bed, they'd be soaked now.

All I can picture is Ahren and me naked, doing filthy things.

How can this fae be so incredibly tempting when most conversations with him leave me frustrated as hell? Yet here I am imagining myself with him. Thinking of what Ahren would be like makes it so I can barely breathe, and a thick lump lodges in my throat.

I stare at this prince palming his cock, pumping his hand up and down.

A keening, satisfied groan spills from his lips. His dick stiffens and his balls contract, then thick ropes of cum spew from the head.

Sucking in a sharp breath, I clasp my hand over my mouth.

Ahren jerks his head forward as if hearing me. I jolt back, turn, and run. I don't stop, don't dare stop.

God, please don't let him have seen me.

I look behind me as a shadow spills from inside the room. Throwing myself around the corner, I sprint, unsure exactly where I'm going, but somehow I find my way back to my room. I rush inside and close the door silently, then lock it.

Running to my bed and jumping under the covers, I lie there, my whole body thumping with each heartbeat.

The reality that he might have seen me blasts through my mind like a storm. My cheeks are burning with the shame of being caught. I'm breathing so hard, I might be hyperventilating. I lie in utter silence, expecting a knock at my door, but it never comes. All I can picture is him filling me, stretching me to the point where the pain twists with pleasure, where I scream for more.

The image of his hand stroking the thick length of his cock stays with me. It never leaves me, even when I fall into sleep.

Sitting on a balcony with the three princes sends shivers up my spine. I barely know them, yet they stare at me hungrily from their seats in front of me.

A servant comes in carrying a silver platter and hands Ahren a drink in a jewel-studded crystal goblet, the rest of which he hands to the other two princes, then me. I accept and drink two mouthfuls, quenching my dried throat. "So, I'm a lost girl from this world, you say." I press the goblet to my lips, finishing the refreshing minty iced tea. The man refills my drink from a golden pitcher.

"Something like that," Luther adds.

I shift in my seat. They might be the most beautiful men in the world, but they lie through their teeth and keep secrets. The truth hides behind their gazes and their clipped responses.

"If I'm from this place, where are my parents?" I ask.

Something shifts behind Ahren's eyes but vanishes as quickly as it came. "There's no news on your parents. We've searched." The corner of his eye twitches.

Liar. Big, fat liar.

My breath comes too fast, and I can't hold back the words. "If you don't intend to tell me the truth, don't mock me with lies," I retort. "Speak honestly."

Never insult them, the maid told me earlier.

Ahren bristles, his nostrils flaring as he glares at me with narrowing eyes. "Do not challenge me," he roars, his hands gripping the arms of his chair. "On your knees."

Fear strangles me, and I look to Luther for help, but he sits back with a curious expression, like he's goddamn enjoying himself.

I shouldn't have said anything when I have absolutely nothing nice to say, but the response flew out. "Like I told your brother, I'm not yours to control. You hide so much behind that smile, but like someone once told me, we all have shadows. I'd rather we speak the truth."

Never say no to the princes, the maid also said.

Ahren shoots to his feet, his expression twisting and warping. It darkens, but his gaze never leaves me. He marches closer, and panic soars through me. I jolt to my feet, but he moves too fast. His hand juts out and seizes me by the throat, squeezing.

I grasp for his hand, pulling at the fingers that block my breathing. Terror... real terror locks around me like a straitjacket. This is real, and this madman will kill me. Tears spring to my eyes.

"Little girl, you keep pushing me," he spits. "Next time, you'll learn how to fly off my balcony."

~

MY EYES FLUTTER open to a loud banging at the door. It takes me moments to remember where I am and what happened last night. My mind is still drowning in a dream I had of the princes. Like previous visions I've had since arriving at the kingdom, this one stays crisp and clear with me. I remember the moment like it just happened... I can't remember the context of how we came to be on the balcony, but the moment definitely happened.

Why doesn't it surprise me that when I met Ahren for the first time, he was a standoffish ass who threatened to kill me? I know those visions are snippets into my past and memories that refuse to completely unlock for me. Now, I can't get the image of him naked out of my head.

Sunlight pours in from the gaps around the curtains on the windows and even more floods in through the doorway from the main room.

Knock. Knock.

I flinch.

God, please don't let it be Ahren.

I scramble quickly out of bed, pushing aside the blankets, and drop my bare feet to the cold floorboards.

"Who is it?" I call out as I rush toward the door.

"My lady, it's Dana. I've come to take you for your morning bath."

"Bath? I don't need a bath." I unlock the door and pull it open.

A huge brown dog leaps at me. I scream from the shock and reel backward as the animal bowls into me. My chest heaves for air as I scramble away, unsure if this thing is friendly or wants to eat me.

"Do you remember Sir Wolf-A-Lot, my lady?" Dana asks from the doorway, her smile wide as if she planned this so-called surprise.

"Is he going to eat me?"

She laughs and claps her hands. The dog sits in front of me obediently. He's larger than a big German Shepard. He stares up at me with black eyes, his long sharp ears upright, and his thin tail swinging side to side. The end is tipped with a barbed club.

"Is he a hellhound?" I ask, gaining myself a puzzled look from Dana.

"He's an ordinary dog, my lady."

Ordinary my ass, but I smile regardless.

"He belongs to Luther. On your last visit, you and Sir Wolf-A-Lot bonded."

We did? I look down at the dog, who seems to be waiting for a response. I reach over gingerly and pat his head, his dark fur feeling coarse under my hand.

"Hey, boy, do you remember me?" At my voice, he's on his feet and nudging his head into my arm to keep scratching him. Okay, maybe he's not so bad after all.

"Are you ready for a bath now?" Dana asks, impatience growing in her voice.

"Give me a moment."

I hastily dart back into the bedroom and check on my little blue-winged fairy.

"Hey, little one. How are you feeling?" I cross the room, only to find her little nest is empty. I stiffen. Where is she?

I scan the walls and ceiling, then kneel next to the bed and look underneath. Nothing.

Maybe she went into the other room. Frantically, I rush back out, worried about the dog spotting her.

Dana looks displeased in the doorway, arms folded over her chest, but the room shows no sign of the fairy. My gut tightens as I remember the king's warning. *If I find any vermin fairies in my kingdom, girl, you will be held personally accountable.*

Just great.

"Are you ready, my lady?"

I turn to Dana. "Did you see anything rush out of the room while you were standing there?"

Her brows pinch together. Of course she'd remember seeing a fairy fly out of here. God, what if she snuck out last night when I went for a drink of water? This is all I need. The only positive is that the king doesn't live in this mansion. I pray the little fairy didn't leave this building and get caught up where she shouldn't.

"This way," Dana commands as she hurries me with a wave of her hand, being rather pushy. I shut the door once Sir Wolf-A-Lot comes out, just in case she's hiding somewhere in there.

The bathroom is across the mansion. Inside the small room is an elaborate white freestanding tub with golden clawed feet, half-filled with water, but my first thought goes to the princes.

"Any news on Deimos?" I ask as I step into the room, which smells like burning incense. Two light globes dangle from the ceiling, illuminating the space.

"No change yet," Dana answers. "It's so tragic. Deimos is the most mischievous of the princes, but also the one who jumps into any battle first. Poor boy. He might lose his life, and all before he finds a princess to share it with. You know, my lady," Dana continues as she picks up several towels from the shelves on the wall and places them on a table near the tub, "before the curse was placed on our kingdom, the king was arranging a grand ball for the princes to find their prospective wives. He invited all the other royal families. It was going to be the biggest and most elaborate celebration."

I'm lost for words as my mind bounces back and forth like a tennis match between the potential of losing Deimos to the infection and his marriage plans if he survives.

"Once the mages find a way to eradicate the curse, the king will marry off the princes. It's how he secures his allegiances to other family houses."

After a long pause and hesitation, I say, "I'm happy for them."

Except in all honesty, I'm not. The thought of the king finding the princes future wives carves through me like a blade. I shouldn't be jealous, as they are royalty. I'm from the enemy court and don't even belong in this realm. And it's not like I can have all three of them. Even if I could marry one, that's still only one of them, and I'm not sure I'd be okay with that, based on the feelings I seem to have for all three.

I'm barely getting to know them, but I can't ignore the way my heart bangs in my chest in their presence. How I can't stop thinking of Deimos' and Luther's lips on my mouth, how my mind fills with images of Ahren naked.

"Quickly now, before the water gets cold," Dana reprimands me, and I begin to undress.

"What about Luther or Ahren? Have you seen them this morning?" Just saying Ahren's name floods me with a burning desire. I'm not sure I can ever look at him again without picturing him with his hand on his huge cock. My cheeks burn from the memory alone, so how am I meant to act normal around him now? Worse, I'm still praying he doesn't know it was me spying on him last night. I know I'll see the answer the moment I look him in the eyes, but at this moment, I decide on three things.

One, I won't hide from him.

Two, if he did see me last night, then I'll act like it never happened.

Three, no more sneaking around the mansion at night.

"Only Luther, my lady," Dana replies. "He instructed me to bathe, dress, and feed you."

I may as well do as she commands and enjoy it while I can.

"HONEY WITH YOUR PORRIDGE?" Dana asks as she fills my silver cup with more orange juice.

"Yes, please."

She pours some thick honey over my porridge and then heads back into the kitchen while I sit alone in a dining room at a large, round table in the middle. The surface is polished to a shine while the edges are carved with tiny wings. Silver vases overflowing with flowers fill the shelves against the walls.

A fire roars in the fireplace. Across from the table, the windows are floor-to-ceiling with no curtains, just the most spectacular view of mountains coated in white. Pine trees sparkle in the sunlight from the snow dusting them. I eat the porridge while staring outside, daydreaming that I'm not in a dangerous place.

"Gainy, what an opportune moment to catch you," a man murmurs.

I twist around in my seat as Jasion walks into the room, his presence making me stiffen.

His long, black robe-skirt sashays around his ankles, and the crystal eyes in the skull hanging from his chest seem to glint in the sunlight. He's bare chested and not a masculine man, but toned. Just looking at him bare-chested makes me cold.

I'm wearing a long-sleeved dress with buttons running from my cleavage to my stomach, cinched in around the waist, and my skirt flows to my ankles in soft waves. The fabric is thicker than it looks and comfortably warm. Still, I feel cold at the thought of being as exposed as this fae.

"Can I join you?" he asks.

"Of course."

He sits one seat away from me just as Dana returns. She freezes in the doorway to the kitchen after seeing him.

"Tea, please," he calls out, lifting his chin in her direction.

She nods nervously and darts back into the kitchen.

"She seems scared of you," I say.

Jasion laughs softly, like my comment somehow makes him proud of the maid's reaction. He's a handsome man with dark eyes and long lashes, full lips, and a wide jawline. Tiny black feathers twist through white hair cut short that sits messily around his face, and his pointy ears poke upward through it.

"And you look at me like you've never seen a mage before."

"I've seen you around, but many down in the city know that it's not wise to approach a mage," I lie, going purely on instinct and Dana's reaction.

"Are we that horribly thought of in the city?"

"I wouldn't say horribly, but you have to admit your image alone is intimidating."

Maybe I've said too much, as he raises a brow. "The ritual garb can make others wary of us. But it also lets them know we are here to keep the kingdom safe from the curse and Bloodcursed surrounding our home."

I bite my tongue in response. As a supposed local, I should watch my words and perhaps play the meek female.

Our gazes lock.

Does he see through my thoughts?

The door slaps shut, and I flinch as I look up. Dana rushes over carrying a tray with a teapot and two cups. She sets them before us without a word. I catch her cutting me a side look before she hurries away, her eyes holding a warning I can only imagine relates to Jasion.

"Thank you," he says, watching her head back into the kitchen before taking his time to pour us each a cup of tea. It smells overly sweet. "You're a fascinating woman, Gainy."

I cringe on the inside at the way he says my fake name. Instead of letting him see my discomfort, I stare at this dangerous man who sends shivers over my skin. Ahren trusts him, though I doubt the man's loyalty would extend to not reporting an enemy in their court to the king.

"You don't have to compliment me." I reach for my cup of tea and blow over the top of it. My attention lingers on the symbols inked on his cheeks.

Catching me staring, he says, "They are ancient runes, and each one represents an ability I master."

I look closer, having no clue what any of the patterns mean. "It must have hurt getting them."

"Rewards don't come without pain."

I hadn't planned on getting into a full-on conversation with him, but the questions keep rolling off my tongue. "So you're saying the markings are more than just decorative?"

A smirk touches the edges of his lips. "Correct."

I raise the cup to my lips and sip the honeyed drink. The mage watches me as if trying to decipher me.

"Does it ever worry you that your enemies can learn of your power by reading the runes before a great battle?"

He breaks out laughing again. "You have a tremendous imagination. Mages never go to battle. We are the foundations behind the scenes." He leans closer. "Excuse my bluntness, but how does a simple healer from the city attract the attention of the princes? These are deadly times, and trusting the wrong person can be a horrible mistake to make."

There's so much being said between us without words.

"I've known Ahren for a long time, and he's never held back secrets from me...until now." His gaze burrows through me. What I see reflected back at me is determination and jealousy.

I swallow the thickness in my throat. "Luther saw promise in my ability. And he offered to pay me to help him." I lower my eyes to let him think he's intimidating me. Hell, I am squirming in my seat, but he's trying to get me to tell him the truth.

"Perhaps he saw a few things in you." The corners of his mouth quirk as he implies I am more than a healer to Luther. I seethe on the inside but say nothing.

He reaches his hand over, palm side up. "Please, may I have your hand?"

I swallow hard. "Why?" My voice comes out as a whisper.

"I saw you handling the fairy, and I haven't yet met anyone capable of doing so. I want to feel the strength of your healing ability."

When I don't offer him my hand, he says, "Legends tell us the fairy race is older than fae and their magic comes from the gods themselves. The power was given to them by the gods back in the days when fairies ruled this world."

My interest is piqued. "Then why do they attack fae?"

"There's an old account I read in an ancient text that told one version of the story. When fairies first appeared in the Wandering Realm, they were full-sized, like you and I. Many centuries later, the first fae came into existence. The king of the fae was said to have fallen in love with the queen of the fairies. When she rejected his offer of marriage, he kidnapped her and raped her. But it wasn't enough for him, so he kept her imprisoned as his own."

"What a fucking monster."

Jasion nods. "It wasn't long before she fell pregnant, and on the day her daughter was born, she used the child's placenta to cast a deadly curse on the fae. She hexed them to be forever hunted down. But curses born of fury are temperamental things, and the curse turned the queen and her people into the fairies you see today. Ferocious creatures who live off fae flesh."

"That's a tragic story," I say, so captivated by the story that I only now notice my hand sitting in his grasp.

"Legends usually are."

I jerk back, but his grip tightens and holds me still. "Luther is right—your power is incredibly strong."

Suddenly, his eyes roll back into his head, leaving behind only white. A spark races up my arm. Blue lines erupt and jump from my hand to his.

Flinching, I rip my hand from his with such force that I fall backward out of my seat. Scrambling quickly, I get to my feet. My heart is beating too fast, and panic claws at my insides. I can't have this mage know I can open portals.

He's on his feet, his eyes back to normal, and the look on his face is indescribable.

Confusion.

Fear.

Determination.

He scans me head to toe as if he's seeing me for the first time. "Who are you?"

"I-I told you already. I should go." I back away toward the kitchen door, not lifting my gaze from Jasion.

He moves with such speed, all I feel is the movement of air buffeting into me. Towering over me, he brings his mouth to my ear. "Gainy, there are fae in this kingdom way more dangerous than me."

What does he know about me? Has Ahren said something to him? I can't bring myself to ask without somehow sounding guilty, though the questions bubble in my mind.

"Don't do anything stupid. You can trust me," he says.

I want to laugh in his face at the idea that he'd think I am that foolish. If someone needs to ask to be trusted, then my alarm bells go off.

Just then, Dana walks into the room. Sighing with relief, I use that moment for my escape. I spin toward her and take fast steps into the kitchen.

I just need to get away from the mage before he learns the truth about me.

EIGHT

"Deimos has a week," I announce as I march into the council room.

The king stares at me with frustration in his eyes. He's alone, sitting on a golden chair behind a round desk. It's made of timber from Alethian trees. The wood is as black as the night and said to be as ancient as the fae race itself. These trees only grow in the east in a secured woodland where chopping them is prohibited. Queen Titania runs one of the two kingdoms in the east. She gifted my stepfather the table as a gesture of expectation that we would continue trading for our precious stones. Shadow Court's riches come from the wealth under our feet. In exchange, our court receives a constant supply of farm animals, food, and spices for our growing population.

Titania also has her eyes on bonding our courts and is known for collecting husbands. Those poor suckers have a tendency of mysteriously vanishing after a few years of marriage.

"A fucking week," the king growls, his lips twisting. "Fuck."

There are moments when King Tibout surprises me and shows he cares for us. Like now, his level of anger isn't what I expect. Not from the king who's been known to not speak to us for a month, or sends us orders through advisors, or goes on visits to other kingdoms that we don't find out about until weeks into his trip. He's not the most thoughtful of stepfathers, but seeing him give a fuck about Deimos gives me hope that he's not another asshole like our biological father.

"There's only one solution," I respond. I've been thinking about this most of the night, and it's the only way.

The king locks eyes with me. "You're talking about going to Ash Court, aren't you? It has crossed my mind as well. With Gabel gone, I know only one other person in that court who can possibly help." He sighs heavily and gets up from his seat. Pulling down on his gold, embellished tunic, he sighs once again as he turns his back to me. A black cloak with fur lining hangs from his shoulders. He stares out the enormous arched window at the royal gardens that include a small hedge maze. Snow covers everything in sight. Only the king and my mother frequent the location, but even during winter, the paths are swept. No one else would dare go into the royal gardens.

"Who's your contact?" I ask.

The king turns to me abruptly, his nose wrinkled. "You aren't going on this mission."

"Like hell I'm not. My brother's life hangs in the balance. I'm not trusting anyone else." I hold his stare and see the fury burning behind his eyes. "Who else do you trust to go into the enemy court and not fuck it up or change allegiances if they're caught?" I'm not backing down.

He grits his jaw. "You're just as infuriating as your mother. I'll think about it."

"I'm going on this mission, no matter what you say," I declare, standing my ground.

His gaze narrows, a determination washing over his face. No king accepts being challenged, but I don't give a shit. Not this time.

"Fuck! Fine, but take Luther." He huffs loudly. "That boy can fight better than my best soldiers. But if either of you get killed, your mother will cut my balls off, and I'll come after you in the underworld. Understood? Just don't get hurt."

"We'll try not to die." I hold back the gloating grin tugging the corners of my mouth. There are only two other times where the king showed us concern. When we first arrived at the kingdom and he offered us anything we wanted. And when my real father threatened to kill us because he's a fucking asshole.

"Sit," the king orders, and we sit across from each other at his table.

"In the Ash Court, there's a woman by the name of Relle." His mouth tightens, and the way he licks his teeth, delaying the information, tells me everything.

"You keep a lover in the enemy court?" I growl.

He scrunches up his face as if I insulted him. "Nothing like that. Relle is someone who helped me when I visited Ash Court."

I have so many questions about why he'd risk going to the enemy kingdom, but I don't ask.

"Relle used to provide me with some insider information," the king says, "but it has been years since I last heard from her. I don't know what happened to make her fall silent."

"Would she still help you?" I ask.

He pauses, thinking my question through. "I'll arrange to send her a bird carrier. If she responds, then she will be your key to get into Ash Court. If not, then you'll need to break in. Speak to my mages for a masking spell for concealment when you enter the Ash Court." He reclines in his seat. "So once you get inside, what's your plan? Find the mage who cast the spell and bring him back here so he can create a cure?"

I stiffen. "I'll cut open his throat after he gives me the cure then and there."

"Risky." The king clicks his tongue again.

So is kidnapping a fucking mage, but I say nothing. "I'll ask Jasion for a trapping spell, something to help me incapacitate the mage while I find out where he keeps an antidote."

Jasion told me once that Shadow Court mages keep cures of every spell they cast as backup should anything go wrong, so I just need to pray Unseelie mages follow this rule as well, then track the potion down and bring it back home.

"And what about the girl who unleashed the curse two years ago? Guendolyn. Any news on her whereabouts?" He cuts me a hard stare. The king's eyes narrow, and I know the look.

Everyone knows of the fae girl who was taken from our world as a child, along with her prophecy. There are so many theories about who exactly she is, but no one knows the truth except that she came from Ash Court.

But revealing that Guendolyn is in our kingdom comes with too many complications. My stepfather will imprison her until we find a cure, then kill her afterward for being an Unseelie and cursing his kingdom. The mages, including Jasion, won't stop until they have her to experiment on. They are obsessed with magic, and Guendolyn has a rare power I haven't seen others carry—opening portals between realms without the use of potions, not to mention her connection to fairies. Then there's the fae of Ash Court. They want her dead because if she dies, the curse over our kingdom can never be broken.

I look up to see the king watching me, waiting for a response about Guendolyn. "She must be hiding somewhere," I suggest. "If she's dead, we would have felt her death from the magic around us."

This is the reason we brought Guendolyn back to the Wandering Realm, the reason we risked so much. To ensure the Ash Court didn't get to her first and kill her.

I won't deny that there's also a fear I hold on to that anyone else who finds her will break her. We live in a brutal world where trusting anyone is the quickest way to get killed. And there's a vulnerability, an innocence to Guendolyn, no matter how much she fights back. She's not used to the cruelty of our world, and part of me just wants to shield her.

As much as that girl infuriates me, I'm fucking obsessed with her. I hate that I even have that thought, but she's managed to wriggle under my skin. Just last night she spied on me, and I put on a fucking show for her. I sensed her at the door, peering in, watching me, devouring me with her eyes. Every tug, every moan came from imagining it was her sweet pussy riding me.

"All right." The king's voice rips me out of my thoughts, and he straightens his posture. "Is that all?"

I clear my throat. "Yes. I'll talk with Jasion and start arranging the trip."

My stepfather grumbles and huffs an expelled breath. "Are you certain you trust Jasion?"

"I don't understand your dislike of him," I suddenly say. Bravely or foolishly, I want to understand. If I one day take the throne of Shadow Court, I want Jasion by my side as my advisor. That means I can't have the king getting rid of him in the meantime.

"He questions everything I say," the king finally responds. "And I don't trust people who challenge me in public like they hope to humiliate me." He leans closer. "I know you think he's your friend and you two get along, but the fae who appear the most helpful are the first to stab you in the back. Don't you forget that, boy." He sits back. "I don't get close to my mages for that exact reason. Mages are starved for power. They'll do anything to get more and destroy anyone in their way. You think the ones who work for me haven't eyed Jasion and the favors you give him?"

"Maybe they need to be reminded of their place," I state, not wanting to believe Jasion is like the others. We grew up together, saved each other's asses more times than I can count. So to think I can't trust him leaves a bitter taste in my mouth. He's more than a mage, he's a good friend.

The king is notoriously paranoid, so I decide to take his advice with a grain of salt.

I stand as the door swings open and my mother walks in.

She smiles at seeing me, her crystal green eyes bleary from crying by Deimos' side. Her attentiveness over him reminds me of the times she'd lull us to sleep by telling us tales as children. My mother is strong and may not be well-liked by everyone, but after our father left her, she never gave up on us and did everything to protect us.

She spins to shut the door, her long, red velvet dress swirling around her ankles. It's a plain gown with no embellishments, and she wears no tiara today. Her white hair falls over her shoulders in curls.

"Ahren." She walks over quickly, cupping my face. "You need some sun, my son. You are looking pale today." Her thumb slides over a healed cut under my eye.

The king growls, "Don't baby him."

"I will keep that in mind, Mother," I say as I kiss her on each cheek. "I must go."

She releases me and turns to my stepfather. "Any updates on a cure for Deimos?" The pain in her voice has me curling in on myself on the inside. This is why I have to be the one to get the cure. I trust no one else.

I growl under my breath and march out of the room, my mood suddenly soured.

Guen

A FLUTTER of movement catches my attention from down the hallway. Something blue, to be more precise.

Blue wings.

My heart skips a beat as I whip around and race after the fairy. I've been searching the halls for her most of the day, and now that night crawls over the land, she finally shows.

The light globes that hang low from the ceilings throw shadows everywhere, but her blue wings stand out amid the marble and dark marble statues.

On quiet footsteps, I hurry toward her. In moments, I'm peeking around the lion statue. Only one wing sticks out from the shadows. She's balancing on the edge of the lion's tail, leaning over, stalking something.

I lash out and snatch her, my hands coiling around her body.

She startles, jolting in my hold, and her wings beat frantically. She twists her head toward me, teeth bared, lips peeled back. Even for her tiny size, she's intimidating.

"It's just me," I say.

Her fear morphs into a furrowed brow, her nose scrunching up. She looks back in front of her just as a gray mouse scurries away for its life. The fairy makes a huffing sound as she looks up at me and hisses her disapproval.

"If you didn't run away, I could have fed you," I say. "Something a lot tastier than a mouse."

She shakes her head as if she understands me.

"You scared the crap out of me. Thank god you didn't venture into the palace. The king would have had us both killed," I whisper.

She hisses at the mention of death.

"Agreed. But the good news is you're looking much better now. Your wing has healed." Perhaps my earlier touch helped her after all, or fairies naturally heal fast? All that matters is that I found her. "Now we're going back to my room, and I'll get you some food."

More hissing.

"Is that the only sound you make? Hmm... Maybe I'll call you that from now on. Hiss. How does that sound?"

She shakes her head, hissing once more, and I laugh at how adorable she looks.

When the murmur of voices comes from somewhere down the hall, I pause and we both stare in that direction. No one's there, not yet anyway.

Bringing the fairy close to my chest, I rush us back toward my room. Through turn after turn down dark hallways filled with statues and paintings, I check for anyone around while the little fairy wriggles for escape.

"Hold on, Hiss. I'll get you food. You can't be caught, or we're both in big shit."

Her wings flutter wildly as I navigate around another corner to my room.

Footfalls strike the floorboards farther behind me, and I glance back.

Shadows emerge from a corridor. My heart is racing and I throw myself into my room and shut the door. My heart pounding, I press my back to the wall for a moment to catch my breath. Hiss takes off from my grasp and flaps wildly around the room, swooping all over the place before hovering near the window. She stares outside, pushing at the glass with her tiny hands.

"You want to go home, don't you?" I cross the room and reach for the lock. One twist, and I push open the window. A cool breeze swishes into the room, fluttering through my hair.

"Well, if you're ready, you are free, little one."

She darts closer, holding something sparkling in her hands. A nice-sized ruby.

My eyes bug out as I imagine her stealing it from the king's crown or something.

"Where did you get that from?" I reprimand.

She hisses at me, her lips peeling back as she draws the crystal tightly to her chest.

"You can't take that!" I jut my arm out as she buzzes right past me to the window.

Frantically, I grapple to snatch her out of the air before she escapes. I catch her arm, but she freaking bites me. Those sharp teeth sink into my thumb.

Crying out, I flinch back.

Hiss zips right out the window with the ruby, like a little klepto. She looks back at me as she hovers out of reach, licking blood from her teeth. I wipe my stinging, bloody thumb.

Eirian.

The word floats over my thoughts like a cobweb, leaving me shivering.

Hiss' wings beat as snowflakes land on her head and shoulders. She stares at me with such intensity, I expect her to speak to me.

Eirian.

The word comes again.

A sudden, loud crack erupts behind me.

I jump in my shoes and spin around as Dana shoves open the door with the wheeled cart in her hands. She raises her head to see me and startles.

"My lady, you scared me. I didn't expect anyone here." Her gaze flips to the window. "It's freezing outside."

I nod and quickly turn to shut the window, searching for Hiss. But she's gone with the jewel and all she's left me with is a cryptic word that makes me wonder if it's her name.

"It looks like a storm is coming in tonight," Dana explains as she bustles inside with fresh bedclothes, a bowl of fruit, and a silver jug of water.

I stand near the fireplace to chase the cold from my hands.

"Dana," I say as I turn to face her, warming my back against the flames. "Have you heard of the word *Eirian*?"

She looks up from her cart, her eyes drifting farther upward as she thinks about it. Then she shakes her head. "Is it a location, my lady?"

"I don't know."

"Well, there's a small library in the mansion that might hold the answer."

I perk up at her response. "Where is it?"

"It sits one corridor down from the kitchen. I can take you there once I'm finished."

"No, that's fine. I can find it." I'll visit the library. There are so many things I intend to research - including the word *Eirian*, to see if it is a name or maybe it's a type of fairy. Then I want to find some background on mages to better understand their role. The conversation I had with Jasion still sits heavily on my mind. I like to think I'm a good judge of character, but with him, my instincts are all over the place.

Most days are fucked, but today is fucked up gloriously.

I've had enough of company. Enough of royal bullshit, of mages, of arranging transport for our upcoming trip to Ash Court. The only saving grace has been Luther, who stepped in and aided with securing a brand new carriage said to be impenetrable if we're ambushed by Bloodcursed. The problem will be getting it out of the kingdom without detection.

I round the corner back to my room and pause when I notice who's lingering near my shut door. I don't hold back the smirk tugging at my mouth, or the punch of my cock against my pants.

Guendolyn doesn't strike me as the type of woman who wants to sleep with just any man she crosses paths with. Yet she's back again.

I step up behind her, but she doesn't hear me. She's mumbling in conversation with herself.

Suddenly she freezes, finally sensing me.

"Is there something you're searching for?" I say, my words growing deep. "Are you lost?"

She whips around, drawing in a quick breath in surprise. Her cheeks blush as she looks up at me.

Fuck, she affects me like no other woman ever has. All I can picture is that tight little body against mine, her legs and arms wrapped around me, and her moans in my ear as I fuck her until she begs me to stop.

When she tips her chin up, she attempts to look unaffected by me catching her. She scans the hallway behind me as though expecting someone. Except we're alone.

"I…um…" she stammers, unable to come up with a response at first. "I…I took the wrong turn."

From the moment I caught her spying, I knew there was no way I could walk away from her.

I stand in front of her as she straightens her spine, sticking to her lie. Her feistiness draws me to her more.

"I have a particular way of dealing with liars," I say.

"Yeah, and how is that?"

She's so damn good. Her comeback is delivered instantly without a flinch of hesitation, and she stares at me with a twinkle in her bright blue eyes. Guendolyn is perfect in so many ways I had refused to admit before. From the way her lips quirk when she's indecisive to how she plays with the tips of her hair, and then there're those curves of her chest, her slender neck, those lips… Gods have mercy, but I want those red lips on me.

"You will see," I mutter.

She shrugs nonchalantly. "I don't know what you're talking about."

"There you go again, opposing me. Challenging me. But in the end, I always get the truth."

Of course, she studies me with a look of determination, but all I can think about is making her mine and forcing her to submit.

"I better go," she answers, starting to turn away.

"You never answered my question," I say, leaning closer, a smile spreading my mouth.

"I'm sure you can work out whatever has you confused." She tilts her head arrogantly and walks away.

I clench my jaw and lash out, snatching her arm. I don't turn her toward me but step closer to her and press my chest flush to her back.

Her breath catches.

"I saw you watching me last night," I whisper in her ear. "And I know you came back for more."

She inhales a fast, shaky breath. When she looks at me over her shoulder, her gaze is challenging. She doesn't realize that I play to win and will never back down. I lean closer to her and rasp, "It's your turn to give me a show, angel."

She flinches against me and fights to pull away. "L-Last night was an accident. I hardly saw anything."

"You saw my cock, right?" I spin her by the shoulders to face me. Her cheeks are burning up, but her stubborn gaze is on fire as her eyes meet mine.

"Have you lost your mind?"

"Perhaps, but I get what I want."

I don't give her a chance to say another word. I drag her to me and kiss her fiercely. Part of me half expects a portal to open up like it did when she kissed Deimos, but it never does. Perfect, as I need no distractions.

She fights me with her hands and body, but her lips kiss me back in kind. Her mouth shows me her fury as she takes sharp nips of my lips. It won't dissuade me, and I groan with pleasure.

"Now you're fucking mine."

Guen

I PUSH against Ahren as our lips remain pressed together, his tongue slipping into my mouth. I'm weak and melt against him, even as my head screams to run. I need him like I depend on oxygen, but I also want to shove him into a wall to show him I'm not a pushover. My intention had been to visit the library, but when I spied the corridor leading to Ahren's room, I couldn't help myself. I wanted to check if he was there. The previous night has been on my mind all day, and...well, I'm clearly weak when it comes to my sex drive.

Strong hands grip my waist as he pins me to the wall, and my nipples pulse in response. He lifts me and slides a hand down my thigh, guiding it around his hip, then the other. I hold on to round, muscled shoulders, our mouths never parting. He kisses me like he's been waiting for so long to do this.

Passionate.

Dominant.

He pushes himself between my thighs, his erection pressing against my heat. Thin layers of fabric are all that stand between us, but his thrusts are forceful, his dick hard and thick.

"Is this what you want?" he growls with the deep timbre.

"I..." is all I can manage breathlessly.

"What do you suggest your punishment should be?"

"I don't—"

He grinds into me, stealing my words, and I'm left moaning. He takes that as my yes, and his tongue traces the length of my collarbone. His fingers slip under my skirt and move up the length of my thighs. They curl under the fabric of my underwear, and he rips it off me with such ease, I'm left gasping.

"Wait—"

"This isn't what you want?" he asks, his voice dark and sensual. "I think you're lying again. Each time you lie to me, it lengthens your punishment."

My body shudders with arousal, and I can't even think straight, let alone string a sentence together.

"Ahren—" My protest is cut off when he pushes his hand between us, his fingers dipping to my wetness.

I'm drenched, and his fingers slide along my slick. It feels incredible. He pushes two fingers inside me, and I arch my back and groan with desire as he enraptures me with his delightful torture. My hips move of their own accord, rocking forward with each thrust of his fingers into me.

I shouldn't enjoy this so much, shouldn't encourage him with my whimpers of delight. But pleasure coils around me, wiping my mind clean of any thoughts other than what I need him to do to me.

His teeth latch around my earlobe, gnawing. I'm lost and high on him as he fingerfucks me, and moans escape past my lips.

"Was this what you imagined last night as you watched me? Me touching your tight, juicy pussy?" His voice gets quieter. "Why did you stay and watch?"

I have no idea how to respond. I can't speak when my only focus is his fingers plunging into me.

"It's all right. I know why you stayed." His words send me closer to the edge, my climax building inside me.

"Ahren, maybe we shouldn't," I say. All I can think is that once I've gone down this path, I won't be able to go back. Ahren is hard enough to deal with, let alone having *this* hanging over my head. How am I meant to ever look at him again without burning up on the inside as I remember the way he kissed and touched me?

"Your body tells me how much you want me."

His tongue finds my neck, and my resistance is non-existent. Instead of pushing away, I tug at his shirt. Everything about him calls to my arousal. He smells of pinewoods and fresh soap. I've come this far, and I want him ridiculously bad.

"You can't resist," he mocks me as he fingers me harder, faster. My mind is spinning with so many emotions.

"I hate you for saying that." I moan the words rather than deliver them with strength.

He laughs in my face then captures my mouth with a starved kiss. I return the passion, looping my arms around his neck and clinging to him. God, this fae infuriates me, but I crave him insatiably at the same time.

We rock together, our bodies tangled. Part of me wants to recognize how wrong this is, how I also desire his brothers, how I should resist. Except I'm too far gone to believe I have any power in stopping this. For all I know, this might be my first and last time with Ahren, so I intend to take advantage of the pulsing arousal flaring through me.

"How much do you hate me?" he insists.

"Sometimes, a lot," I admit between pants, barely able to catch my breath.

Not much else registers in my mind—just how damn good this feels. How his deft fingers work into me, how his thumb finds my clit and rubs it in small circles. I thrash and moan louder, needing that high that will take me into the heavens. I should care about the noises I make in a silent hallway, but I can't be bothered to worry right now.

He draws his fingers out of me and I groan in protest, needing them back. My skirt falls back down my legs as I stare at him bewildered. He steps away from me and opens the door to his room.

I inhale rapidly, my mind just coherent enough just to think he's taking me into his room to have his way with me. His cock tents the front of his pants and he lifts his hand to his nose, his nostrils flaring as he breathes me in.

"Hell," he curses under his breath. "Your smell alone makes me so fucking hard."

Seeing this powerful fae so turned on by me is exhilarating. I stare into those pale green eyes, at his white hair flowing over his shoulders, at the redness of his lips from our kisses, and I melt before him. Slick heat drips down the inside of my thighs.

"Your decision," he finally says. "Join me and I will fuck you, I promise you that. Or use that hate you're holding onto to finish yourself off. Think of me while you're doing it."

My words are trapped in my throat at the way he talks to me.

He turns away and disappears into his room, pulling the door to leave it ajar just as it had been last night.

I clench my jaw, left high and dry as he plays this game. I sure as hell shouldn't be kissing the heir to the kingdom, let alone allowing him to maul me out in the hallway when he's clearly an asshole. I release a long breath as I glance over to the gap in the door.

Think of me while you're doing it.

He's such a prick! Still, my lips buzz from our kiss. I squeeze my thighs together, and a rush of heat shoots sparks of desire through my body.

The intensity of the moment crawls up my spine. My mind yells at me to get out of there while my body and heart tug toward the door. I'm not prepared for this moment, and shock clings to me. I have to get out of here.

My heart pounds fast like it might explode out of my chest, and I don't wait for a second longer. I turn and bolt down the hallway. This never should have happened. I glance over my shoulder, but Ahren doesn't come after me.

I trip over my own feet on the way, but I don't stop until I reach my room. Shoving the door open, I step inside and slam it shut behind me. Shaking all over, I hug myself and move toward the fireplace that does nothing to get rid of the shivers.

And that's when I realize something that leaves me completely confused. I'd been so caught up in Ahren and what he made me feel that it never crossed my mind until now.

Why didn't anything magical happen, like a portal opening when I kissed him?

"So what's the plan to help Deimos?" Guendolyn asks before eating another mouthful of venison served with a side of roast vegetables. She's on her second helping, and I admire a girl who isn't shy to eat, but I wonder if she's being fed enough during the day.

She lifts her gaze to me, waiting for a response, but she doesn't give me the chance to speak. "I spent most of the day with Deimos, and I didn't see any healers or mages come to check on him. I'm worried."

The bridge of her nose creases slightly, like it does every time she tries to hide her emotions. Anyone can tell with a glance how much she cares for Deimos, how much the two bonded when he went to Earth to collect her. To say I'm not jealous is a fucking lie, but I have no issues with sharing with my brothers. We might very well be all her mates. My issue is her not retaining her memories of the two of us and staring at me like I'm a stranger. That is a dagger to my heart.

Ahren eats his dinner, not having said a word since we arrived in the dining room. A dark shadow seems to sit over him tonight. Something is going on with him, but he isn't the kind of fae one can push for answers. He'll talk when he's ready.

"We have plans to obtain a cure," I explain.

Her eyes widen as a smile captures her gorgeous mouth. "That's fantastic. Where do we get it from? Can we go tomorrow?"

"You're not going anywhere," Ahren responds sharply. "And it's complicated. Leave it to us."

She glares at him as he returns to his food, and the tension ripples in the air. What the hell happened between them? My brother can be fucking infuriating, but Guendolyn has a fiery side to her as well. Since the portal incident, I've kept my distance from her and come to the grave realization that me chasing her like a lovestruck kid is fucking pathetic. She barely remembers me from two years ago, and as much as that stings like a bitch, I'm not going to chase her or live in a dream world. The priority is healing my brother, then sorting out the mess of the curse on our kingdom. Until then, I'll be sure to show her the real me, and if that means starting over, so be it.

Guendolyn fills her silver cup with peach juice before setting the jug back on the table. "Surely there's something I can do to help?"

"Stay in the mansion," I respond, sounding matter-of-fact because there is no way she is leaving the building until we get this mess sorted out.

She brings the cup to her lips and glances at Dana as the servant walks into the room, carrying a plated cake with white icing and decorated with wild berries and figs.

"That looks delicious." Gwendolyn eyes the cake as Dana smiles proudly and sets the dessert on the round table already filled with plates of food and drinks. One of the other female kitchenhands with short blonde hair rushes in after her and begins collecting our plates. I haven't seen her before.

"This recipe belongs to my grandmother, Gods bless her soul," Dana says, the joy evident in her voice and her beaming grin.

"I can't wait to try it," I add as she places a plate with a large piece in front of me. I eye the layers and smell vanilla cream. Dana serves Ahren and Guendolyn with slices.

The smile Guendolyn offers me is a temptation sweeter than any cake. She starts eating, and her eyes widen with surprise, after which she hurriedly eats more of the cake. She's making a satisfied moaning sound that has both Ahren and I staring at her like a pair of wolves stalking a lost deer in the woods.

Guen

THE MEMORY of my time with Ahren has haunted me all day. Not even this heavenly cake distracts me. Well, maybe a little.

He sits across the table from me, watching my every move from behind his hooded eyes. Tonight he's dressed in all black—tight black pants and a shirt with shiny matching buttons. Against the darkness of his clothing, his white hair seems to almost glow. He has it tucked behind his ears today, showing off his very elven facial structure.

He takes a drink of his wine, then licks his lips. On a scale of one to ten, he is easily a fifty, but there's something scary about him too. The way he needs to control and dominate, to prove his point. If I were back home, my best friend, Nickie, would talk some sense into me. Who am I kidding? She'd tell me to fuck his brains out, then walk out on him. And the thing is, I probably wouldn't fight her that hard.

Not when I think of his perfect body, his kiss, his touch. All of it flashes through my mind as I sip more of my juice. My heart thumps faster, and I can't help but wonder if someone can have a heart attack from being constantly turned on.

I can still feel his fingers inside me, and a shiver of excitement lashes over me. I hate him for walking out on me like that, but I also crave his touch. Hell, I'm all over the damn place. I scold myself for having such thoughts about him, for the raw desire surging through me.

Looking up at him through my lashes, I see the storm in his eyes. I eat another bite of cake and try to pretend he's not in front of me. I spent the whole day in the library to avoid Ahren and do research. Except, the books available were limited to history of fae royalty and their entire boring life story. No mention of fairies; it's as if the fae don't want to admit they exist. Nothing on the word *Eirian* either. So that was a waste.

The priority is helping Deimos, then uncovering who my parents are in Ash Court are. Lastly, I want to get a handle on my ability, then I can work out where in all these worlds I actually belong. If portal opening is my thing, there has to be a way to activate it and determine where a portal should open. Oh, and work out the small complication of why that only happened in Deimos' company. I really like the idea of being able to touch and kiss him without worrying about letting in a horde of Bloodcursed.

Luther sits between Ahren and me at the round table, quieter than normal. My gaze searches his ridiculously handsome face. I have never met a man this gorgeous in real life. As far as I'm concerned, they exist only in fashion magazines and are completely photoshopped. But Luther is real, primal, and intimidating. His impeccably straight dark hair falls to his shoulders, framing piercing, fiery eyes and a hard jawline. Everything about him is brooding and sexy. I feel a pull to him, and in truth, it terrifies me to have such an attraction. To not remember our past is like having to live with a blade permanently stuck in my chest. When I look at Luther, I can't take a deep enough breath and my emotions confuse me, so I pull away, scared of the depth of feelings he stirs inside me.

Mael, Ahren's advisor, enters the room. The candles in the orbs hanging from the ceiling flicker from his hard, fast steps toward us.

"What is it?" Luther asks, as if sensing his unease.

"His Majesty requests the lady's company." He gives the princes a small bow of his head, then looks my way.

"What for?" Ahren mutters.

"He didn't say." He doesn't say anything else but stands there, waiting for a response to give the king.

"Then I will attend with her," Ahren announces.

"Your Highness." Mael bows his head. "The king specifically said he wants to talk to her alone."

I stiffen, the cake in my stomach swirling, and I shove my spine against the back of the seat. "I-I don't know if that's a good idea," I murmur.

"You can't deny his request, my lady," Mael explains to me with a gentle voice.

"What does he really want?" Luther asks Ahren.

A shiver races up my back at the thought that the king knows who I am.

Ahren tilts his head up, his lips thinning. "Mael, please advise the king that Gainy will join him after her meal. Perhaps imply we have just started eating."

The advisor nods vigorously and retreats quickly back into the kitchen.

I meet Ahren's stormy irises and ask, "Is this a good idea?"

Ahren

"If you don't go to the king, things will end badly for you," I explain, my words clipped and fast. I'm agitated about why he wants to see her. Did he see something during the battle? I shake those thoughts away. I won't panic. The king has always been an inquisitive man and often invites new people in his court for a casual conversation to get to know them.

I look over to Guendolyn, who's studying her half-eaten cake slice.

Ever since last night, she's been on my mind. In my veins. In my dreams. I can't get her fucking out, and sitting so far from her has me knotted up. I want to roar the anger out of me.

I expected her to follow me into my room, to finish what we started. Instead, she left. Now I meet her stony stare while an inferno blazes in mine.

Her scent still clings to my nose and fogs my mind. All I can think about is imprinting myself on her, biting her, anything to remind her she's mine. To rip that pretty blue dress she wears off her body before I sink into that sweet pink pussy and fuck her balls-deep.

I huff out a deep, frustrated breath, then take my chalice and down several mouthfuls of wine. Luther watches me. He knows I'm agitated. Hell, I've been so fucking horny since yesterday that my balls are swollen and aching for release.

Guendolyn shifts in her seat uncomfortably. "What if he suspects something, asks me questions? God, what if he insists I'm to do...stuff with him?" Panic surges like a tidal wave in her eyes, and she pushes the plate of cake away from her. "I can't do this. I say lots of shit when I'm nervous."

A nerve ticks in my neck at the thought of the king touching her.

"He's not going to touch you," Luther says, drawing me out of my thoughts. "He can be a bastard, but I've never seen him hurt women. Stick to the story we discussed about why you're here. Ask him questions, as he loves to talk, and then he'll forget to pry into your affairs."

I slide my gaze to her as she nods enthusiastically. She wears a crooked smile, that vulnerable side of her coming out, touching me. A nerve pulses against my temple at how much she distracts me.

She'll hate my pity, but right now, she only has us two to help her in the Wandering Realm. "Look, I'll walk you to the palace and give you some more tips along the way."

Her chin raises, her eyes opening wider for a moment, looking at me as if I have an alternate motivation. "You don't have to."

"I insist," I reply.

"I'm sure you have better things to do," she sneers, looking me up and down. This firecat challenges me again, and I lick my teeth, staring at her with so much promise of what's to come.

"When I make a promise, I keep my word."

Her brow furrows. "There were no promises made. Just an offer for me to decide."

She is seriously getting on my nerves to the point where I will tan her ass until it blushes with my handprint. "And you decided wrong."

She gasps, stunned at my response. Did she really assume I didn't want her to join me? Had I not made it clear enough? I search her expression for an answer, but I'm interrupted by Luther clearing his throat.

"Am I missing something?"

I huff and snap to my feet. "It's nothing." I swing my attention to Guendolyn. "I'll be in the hallway when you're ready." She blinks at me, but I turn and make my way to the door before I say something fucking stupid.

I'm letting her get under my skin.

I press my back against the wall in the shadows of the hallway. Around her I react purely on instinct, shoving aside all rational thoughts. This isn't who I am, and especially not when I need to keep my head straight. Except she's gotten to me and has become my obsession.

After a long moment, she steps out of the room and walks right past me without a second thought of where I might be. I snag her wrist, and she flinches around in surprise before tugging her hand back.

My grasp tightens. "You're with me." I stride forward, dragging her alongside me. We march down the hallway and are swallowed by empty corridors, the maids' voices sounding in the distance. We leave the dining room far behind us as my boots thump on the black rug leading us across the mansion.

"What the hell is your problem?" she snaps at me.

"You speak with such disrespect. You talk to the king this way, and you'll lose your head."

"You demand too much of me."

I glance around and haul her across the hall and into an empty room. There are so many barren rooms in the mansion with only my brothers, me, and the servants living here. The intention is to fill this place once the three of us find brides and marry. Fuck, that's the last thing on my mind right now. I can't imagine marrying someone else when *she's* right here in front of me.

As I kick the door shut behind us, the globes light up the large room. I swing Guendolyn around, pushing her back to the wall, and a small squeak escapes her mouth. Her hands instinctively fly up to my chest, pushing against me. I feel the tension in her as her surprised expression dissolves to anger. Bracing my hands on the wall on either side of her head, I lean in, giving her no chance to escape. I inhale her sweet scent, and my cock hardens.

"What part of last night didn't you understand?" I ask.

She stares at me, bewildered.

I endure a moment's hesitation as she inhales sharply and exhales out a long sigh. I smell the peach juice on her breath as my gaze falls to her full lips.

She licks them, staring into my eyes. "Are you always this rude and pushy?"

"When you don't listen to me I am."

Her teeth dig into her bottom lip. "There's nothing to tell. I—"

"Don't lie to me."

Her eyes narrow, and the corner of her mouth quirks, her every move calculated.

"Do I need to remind you of my punishment for lying?"

"I—" She struggles to talk, and fuck, that drives me wild. I want to give it all to her, and now. To rip away that smug look on her face and replace it with one of absolute ecstasy.

"You want to know the truth?" she blurts out.

"Yes," I growl.

"You scare me. The things you made me feel scare me."

Her words catch me off-guard like a slap to the face as she tells me the truth—how her desire for me leaves her frightened. Has she never been with a man before?

She suddenly pushes forward, and her lips graze mine. I breathe against them, slide my hand to the back of her head, and kiss her hard.

I lose myself, a growl rolling over my throat, and I let myself fall to the savage hunger inside me. Around her, I'm losing my mind. I taste her swollen lips and explore her mouth. "You make me crazy with need," I murmur.

She kisses me again and slides her tongue into my mouth. I wrap my arms around her petite frame, pressing her to me, feeling the swell of her breasts, the tremble of her body. I move my hands down her back and over her perfect ass. The new blue dress she wears tonight is long and has too much fabric for my liking.

The small sound in her throat pushes me closer to the edge where I won't be able to stop. I suck on her tongue, on her lips. I'm so fucking starved for her. No woman has ever done this to me before.

"How much do you want me?" she whispers against my mouth.

"I'd climb into the heavens and carve the moon out of the sky for you," I admit, as corny as it sounds in my head.

Her hand reaches between us and slides over my cock in my pants. I growl as my pulse zaps through my veins.

Our kiss deepens, and I'm falling so fast and deep, I'll never find my way back out.

Loud footfalls resonate on the hallway floorboards outside the room. "Where the hell is she?" Mael's voice pierces the perfect moment. "Find Luther; I'll search for Ahren. The king's patience runs low."

"Fuck," I whisper under my breath as I break from Guendolyn.

Those gorgeous lips are bruised red from my hard kisses, her eyes imploring me to continue, her parting mouth demanding I fuck her up against the wall.

"I need to take you to the king," I mutter.

"Right now?" Her cheeks glow.

"Yes, now. We need to hurry," I growl, fucking frustrated that we have to leave this unfinished.

The walk to the palace is silent.

Ahren leads me over the bridge between the two buildings. The night is icy and snow falls feathery soft, covering everything. By the time we reach the palace, I'm trembling. Warmth encases me as soon as the doors are shut behind us, as though the building has insulated heat. Unlike the dark colors of the mansion that remind me of a gothic church, everything here is elegant with gleaming white marble and polished gold. Golden framed portraits of fae fill the walls, each subject more spectacular and gorgeous than the last. Is there such a thing as an ugly fae? I have yet to meet one.

Guards are posted at every turn, standing tall in their midnight blue uniforms, their fitted jackets with gilded buttons running diagonally from their waist to a shoulder. An insignia of a golden wing pierced by an arrow sits on each of their left arms.

Finally, we reach two grand doors the color of snow with ornate golden handles. I assumed we would go to the throne room, except this is a different room. Uniformed guards draw the doors open, revealing an opulent sitting room that has me frozen on the spot, as if I just walked into Disneyland.

Arched mullioned windows with golden frames cover three of the walls, and the corners are laced with frost from the frigid night. Dozens upon dozens of the glass globes hang from the lofty ceiling, each glowing a different color. My insides beam at seeing the rainbow of turquoise, magenta, marmalade, and so many other colors across the ceiling over-head, and I can't stop looking at them. It feels like I've walked into the kind of fantasy world I'd expect in movies. At the end of the room is a golden fireplace, intricately carved and flanked by two giant statues of beautiful women with wings. They seemed to be reaching for the sky. There are four guards near the fireplace and couches, watching over the king.

Ahren places his hand on my lower back and ushers me inside. I stumble forward, my shoes tapping at the golden path that will take me to the semi-circle of black leather couches facing the fire. The door shuts with a decisive thud, and I whip around to find myself closed in here without Ahren.

"Come over already, I don't bite," the king barks from over at the fire-place. Looking closely, I can only see the top of his head from where he sits on the couch.

My insides twist as I walk closer, and I feel like I'm heading to the slaughter.

I'm worried that he suspects something of me. That I might not be from his kingdom, or he knows who I really am and is planning to offer me an ultimatum. Considering the outcome of that, part of me wants this to be as simple as him believing he can make a move on me. That I can deal with.

I swallow past the lump in my throat.

Just get this over with. I march across the room, my steps echoing like hands clapping. I keep looking up at the colors that twinkle with every move I make. As I step alongside the couch, I suddenly find it's not just the king waiting for me, but Jasion too.

My mouth dries.

Alarm bells ring in my head at the possibility that the mage knows something and now they're about to confront me. The princes told me the king doesn't think highly of Jasion, so what reason can there be for both of them being together?

"Ah, Gainy, good of you to join me. Take a seat." The king jerks his chin to the couch adjacent to his.

My feet refuse to move at first, as my gaze sweeps from the king, then to Jasion.

"Evening, Gainy. It's good to see you again," Jasion states formally, his attention dipping to my lips. Can he tell I've just been kissing Ahren? Is my face blushing wildly? When I meet his stare, all I see is hunger—a fae who believes I'm a stepping stone for him to grow his power and standing in the court.

He turns to the king as he straightens his back. He's still wearing the robe-skirt and no shirt with heavy black boots too.

"Your Majesty, I will take my leave, and we can resume our discussion on the morrow."

"Yes, yes." The king waves him off, his eyes locking on me.

Jasion bows his head and walks away toward the door. As if sensing his presence, the doors open and the guards are there to greet him as he marches past them and vanishes around the corner. Then the doors shut once again.

"Sit," the king reminds me.

I do so on the next couch, sitting in the corner closest to him to avoid looking like I am scared by keeping my distance. Even though I'm shaking, I hold myself still since I don't need the king to suspect me of being afraid.

The king is handsome for his age, and has a slight ruddy glow on his face, which is framed by white hair. Unlike the previous time I met him, now he wears a simple deep burgundy loose shirt with a lace up tie at his chest that's sitting undone and black pants with lace-up boots. He sits with his legs wide, arms by his side. In front of him is a small golden table with two golden wine chalices on top and a matching jug behind them.

"Don't look so frightened, girl." He shuffles forward in his seat and collects the jug before filling both of the cups. He hands me one. "This should warm you up. Winter seems to have sprung on us early this year."

I accept the cup, my hands trembling.

"Well, drink up," he says, then presses his chalice to his lips and swallows several mouthfuls.

I look down at the deep red wine, the strong aroma of berries and fermentation filling my nose. It smells like normal wine, so I tilt the chalice back, and the liquid rolls into my mouth. Sweetness and honey hit me first, then a strong peppery punch at the back of my throat. I cough, and the king laughs at me.

"Weren't expecting that hit at the end, were you? It will warm you on nights like tonight."

I nod and finish the drink, which is growing on me, despite the heated aftertaste. "Your Majesty, what would you like to talk about?" I figure the quicker we start, the quicker I can leave. It's awkward enough as it is.

"The cold weather always brings on pain from an old injury on my shoulder, and nothing the healers do helps. Jasion suggested I give you a try."

I stiffen, confused by Jasion's actions.

"I can definitely try. My touch seems to have helped others."

"Good." He leans over and takes the jug before filling the cup in my hand.

"Oh, I think that's enough for me." Last thing I want is to end up drunk... but maybe that's the king's intention.

"Nonsense. I need your hands warm before you touch me." He winks like that's a joke, or does he mean something else?

I am struggling to make sense of the king and what his intentions are. In his position, he is probably the master at holding a poker face, having dealt with lots of royals.

He watches me, so I sip down the second helping of wine and set it on the table before he fills it up once more. Heat rushes down my throat and into my belly, kindling my insides to a warm blaze. I rub my hands together to ensure they are heated too.

"You know what's strange," he begins, "is that none of my healers have sensed you in the city the whole time you've lived here."

Shrugging, I put on a small smile. "I mostly keep to myself. I only help a couple of neighbors who need it." What little Ahren's and Luther have told the king about me comes to mind about what they've told the king about me. The less I say, the better. Just get this over and done with, then I can get out of here.

"The healers do a regular sweep of our population for anyone with abilities. We coud use every able hand in our kingdom in the current circumstance. Perhaps they missed you, somehow."

"They must have." Nerves kicking me, my knees start bouncing, so I inch to the edge of the couch. "Would you like me to try healing your shoulder, Your Majesty?"

There's hesitation in the king's response. He's watching me, and I can see the thoughts swirling behind his eyes. I suspect he doesn't believe the story of my abilities not being picked up.

"When I spoke to Jasion, do you know what he told me?"

I freeze all over and hate where this is going, hate that I feel so trapped. I don't know how many lies I can make up without trapping myself in a web, as I don't know much about this kingdom or realm.

"He told me your power is unlike anything he's felt before. Something he'd like to better understand... And he can't for the life of him understand how he missed you in the city, as he regularly walks through there to detect any strong powers. You know what he thinks?"

I shake my head, not trusting my voice right now.

"He insists that the princes brought you into our kingdom from else-where." He tilts his head to the side, studying me, leaning closer. "So, my question is, who would my princes bring into our home unannounced, and why would they lie about it?"

I suck in a ragged breath as fear pummels me, and I grasp onto every ounce of bravery I have. I loathe Jasion, I decide at that moment. And to think, the last time we talked, he asked me to trust him. But this isn't the time for me to lock up and freeze. Instead, I push out a laugh. It helps that I feel super relaxed from the wine.

"It sounds to me like Jasion is looking for a way to cover his tracks for not detecting me in the first place. You can ask the princes. They stumbled into me about two years ago. Before that, I usually kept to myself and didn't go out much. I'm sure you place more trust in them than a mage." This time I shift closer, leaning my arms over my thighs, holding his stare. The wine's gone to my head and fills me with bravery.

He watches me with a gleam in his eyes. "That so?"

"You know what I believe?" I ask.

"What's that?"

"Jasion is threatened by me."

The king huffs as if surprised, then processes the information. All the while, I'm wracking my brain for what else I can say to turn the tables on Jasion and still sound legit.

"But he's not a healer. Why would he care?" The king fills our cups once more.

Sweat rolls down my spine. The king is indeed inquisitive, and I can tell now this summoning is much more of an interrogation about the red flags Jasion raised about me. I remember everything Jasion said to me over breakfast, well-aware that if he hasn't told it all to the king yet, he will soon enough. So, I'd better to be one step ahead.

"Because of my affinity with fairies." I hold my breath.

He doesn't respond or show any sign of shock. That tells me Jasion has already told him, which I can work in my favor.

"Jasion asked me how I handled the blue-winged fairy who'd been injured during the battle. He was pushy and anxious. He mentioned he hasn't met anyone else who can do that before." I shrug and reach for my chalice. "I can only imagine that's what he's threatened by." I drink down the wine, chasing the lies on my tongue, and set the cup back on the table.

He blinks at me. "Did you call the fairies into the kingdom?"

I gasp on purpose, though on the inside I'm squirming. "I have no idea how they got in, but it's a good thing they did, don't you think?"

The way he studies me sends a shiver up my arms.

I'm suddenly burning hot, and my face feels like it's glowing. Why did I drink that third round of wine?

Finally, he nods and reaches for his cup. "Come, try your healing on me and tell me more about how your affinity with fairies works. Do they listen to your command?" He collects his wine and reclines back on the couch as he pushes down on the fabric of his shirt to reveal a broad shoulder. He grimaces, clearly in pain. There are healed scratches across the white flesh.

"Oh, it's nothing elaborate at all, but more of a coincidence when they seem to help me." I laugh a bit as I get to my feet, and the room tilts around me. Note to self; no more wine.

Navigating to stand alongside his couch, I try to concentrate and remember what I did with Ahren when I healed him. Not much, so I'm going to try the same tactic.

"Is it alright if I sit next to you, Your Majesty?"

"Of course, girl. Tell me how you first encountered fairies."

I slide down on my bent leg so I'm facing him. Lifting my hand, I gingerly set my palm and splayed fingers over his shoulder. His skin is fiery to the touch, but he doesn't react.

For a few moments, I focus on the room to try and stop it from revolving around me. Then I begin making up a story about the fairies...keeping it simple and as close as possible to the truth.

"When I was much younger, I was collecting wild mushrooms outside our walls. Suddenly, two Bloodcursed came out of nowhere and attacked me. I was running for my life when I bumped into the fairies' nest. They swarmed over me, but in all honesty, I was too scared of the Bloodcursed at the time to be too afraid of the fairies."

"Two demons coming at you at once," the king says, nodding his head as though he understands, and drinks his wine.

"But here's the thing. As soon as the Bloodcursed came at me, the fairies turned on them and devoured them down to their bones before my eyes down. Then they let me run back home without coming after me. And ever since, if I see them, it's like they acknowledge me and leave me alone."

"Fascinating. You've heard the story of how fairies came into existence?"

"Of course. Haven't we all?" I snort a laugh then curse myself for snorting in front of a king.

He raises a brow in my direction. "Personally, I've always wanted to believe they are benevolent creatures. They are spawned from revenge after an injustice." He grunts and finishes his wine. Then he leans forward to grab the jug for a refill, and I pull my hand back as he does. When he returns, I don't miss the reddening handprint on his shoulder.

Hopefully, that works on his injury. Ahren's mark vanished after a short while.

"The queen of fairies didn't deserve to be treated the way she was," I say. "And I also think if the fairies can feed just as easily on the Blood-cursed, what if there's a way to make them focus on eliminating the infected?" The room suddenly feels like it's swaying around me.

He turns to me, a grin tugging the corners of his mouth upward. "I like the way you think. Maybe there's something here you can help us with besides healing."

I nod, strangely eager to make this man smile approvingly. I've clearly had too much wine.

"My first encounter with fairies is embarrassing," he begins. "I was using the outhouse when they burst in on me to hide from a greater danger. You can imagine all of our surprises."

"There's a greater danger to fairies?" I ask, half grinning at the image he just described.

"Definitely." He drinks half his wine, then breaks into his story about fighting off underground beasts that sound like goblins. I'm utterly captivated at learning more about this world. He reminds me of my foster mother's boyfriend, who loved telling tales, but what he loved even more was having an audience. So I provide that for the king, pushing away all other concerns—including my worry that the king thinks I am anything but a local from his kingdom.

CHAPTER

TWELVE

GUENDOLYN

"You waited for me," I say to Ahren as I step outside the king's room, the guards shutting the doors behind me.

He greets me with a grin, leaning a shoulder on the wall with his arms folded over his chest. Maybe I've had too much to drink, but to me, he looks like a god...a sexy-as-hell god.

"I wasn't letting you go back alone." The firelight from the torches attached to the wall dances across his gorgeous green eyes.

My knees tremble at the thought of being with a fae who takes so much pleasure from being in my company. Back home, I struggled to get a date, so this feels surreal, overwhelming, and exhilarating. Now I'm feeling all kinds of warm fuzzies on the inside.

"I—" Licking my lips, I step toward him, only to trip over my own feet, so I hastily straighten myself. "I wasn't sure if you would be here."

He arches an eyebrow at my misstep. Then again, my mind is spinning like a tornado. Whatever wine the king gave me is now in full effect.

Ahren reaches out and takes my hand in his, then pulls me into a walk. "Let's go."

I take quick steps to keep up with him. There are are watching us everywhere, and Ahren doesn't say a word, not until he leads me straight to his room. Which is just as well, because it's taking all of my focus to keep from stumbling again.

Ahren lets go of my hand and shuts the door. "I expected you last night, so I had to make sure you didn't run out on me again."

I swallow hard. "Well, I'm here now. Why dwell on the past?"

Ahren strolls over to the fireplace and bathes in its warmth, studying me.

Like my suite, there is another doorway that leads to the bedroom. In this room, swords and shields cover the walls, along with paintings of a valley with a smaller mansion. It's surrounded by woodlands with a river winding behind it, and there's something simple and calming about the scene. I move closer to one of the paintings, concentrating on each step to avoid falling over. It's taking every ounce of strength to hold it together and not just sit where I am until the room stops whirling.

"Where is this location? It doesn't seem familiar," I say, proud of myself for asking a real question without slurring my words.

He steps up behind me, looming over me and burning me up with his heat. Suddenly, I can't breathe. All I can think about is how close he stands, how my skin tingles with anticipation of his touch. I'm no fool, and I know exactly why I allowed him to bring me back to his room.

"It's a painting of the home I grew up in," he explains with a melancholy sound in his voice.

"So you didn't grow up as a prince?" I glance over my shoulder at him.

"Oh I did, but Mother insisted we stay there instead of the palace. But that's all in the past." His hands go to my shoulders, and I let out a tiny whimper of need, then he turns me around to face him.

I can't think, I can only see this god-like man staring down at me while my insides soften in his presence.

"Please," I whisper, unsure exactly what I'm begging for. His kiss? For him to take me already? Or for his kindness? Maybe all three.

I reach up and loop my hands around his neck, my fingers interlacing, while I lift myself onto my toes. He tips his head forward, and our mouths clash. Chest to chest, I push my body against him, my nipples hardening.

His hand splays wide over my back and sweeps down to my ass. The size of his palm easily covers a decent portion of my asscheeks, and I shiver at the memory of his fingers inside me, stretching me. His other hand glides to the back of my head, fisting my hair and holding me in place. His beautiful assault on my mouth sends desire through every inch of me. I return the kiss, desperate to jump right back to where we ended yesterday. I shift to slide against him, and his huge erection presses against my lower stomach, pulsing in response.

It tickles me, and I can't stop the laughter from bursting out.

He breaks from me, pulling my head back, and stares at me. "Is something funny?"

I gasp for air between my laughs. "It's just your cock is tickling my stomach." I reach down to touch him over his pants, but he seizes my wrist.

His eyes narrow. "How much have you had to drink tonight?"

I lift my hand and show him all my fingers, then frown. "No, that's not right." I bend two down. "Three chalices."

"You're drunk," he accuses. "I need to take you back to your room. I won't spend a night with you if you're drunk."

"Am not!" In one swift move, I pivot away from him and saunter to his couch before throwing myself down on the soft cushions and rolling onto my back. "Gosh, is the ceiling twirling?"

"Fuck, Guendolyn," he hisses. The way he looks at me is one of judgment.

"Come to me. I have something to show you, something you'll want to see." In my head, I am sounding sexy as hell, yet this fae stares at me with that arrogant demeanor he often wears.

"You need to go get some sleep," he growls, clearly disappointed in me.

"Take me to *your* bed, Ahren?" I plead. "I don't want to sleep alone."

His shoulders soften, and something washes over his face at my request, making him look at me with endearment.

"You know, I like this side of you most of all," I say. "There's no furrowing brow, and that brooding look you usually have is gone."

He steps closer. "Brooding?

"Yeah, where you look permanently angry or constipated...and like you're ready to punch someone."

He huffs heavily, then sweeps me off the couch and lifts me into his arms. I laugh out loud at how fast he does that as he carries me across the room and toward his bedroom.

"Now, that was fun. Let's do it again."

"You don't hold your drink well," he reprimands me, as if that's meant to be insulting.

"Hello, I'm the queen of being a light-weight drinker. I even got drunk at my friend's party on two shots of her vodka."

"Not sure why you think that's a good thing."

"Wow, you are a master at insults, aren't you?"

He shakes his head, exhaling louder.

"You're not perfect either. What you did last night was a dick move," I blurt out, shoving my free hand against his muscles. Oh, so many of them. I run my hands up his rounded shoulders and biceps as I slip my lower lip between my teeth. "You definitely work out."

"I told you there'd be punishment, but apparently, that will have to wait for another night."

"Your punishment is teasing me, then taking the supposed discipline away." The words rush from my mouth. "It's not just me you're punishing then, is it?"

"The difference is, I have control."

"Hey, I came here because you made a big deal of it. Plus, I've been so freaking horny since last night." My eyes pop open wide. "Oops, I wasn't meant to say that last bit out loud."

Something flashes over his gaze that looks like, a primal hunger, but it's gone as fast as it came. "If you weren't so drunk, I'd tan your ass for drinking so much."

I wave my hands in the air. "Well, your father—"

"Stepfather," he growls.

"He's a great man who has the best stories and made me laugh so much. He told me he loves you and your brothers as much as he does your mother." The king has grown on me, and I can't help but feel differently about him.

"You don't know what you're talking about," he mutters, and walks us into his bedroom.

We enter an enormous room with heavy velvet curtains parted over arched windows. Moonlight streams over the king-sized bed with a monstrous headboard carved into the shape of a huge oak tree.

"Is that made of gold?"

He doesn't respond but lays me in the bed, then covers me in a red blanket. I soften into the cocoon of the mattress and puffy pillows.

"This is so comfortable." My eyes flutter closed and open, and I'm struggling to think as sleep crashes over me.

He brushes the hair off my brow. "Sleep," he orders in a husky rasp.

"No, I..." Dreamland tugs at me, and I can't remember what I was going to say.

"You're going to be the end of me, Guendolyn. The sweetest, most tempting end."

***

"Have you been watching me sleep? It's kinda creepy," I murmur, trying to wake up as I turn onto my side in bed to face Ahren. He's lying on his side on top of the blankets, still fully clothed, studying me.

"If keeping an eye on you is creepy, then I'll accept the title," he responds in a soft tone, as if he's just woken up himself and his walls haven't locked into place yet.

I study him through hooded eyes as the silvery hue of moonlight lights up half of his gorgeous face. I shake my head, clearing up my thoughts this time. "No. That was wrong of me to say."

He reaches over and strokes the back of his fingers down my face. I can't help myself, and my hand automatically goes to his chest, his muscles flexing against me. Something about him makes me want to always touch him.

We've had so many confrontations, and he isn't the most patient or understanding of men. He's quick to speak his mind and criticize, not to mention his issues with being controlling. He is the opposite of what I've always thought I wanted in a man.

Except, I was wrong. So fucking wrong because he is exactly what I desire.

"What are you thinking?" I ask.

"How I never thought I'd have you all to myself," he answers bluntly without any hesitation, but that's Ahren in a nutshell.

My cheeks burn at his confession.

He leans closer to me, his hand on my neck, his gaze sliding to mine. "How's your head feeling?"

"Much better. The wine completely knocked me out."

"Its side effect is heavy sleep. The king drinks it most nights."

"Good to know," I say, our faces so close now. He bends forward and captures my lips with his, soft and demanding at once. His delicious tongue plunges into my mouth almost instantly, and I press myself toward him, kissing him back. He tastes of honey and whiskey.

I'm utterly lost under his spell, knowing where this is going, and I hungrily grasp onto his shirt to hold him in place. Too much has come between us, and I need this. I need him. So I let myself fall, forgetting where I am and the danger all around me, the worry for Deimos, the confusion with Luther. All I care about is about Ahren and me. The other stuff can wait.

Right now, there's only us floating together. It's incredible. Addictive. And I need more.

His hand slides down my shoulder, feather-soft, then peels back the blankets covering my body, and a chill encases me. His large, warm hand finds my breast and squeezes. Flesh to flesh...

Whoa, wait up!

I break from his melting kiss and look down to find I'm not wearing anything, then I shoot a glance back up at him. "Did you strip me?"

"Of course. You can't sleep with clothes on comfortably. Is there a problem?"

I raise a brow. "You can't undress a woman while she's sleeping! Now, *that* is creepy."

He grins mischievously, his eyes almost darkening when he looks at me as if he took a lot of joy in getting me nude. "You worry about strange things. Now will you let me have my way with you and do as I please, beautiful?" His voice carries a longing.

There is no way I can say no to such an offer, so I nod. "I'm yours."

He takes my hand and presses it to his mouth. His tongue traces the length, from the base of my palm to the tip of my fingers. I tremble with exhilaration, wanting that tongue all over me.

"It's only fair that you take your clothes off too," I murmur, my voice barely a whisper.

There is no hesitation in his actions as he climbs out of bed. He stands tall, staring at me the whole time as his large hands pull at the buttons on his midnight blue shirt and part the fabric. My gaze dips to his washboard abs, then to that sexy as hell, sharply-cut V at his hips while his shirt cascades off his shoulders and to the ground. He pops open the button on his pants and bends down, dragging them to his ankles, then kicks them aside. When he stands, my attention falls to his cock.

Erect.

Large.

All mine.

The tip glistens with pre-cum, and he strokes himself a few times, his upper lip curling up as if he's barely holding on.

I shuffle across the bed to his side and reach over to grasp him. He lets go of his hardness, and I wrap my fingers around his thickness. It's so warm to the touch, and the skin is silky soft, yet hard as rock underneath. I slide my hand over him, and he hisses, his eyes rolling back. He moans, and it sounds so incredible. His noises alone have me shivering with need, and the apex between my thighs pulses in eagerness to have him.

One swipe with his hand, and he nudges my hand away. "Enough. Tonight is going to last. With no more interruptions, you are mine to do with as I will." He moves to stand at the end of the bed, facing me.

He's tall and broad... Seeing him standing over me reminds me just how much larger he is than me. How small I actually am in comparison. Bending toward me, he grasps my ankles and yanks me down the bed.

"Whoa!" My stomach lurches from the movement.

Moonlight catches on the healed scars that run over his shoulders from where he was whipped as a child. My heart clenches as I remember his past, except the man standing before me is fucking powerful despite what his asshole father did to him. I can't help but admire someone who can go through so much shit and still hold it together. Half the time, I feel twisted on the inside after growing up and moving from one foster family to another until I found my forever family. Still, I always felt like I didn't belong with them...or anywhere. Until I arrived here. A strange sensation coats my insides, like somehow, this is a homecoming.

"I can see your mind spinning with thoughts. What distracts you from me?" He lays his hands on my knees, forcing them open as he drops to his knees before me at the end of the bed.

That gesture covers me in goosebumps, and I forget everything on my mind.

I gasp as his breath finds my slick heat.

"Fuck, you're so beautiful," he mutters and leaves a trail of kisses down my inner thighs, his lips as soft as feathers. "I'm going to eat you now."

I'm not sure how to respond, but the word "Yes" slips from my mouth. I chew on my lower lip, my heart thumping in my chest faster, louder.

This gorgeous fae, a freaking heir to the throne, is going down on me!

His mouth seals over my pussy, ,then he sucks, and I cry out from the pleasure crashing into me. He licks me over and over with the hard tip of his tongue, and I spread my legs wider, my whole body quivering. Relentlessly, he tugs at my inner lips, keeping his focus on my clit.

I arch my back as he savagely helps himself to me, as he satiates himself. With one hand, he reaches up and grabs my breast, then plucks at my nipple. His other hand presses a finger inside me, and I run my hand through his hair to the back of his head, then push him deeper into me. Arousal aches deeply in me with such intensity, I can barely hold myself together. I'm going to explode any moment.

My body shudders, my hips rocking back and forth. He takes my eagerness well and lashes his tongue over my silky length. When he adds a second thick finger into me, I lose it. I'm shaking, and all I see is white as I scream through the most incredible orgasm I've ever experienced.

Ahren tugs on my clit, elongating the climax and teasing me. I shut my eyes, clasp the bedsheet, and convulse as he takes me into his mouth. I don't know how long I'm floating, but I try to hold on to the pulsing sensation for as long as possible. I'd give anything for more moments like these, when I can't remember real life.

Finally, I float back down to reality and open my eyes, my body vibrating with elation. I can't stop smiling, and find Ahren watching me from between my legs, grinning. His lips and chin glisten in the moonlight, and lust fills his eyes.

I shuffle back on the bed as he climbs on and crawls to me on all fours. Lingering over me, his arms plant on either side of my shoulders, and he smiles down at me.

"Guendolyn, I'm going to make you forget about everything in the best way possible." He leans in and kisses me, tasting me, claiming me. I can feel it in the way he takes control so possessively. I taste myself on his mouth, my sex smell intoxicating.

"I need to know," he begins, whispering in my ear. "Am I to be your first?" He pulls back and looks at me.

For a long pause, I'm at a loss for words, as that's the last thing I expected to hear from him. With me beneath him, it's a bit too late to feel shy about these things. "No," I say. "You're my second."

He nods. "I wanted to make sure, angel, because I don't want to hurt you and—"

"Please stop talking," I manage. "Just take me. I'm stronger than you think, and I won't break. I promise."

The growl in his throat makes me smile.

"Fuck me," I plead.

"I love when you speak to me that way. Now let me make that pretty pussy of yours purr."

He guides the tip of his cock against my heat. His flesh is scorching hot, and I moan from the touch alone. He presses his cock into me slowly, and I hold on as he inches in deeper and deeper, widening me. God, he's big, and pleasure washes through me at the feel of him inside him. He presses his face to my neck and inhales me.

I gasp loudly and grip onto his muscular arms. I crave this fae who bucks his hips, sliding smoothly in and out of me. Flooding me, stretching me, owning me as he swings back and forth into me. The faster he goes, the more the friction between us ignites. With each plunge, he presses against my clit, as if he does it on purpose. He drives harder, his balls slapping against me.

"Fuck!" he grits out, fucking me so hard, my whole body jerks, my heart matching the rhythm. "You see what you do to me, angel?"

He's so hot, and I'm breathing quicker, practically panting. He growls, and I can tell he's going to come any moment now.

"Come for me again. Scream for me," he whispers in my ear, his hips pounding into me, never stopping his gorgeous assault.

A wave of explosions slams into me, dragging me under. I shake uncontrollably as my whole body contracts, and I groan from the pleasure wrapping around me. My muscles clench around his dick, squeezing him as he shoots hot cum inside me, and he roars like a lion as he comes. I scream my own pleasure, and our voices twist together into something beautiful. I don't know how long we stay locked that way, but when he finally pulls out of me, my body feels tender and a bit sore. I sag back on the bed, sweating and breathing heavily.

With a devious smirk, he stands up from the bed and turns to walk out of the room.

"Hey, where are you going?" I tilt my head up, staring at that firm ass.

"Be back soon." He glances at me over his shoulder. "I'm getting something to clean you up, then I want you on your hands and knees. Ass in the air, legs spread, and your tight little pussy exposed. We're going again." His words undo me, and already my heart beats in the pulse between my legs.

I may never walk again after tonight.

THIRTEEN

LUTHER

I swallow, my throat growing dry. Deimos lies in bed where the magic keeps him alive, but for how long? His time is ticking, and we're still waiting for the damn message from the king's contact in Ash Court.

I'm losing my grip, because my brother has one week and we've already lost three days. If we don't get a response today, Ahren and I will depart for Ash Court tonight. I'll tear down the entire Unseelie palace if needed to find a cure for Deimos.

He's so pale. All I want is to hear his voice and for him to tell his stupid jokes. I swear if he survives this, I'll laugh at every one of them.

Worry strangles me. What if we're too late? What if...? Fuck, Deimos can't die. I can't lose him. Barbed emotions drag through me, cresting easily, and too many things come at me, overwhelming me. I clench my hands and grit my teeth, lost in my thoughts and staring down at the floor, when the door behind me creaks open.

"Luther, there you are," my stepfather says with impatience in his voice.

I don't turn to face him as his footsteps close in. He joins me, staring down at Deimos, and says nothing at first.

"The bird carrier just arrived from Ash Court," he states abruptly.

With the realization of what he's implying, I glance at him, locking my gaze on his face. He's not smiling but not frowning either. I bristle on the inside, wishing that maybe for once, he could just show some fucking emotions.

"What did it say?" I ask rapidly.

He lifts a rolled-up piece of parchment in his hand and opens it to reveal a few words, which he reads aloud. "'East entrance to servant quarters.'"

"That's all? You sure this isn't a setup?" I ask. The king's delivered letter could have been intercepted by anyone at Ash Court.

"It's Relle's handwriting, and the location is where we always used to meet. She is most likely expecting me, as I only sent her one word, which was our code for when I had to see her urgently."

I nod, processing everything he's telling me, though I have so many questions. Questions we've been told never to ask him, as we must always let a king keep his secrets. But if we're going to risk our lives, I want to understand the relationship he has with those in Ash Court. "I don't understand why you used to visit Ash Court when the Unseelie would kill you if they found out."

He snorts, completely frustrated with my question. "Concentrate on the mission. My friend Relle is helpful, and you will need to give her this." He sticks his hand into the pocket of his gold and purple surcoat and pulls out a diamond-studded bracelet.

I frown when I look up at him, my eyes narrowing.

"She's not my lover. Fuck, Luther, focus! I've always gifted her jewels to help her provide for her family, and this will also let her know you are with me. Explain to her what you need, and she can demand her price. I'll pay it if she gets us the cure for Deimos from their mages."

My mind races with scenarios of who this contact could be. The darkness sweeping over my stepfather's eyes tells me he won't reveal anything, so maybe we'll uncover the truth from Relle.

"Anything else we should know?" I ask, thinking of the carriage I arranged earlier for our trip, the horses selected, supplies and weapons packed. "Does Ahren know?"

"I can't find Ahren, so let him know and head off this morning. No delays, understand? Tell no one where you two are going. I have asked my mages to create a cloaking spell for your carriage, and one for you and Ahren to enter Ash Court grounds." He pauses, staring at me but seeming to look right through me. "There's a huge tree along the east wall that allows for an easy climb up and over."

I nod and straighten, my mind going over anything else we might have missed for the trip, but we're ready.

"Of course." Part of me plays on the notion of visiting Guendolyn for no other reason than to see her one more time...just in case. Just in case the worst happens. Hell, that's a terrible idea. She will ask questions, and I'll cave. "I better go."

When I turn away, my stepfather seizes my arm.

I face him, expecting him to have forgotten something crucial. Except he's staring at me with a strange look in his eyes. Is that concern swimming in his gaze? I must be imagining things.

"Luther, I may not have been the best father to you and your brothers, but I've only ever wanted to give you all the best."

"You don't—"

"Just fucking listen for once," he growls, then exhales loudly, the anger fading from his face. "I screwed up when you all were young, by not spending time with you and pushing you all aside. But I'm going to fix that. When you return and Deimos is healed, I want us to spend more time together. I want...I want to be a real family."

I'm lost for words. Utterly lost. This isn't the king I've known most of my life, but a man eager to make amends. Before I can respond, he hauls me against him in an awkward hug and slaps my back twice before breaking away.

He clears his throat. "Good luck, my son."

Then he marches out of the room.

I'm left standing bewildered for a few moments, then I look over at Deimos. "Did you hear that? Maybe the bastard is getting soft in his old age."

***

Ahren

"I don't trust Gainy," Jasion mutters with such distaste in his voice that it sickens me. "She's lying and can't be trusted. What if she's here from Ash Court? I know she's not from this kingdom, so she has obviously lied to you."

Jasion marches back and forth in front of the window in my study. I remain in my seat, as the hearth nearby keeps me warm. Shelves full of books line the walls, and I often use this room to take my time away from everyone.

The snow has stopped falling and the sun peeks out from behind the heavy cloud cover. Maybe today will be a day of good fortune and we'll finally hear news from the king's contact. Luther insists we are leaving tonight if we hear nothing, and I can't agree more.

"Ahren, are you even paying attention to what I'm saying?" Jasion growls, and I groan under my breath at his rant.

"You don't need to worry about her, trust me on this. She is safe. Now, is there something else you need to speak to me about?"

My patience wanes today, and concentrating on the mage's skepticism is wearing me thin. He's too close to the truth of discovering who Guendolyn is, which annoys me. He's always been paranoid about every small thing, watching the other mages, believing they were conspiring to kill him, scrutinizing anyone I speak with. I have accepted this is part of his personality, but maybe his behavior is my fault for not putting an end to it when it started. By letting him think I tolerate his paranoia, he's crossing the line right now with Guendolyn. I want him the fuck away from her. There's enough shit going on without dealing with a neurotic mage.

He huffs and fiddles with the skull around his neck. I've always disliked that thing, but I also know the mages use some of the fairy skulls' energy to enhance their own. There's magic in their bones, ancient sorcery from times long ago. That's the real reason Jasion has suddenly been paying so much attention to Guendolyn—he witnessed her ability to control a fairy. And in his eyes, he sees the potential of power she might possess, and that's exactly why I want him away from her.

"You can't trust her," he reiterates. "I'm going to find out exactly who she is and her intentions."

I stand up from the seat and approach him. "I'm saying this as your prince, not your friend, Jasion. Don't go near her. Don't talk to her. Don't let me hear you did anything foolish." Fury burns through me, and I grind my back teeth. I've never seen him this worked up before about anyone. Usually, if I tell him to leave something alone, he backs down. What the fuck is wrong with him today?

His upper lip curls with a hatred I've never seen before. "You trust that whore because she spreads her legs for you, when I've been by your side from the beginning."

My anger nearly explodes through me, knowing he's spied on Guendolyn and me. He must have caught us in the hallway, but I don't fucking get why it bothers him so much. "Be careful, Jasion." My hands curl, and I'm seething.

His face screws up, his chest rising and falling fast. "I don't understand why you're so protective of her. I've told you that I'll always have your back. I'm just trying to protect you. Let me take her into questioning. You know I can be very persuasive." His deplorable smirk has me loathing him. I've seen him enjoy interrogating others before and taking it further than it needs to go.

I get in his face and lower my voice to a growl. "Listen carefully, because you are having problems hearing me. I'm telling you to back the fuck off. Touch her, and I'll kill you myself. Is that clear enough?"

He flinches at my threat, his brows pulling together into an angry knot. Fire flares behind his eyes, and I can physically see him warring with himself in his expression.

With tight lips, he gives me a perfunctory bow of his head. "Of course, Your Highness."

My heart is pounding in my chest at how furious he's made me. I'll set a guard outside Guendolyn's room and ensure she no longer walks around the mansion on her own. Something about Jasion is off, and I can't risk him doing something stupid. There's enough shit to worry about without this added to the heap.

Jasion tilts his head up, meeting my gaze. "You would tell me if she's anything but a local healer, wouldn't you?" His neediness grates on my nerves.

"Get the fuck out of my room," I growl.

He nods and starts to turn away, but looks at me once more. "She's just a whore you're infatuated with. I know plenty more who are better and—"

My fist flies at him, clipping him in the side of the face. I'm furious and can't hold back any longer.

"Get the fuck out!" I bellow before I murder him.

He snarls under his breath as his hand goes to the blood trickling from beneath his eye, staring at me defiantly for a moment. Then he marches out of the study, shutting the door behind him with a bang.

"Fuck!" Jasion has always been loyal, so what the hell?

The door swings open, and I jerk around with fury, only to find it's Luther.

He gives me a weird look, but still asks, "What the hell's up with you?"

I heave each shallow breath and calm myself. "What do you want?"

"I have good news, brother." He crosses the room.

"About fucking time, I could use some."

"We received a response from the king's contact in Ash Court, and we need to leave now." He speaks quickly, reminding me of the times he went hunting, full of adrenaline and fueled to fight. "Deimos only has four days left, so we need to hurry."

"About damn time. I have something I need to do first, so I'll meet you down in the stables."

Luther nods, eager as fuck. "Oh, and the king said not to tell anyone where we're going. I don't think we should let Guendolyn know either, in case she lets it slips to someone."

"Agreed." Plus, she'll insist on coming with us and I don't want to leave on a bad note with her. It's crappy enough I left our bed this morning without saying a word. I should have woken her with a kiss, except I'm just fooling myself thinking there can be more between us. I don't fucking know where my mind is. It's bursting with so much information about what's going on, I'm not coping with the emotions as well as I usually would.

First, I need to help Deimos. Then I can sort out things with Guendolyn.

"Alright," Luther throws over his shoulder as he charges out of my room. "We leave as soon as possible, so get your ass down there immediately."

He vanishes, and I'm left in the room, stewing over Jasion, over needing to keep Guendolyn safe while we're gone...and then reality finally sinks in. We're about to break into the enemy court, and should anything go wrong, it could spell our deaths.

"Are you ready for your surprise?" Luther teases.

"What is it?" I squeak.

Something looks different about him tonight. Why is he so excited? He's smiling too much, and his touch warms my body. I long to sit with him and just talk about us, learn more about him, but when he excitedly burst into my room in the mansion, insisting we had to leave right away, his exhilaration was like a fever enveloping me. Talking could wait, I guess.

"You'll see," he says, his grin captivating as we run through the woods. With him, I don't feel scared. Maybe I should, but not tonight.

When he finally comes to a stop, we stand in front of a square wooden platform with railings on three sides. It's big enough for two or three people inside.

"What is that?" I'm breathing heavily, while he's barely broken a sweat.

He steps inside and guides me to follow him. "Welcome to my Ferris wheel."

I eye him suspiciously, but on the inside, I'm squirming with joy. Not only did he remember what we'd talked about when he spoke to me in my mind, but he made one. It looks nothing like the ones back home, since this is a simple platform that I assume just takes us upward, but he's never seen a Ferris wheel. He based his creation on my description, so I am excited to see what he made, and my stomach somersaults at the notion that he created this for me.

"I'm at a loss for words." I step onto the platform.

"That'll be a first." His hand finds my lower back, drawing me closer, and I sag against him. "Now hold on."

He stands so close now, I can feel the hard muscles of his chest and smell his breath, honey and blueberries and all masculine. He tugs hard on a rope with one hand, and in a heartbeat, our platform lurches and catapults upward. A whirring sound buzzes, like rope running over a metal wheel. My stomach pitches, and I shudder while clutching on to him, my hands bunching up his shirt as I plaster myself to him.

He laughs as the wind brushes against us, one large hand holding me in place the other gripping the wooden railing. We might end up soaring through the skies with how fast we travel as we slide up alongside lofty pine trees, their scent wafting on the breeze.

"Do you like my Ferris wheel?" he asks, his voice buffeting against the rush of air.

I hold on to him for dear life, the heat of his body pouring over me. "It's fantastic."

***

I RUSH DOWN the mansion hallway in yesterday's dress, and morning sunlight harshly cuts across my path from the windows of open rooms. Last night's dream of Luther's homemade Ferris Wheel still clings to my mind. The memory from the dream comes alive in me and leaves behind a tenderness from the reminder that he did such a thing for me. I just want to remember everything so I stop feeling so lost. I promise myself to ask him about it when I see him next.

The open rooms I pass are empty—no sign of the princes.

How long did I sleep in? I woke up in Ahren's bed, and his side was cold. After the most incredible night of my life, I expected to wake up in his arms, but maybe I was fooling myself.

No, I refuse to go down that rabbit hole, thinking that this was a one-off thing for him. Sure, he's the heir to the throne and there are expectations for him. That must be why he left me alone in his bed after a night of unbridled Kama Sutra.

Seriously, Ahren was insatiable, and every step I take now brings a delicious ache between my legs. It reminds me of him devouring my body for hours last night, and fucking me in so many positions, I lost track. If that was the typical libido of the fae, I am in for a massive rollercoaster ride.

Darting into my room, I've just shut the door, when seconds later, someone knocks on it. I pivot and run to it, expecting Ahren.

Dana stands in the doorway, and my heart sinks when I realize it's not Ahren waiting for me. It annoys me how much he's affected me after one night of sex. I should know better, because from everything I've learned about us, we can't be together, yet I fell prey to my sex-driven body.

"My lady, your bath awaits you." She delivers the words with a delighted grin, as if she loves to boss me around.

I blink at her, trying to calm the disappointment jabbing at my insides. "Have you seen Ahren this morning?"

Dana shakes her head, her brown curls bouncing across her shoulders. "We will find him after your bath, now come with me. You can't see the princes looking like that." She takes my wrist and tugs me to follow her. Reluctantly, I cave in and go because a bath sounds perfect. I glance down at my wrinkled blue dress and can only assume my hair is a mess.

"I have a surprise for you," she says, glancing across to me as she fights to hold back a smile.

"What is it?"

"I have filled your wardrobe with over a dozen outfits suited to royalty. The princes ordered them so you will have a selection to pick from."

My eyes widen. "Really? They did that for me?" Then the thought crosses my mind that Dana must have come into my room this morning when I wasn't there.

"I could never save enough money to afford to purchase such a wardrobe in my entire life, so count yourself lucky."

All I can think is that she's been in my room and noticed I didn't sleep in my bed last night. What does she think? That I'm the girl the princes are enjoying for payment in the form of clothes? "Dana, I'm only here to help heal Deimos."

"Of course, my lady." But she won't look at me when she talks.

I grind my back teeth, well aware she doesn't believe me. All the staff in the mansion must be gossiping about me as the princes' latest conquest. Fuck! I shouldn't care because it's better than everyone here knowing the truth, but it makes me wonder how many females the princes have brought into their mansion. A fire flares in my chest at the mental images the thought creates.

In the bathroom, we make a beeline for a tub filled with water. Wisps of heat curl upward, and the air is ripe with a pine scent. I'm ready to wash myself clean and start a new day. I swear I can still smell Ahren and his musky cum on me.

"I hope it's not too rude of me to say," Dana begins, "but I see the way the princes look at you, my lady."

After undressing, I climb into the tub, then slide down into the hot water and wrap my arms around my bent knees. "I'm sure they're just being nice, Dana. They are royalty, and I'm just a commoner."

She laughs and moves to stand behind me before starting to wet my hair with a pitcher. "I've seen them with other ladies, and they never looked at them this way. What a heart wants doesn't follow the rules made by a king."

***

BREAKFAST COMES AND GOES, and there's still no sign of Luther or Ahren. Now I'm in a sitting room with two walls of windows that overlook the picturesque mountains coated in snow. I stand in front of the spectacular view to try to distract myself, except it takes everything in me not to burst out of this room and demand someone tell me where the princes are.

Dana promised to track them down...that was over half an hour ago. If I hadn't spent the night with Ahren, I probably wouldn't care, but something at the back of my mind nags me that the night means something different to him than it did to me. I hate thinking that way.

I turn abruptly on my heels when Jasion strolls into the room. His shoulders are broad, chest bare, and his robe-skirt sashays around his legs. My heart bangs loudly in my ears. What's he doing here? Ahren wouldn't have told him what we got up to, would he? I lick my lips nervously.

"Morning," he says with a grin. "How are you feeling?"

"I'm fine." I look around, avoiding eye contact so he gets the hint that I don't want his company.

"Dana is worried about you," he says. "Saying you were frantically asking for the princes."

I jerk my head up. He moves to stand in front of the fireplace, warming his hands. I watch him suspiciously, convinced he's making up crap. He's trying to get a reaction out of me.

"You know Dana, she's always so dramatic." I half laugh, hiding my nervousness. "She reminds me of my mother. Always thinking the worst of any scenario, but I know it comes from a place of caring. Anyway, what brings you here?" I'm talking too fast and breathing quicker. There goes trying to play calm.

He doesn't respond right away. When he does, his voice is inquisitive. "You have a different dialect than others from this region," he says with his back to me.

"My mother isn't from this kingdom, so guess I picked up her way of speaking."

"And where is she from?" He turns to face me, the skull on his necklace swinging across his chest.

He's so predictable. I expected him to ask that question, so I use the same lie Deimos told Gabel. "She's from Waverton, a horribly dry place, apparently. They all speak a bit funny there."

He scans me head to toe. The more time I spend with this fae, the more he scares me. "Have you visited Waverton?" he asks me.

I shake my head. "Have you?" I'm not used to this back and forth war of words, and it makes my stomach ache.

He straightens. "No. The heat doesn't agree with me." Such a weird comment.

Silence sweeps between us. "The princes will be gone for a few days, and if you—"

"Wait, they're going away? Where?"

A smirk quirks the corners of his mouth upward. "That's not my place to say, but they may have already left."

They must be going to find a cure or something for Deimos. Ahren didn't even wake me up before leaving this morning? Heaviness sinks through me. "Where are they going?" I repeat.

"Why is that important to you?" Jasion's brow raises, impatiently waiting for me to respond.

Ahren seems like a good judge of character, and he trusts Jasion, but my gut tells me not to.

This time, I pull back my tense shoulders and shrug. "Curiosity, I guess." I'm tired of sparring with this fae who stares at me like a bug. My mind is frantically swirling at hearing Ahren and Luther are leaving the kingdom. I don't want to be left alone in this place.

I move toward the door when Jasion mutters, "I know you are not who you say you are."

My insides tremble, and his warning hits me hard. He's never going to give up... and while the two princes are gone, what's going to stop this asshole from going to the king and convincing him to imprison me, or worse yet... kill me? What if he has a way of finding out I'm from the Unseelie court? The thought of him talking with the king about me last night haunts me, echoing in my mind.

"I refuse to keep arguing with you about this. If you don't believe me, then take it up with Luther and Ahren upon their return."

My gaze locks on the door as I march forward, but shivers crawl up the back of my legs as I sense Jasion watching me.

"There are eyes everywhere in this kingdom, girl. Especially on you."

Shock rattles through my system. "You're having me watched?" Spinning around, I face the mage, tired of his threats. I don't even know him, but he treats me like a criminal. My gaze searches the darkness behind his eyes, leaving me feeling uneasy. There is something not right about him.

"Of course." He snorts. "And do you know what my priority is?"

I don't respond as I study this monster who wants a reaction out of me.

"Ensuring Ahren isn't harmed. All I ask is that you're open with me before this escalates. If you care for Ahren, you will tell me the truth and let me help you."

The only person who will take this further is Jasion. I don't trust a single thing about him.

"Help me with what?" I snap as a shiver slithers down my spine. How much does he know? Or is he simply bluffing? "Sorry, I thought you were Ahren's friend, not his bodyguard."

He tilts his head to the side. "I assumed you wouldn't cooperate." His gaze lifts to mine, and the warning is plain as day in his expression.

I suck in a breath, feeling like I've been punched in the gut.

"Have a pleasant day, girl," he patronizes me, then marches out of the room.

Alone with my drowning thoughts, I drag a hand down my face and sigh, feeling sick to my stomach. Jasion's threats swirl in my mind.

There are eyes everywhere.

What have I gotten myself into?

I glance at the door where he left, and my skin crawls. Staying here spells disaster for me, as Jasion seems to know so much more than he's letting on. The threatening nature of his words lift the hairs on my arms. I'd be an idiot to think I'm safe here on my own, and that means I need to catch the princes before they leave.

Marching across the room, I know this is the right decision. I run the rest of the way to my room, and grab a long coat and boots, then I'm off toward the kitchen, where I remember seeing a back door that leads outside. With no one in sight in the hallway, I dart left and into the main dining room. It's empty, and in the kitchen, I find the cook with his back to me, stirring something on the fire stove that smells like stew. Quick feet carry me to the back door, and I inch it open, then slide outside where the snow is coming down like a curtain. I can't see or hear anyone, and I pray I'm not too late.

FIFTEEN

LUTHER

Gusts of wind barrel into the carriage, but the cold is kept away by the fur blankets on our seats, our coats, and the sealed doors. We jostle from the bumpy terrain, but otherwise, it's an easy ride so far. Two horses harnessed to the coach wear a protective spell to aid with the freezing temperatures, and they have instructions on where to take us, so no need for a driver. Courtesy of one of the king's mages.

We've traveled for most of the day, cutting through the forest, and my ass is fucking numb from sitting so long. Ahren, who sits across from me, stares out the window at snow-covered trees.

"Any Bloodcursed out there?" I ask with sarcasm in my voice. The king's mages created a diversion on the opposite side of the kingdom to aid our exit. A few stragglers came after us, but we moved too fast for them.

Ahren shakes his head but doesn't look my way.

"What's wrong with you? Are you scared?" I throw at him.

He sneers at me, his nostrils flaring.

"Look, I tolerate you most of the time, but I'm not dealing with your moody shit today," I explain. "This mission could get us killed, so whatever's gotten to you, spill it."

Ahren responds with an intimidating frown, and I stiffen. If we were anywhere else, I'd push those buttons until we fought to get him to talk, but we don't have that luxury here.

"I've got lots on my mind."

"This isn't the time for distractions, brother."

He nods, almost conceding. This isn't Ahren. He stares out the window, his profile a mask. The air is tense around him, filling our carriage.

So I change topics to take a different approach. "Heard anything about the king's meeting with Guendolyn?"

"He got her drunk." Ahren looks at me, his lips thinning with disapproval.

My pulse races at the news. "He didn't try to—"

"Fuck, no," he answers with confidence. "The girl just can't hold her wine. I bumped into her in the hallway."

"You ended up making sure she got to her room safely last night, right?"

"What's with the interrogation?"

I bristle but don't jump back down his throat. Something else is going on here. "What the hell's up your ass?"

He turns away from the window to face me, his arms stretching out on either side on the back of his seat. "So much could go wrong. I'm just trying to get my mind into that headspace."

The wind howls again, buffeting the carriage and sending the whole vehicle into a sideward sway.

I cross my legs, an ankle over a knee, and run a hand through my hair. "I told Mael to keep a close eye on Guendolyn while we're gone."

"What if we don't make it back? What happens to her?" His voice is gentle, like he's given this a lot of thought, and he lets out a frustrated sigh. So it's fear that distracts him today—fear for Guendolyn.

My brother's feelings for her are stronger than I realized. Did sharing her company in the mansion affect him so much?

"You really like her, don't you?" I ask, locking my gaze with his. If my brothers are drawn to Guendolyn, there's nothing I can do about it, but I want to know. His expression turns thoughtful, as if considering my question for a sliver of a moment.

Then his upper lip curls. "Why the fuck are you asking me so many questions about her?"

"I'm not pissed, if that's what you're thinking. Hell, you know I'm head over heels for her. Have been even before I met her two years ago. Deimos lost his heart to her when he went to collect her from the human realm. So why are you so reluctant to admit it?"

"Since when do you openly talk about emotions?" he growls, his eyes narrowing.

I break out laughing and slouch back into my seat. "Touché, brother."

That rouses a smile out of Ahren, and he stretches his legs out at an angle so he doesn't hit mine.

"What's our backup plan?" I ask. "You fly us out of there?" I arch a brow and gain myself a grumpy look. "I don't remember the last time you used your wings."

"And you're not going to, so leave it the fuck alone." He clears his throat. The wings hidden inside his back are a touchy subject, but where we're going, any option to escape should be on the table.

"If shit goes south, then we fucking run for our lives. I've got explosive spells that will help us escape."

I nod, well aware that the Unseelie have their own range of powers, and there's a reason most fae keep their abilities private. Once the enemy knows, you are easily overpowered, but none of that matters if we can't find a cure for Deimos.

"Do you trust the king's contact that we're meeting in Ash Court?" I ask.

"How much do you trust any fae?"

"Fuck, not at all."

"Then you know what we're dealing with. Our guards stay up. In and out fast."

A short, explosive sneeze echoes faintly in the carriage.

Ahren's brow lifts.

I frown and look all around us. "What the fuck?" My thoughts fly to those damn fairies. Could they have hitched a ride with us?

The sneeze comes again, directly below me. I jump to my feet and shove aside the fur blankets. I grab the edge of the velvet seat and push it up to reveal the storage compartment.

Bright blue eyes stare up at me, face swallowed by shadows, and she sneezes again.

"Guendolyn? For fuck's sake." Fury barrels through me.

Bent low so as not to hit my head on the ceiling, I turn to Ahren who shuffles into the corner of his seat to give me space. He's seething.

"You told her, didn't you?" I bark. "We agreed not to tell her for this exact reason, but—"

"I didn't tell her anything," Ahren snaps back.

She pushes herself up to get out of the tight confinement, and I reach down, sliding my hands under her back and knees, then lift her out. Ahren shuts the lid, and I set her down, then squeeze in alongside Ahren. Both of us are staring at her.

Groaning, she stretches her arms into the air and twists her back until a bone cracks. She was squashed in there for a while, no wonder she's all cramped up, and possibly bruised, from the bumpy ride.

"Surprise!" she says, half smiling, half nervous. "And for your information, Jasion told me that you were leaving." She glares at Ahren more than me.

"We couldn't tell you for this reason," he reprimands.

"I—" She licks her lips and pulls the black coat tighter around her throat. "I didn't want to be in the kingdom alone. Jasion threatened me, and I didn't feel safe. Plus, I don't see why I can't come with you to get whatever is needed for Deimos' cure."

"Wait, what did Jasion do?" Ahren leans forward.

She reclines in her seat, glancing outside momentarily. "He said I was being watched and that he didn't believe my story about who I was."

"How is that a threat?" I ask.

Guendolyn rolls her eyes. "Really? When a man says that kind of shit, that means one thing—someone wants to hurt me."

"I have to agree with Guendolyn on this one," Ahren says. "Jasion is by nature a very paranoid person. It takes him a long time to trust anyone, and he goes out of his way to find out the truth when he thinks he's being told lies. He won't harm you, though. I've spoken to him already about needing to keep away from you, to ensure you are not harmed."

She folds her arms around her middle. "I guess you had to be there to feel the evil vibes shooting off him. And he wasn't keeping his distance. He might be nice to you, but he hates me. I saw it in his eyes."

I butt in. "Jasion has always been attached to you, brother. And I've seen him get jealous when you spend time with women."

Ahren stiffens. "No, you're wrong. We're friends. We've always been friends and he's just protective."

I shake my head. "Brother, I should have seen this earlier too. It makes sense as to why he'd have tantrums when he couldn't find you, and why he's constantly in our mansion and not with the other mages. You know he once secretly paid the seamstress several gold coins to leave and never return or there'd be consequences? I thought he was just being a prick, which is normal for him, but he did that after the woman spent the morning with you alone to measure you for a new coat."

He broods and shifts his angry stare from Guendolyn to me. "Why the fuck are we talking about me?" Ahren swings his attention back to her. "You can't come with us."

"How do you know you won't need me?" She smirks in mischief, and if I wasn't so furious that she joined us on this perilous trip, I might sit back and enjoy the show. She's quite the performer.

Ahren's glare deepens. "I don't want you hurt. You're not coming."

"So what, you're going to turn around and head back to the kingdom and waste precious time Deimos doesn't have?"

He shakes his head. "We're dropping you off in the next Seelie town to wait for us."

Her mouth drops open. "You wouldn't!"

"You think that's a smart idea?" I ask, unsure I want to leave Guendolyn with strangers right now.

"It's better than her joining us," Ahren snarls.

"I'm not getting dumped in some town. I bet all the men there leer at females like that last town we stopped at."

Ahren sighs, and I'm not sure what the fuck to do.

"Fucking fine," my brother growls. "You stay in the carriage this whole trip. If things go bad...well, then we're all pretty much fucked anyway."

Her gaze widens, stunned at his reply.

Exhaling a heavy breath, I offer her a half-smile. "You being here is a really bad move, little wolf."

She studies me for a long pause. "Well, so is being stalked. I'll hedge my bets and choose you two over Jasion. You can't blame me for not wanting to end up in prison." Sullen, she curls toward the window.

Except she has no idea how wrong she is. She's joined us on a trip that might be our last.

I don't know what to feel.

They clearly aren't happy to see me, but I don't care. I'm not being left behind. Eventually, Luther moved to sit on my side, while I have my legs curled in under me. I lean against the carriage window and stare outside, though I keep sneaking glances over to Ahren who has that angry look on his face. I can sense him watching me. Is he thinking about us last night or what a douche he was for not even coming to see me this morning? They're both asses for heading off on a hazardous journey without saying goodbye.

Forests and mountains fill my view, and half the time, I still can't believe I'm in such a beautiful place...but even a rose has thorns, right?

The carriage suddenly comes to a halt.

I straighten in my seat and swivel around. Ahren pushes open the door on the other side, and a gust of icy wind rushes inside, biting into my flesh. He climbs out and sends the carriage rocking.

Luther turns to leave as well, but I grab his arm. "Hey, can we talk?" I ask.

He pauses as if considering my question, then sits back down. "What is it?"

"I get you're both pissed at me, but I was seriously scared for my life with Jasion. That's why I came. I figured I could help if you're just picking up ingredients or something for the cure. I had no idea you were going to Ash Court."

"This trip is perilous, especially for you." A touch of paleness touches his cheeks.

Deimos' words from when we first arrived outside the Unseelie castle come to mind.

They find us on their land, they'll kill us in the most painful way possible.

But with that memory comes another from the Unseelie who attacked me in the elevator back on Earth and what he said.

The King of Ash Court has called for you.

Why would the king send those monsters to bring me to their court if they intend to kill me?

"My parents live there," I say. "This could be a chance for me to find out who they are."

Luther shakes his head and laughs hysterically, but it's fake. "Do you have a death wish?"

"It's not funny. My whole life, I've wanted to know the truth of who I am."

"Little wolf, listen carefully. Whoever your parents are, they are not nice fae. I'd give my right arm to say otherwise, but they gave you up so the mages could use you as a carrier for a curse to destroy Shadow Court."

I try to swallow his words, but they punch me straight in the chest. My parents sacrificed me, that's what he's saying. That I wasn't important enough.

"Then why did they send me to Earth? Why not just release the curse and be done with it? Why this elaborate show?"

He runs a hand through his hair, a softness sweeping across his expression as if he pities me.

"Don't feel sorry for me," I argue. "Help me understand what happened."

"The Unseelie liked to have a constant reminder of the curse they placed on us and the threat of unleashing it if we didn't submit to them. They were the ones who spread the rumors of your prophecy in the first place, to scare everyone."

I nod, my throat thickening, and I swallow past the growing lump. "I'm a nobody then. A throwaway child."

I glance away, and he touches my hand in my lap.

"Not true."

I blink away the tears as my stomach sinks. Am I really just a pawn in a game between two kingdoms? With a tilt of my head, I look up at Luther, this gorgeous fae who whisked me from my oblivious world and brought me here. "Maybe it was a mistake to bring me to the Wandering Realm."

"You didn't have a choice, little wolf. The spies from Ash Court had found you. It was the only way I tracked you down, or we might never have crossed paths."

"Then why would they still kill me if I return to their kingdom? I've unknowingly completed whatever mission they sent me on me, right? So why not embrace me back into their court?"

He sighs heavily, lifting his attention to the window and away from me.

"What do you know?" My voice deepens. "Please, Luther."

His big hand reaches over and strokes the side of my face, but I have no patience today. I push him away. "Tell me!"

He huffs a loud breath. "If you die, the curse on our kingdom can never be removed. We will forever be plagued by the Bloodcursed until every last Seelie fae is killed."

My head feels heavy, and my chest aches. I'm consumed by the horrible thoughts that my own parents used me and are now happy to dispose of me. "The final nail in the coffin. Fuck!"

He starts saying something, but I don't hear the words. I just keep thinking over what he's told me and everything that's led me to this point. All the information amplifies my curiosity. If the Unseelie wanted me dead after I unleashed the spell, why send me back to Earth with no memories? Why not kill me then and there? Hell, why not kill me as a child? What am I missing?

But part of the answer forms over my mind like a cobweb.

I swipe at the tear sneaking out the corner of my eye and interrupt Luther. "I think someone at the Ash Court tried to save me. Maybe they botched the spell." I give Luther a rundown of my thoughts. "Why else would I forget my past? It's so they couldn't find me on Earth. Except, I was lucky that you and your brothers found me first."

His brow furrows as he prods a finger at his chin.

"You think it might have been my parents?" I ask. "Maybe they were forced to give me up." I feel hope creeping into my chest.

"Oh, little wolf." Luther's face falls, and he gathers me into his arms.

I soften against him, inhaling his woodsy, masculine scent that carries a splash of clementine, as if he'd eaten them for breakfast. He holds me so tight, making me feel safe.

"What's going on?" Ahren's words slice through the moment.

I break away to find him watching us from outside the carriage and expect some kind of jealousy, but he stares at us with admiration. I have been way off base with these princes since I first met them. They all confuse me with their emotions and reactions.

"Where are we going?" I glance out through the windows and see nothing but forest.

Ahren stretches out a gloved hand toward me. I pull myself out of Luther's arms and take Ahren's offered hand as I step outside into the cold. Tugging my coat tighter around me, I stare ahead at the enormous bronze fence woven intricately with swirling patterns. They open before us, revealing a dirt road and more trees that layer the land beyond the gates.

A man in a black coat with a hat pulled down low on his head waves us in to join him.

"Where are we?"

"Lockinge, a small town aligned with Shadow Court. We send them protection and whatever else they need," Luther explains. "In exchange, they provide us with information on what they see in the woods. Most living here are scouts or forest wardens."

"What's that?"

"Fae entrusted with the oversight of the forest and its animals."

"So like rangers. That is really impressive."

"You two go ahead," Ahren orders. "I'll take the carriage and horses inside."

Luther and I move forward, the snow crunching under our feet with each step. "Is this town similar to the other one we stopped at when we traveled to the kingdom?"

He shakes his head. "Nothing like it. Here, people work for the good of the fae, and we are always welcome without payment."

It warms my heart to hear that for once we're not looking over our shoulders.

"The local tavern serves the best deer stew and fresh poppy seed bread."

Considering I haven't eaten at all, I'm ready to eat anything they put in front of me. "Sounds good. I'm starving."

Luther walks tall beside me. From the way he carries himself, it's easy to recognize that he's royalty. He pushes up the collar of his deep blue coat, and we stride quickly down the path, fighting a horribly icy wind.

Up ahead, there's a small wooden hut that's round with a pointy roof. The whole thing is a deep green color. There's a front door and two windows, along with a chimney pumping out smoke from a fireplace. Amid the trees, I find more homes similar to that one, but no one's around, and I don't blame them. It's too cold.

Luther directs me to another enormous round hut. No windows, just a large arched door.

I glance back but see no sign of Ahren. "Do you think your brother will be alright? Maybe we should wait for him?"

"He's more than capable. Plus, he has to meet the town leader."

Luther doesn't seem worried about the fae living here, so I breathe easily. "That doesn't sound like fun," I answer.

"Not that much fun, not when it comes to royal requirements and etiquette."

A wall of heat smothers us the moment we step into the building. Rows of long wooden tables and benches fill the large room. At one side is a bar-like counter and a door that goes into what I assume is a kitchen. On the other side is a monstrous fireplace made of black stone, flames snapping and crackling within.

The man behind the counter lifts his chin to us, his mouth dropping open, then he bows his head. He sets the dishcloth in his hand on the counter and rushes over to us, running his hands down his white apron.

"Your Highness," he says. "I didn't know you were paying us a visit today."

"Bracken," Luther greets him. "It's great to see you again. How long has it been?"

"Two years." He lifts his head to look at the prince, not even noticing me. There's admiration in the fae's eyes, as though he's fangirling over the prince. "The king paid a visit several months ago, but it is wonderful to have you join us. Unfortunately, this weather does not permit for a hunting challenge like on your last visit."

Luther breaks out laughing and slaps the man on the shoulder. "I believe I won that round. Do you really wish such torment on the locals again?"

His smile is wide and contagious, and I find myself doing the same. "That you did, Your Highness. Now, please have a seat. I'll bring out hot stew and bread for you both." The man turns and hurries toward the back door.

"Make it for three," Luther calls out. "My brother Ahren will be joining us."

Bracken's eyes almost bulge out of his head, and he's practically bouncing on his toes. "Of course."

Luther undoes the buttons on his snow-dusted coat and takes it off before placing it on one of the dozen hooks on the wall beside the front door, and I do the same with mine.

He smirks when he looks down at me. "What?"

"Does everyone gush over you?"

He leans in close and whispers, "The only fae I want falling before me is you." He winks, reminding me how much he affects me. My heart races when he flirts like this. I may not remember our past, but what I feel now is a storm of emotions and attraction to this fae. I tried my best to push him away until I sorted out my thoughts, but was I just fooling myself? The magnetism between us is impossible to resist.

God, all I can think about now is Luther's remark in the carriage about all of them wanting to be with me. There was no sound of jealousy in his words, so does that mean they want to share me? It should scare me how much I love the idea of three princes ravaging me. Suddenly, I'm feeling extremely hot.

Without waiting for my comeback, Luther leads us to a table all the way at the back and sits with his back to the wall. I sit on the bench across from him.

"What did you do in the hunting challenge?" I ask out of pure curiosity and to get my mind out of the gutter. There is such a calm vibe in this tavern compared to the last one, where women had to be carried inside or they were good for all men to make a move on. I still seethe at the memory that women were for only one thing.

"Boar hunting," Luther answers as he scrunches up the sleeve of his silvery blue top to show a healed scar the length of my hand. "The bastard got me, but I got him back. He tasted delicious later that night."

The door creaks open with a gust of icy air, catching my attention. Ahren enters and spots us. I can't stop staring at him as he leaves his coat on a hook and saunters over like a god, all shoulders and power. He's dressed in black, his white hair sits ragged around his gorgeous face, and his green eyes are wild. His beauty radiates in any room he walks into, and I'd be lying if I said he doesn't affect me as much as Luther and Deimos do. My body responds to them intensely, my heart racing, my core burning up. He's so different from his brothers though...always serious and needing to be in control. Our night together revealed a different side to him...a side I longed to see again.

I turn to find Luther watching me. He's got a stronger jawline and is more rugged, but he's just as utterly sexy.

"Did you order food?" Ahren asks as he sits next to me.

"Sure did," I respond and glance back at Luther, who has a strange look on his face like he's about to ask me a question.

I pinch my lips at him and mouth, "What?"

Last night you let Ahren take you. His words flare in my mind. *Tonight, you're mine.*

SEVENTEEN

GUENDOLYN

Luther grins at me so sexily that a shiver zaps south and hits me right between my thighs. He stirs arousal inside me with just a few words.

Tonight, you're mine.

The look in his eyes belongs to someone who's ready to shove aside the table between us and toss me over his shoulder. I swallow hard and look over to Ahren, who studies the room and isn't paying attention to the sexual tension about to turn me into a puddle.

You're so cute when you're startled.

I narrow my eyes at Luther to show him I'm not falling prey to his seductive stare. His grin widens as we face each other, neither of us moving. I'm at a complete loss for words. Luther likes me—more than likes me, I know this—and I'm madly attracted to him, but he's pulled away from me since we arrived at the mansion. I also can't remember why I feel so strongly toward him, but that doesn't make me less infatuated with him. We just never really got the chance to spend as much time together as I have with Ahren and Deimos.

Long ago, darkness and light came together and created beauty...a beauty that will destroy this world.

I give my head a small shake to imply I don't understand.

A proverb from the ancient fairies. It reminds me of you, except they've got it wrong. You're the beauty who will save this world.

He's definitely a sweet talker.

Ahren gets up from the table. "I'm ordering drinks. There's no one serving at this place."

"All right," I say.

He heads across the room, not glancing back.

"Why didn't you tell me?" Luther asks immediately, his voice deep. "About you and Ahren?"

I swing back to him. "He told you?"

With a tilt of his head, Luther's voice streams over my thoughts. *Brothers share.*

Heat curls up against my neck and over my cheeks. How much, exactly, did Ahren reveal? How many times he brought me to orgasm? Was it just chest-pumping bragging?

"It just happened," I whisper, my breathing growing shallow. "What do you want me to say? That I'm sorry? I won't apologize." Something isn't right with me, but my heart is pounding too hard to stop, and I don't want to apologize for something I enjoyed. Plus, I don't really know where I stand with Ahren. We haven't properly spoken since last night. "I'm sure it was a one-off thing. You don't need to make a big deal of it."

His eyes darken. Sure, he's tall, handsome, and goddamn sexy as hell, not to mention a smooth talker, but that doesn't make him less of an ass for grinning at me as I squirm.

He looks up and over my shoulder, then back at me. "One-off thing? That's not what Ahren said."

My stomach plummets right through me. "W-What did he say?"

A gleam of determination lights up in his gaze.

Just then, Ahren returns and places three wooden jugs on the table. Drops of red wine splash out over the rim and onto the table.

Remembering my night drinking with the king, I say, "Thanks, but I'll pass."

"It's not wine, little wolf," Luther murmurs. "It's a berry juice known for helping boost virility." He snorts a laugh, while Ahren shakes his head and laughs too.

I roll my eyes and push my cup away. Luther drinks his in one go, then takes mine and finishes it off while holding my stare. Oh, I know exactly what he's thinking before he even says anything.

All for you, little wolf.

I want to smack that smirk off his face. He's such a smartass today.

Bracken turns up at our table with a tray and places bowls of stew in front of us, along with a wicker basket filled with sliced bread and butter, then he sets down a cup of water for me. Another waiter, a young man with short dark hair and head held low, joins us and leaves large goblets of wine for the princes.

"Enjoy. There is plenty where that came from." Bracken gives us spoons and a knife for the butter, then bows as he and the other server leave us in peace.

"Thank you, Bracken," Ahren responds, then he turns to his food, stirring his spoon through the stew. All business, he speaks to Luther and me. "We'll leave at dawn and should arrive at Ash Court by midday."

I stare down at my meal and take a spoonful with a piece of meat and potato. Thick and heavily spiced, the savory taste fills my senses, and I swear I'm back home eating one of my foster mom's homemade meals. "This is so good."

"Try it with the bread," Luther suggests, handing me a slice generously coated with butter. I take a bite and moan. It's still warm and salty and creamy.

"Told you it's good."

We all eat without talking until our bowls are empty. Ahren orders another serving, and I'm not too shy to hold back. But when the princes go for a third round and a new loaf of bread, I shake my head.

"That's the best dish I've had in ages." I sip my water.

Ahren glances over at me, then pauses, and I can see the wheels spinning behind his gaze. "This town is very safe, Guendolyn," he points out. "Maybe you staying here isn't such a bad idea until we return?"

"No!" Luther and I say together.

Ahren frowns at his brother, but I'm glad someone agrees with me.

"Worst case scenario," I begin, "I can try to open a portal for us to escape through."

"Except Deimos isn't here to help you with that," Ahren snaps back.

"But she activated and closed the portal for the fairies without kissing Deimos." Luther says, stealing my exact response.

"I just need to concentrate."

Ahren asks, a bit too loudly, "If you do open a portal, how will you close it quickly?"

"Well, I learned a little trick from the blue fairy for closing a portal. I think it should work."

"Think?" Ahren asks.

I don't waste a moment and reply, "If we end up needing a portal, then we're caught anyway, right? You said so in the carriage. We're fucked. To me, it makes sense that I accompany you into Ash Court."

"Hell no," Luther bites back.

Traitor. I eye him intensely, and he winks back. Something flutters in my stomach.

Ahren groans, shadows dancing under his eyes. "Fine. You can join us on the trip, but you wait in the carriage. No compromises on that."

I shrug. "Fine." It's better than being abandoned in a strange town.

The princes finish their meals just as Bracken returns. "Your Highnesses," he says with a bow. "We have a house prepared for your stay. It's the third one behind us in the woods."

"Thank you," Ahren responds, radiating waves of formality in his voice and stiff posture. "You have been too kind to us."

"There is a small matter I wanted to follow up on. The king, His Majesty, promised to send us a supply of horses and extra workers." Bracken grimaces. "I'm sorry to bring this up, but the delivery has been delayed for close to eight weeks."

"Well, that is my cue to take the lady to her room," Luther says, getting to his feet and eying me to get me to follow. "Thank you for everything, Bracken. I will let you discuss these matters with Ahren."

I'm on my feet and step over the bench. "Thank you," I say to the fae before glancing momentarily at Ahren. He's holding the man's stare, that stoic, regal expression sitting on his face, his shoulders broad.

Luther leads me across the room. We collect our coats, and I slip into mine as we walk outside. The icy wind makes me shiver as Luther shuts the door and takes my hand in his, then guides me around the side of the building. Night spreads its wings over the landscape, and the only thing visible is a flickering torch in the distance.

"Quickly," Luther says, his voice sharp.

I wrap an arm around my middle and keep my chin low as we rush down a path between the trees. We pass two homes with bright lights beaming out of the windows, then finally come upon a dark hut. Luther pushes open the door and waves me inside.

Warmth greets me, wrapping around me in an instant and vanquishing the cold clinging to my skin. The door shuts with a thump, and I step into a large living room. The fireplace floods the room with heat and light. Above the mantelpiece sits a painting of the king sitting atop a black stallion. A long couch sits in front of the fire, and two matching single chairs are on either side. I guess with no television, the fireplace is the best they have for living room entertainment in this world.

"This looks nice," I say.

Luther shrugs his coat off to hang on the hook near the door, so I unbutton mine and take it off before handing it to him and toeing off my soaked boots. He does the same. Stepping toward the fire, I head for the lush, brown rug.

Two doorways exit off the main room, leading to a kitchen and a bedroom. Looks like we'll be sharing tonight, and considering the cold, I have no problem with that. Well, and the fact that I'll be with two incredibly hot fae.

Luther stands behind the couch, his amber eyes piercing into me. My heartbeat is rapid, and I'd be lying if I said I didn't like my reaction to him. If anything, I want more. Of course, we have a history together that I don't remember, and I desperately long to... But I can't change that, and I can't ignore my growing attraction to him, either.

"How did you find the meal?" he asks to break the silence.

"Really good," I answer. "I could eat that most nights."

He leans his hands on the back of the couch. "I've asked our cooks back at the castle to replicate it, but they just can't get it right. Just like the berry drink, which you missed out on, little wolf, but I can take a bottle with us on our trip."

I shake my head and don't move from in front of the fireplace, as my back is nice and toasty. "No thanks. I'll stick to water. The last time I drank something I wasn't used to, I was left with my head spinning." Not to mention in Ahren's bed.

He quirks a corner of his mouth upward. "Spinning like a Ferris Wheel?"

I stiffen and remember my dream with Luther and the Ferris Wheel he made for me, and how he'd gone to all that trouble. I can't hold back the smile. "My dream the other night was about you showing me something you created for me in the woods. You insisted it was a Ferris Wheel based on something I'd told you."

His eyes widen, flashing with a fiery light. "You remember our past?" He's upright and alert.

I hold up a hand, not wanting to give him a false sense of hope. "It's only bits and pieces in my dreams of my past in the kingdom. Like a puzzle I still haven't put together."

He emerges from behind the couch and approaches me. "This is fantastic news." He looks at me as if he might suddenly break into cheers, which leaves me beaming on the inside.

"Can you tell me more about the scene in my dream?" I ask.

His smile is contagious, and he flops down on the arm of the couch, one foot propped up on the cushion, his arm draped over his knee. "Before we first met, I spoke to you for a long time in your mind. We talked about things you liked, your fears, your dreams, even other men you admired at your school."

"We did?" I swallow, quite unsure what to say. Did I think I was going crazy with a voice in my head? Was that why I had told him so much back then? Now, I feel a little exposed, because he knows so much about me while I know so little about him.

"And one night you spoke of Ferris Wheels." He breaks out laughing, as if he's picturing the conversation in his mind, and I can't help but grin. "You described them to me and said that's where couples go to kiss. So, when I finally found you and brought you here that first time, I created one for you." He chuckles even louder, and the sound he makes is up there with some of the best sounds I've ever heard.

"You know when I first heard 'Ferris Wheel,'" he says. "I thought it was either a weapon or a sex toy."

I can't help but burst out laughing. Those were his only two options? "So I'm guessing you built it as an excuse to kiss me?"

He studies me, tilting his head to the side. "It worked." He blows me a kiss, and my knees quiver beneath me. I'm not used to having such gorgeous men flirt with me. "I think you said I didn't quite get the wheel part right. But it was worth it for that kiss."

Part of me wants to have him kiss me and see if it sparks anything because I so want to remember more of this fae and our past. Instead I say, "The memories you describe sound incredible."

"You know, our conversations made me fall for you before I ever laid eyes on you."

His confession curls around my chest, and sorrow bites into me at the thought that I've missed out on these pieces of him. "Will you tell me more about our past?"

"Of course."

"And about your ability. There's so much I want to know. Can you go into anyone's mind anytime, including animals? What about fairies?"

He arches a brow, caught off guard by my questions. His eyes flick over me, and butterflies burst in my stomach, beating their wings. His expression denotes intrigue, like I've finally opened a door between us.

I search my mind for something to say. "I met your dog, Sir Wolf-A-Lot. He's adorable, in a if-a-hellhound-could-be-a-pet kind of way."

"I don't want to talk about hellhounds." Luther gets up and moves toward me, looking like he only wants to focus on me. I watch his every move until he stands in front of me. Without my shoes, I feel even shorter next to him, and I have to crane my head back.

He grabs my wrist and draws me to his body. My hand comes up and presses flat to his hard chest as my insides tingle. We look into each other's eyes, and his attention dips to my lips as I bite them. "What does my touch do to you? Stir any memories up?"

"No."

His expression softens. Maybe it's about time I come to terms with the fact that I may not remember my past, but with Luther's help, I can try to recreate it.

When he glances up again, he holds the sides of my face, then slowly leans in and kisses me.

"And this?"

My breath hitches, and my knees threaten to buckle. Holy hell, I'm about to swoon. "Nope, nothing. I think we need to keep trying."

His eyes search mine before he dips his head and lightly brushes his lips across mine again, making my entire body buzz. His tenderness undoes me. I kiss him back, our mouths pressed together, our tongues dancing. I want him so intensely that I forget everything else, possibly even my name. One hand pushes into my hair, and he kisses me deeper. I fist his shirt and wrench him closer, holding him tightly to me, as the hard line of his cock through his pants nestles against me.

"You are breathtaking," he whispers.

I'm drunk on his kiss, swept into another world, so far away from reality that I feel like I might pass out if he were to leave my side. My feelings for him overwhelm me and crash over me. I'm burning up as if the sun has taken residence in my chest.

He breaks our kiss, and we face each other, our foreheads touching.

"In truth, little wolf, I don't know if I'm right for you at all. Promising anything is a disaster waiting to happen. We're from enemy courts, and will never be allowed to be together," he admits, and his words sink into me like fangs.

My stomach tightens. Why is he saying this?

He continues, "I can't make you remember me, but if having you means starting over and breaking the kingdoms' laws, well...I'll risk it all to keep you."

His warm breath skates over my face, and his words tangle around my heart. An ache flares in my chest at the thought that any future I may have with the princes is rife with thorns and heartache. But staring into Luther's dark amber eyes, I realize he's offering me a chance to follow my heart. I don't care about stupid rules, only my feelings for these three princes that deepen with each passing day.

"Luther, I..." I struggle to find the right words. "That is the sweetest thing ever."

"We finally met in person two years ago, but I just didn't know how much you meant to me. Not until you stepped over the Ash Court threshold and disappeared from my arms." He kisses my nose.

"Ahren told me you blame yourself for bringing me here," I murmur.

He studies me, not showing any reaction on his face.

"What I'm guilty of is not keeping you more protected when I brought you into our realm. One of the Unseelie snuck into our mansion one night and lured you to Ash Court. They intended to have you cross the threshold into their Court, then kill you. I came after you, but everything happened so fast." He sighs heavily, shadows gathering in his eyes. "I tried to save you, but you stepped onto Ash Court during the battle, and the curse was released. Then you disappeared from my arms and back to Earth."

We fall silent after that, my chest aching at hearing the pain in his voice. He's lived with that for the past two years, and I don't know how to console him when I can't even remember the events. But with the dreams I've been having and more information from Luther, I'm starting to piece together the mystery of my past.

I cup his face and kiss him, wanting to take away his agony, and the wall I tried to put up between us comes crashing around my feet. I shouldn't rush into this, but I want to stop the hurt. I want to somehow feel like I belong here.

He kisses me back with hunger this time and drags his hands down my back, lighting me up with every stroke. His fingers trace the skin under my clothes and slide around my waist to the front of my pants. There's a desperation in us coming together, like we both want to lighten the burden we feel.

I gasp at his touch, my body thrumming. He pops open the buttons and begins to tug the pants down my hips. Our mouths draw apart, and I glance over to the door. What if Ahren comes in?

"Should we be doing this here?" I ask.

"Fuck, I don't care where we go, little wolf. I need you."

I could drown in the sexiness behind his gaze, my entire body trembling with heightened desire. If Ahren walks in on us, I don't care. Maybe he can even join us. So I pull down my pants and underwear and step out of them, offering myself to Luther because I crave him.

He reaches for me, his attention lowering, but I smirk and nudge his hand away.

"No." I fall to my knees before him and reach for his belt and undo his pants.

"Guendolyn, little wolf, you don't have to."

"But I want to do this so much." I yank down his pants, and his cock explodes out, making me gasp with delight. He's so damn erect and big, and his scent is intoxicating. There must be something to what he said about the berry juice.

I wrap my hand around his cock, and he groans as I slide his tip into my mouth, his taste salty and sweet, then push him in deeper. My tongue runs over his shaft, leaving no part untouched.

"Oh, fuck!" He shudders beneath me.

Glancing up, I meet his eyes. I love seeing this strong fae fall at my mercy. I glide him in and out of my mouth, sucking on him. His hips start rocking back and forth, his sounds driving me to take him deeper. I want to see him lose control under my touch.

God, he is so gorgeous.

Suddenly, he nudges my shoulders back and slides himself out of my mouth with a pop. I lick my lips and take his hand as he brings me to my feet.

"Now it's my turn." He picks me up and places me on the fur rug in front of the fire. "Lift your hands." I obey him, and he tugs my shirt and the one underneath up my body and over my head. The fireplace warms me instantly. Still, my nipples harden, and I lay an arm over them.

"Don't cover yourself. You are so much more beautiful than I could have imagined." He prowls over me.

I lower my arms and lay on my back on the rug as we kiss like it's our first time, fast, exploring each other's mouths. I grasp on to his muscular arms when he dips his head to my neck and chest, licking his way to my nipples. He takes one into his mouth, drawing me deeper in.

Delicious aches pulse through my body, curling around my core. He greedily pays the same attention to my other breast, sucking on me, gently gnawing on my hardened nipple. When he comes up for air, he grins. "You smell divine. Your fragrance reminds me of honey. Will your pussy taste like honey when I lick it?"

I quiver all over. "Oh hell, Luther."

He makes his way lower, tracing my stomach with his tongue, and pushes himself to kneel between my legs, nudging them wider.

His gaze flicks over me. "I love you like this."

Fingers slide over the seam of my pussy, and I moan, my hips automatically rising.

"So wet for me." A finger finds my heat and pushes into me.

"Ahhh." I arch my back in response.

"Good girl. Coat my fingers." He draws them out of me and pushes back in, then he leans down and licks my pussy. His tongue expertly traces my slick length while I lose myself. He wastes no time and presses his mouth to my center, devouring me as his tongue glides over my clit again and again. I fist the fur rug, moaning louder when he pulls back.

Breathing heavily, I plead, "Please don't make me wait."

The corner of his mouth tugs upward, his grin lopsided in the most ravishing way.

"Come to me." He gives me his hand, which I accept, and I'm up on my ass in seconds. Then he draws me up on the couch where he takes a seat. He pulls his top up and over his head, then tosses it aside. He has so many muscles, I am in paradise.

"I want to see you, watch your breasts bouncing in my face." His hands fall on my hips as he guides me to straddle him, then he firmly pulls me to him. We kiss as his hand slides between my thighs, sweeping over my pussy. He presses the tip of his cock to my slit, then slides it up and down.

Hell, if he doesn't take me soon, I'm going to scream.

I adjust to take him and widen my legs more to meet his movements. He sucks on my tongue as he pushes down my hips so I sit on his cock. He goes slow as I widen inch by inch for his size, but my cries of pleasure have him pushing in quicker until he's completely plunged into me.

Gripping the couch behind him, I begin to move up and down his length. His chest heaves for each breath as he watches my breasts bounce. He looks up at me as he raises his hips to meet each of my thrusts, slapping into me harder and harder. I ride him wildly, groaning, loving every second of feeling him so deep inside me.

He growls, his fingers digging into my hips, and pumps faster. I see the primal need in his eyes. He suddenly lifts me, then pivots us around so that I'm lying on the couch with him on top of me. Wasting no time, he pummels into me like a goddamn animal. He's relentless and tearing into my pussy, causing the most insane sensations to course through my body.

I cry out as he fucks me, his delicious assault leaving me filled with electricity.

I finally explode with an orgasm. Head tilted back, I scream with an insatiable release as the climax shudders through me.

Luther groans as he halts his thrusts and stays locked to me as he comes alongside me, bursts of his semen filling me. Both of us are gasping for air, smiling crazily at how good that felt.

He collapses on top of me, his breath tickling my neck. I laugh and wrap my arms around him.

"Didn't realize you were so ticklish," he whispers as his fingers find my ribs.

I burst out laughing, my body writhing to get away from him. "Hey, no fair! I'm trapped."

He pulls out and stands before me, studying all of me. "Well then, I'll give you a head start. Once we clean up, I'm going to find every part of your body that responds to my fingers."

My eyes widen. "Don't you dare."

He grins mischievously. "Challenge accepted."

EIGHTEEN

AHREN

The fire crackles and warms my freezing hands. I spent much longer with Bracken than I intended. Guendolyn and Luther are asleep on the bed, and I smell the musky aroma of sex in the small cottage. I've always shared everything with my brothers, and if Guendolyn is happy with that, I have no problem with her decision. As long as it's just my brothers and no one else.

But right now, I need some time to unwind and slow my thoughts. Tomorrow will be a big day, and I can't keep the fear away. Fear that we won't succeed, that we won't save Deimos, that we'll die.

I exhale loudly when a creak from across the room catches my attention. Guendolyn emerges from the bedroom in her black pants and top, her hair messy, but she's still as adorable as ever.

"Can't sleep?" I ask.

She nods and shuts the bedroom door. "I keep having stupid dreams about drowning, and I'm a bit scared about tomorrow."

"Join me." I pat the couch next to me. "I'm hoping my mind stops over-thinking everything."

She takes a seat next to me, and we don't speak for a little while. It's comforting to enjoy the silence with someone and not feel like I have to always perform, to be the prince always on the job.

"Did I hear right, back in the carriage, that you have wings?" she asks with excitement behind her voice.

I grind my jaw, wanting to drive Luther's head through a wall for saying shit he shouldn't have.

"It's nothing," I respond.

She fake laughs, her eyes widening. "Bullshit. Having wings is not nothing. How come I've never seen them before? What do they look like?"

She's clearly wide awake now, as she rattles on with question after question, and I can't help but adore this side of her. When she sinks her teeth into something, she picks at that thread until it comes undone. She has to know everything.

"Do you have two wings like an angel? Or four like a butterfly?" She's on her feet now, her arms animated, and as pissed as I am for her talking about a topic I loathe, she makes me smile. Guendolyn has an effect on me like no other. I don't know what it fucking is, but I feel myself soften around her.

"How about one question at a time?" I respond.

She pauses and lowers her hands. "Show them to me."

"Of course you'd ask that. The answer is no. Try again."

She huffs, and her face scrunches up before she speaks again. "I thought only fairies have wings?"

"It's quite rare for fae to have them."

"Why don't you use yours?" She shoots back. Maybe I was wrong to give her the option of asking me anything, as this can go very bad.

But with the way she looks at me, all I want is to bring back the mischievous smile on her face.

Fuck, what the hell has she done to me?

"Are you worried the wings make you look a bit girly and delicate, you know, like a fairy? Is that why you don't like them?"

I arch a brow. "What the fuck?"

She laughs at me, and I can't stop the blood pumping through my veins with the need to prove her wrong. Girly? I exhale loudly and tug my top up and over my head as I get to my feet.

I tower over her, but she doesn't back away. My shadow falls over her, while her gaze slides down my chest and lower still. She pulls her fleshy lower lip into her mouth, gnawing on it between her teeth. Last night, I took her every which way, fucked her so sweetly, and she cried my name, begging for more. Yet now, she stares at me just as hungrily, just as desperately, and something in me shifts.

"So?" She looks up at me with an arrogant little grin that I want to lick and turn into a moan. She doesn't even know what she's gotten herself into, but she will soon enough. I'm driven by adrenaline, a rising arousal, and burning rage tangling in my gut. I fear that once she sees the truth, she might change how she thinks of me. But I suddenly want her to see all of me just as I am, to see what made me the fae I am today. My pulse rages through my veins like a storm, throbbing beneath my skin.

She needs to understand what kind of world we live in and why I fight so hard to protect her against those who would harm the innocent.

She licks her lips expectantly.

"You want to see my wings?" I growl.

She nods eagerly.

I close my eyes and concentrate, reaching deep inside me. I've kept them away for so long, hidden and unused, that at this point, I don't even know if they'll respond to my call. But I sense them folded up tightly inside me.

Forgotten things.

A tingling starts at the base of my shoulder blades, then rips upward with the sharpness of a knife. I hiss through clenched teeth as my flesh tears and the wings push out of my back. Two bony shadows are cast against the wall on either side of me. They stretch outward, looming behind me like the branches of a tree stripped bare by winter.

The glint in Guendolyn's eyes vanishes, ripped away at seeing the hideous remains of what was done to me. Ironically, even in this form, their magic will still allow me to fly... not well, but it's possible. Except I refuse to use them.

"I'm broken, Guendolyn. Maybe too broken for someone like you." She's too perfect, too good, too innocent, having not grown up in this world.

Her chin trembles, but she doesn't back away, tracing her gaze over my wings.

"What happened?" Her voice is a squeak, and agony threads through her words as though looking at me is too much for her.

Fury surges through me. Why did I show them to her? It was a fucking mistake. I turn around, tucking them against me when she reaches out. Her fingers gingerly graze over the tip of a wing.

"Who did this to you?" she asks.

I stand with my back to her, fighting the emotions punching through me.

For the first time in too many years, I feel vulnerable, and I fucking hate it. I don't need anyone's pity. I ball my hands. Somehow, I thought showing her the truth wouldn't impact me. Big fucking mistake.

All she'll see now when she looks at me is a broken fae.

Tender fingers stroke along my wing, sending a fiery spark up to my shoulder and down my back.

I run a hand down my face, lowering my head. "It was my real father's punishment. He loathed my wings and wanted them cut off my back. When he found out that would kill me, he stripped them down to the bone, and did so every time the feathers grew back."

Revulsion swirls in my chest as I remember my father's grin each time he ripped the feathers off and cut the membrane to leave me with nothing but skeletal embarrassments. The fucking asshole. The ache in my chest swallows me, and I want to kill him for what he did to me. For what he did to my mother.

"I think they're beautiful."

Her words take me off guard. I frown and jerk around, drawing my wings into their hiding place inside my back, the pain quick and bearable as my skin knits up across my shoulder blades. "Don't say that shit." I search her face for the lie, but all I find is her genuine smile.

"Your father is a fucking bastard, but that doesn't mean he's taken anything from you." She pushes herself against me, her arms wrapped around my waist, her cheek pressed to my chest. She holds me so tightly, I can barely draw in a breath, but I don't move or push her away.

I don't know how to feel.

Furious? Embarrassed?

I'm desperate to punch the wall until I no longer feel a thing, but I suck it up like I've been doing for years. That's how I deal with everything, by shoving it down, but one day, it'll all come spilling out and drive me to madness.

My gaze falls to Guendolyn. She's what I need, curled in my arms, smiling and telling me things that make me forget everything else. A beauty like her can take everything away, can let me escape the memories that haunt me, that echo in my dreams. I hate the fucking weak-ass I've become. I despise this side of me.

"You're not broken," she whispers, dragging me out of my thoughts. "You're perfectly put together for me." Her words sing in the air.

"They haven't grown back." I snarl and shake the darkness slithering over my thoughts. It threatens to take me as it has so many times before, bringing me to a place so deep I forget how to climb back out.

The only people who've seen my wings are my brothers and mother. No mages or healers. Not my stepfather. I don't even know why the fuck I showed them to Guendolyn.

Except the truth lies inside me. I've been attracted to her from the first moment we met, and what I didn't know was that I'd saved a special place in my heart for her.

Maybe we are a better match than I assumed. She's cursed, and I'm broken—the perfect mates.

She lifts her chin. "I'm sorry he did that to you." The softness of her voice clutches at my heart.

I wrap her in my arms, my eyes burning, and we don't say anything. It's not needed.

The ride toward Ash Court is bumpy, jolting us about. I stare outside the carriage window at the most incredible sunrise I've ever seen. It illuminates the night as if it's igniting a captivating flame.

My gaze sweeps back inside the carriage to the two princes. Luther slouches in the seat across from me, his arms folded over his chest, his chin dipped low, and his breathing heavy. He fell back asleep the moment we left the town. Ahren sits next to me, and he looks at me with green eyes so pale, they look washed out, like he's cried too many times and the color ran. Except Ahren isn't the kind to cry. He bottles everything inside, putting on a strong front. As the heir to the throne, he can't be weak.

Movies romanticize princes and princesses, but in real life, nothing is ever so perfect and easy. People are broken and have damaged pasts that shape who they are. Despite Ahren's asshole father, the prince holds on to his integrity and stands up for what is right, as do his brothers. Why else would they risk their lives for Deimos? I adore that about the three of them.

"Are you all right?" Ahren asks.

"Yeah. I'm still trying to wake up," I lie. After our conversation last night about his wings, I didn't sleep a wink. Even when he climbed into bed and I lay between two princes, I had a hard time shutting off my brain. I don't need to explain this to Ahren or remind him of the pain he lives with every day. I can't get the image of his bony wings out of my head, or banish the ache coiling in my chest at what he went through. I want to murder his real father for doing that to him.

Instead, I offer Ahren a reassuring smile and do the thing I excel at—changing the topic. "Why do the Seelie and Unseelie hate each other so much? Jasion told me the tale of the fairies and fae, so clearly, the fae all started as the same race."

"We are the same. The difference comes down to our beliefs and abilities," Ahren says, while Luther stirs, groaning. "Unseelie draw their power from the darker gods, but I believe it all stems from a huge disagreement between two kings who were brothers and ruled together. They both fell in love with the same woman, but she was tragically killed, and each brother blamed the other. So much so, that they split their kingdom—the land and the population—in half, and promised to destroy one another. That hatred has continued to this day."

Luther clears his throat from in front of us, his eyes opening halfway, studying us.

Ahren doesn't seem to notice and keeps talking. "Details aren't precise, but one brother was once called an Unseelie, meaning 'unfortunate' in the ancient tongue, so the second king quickly announced himself as a Seelie fae, the blessed ruler. I guess the names stuck."

I absorb every word. "The history of fae is so fascinating, and there's so much I want to learn. Your stepfather told me many stories the night I went to see him. It helped pass the time as I healed him. I mean, most of the stories didn't make sense to me purely out of context, but—"

"Back up," Ahren interjects, while Luther drags himself to sit upright. "You healed the king? How?"

I shrug. "The same way I did with your bite mark." Something in his gaze makes my stomach drop. "Why are you looking at me like that?"

"Did you leave a handprint on his body?" Ahren continues, his posture stiffening. Now I'm starting to get worried.

I nod.

Luther breathes heavily and runs a hand through his hair. He and Ahren exchange a silent look, and I just know Luther is telling him things telepathically so I don't hear.

"Talk to me. What's the big deal?" I ask. Ignoring the way the corded muscles in Ahren's neck tick, I try to tell myself they're overreacting. How can fixing someone be a bad thing?

"If the king or his mages see your handprint on his flesh, it will reveal that you are an Unseelie. Only their healers carry an ability that mars the skin with magic. We have had two Unseelie healers visit our court in the past, so everyone knows how they heal," Ahren explains.

Dammit. Why the hell hadn't he told me this before? "Oh crap!" My mind is running at a thousand miles a minute. "But wait, if they saw it, why didn't anyone come for me while I was at court?"

Luther shrugs as he says, "Maybe he never noticed the mark, or it faded."

Ahren's lips pinch tightly. "Or that could be why Jasion's been buzzing around you." He looks over to Luther. "Jasion has not been acting like himself. What if the king ordered him to uncover the truth about Guendolyn?"

"Except he was acting all suspicious with me even before I healed the king." I don't even want to think about why Jasion is interested in me. The memory of our conversations sends shivers up my arms.

"Guendolyn—" Ahren begins.

"Let's say they know. I won't be able to return to Shadow Court, will I?"

Neither prince answers because they know it's true.

"You are going to return home with us," Luther blurts out. "We just need a way to hide you until we find out what the king and Jasion know."

It's getting harder to smile and pretend I'm fine with the constant barrage of bad things happening. Ash Court wants me dead to complete their curse. Shadow Court will want to kill me for simply being from the wrong place.

Luther shuffles to the edge of his seat, leaning forward, his eyes wild. "If we tell the king her survival ensures the curse isn't permanently placed on our court, he won't kill her."

"No, but he'll imprison her for life," Ahren answers fast.

The food I ate earlier now wants to make a reappearance. I feel sick that my options are either hide for god knows how long or go into prison. If I don't want to die, of course.

I pull back and curl in on myself in the corner of the carriage, staring outside as the white landscape awakens with the rising sun.

The brothers discuss my options, hashing out a plan, but I'm struggling to deal with the news. So much has happened in such a short time. On top of everything, I'm losing myself to these princes, making me question my decisions and motives. When I arrived here, I wanted to uncover who my parents were, but now all I keep thinking about is how I don't want to lose the princes. Which is why my head feels foggy when I should be focused on not dying.

"Guendolyn," Luther says. "We'd never let anything happen to you. Believe me, we will find a way. Once we save Deimos, we'll talk to the king. He will have to understand."

Their words should encourage me, but the knot in my chest refuses to unravel. "We can try. But you're right. We need to focus on Deimos first and surviving this."

To my surprise, Ahren leans closer and drags me into his arms, giving me no chance to wriggle free. Luther joins us, and already, I feel the cold inside me melting. I believe them, that they'll make this work... God, I want this so much. I soften and curl in against the princes, feeling warm and wanted. The sensation is unlike anything I've felt before. My foster mom loved me, but this feels different, deeper and more secure. I can't even explain the sentiment that makes me believe that for once, I am truly where I belong.

The rest of the trip is spent watching the scenery, drinking and eating food packed for us by the town cook, and talking with the princes.

"The king was fucking furious yesterday," Luther explains, grinning with glee. "You know his goddamn stupid throne? It got damaged in the Bloodcursed attack, and he was yelling at everyone to find every missing shard of wood with the hope of putting it back together."

Ahren chuckles, and I can't help but admire how perfect they are. When not bickering, these princes get along so well.

"What's so special about his throne?" I ask, curiosity getting the better of me.

"It's made of Alethian wood," Ahren explains. "It's impossible to replace, as those trees are protected and it's illegal to chop them down."

"Are they magical?" I ask.

Ahren shakes his head. "The trees are said to be as old as the fae race. Only when a tree falls over from a lightning strike, can its wood be used."

"But it wasn't just the throne," Luther continues. "His precious ruby from the chair is gone."

Ahren bursts out laughing. "Fuck, if I never hear about that damn jewel again, it will be too soon."

I stiffen, remembering how Hiss flew out of my window while clutching a ruby. Of course she'd have to take something that belonged to the king. Well, thank fuck that she's gone, and no one needs to know what she did. Everything I touch in this world somehow comes back and bites me in the ass.

The way they keep laughing makes me more curious. "Why is it funny he lost the ruby?"

Luther glances over at me, stretches an arm out against the back of his seat, and draws up a bent leg. "During the first year we arrived at the kingdom, our stepfather sold all of our mother's jewels in exchange for a stone from a witch fae who passed through our court. The king was promised that the ruby would give him affinity with the fairies because the ruby was one of the last pieces in existence from the original fairy queen's crown." He rolls his eyes. "Right, because a random fae spouting lies just happens to carry an ancient relic. But the king believed her, and Mother was so angry, she didn't speak to him for a month."

"He sounds a bit obsessed," I say, offering Luther a crooked smile, while my mind whirs with thoughts of why the king didn't grill me further about the fairies earlier.

"That he is."

The ride goes on for half a day, while outside the carriage, heavy clouds darken the landscape with the promise of another snowstorm.

The carriage curves around a bend on the edge of the hill we're starting to descend when Ash Court comes into view. I press my face to the window and stare out at the enormity of the place. It glints as though it's made of silver, and snow covers its five broad towers with pointed roofs, all connected by fortress-strong walls made of white stone. Enormous arched gates forged of gold sit at the entrance to the kingdom, and stone walls spread out from either side of the gate, enclosing the castle.

I swallow hard, unable to believe we're here. All I remember from arriving here is Deimos and me landing right inside the grounds and how quickly we ran out of there.

Suddenly, panic curls in my gut, and all I can think is...my real parents are somewhere in that kingdom. Danger suffocates this place, and yet something in my chest tugs at me, telling me that maybe I can finally find out who my parents are.

When I glance back, the princes are looking out the window as well. Their smiles are gone, replaced with trepidation.

"Ready for this?" I say.

"Fuck, no," Luther responds.

"It's going to work. It has to, for Deimos," Ahren says.

I agree. For Deimos.

As we come to a stop at the base of the hill, trees surround the carriage and seeing past them is impossible. Ahren steered the carriage to a denser part of the woods on an overgrown path that looks unused. I've been out into the bushes to relieve myself and stretch my legs, and now I'm back inside.

"How far is the castle?" I ask, peering into the forest through the window, trying to spy Ash Court with no luck.

"Far enough that no one will find you here," Ahren answers from outside the carriage where he's guided the horses to stop.

The door sits open, and a chill flutters over me while Luther goes outside too and prepares to cast some kind of concealment spell over the carriage with me in it, so no one finds me while they're gone. My emotions go back and forth like a yo-yo. One minute, I want to join the princes, the next, I want to run as far from this place as possible. Mostly, I worry about the princes' safety and getting a cure for Deimos back in time.

If there is one positive thing about today, it's that we've encountered no problems on the trip here, so maybe we'll be lucky for the rest of the day.

Luther appears in the doorway, snow speckled over his dark hair, a few flakes sitting on his long lashes. I want to reach over and dust them away, but this isn't the right moment. He stands strong and broad, looking ready to leap into battle.

"We're going to cast the spell and get going." His words are soft, like he can't bear to leave me alone out here.

The moment he finishes talking, I'm on my feet in the carriage and rushing to the door, unable to stop myself. His arms loop around me and swing me outside, and Ahren closes in from behind me. They crowd close, and I look up at how tall they both are compared to me. Conflict swims behind Ahren's green eyes, but he never says a word, only settles a hand on my shoulder. He leans in and grasps my jaw, turning my head to kiss me with a passion I don't expect. My toes curl in my boots as his tongue sweeps into my mouth. We kiss like long-lost lovers, like we may never see each other again. Except that can't happen because I may not survive it.

He suddenly breaks from me, and I'm left breathless. There's a kindness in his expression that feels like it's reserved only for me. "Stay inside. Don't leave the carriage until we return, no matter what."

There are days when my feelings overwhelm me, when I want to stand so still that time itself stops and I can stretch certain moments out. This is one of those times. I haven't spent enough time with the princes, and it now feels like I've lost the chance. I fight the urgency tightening in my chest, the need to keep them near rising from the thought that I may not see them again. Still, I swallow the growing thickness in my throat.

"Hey, little wolf," Luther says. "It's going to be all right."

I turn to him as Ahren steps toward the horses.

"We will be back, I promise. I lost you once. It won't happen again." He cups my face, his thumbs running across my cheekbones, wiping away the stray tears. "There's a legend that says that when fated souls meet, the universe will move the stars themselves to ensure their love endures."

"Who said that? It's beautiful," I whisper, clutching on to Luther's strong arms.

"It comes from one of the ancient fairy tales."

"So much of the fae world is based on the fairies, isn't it?" I tilt my head, smiling at him.

He nods, leaning closer. The moment his mouth grazes mine, I forget everything. There's fire in his kiss, and we come together like nothing in the world can touch us. I kiss Luther, trying to memorize every last thing about him—the firmness of how he holds me, the way his tongue explores every inch of my mouth, the delicious taste of his lips.

When we break apart, worry twists in me painfully.

"We need to go, little wolf." He holds me closer and looks down at me.

"If we don't return by night, say the word 'Cilhaj' to the horses. They will take the carriage straight back home."

I shake my head. "I'm not leaving you."

He kisses me, stealing my protest. "Now get into the carriage." Turning me by my shoulders, he slaps my ass hard. I look at him over my shoulder, but he's already walking toward the front of the carriage where Ahren stands. I climb back inside, my stomach churning.

When I shut the door, the whole carriage suddenly starts shaking. In the blink of an eye, a curtain of glinting dust cascades outside, vanishing as quickly as it started.

Through the window, I watch the two princes track through the woods, leaving me behind. Within seconds, they disappear into the shadows.

I slouch in my seat and wish I had my phone to at least play some games while I wait. When I get tired of watching the snow fall, I flop onto my back and stare at the ceiling. What do people do without technology? Is this why they get married so early and have half a dozen children? I close my eyes and try to rest.

Time passes. I have no idea how much, but it feels like forever.

I shuffle back up and reach over to grab the wicker basket of food the town cook packed for us, then peel back the white fabric laid on top.

Everything inside is wrapped in white cloths. I open the first one to find a block of cheese and smile. Rummaging through the basket, I find some more cheese, then a chunk of bread. There are close to half a dozen more things in here. I'm digging deeper when something sharp bites the top of my index finger.

"Ouch." I draw it back and blood is bubbling over the cut. Sticking my finger into my mouth, I pull everything out of the basket to find the culprit —a knife. I quickly wipe the blade and wrap my finger up in the cloth, then I make myself a cheese sandwich. Before I can do more damage, I place the knife back in the basket.

My finger throbs like it has its own heartbeat, but it'll heal soon enough.

Today is not going to end up as a bad day. It just can't.

I bite into my sandwich and curl up, staring outside at the falling snow, praying Ahren and Luther come back safely.

AHREN

. . .

"Don't hate me, brother," Luther whispers over his shoulder at me, his grin telling me he's up to no good. "But Guendolyn thinks I'm the better kisser."

I roll my eyes at him. "Is that what you're thinking about at this moment?" We move with haste through the woods to reach the wall of Ash Court, and my mind is racing with plans for escape should we be caught.

He shrugs. "It's just something you ought to know."

I smirk and nod his way, knowing this is his way of dealing with the situation. Deflection. Even growing up, when shit got too real, too hard, he refocused on something he could control.

But I also know that once we're in battle, Luther turns deadly and will never back down. He's the perfect fae to have by my side on such a mission, and I trust him with my life.

Without another word, we move like the wind, cutting across the landscape and swerving around trees. Part of me expects Bloodcursed or guards, but there's nothing. I strain to listen for threats, but not even the birds are singing today.

Silence. It leaves me uneasy.

Luther scans the woods and scowls my way, then lifts his shoulders in a shrug.

Something feels off. Luther's voice streams over my mind.

I nod and point straight ahead to where I can already see the stone wall through the trees. My stomach tightens at where we have to go.

We're running, the snow crunching under our rushed steps, and as we get to the wall, I scan overhead and on either side of us. Nothing here.

A twig snaps somewhere behind us, and we whirl around, reaching for our blades, my heart pounding.

Not a sound.

Snow cascades all around us. When I find no movement, I direct Luther to follow me along the wall that towers over us like a giant, and I hate how trapped I feel. My mind won't leave Guendolyn, either. We left her deep enough in the woods away from the castle so she won't be found, and I pray she doesn't leave the carriage. While inside the carriage and under the spell, she's concealed from the Unseelie and warm from the cold weather.

Shuffling sounds erupt around us.

Luther seizes my arm, and I swing around. My attention catches on the three Bloodcursed stumbling out from the shadows of the dense woods. This might explain why there are no guards on the east side of the castle.

My blood runs cold, and it has nothing to do with facing them, but with leaving Guendolyn out there. She survived the Bloodcursed bite once, but can they still hurt her? Seething, I tuck my blade back into the sheath on my waist and reach over my shoulder to grab the hilt of my sword. I draw it out, Luther doing the same, and we don't waste a moment.

We charge the creatures who run at us.

Fury drives me to finish this quickly. I turn to the right, where two of them stick close together, grip my sword with two hands, and lift the blade over my shoulder. Mouths gaping, the fiends growl. Their eye sockets are sunken, their teeth missing, their clothes ripped. These poor souls were once fae just like us, but the curse ravaged them. I picture Deimos this way, and my heart clenches.

I swing the sword with all my strength. The blade sings through the air and swiftly slices through both of their necks in one move. I suck in a frosty breath as the heads topple off their shoulders, the bodies falling into the snow like sacks.

I turn to Luther, who has a monster dead by his feet. Half a dozen more are threading through the woods toward us. Where did they all come from?

Blood stains the once-immaculate snow all around us.

Luther glances at me and grins, his eyes alive with hunger for the battle. *We fight, brother,* he growls in my head.

I nod, and we take on the next wave of Bloodcursed. One of them charges toward me, but I pivot out of his way and swing back around, bringing the sword down fast to the back of his head—a clean cut. Turning back around, I swipe wide, catching a fiend across his abdomen and causing his innards to spill out. When a hand slaps down on my shoulder, I drive my elbow into the creature at my back, then whip around. My free hand falls to my belt, and I grab a dagger, then plunge it right into his temple, piercing through to the brain.

A kick to the gut, and he's on the ground. The next two go down just as fast.

Luther's at my side, heaving for breath, his eyes locked on more Bloodcursed coming for us. I slide my sword over my shoulder and across my back into its sheath, then hastily collect my daggers from dead bodies.

Luther takes the lead, and we run.

Thicker snow sits near the wall, so with each step, my feet sink deeper, but there's no stopping. We have to get over the wall. I didn't come this far to fight the infected.

Up ahead, a lofty tree rises ahead of us, its branches heavily laden with snow. It's bigger than any other tree in these woods.

Luther doesn't pause as he bolts forward, throwing himself at the trunk easily, using the blades in his hands to dig into the wood for purchase. He then wrenches each one out and stabs the wood, climbing higher quickly. He's fast. Holding both my knives, I follow suit.

Behind me, I hear the Bloodcursed's shuffling footsteps, their groans.

By the time I reach the first branch that's at least fifteen feet off the ground, Luther's there grabbing my arm. He wrenches me up, and I scramble onto the thick limb and stand tall. I suck in a ragged icy breath, my heart racing.

Down below are close to two dozen creatures charging toward the wall. They hear a sound and those fuckers don't hold back, running to find their next meal. We need these things eliminated from our world, once and for all.

But not today. Right now, I want to survive and rescue Deimos.

Luther's already climbing across to another branch that stretches toward the top of the stone wall.

Beyond that spreads Ash Court, our destination its grand white castle for the Unseelie.

Between us and the castle is a scattering of trees, not dense enough to conceal us should anyone look this way. Toward the front of the enormous castle stand four guards. If the Bloodcursed make enough sounds, they'll draw the guards' attention.

"Do you have the spell?" Luther whispers, glancing over his shoulder at me. There's tightness beneath his eyes.

I tuck my blades away and pull out a small pouch from my pocket. "This has one use, so we have to make it work. And we have one for returning. It won't last long, so we have to make it across the open yard quickly." My eyes scan the lofty castle and find a small door near a garden of vegetables, tucked away near a tree. "That's us." I point to the spot.

"Let's do this," Luther murmurs.

I untie the rope on the pouch, and pour out half the contents in my palm, and the rest in Luther's. "Dust over your head while whispering, '*invisible*,'" I explain.

"Simple as that?"

I shrug and follow the instructions, stating, "It worked on the carriage." An explosion of prickles dances over my head and rains down over my body. I don't feel different, but when I lift my hand I see right through it. It still has a faint outline that looks like a heat wave, but otherwise, the spell has worked.

Luther stares at me with huge eyes.

"Hurry the hell up." I rush to the end of the branch and leap down before landing on parted legs, knees bent the snow softening the fall. Moments later, two footfalls indent the snow next to me and a hand slaps my back.

"What are you waiting for, brother?" Luther teases, and then we're off, darting across the yard, wasting no time.

I swing my attention left and right, just in time to spot the guards racing toward the wall farther away from where we jumped. They've heard the Bloodcursed.

My heart beats faster, but I don't stop, and Luther's breaths are so loud they ring in my ears.

Rounding the tree near the vegetable garden, I throw myself toward the arched door and slam a fist on its wooden surface.

"We're still invisible," Luther grumbles in my ear. "She won't see us."

"Good, then we're covered in case someone else opens the door."

"Do you know what Relle looks like?"

I shake my head, but I'm too focused on no one answering the door to worry about that right now. A quick look over my shoulder shows more guards hurrying to the wall now. The snowfall is light, so how long do we have before they see our footprints in the snow?

I reach over to knock again when the door pulls open.

A small head pops out. It's an older woman with dark hair drawn back into a plait, her cheeks rosy as though she's been running, her eyes wide with fear. I recognize that expression on her face, the one of someone knowing they are breaking the rules. She's wearing a long, black dress with a white apron.

"Relle?" I whisper, praying it's her.

Her head swings in our direction, but she looks right through us. "Is it you?" she whispers. "Tibout?"

"It's Ahren, Tibout's son." I hold still and wait. Luther grumbles behind me at my saying son, but I ignore him.

Relle's face blanches, and she quickly draws back indoors.

I lunge after her, my hand lashing out to snatch her wrist as I say, "Please, the king sent you the message on our behalf. He said you can help us."

She's trembling against my touch, looking down at where I hold her arm as the concealment spell fades and my whole body appears in front of her.

Her eyes widen as she looks up at me, then she glances back into what a room that looks like a storage room. When she looks over to Luther, she's shaking her head. "No, this is a mistake."

"Please," I plead. "We're brothers and won't hurt you. We need your aid desperately."

For those few moments, she just watches us, her gaze swinging from us to the yard with the guards, then behind her.

"If you hurt me, I'll come after you both in the underworld," she threatens under her breath.

I smile. "The king threatened me with something similar, and now I know you two know each other well."

She sighs, her gaze frantically swinging out to the yard. "Quickly then. Enter." She opens the door wider and steps aside as she whispers, "My king and queen are on a trip to the east court, so there aren't as many guards around the palace as there normally are. This is good timing."

Luther and I slip into the dark room, and I pray that our luck holds out.

Guen

THE CARRIAGE SHUDDERS.

I snap awake, my eyes fluttering open. My heart pounding, I scramble up from the seat and move over to the window. "What the hell was that?" I mumble. Have the princes returned? That would be the best news ever. When I see no movement outside, I check the other side of the carriage, where the doors are still shut. The coast is clear.

On the floor lies the kitchen towel I used to wrap my cut finger, stained with blood. My finger has stopped bleeding, though some dried blood remains on my hand. I only slept for a few moments, I'm sure.

Bang.

The sound reverberates, and I'm sent into a tumble once again as everything shakes. A shard of ice skitters down my spine.

I reach down and grab the knife from the basket. Tucking myself into the center of the long seat, I begin trembling. What the hell is going on?

A sudden explosion comes from the window, the sound ear-shattering.

I scream and flinch away, the blade shaking in my grip.

A brown bear-like animal tears right through the window, sending pieces of glass and wood in every direction. The creature snorts, scrambling to find purchase as it rips its claws through the wooden wall of the carriage.

I'm on my feet and lunging at the door on the opposite side. I rip it open, then leap outside and run, sucking in ragged breaths as I look over my shoulder. The monster lunges out of the carriage, shaking off the window frame that hangs around its neck, the kitchen towel I used on my cut in its mouth. It spits it out and sniffs the air.

Oh, hell. My blood must have drawn this thing to the carriage. So much for trying to stay invisible. Maybe the spell should have blocked out smells, too.

The creature lowers its head, its ears pressed flat to its skull.

Fuck! Brandishing the knife, I raise it at the monster. "Get the hell away from me!"

I retreat and quickly whip around to sprint into the woods.

Except I run straight into a solid wall of muscle.

My heart is going to burst out of my chest. I tilt my head back to find a man with pointy ears and white pearlescent hair that drapes over his shoulders. He's young and has scars down the side of his face. He stares at me with a filthy grin.

He greedily seizes my hand that grips the knife and squeezes. "Drop it," he snaps.

I writhe against him, crying out, but my hand gives, and the blade slips from my grasp. A flash of brown shoots past us as the animal that attacked the carriage is chased away by two other men also dressed in black uniform.

I shove my fist into my captor's arm and push against him. "Let me go!"

Only then do I see the gold on his coat, sitting above his heart. A long broadsword with wings spanning out from the hilt.

Oh, crap. I'm standing in front of an Ash Court guard.

TWENTY-ONE

"Get inside," Relle whispers abruptly as she shoves a hand into Ahren's back, causing him to stumbles into a small bedroom with me. There's only a single bed, a wardrobe, and a dresser in here. The curtains are pulled over the window, letting in only a faint stream of light. There are no paintings or decorations of any kind on the walls, making me think this may be a spare room.

Relle rushes inside and shuts the door, then turns to face us. Her cheeks are flush, yet she stands tall. She's a plump, older woman with eyes the color of midnight. The deep lines around her eyes and hardness in her gaze tell me she's witnessed a lot of tragedy in her time, but there's also kindness in her expression, just as my stepfather said.

Suddenly standing here under her scrutiny, I suddenly feel like I'm a child about to be reprimanded for doing something wrong.

"What could be so important for King Tibout to risk the lives of his sons?"

I smile. "We come for something of *great* importance."

"Well, let's hear it then." She grips her hips, reminding me of Dana, who bosses everyone around.

I have to remind myself I'm in the heart of the enemy's stronghold and why coming here was a good idea in the first place. The king insists he trusts Relle, so we go against our better judgment. I don't feel comfortable with this decision, but I tell myself that we are stuck, so it's worth the risk of her betraying us to save Deimos.

"Our brother Deimos has been bitten by a Bloodcursed, and he doesn't have long. We all know there's only one way to save his life."

She shudders a breath, nodding.

Voices come from somewhere outside the room.

"What do you expect me to do?" she asks, her voice low. "Go into the mage's work chamber and find the potion for your brother?"

"Well, yes," I reply, still smiling slightly. My heart's racing, knowing that any moment she could call for the guards and we'd be slaughtered.

More noises come from outside in the hallway. It sounds like guards running. I guess most are going toward the Bloodcursed near the east wall, meaning escaping that way may prove trickier than breaking into the kingdom.

She shakes her head again. "I'm sorry, but you've both wasted your time."

"Please." Ahren steps forward. "The connection you have with King Tibout must be worth something."

Relle scowls. "I have no connection with your king. He came into the kingdom, and I was simply the fae who ensured his arrivals and departures remained concealed."

I slip forward, my hand sliding into the pocket of my pants. Relle isn't exactly the helpful fae I expected from what the king had said.

"I have something for you if you help us today." I pull out the diamond bracelet. "King Tibout insisted this was for you. He also said to name your price to help us, and he'll deliver it afterward."

She feverishly licks her lips, and I pull back my hand with the jewelry, pocketing it once more. "Your king knows exactly what I desire," she says.

"And that is?" Ahren asks.

"Enough gold to buy my own land away from every damn kingdom in the Wandering Realm." Shadows crowd across her expression.

Does she dislike this court that much, that she'd leave in a heartbeat?

"Deal," Ahren states. "In exchange for the antidote for our brother. No cure, no payment."

She eyes my brother for a moment, and silence echoes between us.

"Done." She draws a small knife out of her pocket, and she slashes the thick, meaty part of her palm. She lets a few drops fall onto the stone floor between us, then hands me the blade.

"Blood oath," she insists. It seems this woman is a lot more cunning than she first appeared.

It's basic magic usually done as insurance should one person not hold up their end of the bargain. Break a blood oath and Relle can demand my punishment any way she sees fit. No one can save me, not even a king because our blood connection will reveal she's right. It's one of the rules in Wandering Realm carried on from the old days and has never been changed.

I cut my thumb and squeeze a bit of blood onto the floor to merge with hers. The cut stings, but I suck it up.

She mumbles a few words under her breath, and the blood fizzles and burns up right before us, then vanishes. She then lifts her gaze to me. "You come with me. If I take you both, it'll raise suspicion."

"I'll go instead," Ahren states, and I know it's because he's spent more time with Jasion and knows mages very well. I've watched mages long enough to know exactly how they work after the king insisted he's appointed one of his mages as mine. But I've resisted and kept my distance from them.

"No," Relle snaps. "I did a blood oath with him, so he joins me. You stay here."

Ahren looks over at me and I say, "Is it safe for my brother to stay in this room?"

She frowns, as though I've asked the dumbest question in the world. "He'll be fine. When I give my word, I keep it, son. Now before we go anywhere, you need new clothes." She eyes me up and down, then rushes out of the room.

"Do you trust her?" Ahren faces me.

"What choice do we have?" I swallow hard. "Just stay hidden in case it's some kind of setup." Unease churns in my gut, because I hate the rushing, the unknown. "We get the cure and bolt the hell out of here."

Ahren nods. "This place gives me the creeps."

I blow out a long breath. "We can do this. We give her what she wants to save Deimos."

"Just be careful. And don't use your mind-reading. We don't know anyone's abilities, and they might be able to sense you probing." Ahren runs a hand through his hair, his lips thinning, and I can tell he's attempting to cover every possible angle.

"Agreed."

He digs into his pockets and pulls out two fabric pouches of magic herbs and powders from our mages back home. We brought a variety to use in case Relle wasn't able or willing to help, not fully trusting the king's contact or methods. "Just in case, brother."

I tuck them away in my pockets, remembering where I placed each concoction.

The door opens, and I draw back, my heart pounding as I finger the blade on my belt, but it's only Relle. She's carrying dark clothes and pushes them into my arms.

"Quickly, boy. Get changed. The guards seem occupied, so this is our chance."

I move to the bed and start stripping. From the corner of my eye, I catch Relle staring at me. I don't give a shit if she wants to see me naked, as long as I get my brother's cure.

In no time I'm dressed in a black guard's uniform. The pants are too tight, and they ride high up my groin and threatening to split my boys in half. I drag the long-sleeved tunic down over my body, then tie the leather belt around my middle. I push my hair off my face and tuck it behind my ears.

"Fits you well," she says, eyeing me a bit too closely.

Ahren curls his lips upward. "Keep your head low and be quick." He claps me on the shoulder.

I tug down on the pants riding up my ass. *Goddamn.*

"Stay close," Relle says as she opens the door. She sticks her head out then steps outside and waves for me to follow.

I give a final nod to Ahren, then I'm out. He shuts the door behind us, and I'm marching right on Relle's heels down a dark corridor with lack stone on the walls, flooring, and ceiling. There are no portraits or statues of animals; only weapons adorn the walls.

There's no sound coming from around us. The place looks empty, though I can't stop looking over my shoulder as if being watched. I study everything we pass, every shadow and corridor. There's not a soul in sight. We suddenly turn and head down a sweeping staircase, making me feel even more exposed. The place smells pungent down here. There are cracks in the walls, and plants grow through those gaps—thorny vines with tiny red flowers and deep green leaves. The place is being swallowed by nature. I've heard tales that where magic is used, nature will always try to reclaim the energy it believes is hers.

My shoulders stiffen with each step I take, and my pants ride up so high that I'm certain they'll vanish up my ass. Fuck. I shuffle as I yank at the fabric.

"Stop that," Relle scolds over her shoulder at me.

Breathing heavily, I hurry down the remaining stairs. We turn right, and coming right for us are two guards preoccupied by heady discussion, barely paying attention to us.

Keeping my head low, I march close to Relle, praying she keeps her word about helping us.

"Fucking lucky bastard. The king will reward him well for that catch," one fae says, and the other chortles like a pig.

I'm so engrossed in watching my steps, I don't notice Relle is no longer in front of me. I halt and spin around until I see her in a doorway, waving me over. She's frowning like a demon at me, so I dart toward her and into a room that smells of dried herbs and death.

Several candelabras illuminate the room. A counter runs the length of two walls, while the third is lined with shelves. Jars filled with all kinds of ingredients are crammed into every available spot.

"Is this it?" I ask.

"Yes," Relle says as she takes a seat on a wooden chair in the corner.

"What are you doing?" I whisper.

"I brought you here. Now go find the cure." She waves her hand at me.

My mouth drops open. "That wasn't part of the deal. How would I know which it is?"

She feigns insult and touches her chest with her hand. "What makes you think I know a mage's magic?"

I eye her, grinding my teeth. "Are you seriously going to just sit there?"

"Look, boy. I don't know what you're looking for, so I brought you here. Now find what you need because we don't have long."

Fury pummels into me, but I can't force her, this much I know. So I swing toward the chaotic room and think this through. I've watched mages back home work their potions enough times to understand that for each spell or curse to last, a portion of it must be kept. If I can find the cure, our mages can test it out ,and then cast it on Deimos. Also, if 'm lucky, I might even uncover the spell cast on Guendolyn that caused her to forget her past. So I dive in and start searching every damn jar and workspace and ingredient. Most of the jars have labels, which makes the task slightly easier.

I've searched half the room when I look over to Relle, who's staring at the door, chewing on her fingernail nervously while still in her seat, her knees are bouncing up and down.

"Relle," I say. "Why did the King of Shadow Court come here?"

She doesn't respond right away, but when she does, she sighs. "If he hasn't told you, it's not my place to say. You'll need to speak with him, as I have sworn secrecy to him."

I return to searching the shelves, determined to get my stepfather to tell us what is going on. We've come this far and risked everything, so we deserve to know what he was doing in Ash Court.

"We should go," Relle whispers, her voice shaky.

"No. I still haven't found it. Maybe if you helped me, we'd be faster."

She's on her feet, her gaze swinging from the door to me. "We go now and come back later."

I refuse to leave, not when I'm so close. The next bowl I look into has half a bone and white power, and I'm curious about what that's used for.

"You don't understand. The mages in the Ash Court are dark." Relle is pacing in the room, her attention locked on the door. "They do death magic, and that comes from lives and blood. If you're caught, we're both dead. So we go now and try again later."

My response is stolen by the door opening as someone enters. My heart slamming in my ribcage, my instincts take over, and I lunge for the door, moving like the wind, drawing a blade from my waist.

Relle backs away with fright, and I don't waste a single moment.

A mage with a bald head sees me at the last moment, his eyes bulging. His mouth opens to cast a spell, no doubt, his hand grappling to one of half a dozen charms hanging from his neck.

I slam a fist right into the middle of his face, the pain racing up my hand. The mage groans and clutches his bloody nose. I snatch his arm and haul him inside, then kick the door shut. Swinging him in front of me, facing away from me, I press my blade to his throat. With my other hand, I grab the charms around his neck and rip the leather cord right off before tossing it aside. Every mage concentrates their power in objects for easier access, and the natural energy in some objects can strengthen the power the mage pours into it. None can do spells or curses without such charms or potions.

"Keep quiet, mage, or your head will roll." I growl in his ear, then I look over to Relle. "Grab a rope or something and come tie his hands —now."

The mage stills, blood dripping from his nose and onto my hand. "I'll turn you into a rat."

Relle drags his arms behind his back and ties his wrists harshly. She's shaking, her breaths racing, knowing too well that if this mage lives, her cover as a spy is blown. I'll have to do something about that.

"You're going to show me the antidote I'm after, or you die. Try anything and you die. You seeing a pattern?"

"This isn't my workshop," he hisses.

"Don't give a fuck. Find it or you die."

I shove him forward, and the bastard fights me. I press the blade to his flesh, cutting skin enough to make him groan with pain.

"Tell me where to find the cure for a Bloodcursed's bite," I command.

He laughs. "Too fucking late."

From the corner of my eye, I see Relle hasn't moved. I dig into my pocket and drag out the pouch of herbs I stuck on my right side, as they're exactly what I need. I stick the pouch out for Relle. "Open it now," I roar.

She rushes over and does so, then gives it back.

"You will pay for this, Relle," the mage warns, his whole body vibrating. The walls and floor shake with him.

My heart is pounding in my ears.

I toss the mixture of herbs over his face and whisper, "Truth."

He shakes his head.

The mage chokes, but I don't ease my hold.

"Let's try again. Where is the cure for a Bloodcursed's bite?"

He groans and shudders against me, fighting the magic. "C-corner." He splutters the word along with spittle.

I walk us to the back. "Which corner?"

He lifts his chin to the right, and I shove him there.

"Where?" I snarl, pressing the blade harder to his throat.

"G-Gold box. First shelf." He thrusts against me.

I pivot us around and reach out, shoving the other jars aside until I discover a small golden trinket box. I snatch it. "Is this the box?"

"Y-Yes!" he barks.

"See, that wasn't so hard, now was it?"

I swing him around toward the room, but Relle is suddenly there plunging a long knife into the mage's gut.

Stunned, it takes me a few moments to work out what just happened.

"What the fuck, Relle?"

The mage cries out, gurgling blood, and slumping against me. I shove him aside and he collapses to the floor. Blood spills from his wound, his body convulsing.

"You could have waited until I finished," I bark.

Relle's face is twisted with hatred as she kicks the dying man in the ribs. "Fucking pig, you raped my daughter. You killed her, so now I take your life." She shakes, her cheeks drenched with tears.

My heart clenches at seeing her agony at what this monster did.

I pocket the gold box, and while I would have liked to ask the mage for other magic spell cures, I guess that's not going to happen now. I wipe my blade on the mage's pants and put it away.

"Listen, Relle, if you want, you can come with us. Leave this castle," I offer.

She's shaking her head, swiping at her tears. She doesn't even look at me. "No, I'm not finished here yet. Go. You got what you want." Her expression focuses on the mage, her expression darkening.

I pull out the diamond bracelet from my pocket and place it in her hand. She nods, and I retreat, knowing everyone deals with revenge in their own way. And what happened to her daughter is devastating. So I walk out of the room, straighten my tunic, pull my pants out of my ass and take hasty steps along the hall and up the staircase. I keep my head low as I pass other guards then speed up until I reach Relle's room.

I knock three times fast, then add a slap at the door—a small code I developed with my brothers when we were younger. The door opens, and Ahren is standing there, gripping his weapon, so I hurry inside. His gaze bounces to the door I shut. "What happened? Where's Relle?"

"Long story, but we need to leave now. I have the cure."

His face beams. "Thank the gods something's going right for a change."

I stick my head outside the room, finding the hallway empty. Then I push open the door and slip out. Ahren is on my heels, and we're running left. I remember the path Relle used to bring us to this room, as I'd counted how many passages we traveled and rooms we passed. I rush down a set of stairs and round the corner to a long, dark corridor.

"You sure this is it?" Ahren murmurs in my ears.

"Yes. It looks the same." We're running toward the end, and I push open the last door. We step into a linen room. Shelves and shelves of folded bed sheets and towels.

No exit door to the outside.

"Fuck, we took a wrong turn somewhere." Ahren growls behind me.

"I must have miscounted. I was sure it was seven corridors we passed before—"

"I think it was six. Hell, everything looks the same in this court," he says.

I go back to the doorway and check. "All clear. We just retreat and take the other path."

We're moving with haste, when I swear the floor trembles beneath me.

Backtracking, we dart into what I hope is the correct corridor. Gods, please let it be correct.

I slam right into a guard, and ice washes down my spine.

Ahren and I are shoulder to shoulder, and we jump the fae, punching him to shut up his cries. I restrain him in a chokehold until he's knocked out, then I dump his body.

"Shit, that was close," I murmur. I totter on my feet, my shoulder hitting the wall as though I'm drunk. "Was that an earthquake?"

Someone clears their voice behind us.

"Fuck!" Ahren groans as we both turn to find a dozen Unseelie guards with swords out, standing feet from us.

TWENTY-TWO

GUENDOLYN

A meaty hand slaps down on my shoulder, and I wince under the pressure. Another hand shoves me in the back, and I'm pushed through open doors into an enormous hall.

The walls are made of gold, while overhead, candle chandeliers are dripping with crystals. Pillars flank a path that cuts down the middle of the room, leading me to a woman sitting alone at one end of a grand dining table with no tablecloth, just platters of food and candelabras.

The clang of her cutlery echoes through the hall while guards stand tall along the walls, watching my every step. Marble glints beneath my feet while balconies sweep around the walls, and I suspect this location is typically used for grand announcements rather than a woman eating her meal.

"Move!" the guard behind me roars, driving me forward.

I stumble onward, unsure what to expect. Well, in truth, I thought they'd take me to the king for punishment. But maybe they sense I have Unseelie blood. The way my luck goes, though, I'll be lucky to keep both my hands.

My heart is beating loudly, my gaze swinging between the guards and the woman, who hasn't stopped eating. Each clang she makes is a bang in my ears, hammering away. I shudder in a breath, trying to swallow the fear surging within me.

Dread flares over me as I come to a stop in front of the table filled with fruit and roast vegetables and a whole suckling pig in the middle. The woman's gray hair is drawn off her face. She appears to be in her seventies, age pulling at the lines edging around her mouth and eyes. Though she's very beautiful now, she would have been even more spectacular in her younger years.

Lowering the golden fork and knife in her hands, she lifts her head and glances at me.

"Kneel," the guard barks behind me.

A kick to the back of my knees sends me sprawling to the floor. I whimper under my breath at the brunt of the marble floor against my knees. I stay down on my heels, my head tucked low.

"Leave us," the woman cries out, her voice croaky. Maybe she'll have sympathy for me.

The marching beat of footfalls fades behind me, followed by the thump of the doors shutting.

Pointy sapphire blue boots step into my view, and a shimmering dress in the same shade cascading to her ankles.

"What's your name?" she asks.

"G-Gainy." I hold tight, drawing on all my bravery. This isn't the time to show fear. I need to be smart and somehow get out of this tangled mess without losing my head.

"Stand."

Shudders ripple through my body, but I push myself to my feet, never eyeing her. I recall the king's anger at me looking him in the eyes.

She grips my chin and tilts my head back. "Let me see you better."

I meet blue eyes, so bright, that they might be a cloudless sky on a summer's day. They evoke something inside me...a feeling of warmth, and all I can think about is the hot days when I used to visit the beach with my foster mom. They were moments I'll never forget, filled with laughter and fun and getting sunburned. It was also the first time I kissed a boy—a surfer, to be more precise.

"Interesting." The older woman's voice snaps me out of my thoughts, leaving me feeling dizzy.

I shake the strange fog from my head and refocus on the fae, who stands at about my height, built slightly thinner, and wearing so many jewels around her neck, I'm surprised she's not weighed down. The crystals glint against the candlelight overhead, drawing my attention to the varied colored stones.

"What is your real name?" she asks, her voice clipped and short.

I try to stop shaking, but with her question, I'm left wondering if she somehow just brought about my vision of the beach and viewed it as well —meaning she knows full well knows that scene is not from the Wandering Realm.

So I decide to take the lead, intending to live through the day. "I did nothing wrong and didn't trespass on your land."

She cocks her head to the side, her rose lips thinning into a grim smile. I already dislike the look of her expression, because something doesn't feel right. Does she know who I really am? Can she sense I am Unseelie? Shoot, what if she can read my mind... had I just let her know who I am? Can she read minds?

"Come. Take a seat with me and let's enjoy a drink." She turns back to the table.

My feet won't respond. Instead, I glance over my shoulder, noting it's only her and me in a huge room. Arched windows made of colored glass that distorts the outside view, making it impossible to decipher what's out there.

My insides tighten, and I want to run from here, but the guards will be waiting outside the doors, so how far will I get? And what about Ahren and Luther? They'll find the carriage destroyed and me gone once they get back to it.

In a blinding flash of movement, the woman pounces. She's in my face so fast, I can't respond quickly enough to defend myself. She's on me like a predator, her fingers iron strong, digging into my arms, her teeth on my neck, biting. Breaking flesh.

I scream and instinctively move to shove her, but she's already back by the table, taking her place at the head. My hand clasps my bloody neck, and I'm stumbling backward. Why the hell does everyone in the realm want my blood? Bloodcursed, fairies, this crazy bitch.

She's licking my blood from her lips, her eyelids fluttering, and for those few seconds, I'm seeing someone else...a much older woman, disfigured, heavily wrinkled, and smoke wafting up from the corner of her mouth.

I don't want to be here.

"What did you just do?" Fear buckles through me, wrapping around me like a straitjacket.

"I had to be sure it was you. Now, take a seat, Guendolyn." She growls, the sound reverberating around us.

The room tilts. She knows my name from tasting my blood? Fae have abilities, different kinds. If Luther can send his thoughts to my mind, why can't this demonic fae determine who I am by tasting my blood?

"W-Who...?" My voice dies on me.

She laughs hysterically, and I already hate this woman. I loathe her.

"Do you know how long I've been searching for you? Then those idiotic princes took you from me."

"Who are you?"

"Sit!" She offers me a wry frown. "It doesn't matter who I am."

I drag myself closer and flop down on a chair. The smell of the food sickens me, and I feel like gagging. Luther told me those in this court want to kill me. I have so many questions, and I'm walking on a blade's edge as I try to determine the best way to survive while uncovering the truth.

I blink at her. "What do you know about me?"

Her eyebrow arches, and she leans forward, looking at me with those hypnotic eyes, but I look away, refusing to let her into my head again.

"I know enough," she answers.

I shift in my seat, unease pricking down my arms. I'm exhausted from her games and just want to know the truth.

"Who are my parents?" I twist my hands in my lap. "Are you my mother?"

"Don't be ridiculous," she snaps back as she pours herself what looks like wine from a golden pitcher into her chalice.

"Then who is she? What about my father?" I sound desperate, but I've wanted to know the truth from the moment I was old enough to understand what having no parents meant. This is my one chance, because I never plan on coming back to this court if I escape.

She eyes me suspiciously. "You don't know about your father? Even after you've been at the Shadow Court?"

A chill runs down my back. "What does that mean?" My mind is running at a thousand miles an hour as I try to piece everything together.

My father is at the Shadow Court?

"Growing up on Earth has made you slow." She shrugs. "Doesn't matter now, does it?"

"Stop talking in riddles." It's either bravery or stupidity that makes me talk so brazenly to this fae.

She sips from her gold chalice, then places it back down on the table. Standing, she eyes me like I might have said the worst thing in the world.

Rapidly, I scramble onto my feet as well and back away from the table. "Please. I just want to know who my parents are, then I'll leave."

She shakes her head and juts out her arm toward me. "Too late."

An invisible punch pummels my chest, sending me reeling backward and onto my ass. I gasp for air, looking up as she saunters over to me. Who in the world is this woman? Her powers are crazy strong, and now I understand why she sent all the guards away. She doesn't need anyone's protection.

"It's opportune that you happened to turn up when I've been trying to find a way to bring you back to our court." She speaks with a smile as though everything is rosy. Except I know the truth—that I'm the one thing that stands in the way of Unseelie completing their curse on the Shadow Court.

My skin crawls as she studies me. Shadows dance around her face, signaling that I need to tread carefully. We may both have Unseelie blood in our veins, but she is my enemy. I see it in the pleasure she takes out of bringing me pain, hear it in the unsaid promise of my death on her lips.

I push myself off the ground and stand tall, remembering that the power I open and close portals runs inside me.

Another invisible punch to my gut has me groaning and bending over to clutch my stomach. "Enough," I cry. "I never asked for this. Never asked to be your curse carrier so you could get revenge on your enemies."

She doesn't move for a moment until she sits back down on a seat and faces my way. "You're right. You never asked for it, but your very presence is an abomination, and we should have disposed of you when you were born. Then none of this would be necessary. This is why Seelie and Unseelie can never be together." She wrinkles her nose at me as though I am used gum stuck to her shoes.

My mouth drops open. "You are so vile. How can you speak like that about me?" I can't work out why this woman, who is clearly someone important, would take so much interest in someone like me. If she's telling the truth, not even the princes knew about my father, as they insisted my parents lived in the Ash Court.

She shakes her head as if I'm inconsequential.

"At least tell me what happened to me if you're going to take my life away," I implore, stalling while concentrating on drawing out my power and working out how to open a portal with the ease the fairy showed me.

She cocks her head to the side. "Who's in charge of the magic in Shadow Courts these days? Is it still Jasion?"

My blood runs cold at her knowing his name and asking about him, like she's had dealings with him before. Except I won't give this woman any information that might harm the princes.

"You keep changing the topic." I push through the pain. "Tell me about my parents. Why was I sacrificed?"

"You know the sad thing?" she says, like I ought to know. "It's that you most likely saw your father, maybe even spoke with him in Shadow Court, since he's an asshole who takes too much interest in every woman who crosses his path. But what's even sadder is that he never even knew of your existence. So it will be no real great loss to the world once you're dead."

Fury courses through me at the way she speaks, like I mean so little. But my attention bleeds over her mention of my father, who I may have spent time with. He must be someone important enough for her to assume I spoke with him; it would have to be a crucial figure to take the interest of this fae. The answer slides into my thoughts like it's been there all along, but I was blind to it.

Dread falls right through me.

"No. No... No! He can't be my father." I suck in a jagged breath and the room spins.

"It took you a while, but you got there eventually."

I want the world to crack open and swallow me whole.

My father is the King of Shadow Court. I am part royal.

She swivels her head upward at me, screwing her pouty lips into a grin. "Yes, I would be shocked to have Seelie blood in my veins too, let alone to be a child of that pathetic king. Now you see why you are a mistake. So I'm doing what should have been done long ago if they'd listened to me."

I can't speak, torn apart by the news. Shock runs like lightning through my body.

Silence drags between us, then I finally find my voice. "Who's my mother?"

She's on her feet. "Does it matter? Let's put you out of your misery and be done with this. It's dragged on for too many years as it is. I've wasted too much time on this nonsense."

"Nonsense?" I can't stop myself. "This is my life!"

In a heartbeat, she hurls her hands outward, and I fly across the room. My back slams into the wall, my head cracking. I cry out in pain and slide down to the floor. My feet crumble under me, and I sink to my knees as I taste blood at the back of my tongue.

"Death is imminent for you."

More attacks collide into me. I'm thrust into the air, screaming, but none of that matters. No one knows where I am. No one will save me.

She stares at me, unblinking, as I'm suspended in the air, her eyes darkening. The room turns icy cold like someone has opened a window. My heart is speeding, and a heaviness is swallowing me from the inside out.

Hatred bathes her face when she looks at me. I doubt this fae has ever felt any sympathy for me... Not when I was a baby, and definitely not now.

I've spent enough time with the fae in Shadow Court to see their hatred for the Unseelie, but what I'm witnessing now is on a very different level. This Unseelie fae will kill thousands and not care.

Not even the king would... I choke again on the realization that he is my father. There is so much I need to talk to him about.

Frantically, I fight against the invisible bonds holding me in the air, but it makes no difference. My mind lurches in every direction, but focusing is impossible. I've forgotten words, forgotten everything but the trepidation claiming me.

"You have a shadow on your heart, Guendolyn. You always have. A curse. That's what you are."

"Because your mages cursed me!" I shout.

One corner of her mouth quirks upward, as if proud of her handiwork.

"It was you, wasn't it? You did this to me!" I cry out.

"I am rather proud of how well it worked out. Payment and revenge against the Seelie."

I'm seething, my insides burning up. "What did my parents do to you personally that you hate me so much? I'm guessing you're someone important considering how the guards do your bidding, but that gives you no right to treat anyone like shit."

"You speak to me with such disrespect. But I guess I shouldn't expect anything less from someone brought up by humans." She tosses her hand outward.

I'm flung sideways, slamming into a pillar, then I fall to the marble floor. Every bone in my body screams with pain.

A shadow falls over me, and she snatches me by the hair, drawing me to my knees. "The two races of fae are nothing alike," she spits in my face. "The Unseelie bloodline comes directly from the fairy queen herself. The Seelie are the fae who tried to murder her. I will cut your tongue out for saying we are the same."

My scalp stings from where she tugs on my hair, wrenching my head back. "Who are you?" I wince from the pain.

"I must thank you for coming in today, while my son and his queen are away from the court. It's like the gods have blessed me to finally fix the horrific mess your birth caused."

Her words slam into me. She's the king's mother! "Fuck you!" I shove against her, fury radiating over my body, not caring if she's god.

She snarls and drags me by my hair across the room and toward the table. "I'll take your tongue first, so you can learn a lesson before your death. You see, I even try to teach you something when I shouldn't waste my time. And this is why I have to fight so hard, to remind my son he needs to do anything in his power to stay king and take over all of the Wandering Realm. And with your death, little girl, you will eliminate one of our biggest obstacles. Your father."

"Why do you hate me so much?" I urge, scrambling on my feet so I'm not hauled forward like an animal.

"Have you even been listening to me? You are a mistake, and I am giving your life purpose. You will make every Unseelie proud when you die. Take comfort in knowing that you will have songs written about your sacrifice."

"Sacrifice?" I'm terrified, and I sure as hell don't want to die.

With incredible strength, she slams the side of my head onto the wooden table. Plates and cutlery clatter to the floor as my mind spins.

I cry out, pain biting into me where her fingernails dig into the flesh at my neck to keep my head pinned down.

"Hold still. It will be easier."

Terror crashes into me like waves, and one after the other, dragging me deeper. She's going to murder me, right here.

Her grip tightens around my neck, and her other hand clutching a long, sharp knife.

I feel sick, darkness smothering me. "Please no," I whimper, and she laughs at me.

I can't reason with her. She's the devil, so foul she's manipulated the Wandering Realm into a war. So much hatred, so much fear, and all because of this woman's need for power... she needs her son's to rule over the realm. Is he any different than the crazy dictators back on Earth? I guess greed and power may wear a different mask, but they're the same sadistic sonsofbitches. I realize then that fae like her will never understand peace or sympathy. I am a means to an end to her, and I clench my hands into fists.

I'm trembling and sucking in raspy breaths as I fight against her hold, but with it comes a power that scrapes over my flesh and balloons in my chest.

Digging my fingernails into her arm, I tear at her flesh. But she only laughs and lowers her blade closer to my face.

"Stop! Please don't do this." Panic swallows me.

A brush of energy comes at me fast.

The table beneath me shakes, walls groan, and I embrace the power. I unleash all of the energy I have with tremendous speed.

A thunderous sound booms around us.

The whole room quakes violently, chandeliers swing, dust falls from overhead, cracks zigzagging down the walls.

She pauses, glancing up at the disturbance, and I shove her hand off me, scrambling away.

"Don't ever touch me again!" I yell bitterly.

She scrunches her nose up in a grimace, looking ready to skin me alive. She throws her power at me, but I scream involuntarily, and with it comes every thread of power inside me.

It booms outward, and the air shimmers. Windows burst open, shattered glass tossed like rain in every direction. I cover my head as the shards pebble down on me.

The vile fae is thrown backward. She grabs a chair but instead of finding a source of stability, she takes it down with her. Huge cracks open up the walls, the ground rupturing, and I'm teetering on my feet. The main doors explode off their hinges, and an army of guards bursts inside.

I heave for each breath, my body humming with power, as though I'm alight. I force every inch of me to dance with the power I embrace. Anger punches through me. I want to bring this whole damn castle down around my feet.

"Guendolyn?" Luther yells out, and I rock on my feet as I turn to see him by the door, held captive by guards with Ahren at his side. More and more fae are pouring into the room as if it's a spectacle to uncover what the hell I've done in here.

Desperation twists with fear in my gut. I glance over my shoulder at the woman who wants me dead, dragging herself to her feet.

Except I'm not finished. Not even close.

She attacks me again, catapulting what looks like a fireballs right at me. She snarls with pure hatred.

I hold my arms out, and power shoots from my body in waves. It collides into everyone in the room, shoving them off their feet. They groan and cry out, but I don't care anymore about playing nice.

The fireballs fizzles, but not quickly enough. One strikes me in the chest and drives me back against the wall. Heat engulfs me, and I frantically flick the flames off me, patting them from my coat.

The clang of metal resonates across the room where the princes are battling the guards, backing toward me. Except more guards pour into the room. How far will we get if we manage to escape?

"Kill them all!" she orders. "They don't leave this room alive."

Exhaustion floods me, and I exhale as my power flatlines. I suck in the cold air sharply as a grim reality swallows me. We're trapped, and I only have one possible option.

Through labored breaths, I stand tall.

Luther looks over at me, fear twisting his expression.

Open the portal, little wolf. Do it now!

Back in the throne room, it was as simple as a single thought, so maybe my problem has been over-concentrating. Lifting my hand to my mouth, I tip the fingers backward, then exhale.

Nothing.

I growl under my breath, fiery anger lashing at me at my inability to get this to work. So I dig deep and draw on the electricity that lingers in my veins.

Glancing over at the princes battling the guards, I realize they aren't going to last much longer. I collect everything I have left within me and open myself so the energy just rushes out of me. A tremor tears through the room once more, and panic rises on the woman's face. She stares at me with an unbelievable expression that someone like me, an abomination, can hold such strength.

More cracks snake down the walls. Wind blows in through the shattered windows, whistling, tugging at my clothes. Energy laces around me, the hairs on my nape lifting. This isn't a battle of brawn, not for us, but one of abilities. I can't stop searching the masses, scared the mages will show any moment now and take me down.

Urgency swells within me, and I call to the portal, thinking of the Shadow Court castle. Of Deimos. Of survival. Of my power.

A storm of wind and quakes surges through the room, ripping it apart. It grows worse the more I attempt to draw on my power. Chunks of walls fall over, guards darting in every direction to escape death. Before me rise shadows and fog, growing in size to loom over me. The center opens up to pure darkness.

I turn my head to Ahren and Luther, who are running toward me at full-tilt, guards on their heels.

"Go through!" Ahren yells.

With a quick look behind me, I meet the fae woman's startled gaze. She had no idea of my ability... not until now. This is my power to master, and

I'll find a way to strengthen it. There's no hiding now; I know that she'll tell the king and queen, and then they will come for me. But with so much happening, the terror of what's to come sits heavily in my chest.

Luther reaches me first and shoves me to get going.

I whip around and lunge into the pitch blackness of the portal.

The emptiness engulfs me... and then I'm gone.

TWENTY-THREE

GUENDOLYN

I stumble out of the darkened portal. Bright light blinds me momentarily as I try to find my bearings. Cold droplets of snow land on my face and coat the woods around me, yet I don't recognize this place.

Ahren bursts out of the portal next, blinking against the light, stumbling to catch his footing. "Where are we?"

Luther darts out just as fast, grasping his sword, glancing around. "Where'd you bring us?"

"I don't know. But please tell me you have the cure for Deimos."

"We got it," Luther states.

Unease clings to my ribs as I see no sign of any castles nearby. Where exactly are we?

When another figure emerges from the portal, Luther pushes me away and raises his sword. He and Ahren wait on either side of me, weapons raised.

"You better be working on closing this portal fast." Ahren growls as an Unseelie guard stumbles out. The prince grabs him by the neck, then plunges his sword into his chest. There's no hesitation or remorse. This is life or death, and the princes are trained to battle until the end.

I lift my hand just as I did back in the throne room and picture the gateway shutting.

Three more guards shove forward, bellowing their war cries, swords drawn.

I extend my hand and blow out a long breath. The hairs on my nape shift as I feel the magic rippling on the wind. Blue energy shimmers around the portal, but it doesn't vanish. It just sits there, quivering.

"Guendolyn!" Ahren roars.

"I can't get it to shut. I don't know what I'm supposed to do."

Guard after guard comes out, and panic strangles me. How am I meant to help when I can't even control my power? I groan and fist my hands, wanting to scream in anger. Snow falls quicker now, its touch icy on my skin.

I turn on the spot, my head whirling with how to fix this. Running won't help, and how long before a mage steps through and annihilates us? If Deimos were here, he'd be able to command the forest to attack the enemy. I feel so damn useless.

Turning back to the portal, I find the princes battling the guards, slaying them. Luther is bleeding across his cheek, and a large gash on his arm drips with blood.

My heart is racing as I lift my hand, trying once again. Shadows rise on either side of me with frantic movements, and I whip around to the fluttering of wings.

Fairies. They're just fairies, and my heart beats with adrenaline, hoping that they're on our side.

A rainbow of colors surrounds us, and there are so many fairies, so many that I'm left intimidated. What if they belong to a different clan and have nothing to do with Hiss? I don't even know where I teleported us, and now fear creeps into my chest that we're in bigger shit than I thought. These fairies could be our enemies.

The swarm rises higher, looming over us like a shadow, baring their sharp fangs. They hiss and dart toward us but swoop back at the last minute.

I duck from one, and fear presses on my chest.

"What the fuck is going on?" Luther snarls as he plunges a blade into a guard's throat, then kicks him aside.

The only way I know to get the fairies on our side is to feed them. It seemed to work with the others back in the Shadow Court.

I rush over to a dead guard and frantically grab his knife. Without thought, I run the sharp end down my palm, the bite stinging like a bitch. I grit my teeth and stagger to my feet while sticking my cut hand out to the fairies.

"Taste!" I offer my blood to them, hoping they will understand and aid us.

But none of them approach me. They flutter about, staring at the dead bodies, at the princes fighting.

I dart up to them. "Take it, please. Just help us." They part at my approach, and only then do I see that behind them lie beehive-type homes hanging from the trees nearby with fairies flying in and out. Then I glance around to really see the forest. Dozens upon dozens of these homes are suspended from the branches.

We're in the middle of a fairy village or nest. No wonder they seemed angry. We just crash-landed in their home.

For those few moments, I don't know what to do, how to get out of this mess.

So I return to the portal and try again. I raise my hand, blood dripping onto the soil, and push out the energy bubbling inside me.

Close. Fucking close.

Something small falls into my palm out of the air, sliding into the small puddle of blood from my cut.

I flinch at first, then carefully inspect it.

A red crystal sits there...a ruby, just like the one Hiss stole.

I jerk my head up, and above me, those beautiful blue wings beat frantically.

"Hiss!"

She glowers at me and points to the portal. Right!

I fold my hand around the stone, and a sharp prickle of power digs into my palm. It zips up my arm, racing through my body as though I've touched an electrical socket.

Bringing my fist to my mouth, I unfurl my fingers and blow over the stone.

A tremendous wind comes out of nowhere and buffets into me. It races past and collides into the guards and princes, sending them stumbling, and fairies flutter crazily around us.

But my eyes are only on the portal. It starts dissolving just as another guard steps out. But he's too late... The mouth of the portal vanishes with him in mid-transit, and all that's left of him is his chopped-off leg. It drops to the ground, his blood soaking into the soil.

My hair billows in my face, the wind's whistle deafening in my ears, and I curl in on myself.

But something feels different inside me. A burning erupts in my chest, deepening, hurting to the point where I can't stand still any longer. Energy rolls through me, the sky overhead snarling.

Something slithers over my flesh, and I scratch at my arms to find it's nothing. Everything inside me clenches tight, and I wrestle to see anything but the chaos of trees blowing, leaves rustling. Fairies are being flung in every direction, and I can no longer see the princes.

I lick my dry lips as the weather rages. "Luther, Ahren, where are you?" I cry out.

In a heartbeat, everything dies. The portal has vanished, the winds quiet down, fairies fly as far from me as possible.

And my princes are on the ground amid the dead guards.

My heart hits the back of my throat as I throw myself toward them, tears already pooling in my eyes.

"Ahren," I cry, snatching his coat to turn him on his back, coldness slicing right through my heart.

This isn't meant to happen. They aren't supposed to be hurt. They, and Deimos, are the only ones who made me feel like I belonged, who captured my heart.

All this is my fault. If only I knew how to use my power correctly... I sink to the ground between the princes. My fingers shake as I check Luther for a pulse, but his skin is cold, and I choke back a sob. No, no—this can't be happening. I can't lose them. Not now, not after everything.

I grasp Ahren's shirt, fisting it, wanting to bring him and Luther back, no matter the cost. Tears flow fast and furiously down my face.

A groan comes from Luther, and I jerk around to face him.

He's pushing himself off the ground, groaning, his hair sticking upward and tangled with leaves.

I throw myself into Luther's arms, causing him to fall back down with me on top of him. I can't stop laughing and kissing him. His hands clasp the side of my face, and the way he kisses me back tells of someone who has been to death's door and back.

"Don't you ever die on me." I breathe the words into his mouth.

"I've no plans to go anywhere, little wolf."

Breaking away from him, I swing toward Ahren, who's kneeling beside me. I throw my arms around him, then tuck my face into the curve of his neck, hugging him tightly. "I thought I lost you for a moment there. Don't ever scare me like that again."

When I pull back, he kisses me, and I'm lost to his touch. It amazes me how much almost losing them reinforces what my heart wants.

I glance around to find the fairies have returned, but it's Hiss who hovers near to us, looking at me with a strange expression.

Eirian. Her voice trails over my thoughts, just as easily as Luther's does when he speaks in my mind.

Hiss points to my hand, and I open my fist where I'm still holding the stone.

Ahren gasps as he looks down at the ruby.

"Please tell me that's not the missing piece from our stepfather's throne?"

"It doesn't belong to him," I explain. "This is a fragment of the fairy queen's crown and should be with the fairies, not a showpiece in someone's chair."

I'm on my feet and step toward Hiss, my hand stretched out, handing her the ruby. "This is yours," I say.

She shakes her head. *Eirian,* she says again.

All the fairies suddenly flutter closer to me and land on the snowy ground to kneel before me, their heads low, their wings curled around them.

Hundreds of fairies fill the land.

"What did you do?" Luther asks.

"They won't take back their fairy stone. I don't understand. But Hiss keeps saying the word 'Eirian' in my head."

"You can hear it talk to you?" Ahren asks in disbelief.

I glance over my shoulder at him. "Well, I'm not sure I can count one word as speaking to me." I offer him a crooked smile, imploring him for any kind of help.

"Um, little wolf. Do you know what 'Eirian' means?" Luther asks.

"Of course not."

"It's the ancient word for fairy queen."

I burst out laughing at his implication. As if things aren't weird enough.

"It's not funny," he reprimands me. "There are legends that speak of the fairy queen's spirit living on through a few chosen. What if—?"

"Don't even say it. I can't take any more surprises." I can barely deal with knowing my real father is the King of Shadow Court, and somehow, I need to break the news to the princes.

"We need to go home," Ahren interjects. "Deimos doesn't have much time." I turn to the sea of fairies bowing before me, and I feel anything but prepared or worthy.

"Hiss," I murmur. "We need to go back to the kingdom." I don't know if she understands me, but she looks at me, confused.

I point at myself and the princes, then into the distance.

She nods, then flutters over to me. Her huge, dark eyes study me, then she speaks to me in my head...but the words make absolutely no sense to me. She then points to the stone and nods.

I think she might be telling me I can use the stone to contact her? I have no clue, to be honest, but I smile. "Thank you."

Once more, she studies the ruby and then her hand sweeps to where I indicated earlier about traveling in the distance. This I understand—use the ruby to get home. She leans over and lowers her head to the cut on my hand, licking the blood. I wait until she's had her fill, then she pulls away.

She sings, and her soft tune is like a maiden crying with loss. The other fairies raise their heads and spread their wings, then break into the same song. The sound grows louder, hypnotic and beautiful. As they all fly back into their homes, the area turns magical with gorgeous colors everywhere.

I turn toward my princes, and they're both staring at me with awe in their eyes.

"What?" I ask.

"I think you're so much more than any of us realize," Ahren admits.

Shrugging, I saunter toward them. "You don't know how true that is. I have lots to tell you both, but let's get to Deimos first."

I raise the hand that's holding the ruby, and I blow a lungful of air over the crystal, picturing Deimos in bed.

Before us, shadows rise and quickly form into a portal. "Are you ready to go home?" I ask, feeling more confident than I have in a very long time.

"Fuck, yeah." Luther takes my hand and leads me to the portal.

I step forward, and in that moment, I realize why that portal opened up in the throne room, across the grounds from where I was, on my first day at the Shadow Court castle. It was because of this ruby. It called to my power...

TWENTY-FOUR

GUENDOLYN

In one heartbeat, we're in the snow-covered forest surrounded by fairies, and the next, we're in Deimos' bedroom back at the mansion. He's over in the palace, but who the hell cares if I got the room wrong? We're in Shadow Court. The portal brought us here and not somewhere across the Wandering Realm.

I turn back to the portal and close it with the simplicity of blowing my breath over the stone in my palm.

"Thank the Seven Hells we're back," Luther mutters.

My emotions are all over the place, so tangled and chaotic that I don't know what to feel. Fear from everything we've gone through, elation that I managed to control the portal for once, and an undulating surge of anxiety about meeting my father again. How will he react?

Ahren steps alongside me, his hand sliding into mine. "Are you all right?"

I nod, but my insides are jumping. "We need to go to Deimos now."

"Agreed." Luther opens the door and we rush into the hallway. It's silent with not a soul in sight, but all I can think about now is Deimos. About seeing him smile again.

Please let the cure work.

As we cross the bridge, we're battered by a snowstorm, the day darkened by bruised clouds. I push ahead, one step in front of the other. It isn't long before we enter the palace and race down the corridor, Luther taking the lead.

But something is wrong. Really wrong.

Why are there no guards around? Where is everyone?

Luther leads us to a set of grand marble stairs that sweeps upward in an arc.

When Luther pushes open a door to his right, we hurry in behind him. My breaths are raspy, my lungs aching from sprinting here so fast.

Across the room stands an elaborate poster bed made of black wood. Magic encases Deimos, just as it did the last time I saw him. I step forward eagerly and gasp at how far gone he looks. He's so much paler...almost gaunt in his face.

"Is he okay?" I squeak as I swallow past the boulder in my throat.

"He's deteriorated faster than I hoped. He should have had another day, but..." Ahren's fear goes unsaid, but we're all thinking the same thing. Deimos has run out of time. We do this now, or he will slip from us.

Invisible claws clench my heart at the thought of losing him. I can't live with that. I won't live with that.

Luther digs into his pocket and pulls out a small golden box, flipping open the lid. He stares down at the contents, and his brow furrows with worry.

"What's the problem?" Ahren asks, looking down at the box.

"Is that the cure?" I ask.

Luther licks his lips and glances over at us. "It's a powder. How do I get this into his system? I don't know the magic words. Fuck." He shuts the box with a snap and starts pacing. "I should have asked the mage for the words as well. I know better. Magic comes with words," he bellows, his voice echoing around the room.

"Luther." I walk up to him and take his hand into mine. "There's always a way."

"Jasion," Ahren says. "He'll know!"

My stomach drops at hearing his name, at remembering the Unseelie king's mother speaking of him.

"Ahren, no." I turn toward him, but he's darted through the doorway and left us alone. "Shit." I glance up at Luther. "We can't trust Jasion."

He doesn't seem to hear me, only staring at his brother. Blood drips from the wounds on Luther's arm and cheek, but there's no reaction, as though he can't feel the pain. I leave him with his thoughts as I move to the window and look outside. The view is of the kingdom city, the people wandering about, shutting down stalls.

I don't know how much time passes, but Ahren still hasn't returned. I finally turn, finding Luther hasn't moved from his brother's bedside.

"Maybe I can try healing Deimos?" I suggest.

I open my hand that still holds the ruby, blood dried on my palm and the stone.

Luther shakes his head.

"Hear me out. What if some of my ability comes from fairies? You saw what happened back in the woods. So, what if I can use the stone to heal Deimos?"

He glances over at me, his eyes looking straight through me, and I can't even tell if he heard a word I said.

The door creaks open, and I jerk around just as Ahren marches inside. His cheeks are red from running, his brow streaked with blood from the earlier battle.

"I can't find Jasion or any of the mages." His words are panicked and aggressive.

"Guendolyn will do it." Luther finally speaks. "We have no other option. The sun is going down, and our brother's life ticks away."

Both princes look at me, and I squeeze the ruby tightly in my hand, suddenly doubting myself.

"I can try."

Luther steps toward me and opens the golden trinket box. I look inside to see a small amount of powder that smells like dried herbs and something acidic that burns my nostrils.

"Any recommendations on the best way to do this?" I ask the princes.

"When I've watched Jasion work, he dusts the powder over the person he's spelling while speaking words of what he wants to happen."

"And the ruby?" I ask, studying their faces for some kind of indication that this will work, but they offer me nothing but worry.

I can't sit back and do nothing. "I'm going to try. We have enough powder for what looks like two tries."

"I don't think we should split the potion," Luther says. "Half might not be powerful enough."

Grimacing, I chew on my cheek.

"We get one go." Ahren breathes the words as though he can't bring himself to say them. He stares at the door, then at me. "I'll be right back. I have to try to find Jasion again."

"Ahren, no," Luther barks. "What if Guendolyn is right and Jasion can't help Deimos? What if it isn't in his best interest to heal Deimos?"

Ahren's brow tangles. "Not this again. I know you've always hated him, but—"

"The Unseelie king's mother asked me about Jasion," I say, butting in. "Why would she ask about him by name unless there's something going on?"

Both princes look at me with dread in their eyes, and I can tell what I revealed sits heavily with Ahren. He trusts Jasion, has all his life, but I don't.

"Are you ready to do this?" Luther asks.

"Yes." Not really, but I hide the fear and wear my bravery. This isn't a time to let trepidation into my mind.

We move closer to Deimos' bed, and I take my place alongside him. I have no idea what the right way to complete this is, so I follow my instinct. I offer Luther my free hand, and he pours the contents from the golden box into my palm.

If I do possess some trickle of fairy magic, then maybe that's where my healing ability comes from. Maybe the fairy queen's ruby will enhance my healing magic like it did with the portal magic, allowing me to treat Deimos' wounds once the powder has counteracted the curse. In theory, this should work.

I slide a hand through the magic bubble encasing Deimos and place the ruby over the bite mark on his shoulder, the stone sitting between him and me. Before I say a single word, a fiery heat erupts across my palm, unbearably hot. But I won't move. I don't dare. In my mind, I am healing him. It's all I can picture—the poison leaving his body.

I bring my other hand with the powder over his face.

Please let this work. Please.

I tip my hand, and the herbs sprinkle over him. "Heal the poison from his body."

Silence falls over us, only my heartbeat singing in my ears.

Heat curls over me like flames licking at my flesh. I try to find a memory to hold on to where Deimos is healthy and untainted. That's what I picture in my mind, coupled with my deepening emotions for him, and I drive all those feelings into him.

Heal.

Scorching heat engulfs my hand and slithers up my arm. I know that's the venom from his body. I feel the ache, the way it cuts into me like blades. The toxin fills me, swallows me. Still, I stand tall and don't back down.

Energy crashes over me, and I grit my teeth as I drive the poison out of me with thought and strong will. I embrace every inch of my power and pummel the full force of it into the infection.

Blue threads of light curl around my arm and over Deimos, binding us, driving the power of healing into him. I feel the river of electricity over my skin, and the stone beneath my palm pulses faster.

My breaths quicken, and the pain gathering inside me is becoming too much. It's a fire burning me from the inside out, leaving me barely standing, my whole body shuddering.

Deimos releases a loud exhale, his body arching upward. His brothers are by his side, and I hold on with all my strength as the thread that binds us throbs, thinning with each second it eliminates the poison.

My legs shake beneath me, my whole body weak. When the last thread vanishes, I let go, unable to hold on for a moment longer.

A scream tears past my lips, unleashing a heart-shattering sound. Black smoke curls out from my mouth into a wisp, fading away. My stomach churns and roils while my knees give out from under me.

I fall to the ground, gasping for air, every inch of me shaking with exhaustion. The ruby is still in my hand, and I grip it tight, refusing to let it go. All I can picture is Deimos' response to the healing, praying he's okay. My whole body buzzes, and each exhale rips from my lips.

"Guendolyn." Luther crouches next to me, his hand on my arm. His touch is like a spear through me. I push his hand away, but it's too late. His touch has done something to me.

I scream with pain again, and I'm swallowed by blackness.

Images pop into my mind like lightning, flashing in and out. They're of me at school, Luther speaking to me in my mind, teasing me, flirting. Then I'm carried in his arms into a dark world...the Wandering Realm. We're running, always running.

The snapshots come at me so fast, all I can catch are glimpses. But the memories spread over my thoughts like a web, filling in the missing gaps of the past few years.

Meeting the three princes. Luther keeping me hidden in the mansion from the king.

Luther showing me the Ferris Wheel he made for me, then our first kiss. I melt at the memory, at the intensity of our first connection.

The image vanishes, and in its place is the blonde Unseelie fae who tricked me into leaving Shadow Court and going with her to Ash Court. Me stepping into their kingdom and unleashing the curse.

Heartache shreds me to pieces. The emotions for the princes I haven't had access to all this time because I couldn't remember them come at me. Hitting me, ripping me, taking everything I held on to until there's nothing left. Nothing but me, the woman who lost her life the moment she was born. Who fell for a fae prince way before she ever met him. Who then lost him...and now those memories are a blade slicing into me.

I'm crying, agony and rage filling me at what I lost. I cry for the hunger in my heart that I was denied feeling until now. All those times I went to a therapist over the last two years about my confused feelings only to be told it was hallucinations or something. This explains why I felt this pull toward him, but I didn't really know why... not until now.

"Guendolyn," Luther calls.

My eyes spring open, but his face is blurry behind my tears. I can't stop crying, and I feel like my chest is splitting in half from the heartache I caused Luther, from getting Deimos bitten.

"Are you hurt?" Luther collects me into his arms, and I curl in against his hard chest. I fist his coat, holding him tightly against me.

"I'm sorry," I murmur. "For so long, I didn't remember us." I can't stop the tears.

He cups my face and looks down at me, his thumbs wiping my wet cheeks. "What's going on? Why are you apologizing?"

"I remember us. I remember our past, Luther. Everything, from you taking me from my home, to our first kiss, to you saving me from the Blood-cursed before I stepped into Ash Court." My voice trembles because it's not just the loss of the memories of the events themselves, but the emotions that accompany them, that has me hurting. For two years, Luther suffered while I vanished, and when I did return, I didn't recall our past.

I suck in hard breaths.

"Little wolf," Luther says with a smile, his eyes glistening.

He helps me to my feet, and Ahren is by my side, pushing the hair off my face, looking at me as if searching my face for some kind of answer. Except the truth lies in the ruby that opened up my memories after all this time.

"Why the fuck does it feel like I've just eaten a rat?" Deimos croaks.

We all turn toward him, and I choke on a laugh.

Deimos pushes himself to sit up in bed, shadows still caught under his eyes, but the glint in them has returned.

A cry falls from my mouth as I rush toward him and throw myself into his arms. "You're back." I hold on tightly, not planning on letting him or any of these princes ever leave my side again. I'm tired of death being around every corner in this realm. For once, I want calmness and peace. And I'll claw and scrape for every second I can get.

"How are you feeling?" I ask.

Ahren and Luther sit on the bed next to their brother. Deimos clears his throat and looks at us, bewildered, taking in our disheveled and bloody appearances. He has no clue what we all just went through, but I'd do it again in a heartbeat.

"Have I missed much?" Deimos mutters.

"Brother, you have no idea," Luther says. "Get better, and you'll hear all about it."

The thundering sound of the door thumping open has me jumping in my skin.

Mael, Ahren's advisor, bursts into the room, his gaze petrified and wild. "Your Highnesses," he begins, his voice trembling.

"What's wrong?" Ahren asks, standing up from the bed.

My heart does that thing where it knows something bad has happened and it's preparing to break out of my chest.

Mael's face grows three shades paler. "The King of Shadow Court is dead! He's been murdered!"

TO CLAIM A FAE

WINTER'S THORN, BOOK 4

TO CLAIM A FAE

The king is dead...

...and now my future, as my heart, hangs in the balance.

With the kingdom in chaos and my powers still fighting me for control, I'm left to wonder if there's even a place for me among the fae.

Or among the three men who have been there since the beginning of this journey.

Because even they feel like they're slipping away...

Especially since the court mage hates me and is conspiring against me at every turn.

But those aren't my only problems.

Finding the truth of who I am and what my destiny will be is consuming me and threatening to ruin all that I have and all those I love.

If I can't find a way to stop my enemies, we are all doomed and the fae realm will be lost.

And I can't let that happen. I won't. Even if it means a fight to the death...

Captivating conclusion to the 'WINTER'S THORN' saga.

FAE LEGENDS

The girl made of ash and shadows.

PROLOGUE

19 years ago

The world smells strange. Smoke. Rotting food. And sorrow. It leaks into the air like pollution. How can these humans live in such decay and filth? I scrunch up my nose.

These are my first steps on Earth, and I pray they'll be the last. Trees behind me sway from where I've emerged, and before me lays a flat road with lamps lighting the quiet area.

Soft gurgling sounds draw my attention to my baby in my arms, cradled against my breast. Her eyes are shut, and she sucks on her thumb, her nearly white hair laying across her forehead. So peaceful and perfect. My eyes prick, but I blink the tears away. The time for falling apart has long passed. This is for her. Everything is for her.

Hurriedly, I cross the road. The wind is vicious tonight, tugging at my cloak, ripping it off my head. I glance back into the silent woods, at the heavy moon that hangs low like a pregnant belly.

"Please Goddess, protect us," I whisper under my breath and rush forward. Old, worn buildings like square blocks line the sidewalk, and up ahead I see exactly what I'm after.

A bright yellow sign with the words *Women's Refuge.* The 'W' in the first letter flickers like it might snuff out.

My heart beats fast as my feet slap the ground.

Relle, my maid, found this place. She came to Earth and said no one would find it. When I glance around to the barren road, the decrepit homes, I have to agree. There is no way they'll find her here. No one will know.

She stirs in my arms, and my heart breaks when she looks up at me. Crystal blue eyes akin to mine. She smiles at me, and a tear escapes from the corner of my eye.

"Oh, little one." I choke on my words and press her to my chest as I flee toward salvation. The lights are on inside, and I stand in front of the white building. Three steps lead up to the door, but I can't get my legs to move.

I stare down at my baby, and tears keep falling. She makes gurgling and cooing sounds, and they have me choking up. If only she knew the truth of why I can't keep her. Except, she can never find out or it'll kill her. Here, in this backward world, she stands a chance. In the Wandering Realm, her end is already planned.

"This is all I can give you." I move to sit on the steps and hold her on my lap. I draw out a small ribbon from my cloak pocket and wrap it around her tiny ankle. Her skin is so soft and warm against my fingers. I tie the knot loosely, leaving her embroidered name on the fabric. The least I can do is leave her with her nickname to make it a bit harder for her to ever find her way back home.

Guen.

Lifting her into my arms, I kiss her brow and inhale her beautiful powdery baby smell. I take in every bit about how she feels against me, the soft sounds she makes; everything I can, I memorize. It's all I'll have left of her.

I wipe my eyes, knowing I need to get going. The longer I'm gone, the more suspicion I'll raise.

On my feet, I turn toward the door just as it opens. Bright light beams from the hallway, and a middle-aged woman with the kindest eyes greets me.

"Hello, do you want to come in?"

I lick my dry lips, barely able to find my words. My chest is cracking in two, and it takes everything to not fall apart. I can't fall apart, at least not yet.

The woman motions with a hand for me to enter the house and steps aside in the doorway. Her aura swims in kindness. There's not a mean bone in her body, and I know now why Relle selected this house for my babe.

Up until now, I haven't cried, as I was too busy trying to not be caught, but now I can't seem to stop. My arms cling to Guendolyn like somehow I can keep her. The idea of staying here with her plays with me, teases me, but it's useless. My family will find me—they know my aura, and it'll lead them directly to me. But not my girl. I made sure no one would ever find her. As long as she stays here, the curse put on her should never come to pass. The glint of my magic, which will keep her concealed, still sparks in her. On Earth, she can just be a normal human and live a simple life rather than be hunted down.

"Is everything alright, ma'am?"

Startled by the woman's words, I lift my head and blink. I don't think as I hand my baby to her. "Please, will you hold her for a moment for me while I pull myself together?"

"Of course." She's a beautiful soul and scoops up Guendolyn, already cooing her a lullaby, rocking her in her arms.

My chin trembles, vision blurs with too many damn tears. Empty and barren is how I feel, my arms growing heavy from the loss.

When she's busy looking at the child, I slip away with the speed of the wind and pray I've done the right thing to keep Guendolyn safe.

When I'm across the road in the shadows of trees, I look back. I can't stop myself. The woman is in the doorway holding her, searching, calling for me. Then I turn and run.

I love you, my little fairy.

"The King of Shadow Court is dead! He's been murdered!" Ahren's advisor, Mael, declares from the doorway, his face pale and stricken with grief.

Silence falls over the bedroom. This has to be a mistake. So this... god no, please no, this has to be a mistake.

"What are you talking about?" Deimos asks, his voice still croaky from having just recovered from a Bloodcursed's bite.

Ahren suddenly bolts out of the room, Luther on his heels, their thumping footfalls fading somewhere in the corridors.

Just like that, in the span of a few seconds, our world crumbles, and my stomach drops right through me.

The King of Shadow Court is dead.

My real father.

I finally found him, and he's been swept away. I can barely make sense of it.

Deimos stumbles from the bed, but the reality of what I heard from Mael collides into me. It crashes over me like powerful waves.

My whole life I've longed to know who my parents are, and when I find one, he's been murdered.

What the hell, universe? You hate me that much?

I had cured Deimos from the Bloodcursed's bite. Coupled with my memories from my past coming back to me, this should be a time to celebrate.

Instead, my knees wobble out from under me and they hit the floor, my stomach churning like I'm going to be sick. I can't even cry, because what stirs inside me isn't heavy grief but shock, sorrow and heartache of what's been ripped away from me. It's like I looked away for a few seconds and someone went into my room and stole everything I owned.

To have him ripped away breaks me. I spent one night with him, drinking and listening to his tales about fairies and fae, but it isn't enough.

Did he know who I was, or was he as oblivious as me?

Deimos is kneeling next to me, his arm around my lower back, drawing me toward him. I should be the one helping him, seeing as he was on death's door just a few minutes ago. Instead, I'm falling apart against his side and tucking my cheek to his chest. The moment he embraces me, the tears fall. He takes my hand and gives it a squeeze. His touch is overwhelmingly warm from being in bed so long, and he smells of perspiration, but I don't care.

Each breath comes hard. I never asked to be abandoned. Never asked to be born, either. And I hate those old feelings rising through me again. I worked for so many years with counsellors to learn to love myself and accept myself as I am, to convince myself that I'm not 'less than' because my parents left me alone in the world. Now, the familiar sensation of being abandoned forever claws through me, unravelling it all.

"It's going to be alright," Deimos whispers.

I look up at him, at this perfect man who barged into my blissfully unaware life on Earth and brought me back here to remember how royally screwed my life is. But when I meet his gaze, my heart melts like ice under the summer's sun.

"What's going on? I didn't realize the king meant that much to you?" he asks softly.

"I don't know what to do. Tell me what I should be doing, Deimos." Confusion and agony rip through me again and again until I can't breathe.

He cups my face, his thumbs rubbing away my tears. "I don't understand, Guendolyn. What do you mean?"

I can't stop the growing ache in my chest, the one where I miss a man whom I barely knew and who I've searched for my whole life. But I shake my head. "Go see your father." I pull back, desperately wanting to drown in my loneliness, to let myself grieve and fall into the sorrow hacking at my chest. To be left alone as I come to terms with so much that I don't know where to start or end.

Deimos doesn't know that the king was my biological father. And this isn't the time to mention it, either.

He climbs to his feet and takes my hand gently. "Come with me to find out what happened."

I lower my gaze to my hands in my lap. "You go."

Silence.

I expect him to heave me to my feet and force me. Instead, the soft thump of his heels against the floorboard fades as he crosses the room. Seconds later, he's gone, and the door shuts behind him.

Everything happened too fast. I get up onto the couch and curl in on myself, hugging a pillow to my chest.

Snow drifts in slow motion outside the window against a backdrop of dark clouds. For years, I assumed when I found out who my parents are, I'd have closure. The likelihood of finding they had died was high, I'd told myself this. But at the end of the day, loss is loss, right? And still, it stings.

I don't remember how long I lay on the couch feeling sorry for myself, and when no one returns, I decide to head out and join the princes.

This isn't about me, now is it? It's about someone murdering the king. So, I open the door and find two guards swinging around to face me. Tall fae in dark uniforms who keep looking over their shoulders. They look just as worried as the rest about the king's death, and I don't blame them. I don't know enough about fae royal rules, but when a king falls, doesn't that make a kingdom vulnerable? I should have gone with Deimos in the first place.

"Can you take me to the princes, please?" I ask.

They nod, and we start walking fast along the dark hallway. It's like they'd been waiting for me to finally get my act together.

We cross the bridge between the princes' mansion and the royal castle. The breeze is icy against my skin. I hug myself, and quick steps bring me to the warmth of indoors. The mood in the castle hangs heavy, and guards run past us frantically. Other fae in silks and embroidered gowns and suits dart into rooms, their faces ashen. Their fear is palpable.

Moments later, I'm standing outside the doorway to the throne room. I hate this room. It brings back memories of me accidentally opening the portal to the Bloodcursed that hurt Deimos, and then another to the fairies. And now, the king has been killed here.

I don't move inside, a strange sensation crawling up my spine like I don't belong.

Luther consoles his crying mother, who buries her face against his chest. Ahren crouches near the body of the king, who's covered in a white bedsheet. Blood stains the material in large blotches, the red against the white a stark reminder of the loss. Deimos, still in his blue pajama pants and top, stands over the dead king, arms dangling by his side.

Mages are there too, including Jasion, along with a host of other men I don't recognize. Maybe close to thirty people are in the throne room, and no one pays me any attention. But all I can do is stare at the body.

He's the king.

My father.

I tell myself I have every right to be there and say my final words, but I can't get my legs to move.

So much blood.

Do I really want to remember him this way? I have so few memories of him, and the one night we did spend chatting, I cling to. That's the father I want in my thoughts.

I step back and bump into the guard who brought me here. "Please take me back." My voice trembles, but I don't care. This is too much.

"Follow me."

And I do just that. Hurried steps carry me away. I take one last look at the room and lock eyes with Jasion, who stands in the doorway to the throne room.

Did he play a hand in the king's demise? The Ash King's mother asked me about him specifically. There are traitors in this castle, and for all I know, I could be the killer's next target.

His stare darkens, and a shiver runs down my spine.

Jasion must be involved... I know it in my bones, and I'll find a way to prove his guilt.

Deimos

"THIS IS a shit show to wake up to." My attempt at lightening the mood in Ahren's study fails miserably. Neither he nor Luther respond. Ahren stares out the window, his back to me, while Luther sits in the middle of the room, his feet up on the table, crossed at the ankles and rocking back in his seat. He's miles away, staring into oblivion.

I'm in a strange state of both cheering that I survived the Bloodcursed's bite and my chest clenching with what we've lost. The king was the closest thing we had to a real father. Sure, he often kept his distance from us, but he tried, and it was more than we could ask for. Now, the grief pulsing through me is for a fae's life taken too soon and the agony my mother faces in losing her husband.

A knock comes at the door, and I turn. My brothers don't move, so I stroll over to find a maid in the doorway holding a silver platter with a jug and chalices. The sweet grape and cinnamon aroma finds me instantly. Spiced mead, only served when someone passes. My stomach growls at the smell, as it's been days since I've eaten.

"Enter," I instruct.

Not wasting a moment, she rushes in, places the offering on the table, and retreats.

Once she's gone, I serve myself a cup and take a drink, its warmth coating my insides as it slides down my throat. Still in my bedclothes and needing a bath desperately, I flop down into a seat at the head of the table and take my fill of the wine. I don't recall much from my time when I lingered on death's door, but I'm grateful the lethargy is gone. I doubt I'll be able to sleep for a week straight from the energy buzzing in my veins.

"Any thoughts on who killed him?" My voice slices through the silence.

"Many hate him," Luther muses. "Both in the court and outside."

"The killer was brazen. He got him in the heart, the blade driven down to the hilt. Whoever did this stood in front of him as he committed the murder," I state.

"There was no sign of a struggle," Luther adds. "Means it's someone he knew to get that close and for guards to see nothing."

"Unless they're in on the attack?" I suggest and glance over to Ahren. "What do you think?"

He doesn't look our way, just keeps staring out the window.

Luther cocks a brow. "What's the plan then?" he asks. "We all know what's coming next, right?"

Ahren turns his back to the snow-stained glass and leans against the frame, arms folded over his chest. He stares at me with contempt, but it's not aimed at me. He's the one that's going to save the day, and that means a massive sacrifice, whether he likes it or not.

"We delay the ceremony for as long as possible," Luther suggests.

Ahren growls under his breath. "How long? Less than a week at most, then the vultures will pounce. The king's sister will race to our kingdom to claim the throne the moment she hears her brother has died."

I slouch in my seat and drink more of the warm wine, helping sate my empty stomach.

Luther drops his feet from the table and asks the question we've all been thinking. "You're the heir to the throne, Ahren, and to take ownership, you must be married. Who will you take as a bride?"

Guendolyn pops to mind. Mother will ask a million questions if we suggest her, as will the royal council. She'll need to know Guendolyn's family heritage, and Luther can't marry a non-royal. The big issue will be that Seelie and Unseelie are forbidden to wed, so that's not going to work.

Ahren knows this. The bitterness is scribbled over his tight expression. Each of us have fallen for Guendolyn, so how will she react to Ahren marrying someone else?

"I don't know the answer," Ahren answers truthfully. For once, he's not the older brother in control of every situation, but someone adrift in the chaos surrounding us. To lose someone and be forced to make such immediate decisions is fucked up. Letting another family member take the throne from Ahren will mean we lose our home and most likely will be kicked out of Shadow Court. So really, there is no other solution.

Ahren must marry a royal.

Footsteps echo outside the room, and the door suddenly swings opens.

We all glance at our mother as she steps inside. She pulls the black cloak tight around her neck, the embroidered golden swirls along the lapels glinting under the fireplace's blaze. It falls to her knees, and a blue dress dances around her ankles with each step she takes. Her crystal green eyes are red and puffy from crying, while bright white hair tumbles over her shoulders in curls. She holds herself tall and regal, even while her heart breaks. The lines around her mouth and eyes deepen, the signs of her aging more apparent today than previously.

I'm on my feet and reach her side, then take her into my arms. She softens against me and cries gently. Growing up, she'd always been a strong figure, someone who fixed our problems, who never gave up on us three. Now, she feels so small and weak in my embrace. I hold her tighter, needing to be there for her. We all do, just as she did for us when our father treated us like shit.

She breaks away from me and wipes her eyes. "These ridiculous tears refuse to stop. I left the mages and haven't been able to cease crying since."

Her crooked smile shatters me. She loved King Tibout dearly, and this kind of loss is gruesome.

"Come, sit down," I offer. Once she's comfortable, I pour her a serving of warmed wine. "You'll always have us."

She holds the goblet, running the tip of her finger over the rim, then lifts her head toward Ahren. He joins us at the table. The four of us sit around in silence. The last time we were in this state was when our mother announced she was leaving our real father and we had to leave our home that very night. It happened long ago, yet it feels like just yesterday when we were on the cusp of being homeless.

Ahren reaches across the table and places a hand on hers. "Everything will be alright. I will make sure of it."

She nods, but more tears thread down her cheeks. Luther's on his feet and retrieves a napkin from the cabinet behind him, then hands it to our mother. She wipes her eyes as he crouches behind her, hugging her, his chin propped on her shoulder.

"I've sent a message by crow," she finally tells us. "We can't waste a single moment." She sips the wine, all the while her eyes never leaving Ahren. Her hands shake.

He knows as well as we do that if Ahren doesn't marry, he'll lose the throne and we'll be out on our asses. Mother married into this family, so her taking the throne isn't an option.

"Who did you send it to?" he asks, stiffening in his seat.

"Our closest allies. Queen Titania."

I groan, as do Ahren and Luther on cue. She runs one of the two kingdoms in the east with her king.

"She's on her fourth husband," I quip.

"And the previous three all mysteriously vanished," Luther murmurs, glancing at our mother with raised brows.

"You believe those rumors?" She shakes her head. "I'm not marrying my son to the Queen, but her daughter. She is said to be a beauty unlike any other in the east. She will make a perfect partner and ensure your claim to the throne." Her words are directed at Ahren, even if he hasn't said a word. "The Queen has been eager to merge our two kingdoms for a while now, which means the offer should be accepted before your stepfather's sister arrives to take the throne. I've postponed the funeral and forbid anyone from spreading the news about the king for a few days."

Ahren doesn't speak but pulls back his hand from Mother's while Luther moves back to his seat. Tightness gathers under Ahren's eyes. He holds himself composed, and I doubt anything could rattle his outside appearance. Different story on the inside.

This isn't an easy choice. Nope, not a choice at all, is it? He has no other option, and it kills me to watch him drown while there's nothing we can do. To save all of us, he has to carry the burden. And that's why he says nothing. Arguing won't change the situation we knew was coming, and any match he's paired with won't bring him closer to Guendolyn.

He wants her, like the rest of us, and his silence is the realization that he will lose her.

"You will be fine, Ahren, you'll see," Mother explains. "I barely knew King Tibout before I married into Shadow Court, and now I love him." She stands and pats down her cloak, her cheeks blushed, her eyes still spilling with tears. "Please keep this to yourself for now. Only a handful know. I will begin arrangements for the wedding in the meantime." She lowers her head and no one responds, plunging the room into a stifling silence.

His face reddens with fury, but if he says no, then we lose our home. And while he's alive, the second son can't take his place. I pity him, but I'll never show him that.

"We have a few days to the wedding," she states, her posture strong. Gone is our nurturing mother, replaced by a woman forced to take the lead to protect all of us. "We must be diligent and cautious until the killer is found in case they want you dead too, Ahren."

She turns on her heels and heads out of the room.

"Hell, Ahren," Luther blurts first. "What the fuck, man? Are you alright with this?"

Ahren's gaze narrows and he jolts to his feet, his chair scraping against the stone flooring. "What do you think?" he growls. "I'm fucking pissed, and I sure as hell don't want to marry someone else." His voice chokes. "But I don't have a choice, do I? I won't let our mother end up homeless." His pale green stare turns cold, his long white hair windblown, giving him a wild appearance. I swallow the boulder in my throat for him, as I can't begin to imagine how I'd feel if I were in his shoes.

"We knew this would come to pass one day. It's not a surprise," he says like he's trying to convince himself. Moments later, he says, "We don't tell Guendolyn, understand?"

"But—"

"No!" Ahren shuts down Luther. "Not yet, and I'll be the one to let her know when the time arrives." He marches out of the room, the door banging shut behind him. Luther clicks his tongue.

"This is cruel torture for him. You know he'll lose it and end up doing something stupid in his rage."

"Most definitely." I'm on my way to the door. "I'm going hunting or something. I need to get away from this shit."

I can't stand still, drowning in my thoughts. Ahren is fucked, and I don't know exactly how strong his bond is with Guendolyn, but from what I've seen, the news will break her.

CHAPTER

TWO

GUENDOLYN

I roll the red ruby over the back of my knuckles and flick it over my palm with a thumb, then repeat. Over and over. It's calming, in a strange way. The stone is cold against my touch, no matter how much I hold it. Then again, this isn't an ordinary rock, now is it?

It's the last crystal from the fairy queen's crown and belongs with the fairies, yet Hiss insisted it stay with me. Not to mention, it helps me open up portals with ease. Luther had said that the king had sold all of his mother's jewels in exchange for this stone from a witch fae who passed through Shadow Court. The king had been promised that the ruby would give him affinity with the fairies, which makes me wonder why he insisted on having it. Pure obsession, or something more?

Sitting cross-legged on the couch in Deimos' bedroom, I keep looking outside where the winds lash against the window and snow falls fast and heavy. The weather howls, and all I can picture are the tiny hive-style homes hanging from trees in the fairy village swinging wildly in the storm.

Since arriving in the Wandering Realm, if there's one thing I've learned, it's that nothing stays calm for long. Then there's the whole fairies helping me and calling me *Eirian*, a word for fairy queen, which confuses me even more.

I keep rolling the ruby over my knuckles, my thoughts wandering to Ash Court.

This is why Seelie and Unseelie can never be together. The Unseelie king's

500

mother had said those words to me. She also added that the Unseelie bloodline comes directly from the fairy queen herself, which might explain my connection with them. And everything else she told me confirms the late king of Shadow Court had an affair with someone from the enemy kingdom. And yet, the king never knew he had a child. Why didn't my mother tell him?

The Unseelie king's mother had reveled in that announcement. I hate her for that alone… and the fact she then tried to kill me, of course.

But I'm no fool. Whoever my mother is, she must be someone important. Why else would there be a war between the courts with me in the middle of it? I just hope she's still alive.

For so long, I was a pawn in their games.

The Unseelie king's mother had put the curse on me as a baby, and she gloated about it. I grit my teeth, as I barely escaped with my life… with the princes' lives. Something must be broken within me that the king's mother calls me an abomination. Or is that her demented view on anyone born to Seelie and Unseelie parents? The thought brings with it a reminder of the demented king's mother from Ash Court. Will she come after me again?

A groan from the doors sounds.

I quickly tuck the stone into the pocket of my pants and glance over my shoulder to Luther entering the room.

My heart pounds, while my stomach bursts with butterflies. I shouldn't be this excited about seeing a man I've been spending weeks with. Though, things aren't the same anymore. Not since I cured Deimos and Luther touched me while the magic still filled me. That touch had broken the spell that hid my memories from me. Now, my past with Luther is crystal clear in my mind, from his voice in my thoughts back on Earth, to the dirty things he'd say. There were the endless nights we spoke about stupid things, yet he captivated me all the same.

I know this fae inside and out, and the ache growing in my chest for him has everything to do with what he went through. He suffered on his own with our memories, and I couldn't do a thing to help him.

His keen gaze scans the room and rests on me. We're alone, and he kicks the door shut behind him. The gleam in his eyes calls to me. He looks at me differently, like we're long-lost lovers and we've finally found each other. The mischief in the quirk of his smile ignites the blaze in my chest. It's strange to think that I fell for his charm twice. Once before I even met him. And again while I couldn't remember much about our past.

We are meant to be together.

"I have a surprise for you." His deep baritone warms and comforts me.

I'm on my feet before I can make sense of how much influence he has over me.

"Luther." I rush to him and he collects me into his arms, lifting me off my feet.

Our mouths clash in an explosive match of emotions.

Arousal.

Desperation.

Unbearable need to make up for lost time.

His hands grab my ass, and his tongue slides into my mouth, dancing with mine. I lace my hands behind his neck and hold onto him, my legs wrapping around his hips. Our kiss is deep and passionate, the kind that knocks the breath out my lungs and leaves me dripping wet.

"You were saying?" I breathe the words.

One corner of his mouth curls upward into a lopsided grin with mischief gathering behind his gaze. Instead of answering, he kisses me and walks me back to the wall, where he pins me in place. The world fades around me; it's just us two at this moment.

No deaths.

No confusion.

No worry.

Only Luther and I.

Unable to resist or concentrate on anything, I run my hands through his long, dark hair, drawing him closer. He's like a wind sweeping through my mind, awakening our past from the first time I laid eyes on him. Dark and menacing, and even then my knees wobbled in his presence with a desperation to connect. For so long we spoke in my thoughts, and I should have known then he'd always be in my life.

I grip onto him, gliding my tongue into his mouth, bucking my hips against his growing erection. Despite everything, if there's one good thing to come out of me discovering where I came from, it's finding three fae whom I adore and who want me just as much. I don't think I could bear to lose any of them.

They are my lifeline in this crazy realm. And I need more... so much more of each of them.

His lips drag over my cheek and to my neck, where he nibbles on the flesh before he pulls my earlobe into his mouth. Fingers slide under the fabric of my top, finding skin.

I arch and moan as his hand slides higher and cups a breast. I tip my head back against the wall and close my eyes as he grinds his cock against my heat.

This is where I long to be every day. I suck in ragged breaths as he devours me, pinches my hardened nipple.

I cry out as he tugs on it, and my control is destroyed by his passion. Our lips once more merge. I kiss him with depth and passion, our tongues at war, then his teeth pull at my lower lip, the pain and pleasure a cocktail that leaves me dripping.

He draws back, our breaths racing, and slowly eases me back down on my feet, like that moment of fire was nothing more than a welcome kiss.

"What in the world was that?" I gasp, pulling down on my shirt to cover my stomach.

"You come running at me and I'm going to kiss you until you forget yourself." He slides a loose strand of hair behind my ear.

"That was so much more than a kiss, and you know it. You're an evil tease."

He lowers his hand from my hair, his knuckles gently brushing against my erect nipples. I gasp with a renewed flare of desire coiling tighter deep in my gut.

"Now *that* is a tease." He winks sexily at me. "What we did was different. I was preparing you."

I stiffen and narrow my gaze at him. "For what?"

"Told you I have something for you. And while I have every intention of fucking you, this isn't the right place... or maybe the time."

He cups my face and kisses me softly for a change. I consider protesting. Instead, I let myself fall for the distraction at a time when we need it most. His tongue licks over my lips, and I lean into his chest and whisper, "If you keep kissing me that way, I'm not responsible for what happens to your cock."

A burning gleam passes over his eyes, and the twitch of his erection pulses against my stomach.

"And you smell good enough to eat."

I draw in a shaky breath, waiting for my libido to stop sending waves of delicious arousal over me. "Damn, you're good."

He laughs, and I adore everything about him, but that sound he makes is extraordinary. "Remember who you're dealing with, little wolf. I'm the prince of darkness, a lord, a master." That grin brings back those exact words he'd said to me before we came to this realm.

"You're just as cocky as when you said that the first time." I lift my chin to him and smile back.

"It worked, didn't it? You melted over me. I remember when you first laid eyes on me; I saw the instant attraction you felt for me, the hunger in your eyes."

I half-laugh, refusing to let him know how right he is. "You're mistaking that for utter shock. I mean, at first, I almost mistook you for Dracula." I poke my tongue at him.

He grasps me by the arm and tugs me against him. "Who is Dracula?"

I burst out laughing. "It's a fictional character who's all dark and broody like you, but drinks people's blood to survive."

"Like the Bloodcursed?" He blinks as though trying to make sense of my ramblings.

"Yes and no. Anyway, I remember you once saying to me that long ago, darkness and light came together and created beauty... a beauty that will destroy this world. You were talking about me. Why didn't you tell me back then I was a fae?"

"Would you have believed me?"

I shrug and want badly to say yes, but it'd be a big fat lie. "So, where's this surprise you promised me?"

His hand slides into mine and our fingers interlace. He guides me toward the door and out into the hallway. "Patience," he says.

"Will you stay with me today?" I ask as we stride down the corridor where a maid shuffles past us, her head low.

"I'm not going anywhere. Now or ever. Just remember that, little wolf. No matter what happens, you will always have me by your side."

I glance over at him—his words are peculiar, but I think nothing of it once we pause in front of a black arched door.

"Hmm, should I be scared?" I ask.

"You tell me." He pushes the door and it swings open.

Before us lies a round room with white stone walls and floor, along with long narrow windows akin to the ones in the bedrooms. In the middle of the room sits a round pearl-white tub, big enough for five or six people to sit inside. It sits flush on the floor with no feet, and it must weigh a tonne. A small set of wooden steps rests on one end of the bath, and the other has a table with an array of fruit and breads and cheeses.

Steaming heat curls up from the water, waiting for us. "This is so perfect. But seriously, what is it with fae and baths?"

"It's a luxury not many have, and we use it to relax. Now, are you stripping, or am I doing it for you?" He releases my hand and starts grabbing at my top.

I slap his hand and push him away. "Are Ahren and Deimos joining us too?" With the tragic news, I want us all together.

"Deimos has gone hunting, and Ahren needs time alone right now. So you're stuck with me."

I guess everyone deals with death differently, and I welcome a bit of luxury, so I fumble with the buttons on my pants and take off my shoes.

When Luther doesn't move, but stares at me, gaping like he might drool, I say, "You just going to watch?"

"Is that a problem?" He strides toward me, and I back away, recognizing the look on his face. My insides burn up from his intense stare.

"I can get undressed on my own."

"Then hurry." His voice grows deep, like his control is on the verge of vanishing.

I force myself to turn away from him to not give him the satisfaction of seeing everything. Then I muse, "Any chance you could arrange for a drink? Something warm?"

Over my shoulder, I find him looking at the platter of food that lacks drinks.

He narrows his gaze at me and huffs. "I'll be right back."

The moment he shuts the door behind him, I sprint to the bath while ripping my clothes off in record time, leaving a trail in my wake. Up on the steps, I step onto the seating platform that runs along the inside wall of the tub. The water is scorching hot, but at the same time it feels incredible to sink into its embrace. The water is like silk, gliding over my body. I slip my head under its surface and stay submerged for as long as I can hold my breath.

It's a strange thing to crave numbness. I keep telling myself the king might have been my father, but only by blood, yet I also think I should grieve more than I am.

I push my head up and out of the water, my eyes flipping open only to come face to face with Luther staring down at me.

He drags his top up and over his head before tossing it behind him. Then he's pulling at the buckle on his pants as his gaze travels over my body in the water. It's nothing he hasn't seen before, but it doesn't ease the blush spreading over my cheeks. Seconds later, he's naked and climbing in. I tell myself to look away but fail miserably—I can't help but take in his cock, large and partially hard. I recall how big he gets once he's at full mast, how incredible it feels inside me. A shiver curls over my clit just at the thought.

I splash around as I attempt to maneuver as far from him as possible to give him space, only managing to slide on the smooth surface of the tub and dip underwater.

Frantically flaying about to get my balance like the most uncoordinated goldfish in the world, I grab for the edge of the tub. Strong hands snatch my ankle and haul me across the tub, dunking me further.

Holding my breath, I struggle and finally burst out of the water, gasping for air.

Luther's sitting on the ledge in the bath, legs spread and me between his thighs, laughing at me.

I wipe my eyes and push my hair out of the way, then splash him in the face. "If you're trying to drown me, you're doing a fine job."

"I thought you could swim?" He mocks me with his words and mirth.

With a roll of my eyes at him, I spin away from him. Strong hands grasp my hips, and he drags me backward until I'm sitting right on his lap. My bare ass on his thigh, his cock nestled against the side of my leg as I am turned to my side.

"I want you close to me." An arm locks around my stomach, and he's pretty much eye level with me. "You don't need to be shy around me, little wolf. I adore every inch of you, and if I could have my way, I'd spend every second in your company. And you would be naked, of course."

"Really? And you?"

"I'd be at your mercy." He blows me a kiss.

"You're such a sweet talker."

He shuffles us around so we are sitting on the ledge sideways, and I slip down to sit right between his legs. My back presses against his hard chest, his cock cradles my back, and his arm coils around me like he has no intention of letting me go. He brushes my hair over one shoulder, then kisses the back of my neck and shoulders. My skin pricks with goosebumps from the excitement building within me. But he never does anything more.

At first, I'm confused. I had this impression he carried every intention to finish what we started in the bedroom. Except, he holds me tight like he just needs the company.

A knock raps at the door, and I straighten. Luther draws me back as the door opens. His arms lower to cover my breasts, which I appreciate. My knees are bent in front of me up on the ledge.

Dana waltzes in, the older maid who remembers me from last time.

"Excuse me, Your Highness." She comes in with another maid, both of them carrying bundles of towels and clothes and shoes. They place the items at one end of the room on a side table, then they retreat and shut the door.

"Thanks for covering me up." I glance over my shoulder at this smoldering hot fae, whose dark hair is wet and pushed off his face. Thick brows crown the most spectacular amber eyes. My gaze drops to his full lips, tempted to lean in and taste them again.

"You got it wrong," he murmurs. "I wasn't concealing you, little wolf, but making it very clear that I've claimed you as mine by holding onto your gorgeous breasts in front of them."

My breath catches as I remember he's mine now too, and I can't help but love how protective and proud he is of me. I almost lost him because I couldn't remember our time together. Now, I want to soak him up and not lose another moment.

"The more I learn about your ways, the more you remind me of a hierarchy of wolves." I soften into his arms, the hot water brushing against my shoulders.

He kisses my head. "That's probably the most accurate way I've heard it described. And there are many factions vying for power." He traces his fingers across my palms, sending shivers through me. "When I find the person responsible for today's atrocity, they won't die a quick death."

I hold onto Luther's arm around me, my mind racing in dozens of directions when a thought slips past my lips. "Why would someone kill the king?"

"Usually power," he answers. "Or revenge, but I'm suspecting it's about power to weaken our court more than it already is."

"Between us," I begin, "I wonder if Jasion might be capable of such a gruesome act." The moment the words leave my mouth, I regret them. I'm pointing fingers to the mage based on my instinct, on my dislike for him, but does that make him a murderer? Maybe... hell, I don't know.

"Jasion has been part of our inner court since a young age, as were his father and father before him." Luther frowns. "But I don't trust him. Haven't liked him since we first met so long ago. He'd always make snarky remarks at Deimos and me when Ahren wasn't around as we grew up. But I'm not sure he is a killer type."

"No, forget I said anything." Maybe the Unseelie king's mother was trying to get under my skin. Make me see guilt where there was none, to cause derision. And just because I don't like the guy doesn't mean that he's a murderer.

"What would he have to gain?" Luther continues.

I shrug because I don't know the answer. "Anyway, let's not talk about that. I'm starving."

He reaches over to the table and collects a bunch of black grapes. He plucks one and places it into my mouth, the fruit exploding with sweetness over my tongue.

Not for a moment do I mind. If this Adonis wants to feed me and treat me like a princess, then I say *more please*. Maybe for a change, things might finally calm down so I can wrap my head around where exactly I fit in the Wandering Realm.

Candles flicker wildly across the dining table, and darkness cloaks the rest of the room. I'm sitting next to Deimos, with Luther directly across from me and Ahren on my right. Since arriving back at Shadow Court, I've longed for us all to be together, but there's a strange feeling in the air tonight. A sense of tension which I put down to the shitty day. Still, it nags me, as I hoped being with the three princes would help us all. But it isn't.

I reach over and fill my plate with a slice of roasted rabbit and vegetables. My mouth waters, and I scoop a bite into my mouth. Maple glazed, I moan at the crunch of the potatoes and how fluffy they are on the inside, Quickly, I collect four more with the serving spoon.

The princes don't seem to notice. Deimos eats directly from the platters, unable to put enough into his mouth. He has a fresh cut across his cheek, blushing pink, but I don't ask him what happened. Luther had told me he went out hunting, and if that's his escape, I respect his decision.

Luther only eats meat, nothing else, and when I watch him cutting slices and eating them hungrily, all I can remember is the two of us in the tub earlier today, talking, laughing, embracing. He fills out his deep mocha-colored coat so well, leather buckles taut across the front instead of buttons. There's no mistaking the attraction I hold for him. His black hair is draped off his shoulders, a thin layer of growth on his jawline, and my body awakens at the memory of him naked against me. My stomach flip-flops at how much I crave him... crave all three princes.

Ahren isn't eating but staring into the darkened corners of the room.

I lower my fork to the table. "Ahren, are you alright?"

He doesn't respond but remains distant. The other two glance up, looking over to their brother.

"Ahren, you with us?" Luther asks with a calm voice.

The eldest prince blinks and turns his attention to the three of us. "What did I miss?" He helps himself from the ceramic bowl of stew and begins eating as if none of us are watching him.

Luther looks my way. The corner of his mouth quirks, coaxing my own smile. His feet under the table clasp around mine. Every inch of me responds to him, screams for more.

Deimos tilts his head in my direction, his hand sliding onto my thigh, fingers pulling the fabric of my skirt up my legs.

I tense and push his hand away, tucking my legs back from Luther's reach. I'm not a prude, but right now, I am more concerned for Ahren and need to know he's okay.

"Ahren, do you have plans tomorrow?" I ask just as the door to the great hall opens. Footfalls echo around us as several maids hurry inside with platters of cakes and fruit and cheese.

"I'm busy," Ahren replies, not even looking at me.

I swallow hard and try not to overthink his reaction. Everyone is quiet tonight, and it's understandable, so I let it go. Sorrow is a close friend of mine. I focus on my meal while the maids squeeze the desserts onto the table. I've always been a sucker for sweets, and the three-tiered chocolate cake has my name written all over it.

"Would you like a piece?" Deimos asks, having seen me drool over the treat. "It's the sweetest plum cake."

"Plum? Not chocolate?"

Luther leans back in his seat, grinning like the Cheshire cat, which feels appropriate for the realm I've fallen into here. "There's no such thing as chocolate here, little wolf."

I frown. "The cake looks like it could be."

Deimos places a wedge on a clean plate, and I have my fork ready when he hands it to me. Even before it touches my tongue, I smell the fruit, but I don't care and stuff it into my mouth, wanting it desperately to be chocolate.

Sweetness spreads over my mouth—super sweet—the icing buttery and more like blueberry jam than chocolate. I won't lie, disappointment sweeps over me, but beggars can't be choosers, right? I finish the slice.

Ahren's on his feet. "I'm calling it a night." Without another word or even a glance my way, he turns and strides toward the door.

Nothing feels right about his behavior. I get he is grieving, but so are his brothers, and they can look me in the eyes and talk to me. They are super affectionate—in fact, more than before—so what's up Ahren's ass?

I stew over his behavior. When the door shuts behind him, I push away from the table. My chair scrapes on the stone floor and I scramble to my feet.

"Guendolyn?" Deimos asks.

"I'll be back. I just need to do something. Don't eat all the cake," I tease as Luther reaches for a slice.

Out in the hallway, Ahren strides down the corridor quickly, his shoulders curving forward like he carries the world's problems on them. We've been through too much together, he's shared personal things about himself with me, and I want to be there for him. Whether he wants it or not.

Guards are stationed along the marble hallway and down every passage I travel. With Ahren moving faster now, I quicken my pace.

He suddenly glances over his shoulder at me, shadows dancing his darkening eyes. "You have no subtlety when you track someone."

"Yeah, well, I wasn't trying to sneak up on you." I close the distance between us as he slows down but never stops completely.

I look up at him and wait for him to say something, but he never does. I reach for his hand, my fingers finding his warm skin. He doesn't flinch, but he doesn't hold my hand either. Worry coils at the base of my gut, and with it comes a fear that he doesn't want to be with me. A lot of things scare me, and I've conquered many of those fears, except when it comes to the princes, my bravery dissolves.

For now, I tell myself it's him grieving.

"Was thinking we can spend time together to talk," I offer.

It's only when we reach the door that leads to the bridge between the castle and mansion that he pauses. Two guards flank the door, and I feel uncomfortable having them listen to us.

"It's best you return to my brothers for dinner. With the king's passing, I won't have time for you." His voice is flat and cold. Icy shards spear through my chest as he stares right through me.

This isn't Ahren. "What's going on?" I hate that my words come out as a whisper, that the guards are witness to my despair.

The prince turns away from me and shoves open the door before stepping into the windy night across the bridge.

I shudder at the way he dismisses me. Heavy layers of dread drag through me that something else is wrong here. I look over to the guards, who glance away at my stare.

I don't even wait for the door to shut before I rush out after Ahren, fury burning me that he'd treat me this way.

"Hey!" I call out.

He pauses on the bridge, keeping his back to me.

Night drapes the kingdom around us, the sky bright with stars where the clouds have parted.

Hair blows in my face, and I push it behind my ears. My skin ripples from the freezing wind buffeting into me.

"You want to tell me what's going on?" My steps toward him are awkward as I hug myself. The skirt whips around my legs, and despite the cold, my insides are on fire with emotions.

"There's nothing to tell, Guendolyn. Don't make this harder than it is."

The words slice into me like blades. "What are you talking about?" I grab his arm, but he pulls away. My heart splinters, the ache in my chest deepening. "You don't have to go through the loss of your stepfather alone. Please Ahren. Let me in."

He keeps his head low, his breaths deep and ragged. The dull ache rising through me deepens, and I know in that moment without a shadow of a doubt that his reaction has little to do with the king's demise. It's about us. I feel it in my body.

"Did I do something wrong?" I whisper, hating that I sound so hopeless. Except this isn't anguish, but the tearing of the bond I thought we shared. In those few moments when he doesn't respond, a storm of feelings sweeps over me.

Sorrow that I'll lose him.

Pity for myself.

Fury at him for pulling this shit.

And most of all how I want to force him to look me in the eyes and tell me the damn truth of what's going on.

"Over the coming weeks, there will be changes in the court. I'll take the throne, and..." His voice fades, and at first I don't think he's going to respond. Then he says softly, "I can't do this, Guendolyn."

I tremble, fighting the panic clawing at my chest. I lash out and snatch his arm, forcing him to face me. "So you won't have time for me? Is that what you're worried about?"

"I'd rather you hate me. That I can deal with, but your tears will destroy me."

I stare at him, bewildered. I want time to stand still, to pause everything and let myself catch up on what's happening. But my mind is melting, and the words slip past my lips like unstoppable lava from an erupting volcano.

"Are you breaking up with me?"

Does he even understand that concept? I don't know, don't care as everything inside me starts to fall apart.

"I have a responsibility," he says, like I'm his guard or one of his servants.

"Fuck responsibility," I snap. "I thought we had..." My eyes prick with the tears pooling and rolling down my cheeks. "What's happening, Ahren?"

He doesn't move to take me into his arms as I expect him to. It's only us two, the wild weather roaring around us, and the crack of my heart.

"Look around to where you are," he starts with a frustrated tone. "I'll be in every council meeting, visiting other courts, dealing with Ash Court, the Bloodcursed, never being home. I'll have to make hard decisions that I already hate myself for, that you will hate me for. Fuck, this isn't what I want, and I wish I could tell you we'll make this work, but I won't break your heart by keeping you in the shadows. You deserve so much more."

The anger fades from his face, his eyes shining in the moonlight. This gorgeous fae captured my attention from the first time we met. He shared with me his past struggles, his agony, his dreams, but maybe I was a fool to believe anything could happen between us. I had known he was destined for the throne as the heir, but everything happened too fast to truly acknowledge what that meant.

He's already made up his mind.

Clouds slide over the moon, stealing the light and darkening his expression. He looks angrier now. My stomach clenches as he draws in sharp breaths.

"You are wrong," I whisper. "Because you've already broken me."

"Oh, Guendolyn." His voice shakes. But a split second is all it takes for the stoic prince to return in front of me. He straightens his posture, standing stiff against the strong wind tugging on his coat and long white hair. It flutters in the air like a flag. "You'll understand soon enough. And then you'll hate me."

My chest clenches at his words. As much as it kills me, I do nothing as he turns and marches away. Desperation blooms through me once more, stronger this time. I curl my hands into fists, refusing to be the one who runs after him. I may not make sense of his reasoning, but he's made his choice, hasn't he?

My first instinct is to leave this realm, but I've given my heart to three fae. And I refuse to lose Luther and Deimos because Ahren is being an asshole. They mean the world to me. And today... well, today is just too much for me.

I've lost my father and one of my men.

I rush across the bridge and make a line for my bedroom, tears blurring my vision, my throat tightening to the point where I can barely breathe.

I lean against the wall outside Guendolyn's room. No idea what time of the night it is, but there's not a soul in sight. It's too late, but I can't sleep or silence my mind. Add to that my gut aches and twists in on itself, and I feel like utter shit. I'd been unprepared for this catastrophe, and now I'm drowning.

This wasn't how anything was meant to go. In truth, I still hadn't worked out how to keep Guendolyn with us for a future together, but letting her go had never crossed my thoughts.

Now I can't get her sweet voice, the tears in her eyes, the devastation on her expression out of my head. It strangles me, and I came here to try to do something. To make it right somehow.

A guttural moan rips from my throat, hands curling into fists. My emotions whip back and forth between the grief of letting her go and fondness at memories I will cherish forever. Those lips so sweet, so soft, so captivating, just like her.

I should be paying this much attention to uncovering the king's killer and making them suffer. I'm fucking furious for having the one thing I desperately want taken away. My priorities have changed now to Guendolyn.

I turn to the door, staring at the handle, and I play with the idea of going inside, breaking down the door if I have to for one last kiss, one more everything. Who the fuck am I fooling? There is no 'one last' anything, is there? It will never be enough.

Pitching one hand to the wall, I can't see straight through the fury burning within me. Revenge bubbles in my chest. When I find the sonofabitch, I'll rip them apart with my bare hands for putting me in this spot.

Except, what I want doesn't matter anymore. Not if I want to keep a roof over my family's heads. It's what mother wants, what the king had insisted on. And something I've dreamed of since we moved here. I was so young then, and I trained endlessly for this position, aspired to take my place on the throne. Now, I'm torn.

I never expected Guendolyn to sweep into my life and steal my heart.

Fuck!

I suck in one raspy breath after another, nails digging into my palms as I squeeze my fists. Wrenching my gaze from her door, I turn away.

This is for the best.

I goddamn hate those words. Nothing is better for me than Guendolyn, and it cuts me deep to make this decision. When the hell had she crept into my heart so much, anyway?

I blink and wait for my reasoning to catch up to the heartache of hurting her. I'll accept my pain, but it's unbearable to watch her cry.

One last look toward Guendolyn's room and I stride away. My presence won't help. It'll make it harder for both of us, and I won't entertain that idea. I'll keep my distance, as much as it kills me. I'll follow the rules and do the right thing for everyone else.

I'll sacrifice my heart.

Guen

BRUISED CLOUDS SHIFT over the sky, stealing the morning sun outside, the view spectacular through the floor-to-ceiling windows in the dining room. I stir honey into my porridge and take another mouthful. The room is empty. No signs of the princes this morning.

Rage roared inside my head and chest at Ahren for most of the night, and when I finally slept, my dreams were filled with me running from darkness. Out of that darkness, a voice came, calling for me. It reminds me of the dreams and visions I experienced growing up. The twisted woods and lurking danger. The images I painted of them, having no clue how much of a significance they had to me. Guess the truth has been dying to come out all along.

Now I sit here drifting away in sorrow, my mind heavy with questions I have no answers for. But I force myself to finish my food and wash it down with juice.

I refuse to accept Ahren's decision to push me away, and his brothers are bound to know what's really going on with him. But I also need a distraction before I wear a hole in my bedroom from pacing.

Outside the dining hall, my guard waits for me. "Michae, can we visit the throne room, please?"

He nods without pause, and we stride down the corridor. Michae is a tall fae with short blond hair and pointy ears. Like most of the soldiers, he's broad and intimidating. Luther appointed him as my personal watchdog, and if anyone questions who I am, I'm to continue the ruse that I'm the princes' personal healer.

Like the previous day, there are fae darting about the castle in a frenzy.

I wrench my gaze toward the throne room as we approach. The door is shut. Michae pushes it open, and I step into the empty hall made of marble. The place is spotless, without a hint of blood or the chaos that took place here. It's a grand, large space with columns creating a passage down the middle leading to a wide staircase.

"Have they found anything on the murder?" I tilt my head back to look at Michae.

His attention sweeps to the top of the marble steps to an empty black throne. "Still can't believe our king is gone."

It's where Ahren will sit as he rules the Shadow Court, and with that thought comes the ache in my chest. He pushed me away. Insisted it's due to responsibility, but I listened to the cracks in his voice. This isn't what he wants, so I need to dig and find out the truth, to make him understand there is always a way to make us work.

I refuse to walk away. We were just beginning to bond, to get closer, and I will break down the gates of hell itself if it means I can claim him back.

"Not much," Michae says, pulling me out of my thoughts. It takes me several moments to remember what I had asked him. "But you know what's strange?" He leans in close to me. "Apparently there were traces of clove powder near his body. Either the fae who did this is clumsy or it was a deterrent."

"Clove, the spice? That's unusual."

"The kitchens and staff working there are being investigated by the mages."

The clue leaves me confused, but a clue is a clue, so maybe they'll find the person responsible soon enough. The idea of a killer roaming the castle who may have his eye on Ahren next makes me sick to my stomach.

Michae walks deeper into the throne room and pauses at the base of the steps, lost in thought.

My hands are in the pockets of my riding pants, since it was all the maids had available and I was tired of how inconvenient dresses were. Clasping the cold ruby calms me. It has this way of bringing all my focus to the middle of my core rather than to hundreds of other distractions.

Sniffles sound, and I tilt my head sideways to gain a better view of Michae. I am convinced he is crying for the loss of his king.

I step closer to the spot where I remember seeing the late king on the ground, rolling the ruby over my knuckles. To lose my father sits heavy on my chest. I grieve the notion of losing him, not necessarily the man himself, who I didn't know well enough. Which makes me want to find my mother so much more. To uncover what happened between her and my father, why they gave me away, and so many other whys that the muscles in my shoulders bunch up.

Don't get your hopes up, I keep telling myself.

"Are you permitted to be in here?" a male's voice barks.

I flinch at his abruptness, the ruby almost bouncing out of my hand, but I snatch it out of the air and stuff it into my pocket.

Behind me stands Jasion, and a shiver crawls down my spine. He's wearing his mage clothes—a black robe-skirt that falls to his ankles, metal chains around his waist, and a fairy skull that is fist-sized hangs from his bare neck. After meeting Hiss and having the fairies save me several times now, I sneer at the way he carries that skull like a trophy. I want to rip it off him. I hated this mage from the first time I met him, and my distaste for him hasn't changed.

Michae steps alongside me. "We were just leaving," he announces and takes my elbow to rush me out of the room.

I hold Jasion's gaze as we pass him, and if someone could spew hatred from their stare alone, this mage would be loathing me to the moon and back. It has to do with Ahren, this I know. Luther mentioned in the carriage on our way to Ash Court that Jasion might have a crush on Ahren, which would explain his evil eye at me.

With hurried steps, we make quick work on vanishing down a corridor that takes us straight to the bridge outside.

I glance over my shoulder, almost feeling Jasion's eyes still on me.

Michae murmurs, "He sneaks around the castle, but no one knows what he does." My guard finally lets go of my elbow, and we walk at a normal pace through the hall.

"Hasn't he been working at the castle for most of his life?" I ask, recalling the bits of information I learned from the princes.

Michae cuts me a sarcastic look. I'm starting to really like this guy. He leans closer, whispering, "The maids tell me they find all kinds of dead animals and birds in his room, that he tortures them."

I gasp. "Have they told Ahren?"

Michae stares at me as if I've grown horns. "Unless the maids want to suddenly disappear, they keep quiet. Jasion is a very vengeful mage."

The truth of his words doesn't surprise me, but it worries me. "Did the king and Jasion get along?"

Michae raises a brow. "The king didn't like his wildness and disobedi-ence, but he appreciated that Jasion carried strong powers, more so than the other mages. It's that old saying, *sup with the devil.*"

I nod as the shivers return to my skin and remind me to keep my distance from the mage even more.

When I reach my room, I head inside and kick off my shoes while Michae stands guard outside.

A hard knock raps on the door, and I snap around, expecting my guard to tell me I forgot something.

Instead, it's Jasion standing in my doorway, glowering.

Oh, hell. What does he want?

"My apologies for not coming to you earlier," Jasion says. "May I come inside?"

Michae stands behind him in the hallway to my room, waiting for me to respond so he can have any excuse to get rid of Jasion. Except, is it a good idea to anger a mage who tortures animals in his chamber? *Keep your enemies closer*, floats in my mind.

I nod. "Michae, please join us too." Which he eagerly does, leaving the door open.

Jasion cuts the guard a hard side look. "These are not matters to be discussed in front of you. Wait outside," he commands.

I stiffen. "Michae, you are fine to stay," I reconfirm.

Jasion's lips thin, but I don't care. This is my room, and I honestly don't want to be alone with him. Every time I've spent time with him in the past, I ended up feeling like a bug under a microscope.

He steps into my room, chest sticking out, distaste twisting his lips.

I retreat and lean up against the back of the couch, hands on either side of me, gripping the wooden frame. Where I am as far from him as possible without it looking obvious.

"What did you want to see me about?" I ask, grasping onto every thread of confidence I have.

"I like to get to know anyone who works closely with Ahren. As you can appreciate, since he is going to be the king soon."

I lick my dry lips, trying to make sense of what exactly he wants. "You are worried about him?" I ask.

He bows his agreement with a small tilt of his head, the fairy skull around his neck swinging slightly. "I knew you were smart."

I bristle at his patronizing tone. Stupid asshole. But I smile because I'd rather he think I'm some dumb female healer.

He rubs a hand over his mouth as he strolls toward the window. "I've been told you are getting close to Prince Luther as well. The walls in this kingdom have eyes."

Michae stands tall near the door, shrugging when I glance his way. I turn to Jasion, who remains with his back to me. The wind howls bitterly outside. The storm may have passed, but even with the fireplaces, these large rooms and halls never fully warm up. What I wouldn't give for my electric blanket and an outlet about now.

"I'm not following your point?" I play the person he expects of me.

"Of course not." He pivots toward us, the material of his long mage-skirt flaring around his ankles. "Many who come to the kingdom to work for the princes dream up ideas of how to stay here longer." He closes the distance between us. "You're a pretty girl who I'm sure spreads her legs easily, but—"

"Don't speak to me that way," I snap, squaring my shoulders, facing this mage. I don't give a shit who he is, I have powers too, used them with the king's mother in Ash Court, and I won't bow down to this prick.

He raises a brow and doesn't show a hint of being taken aback by my retort. He's good, I know that, and he's rattled me, but I won't show it. No matter how much my heart hammers in my chest, how much my knees shake.

"Remember your place," he says calmly, like I have no control of myself.

Fire lashes over my chest that he says that to me. Fucking asshole.

"I witnessed the tension between you and Ahren last night, and I'm here out of the goodness of my heart to help you."

The moment between Ahren and I on the bridge flashes in my mind, the time when he tore my heart to shreds. Jasion had been watching us? The prick!

I scoff a bit too loudly, which has him straightening his spine.

His eyes narrow at me. "I realize I'm wasting my time, so I'll make this short." He steps closer to me, as does Michae from his spot by the door.

A shiver worms its way down my spine, but I won't retreat, no matter how desperately I want to. I loathe how close Jasion stands in front of me.

It's intended to intimidate, and for that reason, I dig in my heels and raise my chin to face him straight on.

"Ahren and the princes are royal. They have slept with many commoners like you in the past, but that is all you are to them, little girl. Ahren needs someone stronger by his side. Someone with the ability to guide him, someone with a royal bloodline. You are not worthy, and I recommend you pack your bags and leave before it's too late."

My blood boils, rage pulsing in my ears. I want to wipe the smug grin off his face. "You're a petty asshole, but let me give you a piece of advice while we're sharing. Ahren loves women way too much, so if you think you have a chance in his bed, then don't waste your time. He'll reject your ass so quick, you won't know what hit you."

I suck in each sharp breath, my pulse raging in my veins. This isn't like me, but right now he has me so angry, a faint thread of power sweeps over my chest and down my arms like it did back at Ash Court. What would he do if I tossed him through a window?

My lips quirk into a grin.

His face flushes red, shoulders rising.

Oh, shit, I definitely hit a soft spot.

The air thickens in the room. Michae clears his throat uncomfortably, while I wonder if I can even draw on whatever power I have before this mage attacks.

Jasion's hand lashes out and snatches me by the throat. He's so fast, I barely have time to raise my hands to stop him. Iron fingers squeeze, and the pain is excruciating, like he might tear my head right off. Panic slams into me as I glare into his darkening pupils. Michae rushes to us.

Jasion hurls his hand in the guard's direction, and a spray of powder splashes Michae. He flies backward, colliding into the wall.

I dig at Jasion's fingers around my throat, my lungs burning for oxygen. This isn't how I was meant to die, and with fear curling around me, I can't even focus on my power.

I strike my hand at his face and claw my fingernails down his cheek, breaking the skin.

He growls and throws me aside with such strength, my legs crumble under me and I smack the ground with my hip hard.

Scrambling backward, I don't feel the ache; only how fast my heart beats, how I was stupid to think I stood any chance against this monster. I'm gasping for each breath, my gaze never leaving him.

He turns to me with fury burning in his eyes. Blood drips down his cheeks from the two scratches I gave him. The bastard deserves so much worse.

Nostrils flaring, he comes for me, fist raised. His face darkens, and he resembles a demon in that moment, ready to strike me repeatedly until I can't take another breath.

I frantically dig my hand into my pocket for the ruby, my only thought to escape, to get out, or even call the fairies. I don't know exactly how to do that, but it doesn't stop me from trying. Power erupts deep in my chest.

But he moves too fast, and panic takes me.

I cover my head, cowering, the stone clasped in my fist.

Someone darts into the room in a sudden flash.

Deimos.

Oh my god, thank you.

He snarls and leaps onto Jasion's back, locking an arm around his throat and wrenching him backward.

Jasion jerks his head back, his hand diving into one of the small leather bags hanging from his belt. But when he glances up to see it's Deimos, his face turns snow white.

His body slackens, and he slips his hand free from the pouch.

"Your Highness," he gurgles.

"You like to hurt women?" Deimos snarls like a lion. He releases the mage and spins him around by the shoulder.

Then his fist flies at Jasion's face. Over and over. He knocks him off his feet. Deimos is wild and never stops. He drops to one knee and pounds like a machine.

Blood and groans.

I don't look away, not for a second. I'd like to say it's too gruesome and violent, but Jasion deserves that and so much worse. My chest blooms at seeing my prince fight for me. There's no hesitation, and I adore him in that moment more than I thought possible.

Michae stumbles toward them, shaking his head as if his vision is blurry.

The mage cries out, his hands pushing against the prince, but he never strikes back, never uses magic. Guess he knows that's instant death.

Michae firmly sets a hand on the prince's shoulder.

Deimos finally stops his assault, his fist bloody. Jasion draws in raspy breaths, his eyes puffy, lips torn open. There's so much blood. I should feel pity, but I am cheering on the inside.

Deimos gets to his feet and looks over to Jasion. "Get the fuck out of my

face before I rip your spine out. You touch her again, and I'll keep my word."
He swings his attention over to a bewildered Michae. "Get him out of here,
now!" Then my prince takes long strides toward me, his eyes flooded with
worry.

He cups my face with a clean hand, studying me. "Did he hurt you? I'm
going to murder him if he did."

I shake my head but his gaze falls to my neck where it burns from
Jasion's fingers. "I'm fine. You arrived before he could do worse."

He draws me into his arms, holding me so tight I can't inhale, but I
don't want to push him away. Not when I'm shaking all over from the
attack.

Deimos breaks from me and watches as Michae drags the mage out of
the room. "Why did he attack you?"

"He came here to tell me I wasn't worthy of royalty. He pissed me off, so
I provoked him by saying Ahren is into girls and he doesn't stand a chance."

Deimos bursts out laughing. "That's my girl. There's no doubt now
Jasion is so head over heels infatuated with my brother that he'd do
anything to get rid of the competition. So, he's staying locked up until all
this shit is over."

I blink at him. "The funeral?" My mind echoes with Jasion's words
about not being worthy, about royal blood. But I won't let him get to me, I
just won't.

Deimos looks at me for a long pause before he nods. "Come, I want to
get cleaned up and take you away from everything for a while."

"I'd love that." He collects my hand and we slip out into the hallway
and make our way to his room. "Thank you for helping back there."

His lips pinch to one side, and his hold just squeezes slightly. "No one is
going to hurt you again."

I smile to myself because I never expected to have men in my life who
cared and protected me so much.

Once in his chamber, he heads into his bathroom where I hear the
splashing of water.

Unlike my room, Deimos has a huge bed, a couch, fireplace, even a
table, all in the main area. It's twice as big as mine.

Deimos emerges, wiping his hand on a towel while wearing nothing
but dark pants that sit low on his hips. Muscles ripple across his chest and
arms, his abs rock-hard with a thin line of hair trailing down into his pants.
With everything happening so quickly since I arrived in this realm, with
Deimos falling sick, we never got a chance to be together. The way he looks

at me now is temptation on steroids, and my nipples pebble at the way his stare devours me.

"Come over here, kitten."

I involuntarily move toward him, my body now listening to him, apparently. I slide right into his arms, and he embraces me, nestling his face into the curve of my neck. Each breath I take fills me with the masculine scent that is all Deimos and has me melting against him. Looping my arms around his chest, I know my heart is in a good place with him. It sounds corny, but after he collected me from Earth and all the things we went through, the cure and magic I used to heal him, there's a bond between us.

"You always smell like delicious berries," he whispers in my ear, then draws my earlobe into his mouth with his tongue.

My toes curl in my boots, and every inch of me shivers with anticipation. This whole time, I've only kissed Deimos and done some heavy petting, but nothing more. Now, I can't get the image of us naked and together out of my mind. I crave it, long for it...

He lifts his head to look at me, and my attention goes to the cut under his eye. It's healed, even if blushing pink.

"How did you get that wound?" I ask, knowing he went out hunting yesterday. I skim my fingers underneath the wound lightly, then kiss his cheek.

"I want to say it was from a fight with a bear in the woods within the kingdom grounds, but the truth is we don't have anything wild in here. Only pheasants and deer. I tripped over a tree root and a low hanging branch whipped me in the face."

A laugh erupts past my lips and I regret it at once, but I can't stop myself. "I'm sorry, but that's hilarious."

He raises a brow, then his fingers find the bottom of my top and slide under to tickle my ribs.

I flinch and cry out as he tickles me like a mad man playing the piano. Slapping his hand, I shove him away playfully and leap out of his reach.

"Come back here, I'm not finished," he teases.

"Don't you dare or I'll scream. I'm ticklish."

His lips quirk upward. "I know." Then he lunges after me.

A yelp flies past my throat and I spin away, darting across the room. I jump up and scramble right over his bed, making a mess of it, then hop down, snatching a pillow for a weapon. Giddiness claims me; I can't remember the last time I just acted silly and laughed at nothing.

He comes at me, careening around the bedpost. I slap the pillow into his head, and he shoves it aside. Then in a flash, he swoops an arm under my knees and another around my back, swinging me up and off my feet.

"You cheat!" I declare.

"How is that cheating? I caught you and now I get to have my way with you."

I cling to his neck, pressing my lips to his collarbone. "There were no rules about this, so it doesn't apply."

He tosses me onto my back on the bed. The mattress bounces beneath me, and he crawls over me, making his way up from my legs to my face. "That's where you're wrong, my kitten. I always get my way, even if I have to play dirty."

I push myself up and reach for a pillow to whack him in the head, but he matches my attempt with a kiss. Our mouths come together; they mash, our tongues craving one another. He kisses me deeply and hungrily, and I don't blame him. This has been way too long in the making.

His hand reaches for my shirt, and he tugs at it aggressively, the buttons popping. He's so strong, all angles, and looks spectacular.

And in that split second of meeting his gaze, a memory I'd forgotten slams into me.

Every time I've kissed Deimos, my power shot outward and opened a portal. As if thinking the same thing, his eyes widen, and he gets off the bed in a heartbeat. His hand meets mine and he pulls me to my feet.

"Shit, did you open a portal again? Can you feel it?" Frantically, he scans the room like somehow the answer lays in here somewhere.

My mind is reeling at a hundred miles an hour, and for the life of me I can't remember if I even felt a surge of power. Arousal, yes, in bucketfuls. Power? Not sure.

"Guendolyn," he prompts me, holding onto my arms.

"Don't rush me. I'm trying to think. How could I forget about this? It only happens with you, not your brothers, but why?"

"So, you kissed my brothers while I was close to death in bed?" His brows pinch, his shoulders curving forward almost in a defeated pose.

I cock my brow at him. "Really? That's what bothers you right now? Anyway, I'm convinced there was no power energy when you and I just kissed," I state. His brow remains furrowed, and I can't tell what upsets him most. Me kissing his brothers or that I might have opened another portal somewhere.

"You sure?" He's already leaving my side and crossing the room in long strides, his arms swinging at his sides.

"Yes. Last time it was unmissable. There was no shaking of walls now."

He opens the door. "I'll be right back." And he's gone in seconds.

Oh, shit. Why can't things just be normal? Like kissing my boyfriend shouldn't always come with the potential of hell unleashed.

Deimos returns so fast, I haven't moved from where I stand. "My men are doing a sweep of the kingdom just to be on the safe side." He strolls closer. "So, you're certain you didn't feel any tingling of power."

The more I think about it, the more I'm positive. "Yes."

"Why? What's changed?"

The same thought crosses my mind, and I shrug, going through everything that happened recently. But with regards to controlling the portals, something has changed.

"Hmm, well actually." I reach down to my pocket and pull out the ruby.

"Is that fairy stone from the king's throne?"

"Yep. And when I hold it, I can now control opening a portal. So—"

"So that's the answer. It's got to be next to you." His hands settle on my hips and he tugs me toward him. "Thank fuck, as I can't take any more shit, especially if it means not taking you as mine."

I stare up into his gorgeous eyes, and the panic attack we both had fades. He guides me back to the bed and kisses me, softly this time. My arousal spikes in moments. Our mouths part, and I lean toward the dresser and place the stone down.

Deimos is right there, picking up the ruby and pressing it back into my hand. "Hold it just to be on the safe side." There's a serious tone in his voice, a worry that somehow I'll unleash another wave of disaster on the kingdom.

I can't even roll my eyes at his concern because last time we kissed, it ended in him being bitten by a Bloodcursed. I almost lost him, and the panic and danger we faced to save him is not something I want to experience again. Wrapping my fingers around the stone, I flop back onto the bed and call him to me with a bent finger.

My heart is racing, a flush flaring over me as I pull off the remainder of my top, along with the undergarment. Nipples pebbled from the sudden coldness, the anticipation of what's to come hums through me.

Deimos groans his approval as he stares down at me, the sound sending a spike of desire between my thighs. My prince leans over me, his lips on my breast, kissing it all around, making his way to the nipple. He accepts it greedily into his mouth, sucking on it like he's starved, like I'm the air he breathes and he can't get enough.

I moan against his touch, running my fingers through his long blond hair. He's captivating, everything I always wanted. I always thought men like him were not in my league—turns out I was wrong.

Closing my eyes, I soften into the mattress and feel every kiss, every mock bite, every lick as Deimos adores my breasts. I wrap my legs around his hips, lifting my pelvis up to grind myself against the erection in his pants. The stone in my hands feels still cold.

When his mouth is on mine again, I flip open my eyes and wrap myself around him, kissing him back. I can't get enough of tasting his lips.

His hand dips between us and pops open my pants. My stomach flip-flops—I'm so horny and yet at the same time, slightly shy. I'm not the most practiced girl when it comes to sex, and well, this is our first time.

A sudden rapping on the door has us both freezing. We exchange worried looks.

"Must be my men," he murmurs before he jumps up to his feet and rushes across the room as I tug the blanket up to cover myself.

Please don't let there be a portal I'd opened. I love kissing Deimos, so universe, don't take that away from me.

I wrench open the door to my bedroom. Two of my guards stand in the hallway, and their faces show no traces of shock or terror. "Did you find anything?" I ask.

"Nothing. All is fine," Reinland says, the taller of the two.

"Are you certain?"

They both nod, and relief washes over me. Maybe Guendolyn was right that the fairy ruby controls her magic when she's with me. Though it begs the question... Why did my kiss trigger her power in the first place?

"Alright. Let me know if it changes," I instruct my guards and shut the door. My sexy kitten lies in my bed, wrapped up in the blankets, only her head poking out.

"Sounds like we're all clear," she says, climbing out of the nest she made for herself.

My gaze dips to her gorgeous bouncy breasts tipped with the most perfect rosy nipples. She sees me staring, and her cheeks blush. I love how easily she responds, how innocently she reacts when she's normally feisty. Both sides of the same coin, and I adore everything about her.

"I'm disappointed," I state. "You're still wearing your pants."

She grabs a pillow and tosses it at me. "You can't talk. Take off yours first."

I grin and march over to her as she draws another pillow to her chest.

"You're mine." I snatch the pillow from her grasp and throw it behind me. Then I grab her by the waist and haul her to me, my fingers tearing apart her buttons.

Her eyes widen. I let my arousal take the lead, and I hook my fingers into the top of her pants and yank them and her underwear down her legs.

She takes a deep gasp of surprise.

The pants jam at her ankles, as she's still wearing her boots. I tsk, meeting her sheepish expression.

She shrugs and sticks her tongue out. "That's what happens when you rush."

I can't deny, I enjoy her fighting against me. As I reach down to grab her foot and rip off her boots, I take in her gorgeous body. Round breasts, her waist cinching in then beautifully curving to follow her hips. The small mound of light hair between her legs glistens, and already her arousal perfumes the air.

My cock twitches, growing. Frantically, I drag the boots and pants off so I can reach my girl.

"Don't make me wait too long," she teases me, her eyes batting as she lays there looking spectacular.

She looks at me with wide eyes, lips parted, her knees locked together as she lies on the bed, propped up on her elbows. My balls ache with a desperate need to claim what I've wanted for too fucking long.

I reach a hand down to her knees, and her breath quickens at my touch. I pry them open. She gives no resistance. Her sweet pussy is slick, and I run my thumb over the seam of her heat.

She trembles, her thighs falling wider. Her hips rise slightly in response to my strokes. Unsure how much longer I can hold on, I lean forward and sweep my hand to the back of her neck and bring her up to kiss me.

Her gasp makes me want to protect her from the world.

"I missed you so much," she whispers, struggling for breath through her emotions.

"Today I will claim you, mark you, show you what you've missed." Let her see that no matter what the future holds, she will always have me by her side. To keep her in our kingdom, I may propose to my brothers that Luther or I marry her under the court's rule to avoid hiding her. We'll need to work out how to create her a Seelie identity, but I drive those thoughts aside.

I can't believe I just thought of marriage when I vowed to never settle down.

"Stop talking, just kiss me," she demands.

Her mouth melts against mine. She's soft and smells so good, and hell, all the things I want to do to her... We fit perfectly together, and I'm not just talking about sex. I intend to get to know her better, to show her life here can be magnificent with Luther and me by her side. I want to protect her, wrap her in my arms and keep her close.

Her fingers thread through my long hair, drawing me closer. Need claws through me, and our mouths part. Her cheeks and lips are rosy, and the heat in her eyes calls to me.

"Take me," she says, and my cock twitches at her words.

I lay her back on the bed and pull back, tugging my pants down my legs and stepping out of them. My erection sits stiff and so hard it aches.

"Touch it," I ask, and my kitten obliges, sitting up, her lower lip between her teeth, gaze locked on my cock. She grasps the shaft, and I hiss at the sensation. Her long fingers curl all the way around, and she tugs.

"Fuck!" I've waited for this so damn long.

Soft wetness presses around my tip, and I glance down to that sweet cherry mouth wrapped around my cock.

My chest rises and falls quicker, my blood racing south, balls tightening.

Oh, hell! My eyes flutter upward as she takes me deeper and deeper. That wicked tongue lashes over my erection, the sensation driving me insane. I rock my hips forward and back, slowly at first, but the intensity escalates too fast.

I slip out of her mouth with a pop, and she simply looks up at me with doe eyes. She kneels on the edge of the bed, naked and spectacular. I can't stop focusing on her perky breasts, the way her waist draws in, the small thatch of light hair between her legs. I need more. So much more.

"Lay on your back, kitten," I order, and she slips down onto her side, untucking her legs and laying back. "Show me everything again, wider so I can see those glistening lips."

Her breaths quicken and she lifts her legs, widening her bent knees. "I love when you talk like this to me," she purrs.

I fall before her, staring at the pink slit, her arousal so obvious. My dick twitches.

Kissing her inner thigh, I make my way higher. Her sexy, musky scent is intoxication. I take it deep into my lungs, arising a primal hunger inside me. Before I even reach her juicy lips, she moans.

I groan at the sight of her spread before me. Then I flick out a tongue and lick her length. She arches her back, her legs widening, giving me everything she has. Taking her into my mouth, I suck on her and ravage what is mine.

"Oh, fuck! Deimos!" she screams.

She's so wet, her pelvis rocking back and forth. I devour my sweet kitten, wanting her so close to the edge she'll beg me for more.

I tongue her, my fingers gripping her hips as I shove myself deeper, pinning her to me.

Her cries of pleasure rile me up; they make me so fucking horny, holding back is killing me.

I pull back as she cranes her head up to look at me. "Why are you stopping?

Up on my feet, I laugh, because this is how I want her. Spread open, craving me. "Neither of us are going anywhere, kitten." I cover my body over hers and our mouths clash. My cock presses to the heat between her thighs, finding the place I need to bury myself into. She's an addiction I can't get enough of.

Taking her tongue into my mouth, I push my dick into her. She adjusts her hips, making it easier to slide inside. She's tight, her walls clenching, and holding back grows harder.

"Let me in, angel," I breathe against her. "Just relax, I won't hurt you."

She nods, and I physically feel her softening.

I growl as I slide in all the way, my heart pounding.

"Deimos," she cries.

I pull out and go back in, slow at first so she adjusts to my size, then I move faster. Fucking her, pumping.

Her breasts rub against my chest with each thrust, her eyes never leaving mine. I adore the way she moans, how her body responds to me, curling around me like we are one.

"This feels so right," she says. "I missed you."

I kiss her, never stopping myself from burying my cock in her. With one hand sliding between us, I reach for her clit and rub it.

Her breaths rush and she moans against my mouth.

"Come for me, kitten," I whisper, then dip my head lower and grab her nipple between my teeth. I gnaw on it gently, then suck on it.

Her breaths labor, and in a heartbeat, her body shudders beneath me. She cries out, convulsing with the orgasm tearing through her.

Her pussy squeezes my cock, and I let myself go this time, rip open the floodgates as I explode inside her. I growl, pulsing, feeding her my seed, both of us gasping for air.

Clasping the bedsheets, her head tilts back with her beautiful screams of pleasure. Fuck, she's gorgeous.

By the end when we're both floating down, I press my mouth to hers softly. "I want more."

She breaks out laughing, then cups my face and kisses me. "Yes, please."

I draw out of her and push up to my feet. Her pussy glistens, her lips full, and I fucking love seeing the white seep of my seed at her entrance.

"I'll get something to clean you."

She winks and stays there. Her hand outstretches and she opens the fist holding her ruby. "I feel like this stone should have been with me all along. I mean, I can open and close portals with it—though I'm not sure yet I can control where I'll end up—but it's an improvement. And well, I can kiss you to my heart's content."

"I need to find a solution so you don't have to grasp it each time I want to kiss you."

"I'd love that," she answers from the bed.

In the bathroom, I collect a towel and moisten it slightly at one end, then return to my kitten. I clean her delicious pussy, then I climb into bed with her, taking her into my arms.

"This is how our future is going to be. Freedom to be together, to share our lives."

She's curled up against my chest, face to face, then she glances up at me. "It's strange how I feel more at home here than I ever did back on Earth."

"That tells you everything," I muse.

"I really thought I'd lose you," she begins, her hand on my bicep trembling.

"You risked so much for me, and I don't doubt for a moment how much you feel for me. But promise me you won't ever put yourself into such danger for me again."

She scrunches her nose like she'll never do that, and it doesn't surprise me.

"If I didn't go to Ash Court, I never would have discovered so much."

"Oh yeah?" I massage her lower back, encouraging her to tell me more.

"Like meeting the king's mother; finding out that my mother must be important, whoever she is; or that I have more power inside me than I first thought. Plus, I never would have bumped into Hiss to get the ruby. And then, then there's who my real—"

"Hiss?" I query, and she gives me a quick rendition of what happened while I was sick, and I merge it with what my brothers told me. "The fairy with blue wings, right?"

She nods. "But there's something else." She swallows hard, and I see the trepidation in her expression.

"What is it?"

A pounding knock erupts at the door, and she flinches in my arms.

"Let me see who that is. Get under the blankets."

I drag on my pants and stride across the room. Once Guendolyn is covered, I open the door.

My guard stands before me, his gaze never drifting into my room. "You've been summoned by His Highness, Prince Ahren, to his meeting room immediately."

I groan and run a hand through my hair. What the hell now? With a quick nod, I reply, "I'll be there shortly." Then I close the door and turn to my kitten, who again has only her head sticking out from under the blanket in my bed.

"Stay here." I close the distance between us and lean over her, then kiss those full lips. "I'll be back later and bring you some food."

"Sounds like a plan. Don't be long." She snuggles deeper under the blanket like she might go to sleep.

My heart thumps in my chest. What has she done to me?

Fuck!

She's constantly on my mind, and my cock hardens just at the thought of her. I should have known from the first time I went to collect her from Earth she'd captivate me. I insisted my job was just to bring her to Shadow Court, but I'd been fooling myself.

She had always been mine. I just had to admit it to myself.

I slide into the scorching hot water before reaching over for grapes from the platter of fruit near the tub while the morning sun shines gloriously. Yesterday, after a while when Deimos hadn't returned, a maid delivered my early dinner in the room. After which I crashed on the bed and slept all the way through. Deimos still wasn't in my bed this morning so I decided to get on with the day, starting with a wash.

I made my way down to the baths because I can't wait around doing nothing.

My guard waits for me outside, and right now it's better I stay low. The princes are most likely talking about the king's funeral, about Ahren taking the throne, so I can wait.

Though it keeps playing on my mind about the king being my real father, and how much I desperately wanted to tell Deimos. But I feel selfish doing so.

The throne is Ahren's, even if he's not the king's son by blood. And if I announce this now, will I come across as someone trying to steal the throne from him? In all honesty, I don't know enough about royal rules and politics to know if that's possible. Can a female take a throne in fae courts?

Regardless, I don't want such a position, and I'm already so close to losing Ahren. I won't do anything to jeopardize pushing him even farther from me.

A stupid thought pops into my mind, one of marriage, and I almost laugh out loud. Right, a court that hates Unseelie will never allow one to rule over them. Even if only half an Unseelie, I don't really belong in their court, now do I? And technically, it means the princes and I are step-siblings.

Nope, I'm not even going there. There is no bloodline shared between us.

It's why I contemplated asking Deimos' opinion, but is that a smart decision? What's to stop him from making a big deal of this and telling Ahren?

I slip deeper into the water, deciding to say nothing for now.

Sucking in a deep breath, I relax and think about the incredible time with Deimos and how I don't know what I'd do if I lost him and Luther. It shocks me how quickly they've grown on me. I let myself linger on those thoughts and not what I'm losing.

When the water temperature falls and my fingers resemble prunes, I climb out of the tub and grab a towel. The maids had taken my clothes and left me with a dress. I pick up the deep blue fabric pebbled with tiny crystals and find no underwear. I sigh, tired of going around with no panties. Is this a fae thing?

What I miss desperately are slack pants and a hoodie. These gowns may look spectacular, lift my breasts, cinch in my waist, but they aren't uber comfortable.

Dressed, I pull on the square neckline that sits a bit too low over my chest, then tie up the laced corset across the front, squishing my breasts together. No need for a bra when the ladies are constantly pressed inside a corset or tight dress.

Stepping into a pair of ankle boots, I run the wide-toothed comb through my hair. Then I head into the hall.

Michae greets me with a smile, standing taller. He has a healed cut on his upper lip that only reveals itself when he grins. He's growing on me, and it's nice to have someone to talk to. "Where to, Miss?"

"The dining hall, please. I'm thirsty." He nods, and we head through the mansion.

Two maids rush past us, holding their skirts for ease. I glance back to see them vanish around a corner. A man in a black suit pushing a silver food trolley races down the corridor, coming toward us.

He waves a hand for us to get out of the way.

We do, and he's a storm, exploding past us.

"What's going on?" I mumble to myself.

More maids carrying baskets of fruit dart past. Another woman behind them has her arms filled with flowers. Then two men roll more trolleys piled high with beautiful gold plates. Their rattling sounds have me cringing as I picture them falling over and smashing.

I blink at the commotion down every hallway. "What are they preparing for? The funeral?"

"His highness Ahren is set take the throne in a few days."

"So this is for a celebration then?"

When Dana marches past us with bundles of linen in her arms, I reach out for her, stepping in her path.

She bows and darts past, the older man huffing and vanishing into a room.

"Guess it's not every day a new king is crowned," I murmur. Of course, I don't expect to be invited, though I do hope Deimos or Luther sneak me in. I want to see the throne room decorated elaborately, to witness the ritual and party to understand fae culture. To see if they are anything like medieval festivities in movies.

Leaving behind the commotion, we enter the dining room in the mansion. The beautiful wall of windows always draws my attention to the ocean of trees and mountains. This has to be one of my favorite rooms.

"I'll request a drink for you," Michae states and heads through the back door that leads into the kitchen.

Returning my attention to the window, I glance out there and try not to overthink all the commotion that makes me feel like I'm being left out. This isn't about me, I keep telling myself.

Footsteps close in behind me, and I turn, expecting Michae, except it's Luther. Where did he come from?

My chest swells with the way his mouth spreads into a delicious grin. His dark hair is swept off his face, and his cheeks glow like he's been outside in the cold. The black tunic he wears hugs his strong chest and broad shoulders, gold dots embroidering the round neckline. A leather belt sits loosely around his waist, and his leather pants hug muscular thighs. His boots are speckled with snow, confirming my suspicion.

"I've been searching for you," he says, taking my hand in his and drawing me toward him. "I have a surprise."

"What is it?" I can't help but grin widely, lapping up the attention he gives me.

"You'll see."

Just then, Michae emerges carrying a glass of juice and places it on the long dining table for me.

"Order the chef to arrange a packed feast for me. We don't have much time to wait," Luther orders.

The guard taps his chest just over his heart twice. "Of course, Your Highness." Then he returns to the kitchen.

Luther looks devilishly handsome today, and I love how his greedy fingers hold onto me, never letting me get far from him.

"Did you just come out of the meeting with Deimos and Ahren?" I ask, curious about what they discussed and if it had anything to do with finding the king's killer.

"It dragged so long. They didn't even serve us lunch, and I'm starved. Deimos will most likely find his way here soon. He eats like a lion."

"And Ahren?" I query.

He slides strands of hair caught in my eyelashes behind my ear, and something crosses his gaze. Is it pity? Does he know Ahren pushed me aside, that now I pine for him? I hate myself for coming across that way, but I can't control how I feel about these princes.

"He's busy," Luther explains. "He'll be busy for a few weeks, at least." His hand falls to my lower back and nudges me to the table. "Come, let's sit as we wait."

But I don't budge from my spot. "Is that how long crowning a king takes?"

He swallows loud, his Adam's apple bobbing up and down his throat. He hesitates, and it only strengthens my suspicion that there is so much more going on here. Why am I being kept in the dark?

"Luther, what's going on with Ahren? Why is he turning away from me?" I don't want to bring this up here and now, but the way he stares at me draws my emotions to the surface. I fell hard for three princes, but in truth, I'm still getting to know them. Still discovering their secrets. So what exactly is Ahren's?

Luther licks his lips, looking like he's deciding what to tell me. "He needs to talk to you himself. I'm sorry, little wolf. I'm surprised he hasn't, but I'll mention it to him."

My stomach drops and hits the ground. Just great. So there *is* something beyond him having extra responsibility or whatever else he insisted. They were lies.

Now my mind spins with horrible scenarios, like he's sick and going to die, or he needs to go live across the realm for years as part of taking the throne, or... god, I need to stop torturing myself.

"Little wolf, you will always have me and Deimos by your side."

Why does he keep saying that? I pull from him and turn to the window, wishing more than anything I had wings like a bird and could fly out there. To feel free and not be so confused and trapped.

In this realm, I'm the stranger.

The foreigner who is vulnerable and gullible.

I rely on the princes, and I hate that. I see that now, because they can walk away just as easily as Ahren is. Where does that leave me?

Luther stands at my back but doesn't hold me. The heat from his body engulfs me like a warm blanket.

"Why can't you tell me what's going on with Ahren? I hate this. I don't even know where I belong. I keep getting brushed aside, needing to hide who I am. Is that who I will be? The person swept away when things get too real?" Anger and frustration tighten around my throat.

Luther takes my shoulders and spins me to face him. My back presses against the glass window, and I glance up at him.

"That's not fair, little wolf. We have to keep you safe until we find a way to make your stay here more permanent. I've told you before that I'll do anything to protect you, and you need to trust me, now more than ever."

There's truth in his warm eyes. I glance down, feeling heat in my face, loathing that I sound like a spoiled brat. "I just feel lost," I whisper.

His finger glides under my chin and lifts my head so I meet his gaze. He's inches from me, his expression heartfelt, his scent musky and spicy and so delicious. "You'll never be lost at my side."

His words are like a fresh spring breeze chasing away the winter blues, and my eyes prick. I melt against him, and he embraces me. I don't even know why I'm crying, but all the emotions building inside me finally rush out. The news of my father. Not knowing who my mother is. Ahren pushing me aside. Not knowing where I belong. And who exactly am I, anyway? Am I better off back on Earth where I'm nobody and I can pretend I have a life?

Luther rubs my back and holds me close. There's something about him that always calms me. Maybe because I've known him the longest. He's seen the worst and best sides of me and still sticks around. For those reasons, I embrace what he offers and believe him when he says he'll always be by my side.

Luther

MY HEART HURTS.

From what I've seen, Guendolyn has faced challenge after challenge, and she always fights back. She's never once demanded to leave.

Not my little wolf.

She doesn't give up, I see that now. Her eagerness to uncover the truth of her past drives her, and I admire that more than she'll ever realize. Too many fall complacent, retreat from fear... but not her.

I embrace her as she softly sobs against my chest. Running my hand over her blonde hair, I don't rush her but let her settle down in her own time. We all need to regroup and reassess our next decisions when all hell breaks loose, and while her way of dealing is crying, mine is smashing anything in my way. Similar, in a way.

The heat from the fireplace engulfs us, while outside the sun peeks out from behind the clouds. The snowfall fades, as do the gray clouds.

This is what she needs. Time away from everything. Because once she finds out about the wedding, she will be heartbroken. Until then, I intend to make her smile so she has something to hold onto.

Guendolyn breaks from my embrace, her cheeks rosy, eyes still puffy.

"Change of scenery and fresh air, how does that sound?" I offer.

Her sweet lips curl upward as she nods. "I would love that." It warms me to see her smile rather than cry.

The maid appears from the kitchen, followed by Michae. She hands me a wicker basket covered by a white kitchen towel, and I feel like a servant about to stroll through the woods. But I take it nonetheless from her hand.

"Everything you need is in there, Your Highness." She bows her head slightly and retreats.

"Thank you," I say, and Guendolyn gives her thanks too. Michae bows his head as we leave the dining hall.

By the time we head downstairs and step outside into a courtyard, the expression on my little wolf's face is bursting with excitement.

"Where are we going?" She looks at me for an answer, and there is something riveting about her childlike enthusiasm. My chest tightens as my heart pounds for her. She affects me so easily, so quickly.

"You'll see," I assure her and guide her over the snow-covered yard to the large black sleigh harnessed to a large chestnut horse.

Guendolyn's mouth hasn't closed yet, and she quickens her steps. "Is this really for us? Oh my god, it looks like Santa's sleigh." She mumbles things I don't understand, but her excitement is contagious. Then she turns to me abruptly. "Wait, the Bloodcursed are outside the walls."

"Who said anything about leaving the kingdom grounds?"

She's bouncing on her feet and runs ahead, then climbs up into the open sleigh. She flops down onto the two-seater wooden bench covered in blankets, laughing when she looks my way.

"Hurry up," she calls.

This is how I want her to feel every day. Who would have thought I'd end up such a love-struck sucker. I need my little wolf by my side, always. That's what matters. I reach her and set the basket under the bench in the sleigh and turn to find our stable manager, an older fae with long pointy ears sticking over messy white hair, marching over to me.

"Your Highness, you are all set to go. The paths have been cleared of snow." There's a glint in his eyes just like the maid's and Michae's as he glances over to Guendolyn and back at me. I can't help but get the impression the staff at the mansion are excited for me to be with her. Or maybe it's hopeful thinking on my part.

"Thank you."

Beyond the castle and town and within the kingdom walls lies a woodland safe from Bloodcursed, where fae can hunt game and pick wild fruit and vegetables.

I climb into the sleigh, take the reins, and sit next to my little wolf. "Are you ready?"

"You bet. I'm so excited to do something fun. I still remember the Ferris Wheel you made for me." She presses up against my side, and I wrap an arm around her.

The horse takes off, and she bursts out giggling as we lurch backwards in our seat. We quickly fall into a steady trot, going over small bumps over the terrain. A few maids wave to us from the grounds, and Guendolyn repays the favor. Once we leave behind the castle yard, we start moving faster. I swing the horse right and take the path where pines and firs stripped of leaves and pine needles fill the landscape.

Behind us lays another path that leads into the Seelie Shadow town, but today I want us away from everyone and the fucking drama of royal life.

We jostle in our seat, but Guendolyn doesn't dislodge herself from my side. "When I was young," I begin, "I used to go into these woods and stay out here for a week at a time. I'd camp out here, catch my own meals and build fires, and I usually only returned when one of my brothers came to collect me."

"Escape?" she asks.

Sort of. A faint tingle of energy brushes over my skin, like it always does when I send her my thoughts.

She looks up at me, and it's strange to sense her emotions while also seeing them dance across her face. That's part of my ability... I may not clearly hear all of her response, but I do pick up on her feelings when she opens her mind to me. And right now, she's beyond curious.

I beat her to the questioning as we head through the woods, jumping about in our seat from the bumpy land. "My second sight came from my grandfather on my father's side. When we first moved to Shadow Court, I struggled to shut out the thoughts of people who had no idea how to guard their minds. You'd be surprised what people give away if I prod just enough. And I was young, still unable to control my power. So I used to hide here where I could keep my mind silent."

"Didn't your grandfather teach you to manage your power?"

I stare straight ahead at the path that starts to curve right and upward. Snow covers everything in sight, reminding me of the last time I saw my grandfather. A week before my tenth birthday, he'd entered my father's mind a few too many times to steal guarded information. When my father caught him, he killed my grandfather for it. Knowledge is power and makes people gruesome beings.

"Not really," I answer. "He wasn't the friendliest or most helpful fae." Which was the truth. He used to beat our real father as a child until he was bloody. Guess the whole apple not falling far from the tree applied here since Ahren was then treated the same. But the three of us made a pact to never become our father. And if we started down that road, we pulled each other back on track.

"That's a shame." She loops her arms tighter around my middle and nestles closer. "It seems to me you have it down pat if you were able to track me down on Earth."

"With the use of magic," I remind her.

"Still, what you can do is incredible."

I lean down and kiss the top of her head. "Says the girl who can open portals and heal fae, not to mention communicate with fairies."

"I think I have another ability," she tells me and goes on to explain about the energy she used to combat the king's mother in Ash Court.

My heart jackhammers at hearing she used energy to drive the Unseelie across the room. "You are incredible, my little wolf. And part of me wonders if you may even make a good mage."

She stiffens and pulls back. "Don't even say that. I've seen the mages in this court, and they are terrifying. I am nothing like that."

"You're right, you're different, and this is why I vow to protect you with my life."

She smiles and buries her head against me as we make our way forward. Birds chirp, and a deer darts past our path. Finally, I guide our horse to a stop in a small clearing where the white snow on the ground looks untouched. It glistens under the sun that's warmed up the icy day.

"We're going on foot from here. I have something to show you. Bring a blanket to keep you warm."

I jump out of the carriage and help her down as she holds onto the blanket from the bench. As she wraps it around her shoulders, I quickly give the horse feed to keep him content while we're gone.

Hand in hand, Guendolyn and I trek through the ankle-deep snow, walking past trees and over logs, the land sloping upward sharply.

She's gasping for air. "Are you trying to kill me?"

I laugh and draw her closer to me, helping her up the steep terrain to ensure she doesn't slip. Trees grow thinner, the sun stronger, and I love it up here. Around us, the world seems farther away, smaller; it feels like nothing can touch us.

We rise over the treetops now, following the circular path around the rocky hill. Once we reach the flat platform on the summit, I glance out to Shadow Court. Lofty and dominating over the land, the castle is ancient, stones worn from centuries of wear. Walls rise from the ground and stand protective over the kingdom with steadfast towers to watch over them. The town surrounds it, homes covering the descending landscape. And snow covers everything in sight.

"Oh my god!" Guendolyn gasps at the sight. "It's stunning up here. I need a camera because this is crazy beautiful."

"Little wolf, that view is not what I brought you up here for. Turn around."

She does, and her mouth drops open. "Are you freaking kidding me?"

CHAPTER

EIGHT

GUENDOLYN

Standing on a hill in the woods behind the castle, I stare out into the far distance, over the kingdom wall and another great expanse of woodland. My sight settles on an enormous tree I've never seen before. It towers over the woods around it as though someone placed a skyscraper in the middle of nowhere.

From our position on top of the hill, I can't make out the smaller details, only the branches tangled around the trunk, shooting upward where the canopy springs outward like an oversized mushroom top.

Hundreds of tiny lights speckle along the branches like fireflies.

"So beautiful," I murmur. "What is that tree?"

"Take a closer look." Luther hands me a pair of black binoculars that definitely did not come from this world.

I peer through them, my eyes taking a moment to work out what I'm looking at. Then I lower them because I've been staring at the sky. I zoom over to the tree that glints in the sunlight. The leaves sparkle like jewels, and from the branches hang oversized beehives.

My heart skips a beat as the realization hits me that I've seen these before. After we stepped out of the portal when escaping Ash Court.

"Holy shit! Those are fairies' homes!" I lower the binoculars and turn to Luther, who's grinning ridiculously.

"Why didn't you tell me they lived so close to the castle?" I swing back around to stare at a fairy emerging from a hive, her wings spanning outward in brilliant reds and golds. There are so many of these gorgeous fairies, all buzzing about like bees, popping in and out of the homes and then vanishing into the canopy tops. "We need to come here at night. Can you imagine how stunning this will look?" I lower the binoculars and glance over at Luther. "Can we go there?"

"If anyone gets near the tree, they attack and kill them. Even the Blood-cursed are afraid. Many fear and hunt them down to ensure they don't swarm the kingdom. We're under a kind of unspoken agreement that we each stay on our side of the land." He gives me a wonky smile, almost awkward, almost apologetic.

"They are super protective of their homes. I don't blame them." I turn my attention back in the tree's direction, taken aback by the beauty this realm holds. I think back to the stories I've been told about the fairy queen, the tragedy she encountered, the history behind the fairies' existence. The reactions from fae when fairies are mentioned, including the princes.

They are feared.

But also misunderstood.

I think of Hiss and how she helped me, of the hundreds of fairies that bowed and sang to me. Those are not the actions of a wild, vicious race. They are trying to survive in this terrifying world that hunts them down, exploits them. They are direct descendants from the fairy queen herself, pushed aside by the Unseelie and Seelie alike. I recall the Ash King's mother gloating about her bloodline being directly linked to the fairies. Then why don't they embrace them into their court?

My mind runs rampant with injustice.

Luther closes in behind me, his hard chest pressed against my back as his arms wrap around my waist. His breath is on my neck. "To answer your earlier question, it's only after our recent trip that I realized how closely connected you are to them. They recognize you as one of their own."

The reality of his words is too much, except deep down in my gut, I know it's true. From the first time I encountered them, they saved me. One of them talked to me in my mind. One word, but still—communication.

"Are the fairies known for having abilities other than devouring the flesh from a person's bones in seconds?" I ask.

"Not that I'm aware of, though the fairy queen carried incredible power. She tapped into elemental magic, the legends say. It's why fae have such a varying array of powers. But most have been diluted over the generations."

The more I discover about this realm's history and inhabitants, the more it starts to piece together and somehow seem normal to me.

"I like the fairies," I admit.

"Yes, I know," he answers and kisses my cheek. Warmth spreads over my body from his affection.

Twisting my head, I glance back at him, but he surprises me, sliding a hand across my jaw and kisses me.

Powerful and intoxicating, he knows exactly how to distract me and make me forget about what I'd been thinking about seconds earlier.

When he breaks away, I melt my back against his chest and hold onto his arms locked around me.

"I knew the first time I found you that there was something special about you," he muses.

"Well, of course. I was the girl with a curse," I answer with sarcasm.

His hold squeezes lightly around me. "Not what I meant. When I enter someone's mind, I can feel their aura. I can't explain it, but I sense in my heart how pure their soul is, and you are untouched."

"Untouched?" I turn around in his arms to face him.

"Nothing stains your soul. Everyone has some level of corruption or darkness in their aura. It's part of who we are. Except you. I've never seen that before."

I open my mouth, but nothing comes out. I'm unsure what to ask.

He cups my cheeks and kisses my nose. "I think it means you are destined for something unimaginable."

"That sounds terrifying." My breath quickens. "I have yet to see when anything in this realm is filled with butterflies and rainbows rather than death and blood."

"These hardships will shape your legacy, little wolf."

I half-laugh at the motivational quote. "You are confusing me with someone else. Everyone wants me killed."

He leans in closer and whispers in my ear, "You got that backward, beautiful. Anyone with a death warrant is direly important. Even if you don't realize it yet."

I frown and tilt back my head to look at him. "Do you know something I don't? Tell me; don't talk in circles, please. I've had enough of secrets."

"You are special, that part is obvious. Exactly why or how is still unclear, but it doesn't take anything away from you."

When his mouth grazes mine, I press myself against him and kiss him, tired of the merry-go-round conversations that leave me uncomfortable. I've never been anyone important, and I refuse to believe that somehow that has changed. I've experienced enough to know how the universe works. When it gives me something good in my life, it usually comes with a sucker punch. And I just feel like I haven't felt its full brunt yet. Luther telling me otherwise is his way of distracting me, to placate me.

With no answers, I prefer not to talk about this anymore.

I focus on how amazing Luther tastes instead, how his hands slide to my ass, fingers digging into me with a possessiveness I adore.

On my first time in this realm, I kissed Luther up in the treetops, so it fits perfectly that we find ourselves high up on a hill, overlooking the land, in each other's arms.

An icy breeze washes past, ruffling my hair and tugging on my clothes. Luther holds me closer, our lips still crushed together.

"I'll take you back to the sleigh. The winds are too harsh up here." His face is so close to mine, our noses touch.

I still struggle to believe that I somehow caught his attention. If it wasn't for this wind, I'd insist we remain right where we are.

He takes my hand, and I race alongside him down the slope, staring out to the fairy tree one last time before it vanishes from sight behind treetops and the lofty kingdom wall.

By the time I climb back into the sleigh, my teeth are chattering, and the first feathery snowflakes cascade around us. Then it changes in the blink of an eye. Snow falls in thick sheets, the cold penetrating through to my core. I tuck the binoculars beneath our bench and touch the basket.

"We didn't eat our picnic meal," I remind him.

"It won't go to waste, trust me." Luther slides in next to me, wrapping an arm around my shoulders and gripping the reins, then we are traveling through the woods again.

"The weather changed so fast." The earlier blue sky is now bruised with dark stormy clouds, darkening the woodland.

I rub my arms and curl in closer against Luther, absorbing his heat, though my nose still feels like ice.

The trees blanketed in snow blur past us as we move faster, and with the snow coming down quickly, I can barely see the track ahead of us, let alone anything else. Branches swing wildly in the blizzard, the wind howling around us.

My heart is beating with the thought that somehow we'll get stuck out here in the storm.

"Keep your head low," Luther instructs.

That's when I feel the ice pellets bounce off the blanket around my shoulders and my head.

A sudden gust of freezing air rushes past, colliding into us, throwing us back into our seats.

"Oh shit!" I gasp, and I won't deny, I'm more than a bit scared at how horrible the weather has shifted.

Luther whistles and drives our poor horse forward, then swings down a path toward the right. We're bouncing in our seat, and I can't stop shivering.

Before us, a small wooden cottage materializes through the curtain of snow.

A sharply pointed roof, windows covered by curtains, and a small covered veranda at the front door.

"Where are we?" I raise my voice over the blustery weather.

"Hunter's lodge. It's always open for anyone stuck out here during a storm." He comes to a pause a small distance away. "Run inside, and I'll be there soon. I need to take the horse into the stable in the back."

I nod, already climbing up as I grab the basket from under the bench, then I jump out of the sleigh. My feet sink into the snow instantly.

Not wasting a second, I hug myself, tucking my chin into my chest and shoving against the wind to the front door. I look back as Luther ushers the horse and sleigh around the side of the hunter's lodge.

Quickly, I stamp my feet on the veranda to get rid of excess snow and push open the unlocked door, rushing inside.

It smells stale in here. I shut the door, pushing it against the ferocious gusts that whistle outside, closing it with a thump. I'm trembling and hurry to pull back the curtains to light up the dark room.

It's a spacious room with an enormous fireplace. Table and chairs near the door, a couch facing the fireplace, and a bed covered in furs in the back corner. I move forward and find another door, behind which lies a makeshift toilet. Basically a bench with a hole in it. At least it's not outside, so for that I'm glad. I close that door and make my way to the fireplace and the large stack of wood neatly piled against the wall.

I place a handful into the fireplace, but with no idea on how to start a fire without matches, I turn to the basket of food instead. Underneath the kitchen towel is an array of breads, sliced roast meat, cheeses, chutney, bottles of wine and water, and what looks like half a fruit cake. I lay them out on the table, finding not only plates, cups, and cutlery at the bottom, but also strips of cured meat, tomatoes, eggs I assume are hard boiled, and a small jar of churned butter along with a small bowl of tiny pears and plums. I have no idea how the kitchen packed so much into the basket, but I couldn't be happier to have all this food while trapped here during the storm.

The door opens abruptly, and an explosion of winds rushes into the cottage. The cold finds me, digging claws into my flesh, and I'm shaking instantly.

Luther forces the door shut and shakes his head, sending snow in every direction.

"It's wild out there. We might be stuck here until it quiets down, little wolf." The way he says that isn't with any hint of worry, but more of excitement at us two being alone together. For that, I'm excited too.

"I'll get the fire started, you serve the food," he says and blows me a kiss. My knees soften at the gesture, my stomach flip-flopping. "I'm so fucking hungry right now," he murmurs.

"Then get your ass into gear," I throw back playfully and look over at the lack of fire.

He doesn't take long to ignite a blaze and have it burning. An orange glow lights up the room quickly. The windows rattle from the wild weather, small pellets of ice hitting the glass, but in here, it feels cozy and oh-so-right when I look over to Luther getting to his feet.

He's gorgeous. Built like a bear, and those amber eyes complement his midnight black hair.

My gaze trails over his muscles, at how tall he stands... and why in the world does a fae like him see anything in me? Truthfully, I suspect if we crossed paths in the street, he wouldn't even bat an eye my way. I am ordinary. He is a god and would have every woman stopping in her tracks to check him out.

What drew us together were the years we spent in each other's minds, talking to one another. I may not have realized it at the time, but I fell for Luther long ago. And I believe he feels the same about me.

He turns to the table with the food. At the sight of the mountain of food on his plate, my stomach groans.

I make my way toward the food and help myself before he eats it all— and that is no exaggeration.

We're both on the couch, enjoying our meal. With my legs folded under me, I balance the plate on the wide armrest. Heat from the fireplace curls around us, while the blaze crackles and spits. There's something thera-peutic about eating comfort food and watching logs burning while a storm howls outside.

"If the weather doesn't stop, we'll spend the night here," Luther explains, then bites into a slice of roast venison. He watches me, waiting for my response like his comment is meant to elicit a dramatic reaction. Of course I know what he's implying. One bed, two of us.... and the thought sends a shiver of excitement down my spine.

I shrug and keep eating, refusing to show him my reaction. Mostly to tease the hell out of him. "How far is the castle anyway? Can't be that far."

He eyes me while I get up to fetch some cake. "You want to go back already?"

His gaze sits heavy on my back, and it takes everything I have to refrain from grinning as I walk past him. He's so easy to rile up, it's hilarious.

The floorboard creaks behind me, and his hands are on my waist instantly. His breath is in my ear. "You're not as clever as you think you are, little wolf."

Setting the plate down on the table, I turn, but he forces me to remain with my back to him.

"Yeah, how do you figure?"

His mouth is on my neck, nipping at my skin, then licking up to my earlobe. My knees wobble. He ignites desire within me in seconds. That's all it takes, apparently.

"Because the moment you heard we are staying here tonight, your stomach fluttered and your delicious little pussy pulsed, didn't it?"

I scoff for effect. "If you say so."

His hands fall to my waist, fingers tugging at my pants. "Let's find out, shall we?" he teases.

I slap his hands away playfully and throw myself out of his arms, then pivot around to face him. "Don't even think about it." I poke my tongue out at him.

His expression morphs into one of mischief, clearly seeing my response as a challenge. God, I love that response more than I thought, and the idea of him chasing after me is exhilarating.

He lunges after me, and I spin and dart across the room, but there's hardly anywhere to go. Careening around the couch only brings him leaping over the furniture and straight for me.

I'm giggling as I whip around.

Strong arms snap around my middle and lift me off my feet.

"You're cheating." I love toying with him.

He laughs in my ear, his tone full of mirth. "Only the loser would say that."

I writhe against him. I'll show him who the loser is. But suddenly, I'm flying toward the bed and land face first on the soft mattress where I bounce up and down before settling. Hastily, I roll over, but Luther is there, forcing me back onto my stomach. His body covers mine, holding me in place. Butterflies burst through my stomach, the heat between my legs melting into a puddle.

"You know how long I've waited to have you all to myself?"

"Years," I gasp with sarcasm from under his weight.

He shifts to hold himself on bent arms, still on top of me. "The tiny taste I had in that small town was just the beginning. I haven't been able to get you out of my mind."

"And is squishing me to death part of your plan?"

He gently sweeps my long hair off the back of my neck, and his lips on my skin cover me in goosebumps. "If it means pinning you down."

His weight lifts off me in seconds, and he tugs the fabric of my dress up to my waist, exposing my bare ass.

"Oh, little wolf. Here you are protesting, and yet you've come prepared."

Heat scales my cheeks, and I roll over. "For your information, the maids took my underwear and never brought it back. Then you wanted to go on a sleigh ride, and well, here we are."

His eyebrows rise, as do the corners of my mouth. He tugs on his top and yanks it up and over his head, so he's bare-chested. "Yes, here we are." He grabs my ankles and drags me across the bed toward him.

I cry out with laughter, while hunger sweeps over his expression. "Tonight, you're mine."

I'm burning up, and I'm still clothed.

Well, partially. Luther is only in his pants, and I'm missing my underwear. While I lay on my back on the bed, propped up on my elbows, I can't stop looking at my gorgeous fae. At the way his biceps flex as he runs a hand through his pitch-black hair, the pecs on his chest, the rippled abs. I could very well be staring at a model, except he's a prince and here for me. After everything we've been through, I still need to pinch myself to realize I'm in a relationship with this man.

I don't fully understand the exact level of our dating or courting.... It just happened.

Luther unbuckles his belt, and my gaze dips.

"I could watch you strip all day long," I tease.

"My preference is the other way around." A devious expression sweeps behind his eyes. "Once things settle down in the kingdom, we will announce to everyone we are officially together."

My body tingles at the promise of his words, but they also have me curious. "Like in telling everyone we're dating?"

"Huh?"

"Boyfriend and girlfriend kind-of thing?" I sound like a thirteen-year-old, even to myself.

He nods. "If that is what you call it on Earth, then yes, we will announce to everyone that you and I are betrothed for the sake of rules. This way, no more hiding, and you can easily be with us."

My heart stops, and I push myself to sit up on the bed, crossing my legs. "What?" I suddenly can't speak, and my heart is racing at a million miles an hour.

"It's only to ensure that no one questions your presence in the mansion. And we can arrange for you to marry us as that is permitted."

My entire body is strung so tight. One second ago I thought he was proposing our engagement, and now he's implying it's going to be fake. Does that mean he doesn't want that? My head hurts, especially since this never crossed my mind until now. I adore the guys more than anything, and it kills me that I don't understand what is going on with Ahren. But I don't want to lose them, and I guess that means eventually ending up together for life. My thoughts ramble endlessly, while my chest constricts.

He kneels on the mattress in front of me, still in his pants, and reaches over to cup my face with one hand. "Are you going to be sick? You've suddenly gone pale."

I swallow the thickness in my throat. "So, you don't want to be betrothed to me?" They aren't the words I intended to ask, or the conversation I expected us to have. My cheeks blush that I made such a presumption or put Luther on the spot.

At this point, all I want is to feel safe and keep the three princes with me. To feel their kisses, their touches, their bodies against mine. Yeah, it sounds simple and maybe greedy—the voice in my head reminds me of that constantly—but is it wrong to want happiness?

Luther's smile warms me, but I don't want to talk about this any longer. All I'm doing is setting myself up for disappointment. He takes my hand and guides me off the bed.

"Come with me," he instructs.

I follow him to the window across the room from us. The trees sway wildly in the storm, the snow coming down at an angle now, the wind whistling past.

"Look straight ahead down the path."

Squinting, I tilt my head to the side and catch a perfect tiny view of the castle—the tall towers, the ridged bridges, the arched windows—all smothered in snow. It reminds me of a snow globe.

"It's beautiful."

"Once Ahren takes the throne, Deimos and I will rule the Shadow Court with him, but there are rules that come with such roles. We can't be seen in public with females unless we are courting them with the intention to marry them."

My breath catches in my throat, and I can't turn around as he embraces me from behind. I don't know where this conversation is going, but my stomach is turning. I really can't take any more surprises or disappointments right now.

"Deimos and I have talked about this. We both agreed that to keep you close to us, you will be betrothed to us." His arms squeeze me slightly as he kisses the side of my face.

I blink and twist around in his arms. "So like, a fake engagement?"

He narrows his gaze at me. "Why fake?"

My head spins at what he's saying, and I don't want to jump at conclusions. "Does betrothed mean something else in this world than it does on Earth?"

"It means we have the intention to marry."

The cold shock of his response knocks the breath out of me. Except, I'm missing something. "So, we will pretend to be engaged for as long as..." I don't know how to continue that, because what happens next? I still don't know where I really live or belong.

"You will have a new identity, but this isn't pretend, little wolf."

I stare into his genuine expression, and my stomach twists into knots, my knees close to giving out under me.

"You're asking me to marry you? For real?"

He stiffens and pulls back from me, and my heart stops beating for a few moments.

"You're right. I did this completely wrong." He gets down on one knee in front of me and fiddles with his hands, then looks at me.

Those stunning eyes, crowned by thick brows.

This prince is addictive.

He's royalty.

Everything I would ever want in a man.

And he's about to propose to me...

My eyes prick with tears while my heart clenches. This can't be right... can it? Is he pranking me?

"Guendolyn, will you marry me?" He stretches out his open palm toward me.

Shock hurtles through me. I adore this fae beyond belief... Hell, I love him.

Emotions tumble through me so fast I can't think, and I rush into his arms as he stands, tears running down my cheeks. We collide spectacularly, and he embraces me, lifts me off my feet.

"Oh, little wolf, you are so beautiful. And that's a yes then?"

I'm laughing, and when he finally puts me back onto my feet, I wipe my tears and nod crazily. "You're being serious, right? Like a real marriage, not a ruse just to get me to stay in the castle?"

Luther's face morphs into a serious look, and he cups my face, forcing me to look at him. "I do not joke about these things. My intentions are to marry you for life. I hadn't intended to ask you here and now, or like this, but I love spontaneity. It's been that way since you entered our lives." He kisses me as his thumbs wipe away my tears. "I love you, little wolf."

My whole body trembles to hear those words. I keep my eyes trained on his, at the way he smiles at me with genuine emotion. There's no teasing or assessing, just a fae opening himself up to me.

He lifts my hand, and I look down as he pushes a ring on my finger. A dark metal intertwined on itself like a vine. One line is studded with diamonds, the other filled with an electric blue stone that glimmers like a moving ocean. "This is beautiful."

My heart beats too fast with the emotions building inside me.

"This belonged to my grandmother, and she made me promise I gift it to my future wife. It's black gold with dragon tears and lava from the oldest volcano in our realm, the one they say the first fairies emerged from."

I glance up at him. "Wow, are you sure you want to part with it?"

"I've been carrying it around with me since we got back from Ash Court, trying to find the right time to give it to you. In fact, Deimos and I were meant to do this together, so I kind of stole that from him. Oops."

I run my finger over the surface of the ring that fits perfectly on my finger and throw my arms around Luther's neck, then shower his face with kisses.

"Yes," I assure him. "Yes, I want to marry you and Deimos. I wish he was with us too."

Luther kisses me firmly, his hands gripping my arms as I melt against him. Fingers slide over and cup my breasts, squeezing them. I moan against him as he pulls at the laced-up ties across my chest, loosening the bodice. Then he pushes the fabric down my shoulders and body until it falls into a heap around my feet.

Coldness creeps over my back from the window behind me, and I tuck myself against Luther. With my breasts against his bare chest, the heat is instant. My prince. My fiancé. My husband to be.

This is definitely going to take a lot of getting used to. Maybe for once, things are going to start going right for me.

"You are divine, and I'm going to devour you tonight." Luther steps back and eyes me head to toe, and the erection growing in his pants does not go unnoticed.

My whole body burns while I pull at his pants, needing them off already. The moment I tug them open, his cock springs out like a jack-in-the-box, and I can't help but laugh. He's so huge, the long vein running down the front of his shaft thick, his tip coated in pre-cum.

Not wasting a second, he drops his pants to the floor and steps out of them, then takes me into his arms. Pressed together, I lean in and kiss him as he slides a hand down my leg and guides it around his hip, then does the same with the other. He walks me over to the wall away from the window and cages me in with his body.

"Tonight is just the beginning to all the ways I'll fuck your sweet, tight pussy."

Arousal claims me, consumes me. I want it to rip away everything else so nothing remains but the raw emotions we share. "I'll hold you to that," I answer and grasp onto his strong shoulders, drawing him closer and kissing him. The tip of his erection slides over my heat with the promise of so much more.

"Tell me what you want," he commands.

"God, I want you so badly." I shudder with need and arousal, my body scorching hot, my focus on where we're merging.

He's breathing heavily, teasing me. I shift to better accommodate him— my prince is a very big boy.

"Say it," he demands, his hands to my throat, keeping me in place firmly but not painfully.

"Fuck me, please. I can't wait any longer."

He laughs and starts pushing into me, gradually at first, stretching me. My toes curl and I hiss out as my head falls back against the wall. He never relents, but moves all the way in, all the way to his balls.

He groans, sucking in air. "Fuck, you're so incredibly tight." Slow at first, he pulls out of me then moves back in, his pace picking up. Friction builds between us, igniting me.

Digging my fingers into his arms, I hold on as he thrusts into me, harder, faster now. His muscles tense and shift beneath my body.

"You will always be mine," he groans as he fucks me like nothing else in the world matters. His gaze never breaks from mine, and it reminds me how much I fell for him even before we met, how my heart beat for him even before I ever admitted it to myself. He watches me moan as I bounce up and down on his cock. "No one can even come close to what you mean to me. To how beautiful you are. To how perfect your sweet pussy is. Ever."

"I love when you say those things." My words are breathy, exhilaration building in me. He lets go of my throat, hands on my hips as he grinds into me. Seconds later he wrenches me toward him and walks us to the bed with him still embedded in me. Lying me on my back, he slides off, and I moan my protest.

"On your hands and knees," he orders.

"Oh yes, please." I roll over and prop myself up just as his hand gives my ass a hard slap. "Ouch." The word comes out involuntarily, but there's no denying there was something delicious about how good that felt.

He growls deeply, grabbing my hips and drawing me backward so my knees balance on the edge of the mattress, my ass high in the air and everything I have exposed.

"I love you looking this way." His cock pushes into my entrance, and in a heartbeat, he plunges deep.

I scream from the sudden explosion of pleasure.

"Fuck!" he snarls. "You feel so good." He hammers into me, the slapping sounds a gorgeous song of our love. His hands grasp my ass cheeks, kneading them, spreading them, then he curls a hand around my waist, finding my clit.

"I want to feel you coming with me buried in you."

Groaning, I fist the bedsheets as he spears me over and over. I slide toward the edge fast, my orgasm building with each passing moment, mounting as Luther takes me.

His finger strokes me to the point where I peak so fast that my climax comes at me suddenly. Tearing through me, my body convulses, and I cry out as I fall with the pleasure, my arms giving out as I collapse forward, my ass still high and Luther fucking me faster.

I scream out, orgasming long and ferociously, my whole body clenching.

Luther snarls like a beast, stiffening as he explodes inside me. "Squeeze me, that's it."

We both float on the clouds, attached and shuddering with the desire binding us. I no longer know where I begin and he ends. My heart thumps harder.

When we both come down from the most incredible orgasm, he slides out of me and we collapse on the bed. He draws me toward him, and I roll into his arms, both of us sweating and gasping for breath.

He kisses my brow. "Are you ready for more?" he asks eagerly, and I'm not sure if he's serious, considering we're still both puffing.

"Absolutely," I respond regardless, and he shuffles out of bed.

It seems he was one hundred percent serious, and I'm blown away by his stamina.

"Spread yourself for me," he demands. "I'm going to clean you up first."

I roll onto my back and obey him, adoring the way he commands me in the bedroom. There's nothing more thrilling than a delicious man dominating you when it comes to sex.

He stands before me, his gaze dipping to the apex between my legs. A tingle of desire curls deep in my stomach, even though I've just climaxed.

"Don't move," he tells me. "We're not even close to being done."

My breath catches in my throat—I'm ready to go all night.

A coldness wraps around me, and I open my eyes to the sun beaming into the cabin through the gaps in the curtains. It takes mere seconds for my memories to return, and I lift my hand to stare at the ring on my finger. I still can't believe this is real. What we experienced was pure magic, and I want more.

I'm engaged to a prince. A fae prince, precisely, and butterflies whirl around in my stomach, twisting me into an anxious mess. While hundreds of questions and concerns pelt into me about how it all went down, I shove them away. *Not today, bad thoughts. I've ridden a terrible storm for too long, so give me this moment of joy. Everything else we can work out later.*

I mean, never in a million years did I ever think I'd find a prince, let alone marry one. So this is utterly surprising. It's the things fairy tales are made of and the best thing to have happened to me.

Rolling over onto my side, I reach out for Luther, except my hand falls through the air and lands on his empty side of the bed. I sit up and scan the cottage.

"Luther?" I call out in case he's in the bathroom, but when no response comes, I wrap the bedsheet around my naked body and pad across the cold wooden floor. The fire has burned out, so the air is crisp and cold.

When I knock on the bathroom door and there's no response, I open it.

He's not in there. Suddenly, his absence makes the cottage feel lonely and sad.

I frown and march over to the window. As I draw back the curtain, I see a guard standing outside with his back to me. The storm has passed... has Luther returned to the castle without me?

Why's there a guard outside? First, I need clothes. Quickly, I rush to get dressed, then I pat down my wild hair and open the front door.

Michae stands tall and greets me with a smile. "Morning, my lady."

"Where's Luther?" I groan.

"Prince Luther was called to an urgent matter with his brother at dawn. I am here to escort you back to court."

I glance back at our love shack, a place I will never forget as the place where Luther proposed. Sure, it was the strangest proposal, but it'll always stay with me.

"Are you ready to leave?" Michae asks.

I step outside and draw the door shut behind me. "Should I clean up the room, perhaps, before we leave?"

He smiles so genuinely at me, that I wonder if he must think me strange to ask such questions. "Maids will be arriving soon to clean everything. You don't have to worry."

I track behind him to a horse carriage waiting farther down the snowy path, reminding myself that having others clean up after me is something I will need to get used to. I'm pretty sure the guilt will vanish soon enough.

We ride under a stunning azure sky, no trace of the savage storm that roared all night. As did my prince. The thought brings an electric buzz racing up my spine. That fae has insane stamina. We went all night and only fell asleep in the early hours of the morning.

Once back at the castle, I head down to the baths for a wash, after which I dress in a brand-new, simple straight gown the color of my ruby. This time I include underwear that look more like white shorts.

Once I spot Michae go down the hall for a break from watching my door, I sneak out, hurrying down the corridor of the mansion. I have to speak to Deimos, but I can't have Michae following me and hearing my conversation with him.

I keep admiring my ring, at the way the dragon tears, as Luther called them, sparkle in the light. Part of me feels guilty that Deimos wasn't with us, that he may not agree to Luther having done this on his own. The last thing I want is to create any tension between the brothers, so I need to talk to him urgently. I think of what Ahren's reaction would be, but I don't even know what to make of that situation.

As I approach his room, a maid walks out carrying a bundle of bedclothes and dumps it on the wheeled trolley in the hallway.

On my approach, she lifts her gaze. "Miss." She gives me a small bow.

"Is Deimos here?" I ask.

She shakes her head. "He went up on the roof."

I frown. "How do I get there?"

She wipes her hands down her white apron, then glances over her shoulder down the corridor as if she's expecting someone to reprimand her for her talking to me. "Quickly, I will show you."

"Thank you." I take quick steps to keep up with her as she races down several hallways, then pushes open a door to a set of stairs.

"Go all the way to the top."

The stone walls of the circular enclosure are a dark gray, with narrow slits for windows. My skin pricks with the cold in here.

"Um, what is on the roof, exactly?" I turn back only to discover she's already marching back to the prince's room. If Deimos is up there, likely so is Luther, and even Ahren. As much as my stomach protests at seeing them all together, maybe it's not a bad idea to get everything in the open. To speak the truth about my engagement, about what is up Ahren's ass lately, and for me to tell them the truth of who my father was.

No more secrets. Tightness coils in my chest about such a conversation, but if I intend to marry the princes and join their family, we need to come clean on everything.

I want us to start fresh.

Taking a deep breath, I step forward and make my way upstairs. It's quiet—there's no one else in here. It's only when I look out a window do I see how far up I am. I must be in a tower at the corner of the mansion.

Losing track of how many turns I've taken, I finally reach the top, my thighs smarting. Gasping for air, I pause for a moment to catch my breath so I won't appear flustered.

One last look at my ring, and I push the wooden door open. *I can do this.*

Bright daylight greets me, along with a faint breeze. I step out of the stairwell and onto an outdoor terrace. The mansion sits like a U-shape around the open balcony, which is enclosed by a stone railing. A table and several chairs sit in one corner, filled with platters of food and what appear to be paper scrolls. And there's only one lone figure up here.

Ahren stands at the other end of the balcony, hands on the railing, head low and staring at the kingdom grounds below.

Suddenly, I'm doubting my decision to be here.

"Lingering in the doorway is asking for trouble," Ahren states without looking my way, his voice deep and velvety. Just hearing him brings to the surface so many emotions—the pain of his rejection and secrets, how much I miss him.

I guess that is the best invitation I'll get from him, so I shut the door behind me and go to tuck my hands into pockets, except my dress has none. I've been keeping my ruby on the underside of my laced-up corset where there are layers of fabric. It's amazing what perfect little pockets they make.

Fidgeting, I chew on my lower lip and saunter toward him while my stomach does somersaults.

"How much trouble are we talking about, exactly?" I murmur upon approaching him.

"The kind that seems to follow you around." There's a tenderness in his voice; the words aren't bitter or aggressive. They belong to the fae who made me fall for him.

Maybe this is my chance to finally speak to him, to find out what's going on. I move to stand alongside him and stare out over the town sprawled over the rising landscape. The cottages shine black beneath the morning sun with trims of varied colors around the roofs and windows. In the valley lies a river that seems to divide the town in two, and I try hard to imagine what it would have been like growing up here. But in all honesty, I can't even fathom that lifestyle.

My chance to grow up amid my kind was taken from me by an evil woman in Ash Court, and one day I'll find out why.

"Deimos and Luther should be back later today," Ahren explains without looking my way.

"Where are they?"

"On an errand outside the castle walls to escort visitors past the Bloodcursed."

My stomach clenches at the sound of them facing danger. "Why did *they* go out there instead of soldiers?" I sound protective of them, and dammit, I am.

"Our mother insisted they be the ones to meet with our father first."

I almost choke on my breath. "Your dad, the asshole who left your mother for another woman?" Not to mention the bastard who beat Ahren senseless growing up, ripped his wings until there was only bone left, and left the scars on his back that will be imprinted on my mind for eternity. "Why would you welcome *him* to your court?"

"It's not mine yet, and Mother accepted him for the sake of kingdom alliances. We must all stand together against the Unseelie." This time, the bitterness surges through his voice.

"It's still wrong," I answer.

He glances over to me, the corner on one side of his mouth curling upward, those pale green eyes smiling while the wind catches his long white hair and pushes it off his face.

I lose myself in those few moments in his presence. He's spectacular. Handsome. Rugged. Dominant. Scary. And someone that makes my heart thud in my chest with need.

As much as my hands tingle to reach over to him, I fear I'd be pushing my luck, so I turn back to the view, my hands gripping the cold stone railing instead.

"I admire that you always speak your mind. That's one of the things that I hate about my role. Being unable to do so."

When I glance over to him, I notice him looking down at my hand, at the ring Luther gave me. Luther said it was his grandmother's, so Ahren would know exactly what it means.

A paralyzing dread crashes through me. It shouldn't, but I see how quickly Ahren's demeanor stiffens, jealousy curling behind his narrowing eyes. His breaths quicken, and I lower my hand by my side, feeling like somehow I've cheated on him.

"Ahren, it's not—"

"I'm happy for you. This is exactly what I wanted for you." His words are sour and dark.

I cringe on the inside.

His shoulders bunch up, and the corded muscles in his neck flex.

"You're happy that your brother asked me to be his betrothed?" I hate asking that question, but I refuse to believe he's happy.

"Of course." His voice deepens, yet he refuses to look at me.

My knees weaken. "And it doesn't bother you in the slightest?"

"Should it?" He shrugs.

I study his face, searching for the expression that tells me he's lying, but he's a blank page, so good at hiding his feelings. I'm dying on the inside. I'm no fool; I can tell he's pretending, but it still damn hurts to hear those words from him.

He doesn't even give me a chance to respond before he turns and storms away from me.

What the hell?

I'm moving before I make the decision and grab his hand, forcing him to stop and look at me. There's a buzz that zips up my arm from our touch, and he flinches too, feeling the connection.

"Can you just talk to me, please," I plead.

He pauses and twists toward me, raising an eyebrow. "What do you want from me? To say that it rips me apart to see Luther's ring on your finger? That I want to shove my fist through a wall over and over until I feel nothing but excruciating pain?"

My head spins, and I tighten my hold of his hand. "Then why are you pushing me away?"

He lowers his gaze. "I need to leave. I'm not doing this."

"No," I challenge him, stiffening. "Just fucking talk to me." I'll lose my shit before I let him walk away.

He groans, making a sudden, painful sound as his back unexpectedly twitches while he rolls his shoulders.

"Are you hurt?" I scan his back, which is silly, as he's wearing a black tunic and I can't see through it.

"It's nothing. Look Guendolyn, I'm sorry if you think we had something, but we can't have a future together." His voice is so monotone and robotic, as though he's been practicing this line.

My fingers curl around his when he flinches once more, his face scrunching up as if he's drowning in agony.

"What's going on?" I ask.

"It's stress. I hold it in my shoulders. It's nothing."

My insides are sizzling with confusion, and I don't know what to say or do. Ahren is in obvious pain. Sure, he has too much going on, and it's getting to him. But is that all it is?

"You expect me to sit back and watch you fall apart? Let's go sit down and I'll rub your shoulders. It always helps me."

He tugs his hand free from mine, his face morphing into one of frustration and anger. "How much clearer can I be?" he barks. "I assumed you would have found out by now about me from one of the castle staff."

My back flinches as I straighten. "Find out what? The reason you supposedly want to move on?"

He's heaving, the struggle obvious in his eyes and the way his shoulders hunch, his body curving forward.

"Just tell me. Whatever it is, I'll understand," I persist.

He looks away, darkness swallowing his expression.

I should be mad at him.

Should be furious and storm away.

But I can't get my legs to move when the desperation to uncover the truth pummels through me. I need to know what is going on with him.

"Tomorrow..." he begins, but instead of continuing, he groans and drops to his knees, his back suddenly arching.

My stomach curls in on itself. "Ahren." I reach for him as he slumps forward on bent legs like he might be sick, and in a heartbeat, the sound of fabric tearing has me startling upright. He hisses through his teeth.

Only when I step back do I notice the shirt on his back is shredded and his wings are pushing out for release.

Like last time I saw them, they are mainly bone. And they're stretching outward on either side of him for escape, wrapping around him. My heart cleaves in half to see them this way, to know his monster of a father ripped the flesh off his wings—and yet, he's being welcomed into the kingdom.

I want to scream at the injustice and destroy the sonofabitch for doing this to his son.

Reaching over, I tenderly touch a wing.

He flinches from my touch. "I told you before, I'm broken," he snarls. "How the fuck am I meant to rule a kingdom when I can't even control my own body?"

His voice cracks, and my heart squeezes as though a hand has it in a death grip. All I want is to take away his pain.

That's when I realize that I don't completely have control of my body either, because I'm still by his side after he's repeatedly tried to push me away. But maybe my mind knows something I don't... there is something much deeper going on with Ahren.

My hand traces over the length of the bone in his wing, and I close my eyes, imagining the energy in my body going into his, healing him.

There's no guarantee this will work, but I can't sit back and watch him fall apart. It kills me to see him so broken.

Heat radiates from my chest, right where the ruby sits, so I turn my focus to that. My skin pricks in an instant as power flares over me, lifting every hair on my body.

Ahren roars. "What are you doing to me?"

I flip open my eyes as he rips away from me and climbs to his feet, skeletal wings jutting outward. The shadow of his wings looms over me, making him appear so much larger than usual. It reminds me just how small I am in comparison.

He stumbles about when the first spark of electricity snaps across the bones of his wings. It flares like lightning, dancing across his back.

I hate hearing the agony in his voice, and I don't know what to do. Have I made a mistake by using my stone to heal him? What have I done?

At his side, I wrack my brain on how to fix this, how to eliminate his pain, but I come up empty. None of this is normal.

He roars, his back arching, white sparks popping across his back.

"I'm sorry," I murmur, placing my hands on him, but he pushes me away and I stumble.

Everything I try fails.

Ahren's legs give out and he's back on his knees, hands reaching up over his shoulders to try to reach his wings. I tell myself I tried to help him, but seeing him this way kills me.

"Ahren," I call to him when he curls in on himself, trembling.

Inside, I'm bleeding with guilt, and again I step closer to do something... anything.

Something blue catches my attention at the base of a wing, and I squint to get a better look. In a flash, a sudden wave of violet, turquoise, and pearlescent white rush over the bony limbs.

That's all it takes... a breath, a heartbeat, as a layer of membrane materializes before my eyes, knitting itself over his bones. The colors blend and swirl in playful waves as they weave the fabric of his wings.

My breath catches in my throat, and the sight of him completely healed fills me with a sense of serenity, satisfaction, and fulfillment. They still remain curled around him, like a thin layer of colored stretchy fabric, and I can't stop staring at how spectacular they are.

"Oh. My. God! Ahren." I crouch in front of him, nudging him in the shoulder. "Get up."

He lifts his head to meet my gaze, his face pale, lips tight.

"Your wings," I whisper. "They're beautiful."

He blinks with confusion, then twists his head around to take them in. There's no response at first; he's just silent, frozen in time like the shock of healing is too much for him to bear.

He stands up in all his glory, the colors on either side of him like stained glass. They're captivating and brilliant, like the first blossoming buds in spring. They stretch out, spanning most of the balcony length.

His hand reaches out as a wing curls around to meet his touch. He swallows loudly, his mouth parted, and when he looks at me, his eyes glint with fresh tears. With the agony of seeing something I am sure he'd resigned himself to never experiencing ever again.

"How..." His shaky words trail off, and he grabs me by my arm and hugs me tightly. His heart beats ferociously in his chest, breaths racing, and tears prick in my eyes at his reaction. All I've ever wanted for him is to love himself despite what his asshole of a father did to him. This is the least I can give him.

I wrap my arms around his waist as warmth floods me at having him back. I don't understand how I can be so attracted to three men at once, but I don't care about that anymore. Right now it's just us, isn't it?

His grasp tightens, and my feet suddenly lift off the terrace. My heart thunders. I glance up at Ahren as he stares down at me, smiling like nothing in the world can touch him. The world falls away below us as his wings beat, air buffeting into us, hair fluttering around us, but I never break our stare.

"This is incredible," I gasp.

"I don't know how you managed it, but you've given me something I can never repay you for. You can't even begin to understand what this means to me." His voice cracks, and the sight of his joy loosens at the corners of my eyes.

"I want you to feel whole and not be reminded of what your asshole father did to you. There's—"

He leans and steals my words with a searing kiss, so powerful, so possessive, that it leaves me trembling. This is the Ahren I've missed, the fae who captivated me. I reach up and cup his face, pushing myself closer, kissing him back, showing him how much he means to me.

My heart almost explodes from the sheer happiness of being in his arms. Our kiss is fire; this is how we should always be. His tongue swirls over my lips teasingly while my stomach flutters with exhilaration.

"I've wanted you from the first time you arrived at our court, which was a mistake on my part. You deserve everything and so much more." A flare of uncertainty brushes over his face, and we're floating back down to the balcony.

Unease rises through my stomach, and the truth pushes to the forefront of my mind.

He doesn't intend to be with me, after all.

No, he wouldn't do that. Because the way he just kissed me belongs to a fae who is desperately in love.

My feet softly land on the floor, first my toes, then my heels. Ahren doesn't let me go and says, "I want your happiness." He pauses, and my heart stops for a moment.

"And?" Tears already blur my eyes because my body knows what's coming. I feel it twisting inside me, the agony squeezing, squeezing, squeezing until I can barely take a breath.

"I am to marry the princess of Ember Court in order to claim the throne of Shadow Court."

The sucker punch comes fast and instant, and I can't think at first. Tears fall; there's no stopping them. This is why he's been pushing me away, why he's doing it again now.

I stumble backward from him, utterly broken. This can't be right. It's me he is supposed to be with... how dare he marry someone else!

"Guendolyn, please. I have no choice in this." He reaches out for me, but I push his hand away.

The world freezes around us. There's nothing left.

I'm shaking my head, wiping my eyes, and my mind is spiraling. "I thought..."

How could I have been so blind to not see this coming? Of course he'd have to marry—I should have seen this. But in truth, it never once occurred to me that I'd lose Ahren. In my mind, we were secure and the problem was related to something else. I'm such a fucking idiot!

"If things were different," he begins, but I can't do this. I can't be in his presence.

"Don't."

The heartache in his eyes when he looks at me buckles my knees. My gaze lingers on him a bit longer, tracing every bit of him—his sharp cheek-bones, the fullness of his tempting lips, the strong line of his jaw. But the longer I look at him, the more my body is ready to collapse, but I refuse to cry desperately in front of him.

I turn and run across the balcony and through the door. I don't stop moving as I race down the stairs. Tears drench my cheeks while on the inside I feel pathetic.

Stupid.

Naïve.

Foolish.

My lips feel bruised from his rough kiss. It's a reminder of something we can never have again. Here I assumed we were making up, that I'd given him a gift of his wings and in exchange he'd take me back. But that was just me being desperate, wasn't it?

Our time together was nothing more than a farewell.

ELEVEN

Shock rattles me, digging its claws into me as I rush down the stairs from the balcony. I want to vanish from this whole damn kingdom. Shoving the bottom door open, I burst into the hallway and swing toward my room to be away from everyone. Especially Ahren.

I hate him for making me feel like shit, for rejecting me. And what I loathe even more is that in the back of my mind, I partly understand why he's doing it. That doesn't help me in the slightest. I want to detest him and remove him from my thoughts and memories as if we'd never met.

I wipe my eyes as the tears keep flowing. His decision cleaves my heart in half. How could I not have seen this coming? I've made a fool of myself.

There's no way I can live here and see him with someone else every day. Thinking about the marriage about it makes me feel sick.

I stumble forward, sobs wracking through me, and I bump into the wall where I cry in my hands. My chest burns at the thought of seeing another woman in his arms. He is meant to be mine… and he knows it. I felt it in his kiss.

How did this become such a fucking mess? Do I really belong here anyway? Luther proposed to me, and I haven't even spoken to Deimos about it yet. But now that earlier joy is stained by Ahren's news. I twirl the ring around my finger, not sure what I'm supposed to do.

After everything I've gone through with the princes, I fell in love with them. With each one of them.

Luther.

Deimos.

Ahren.

Except Ahren has broken my heart, and I'm not sure I can recover if I'm reminded daily of what I lost.

I pull out the ruby from the inside of my corset and roll it over my fingers. There's still so much about myself I haven't uncovered, and the plan wasn't for me to fall for three princes.

The more I stare at the stone, the more I contemplate using it to just vanish out of here and return home to Earth. Just to think things through, to feel normal and blend into society like a nobody. I never thought I'd actually crave such a thing. I keep thinking how most of my life was a lie, and that pattern seems to be following me here too. Ahren's secret has ruined me, and I'm not sure how to get over it.

One minute, I'm ecstatic; the next, I want to run away. I'm growing tired of the drama and danger at every turn.

Footfalls resonate behind me, and my stomach clenches as my thoughts fly to Ahren.

I turn to find someone right in my face, and it's not the prince.

"Jasion!" His name rolls off my tongue with a gasp.

I stumble backward, and his gaze falls to my hand as I curl my fingers around the ruby stone.

"What's in your hand?" he demands, towering over me, his mouth in a sneer.

The bastard hates me, and the feeling's mutual.

"Leave me alone." I pivot away from him, my skin crawling in his presence.

Strong fingers snatch my wrist, and he tugs me backward. "I asked you a question."

Everything is getting to be too much for me. I just want to collapse and cry, to try to process what happened with Ahren and not deal with this idiotic mage.

"It's nothing." I wrench my arm from him, but he's not letting me go.

His nostrils flare as he glares down at me like I'm nothing. Arrogant asshole.

"You stole the king's ruby." He spits the words, saliva splashing onto my face, and I cringe.

I wipe my face with the sleeve of my dress. "Gross, keep it in your mouth."

His grip squeezes harder, making me wince.

"I thought I saw you playing with a red stone the other day, and then when I checked the throne and found the ruby gone."

Ice fills my veins that he was able to catch me with the ruby. I've been too careless with it, and now I reprimand myself for not being smarter about hiding it.

"I asked a few questions, and it seems the ruby went missing about a week before our king was brutally murdered."

A cold shiver runs down my spine at his accusation, but there's no way I'm telling a mage of all people that a fairy took the stone.

"Give it to me!" he growls, leaning in closer.

The hatred in his voice triggers something in me. I've had enough of everyone. I'm trembling with anger.

"Fuck you!"

He snatches my jaw hard, hurting me even more after his last attack, drawing me to his face. That's when I see the shadows of guards coming up behind him. Are they escorting the princes? Except Ahren said Deimos and Luther were out of the kingdom.

"You murdered the king," Jasion hisses in my face.

Ice fills my veins at his words. "Are you crazy?" I shove a hand into his chest, but he doesn't move.

"The gem is priceless; you killed him to take it. What was your plan? Sell it and make a small fortune, thinking we'd never find out? That's why you played the princes, isn't it?"

I clench my fists, sick and tired of his crap. Fury flares across my chest, spreading through me like an inferno.

"I am not a killer. And if you want the damn thing, take it." I swing my arm to toss the stone aside, but my hand and ruby slap against the wall.

Crack.

Sharpness digs into my palm, and shards of the shattered ruby fall to the floor as I draw my hand back. Blood spills from the cuts and pieces embedded into my skin.

"Oh shit," I cry, the pain sudden and sharp, feeling like the world's worst paper cut.

"You whore." Jasion shoves me to the side, right into the arms of a guard.

My world spins. The guard's hand is like a shackle on my wrist, and I'm being dragged behind him before I can even respond.

"Let me go," I bellow, punching his arm with my free hand. But it's useless because he doesn't react. He's walking so fast, he's practically dragging me down the hall.

I scream, needing someone to hear me and call Ahren. But the place is empty. The guard shoves open a door, and I'm wrenched in there with him, then I'm stumbling downstairs.

My heart is pounding in my chest as fear collects inside me. Behind me, footsteps race closer, and I look back to Jasion and another beefy guard built like a barrel.

"I did nothing wrong!" I yell at him over my shoulder. I'm so damn furious that he caught me off guard.

Jasion smirks, staring at me with ill intent.

Next thing I know, I'm shoved through another door, and I stumble into a dimly lit room that smells like socks and the horse stables.

"Where are you taking me?"

But none of them answer. The guard hauls me along the dark corridor, then down another set of steps, and only once we go through another door do I realize where we are.

Prison cells line one side of the room. Brick walls divide the four enclosures, all of them empty.

My stomach drops through my body while panic strangles me. Despite my hand stinging and bleeding, I shove my elbow into the guard's gut, but he doesn't react.

"The princes will have your head for doing this," I threaten as I'm pushed into the open cell. A snap of energy strikes like a severe electric shock the moment I stumble over the threshold. I shudder and coil back around to escape.

"That's where you belong, assassin." He shuts the barred door with a deafening bang.

I rush forward and grasp a metal bar with one hand, shaking it. I don't feel the pain in my hand; I can only focus on the terrifying reality of what's to become of me.

"Let me the fuck out of here. I didn't kill anyone." My voice echoes around us.

Jasion steps in front of the door, hands folded over his bare chest, looking smug and proud of himself.

The hairs on my arms rise as a trickle of energy dances under my skin. The same kind I experienced back in Ash Court when I fought for my life.

"Let me out before the princes make you pay severely for this."

He chuckles to himself. "You actually think they'll find you? You'll be long gone before that happens."

Anger skyrockets through me. I grind my teeth as I call to the power as I had once before, but nothing happens... it doesn't respond. I fist my hands, my shoulders curling forward, and death plays on my mind... the death of this fucking sonofabitch.

The hatred in his eyes would kill me if they could form daggers. He's a piece of scum.

"You stand in my way, and that's the problem. But not for much longer."

The prick steps forward, just out of arm's reach, his head cocked to the side. The smugness on his face is infuriating. He tsks and sighs heavily like I'm a nuisance to him. Asshole.

"I'm doing you a favor. Do you know what they do to assassins here? Not even your princes will be able to save you from a brutal, long, and painful death."

"You've got it backward. I'm going to enjoy seeing the princes slice you apart with their swords."

"Maybe I'll change my mind and feed you to the wolves sooner than I thought. I have pieces of the ruby stone." He taps his pocket. "All the evidence I need to convict you. Along with a few witnesses. The princes won't be able to save you."

He whips away from me and storms down the long corridor, the guards on his heels. Seconds later, a door slams shut, and I'm alone.

Fear chokes me as I stumble back, hugging myself. A torch sitting in a metal bracket on the wall outside my cell is all that lights this place. A putrid, filthy, sorrowful dungeon.

I pace back and forth, screaming for help.

But will anyone hear me? We came down so many flights of steps, and... and I'm going to die here! I fucking hate Jasion, and when I get the chance, I will kill him with my own hands.

I stand in the cell, sick to my stomach wondering how the hell this happened.

When I look down at my bleeding hand, I become even more furious. I can't believe that on top of everything, I also managed to smash the ruby, meaning if I open a portal, I could end up anywhere. I want to cry, but I'm too numb. Instead I return to the cell door and scream for help.

DEIMOS

"Fuck, Luther, I thought we were doing it together?" Some days I want to punch my brother so hard for the simple satisfaction of how much he frustrates the hell out of me.

"The moment felt right." He shrugs and stares out at the snow-covered woodland surrounding us.

Guards are behind us. We left the kingdom with help from the mages, making us undetectable by the Bloodcursed for just long enough to race away from the castle where they linger.

"We were alone," Luther continues, justifying himself. "Stuck in the cottage out in the woods during a storm. And well, the discussion came up, and it just happened that I had grandmother's ring on me."

I narrow my gaze at him with pure disbelief. "You've carried that thing with you since you were eight when she gave it to you, so don't fucking lie to me."

He glances over to me from atop his black mare, half smiling, not remorseful at all about asking Guendolyn to marry him without me there. "You really want to do this now, while we're going to meet Father?"

"Fuck yes," I say. "We had agreed, but keeping your word is impossible for you."

"What are you angry about the most, brother?" he snaps back. "That somehow you think you'll miss out, or that I spent a night with her and you didn't?"

"Fuck you." In truth, he's right on both accounts, but I won't admit it out loud. I'm still pissed at the stunt he pulled. I turn my attention to the landscape, keeping an eye out for Bloodcursed. That is the focus, not the fire brewing in the pit of my stomach that I wanted to be there for Guendolyn.

The more I think about it, the more sure I become that I want to hold my own proposal to her, with my own ring. It feels right that she has one from each of us. Once we arrive back, I'll put that into action. In all honesty, I wanted us to do this before she found out Ahren was marrying someone else. For her to know she wasn't alone, that she always had Luther and I.

It's not too late, but we have to escort our dickhead father back to our home. First get this worthless exercise out of the way, then I'll be back in the castle with her.

"I still don't understand why we have to greet the bastard," Luther growls in my direction as our horses trot alongside one another along the wide path.

The sunlight is bright, the sky clear, but being out here is the last thing I want.

"Mother insisted." If it was up to me, our real father would have never been invited to Ahren's wedding... and this is why I detest political bullshit.

Luther grumbles something under his breath, his knuckles white from how tightly he holds the reins. We all hate our father for different reasons, but at the core of the problem, he's an arrogant turd who puts wealth and status before family.

"You think he'll bring his bride?" Luther sneers when he asks the question. The woman is young enough to be our sister.

"Might be awkward, but it wouldn't surprise me."

"I was thinking the same. It's another opportunity for him to rub it in Mother's face. Maybe we can speak to the chef about slipping something special in their meals so they spend the night in the toilet rather than at the ceremony."

"Get it done, and I won't tell a soul."

The evil smirk on his face has me grinning. Growing up under Father's thumb, the only way Luther and I survived was to make jokes, pull pranks —anything other than constantly fear his wrath.

We soon reach a crossroads. Straight ahead goes to Ash Court, and the other two lead toward the east and west kingdoms.

Standing before us are a dozen soldiers on horses, and near them is a golden carriage pulled by two mares. So he brought his bride after all. I sigh.

Our father rides forward on a large chestnut horse. He's filled out, grown stocky since we last saw him years ago. Gray streaks his short, dark hair, eyebrows bushy, and he's dressed in a thick winter coat the color of the blackest night.

"Luther, Deimos," he announces upon approach. Our guards part for him to join us.

Father pauses in front of us, permanently wearing that angry expression like he might strike out unexpectedly. Except we're not kids anymore. He is a lord, while we're princes, and hitting us comes with death, no matter who you are.

"So they sent you two? Not even His Highness can pull himself from his new throne to meet his old father." His nostrils flare, but I don't even speak to the man. The fact I'm out here is more than enough.

"Welcome." Luther sits tall on his horse, taking the high road. "The woods surrounding Shadow Court are dangerous. You will see Ahren and Mother soon enough." There's bitterness behind Luther's words.

Father snorts, his nose wrinkling. "Right, your land is still cursed. Shame, really."

With the vile smile tugging on his lips, it's easy to see he's enjoying every chance he gets to remind us of our downfall.

I grind my teeth, wondering if anyone will notice if we accidentally feed him to the Bloodcursed.

He glances over his shoulder and gives a low, short whistle at his men, and they begin coming toward us.

Father swings back to us. "Let's get moving. My ass and legs are aching from the saddle, and I want to hear everything about how King Tibout died. I've been hearing some strange rumors about your court, like a breach of Bloodcursed and fairies. Boys, maybe my arrival is exactly what Shadow Court needs."

He rides up ahead of us as though suddenly he is in charge. My insides sear with fury, and when I glance over to Luther, the corded muscles in his neck twitch.

Gods, it may not be the Bloodcursed that kills our father after all.

TWELVE

AHREN

"**G**et the fuck out of my room, all of you!" I bellow, fury tightening my chest.

The council members abruptly stop their bickering and jolt to their feet. They look at me like they heard wrong, except I couldn't be more serious.

"Out!" I snap and whip around toward the balcony of my study... the king's study.

I don't have the patience today for their ludicrous ramblings about where different guests are to be seated at the wedding, the whole discussion on how the king will be buried after the wedding, and how I am to be relocated in the palace in preparation for my new wife.

The notion has me feeling trapped, and I'm teetering on the edge of just walking away from everything. Everything I do is for duty, for loyalty, for my family.

But the cost is severe, and it's taking its toll on me.

All I can think about is Guendolyn and our time on the balcony. She healed my wings, eliminated the shadow I've lived under most of my life. And to thank her, I drove her away.

I'm fuming while my heart sits broken, a useless thing in my chest. How am I meant to marry another when the one person I would kill for is just out of reach? The hurt on her face is the worst... it destroys me to see her torn, to know I did that to her.

I clasp the railing out on the balcony and look down at the yard where guards and staff run around with decorations, making sure everything is perfect for something I don't fucking want. I'd give anything to be in their shoes, to just do a job and not have to make every damn decision for everyone. To be with who I want.

Tense, I grind my teeth, hating my life. I loathe getting up out of bed most mornings, and my stomach hurts unbearably. I can't remember the last time I had a full meal—nothing stays down anymore. I'm falling apart.

The door bangs shut behind me, and I twist around, expecting to find an empty room. Except Jasion remains, sauntering over to join me on the balcony, the fairy skull swinging from his neck annoying the hell out of me. It reminds me of Guendolyn. Everything does.

"Why are you still here?" I mutter.

"You're distressed. Good idea to get rid of the lot of them. They're a gaggle of geese going round in circles with no clear direction of what they want."

I return my attention to the grounds below. "And what do you want?"

He sucks in a sharp breath. "For Your Highness to be happy, of course. Remember all those years you spoke about what sort of king you'd become when it was your turn? How you'd make the kingdom a better place, ensure fairness and equality of wealth? I worry you've lost that spirit. Maybe the reality of being king is a lot more stressful than any of us realized."

His voice grates on my nerves, his words like a mosquito, constantly in my ear.

I straighten and face the mage as he leans over the balcony railing to stare at everyone working tirelessly in the courtyard. "Don't give me your pity, Jasion. What do you really want? I can tell when you're leading up to something."

He coils around to meet my gaze and squares his shoulders. His hair is wild today—more than usual—peppered with tiny feathers, which means he's been practicing magic.

"I worry for you," he states, like he does all the time.

But my thoughts sweep back to my discussion with Luther on our way to Ash Court, where he insisted Jasion was infatuated with me. I've heard similar rumors for years, but I never paid them any attention. Jealousy comes in all forms—except when I study the way he looks at me, it makes me wonder.

"What you need is a close advisor by your side who isn't a dusty old rat who'll leak information to anyone for gold coins."

I frown at him. "What are you implying? That my royal council isn't to be trusted?"

He breathes heavily like he carries the world on his shoulders. "Ahren." He steps closer—too fucking close for my liking. "Where do you think I learned that your wings are healed?"

I stiffen, his confession taking me aback. "What the fuck?" I growl.

His shoulders rise and stiffen. "You're missing the point. I am the only person on the council you can trust to have your back, so appoint me as your chief advisor to take some of the load from you. Let me deal with the intricacies of planning your wedding, of the funeral, of our guests. You should not be bothered by these things."

He has a valid point, but my attention remains on someone having watched me on the balcony with Guendolyn. Had they seen her healing my wings?

"What did they see?"

Jasion rubs a hand over his mouth as if having to think this through. "You were seen from the grounds elevating over the balcony, your wings bright and spectacular. This is a new start, like you were reborn, meaning you leave the past as just that."

I almost choke on the words 'new start.' What waits for me feels more like being herded into a corral where I'll be closed away for life.

"Leave," I command. "I need time to think."

"Of course." He bows his head and begins retreating. "Just remember, you don't have to do everything on your own. We've been friends for a long time, and I'm here for you."

His over-affection is wearing thin on me. While he makes some good points, I don't know how much faith I can put in him until I better understand his motivation. He and I may have grown up together in Shadow Court and shared experiences, but that also made me privy to the type of fae he is: manipulative, starved for attention, and in desperate need to prove himself. Those traits don't make him deadly. Yet with Guendolyn's mistrust of him and the conversations I've had with the king and my brothers about him cause me to question things. To look at him in a different light, which now leaves me now doubting Jasion.

Once he leaves the room, I turn back to look outside, needing to find a way out of my damn messed up life.

Guendolyn

An ear-piercing screech rips me from my sleep—if you call slumped against the wall, hugging your knees on the filthy floor of a prison any kind of sleep, that is. I don't even know how much time has passed. A full night? Hours?

Footfalls sound, and I make out the sounds of two people entering the dungeon. My stomach growls, and I'm certain it's starting to eat itself. Aside from water, the guards haven't given me a morsel to eat. And that's if they come to visit me at all. I'm alone down here, leaving me nothing to do but stew on my hate for Jasion. I hate him with every fiber of my being. My throat is raw from screaming, but no one can hear me down here.

The bastard mage is going to get rid of me without anyone knowing what happened. The princes will think I vanished, or maybe used a portal to run away after discovering Ahren was getting married. But I'd never run from Deimos and Luther. My time here has given me perspective. Ahren pushed me away, and it's my choice what I do with that. Not him or anyone else. So once all this bullshit marriage business is over, I'm going to ask Luther and Deimos to move with me out of the mansion, maybe even the kingdom. I don't care where we live, but I can't be under the same roof as Ahren knowing he is fucking someone else. It will rip me to shreds more than it already has.

The murmur of voices hums in the air, but I can't quite make them out, so I push myself up to my feet and quietly tread toward the barred door. I look out, but from my angle, I can't see who it is beyond the brick walls of my prison.

"You did a good job," a bristly, dark voice says in a whisper. I don't recognize who it belongs to.

"Just as you said, the bigger they are, the faster they fall," Jasion responds, and my hackles flare. I clench my teeth when I hear him.

"And Ahren?" the man asks, his voice vicious.

I freeze in place.

"He'll slowly come around," Jasion explains. "Then once you relocate here, he's ours to sway."

I don't dare move, going over and over what I've just heard.

"Come, let me show you the girl."

My heart slams into my throat as their footsteps close in. I throw myself to the nearest wall and slump down onto my ass, head low as though I'm sleeping.

A loud whack of metal against the bars has me jerking and snapping my eyes open. My breath catches as these two murderous monsters stare at me. Jasion and an older man with graying hair, wearing a long winter coat.

The older fae with longer ears leans forward, squinting his eyes to look at me. "So this is the whore who captured Ahren's attention? She doesn't look that special."

I hug my knees tight, unable to find any words that will make a difference to these two.

He tilts his head, studying me. I already detest this man as much as I do Jasion. I don't have a damn clue who he is, but I have to warn Ahren that he's in danger.

"She was found with the ruby from the king's throne. And she will be executed for treason before the whole kingdom the day after the wedding. But there's something special about her I haven't worked out yet."

The man sneers. "Get over here!" he barks at me.

I don't move.

Jasion glares at me. "Do as he says or I'll come in there and force you."

My skin crawls, and I want to scream at these assholes to leave me alone. But I push myself to my feet nonetheless and move toward them.

"Hand," he demands.

I swallow hard, terrified. "Please don't hurt me."

"Give me your hand!" he shouts, and I flinch.

Considering my palm still hurts from my failed attempts to remove the shards of ruby, I stick forward my other arm.

He lashes out and snatches my wrist, dragging my whole arm through the bars. The side of my face slaps against the metal bar, my body shaking.

The bastard sniffs my hand, the sight sickening me.

I'm locked in place, my stomach tight. The man's expression gives little emotion. I get the feeling that maybe he's incapable of showing any feelings.

Jasion is in my face in seconds, smirking like a gutless asshole. "Not so tough now without your prince." He enjoys seeing me squirm.

As I suck in a rapid breath, I take in the scent of strong cloves... a familiar smell I can't place at first.

Then a sharp pain digs into my wrist, tearing skin, feeling like blades.

I scream and wrench my hand back to find a goddamn bite-mark. The old bastard drew blood.

"You fucking pig," I spit as I pull down the sleeve of my dress to cover the bite mark, pressing the fabric against the wound to soak up the blood.

The dickhead licks the blood from his teeth, his eyes fluttering upward for a moment. "You're right, she's more than just a healer. The magic sparks in her blood. She will destroy everything we have worked toward for years. Kill her!"

"No!" I cry out and recoil, my knees buckling. It's only by a miracle that I'm still standing.

"I'll arrange it shortly," Jasion answers, then looks my way with the threat clear in his eyes that he'd prefer to torture me than make it a swift ending.

The older sonofabitch groans and turns away. "I've had enough of this depressing dungeon. I'm starved."

"Of course, your lordship." They both stroll away, the man barking in laughter, until the clang of the main prison door shutting steals the hideous sound.

I can't move, not after everything I've just learned. Fear grips me, and dark whisperings of nightmares coming my way drag me under.

But like a spark, the scent of cloves I picked up on Jasion clings to my nostrils, and the reality of it slams into me like a wrecking ball. Michae said he found cloves near the king in the throne room right after he was murdered. I thought it had been strange at the time.

Fuck! Jasion used magic to murder the king. My father. I knew it.

My stomach drops right through me like a boulder.

And I'm next.

The asshole blamed me, using the ruby as evidence. I'm his scapegoat, aren't I?

My chest burns with rage, my heart beating so fast and hard, the room tilts around me. They killed the king in cold blood for Ahren to get into power, to use him as a puppet. But my prince isn't that stupid. He can't be.

I pace mindlessly in my cell, both hands now hurting terribly.

Anger surges like a tsunami through my chest, and nerves dance across my temple. Darkness begins to linger inside me. My time is coming if I don't get out of here and warn the princes.

All I can think about is them, my throat thick with terror that I won't get a chance to stop this.

I close my eyes and take deep breaths to still my raging heart, and a flare of power erupts down my arms. My power sparks as a sharp ache digs into my cut palm from the ruby. Is my ability fluctuating because I shattered the ruby?

There is only one thing to do and it's risk, but sitting here is not going to help me. I raise my hand covered in dried blood and bits of stone too small to remove, bringing it to my mouth and focusing on the image of a portal opening to my room in the castle. Then I blow out a breath.

A surge of energy rises through me and rolls out past my lips. A pale blue fog puffs out into the air, billowing all around the cell until it concentrates in a corner, darkening until all that stands before me is a black opening just large enough for me to enter. I don't wait a single second longer and lunge toward my escape.

As I step through the portal, I whisper, "Please don't let this be a mistake."

THIRTEEN

I step out of the portal and emerge out into an oversized sitting room with pearlescent wallpaper. Long, narrow windows flood the room with natural light, while a fire roars from the hearth in the corner. Ornate wooden furniture decorates the space, and carved display cabinets are packed with all manner of books and colorful gems. Only when I look over to the two couches facing each other do I notice the back of someone's head.

My heart beats frantically because nothing in this room looks familiar. I've seen enough of the princes' mansion to know they don't have windows like these.

I'd been trying to get the portal to take me to my room, but obviously it didn't work. So where the hell am I?

I turn back toward the portal, except it's gone, and my insides freeze over.

Please, no! I raise my wounded hand, needing to get out of here fast. I give a quick blow over my palm, concentrating on my room in the mansion, yet not a single spark of energy comes. The more I try, the more I start trembling. This is the worst-case scenario, being taken to a random place. Sure, I escaped the dungeon, but where in the world did I land instead?

Wasting no time, I swing toward the black, wooden door and quickly grasp the handle...

"I wouldn't do that if I was you," a female's voice sweeps around me from behind.

My shoulder muscles bunch up, and I turn around swiftly.

Several feet away stands a jaw-droppingly beautiful woman who looks so familiar. She's older, maybe in her mid- to late forties, long blonde hair falling over her shoulders in soft curls. Delicate round face with the bluest eyes, pale lashes and deep red lips. She's slightly taller than me, curvy, and wearing a teal gown that's tight around her bust and billows outward like she has layers of fabric underneath. If there was ever an image of a perfect fairy tale princess, this woman was the epitome.

There's something quite familiar and calming about her.

"I-I think I've l-lost my way," I say softly, playing the innocent card.

She looks at me from head to toe, then to the door.

"You came exactly where you needed to," she answers. "The portal brought you here because this is your place."

What is she talking about? Looking around the room for anything familiar, I find nothing, and outside all that's in view are snow-covered woods for as far as the eye can see. There are no mountains, which is strange, as I'm used to seeing them from the mansion windows.

"Who are you?" I ask. "What is this place?"

She steps toward me, and there's a daintiness in the way she saunters. She is a woman of higher standing, someone used to always appearing perfect. I've seen the princes' mother, so I know it's not her.

But why is this woman locked in a room?

"Come with me." She offers me her hand, palm upward, the tips of her fingers slightly curled.

I should be afraid, but the energy around her calms me. There's something about this woman that makes me want to curl up and listen to her tell me tales. And she seems to know more about me than I do.

So I reach out and place my hand with the bite on my wrist in hers.

In response, she rewards me with a beaming smile that I feel deep inside me, like she's the sun filling me with a strange tranquillity.

She guides me over to a window, both of us standing side by side, staring outside to where the morning sun is just peering up over her horizon.

Down below is a lofty stone wall surrounding the building, the grounds dotted in trees, and beyond the barrier lies a creek frozen over by winter. Then the forest explodes outward in every direction.

It takes me seconds to realize I've seen this place before. I've been here...

and as the memory hits me, I gasp and pull my hand from hers, wincing with discomfort from the bite.

The yard below is exactly where Deimos and I first stepped out of a portal when he brought me to this realm.

I can't breathe.

I've teleported myself into Ash Court.

Fuck!

The woman smiles. "You remember, good. I watched you arrive that night from up here and have been keeping an eye on you ever since."

"How?" My knees wobble. The last time I came here, the king's mother tried to kill me, and well, will this woman do the same?

"There is so much I have to tell you. We don't have a lot of time—no one must find you here."

"Please tell me what's going on?" I hug myself.

She steps toward me, and I retreat.

"Let's take a seat." She waves for me to follow her back to the couch, where she sits and pats the seat beside her.

Not like I have many other options right now, and she hasn't threatened me, so I go and join her. She sits with her back straight, hands in her lap on the opposite end of the couch, facing me.

"I know who you are because I recognize the scent of your magic," she says. "I always knew you were powerful, with abilities like opening portals, like affecting other fae's abilities or vice versa. To me, you are beautiful, but your presence scares many others. You are a threat to them."

I wait quietly for more information, taking it all in, eager for the punchline to understand how all this ties together.

"What I was forced into doing to you has destroyed me." Her voice chokes. I don't even know this woman, but I lean closer and place a hand on her arm. She trembles under my touch.

"What do you mean?" I whisper, almost afraid to find out the truth.

She lifts my hand and kisses the back of my fingers tenderly. Not in a creepy way, but with a loving nature like I'd expect from a family member... a parent...

Then I see everything clearly, like a door has been opened in my mind.

The similarities I'm looking at are mine. The hair, the body shape, her tenderness. The agony that burns behind the gaze when she looks at me.

Tears prick my eyes. "Are you my mother?" My breath catches in my throat as her fingers tighten around mine.

"Leaving you in the care of the Women's Refuge on Earth was the hardest thing I've ever done, and I still haven't recovered." Tears slip freely down her cheeks. "You were just a baby, and if I didn't hide you, my husband and his mother would have killed you."

My head spins. I can't even respond at first from the shock of what I've just discovered. I try to hold myself strong, but my chin trembles. I shuffle closer, and she hugs me tight against her. I cry against her chest, and she's sniffling, both of us emotional wrecks. I always imagined laughing and smiling crazily when I finally met my parents, not crying.

But to discover I lost my father was devastating enough, and now... I found my mother. Is this why the portal brought me here when I asked for my room? It delivered me to where I belonged. To my mother.

Sorrow and unbelievable happiness twist inside me, tugging me in different directions until I don't know what I feel anymore.

I draw away from her and wipe my eyes with the back of my hand, then remember her last words. "I'm confused by so many things. You say my father wanted me dead, yet—"

"I didn't say *your* father, but my husband. I am married to the king of the Unseelie in Ash Court, but I never loved him. It was a forced marriage to unite two powerful houses."

"You're the queen of Ash Court!" I gasp and blink at her, processing everything I'm learning. "And you had an affair with the king of Shadow Court?"

Fresh tears gleam over her eyes at the mention of my real father, and she nods. "I loved him, but there was no way we could ever be together. Seelie and Unseelie don't mix."

I loathe that saying. I am a result of both, so I must be the most hated person in the world. I hold onto her arm and think how much it hurts to have Ahren taken from me, and I can see that same excruciating ache in my mother's eyes.

"Listen to me very carefully, Guendolyn." She leans in closer. "You are more powerful than any of us. The fairy blood that runs through my mother's family bloodline is the purest, from the queen of fairies herself. It's laid dormant in every generation since her demise, but when you were born, the fairies surrounded the castle in the hundreds of thousands, chanting the word *Eirian*."

"Fairy queen," I whisper.

"Yes, my little one. You carry the fairy queen's power inside your veins. It's one of the reasons the king and his mother wanted you dead. Your power is too great. It's why the king's mother put a curse on you when you were born, unbeknownst to me. She made it so that if you did somehow come back to our realm, your presence in our kingdom would unleash hell on the Shadow Court. A fitting punishment to King Tibout, my husband would remind me."

"So they knew you had an affair with the enemy king?"

She nods. "It's why I've been living under constant security for most of my life."

There's so much information coming at me that I sit back and try to sort through it all. Things are starting to make sense now… like the fairies' attraction to me, why everyone would hate me, and how I ended up on Earth.

"There's something else you need to know," she says.

"In all honesty, I don't know how much more I can take." With everything else that's happened in Shadow Court, all this news is overwhelming.

She continues regardless, "The main reason most fae want you dead is because you are the one true heir to reign over both Ash and Shadow Courts."

My mouth drops open.

She turns to me and grabs my arm tightly, her expression beyond serious. "King Tibout is gone. Before his son Ahren takes the throne, you need to claim that position and marry a royal quickly. Once you hold it, you will lay claim to the throne in Ash Court as well, meaning you can influence this court's decisions while the king and I still rule here. Once one of us passes, then you can claim this throne with your king and reign both courts. You will bring them back into one kingdom as it once was. The other kingdoms in the realms will join as well."

I'm shake my head. "What? You can't die!"

"Hush." She places a hand on my mouth. "I'm not going anywhere. I've waited for this moment for too long, I've lost too much—but now is the time to strike."

"I don't want the throne," I whisper.

"It's not about what you want, sweetie. This is the only way to stop the bloodshed between our courts, to end the deaths, to restore balance in our world."

I swallow past the mountain in my throat, pondering her words, mostly considering my three fae. "What will become of the princes? Can I marry one to take the throne?"

She looks at me strangely and smirks. "Has one caught your eye?"

I smile too widely, unsure how to tell her that it's in fact all three. "Sort of."

"To claim the throne, you must take someone royal as your king anyway, so yes."

There's an explosion in my stomach of anticipation and excitement at what she tells me. I can marry Ahren!

But just as fast, doubt settles in me as I consider the enormity of what she is proposing. "I'm not sure this is going to work. Why would they believe me when King Tibout can't back up my claim? And how does that unite the courts?" My knees are bouncing; I can't believe I'm even contemplating this. I barely understand fae customs, let alone know enough to rule. It's a joke to think that I could reign over anything when half the time I can't even control my own mouth.

"The answer is in your blood. Mages can test your bloodlines with magic—that is your evidence."

The mention of mages makes my skin crawl, because there is no way Jasion will ever help me. But the king has other mages, so maybe I just need to get them on my side. My breaths are coming fast now, and I'm struggling to fill my lungs. Am I really thinking of trying to claim the throne?

I shouldn't feel guilty, though part of me wonders how Ahren will react to this. Me stepping in...

"Maybe this isn't the best thing to do. I just want to fit in somewhere and have a normal life."

My mother stares at me with sympathy and cups a hand over my cheek, rubbing my tears away. "The biggest mistake I made in my life was that I never fought for what I wanted. I let fear rule my decisions. As a result, I lost my daughter and the fae I loved. I don't want you to live with such regret. It eats away at you; it's crippling. This is your chance to take what you want, to make a difference in a world that once tried to kill you just because you were different." She gets to her feet and takes my hand. "It's time to stand and show everyone who you really are."

I don't move at first but look at her, and the question swirling on my mind comes forward. "Did my father know about me?"

Her head lowers, but I catch the glint in her eyes before she whispers, "Yes. But he lost the chance to meet you." Her soft, wavering voice breaks me. She moves across the room to a display cabinet and pulls a drawer open.

I'm on my feet and meet her as she turns around. Taking my good hand, she places a long, pink ribbon in my hand. The fabric is soft like silk under my fingers, and on one side my name is embroidered in white, repeatedly. *Guen.*

"Your father had this made especially for you and sent it to me, but you were already gone by then. I never told him it was too late; I couldn't." She covers my hand with hers, curling my fingers over the treasured ribbon. "I can now say I've kept my word to him." She hastily wipes a loose tear from the corner of her eye, and the ache in my chest intensifies.

Clearing my throat, I say, "I spent time with him in Shadow Court, but I don't think he knew it was me. He made me feel comfortable and welcome when we had the chance to speak."

She reaches over and collects my cut hand, still embedded with shards of ruby, and places it between her two palms. "Sometimes, fate has a way of uniting those who are meant to cross paths, even if they don't know it."

Suddenly, her touch sends a flare of scorching heat up my arm.

I wince, and she lets me go. When I look at my hand, the cuts are all gone, and only dried blood remains. I glance up at her, bewildered.

"I have the power of healing and a few other tricks."

So it's her I gained my healing from. When I look at my hand again, I can't help but wonder if she's sealed the shattered pieces of the ruby inside my skin.

"Call your portal," she says abruptly, her tone rushed. "There isn't time to waste."

"Wait, what about you?"

"The wedding is today," she whispers, "so stop the marriage and claim what is yours. I will be fine. You coming here has been promised to me by the fated fairies, and everything will change from now on. You will see very soon."

"There's already been so much change," I murmur.

"Quickly now, you must go and claim your true heritage. Nothing else matters."

I have so many more questions for her, but she's right. I need to stop Ahren from marrying someone else. I lift a shaky hand to my mouth and blow a breath, blue air misting outward past my lips. *Return me to the Shadow Court in—*

My words fade as the portal materializes before me within seconds. This has never gone so easily before. Is it the ruby inside me, or my mother's help?

"Go swiftly." She nudges me in the back.

I stumble forward and cross the threshold into darkness.

FOURTEEN

"Have you seen Guen...Gainy?" I ask the twentieth staff member this morning, almost slipping up her name each and every single time.

The maid shakes her head, her gaze low. "Sorry, Your Highness, but I've asked around too, and no one has seen her since yesterday."

I snap away from her and march down the hallway, then swing directly into her chamber again, but I don't even know what I'm searching for, what could possibly indicate where she's gone to.

Luther charges into the room behind me, and my heartbeat spikes with hope, with anticipation that he brings news.

But the devastation on his face sinks through me, dragging me to a horrible place where I imagine that she's somewhere hurt. We never should have left her alone.

"Absolutely fucking nothing," Luther growls. "We've searched the palace and mansion, along with the grounds and town. I can't even reach her with my thoughts. Something's blocking her off from me."

I turn to my brother. "How did Ahren take it?"

Luther scoffs incredulously at my questions. "You think I'll tell him on his wedding day that the girl he loves has gone missing? But I did ask him when he saw her last, and like everyone else, it was yesterday."

I trudge over to the window, scanning the courtyard below for her long blonde hair, the adorable way she walks with a swing of her hips. I keep hoping I'll spot her and that this is just some huge misunderstanding. "He needs to know," I murmur as I turn to Luther. "Ahren will murder us if we don't tell him and she ends up hurt." I swallow against the lead ball pressing into my throat.

Luther runs his hand through his hair like he does whenever he's holding onto a secret. He's easy to read like that, plus his gaze is miles away.

"What aren't you telling me, brother?" I lean back against the couch, watching my brother, who stands several feet away by the window.

His head cocks up toward me. "Guendolyn healed Ahren's wings."

My eyes bulge. "That's incredible! He should be in a great mood then."

Luther's face scrunches up as his mouth tugs to the side. "Not quite. He told Guendolyn about his marriage and why he can't be with her. She ran away from him, and it's the last he's seen of her."

"Fuck, Luther, you could have started with that! So it means she's upset and maybe ran away to hide somewhere?"

Luther looks at me in disbelief like my suggestion is improbable. "She loves us," he says. "She wouldn't hide from us."

"We weren't here when she needed us most," I remind him.

His deadpan stare tells me everything. Yeah, we had no say in going to meet Father, but this fucking sucks.

"Alright," I state. "Where would someone devastated go?" Just saying those words out loud has my chest squeezing as I picture her somewhere alone and heartbroken. She needs to be in my arms where I can remind her she's *not* alone and explain why Ahren is in a shitty situation that will haunt him his entire life. I just wish Ahren would have spoken to her earlier as he promised he would.

I curl my hands into fists. This isn't how any of this is meant to play out. Luther and I had spoken about asking Guendolyn to marry us; we'd intended for the three of us to live in this mansion, making a new life together. It's everything I want, but I know she hurts for Ahren. And that's going to be a hard obstacle to overcome.

"We split up," Luther begins. "And we do another sweep, keeping in mind we are searching for places she'd use to escape everyone."

I nod. "We need to find her fast, as Mother will hunt us down herself if we miss the wedding. It's meant to begin shortly, and we're not even dressed yet."

Luther huffs. "I fucking hate this wedding." He pivots on his heels and storms out of the room and into the hallway. I do the same and decide to commence searching from the top of the mansion, then make my way down. There are so many empty rooms; maybe we missed something on the first sweep.

Around the next corner, I walk right into Jasion, who rushes without looking. Stumbling back, I groan while he bows his head.

"Apologies, Your Highness, for not seeing you. This is a manic day, and I have so much to prepare for the ceremony."

As much as I dislike the mage, I don't miss the opportunity to ask, "Have you seen Gu-Gainy?"

He stiffens at my question, piquing my curiosity.

"Well?" I urge him, stepping closer, my gut twisting in on itself. I've always hated him. As far as I'm concerned, no one will miss him if he's booted out of our court.

"This morning," he says and clears his throat, lifting his gaze to me. "I saw her just after dawn."

Hope springs to life inside me. "Where?" I eagerly ask, leaning forward.

"I was looking out the window as I awoke, and she was running through the woods outside the kingdom walls."

"What?!" I shout, unsure if I heard right. "Are you sure you saw right? There are fucking Bloodcursed out there."

He nods, his face paling, and there's fear in his eyes. Fear of me—and this isn't the Jasion I know. His behavior is strange, and that's saying a lot for him.

"I thought it was strange too, but I only saw her for a few moments and she was fine, so I just assumed all was well and someone was watching her back. I thought nothing more of it."

I'm fuming as I snatch him around the neck and slam him against the wall. "Why the fuck didn't you come and tell someone right away?"

He clasps my wrist as I squeeze his neck. How incredible it would be to get this weasel out of our lives for good. I've never liked or trusted him, but what reason would he have to lie about this? And... his story fits perfectly with the notion that she couldn't bear to be here during Ahren's marriage, so she ran away.

An invisible hand seems to wrap around my heart, constricting, the aching sorrow escalating. She wouldn't leave Luther and I... but that's something I struggle to believe, even after everything we've been through.

Jasion is hitting my arm, his face turning blue. Oh, right. Probably best I don't choke Ahren's mage to death on this auspicious day.

I pull my hand back and he falls to the ground, his knees buckling under him, gasping for air.

"The second you see her, bring her right to me, understand?" I growl.

He nods. "Of course, Your Highness," he croaks.

I can't stand to even look at him a moment longer, so I turn and march down the corridor, making my way down to the stables. Looks like I'm taking a quick trip along the walls for any signs of Guendolyn and pray to the gods that she's alive.

I'll tear down this whole fucking realm to find her if that's what it takes.

Guendolyn

I BURST out of darkness and into a dimly lit room. My eyes scan the surroundings, expecting to see my bedroom in the mansion.

Except, that's not where I end up, is it? The stench of the dungeon assaults my nostrils as I stand right back in the locked cell.

"Oh, fuck no!" I spin toward the portal that has vanished and curse the damn thing for never listening to my instructions.

I rub my eyes from irritation, ready to scream. I lift my hand to my mouth, but doubt floods me. God only knows where I'll end up. But when I remember my mother's words, I know I have no time to waste—I have to try.

Part of me just wants to celebrate that I found my real mother, that I finally understand my past. Sure, it was majorly fucked up, but it's a start to piece it all together and attempt to move on. So for that, I'll go in and out of my portal as many times as needed, pushing my limits until it takes me where I ask.

I remind myself that I have fairy powers, whatever that means. If I knew how to wield them, I'd zap out of here in a heartbeat and smite all those who've hurt me and those I love. Though considering how much difficulty I've had with utilizing my power, I somehow feel that it's going to take quite a bit of time to harness them.

Geez, what I wouldn't give for a manual—Using Fairy Powers 101.

A sudden creak of the main door into the dungeon erupts, along with footfalls.

I freeze over, terror clinging to me with the fear that it's Jasion returning.

Frantically, I press the base of my palm to my mouth, sucking in a breath.

"Gainy? What in the world are you doing here?" a familiar male's voice murmurs.

I twist my head and almost cry with happiness when I lay eyes on Michae. "Oh my god, you found me!" I dart across the filthy floor and lunge myself at the metal bars, shaking them. "Let me out, please, before Jasion returns."

"He put you in here?" His voice carries a quiver.

"The bastard accused me of killing the king and is planning to murder me, plus he's in cahoots with some old fae I've never seen before. God, Michae, please get me out." I'm rambling and bouncing on my toes, half expecting the mage to burst in here and murder him before he can set me free.

Michae searches the place but comes back with sorrowful eyes. "The spare key isn't here. I need to it."

I nod, my stomach twisting that he's going to leave me. "Please hurry!"

"Yes, I will," he assures as he rushes out, leaving me alone.

I pace back and forth and pray I'm not making the wrong decision to wait.

FIFTEEN

AHREN

"Where are they?" I ask Mael, frustration bleeding into my tone. "My brothers couldn't have just disappeared."

His brown eyes are wild with worry, and he keeps combing his fingers through his short, white hair in a nervous twitch. Like everyone else, he's dressed for the wedding in black pants and a leather doublet with silver buttons down the front. The fabric pulls across his middle, and his brow is moist with perspiration.

"Your Highness, I've sent the guards for another search through the grounds. We will find them."

I huff and turn away, biting my tongue. It's not him I'm furious at. It's this whole fucked-up situation. I'm here, waiting for the maids to bring my ceremonial clothes, and it's killing me. I want this shit day over with.

Today I will marry a princess, a stranger, a woman I don't desire, and the coronation ceremony will take place immediately after. The kingdom is celebrating my ascension to king, and I tell myself over and over that once I am in that position of power, I can change things.

Well, all things except the ability to have the woman I want by my side.

I had hoped Luther and Deimos would join me today for support, but it seems I've been forgotten, left behind. One more reason to hate this day.

"Having cold feet?" a male voice slices through my thoughts, a voice that sends chills through me.

"Father," I hiss through clenched teeth and turn to find him walking into my chamber.

"I was rather disappointed, son, that it's only now I get a chance to come and give you my blessings. I always knew you'd rise to something big. You just needed the right push."

The corded muscles in my neck tense. "That's not how I remember it," I answer, exhausted of the games—and the day has only just commenced.

He smiles at me, a rarity from the man who reminded me daily that I would never amount to anything, that I was weak, who told me that his beatings would strengthen me.

"Enough. Leave," I growl before I drive my fist into his face.

He doesn't move. "Son, I will admit some of the animosity between us might be my doing. I taught you the same way my father did me. Plus, I should have visited you here long ago to make peace between us. For that I hope you can forgive me, and we can begin a new path of truce."

I stare at him incredulously. Is he fucking joking? Who the hell is this man? My father would never grovel.

"What do you want?" I snarl, my pulse racing, throbbing through my veins.

The usual anger I'm used to seeing on his face is replaced with something pitiful. Has my father gone senile? Or did my mother invite him not just for the sake of diplomacy but because she has accepted the past as just that. Is this a clue that maybe we ought to do the same... if Mother can stand to face this fae for a few days to ensure relations with us and the east of the realm aren't broken, then maybe I can do the same?

"To be with my sons, and make up for lost time."

I struggle with my thoughts about following Mother's direction and blink at him in disbelief. Flames engulf my insides still the same. When I look at him, all I remember are his angry fits, the beatings, and the repeated times he ripped the flesh off my wings until it never grew back. That shit is something I'll never get over or forgive. I should have made it clear to my mother not to invite him.

"I don't have time for whatever scheme you have going, now that you know I'm about to take the throne. Maybe it's fear or stupidity that brings you here, but Father, the bridge between us fell apart long ago and there is no mending it."

He stares at me with contempt, an expression I'm much more familiar with. *There's* my real father. "I hope, over time, you can reconsider."

Without waiting, he lifts his chin high and turns around, his coat whipping around him as he leaves my room.

Today is going to kill me. It pisses me off that Mother insisted we invite that asshole to my wedding and coronation. It's a day I'll never forget, everyone tells me. And I agree, except it won't be for the reasons they assume.

Moments later, several maids appear at my door, looking at me expectantly. The brunette curtsies as she announces, "Your Highness, we are here to finish dressing you."

I huff. I know fighting this is futile. Such events are planned down to the most minute detail, so I wave them in, then let them fuss about with my clothes. I'm already wearing my black pants, and I remove my top to make it easier for the maids, who now flutter around me like fairies.

The thought of fairies brings Guendolyn to mind, and my heart constricts. Neither of us asked for this ending.

When the maids are finished, I look down at my deep blue, cut-velvet coat that drapes down to the floor. The edgings of the front and high collar are richly embroidered in gold, the designs resembling the sun and stars, the river and earth. The elements that combine to make up our realm. A maid takes my hand and pushes golden rings on my fingers, as is customary. Only one finger remains bare, waiting for the bride to adorn it during the ring exchange.

The ladies step back and admire me. They smile, proud of their work, but I feel like a fraud. Am I deserving of this role when I carry such heavy doubts?

"Thank you," I offer, and they bow, then hurry from my chamber.

Before I can take a peaceful breath on my own, my mother walks in. It's like my chamber is an entertainment hall. Is there a line outside my room of everyone in the palace coming to visit me?

"You look spectacular, just like a king should." She's at my side in moments, her embroidered silk gown as blue as the bright sky. Long-sleeved, her dress carries a high collar and follows her form before falling to her ankles. Small white flowers dot her curled hair, and she wears no crown or tiara, showing she approves of passing the position of Queen to my future bride.

"I'm not ready," I admit out loud.

She steps closer and cups my face. I study the deep lines at the corners of her eyes, the tiredness in her gaze, the grief still clinging to her forced smile. Now that she's lost her husband, it's up to me to care for her. Family is the reason I can't walk away from the throne.

"It's normal to be nervous, Ahren. But you've been preparing for this role your whole life. You just need to be yourself; everything else will fall into place. I'm right here by your side." She beams a glorious smile, and for a few moments, she makes me believe this will be incredible. Then I remember the ache in my chest, the emptiness in my heart, and the unbearable decision I've made.

"Are you ready to become king?" she whispers, the glint of tears collecting in her eyes with pride.

I used to dream about the day someone would ask me that question. Now, I wish more than anything I could turn it down.

Guendolyn

"Please hurry," I gasp.

I lift my head to Michae standing outside my cell, fiddling with a metal key he jabs into the hole. Finally, the door swings open. I run out and throw myself at my guard, wrapping my arms around his neck.

"Thank you, thank you, thank you."

He stumbles and laughs quietly, almost nervously.

"We have no time," he reminds me.

Breaking from him, I nod. "You're right. We have a wedding to stop."

His face blanches. "Umm, that's not what I had in mind. I was thinking of getting away before Jasion can find us, not being incarcerated for challenging royalty."

"You just have to take me to Luther and Deimos, and they will do the rest."

"Yes, miss. Now move quickly and quietly so we can get out of here before the mage returns." He takes the lead, and I stay close behind. Fear bubbles over me with the expectation that any moment now Jasion will curl around the corner of the stairwell. And I worry that Michae alone can't stop him.

Once out of the dungeon, we rush upstairs, my heart banging in my chest. By the time we reach the main door to exit the staircase, I'm breathing heavily.

Michae opens the door, peers out, then waves for me to follow him. I exhale loudly before swinging right to dart down the corridor decorated with animal statues. I've spent so much time in the mansion that I now recognize where we are going... right for the palace.

Abruptly, Michae turns toward me, snatches my arm, and shoves me with him into a room right next to us.

My pulse drums in my veins, and I catch the fear on his face. With the door shut, we both stay silent.

Male voices come from out in the hallway, and when a laugh comes, fire flares over me. It's Jasion.

I inhale softly while I look around the empty room in an attempt to calm myself. I never thought I'd hate someone as much as I do him. Just hearing his voice has my skin crawling. I want to strangle him, except my priority is getting to Ahren. And that means not getting caught by letting anger take me over.

When Michae clicks open the door, I freeze in place as he pops his head out and checks the hallway.

"All clear," he assures me.

I slip out, and we rush forward just as Luther bursts through the door that leads to the bridge between the two buildings.

I don't know who's more shocked—me, who flinches, or Luther, whose eyes practically bulge out of his head.

For a second, we all remain frozen, stunned. Then I push past Michae and run right at Luther. Throwing my arms around his chest, I press my cheek over his heart and don't let go.

His hands are on my shoulders, and he forces me to look at him. "Little wolf, where the hell have you been? We've been searching everywhere, and I couldn't reach you with my mind."

I meet his gorgeous but worried amber eyes. "Down in the dungeon. Jasion kidnapped me."

His body tenses, his upper lip curling. "I'm going to fucking murder him."

"We don't have time," Guendolyn cuts me off. "I have to stop Ahren's wedding before it's too late."

I stare at her, unsure if this is a result of her not accepting Ahren's decision, or if something else is going on. "You know it's the only way he can claim the throne, little wolf." My heart tightens, as I know this is killing her. "You will always have Deimos and me, baby." I draw her closer by her shoulders, but she brushes me away, anger twisting her lips.

"I know that!" she blurts. "You don't understand. There's so much I have to tell you, and fast. You need to be open-minded, alright?" She looks up and down the hallway as if to ensure we're the only ones around. Michae stands several feet away, but we're otherwise alone.

Leaning in closer, she whispers, "My real father was King Tibout. Eighteen years ago, he had an affair with the queen of Ash Court. I am their child. This is why those in power who know the truth want me dead. Because I'm the rightful heir to both kingdoms."

What the fuck?! My head is spinning. This is nothing like what I expected her to tell me. I was thinking along the lines of her sorrow and deciding she can't live here any longer.

I turn to her. "Where is this coming from?"

She grabs my arm, and I feel her shaking. "When we were at Ash Court to get the cure for Deimos, the king's mother told me about my father, and I should have told you and your brothers right then, but I didn't want to take away from Ahren claiming the throne. He deserves it. That's not what I want..." She pauses, breathing heavily, while my mind reels. "The most important thing here is that if I can show that I am the rightful heir to the throne, Ahren doesn't have to marry someone else."

Except she's wrong. The most important thing here is that she is claiming to be the heir to the throne. But how? "Are you sure?" I ask. "How can you be certain? Did the king say something to you when you spoke to him?" Hundreds of questions barrage my mind.

She blinks at me, confused by my questions, and that's when it occurs to me—if she is the rightful heir to the throne, it won't be Ahren, Deimos, or me in line anymore.

I sit with those thoughts for a while. Since moving to Shadow Court, being a prince has been driven into us and we are reminded of it daily. Told that we would hold great power and positioning one day. And suddenly, we're not.

I'm not sure how to react, but my thoughts are scrambling to make sense of it all. It would explain why she was cursed, why Ash Court wanted her dead, why the rumors and prophecies about her spread so fast in our realm. Were they all intended to make her a target the moment she returned home? All those tales about the curse were used to scare anyone from helping her get back to the Wandering Realm, when in fact the curse on the Shadow Court was because of the king's actions.

Fuck! She might be the heir to both thrones. A spell of dizziness overcomes me.

I swallow hard as I take everything in. "So if you take the thrones, you are set to inherit the courts from two of the biggest kingdoms in Wandering Realm. You will be the queen of both."

"That's what I just said."

"It only just sank in." I lean against the wall to hold me up. This changes so many things.

"I want you to know I don't want the throne," she admits. "But I can't cope with Ahren being with someone else."

"To be honest," I tell her, "I doubt anyone truly wants that kind of responsibility. Being the king or queen comes with expectations, and it changes you."

She blinks up at me, and I can tell she's trying to understand, but she won't until she takes the position. And as I picture her as queen—my queen—my breath catches in my throat. She will become the most powerful person in this realm when she claims the two thrones.

Fuck!

She doesn't seem to notice my shock and keeps talking. "Also, stupid Jasion sees me as a threat. I heard him conspiring down in the dungeon with an older fae I've never seen before, about how they killed King Tibout and planned to target Ahren to do their bidding."

"Wait! Back up! Jasion killed the king?" I snarl a bit too loud, my heart colliding into my rib cage. A primal growl rips through me—when I see him next, I'm tearing his head from his body with my bare hands. "That sonofabitch. That insignificant rodent has been playing Ahren all along."

"There's more. When I was in the dungeon, I used a portal to escape but ended up in Ash Court. In the Queen's chamber. And that's how I found out she's my mother." She digs her hand down the front of her dress and pulls out a ribbon. She stretches it out, and on it is embroidered her name, Guen. "She gave me this—it's similar to the one that had been on my ankle as a child back on Earth."

I rub my eyes as the truth settles in my mind. I'm still struggling with this news, and the implication is massive. "We need more evidence than just a ribbon." Sure, she's always had a bit of an otherworldly feel about her, and her power with the fairies is very uncommon, but the court will need more to prove she is the rightful heir.

"I know," she whispers, as if it's all too much for her too.

I draw her into my arms, a protective surge rising through me. I need to keep my little wolf safe from all the monsters who'd harm her.

"Will you help me?" she murmurs, staring up at me. "I need to claim the throne so I don't lose Ahren or any of you. I know how to get evidence to prove who I am... Well, sort of."

"Of course I'll help." There is no other answer.

"Good, then we need to use one of the mages—not Jasion, obviously— to test my blood. My mother said they have a magic test they can perform that can reveal my true heritage."

"I think that's true."

She holds onto my arm. "I have no other choice. We have to do this; it's a risk I have to take."

"I befriended one of the other mages years ago; he can help us. But I need to go stall the wedding or this is all in vain, so Deimos can take you to the mage," I murmur, then turn to Michae. He's my most loyal guard and has done everything in his power to protect my little wolf. "I saw Deimos riding his horse madly near the perimeter of the walls surrounding the castle. Go fetch him urgently."

He taps his chest over his heart twice, bows his head forward, then rushes down the corridor and vanishes around a corner.

"How long before the wedding?" Guendolyn's talking fast, panicking.

"Ahren should be already headed inside, but tradition has it that the new queen must delay her entrance. We don't have much time, but we need Deimos' fast." Even as I'm talking, my mind continues to reel with the news she's dumped on me.

"Will the mages be at the wedding?" she asks, distracting me.

I shake my head. "The old king's mages aren't invited to attend."

"Ouch, that's harsh." She's shaking as she rubs her arms as if cold, and all I want is to wrap her in my arms, for us to talk through what she's just revealed. Her ruling both courts means unity between our kind, the end of war and bloodshed. Mother used to tell me tales about the times when only one kingdom ruled the whole realm, a time when the world lived in the greatest peace in history.

Guendolyn paces in the tight space.

Today's going to go down in history. What my little wolf intends to do will cause an uproar. I can't help but be a little worried, though, because if she's wrong, she will be seen as a traitor, which means a sentence of death I'm not sure even we can stop. But she believes this wholeheartedly, so I have no choice but to believe the same.

I keep glancing at her as she chews on her lower lips. Worry washes over her face, and it hurts to see her so distressed.

"We'll find a way to stop the marriage."

She looks at me like a startled deer, but there's so much more behind those blue eyes. She's gone through such horrific ordeals, and for her to end up in the dungeon must have been terrifying. I tense each time I think about it, and it just drives me harder to destroy everything about Jasion.

"I don't want you to ever think I am doing this to gain power, because I'm not."

"Little wolf." I turn to face her, taking her hand to my lips to place a tender kiss on the back of it, not caring who sees. Nothing will be the same after today. "I don't doubt you for a moment. If that were the case, you would have tried to claim the throne as soon as the king died. Not to mention," I force a cough, "we might not be here right now, as you'd be in there marrying Ahren."

Her expression falls, and she draws her lower lip into her mouth again. "I didn't know the fae rules. I just assumed Ahren would take the throne, not that he had to marry as well. No one told me that part."

I swallow hard, wondering how different things would have turned out if we'd all been open with one another from the start. "You're right. We should have told you right away what was going on. We've all kept things from each other, but that ends here and now. And I also want to know why I can't reach you in your mind anymore?" As I say the words, my energy stretches out to her mind, like I always do when I talk to her, but there's nothing there. It's like I'm lost in a black hole.

"I don't know." She brushes hair out of her eyes and winces.

I catch dried blood on the side of her knuckles. "Show me your hand."

She lowers her hand and looks at her palm. The flesh looks dirty, with dried blood crusted across it.

"What happened?"

"I accidentally smashed the ruby, and shards went into my skin. I think some were still in there when my mother healed the cuts. Ever since the stone broke, I've felt different inside. Could that be why I can't hear your voice anymore in my mind?"

Maybe? I shrug, because I don't have an answer. This is all so new to all of us. She presses herself against me. She's so small and fragile, and I just want to keep her safe. Except she's a lot stronger than she appears—a lot more than any of us knew, apparently.

"You need to know something. The way I found you on Earth was by using magic... a spell that was initially meant to help me track down my fated mate."

"Fated mate?"

"Yes, we are meant to be together. And I'm convinced it's the same between you and my brothers. Our destinies are intertwined."

She smiles like the admittance is something that brings her joy not surprise. "So, does that mean all three of you, in a perfect world, would be happy to be with me at the same time?" She chews on her lower lip.

"Yes. It's not unheard of in our realm."

Her smile widens and I adore the gleam of excitement in her gaze.

Loud footfalls grab my attention. Deimos marches over to us, arms swinging by his sides, the panic on his face sliding away as he gets closer to us. Michae follows soon after.

"Deimos!" Guendolyn pulls away and runs to him. They collide, and he embraces her, lifting her off her feet. They kiss, and I smile to see the happiness we inspire in her, and what she's brought out in us.

They fall into a deep conversation, Deimos' face twisting with anger. And by the look of my brother's dropped mouth and the way he freezes on the spot, he's learning about who exactly our little angel is. Must be precisely how I looked when she told me.

"Deimos," I call out, and he twists his head in my direction as I march up to them. "Now that you're caught up, we have to move fast. Take Guendolyn to visit Ramond in the basement and get the blood test done. I have a wedding and coronation to stall for as long as I possibly can without getting tossed into a dungeon myself. Then come to the great hall, fast." My words are rambling, as panic now spins in my chest.

"Why don't you go to your mage friend, and I'll do the distraction," Deimos offers.

"Because the moment Ahren sees you acting up, he'll kick you out. He won't expect it from me. Now go!"

"Thank you," Guendolyn says.

Deimos gives me a begrudging nod, and I see the questions burning in his gaze. But like me, he knows we don't have the luxury of time if we intend to help Guendolyn.

"Good luck, Luther," he says, and I huff a laugh because if anyone needs luck, it's him and Guendolyn. They're the ones who have to get the evidence to stop the wedding.

I take off and call Michae with me, proclaiming, "Let's go and get into a lot of trouble."

"No matter who you are, you are still my Guendolyn," Deimos states, his fingers squeezing around my hand lightly. That has to be the sweetest thing he's ever said, loving me for who and what I am.

Deimos and I walk hastily through the palace, which is terrifyingly quiet. Only a small handful of guards are here and there.

"You know just the right things to say to make me smile," I answer. "But all this stuff is happening so quickly that I don't have time to really think of the implications. Right now, I'm going on pure instinct, and my priority is to not lose the three fae I want in my life forever."

My thoughts keep swinging back to Luther and Michae having to stall the wedding. My nerves are tight, worried that they are too late.

Deimos half laughs, drawing me out of my thoughts. He always has that effect on me. I will never get sick of hearing that beautiful sound, either. It always lifts my spirit. "*Stuff* like you being a queen of two king-doms? Do you know how unheard of that is? Some would say it's impossible."

I shrug as he hurries me down a set of grand marble stairs. Paintings adorn the walls, depicting numerous royal fae in elaborate clothing, in stiff poses that are obviously staged. They are royalty, while I'm... I feel like the lost girl. How can this be my future when I have so much to learn about this realm? Honestly, I didn't even know Ahren had to marry to claim his throne, and that's just one tiny detail of fae culture. So how am I supposed to rule a kingdom?

"There will be portraits of you, too, before long," Deimos tells me, noticing me staring at the past kings and queens of Shadow Court. "You will be stunning."

"Do you think anyone will accept me as their queen? I didn't grow up here." My voice cracks with uncertainty.

Deimos stops in front of me and takes my hands. "They will love you because you will be the Queen of Ash and Shadows."

I eye him. "Is that a real thing?"

He chuckles to himself and drags me back into a fast walk down the rest of the steps. "Just made it up, but I like the sound of it." The smirk he offers is hypnotic. At the bottom of the stairs, he says, "After all of this is done, you and I are spending some serious time together. Just like you and Luther did. Just want to make sure you are aware of that."

He's referring to Luther's proposal to me... I can tell by the way he glances down to the ring on my finger, and despite the mess we're in, he keeps making me smile. "I sure hope so."

"Good." The next thing I know, we're rushing along a darkened corridor that gives me the creeps. Before I can ask any questions, we stop outside an arched doorway, and he bangs his fist on the wood.

The door opens, and we're greeted by a mage I'm not familiar with—then again, I've tried to not pay them too much attention. Like the rest, he's dressed in the usual mage garb, his white hair short and less wild compared to the others. He looks to be in his thirties, his skin tanned like he spends too much time outdoors.

"Your Highness." He bows his head but keeps his eyes on me.

Deimos steps forward. "Ramond, remember that favor you owe me? I'm calling it in."

His face blanches, and he pauses for a few moments before responding. "Shouldn't you be at the wedding?"

"Can you help me or not?" Deimos persists.

The mage stiffens in response. "Of course, Your Highness."

I look past him and into his room, which contains just a simple, small bed, a bedside table, and a wardrobe, with no window. Just candles. This place is depressing, and it almost feels like the mages are put here to be out of sight from others who might fear them.

"Thought so," Deimos answers. "We need to go to your ritual room."

Ramond's brow furrows into dozens of lines in confusion.

"Can you determine someone's heritage through magic?" my prince asks.

The mage stares at me, studying me. Does he recognize me as the princes' healer, like most in the court? I can't help but wonder if he hates me as much as Jasion does.

"I need blood samples, one from the fae being tested and one from the bloodline in question."

His response leaves me frozen on the spot, and Deimos looks at me for a moment, his lips pinched. My mother hadn't said anything about needing a sample from the original bloodline. Then again, she rushed me out of Ash Court fast.

"It's my blood we need to test against King Tibout's," I admit, my insides jittery with worry that they won't have any samples of the king's blood. If he just died, maybe there's a possibility of still getting some from him? The thought turns my stomach, but a wave of desperation constricts around me. "Please, we don't have time."

The mage's eyes narrow. "What's this really about?"

"Listen, Ramond. I heard a rumor that you keep samples of dead royalty blood."

I glance over to Deimos, unsure if he's making this up or it's a fact. And if the latter, why?

"Who have you been speaking to?" His eyes half hood, shadows darkening around him.

"Jasion," Deimos spits.

"Curse him to the Seven Hells," Ramond snarls.

Interesting to see that even the other mages hate Jasion that much.

"Get what you need; we're doing this now," Deimos growls. "I don't care why you have the blood, just fucking take us to it."

Ramond nods. "Your Highness, it's to keep track of bloodlines through history. It helps us trace which lines are the closest aligned to the fairy queen and those of the first fae."

"I don't give a fucking shit!" Deimos snaps, then unleashes a deep exhale. "Get your ass moving!"

Ramond nods, panicked, then hastily emerges from his room and into the hallway.

"This way," he instructs.

Deimos collects my hand, and we're practically running to keep up with the mage, who takes turn after turn down halls where darkness seems to breed. As many questions as I have, I keep quiet, because everything seems to echo here.

The walls are dark stone, and unlike upstairs, there are no paintings. It's depressing here, but the air also feels charged, the hairs on my arms lifting.

At the end of a long corridor, Ramond stops and fiddles with a bunch of metal keys dangling from the chain around his waist, then unlocks a door.

We step into the room, my curiosity piqued by what's inside. Black walls, mostly covered in shelves and shelves of jars filled with powders and liquids in all kinds of colors. Down the middle runs a long table that isn't too different from science labs back home. It smells musty in here, like no one has ever let in any fresh air, ever. The one large window against the back wall is covered by material that has long ago faded to a yellow color, while cobwebs fill the ceiling corners.

Ramond is in the back corner opening a dusty-looking, vintage cabinet. He huffs while jars clang about as he looks for the right blood, I'm guessing.

Deimos' hand squeezes mine lightly, drawing my attention to him. He blows me an air kiss, and I lean against his side. How did I get so lucky to have these princes fall for me? Everything I do now is to hold onto them.

"Found it," Ramond calls out and sets a black vial on the counter, then sweeps back around and heads to the wall covered in floor-to-ceiling shelves. Two seconds later, the whole wall swings open to reveal a hidden compartment.

My mouth drops open, and I peer inside, but only darkness looks back. Ramond vanishes inside.

"Did you know that secret room existed?"

"Of course." Deimos releases his hold of my hand and marches over to investigate. He clearly had no clue.

Just as he pokes his head in, Ramond reappears and Deimos retreats. The mage is carrying a birdcage large enough to hold a parrot, except he's got a fairy trapped.

My stomach constricts, and I step closer to study the creature fluttering around crazily, trying to escape. It doesn't look well. Its wings are forest green, but the skin on its face and body are sickly pale and streaked with cherry-red veins.

"Why is it imprisoned?" I ask just as the fairy throws itself at the cage, eyes red, mouth gaping open. Razor-sharp teeth bared, it hisses at me. It's nothing like the fairies I've seen before.

"Something's wrong with it!" My insides curdle to see it captured this way.

The mage swings the cage away from me. "It was bitten by a Blood-cursed, but it still holds a lot of power regardless and does the trick, especially since capturing a normal fairy is difficult. By feeding it two drops of different types of blood coupled with the sprinkle of some magic, it will reveal if the blood samples are from the same family or not."

"Bring it all, we need to go. Now," Deimos says as he crosses the room to stand by the door. "I just hope Luther's held off the wedding this whole time."

"We're doing the test at the wedding?" I gasp just as Ramond, carrying everything, rushes past me.

"We need the council and Mother to see the evidence with their own eyes."

I join them quickly as we rush back along the hallway and up the stairs. My breathing speeds up as nerves pinch down my spine. I know Deimos is right, but what if something goes wrong?

Upstairs, we turn onto a wide corridor lit by windows on one side. Farther in the distance are two white doors, like we're about to enter the pearly gates. Is that where the wedding will be held? The thought has goosebumps sprouting along my arms.

I reach over to Deimos just as my sight catches onto a familiar man farther down the hall, talking to several guards. I squint for a better look. White hair, the long coat—I gasp. It's the asshole from the dungeon who conspired with Jasion to kill the king.

My knees buckle as I drown in dread. Deimos feels me falling behind and turns to face me, his expression swimming in concern.

"What's going on?" he asks.

"It's him." I hate that I try to make myself as small as possible to conceal myself from the man.

Deimos follows my gaze to the older fae, then looks back at me. "Who? My father?"

His words are like a blade slicing at my insides. *Crap!* "That old fae is your real father?" I almost choke on the words. The fucking asshole who ripped Ahren's wings.

When he nods, I suck in a shaky breath. "That's the man who had Jasion kill King Tibout," I whisper. "I heard him praise Jasion for it and say how the bigger they are the quicker they fall, and how they planned to conspire against Ahren to get power in this kingdom. He also intends to relocate to Shadow Court." I try to remember what else I heard while my pulse thumps with adrenaline.

Deimos stiffens, his jawline clenching, twitching. "Are you sure?"

"Yes. The asshole bit my arm." I frantically pull up the sleeve of my dress and show him the ugly mark. "I'll never forget him."

His face burns red like he's about to explode. Fists coiled, he turns from me, but I lunge after him, snatching his coat. "No. Not now. We don't have time right now."

The mage stares at us bewildered, holding onto the fairy that starts screeching in the cage, drawing everyone's attention our way.

Deimos shakes me off and storms over to his father.

My heart beats harder, because this is going to go really bad.

I exchange looks with Ramond, who shrugs like he's used to seeing this kind of drama in the court.

"Fuck, we need to stop him," I say.

I race after Deimos, but before I can get to him, Deimos has lunged himself at his father, throwing him off his feet. Both are on the floor, my prince laying punch after punch into his face.

I should cringe, except I'm cheering on the inside, because his father deserves the worst things in the world. He wanted power, a foothold in this realm, and he got Jasion to take a life. Seething, I tense up, loving every hit Deimos delivers.

Four guards stand around watching for a few moments, probably unsure what to do. After all, Deimos is a prince, *their* prince. Someone who can have them imprisoned for harming him.

Except moments later, two of the guards lunge forward and heave the prince off his father. "Deimos," I say from behind him. "Please, we need to go."

He faces me, the anger flaring over his expression. I somehow suspect that attack had a lot more to do with how he was treated growing up, more so than just revenge for King Tibout's callous murder or the way I was injured.

He wipes his mouth with the back of his hand. "You're right." His chin lifts to the guards briefly, then he looks down at his father. "Take him to the dungeon and lock him up."

Then he takes me by the elbow and guides me around his father still on the floor, and together with Ramond we close the distance between us and the white doors.

"Halt!" a male's voice calls out from behind us, and we all instinctively glance over our shoulder just as those same guards now march after us with determination.

Deimos' father stands up. He's not being apprehended, he is brushing down his coat and sneering in our direction.

"Take her!" he growls. "She is an assassin! She killed King Tibout!" Seconds later, he darts down a corridor.

What the fuck?

"No!" I recoil. "That's not true."

When Deimos nudges me aside to take a protective step in front of me, I stumble against the mage, both of us teetering while the fairy in the cage goes crazy. Ramond pushes the cage with the fairy into my arms and turns to face the onslaught. Already I can feel the prickle of magic in the air.

The guards slam into Deimos and Ramond, the momentum sending them all crashing against the white doors, creating a tremendous boom. Who the hell are these guards to attack a prince?

A massive man in uniform cracks his neck, straightens his clothes, and saunters toward me with the promise of retribution.

Oh, fuck!

in from the windows clearly shows every disgruntled face... mostly those from the bride's family.

"This madness is enough," Mother groans in my ear. "End this now before we become the laughingstock of the realm."

I clear my throat, stand from the throne, and march over to my brother, who's swinging his hands wildly in song about getting drunk before a wedding. He's even coaxed one of his guards to participate with him, who keeps beat by clapping.

We have a great band of talented musicians in the corner who can do nothing but stare on in bewilderment.

Stepping down from the platform where my bride will join me—if she ever arrives—I approach my brother.

He senses me and turns to meet my gaze. The look he gives me is one of pleading for me to back off. In his eyes, I see how hard this must be for him, how he is pushing through this, not for himself... So that means it's for Guendolyn.

Of course that's what this is about. What the hell are they up to? I'm torn, because I want to humor Luther another moment longer to find out where it's going, but the tension in the room is about to explode.

Abruptly, the two doors into the hall burst open, one of them breaking off its hinges, wood splintering everywhere.

Someone screams as two bloodied and bruised guards roll into the room, coming to a stop at the line where the seats begin. They don't move.

The crowd breaks into hysteria, several women yelling with shock.

Deimos strolls into the hall with a bloody lip, his double-breasted doublet ripped at his throat. He's not even dressed in wedding attire. One of the mages he knows, Ramond, joins him, also looking roughed-up with messed up hair, a bruise under his eye, and his necklace sitting over his shoulder.

Behind them enters Guendolyn, carrying a large cage with a fairy fluttering around crazily inside. She looks around sheepish, scanning the enormous room filled with people. When I look outside the room and into the hallway, I find more guards laying on the floor, bloodied and unmoving. Why would the guards fight with Deimos?

I move forward, my heart banging in my ears, waiting for this to somehow make sense. Is this another joke to delay the wedding even further? Fury collects in my chest. This wedding is hard enough as it is; I just need to get it over with. This foolishness ends now.

"What the hell is going on?" I demand.

"Is this no longer a wedding, but a freak carnival?" one of the older council members calls out from behind me.

I stiffen as guards from the room close in on either side of Guendolyn and the mage, then I spot my father slipping into the room, sliding in behind the crowd like he's running late.

"Deimos, what the hell are you doing?" I call out, confused and frustrated. I don't fucking want to marry a stranger, but the throne must be mine to save our family.

My brothers know this.

"Ahren," Deimos begins and Luther steps aside. It seems his part in this ridiculous charade is over. "Before the marriage commences, crucial information has come to light." He wipes the blood from his lip. "King Tibout has a child who is the actual rightful heir to the throne."

The whole room falls silent, and I'm not sure I heard him right. I tense, leaning forward slightly. "What are you saying, brother?" I snarl. What is he doing?

I tense as he takes Guendolyn's hand and brings her forward. Ramond collects the fairy cage from her grasp. She stumbles on her feet and stands before me. The girl I love looks at me with uncertainty, with fear on her face. My insides clench. She's everything I want, my dream, my fantasy, my future... but not in this lifetime, according to fate. Being this close to her does things to me, breaks me over and over to the point I no longer know how to be the fae I once was.

"What in the world is going on here?" my mother says, her footfalls closing in behind me.

"It's true," Guendolyn answers, raising her voice to ensure everyone hears her. "King Tibout is my father. I'm sorry to say this in front of everyone, but the king had an affair with the queen of Ash Court, my mother."

The room breaks out in an explosion of gasps and whispers, and my mother pauses by my side. I'm confused.

"Is this a joke?" I growl.

"Brother." Luther steps forward. "Listen to her."

I turn to my mother, whose face pales as she blinks tears from her eyes. I reach over and wrap an arm around her back. "Come, I'll walk you back to your seat."

She pushes me away and whispers, "I always knew he was seeing that fae, and about the child too, but I accepted it for you three to have a home, a future. I was told she was gone and would never return to the realm."

My throat thickens, and her agony shatters me. Living with such knowledge would have torn her apart, but she did it, nonetheless.

And that means I am not to take the throne today.

"We still loved each other," she admits. "In our own ways. Sometimes you do things in life you don't want for the greater good." She looks at me, clearly referring to me marrying the princess from the east kingdom.

When I stare at Guendolyn and my brothers, a fiery surge of anger rises through me. "You had to wait until now to tell me this? Fucking now?!" Why didn't she tell me earlier? If it's true, I could have married her today and avoided all this.

Betrayal washes over me, because if she cared for me, she would have told me this already. I don't understand... Does she want the throne for herself?

Every eye is on us, every ear taking in the drama that will forever be attached to this kingdom.

"There is evidence for this," the mage who came with them announces. "Well, there will be, once we conduct a test to confirm this girl is indeed, King Tibout's daughter."

The murmurs in the crowd quiet down, and it almost feels like everyone is leaning forward to listen. Mother is right. We will become a joke.

But if Guendolyn is the king's daughter, she has the right to claim the throne before I wed. Though she can't claim it without marrying someone herself.

This is why Luther made a complete fool of himself, isn't it? To help her gain the throne... is he intending to marry her?

Hundreds of questions flood my mind, only adding to my confusion.

Except anger keeps surging within me, growing, while an agonizing heartache spears through my chest. I can't believe Guendolyn and my brothers would keep this from me. I've always been there for them, doing what I think is right. I'm burning up, wanting to demand they tell me the truth.

"This is absurd," Jasion's voice streams across the great hall, tearing me from my thoughts. He's marching toward us from the side of the hall, his jawline clenched tight. Fury flares on his face. What the fuck now?

He reaches my side in moments, his breathing fast. "You cannot allow her to turn this most sacred of ceremonies into a spectacle. If you want to know the truth, it's that she is a spy in our kingdom. I have actual proof that she killed King Tibout."

"That's a lie. Jasion killed the king and conspired with your real father to do it," she shouts.

The shock of her words leaves me speechless. I've started to have doubts about Jasion... but to kill a king?

Deimos flies at Jasion, his punch leading the attack. It clips the mage right in the nose, sending him to the ground in moments.

"What the fuck?!" I grab the back of my brother's doublet and force him away from the mage.

"Has everyone gone mad?" I shout, which does nothing to silence the whispers that spread through the room like wildfire. This is not the venue for secrets to be spilled or accusations to be fired.

Jasion climbs to his feet, blood dripping from his nose. There is no way Guendolyn would kill the king... she was with us when it happened, so that alone confirms Jasion lies. Is he covering up the guilt over the death of the king? I glance over the crowd to where my father sits at the edge, watching with amusement on his face. If there was ever a guilty face, it's that one.

An inferno of anger envelops me at the thought that he had something to do with the king's murder.

Guendolyn steps toward me, but I'm shaking with anger. The repercussions of this will be enormous. Not to mention airing out all of this to all the lords of the kingdom, including my father, who must be beside himself with joy to see us like this from amid the spectators. With the way the bride's advisors glare at me, I doubt this union is happening today. Her and her parents are in a room, waiting to be called for the marriage. And of course, there's the king's sister who sits in the crowd too, waiting like a buzzard to claim the throne. I glance over and find her smirking to herself.

My blood boils, but I can't lose control. That's what everyone expects. What I need is to understand what Guendolyn knows about the murder and how it involves my father and Jasion.

"Can we focus on one thing at a time? If the king has a child, we need proof," one of the council members behind me calls out. "Then we need evidence of who killed the king."

An ache starts at the base of my head and spreads fast, the stress mounting by the second.

I turn to the mage grasping the cage with the fairy. "Show us the evidence. And be fast about it. My patience is running out."

"Your Highness," Jasion insists, his voice loud and clipped. "You can't seriously be entertaining this. She murdered King Tibout."

I swing around and grab him by the throat, drawing him to me. I'm barely holding onto any semblance of sanity, and this asshole pushes me by counting on me not knowing he lies.

"Be very careful what you say when I know you're lying," I growl.

His face goes as white as snow, but then I witness his expression morph into confidence within moments, like that's all it takes for him to reconstruct his story. I've always thought he was a friend, but that was a huge mistake on my part. I see that now. I release him, and he stumbles on his feet. Once this is over, I will personally interrogate him. I look over to my guards to call them over when Jasion's voice sears across the room to ensure everyone hears.

"Your Highness," he continues, and my fingers twitch into fists. "Surely you are aware that permitting someone to challenge the claim to the throne comes with repercussions. If this girl, *this assassin*, cannot prove she is the rightful heir, then she will face death in her attempt to usurp the throne."

I swing toward him, my fists tight. His words sucker-punch me right in the gut. I glare at him, picturing how I will destroy him. "You are not—"

"Agreed," my mother calls out from behind me. "Get this absurdity done, then everyone who disrupted this ceremony will be interrogated and face the harshest of punishments. This is enough!"

The crowd cheers in a kind of maddening approval. I look at my mother, infuriated that she's siding with Jasion. But at the same time, I can't begin to imagine how hard this must be for her. To lose a husband she knew cheated on her, then to have his child come to claim the throne from me. To be reminded of his infidelity.

"Guards," I bellow. "Apprehend Jasion and lock him up in the dungeons."

The mage's face falls as two guards from the side of the room carry out my order. Fury twists Jasion's face, hatred pouring from him, but I can't stand to look at him another moment. I curse him under my breath and vow that once this is over, he will be tossed to the Bloodcursed for all I care. No interrogation needed—his fate is sealed in Shadow Court.

I glance over to Guendolyn, who's chewing on her lower lip, fear building behind her eyes. She meets my gaze, and my first instinct is to pull her into my arms, to take her out of here and get her to tell me everything. But I don't move, because that's not going to work. Not when hundreds of fae are invested in this scandal. The only way to douse the flames is with a public display of the truth.

My mind is foggy as I contemplate Guendolyn's intention to take the throne as queen. I won't deny, at the back of my mind, I ask myself if part of her motive is to make me suffer after I pushed her away. To take away the one thing I picked over her...

I shake my head. She wouldn't do that.

My thoughts linger to when we were last together on the balcony and she healed my wings. To her torn expression when I turned her down.

Why didn't she tell me about her ancestry before?

A loud clap draws my attention to my mother. "Perform your test up here for all to see." She's furious and won't even look at me. She fears losing our home if the test proves truthful, not to mention the wolves within the crowd ready to pounce.

The mage carries the cage up the steps and stands in the middle of the stage, looking toward Mother and the council. I move to take a seat alongside her, while my brothers come to stand on either side of us.

Guendolyn climbs the stairs, holding her head high. For her sake, I pray the test proves she is who she claims to be. Not being with her is one thing, but to have her executed will end me. The ache in my gut returns, the muscles in my shoulder blades pinching with stress. It's snowballing, and each breath comes out ragged.

I sit next to Mother, my whole body tense as shit, and I wait. Guendolyn looks so nervous. It's difficult to watch her this way when I want to protect her from everyone—except she's asking to be at the forefront of everything.

She hid this secret from me. It didn't have to end up this way.

"Ramond, you may commence," Deimos instructs.

The mage nods once and sets the cage on the floor near his feet. "I don't carry a blade on me," he says. "I need a few droplets of blood from..." He glances over to Guendolyn, clearly not knowing her name.

"G-Guendolyn," she says softly, her gaze traveling to us before returning to the mage. There are gasps through the room, even my mother's breath catches at learning who stands before her. The cursed girl from our realm.

The mage doesn't seem to bat an eye and pulls out a small wooden bowl the size of my palm from the pocket of his robe-skirt.

I stand and draw a blade from my waist, then approach her. She gingerly offers me her hand palm side up, the mage gripping the bowl close to catch the blood.

She's soft to the touch, and I feel her trembling. "It's going to hurt just for a bit," I whisper.

"It's alright," she reassures me. Like it's me who needs comfort when her life is at risk. I don't even know if I'll be able to help her if she's accused of treason and sentenced to death. And I struggle to breathe at the thought.

"Are you sure this is what you want to do?" I hesitate a bit, speaking softly so the others don't hear.

She blinks up at me with the same heartache in her eyes she carried on the balcony. "There's nothing else I want more than to be with you."

The mage next to us clears his throat, but he remains in place with his bowl. My breath catches, and all the emotions I've shoved deep inside me burst to the surface. The ones that insist I walk away and just follow my heart. To claim the girl in front of me, to be happy for once in my fucking miserable life.

That's when I realize she doesn't want the throne for herself, but to ensure I take it with her.

My throat thickens, and I don't move. Not when I see everything she's going through for me.

"Do it," she whispers. "Please. Just cut me."

Silence permeates the room, everyone seeming to wait with bated breath.

So much rides on this, so many people's lives and futures.

"I hope you're right." I make a quick swipe over the meaty part of her palm, the blade biting into her flesh. Blood bubbles quickly along the cut. She tilts her hand to the side as red droplets roll down her palm and trickle into the bowl.

When a small puddle is collected, the mage says, "That's enough."

Guendolyn pulls back, and I hand her the handkerchief from my pocket. I tuck my blade away and return to my seat. My gut tightens, and with each passing moment, unease curls inside me. I feel like I'm about to watch the world's biggest disaster, and I'm doing nothing to prevent it.

I glance over to Luther, who gives me a reassuring look like we are doing the right thing. How can he be so sure?

The mage retrieves a small black vial from his pocket, uncorks it, and starts pouring what looks like someone else's blood in with Guendolyn's. "This is King Tibout's blood," he announces.

Not a single word can be heard from the packed room. The silence is strangling me.

Once he has the vial closed and back in his pocket, he crouches by the cage.

The fairy inside sits against the back wall, silent, watching him with huge eyes. Opening the small latch at the side, he quickly slides the bowl into the cage before retracting his hand. A light blue energy stretches from his fingers to the bowl, vanishing as quickly as it came.

He lifts the cage and turns toward us. "This fairy has been bitten by a Bloodcursed, and with my magic, when it drinks the blood, it will react in one of two ways. It will either sit calmly, which will tell us the bloods are from the same bloodline. Or it will go ballistic, crashing into the walls to escape, as it'll be momentarily poisoned by the mixed blood."

Guendolyn stands nearby, pressing the handkerchief to her cut, and like the rest, her eyes are glued to the cage.

The fairy wanders over to the bowl, where it drops to its knees. In the silence of the room, the fairy lapping the blood is all that's heard.

Moments later, it jerks its head up.

Guendolyn hugs herself, and I can't move. I'm frozen in my seat, waiting, desperate to see this succeed. *Please, let this work.*

The sudden explosion of the fairy's wings shooting outward on either side of her, green as moss and beating frantically, causes my heart to race and a terrible ache to sweep through my gut.

The fairy starts spinning mid-air inside the cage, faster and faster. She isn't bouncing about crazily though, but remains in one spot, whirling around.

"What does that mean?" I demand.

The mage licks his dry lips and glances over to me. "I've never seen this before."

A gasp falls from Guendolyn's lips, and the whole room bursts into sound. It isn't long before a few start demanding her death.

CHAPTER

NINETEEN

GUENDOLYN

My heart beats frantically, and I try to curl in on myself, wanting to vanish right here and now. My gaze darts between the spinning fairy in the cage and the perplexed mage as the chants for my death escalate.

These fae don't even know me, yet they want me dead? How in the world are they meant to embrace me as their queen when they're tossing me aside so hastily?

Power flares down my arms. It's getting to the point where I don't care about the throne; I don't care about anything but trying to be with my princes. Maybe the answer lies in me taking all three with me to Earth and make a go of things there. But that'd be running away from my problems, wouldn't it?

I approach Ramond and whisper, "Can we try again, please?"

He looks at me with sympathy and nods. Ramond, thankfully, is nothing like Jasion.

Luther and Deimos step forward, while I hold Ahren's gaze. They support me, but he must have doubts that I'm not telling the truth—otherwise, why does he hesitate?

I try to think if my mother said anything else about how to do this, anything we may have missed the first time around. I can't stop trembling, fearful of what will come next.

Luther comes up to me and leans down to whisper in my ear. "Let Deimos and I take you from here safely."

I lift my head and look into his eyes. "You believe me, don't you?"

"Yes, but it's not about us, little wolf. Right now you're in danger. Please," he whispers, his tone shaken.

The sound of something clanging draws my attention to Ramond, who's taking the small bowl out of the fairy's cage. The moment he does, the poor fairy collapses to the ground. It crawls over the side of the cage toward me and grabs the metal bars, staring at me with the most heartfelt eyes. No longer does it look wild and ready to tear into anyone who gets too close. It's calmer, and all I feel is pity for the little thing.

"Guendolyn," Luther persists in my ear.

I face him. "Please, let me try one more time. Give me that."

There's no hesitation. He nods, and I have to resist the urge to hug him. I need to be strong and appear in control, even though inside I'm filled with turmoil.

Luther addresses the royals and council. "Now that our initial trial is complete, we will proceed with the actual test."

Jasion groans loudly. "She is a traitor, and you are openly allowing her to betray you." Why the hell isn't he in the dungeon like Ahren ordered? Several others in the crowd start echoing his words, which was exactly his intention.

"Luther," the queen warns.

The prince addresses everyone in the room. "I don't know about the rest of you, but when someone claims to be a lost heir, it is our duty to give them every chance to prove their stake. If King Tibout were alive, he'd agree, and everyone here knows it." He turns to a guard.

"She's bewitched the prince. You all can see she failed the test. We don't need more proof. She killed the king and now she's trying to take the throne."

"Gag and tie up Jasion now!" he roars.

A guard snatches Jasion and forces him to a seat, tying him up and gagging him.

"My Queen, this has gone on long enough. Please, I implore we push ahead with the ceremonies," a male intones from behind me. It's one of the councilmen, an old, stuffy fae. The others around him nod their heads.

Voices from all around start to rise as everyone chats amongst themselves. Sweat drips down my back, and I swallow hard. The councilmen break into an argument, and the realization of how horrible this is going sinks through me.

I look back to the fairy and reach over to stroke its wing inside the cage. It doesn't look crazed any longer but more like a fairy who's lost, and I'm left wondering if feeding it my blood has had this effect.

"Let it out," I say to Ramond, but he doesn't hear me and is staring wide eyed at something at the entrance to the hall.

An explosion of panicked voices booms from the crowd as attendees scramble away from their seats and spread outward in the room.

Emerging through the doorway is my mother. My mouth drops open. She's wearing a pale blue gown glinting with diamonds, her hair pinned off her face with a glittery crown, lips rosy and bright. She's beautiful. Stunned is an understatement on how I feel. What is she doing here?

Behind her, half a dozen guards in the dark uniform of the Ash Court march in tight formation.

"Mother!" I call out, gaining everyone's stare. The way Ahren looks at me in shock resembles his brothers' expressions as they tried to comprehend who exactly I am, reminding me that Ahren hasn't heard this part of my story yet.

In fact, everyone glares at me that way, disbelief and confusion about how I could be both the daughter of a Seelie and an Unseelie running rampant.

She smiles at me, but before she can speak, someone else steps forward.

"Son," Ahren's father emerges from the cowering masses. "I can't sit back any longer and watch this embarrassment. You are in over your head. It's clear that witch has invited the enemy into our court, and yet you still haven't summoned her arrest?! Has she bespelled you, or is her cunt truly made of gold!"

Deimos throws himself off the stage to lunge at his father, roaring like a beast, face contorted with fury. Luther and Ahren on his heels, seizing him by the arms to hold him back. But by the raging anger twisting their expressions, at first I can't tell if they are stopping Deimos so they can get to their father first and beat the hell out of him.

"Fuck you!" Luther spits, gaining gasping shock from the guests.

This is turning into a spectacle, and their fucking asshole father has to make a show, doesn't he? I steel myself and glare at him, my hands curling into fists. I'm furious at his words, but at the same time panicked at the mounting tension in the room.

"Apprehend the queen!" Ahren's mom bellows, rising from her throne, drawing away from the explosive thickness in the air.

"No!" I cry out, lunging for the steps to reach my mother's side.

"Is that the welcome I get after I had my mage end the curse on your kingdom, under duress mind you? The creatures are no longer lured to your kingdom. They're still around eradicating them completely is a lot more complicated, but the mage with his dying breath was able to stop their bites from transforming anyone into a Bloodcursed." My mother's eyebrow arches, and the whole room gasps. These creatures have plagued these lands for a long time from what the princes had told me, so this is amazing news. "I did it for my daughter, for your kingdom to embrace her, and I risked everything for this to work."

Someone claps in the crowd, then more follow, standing up because she has eradicated a huge problem.

But when a sudden spark booms in the room from our right, everyone flinches with fright. I smell electricity in the air. Magic, to be more precise.

The Shadow Court guards draw their swords in unison and I flinch from the abrupt, ringing sound. They appear stiff, their eyes pale, glazed over like zombies... like they are being controlled.

"Ahren, son, you must be able to see through their ploy to take your throne from you. King Tibout is dead so he can't dispute this. But even I can see it clearly what is happening here."

"This has nothing to do with you, Father," Ahren growls.

One of the guards slashes the cords binding Jasion's wrists and gag, and he's up on his feet, joining the princes' father. They sneer, looking at me. "Change of plans," Jasion declares as more guards dart into the ballroom from the hallway, blocking off everyone's exit. And that's when it hits me that this is all Jasion's doing and why the guards don't apprehend him. He had this orchestrated from the beginning.

"Guards, stand down," Ahren commands, Deimos and Luther moving to his side and drawing their blades. Their mother, along with the council-men, recoil to the rear of the stage. But no one listens... They are under Jasion's control now.

Fear lifts the hairs on my arms. This is going to turn into a bloodbath.

"It didn't have to be this way," his father says. "But maybe this is what this kingdom needs. A clean slate and a new beginning. A new king in charge."

"Father! This has nothing to do with you," Ahren snarls.

But with a single whistle from Jasion, the guards charge, attacking anyone in their way—Shadow and Ash Court alike—as they carve their way toward us.

The screams are ear-shattering, and dread shakes me at the core. Instinct and panic take over, and I race down the aisle to my mother as she runs to me. Fear tightens her face even as she hurls her arm outward, a blast of power colliding into a guard coming for her, tossing him into the hoard of soldiers. She gasps and slows down suddenly. I take her arm.

"I'm not as strong as I once was," she says amid the chaos.

"We need to get you out of here," I shout, grasping my mother's hand, drawing her toward the stage while my three princes and Michae leap into battle alongside the Ash Court guards.

Screams and chaos spread like wildfire. The clang of metal resonates, while fear strangles my heart.

And there it is. As soon as something good is about to happen, the universe says, *Fuck you!*

The air thickens with hatred and death so fast it leaves my head spinning.

"Your Majesty," I address the princes' mother. "Stay close. I'm going to get you both out of here."

I'm shaking furiously as I call to the power inside me. I stare at the palm with shards of ruby inside. *Please work.*

"I'm Queen Sarey," my mother says to the queen, who looks torn, her eyes glinting with tears. "This isn't the best circumstance for us to meet, but please know I have always held the highest respect for you."

"Oh? Did you respect me when you were sleeping with my husband?" she spits while more people run onto the stage, crying.

Shit, this isn't the time for this.

"After Guendolyn, we stopped seeing each other. He truly loved you," my mother explains, stretching her hands out to the queen. "I wish I would have come to you earlier and explained it all."

But I don't have time for this.

Just as I realize I've lost track of where my princes are in the fight, Luther is tossed across the floor, blood streaking his cheek. Jasion throws a ball of energy at the guards standing in his way, while the princes' father pushes a woman out of his path so can he reach the stage faster.

My pulse is a raging storm. Ramond is at the edge of the stage, looking like he's attempting a spell on the battle, except mages need the proper ingredients to empower their magic. Whatever he does will be weak, but at least he's trying. Near him sits the fairy in the cage. And a better idea comes to me.

I lunge for the cage and fumble with the door, opening it. The fairy flutters out instantly, its wings wide and beautiful.

"Please will you help me?" I cry out, outstretching my hand that has the ruby embedded.

As if understanding, it flutters and lands on my wrist.

The princes' mother gasps from behind me. "You have the power of the fairies?"

"Yes," my mother explains. "Just like my ancestors. This is why she is the rightful heir to not only the Shadow Court throne, but the Ash Court throne as well. You don't have to like it, but deep down inside, you know it's right."

The princes' father charges onto the stage, pushing others aside and coming at me so fast I don't react quickly enough. His fist finds the side of my face, and I see stars as I fall backward with a thump.

Wings flutter in my face, and a hissing fills my ears.

"You will ruin everything," he snarls. His shadow towers over me, and I open my eyes as the fairy flings itself to his face, scratching and biting him. He bats at the fairy like a lunatic.

My mother throws her arms toward him, and the fairy flings away from him in that same moment.

An explosion of air punches the old fae in the chest, and he's hurled across the room where he slams into a pillar. He groans and slumps to the ground, and I do a small cheer on the inside.

My mother stumbles on her feet as if suddenly exhausted, barely catching her breath. The queen of Shadow Court catches her around the waist. "I have you."

I get to my feet, trying my best to ignore the pain flaring down my face like it's on fire and concentrate instead.

"Take everyone as far back in the corner as you can." I gesture the queens toward the part of the stage where the gutless councilmen hide like rats. My mother helps keep everyone together behind me, as far from the danger as possible.

The fairy returns to my outstretched wrist once more. The battle spreads to my left, guards against guards, princes, and some of the guests who've harnessed knives to fight against the possessed soldiers.

I can't see Jasion anywhere, but I don't have time for that right now.

Energy flares down my arms and I lift the fairy closer to my face. It mimics me, and we both blow a breath onto our palms. Blue haze spills past my lips.

"Fairies," I whisper, and my little friend makes a sound that sounds very close to *Eirian*.

In seconds, a black portal spreads out before me, growing in size. My skin ripples with goosebumps from the power. The sounds of battle and screams surround me, but I try to focus on what I've opened, praying this works. My fairy takes off and vanishes right into the portal. Oh, crap. That wasn't the plan. Maybe I'll get all the guests to do the same.

A sudden punch drives into my lower back with such force, all the air is knocked out of my lungs and my legs buckle. I drop to my knees, gasping, arching my back from the ache zigzagging up my spine.

An arm locks around my throat and wrenches me to my feet and up against a hard chest. "Got you, bitch!" Jasion snarls in my ear, strangling me.

I struggle against him, shoving my elbow into his gut and kicking my heel into his shin. "Let me go!"

His grip tightens. "You will die today!"

Dread shudders through me.

"This is something I should have done long ago." He raises a blade over my chest.

My life flashes before my eyes, and with it comes visions of everything that will be ripped from me. This piece of scum will kill those who mean everything to me and take away what I've fought to find my whole life—my family and happiness.

When I catch sight of Ahren pinned to the ground by two guards, Deimos is surrounded by three others, and Luther is thrown into a wall, my heart bleeds.

I draw on everything inside me, every thread of power, and call it to the surface just as I had back in Ash Court.

A blast of energy launches from my hands so ferociously that I'm suddenly shoved back into Jasion, both of us stumbling. His grip loosens, and I pivot on my feet, driving my palms against his chest. All the power inside me pummels into him.

He's thrown backward and onto his back in an instant.

His eyes widen into orbs, the blade drops from his grip, and he glances down to his chest. Blood seeps from where my energy hit him. A terrifying cry spills from his mouth as he frantically wipes as more and more blood emerges from his pores.

An explosive flutter of air zooms right past me on both sides.

Wings are all I see at first, violets and greens and magenta, then I make out the dozens of fairies—no, hundreds of fairies—swarming through the great hall.

I yelp with joy at seeing them—they are the most incredible sight.

A group rushes over and attacks Jasion, surrounding him until they coat his entire body. His screams are all I hear, while wings beat around him.

Maybe I should feel pity, but the vindication of giving him exactly what he deserves is the sweetest satisfaction ever. After just a few moments they pull back from their assault, leaving behind the clattering of bones falling to the floor. Clothes. Hair. And a few flecks of blood.

That is all that remains of the fucking asshole mage, and even that is too much. I'm going to make sure every bit of him is burned to ashes.

The guests at the far end of the stage are crying out, ducking from fairies who aren't even touching them. My mother stands before them, looking at me with a wide, approving grin. "Finish this," she says.

A fairy with glinting blue wings flutters in front of me and waves.

I blink to clearly see, and my heart beams. "Hiss!" I can't stop smiling because this little critter is exactly who I'd hoped to call. "You came!"

Eirian. The word streams over my mind, and she swings around and hisses, pointing to the chaos.

I turn to the hall where the Shadow Court guards are no longer fighting but cowering away, falling to their knees before the princes with remorse, with confusion. Which confirms that Jasion did indeed spell them.

Dead bodies litter the floor, fae who lost their lives because of two greedy bastards. And my sights set on the princes' father, slithering like the snake he is to dart out of the room. "Hiss, bring him to me."

She catapults across the room like a torpedo, an arrow of fairies right behind her.

They collide into him, taking him off guard.

He spins around, his face contorted in panic as he sees what's coming for him. His screams are music to my ears.

The gorgeous little creatures swarm him as he fights against them, flinging his arms out, but he's off his feet in seconds. They carry him over to me, then drop him down where he collapses onto his knees in front of the steps before me.

My three princes approach their father, as does his ex-wife. My mother is by my side.

"Ahren," he grovels. "Will you let her hurt me? I'm your father, your flesh and blood."

My prince steps up to his father, his expression one of pure hatred and fury. He lifts his fist and drives it into his father's face, sending him to the floor on his back. "I no longer have a father."

Ahren then unbuttons his jacket and lets it drop to the floor behind him, followed by pulling his top up and over his head.

The Queen on the stage gasps, but I know exactly what he's doing, and I love him for this.

His shoulders curve forward as the back of his shoulder blades split downward. Wings push out of his back, the sound like leather rubbing together. They spread out on either side of him in glorious blues and violets and white. Spanned outward, they a large portion of the room's width. My prince lifts his chin, not ashamed of what his father told him was wrong, and I'm so fucking proud of Ahren.

The whole room is oohing because their prince has the most spectacular wings, which I believe is rare.

He glares down at his father and says, "You tried to break me, but it didn't work. Fuck you!"

He glances at me and gives me a nod of approval, as do Deimos and Luther. I glance over to their mother, who is red in the face with fury. "Kill him!" she demands.

I smile while the worm writhes, crying for escape.

"He's yours, Hiss." I point to him, and the fairies descend on the old fae in seconds.

They are ruthless, biting, tearing skin, gouging holes in his face and body. I refuse to look away, because if I intend to take my role in this realm, I must show strength.

My princes stand by, watching the man who brought so much grief to their lives finally get what he deserves. Though in truth, I do feel like they are killing him a bit too fast. This should be elongated, drawn out a bit more.

The slurping and chewing sounds are muffled by the terrified sounds of the guests. Yep, this is definitely not the wedding that was planned. I somehow doubt anyone will ever forget today. Ahren draws back his wings, and gets dressed, and I catch the smirk on his face. This is something so long overdue for him.

Most in the audience don't know where to look... him or the ruthless end to a horrible fae.

My mother comes to my side along with Ramond, carrying his bowl of blood.

"It's time they saw the truth so you can take your rightful place," my mother reminds me. She grasps a blade and runs the sharp end down her palm in a quick swipe. She turns her hand sideways and lets her blood drip into the bowl that still holds blood from King Tibout and me.

Ramond runs his hand over the liquid, blue energy covering the surface. Then he offers the bowl to Hiss. "This will work on any fairy," he reassures us.

Hiss looks at me, and I nod, praying this time goes better than the last.

My heart beats frantically. Nerves zip up my spine with worry that this will fail.

I remember when I was small, and I once had to wait for blood test results because they feared I might be epileptic. The wait was excruciating. But that doesn't come close in comparison to this. This is a hundred times worse.

Ahren's face is stoic, eyes glued to Hiss, who lands on the mage's arm and leans in, tasting the blood. Seconds later, she is feverishly lapping at the offering.

Her head suddenly jerks up, mouth covered in blood, more dripping from her chin. Her eyes are wide like she's tripping on something really good.

I want to shut my eyes and turn away so I don't have to watch this. All I can picture in my mind is her bursting about wildly. Coldness floods me, and it chills me at the core. My knees tremble.

The fairy dunks her face back into the dish, loving every drop.

My mother takes my hand in hers and leans over. "There is nothing you need to fear. Ever again."

Suddenly, the little critter pulls her head up, and several people in the room gasp in anticipation.

I hold my breath, watching her surge into clumsy flight toward me, her wings stretching out, twitching. The more I look at her, the more I expect her any second now to burst into a frenzy.

My mother grasps my arm.

And I hold my breath while we wait.

CHAPTER

TWENTY

AHREN

Every inch of me aches, including where I'd been kicked in the balls by a fucking guard. But now I can't move as I follow every stiff, jutting movement the fairy makes.

This day will go down in history—the entire realm will talk about this—but all I care about is keeping Guendolyn safe. If she'll have me, I'll take my place by her side.

The fairy suddenly drops out of the air and lands clumsily on Guendolyn's shoulder. Finding her balance, the fairy settles down on her knees. Her head tilts downward, and she begins to snore softly. Guendolyn collects her into her arms, while the rest of the fairies surround us and watch.

"It's a match," Ramond announces loudly, making everyone flinch. "Guendolyn is the daughter of King Tibout of Shadow Court and Queen Sarey of Ash Court. She is the rightful heir to both kingdoms."

No one dares speak or even move with that announcement, and I'm bursting with joy on the inside. I want this for her more than I could have ever thought. "Oh Guendolyn," I say and move to her with haste. "This is everything you deserve."

Guendolyn gasps, her expression one of shock, as if she can't believe her ears. With glistening eyes, she wraps her arms around my middle, and I embrace her, kissing the top of her head.

My mother looks at me strangely.

EIGHTEEN

AHREN

A thunderous boom escapes from behind the doors leading into the main hall, cutting off Luther from his ridiculous singing. A ritual he insists that comes from historic books. I'm not sure if I want to laugh or kick his ass for making a fool of himself in front of everyone.

He sounds like a dying animal. At least the noise has given us a reprieve.

But when the boom doesn't come again, Luther howls another rendition, standing in the middle of the passage that divides the guests into two groups.

Mother glares at me, shaking her head, her perfectly styled white hair bouncing over her shoulders. I hate to see that amount of distress twisting her expression, especially in front of our guests.

"What is he doing?" she hisses.

I know he's stalling, but I can't even begin to understand why. My new bride still hasn't arrived, which I'm guessing is also due to Luther's influence in trying to delay the inevitable.

The great hall is elaborately decorated for the grand wedding of the century. Floral arrangements adorn the white walls, golden vines curl around the marble pillars, while the perfectly white rug that runs down the length of the room is bunched up under Luther where he keeps shuffling about like a madman.

The council members sitting to my right are furious, shifting about, while the guests are more shocked than entertained. The sunlight pouring

"This is who I want to marry," I declare loud enough for all to hear. "If her and the Queen of Ash Court will have me."

"Yes," she answers. "I want to marry all three of you."

There are gasps from the crowd, but it isn't an uncommon event for a queen or king to take more than one partner to rule alongside them. My brothers join us, and I've never been so happy. I never expected to find this kind of joy amid death, never expected that somehow I'd find a way out of the corner I'd been wedged into.

I glance over to where the guests are dispersing around the room and catch the eye of the advisors from the kingdom to our east. I was meant to marry their princess, yet they stare at me with anger burning in her eyes. My first point of call is to address this with them and apologize for how today has turned out. I wave over to my advisor, Mael and instruct him to take our guests from the east to where Queen Titania, her husband and daughter wait in the castle. "I won't be long and don't let them leave." It's a hard conversation I am hoping I can smooth over for the sake of our relations.

"Of course." He bows his head and rushes away. I hate that they've been put in this situation, but I won't change that I finally got what I wanted.

The queen of Ash Court says, "This test confirms Guendolyn's true legacy as a descendant of two royal lines. And by the looks of our winged friends, my little girl also has the fairy queen's power." She clears her throat and looks over to my mother and then the council, who stand amid the crowd of guests, huddled and utterly shocked.

I'm still dealing with learning that Guendolyn is the princess of both Shadow and Ash Courts... and now, added to that, she is now also the queen of the fairies. My mind can barely comprehend this turn of events. If anyone deserves this, it's my Guendolyn.

"There is more," the queen says. "Many know my daughter as the cursed girl in our realm, but not many understand she was cursed as an infant by my mother-in-law and husband so that she would never return to our realm to claim the thrones and to unite our kingdoms. I was never given a choice and did what I could to protect my girl, which is why I hid her amid humans in the Earth realm. But now that she is back, I want to bestow a gift upon her for all the wrongs done against her. To make things right."

She moves to take her daughter's hand. "My bloodline is of the original family that came from the fairy queen herself. I was forced into a loveless marriage. Now I am taking a stand. I am officially abdicating my position as

Queen of Ash Court. The throne is open to be claimed by a family member as I have stepped away. And my husband can't do anything about it as you are the heir by blood." She glances over to Guendolyn, who is crying happy tears.

My stomach knots up, because this is unprecedented. No royalty has ever renounced their throne. Deimos' mouth drops open, while Luther blinks in disbelief.

"Mother," Guendolyn whispers, her voice shaken. She draws away from me and rushes into her arms.

My heart warms to finally see Guendolyn find her family, to know where she belongs. I grew up loathing what my father did to me, so focused on becoming a better king, on what changes I'd need to make in order to achieve some semblance of happiness in the future, that I didn't see that I already had everything I needed. It took a while, but with Guendolyn, we got there. And there's nothing I would ever change... though I do wish the path here wasn't so treacherous or heartbreaking.

I turn to my mother and collect her in my arms, as do my brothers.

"Looks like we have another wedding to plan?" she says, tears pooling in her eyes, glancing up at me, smiling like she used to when life was easier.

"And you're fine with the union between the kingdoms, with us three marrying her?" I ask.

"Of course. I lived too long with hatred; now I just want peace, and grandchildren. And if this brings my three boys what I couldn't have, then I give my blessing."

"About time!" Deimos calls out, drawing everyone's attention.

Guendolyn glances over and laughs like she can't believe this is happening. The rest of the guests and councilmen are silent, clearly lost for words.

I step aside from my family and kneel in front of my queen, my brothers following suit.

"Guendolyn, to make it official, will you have us three as your husbands as you claim the thrones?" I ask, wishing I had a ring to offer her.

The way she looks at us is heart-warming, and a tear slips down her cheek. "Absolutely. It's why we did all this. So we can all finally be together."

In that same moment, the fairies break out into a beautiful song and begin fluttering around the room in a splendid aerial dance.

My heart thumps, and adrenaline races through my veins. We have found our queen. This is the day I've dreamed of... to get what I want in the end. Never believed it could happen, but now that it's here, I will fight to the end to ensure it remains. We will prove ourselves to her.

I tilt my head as she kneels in front of us and she embraces us all saying, "Please tell me this isn't a dream?"

We all burst out laughing, and I lean in to brush my lips over hers. I try to act casual, to pretend my heart isn't pounding in my chest and that I want to scream at the top of my voice that she's mine. Instead, I just whisper, "This is only the beginning of your new life."

CHAPTER 21

GUENDOLYN

One Day Later

'm in my room in the mansion, staring out the window at the landscape. The rolling hills and woodlands coated in snow, the superb sunlight brightening the blue sky, the landscape that I reign over. Me, the lost girl who only wanted to find her family, but instead, I found something more incredible than I ever thought possible.

The notion of who I really am and what this means still doesn't feel real, but I haven't been able to stop smiling or spinning around on the spot each time I think about how things ended up.

I recall a corny saying about how when life gives you lemons, you give it lemonade back. Well, I've just created the fucking golden ambrosia of the gods' kind of drink with my lemons.

Don't get me wrong... I'm nervous as hell to become a Queen. But I get to be with my three princes unquestionably now, and that is what I really care about.

Yesterday's events at Ahren's wedding to a princess turned into a whirl-wind. Everyone keeps telling me, the day will go down in history, talked about across the realm, and my name will be on their lips. The cursed girl who will become Queen. Songs will be written about me, and in truth, that just makes me laugh because it can't be me they are talking about.

The princes had assured me, they are by my side and I will make a strong leader, and while I believe them, the trepidation that I will fail everyone drags heavily through me.

So, I escaped to my room where it's quiet. After all, the princes have been dealing with the guests who came to our court from far away kingdoms for a wedding that never happened, not to mention the princess and her family. Everyone has been welcomed to remain a few extra days so they may attend the real wedding.

A buzz runs down my spine at the thought of my marriage, and those butterflies spring up in my stomach. This is happening.

This is actually happening.

Goosebumps cover me with elation.

A knock at the door has me spinning around to find Michae in the doorway, hands stiff by his side, a relaxed expression on his face. "Prince Ahren has requested your presence." He bows his head forward. "He has something to show you."

"For me?" My nerves start dancing beneath my skin.

Michae smiles calmly, reassuring me. Then he gives me a cheeky grin. "Shall we go, my lady?"

I follow him out into the hallway where it's quiet. Majority of the staff are in the palace to clean up after yesterday. Others are helping with my wedding. Apparently, I don't get a say in how it runs. Under Fae customs, it's up to the mothers of the bride and groom to arrange all the whole event. I am hoping this means my mother and the princes will start to get along.

Michae walks me through the mansion, over the bridge and soon brings me to a small enclosed courtyard with a clear ceiling to view the sky. The castle walls surround the gardens on four sides. Flowering trees of pinks and whites dot the land. Roses and flowers scatter in between, along with shrubs. There's a small vegetable garden to my right, and even a round marble fountain, spouting water. This is a greenhouse, and it's spectacular.

Half a dozen butterflies flutter through the air, and I already want to move my bed here.

"Follow the path," Michae tells me, and when I turn toward him, he's retreating inside and shuts the door.

There's only exhilaration in my veins. The two fae from the court who wanted me dead are gone, and I doubt Michae would put me in danger after everything we'd all experienced recently.

I take a step forward, then another over the cobblestones dotting the ground, while flowers of every color surround me while the butterflies sweep around. I pass trees with gold and red globes like apples, the air heavily perfumed with lilac and vanilla scents. I feel like Alice in Wonderland, my stomach a buzz with adrenaline of what I'll find. And why haven't I been taken to this garden before? Only once I curve around a large weeping tree, does a wooden hut with a pointy roof come into view. No windows, but there's an open doorway.

Curiosity has me lifting my deep red dress that dances around my ankles and hurry forward.

Stepping up to the doorway, I meet Ahren inside, sitting on a black leather chaise lounge that looks more like it belongs in the throne room, rather than as garden furniture. My prince stands at my presence, his smirk captivating. White long hair is combed and parts just over his temple. Full lips pull into a devious grin, while those jeweled green eyes draw me closer. There is a different air about him today. Gone is the sorrow and anger on his face because now he knows he doesn't have to marry someone else. That memory knots in my chest with a surge of desperation at how close we came to having both our lives ruined. But that's the past now, and I refuse to hold onto that fear any longer.

"Is this your secret getaway place?" I ask, stepping inside, taking in the little clear globes filled with lights hanging on the walls, making the place appear magical.

Ahren steps toward me and takes my hand, drawing me into his arms instantly. The magnetic attraction is instant between us as I push myself onto my toes, our mouths meeting. His kiss is hungry and fast like we haven't seen each other in months. I return the passion, grasping onto his shoulders, pressing my breasts against him.

Strong hands wrap around my back, sliding down, cupping my ass.

I can't breathe with the desire of how much I crave him. Mouths join together, our bodies pressed tight, it hits me how much I would have lost if he married someone else. To never feel his touch, his lips, his body would have killed me.

"I never thought I'd be with you again," he breathes against me. His lips fell to my neck, where his licks and small bites sent shivers through me.

His words coat me, as does his fear of losing me. The breath I draw in hitches, mirroring my own dread. I knew this already but to hear it from him means everything to me.

I cup the sides of his face, whispering, "We're never going to be apart again." Then I kiss him with an addictive fever, and he responds with a raw, primal growl, his fingers digging into my lower back. I give a soft moan as he takes handfuls of my dress, bunching it up around my waist. He breaks from me suddenly and kneels in front of me.

My chest heaves with breath as I wait to see what he'll do.

Fingers curl over the top of my underwear and tug it down my legs. I step out of them as his hand, feather-soft, touches me across the apex of my thighs, over the small mound of hair, while holding the material of my dress up. Ahren just stares at my pussy like he's taking in what he hasn't seen for a while, and kisses me there so tenderly, my heart flutters. Though he moans with a hunger that drives me crazy with lust.

He's on his feet in seconds, a hand behind my head, and he pulls me in. We kiss again, his other hand tugging the fabric down my shoulder so harshly, my whole body shakes. But I don't care, not when I'm starved for this fae.

My breasts pop free, and he lowers his head, sucking on my pebbled nipple.

"Please make it hurt," I ask.

His gaze drifts up at me and smiles, then he gnaws on my nipple harder, while his other hand finds the heat between my legs again. Fingers slide between my soaking lips, parting them, and he pushes two fingers into me unceremoniously.

I throw my head back, groaning, giving myself to this fae. He traces his mouth over my collarbones, my throat, and he kisses me, bruising my lips.

Everything about him calls to me.

My hands thread through his hair, holding onto to him as he releases his fingers from within me.

"Fuck me, Ahren," I purr.

His smile is wicked, and I clench my thighs, my clit pulsing just at the way he stares like he's about to devour me. He unbuckles his belt and pants, dropping them so quick, he's naked from the waist down in seconds. His thick cock is hard and moist on the tip. God, he is so big and I want him inside me.

"Come here, beautiful. I haven't been able to stop thinking about your delicious little pussy, and how much I'm going to fuck you."

My ovaries more than approve, and my whole body clenches at the sexiness of his words. I grab hold of his black top to drag him to me but he lifts me off my feet by my waist. I coil my legs around his hips, deftly lifting the skirt of my dress between us with one hand.

"Take me," I demand. "Show me how much you've missed me."

"When I'm finished with you, the whole kingdom will be breathless."

A shiver runs over me, and I shudder from his words alone.

He adjusts me slightly, until the tip of his cock kisses my entrance. I'm wide and spread for him.

"I make you a promise," he says, slowly pushing into me. "That every time we fuck, you will scream and beg for more."

Writhing against him, I tilt my pelvis to take him easier, to fit him. "Then show me already," I challenge him.

Grasping my hips, he sinks into deep in one long thrust. I scream out, partly from the best kind of pain, and mostly from surprise at how fast he takes into me. I grip his strong, round shoulders as he fills me completely. There's no pause as he fucks me standing up, his mouth on my neck

I moan and squeeze him inside me, the friction between us an inferno. He walks us over to the lounge, where he lays me onto my back effortlessly, one of his hands on the cushion, the other on my back. He remains embedded inside me the whole time. He is so strong.

Shifting slightly to accommodate him from this new angle, I lean forward and we kiss.

Our bodies are one, moving in rhythm, our breaths in a dance. My nipples prick the quicker he pummels into me. He's relentless, showing no sign of slowing, and I'm drowning in his passion, our sex scent, in the way he claims me. His lips caress my neck, while his hips drive into me, over and over.

"Oh yes, fuck me harder," I plead.

I'm floating on the clouds, loving every damn second of the way he makes love to me. I surrender completely to him.

We fuck, and I adore those sounds he makes... they are pure bliss. I am so turned on, his thrusts are incredible.

My entire body trembles, and a powerful shudder of euphoria coarse through my entire body so quick it surprises me. The orgasm comes suddenly, tearing through me. I scream out with pleasure, my back arching, as he keeps crashing into me, over and over, shaking the chaise lounge.

A thunderous growl rumbles out of his throat. His grip on my hips tightens, and after a final plunge, he pauses inside me, pulsing. He roars, and I fucking love him. I can't stop staring at this gorgeous man lost in his own lust, buried deep inside me. And he's mine. All mine.

We're both breathing heavy, sweat beading across his brow.

He collapses on top of me. "You are fucking beautiful, and I love everything about you." We stay embraced, locked together for I don't know how long, but I don't want to move. This is where I want to be always.

His breaths brush over my neck as he finally pulls back from me. He slides out of me and goes to collect his clothes, dressing himself. Then with my underwear in his hand, he cleans me up, then tucks them into his pocket. I can't help but adore the way he cares for me.

I shuffle to sit upright, drawing my knees to my chest as I cover them with my dress. He flops down near me, our sides pressing together like neither of us can bear to be apart from each other for more than a few seconds.

"My intention was to talk to you first," he says, half laughing. "But I have no control around you."

Cradling in against his chest, I embrace the contentment that fills me. "That was perfect. I missed you so much."

We don't talk right away. He holds me, and I let myself start to believe that what I have is real. Then I decide I need to tell him things he doesn't know. I clear my throat and say, "I wanted to tell you about my father earlier. But I didn't want to come across like I'm taking your throne. I never wanted it, Ahren. In truth, all I cared about was not losing you."

With the way he looks at me, I see the hurt in his eyes like my words have taken him aback.

"Guendolyn, I would never think anything less of you if you'd told me the truth. And I should have been truthful about my arranged marriage the moment I found out. I kept hoping someone else would break the news to you. I didn't want to lose you, so I put off the inevitable." He wraps an arm around me, drawing me closer. I melt against this big, powerful fae who wants me as much as I do him. "We both tried to protect each other and only made things worse," he admits.

I rest my head against his shoulder, breathing in his masculine scent of fresh soap, pine, and our sex. "Pretty much. But we ended up together in the end. That's all I care about."

"I want to hear everything," he coos, while kissing the top of my brow. "Tell me how you first met your mother, how you found out who you were. I feel like I missed out on so much to make sense of it all."

For the first time in too long, I feel calm. There's no secret to conceal, no worry about what tomorrow will bring, no one hating me. Well, not that I'm aware of.

So, I take a long breath and explain the events from recent days from

Jasion kidnapping me, to visiting my mother, the ruby shards in my hand, and even to Ramond helping us.

His hold tenses, and I sense him stiffening at hearing me. I expect him to bombard me with questions, but he doesn't. When I glance up at him, his expression is of someone distraught.

"You know the rest as you were there in the great hall yesterday," I say, but he doesn't meet my gaze. "Did I say something wrong?"

He still doesn't speak, and the struggle on his face intensifies, slicing through me that something is seriously not right here.

"Talk to me," I prod.

"You were in danger and hurt, and I did nothing," he murmurs, almost as if he's speaking to himself. His voice darkens.

The piercing ache in his voice rips me apart because the point of reflection is to understand and learn, then move on, right?

"Ahren."

"No, I was meant to protect you. I did nothing to stop you from being hurt." His jaw clenches, and he stiffens against me like he's shutting off.

Except we've come too far, overcome so much, to let this get in our way.

I turn to face him.

"I'm alright." He takes my hands and kisses the palms of both. "But I should have been there for you."

"You're here now. That's what matters. We both did what we thought was right at the time." I kiss him, stealing the hurt from him, replacing it with my love.

He doesn't break away, but when I break our kiss, he leans his head against my chest. I hold him like that for a long while. We all deal with pain in our own ways, and if he needs me to just hold him, then I'll do that.

I lose track of how long we stay bound together, and when he finally comes up, he just cups my face and kisses me. Tenderly, filled with love and affection. This isn't about lust or desire, but the true feelings he holds for me inside. That's why he hurts.

"I know I can't undo the past, but I will show you how much you mean to me every single day for the rest of our lives together."

I laugh as happy tears prick my eyes and I hug him. "That means the world to me."

CHAPTER 22

GUENDOLYN

Three Days Later

I stare into Luther's gaze as he stands next to me grinning madly, dressed impeccably in deep blue pants and a doublet jacket, with a gold coat that hangs from his broad shoulders like a cape. The color matches the gold buttons running down the front of his jacket, bringing out the color of his amber eyes. Each time I look at him, my knees wobble... but let's be real here. All three princes have the same effect on me.

Deimos stands next to him who winks my way, rousing giddiness inside me, while on my other side is Ahren. Tall and proud, dressed similarly to his brothers except in a deep red and silvery suit.

His smile is spectacular, the corners of his eyes crinkling, his strong jawline drawing my attention. I am so in love with my princes that it still overwhelms me.

Ahren leans toward me and whispers in my ear, "I'm going to ravage you tonight."

A shiver of delight zips down my spine and curls in the pit of my stomach, recalling our time in the garden hut, and arousing the beast that is my libido. She's completely out of control around them.

So I lean in and repay the favor, whispering, "I'm not wearing any underwear today."

The change in his expression is instant, lust gleaming in his eyes.

Normally I would laugh at him, but this may not be the most appropriate of places. I glance out to the thousands of fae spread throughout the Ash Court grounds, made up of both Seelie and Unseelie, here to celebrate our marriage and our acceptance of the throne. After this, a spectacular revelry is planned. Mother, who sits in the front row next to the princes' mother, arranged this for us.

Looking at the attendees, my stomach flip-flops with nerves. I don't think I will ever get used to this kind of attention.

The late afternoon sun is setting, coloring the sky in an array of bejeweled reds and oranges and pinks. Hundreds of fairies sit in the branches of the surrounding trees, watching and taking part in our gathering.

"Your Highnesses," Michae announces and bows before us. He's dressed in a crisp new guard's uniform, his shoulders lined with the golden stripes of the captain. His new role, which he quickly accepted.

Behind him, several guards drag forward the old king of Ash Court and his mother, hands tied behind their backs, a blue aura around them. Courtesy of Ramond to ensure their magic is blocked.

My mother had them captured and imprisoned the day she arrived at Shadow Court, keeping them locked safely away until we could make a decision.

"Drop to your knees," a guard bellows as he kicks in the back of the king's legs. He falls, and his mother follows suit on her own.

My mother gets up from her seat. She looks incredible, dressed in a pale green dress that flows loosely to the floor, the hems and sleeves made of fabric as thin as a spider's web, her hair pulled off her face by a tiara made of flowers.

She looks at me. "My Future Queen, I realize we are doing this a bit backward, but I don't want anything to interrupt your marriage and coronation. The decision is yours on what we should do with these two."

The old king studies me with contempt, with hatred, while his mother might very well be poisoning me with her glare. I've been pondering this moment for the past few days as we prepared for the event, knowing this was coming.

I step forward on the large dais, the diamonds on my billowing princess dress glinting from the numerous lights strung around the grounds and the fiery torches peppering the land.

"I don't know either of you very well," I say, "but my whole life, up to this point, has been a lie because of you. I grew up without my real family, thinking that I was going crazy. You took away everything from me. And as much as I'd like to think you've learned your lesson and would never harm me again, that's not the case, is it?"

Their deadpan stares answer my question. Not that I'm surprised.

"You are a curse on our realm" the old woman spits. "You will rip it apart and wreak havoc with your tainted existence."

I square my shoulders, lifting my chin, and despite the anger curling around me, I refuse to give her what she wants. To see me lower myself to their level.

"That's where you're wrong. I will unite the fae like they once were, like the fairy queen would have wanted. There will be no more war, no more death and bloodshed, but a realm where fae aren't afraid of their own kind. Your militant leadership ends now." I lift my gaze to Michae. "Take them to the dungeon!"

"No," the old king pleads. "We ruled this kingdom for years; please, show us mercy. There is no reason to condemn us to death."

I feel no pity for him, because he had years to make right what he did to me. I don't trust him in the least. "Take them," I repeat, louder this time. "You tried to kill me, and for that you will have your power stripped and sent to Earth to spend the rest of your days. Get them out of here."

"You're a fucking whore who will destroy this realm!" The old king gets to his feet, writhing against the guards' grip, bellowing curses.

While his mother cries about injustice, then turns on me, "I should have killed you as a baby instantly."

Her words make me sick to my stomach. I turn my back to them and return to my princes, who smile with admiration.

"You were perfect," Deimos says.

Then why am I trembling with nerves of the confrontation in front of a crowd? I take slow breaths to calm myself.

It isn't long before an elderly fae in a long white coat buttoned from his thighs to his neck approaches us. White hair drapes halfway down his back, and he smiles so gently when he meets my gaze.

A soft tune permeates the air, the fairies serenading us as they move from the trees to hover amongst the guests. The sight and sound of their beautiful wings beating, blending with their humming tune, brings a sense of love to my heart.

The guests join in, and I can't stop smiling, because I know what's coming.

My whole life I've struggled. I fought to just feel normal. To fit in. To stop being an outcast. But this feels right—I'm exactly where I should be.

The elderly fae stretches a ribbon of lace between his two hands. "Place your wrists on this band," he instructs.

The four of us crowd together and follow his instructions, after which the officiant proceeds to tie our hands together with a nice little bow.

He then begins to speak in a language I don't understand—an ancient fae language, I'm guessing—but I get the gist. He is marrying us, uniting us as one family as he holds our bound wrists in his palms.

My chest beams with warmth, and that earlier giddiness spreads through me, because this is real. There are no more tricks or secrets.

The girl who was lost, who had nothing, is marrying three princes. Tears prick my eyes, and I blink them away, because I won't cry. My princes all look at me, smiling, and I wish more than anything it was just us four and not so many onlookers. I'm trapped, my emotions bubbling within me to the point of exploding while trying to act as casual about this as possible. But it's a losing battle.

Looking from Deimos, to Luther, and then to Ahren, I know I made the right decision to fight for us.

Once the fae pauses, he lifts our hands and kisses each one in blessing, then undoes the ribbon from around our hands. "You may now exchange rings."

A flash of panic races up my back as I realize I didn't get rings for my princes. With everything else going on, it hadn't crossed my mind.

All three of them drop to one knee in front of me, loving me with their eyes and smiles.

Ahren takes my hand first and presents me with a gold ring embedded with a pink, star-shaped diamond. I gasp. "It's beautiful." And then I start giggling—never in my life did I expect such dreams to come true for me. It sparkles like a disco ball as he pushes it onto my fourth finger. I wiggle my fingers at how perfectly it fits perfectly on my middle finger.

"May it always brighten your path so you never forget you are loved," Ahren says.

I melt on the inside, and I lean in to embrace him, except Deimos takes my hand and I quickly straighten back up.

He slides a ring on my index finger, a white gold band with the reddest ruby in the shape of a teardrop. "A reminder of the beauty that lies inside your heart and that it will never steer you wrong."

I grin crazily at him, chewing on my lower lip. I just want to throw myself at him and kiss him all over.

Next Luther takes my hand, and his half-smirk says it all. We've come such a long way, him and I. From when he entered my mind with his smartass flirting, to bringing me to this realm and fighting for our life together.

He takes my hand and rubs his thumb over his grandmother's ring I wear on my wedding finger. "For my little wolf. Never stop fighting for what you believe. It's one of the many reasons I fell in love with you."

And with that, I completely lose control of my emotions. Tears fall and drench my cheeks; I can't stop crying with happiness.

My princes stand and embrace me, all of us as one. "You don't even know how much this means to me," I manage to say between sniffling and wiping my eyes.

"Yes we do," Ahren says. "I love you so much that it killed me to almost lose you."

"I love everything about you," Deimos says.

"And I loved you from the beginning," Luther adds.

I huddle against them, tears streaming down my cheeks—then I start laughing like a crazy person. "These are all happy tears, you know that."

They chuckle with me, and Ahren wipes my cheeks with his thumbs. "Are you ready to continue, beautiful?"

"Yes. Let's do this."

My mother waits a few steps away, her eyes also glistening, and she hands me a small box. I find three rings inside, all a dark gold with different patterns carved into the bands. I collect them into my palm as I mouth *thank you* to her.

Then I turn to my princes and push my ring on their fingers, one at a time, each beaming with joy.

The crowd cheers—fairies included—as the officiant declares our marriage. It all feels surreal.

The elderly fae has left the dais, and now the head council members, one from each court, step forward.

Behind them are four young girls, carrying a silky pillow with a crown on it.

My heart beats faster, anticipation curling in my chest. Ahren removes his cape from his shoulders and lays it on the floor before me. He then takes my hand, murmuring, "We must all be on our knees."

They kneel down, then I take Ahren's hand and do the same, all of us in a line, and I am the first the councilmen come to.

I shake with excitement, wishing I had my phone so I could take photos of everything and not forget a single memory.

One of the councilmen approaches with a small crystal bowl filled with liquid. He dips two fingers into the liquid, then runs them across my brow and down my cheeks. He speaks fae words again, which I assume are a blessing and the anointment of my new role. A young girl steps forward carrying the most spectacular tall crown, pebbled with rubies and white gems to match my wedding dress. The other councilman, so councils from both courts are involved, lays it on my head. It's a lot heavier than I anticipated, but it sits perfectly.

I can't stop beaming, convinced I'm about to cry again, while I watch the princes receive their crowns, gold and dotted with colored gems. I actually pinch my arm to make sure this is real. I've always heard people say that when they got married, the day flew by at lightning speed. That is how this feels.

"Please embrace our new Queen and Kings of Ash and Shadow Courts," the council members announce in unison.

At that, the masses break out into a cheer, the fairies singing louder, fluttering around us and filling the sky with a rainbow of colors. As we climb to our feet, the fairies' song explodes into its crescendo, and everyone claps louder. The band chimes in, and then an array of staff in white suits come out of the castle nearby, carrying silver platters of drinks and food.

I'm utterly dumbfounded that I am now Queen. It's going to take a bit of getting used to.

"What happens now?" I ask Ahren.

"We have fun and kiss you a lot." He takes my hand and leads me down the steps, and I keep reminding myself—this is my wedding reception. It's time for me to party and celebrate—because I won. I got what I wanted in the end...my three fae.

～

"WHERE ARE WE GOING?" I ask Luther as he drags me down one hallway, then another. "Do you even know this place? What about the guests outside?"

"Of course he does," Deimos answers from beside me. Ahren is at my back, all four of us heading through the Ash Court castle. This is our new home... well, one of two, really, and I still don't know where we will end up living. Part of me is toying with the idea of expanding one of the courts to bring everyone to live in one location, united. Wherever we end up, we'll plant grand trees for fairies to live in, if they choose.

But that comes later. Right now I need to know what my kings have in store for me.

After hours of celebration, they snuck me out, insisting they had a surprise.

We rush quicker, the three of them smiling wickedly while I laugh. Nothing in my life has ever felt so secure. So perfect.

Coming to a halt in front of a grand arched door, Deimos turns toward me. "We spoke with your mother and discovered something you'll find interesting. King Tibout purchased the ruby for his throne because he knew his daughter had a direct lineage to the fairy queen, as did the ruby that might assist with your powers, even though he told nobody. He had intended to give you the ruby if he ever had a chance to meet you. I'm not saying this to upset you, gorgeous, but to let you know he loved you."

His story touches me, and all I can think about was the last time I saw my father. Our conversation over wine. I wish so much that I would have known then he was my father so I could have told him it was me.

Luther's hand is at my back, rubbing small circles.

Deimos swings open the door, and before me lays a beautiful, grand room that whisks me away into another world.

Pearlescent walls dripping with green vines covered in small white flowers. Rows and rows of white benches, as though we've stepped into a gothic church. A fresco of fairies and flowers on the lofty ceiling. There are freaking real trees along the back wall, filled with green leaves and flowers, the ceiling there made of glass to let in natural light.

In front of the trees are four thrones, all black with golden patterns to match my husbands' rings. The high backs are engraved, except one is different. A ruby stone is embedded into the crest.

"Is that—"

"Yes," Ahren answers. "Your little friend Hiss had another ruby the fairies were guarding, and she is gifting it to you."

I want to run outside and hug her. My cheeks are now officially hurting from smiling so much. It's still hard coming to terms with all of this, but it doesn't stop me from twirling on the spot. "You did this for us?"

"Well, magic was involved," Luther tells me and leads me forward by the hand.

Deimos shuts the door behind us, and once I take my seat, it's Ahren who stands in front of me. The other two are to the side—it's like they have their own ceremony planned.

"What's going on?" I ask, finding my throne rather comfortable as I recline and look out into the room. The seat is wide and can easily seat two people, so naturally I picture myself snuggling in it with one of my men.

My crown, along with the princes'—no, kings'—have been put safely away for now, but a girl could get used to wearing it and sitting up here.

"This room is brand new, as are the thrones. And we figured this would be the perfect time to break them in," Ahren announces. The way he stares at me is different from the serious expression I'm used to. Today he is playful and flirtatious, and I completely love seeing him happy for a change.

He falls to his knees before me, and I straighten in my seat. Except, he takes my ankles and tugs slightly so I'm slouching again.

"Whoa." I grip the armrests to avoid tumbling off.

"I remember you made me a promise," he teases, his hand slithering under my gown and crawling up my legs to my knees.

My heartbeat intensifies as heat coils deep in my gut. "Yeah, and what is that?" My breath catches in my throat as his hands pry open my legs as much as the seat allows, which is quite wide, apparently. Is this why they build them so large?

"I haven't been able to think about anything else but you not wearing any underwear." Ahren's touch slides between my thighs, his fingers grazing the heat, the inferno, the melted puddle of what they all do to me.

"Fuck! I need you," he growls and pushes the fabric up as he tucks his head under.

Before I can respond, he grips my hips and drags my ass to balance on the edge of my seat, placing me in prime position.

My heart beats hysterically as arousal intensifies with fury through me.

"What if someone comes in and... Ahh." I throw my head back, clasping the arms of my throne as Ahren's mouth clasps over my pussy.

Unrelentingly, his tongue flicks as he devours me like an animal.

I'm crying out, groaning, while Deimos and Luther close in, both of them bunching the fabric of my wedding dress around my waist.

"We need to see this," Deimos insists.

Luther is already unbuckling his pants, staring down at Ahren eating me out, my legs spread wide.

I pat the fabric down so I can see my kings get off as much as I am. Ahren pushes two fingers into me, tugging on my clit with his mouth. Fire streaks through me, the warm heartbeat between my thighs growing in intensity.

The euphoria rushing over me comes fast, and I'm not sure how much longer I'll last.

"I want to fuck you bending over the throne," Deimos coos.

Now, if being a queen means having your pussy licked and claimed by the three most insanely handsome fae in the world, well... I'm fucking intend to be the best Queen this realm has ever seen.

I look back and love the feeling after the ceremony... After everything I've been through, I finally found my home.

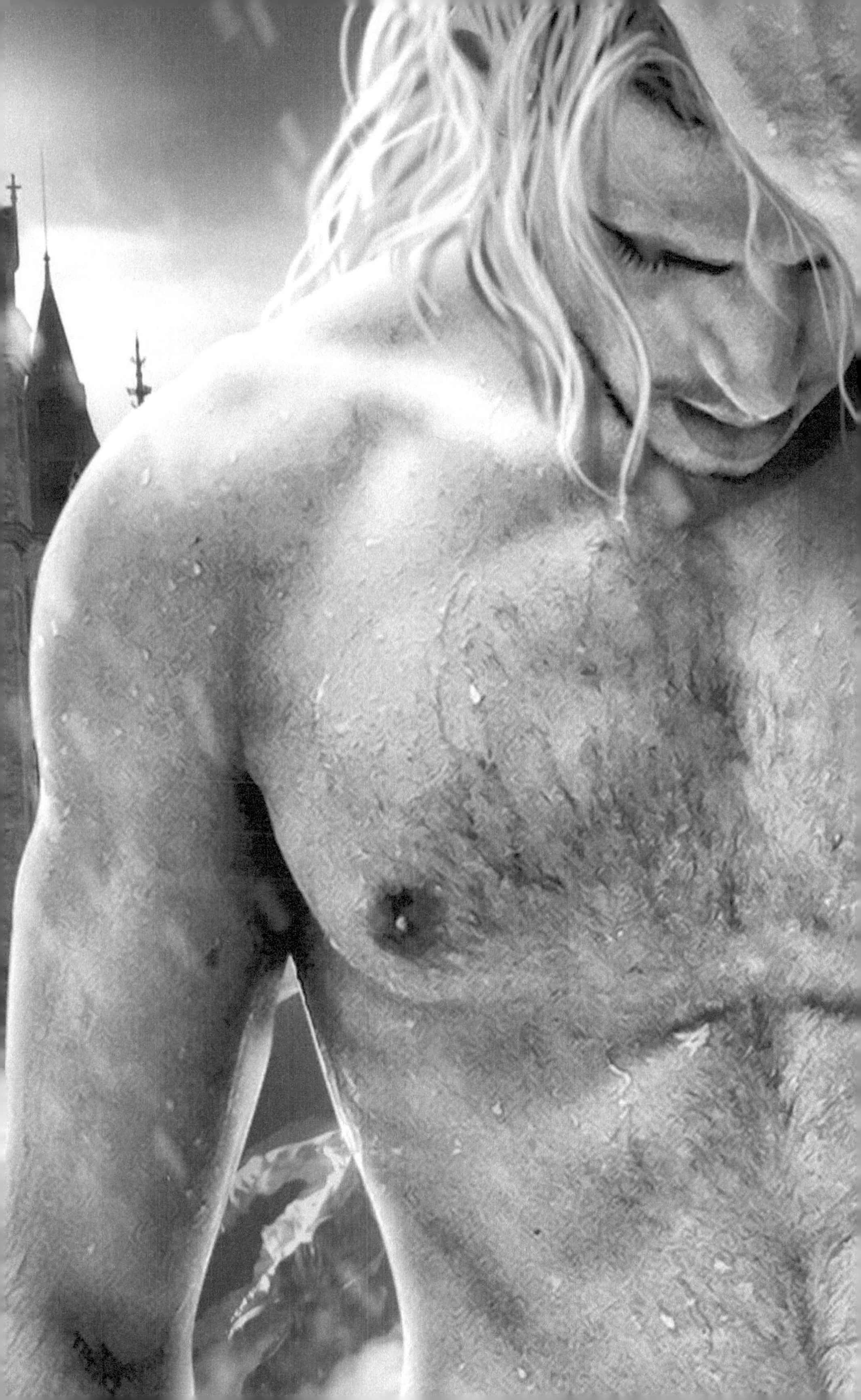

FREE BONUS SCENE
WINTER'S THORN

Five Years Later

"Lucia, not so high," I call out as I pour rose tea in my teacup at the garden table. The sun is glorious, so it makes sense to enjoy breakfast outdoors for a change. Plus, the gardens in Shadow Court were too beautiful to not use, especially during spring.

My little bundle of wings doesn't listen to me, of course, she's beating those gorgeous tiny silvery wings, trying to reach a flower in the tree. She is exactly like her fathers... seriously, with how stubborn she is even at only four years old, she definitely takes after all of them. I see it in the way she jumps into action before thinking anything through.

Her little legs tread the air as she still hasn't gotten the hang of just beating her wings to fly. Yet she insists on flying everywhere.

Hiss buzzes around Lucia, tugging on her blue gown, but Lucia just bats the fairy away. I recently had Lucia's hair cut short... a pixie's hairstyle and it suits her round cheeks so well.

Hiss looks over to me, huffs and folds her arms over her chest, hovering in the air near my baby girl.

I sigh as it's the third time this morning Lucia has gone up into the tree after I dragged her down.

I've been blessed with triplets, each a handful and different than one another, but they are perfect. I see bits of each of us in our three girls. Tasi with her white hair and crystal blue eyes, she has the longest lashes, and is definitely a daddy's girl who loves her gowns and tiaras. Evie is quiet and just enjoys adult company. Ahren tells me she has an old soul. But to me with her dark raven hair cut into a bob style, she'd be perfect as an actress. Then Lucia, my handful with mousy blonde hair, more like my hair is full of mischief.

"Don't worry so much," Lily, my husbands' mother says and sips from her golden teacup, her manicured eyebrows arching over the palest eyes. "Deimos was the same growing up, minus the wings. He was obsessed with a pony we owned, and he rode that thing everywhere, even inside the castle. Nothing we said or did changed his mind, until we gave in and made a small sleeping section for the pony in his bed chamber. Then he got bored with the animal. And if Lucia is anything like that, she won't give up until she gets what she wants."

I grind my teeth as I lift my line of sight to Lucia's hand stretching out and grabbing the flower, then another, and more. Her stubbornness grows every day, but I adore her to bits and she knows it.

If we weren't outside in the gardens of Shadow Court enjoying breakfast, I might have gone right after her and made her sit down to eat her meal.

"Mama," Tasi asks, pulling on my sleeve, sitting next to me, her mouth covered in cream from the scone-like cakes. "Can we get a pet fox? If daddy had a pony in his bedroom, I should have a fox."

She pouts, except that look doesn't work on me as it does her fathers. "Ashamed I'm allergic. Sorry baby, we can't be in the same house." Did I mention Tasi listens to everything we talk about and is an opportunist?

"You could sleep outside," she responds, sending both her grandmothers into a laugh, while I roll my eyes at her cleverness. Evie, my other little one sits in my mother's lap across the table from me, playing with her long, blonde hair.

"How about you finish your berries first," I say, hoping to distract her enough that she'll forget about the fox for a bit. Though I wouldn't be surprised if her fathers buy her one soon.

I pick up my cup of tea and recline in my seat as a butterfly flutters across our table, sending my two girls into bustling laughter and excitement.

I've been living in Wandering Realm for the past five years with my three kings, our mothers and girls, and I still pinch myself some days that this is my life.

I am a Queen living in a castle, ruling two kingdoms, working at constantly keeping peace between two races of fae. Some still consider me an outsider, but everyday things improve. And to me, family comes first above anything else.

I never thought I'd been so maternal, so color me surprised when these three turned up.

"Papa!" Tasi calls out, shuffling down from her seat to run down the cobblestone footpath to Luther. His smile beams as he sees her and scoops her up into his arms, bathing her in kisses, then sets her up on a shoulder, holding her tight.

She's giggling, waving like she is the queen of the land. I chuckle at how quickly they pick up on everything. Technically, she is the eldest by a few minutes, so if anyone gains the throne first, it will be her.

Luther saunters over, looking magnificent in simple black pants and a V-neck matching tunic. It doesn't matter what he wears, he is spectacular, and he knows it with the way he winks my way.

"Breakfast is the most important meal of the day," his mother reprimands him. "Have you eaten yet?"

"Yes, I had an apple," he responds and turns to me. "I have the carriage ready for the ride to the waterfalls," he says and takes Tasi from his shoulder as he sits on her seat. She runs away as Ahren and Deimos enter, half laughing at something.

"We're almost ready," I say and lean in closer to kiss Luther, his hand threading through my hair, holding me in place. Every kiss with my kings is like the first time, like my world stands still and it's only us. My biggest concern is since we are like rabbits in the bedroom every night, I'll end up having more kids. We'll end up with a zoo of children if we're not careful. Ahren insists it would be perfect. But my body may not be loving it especially when these three had me waddling around for weeks before I gave birth.

"Papa, stop kissing mama so much," Evie calls out, and Luther breaks our kiss. He glances across the table.

"And why is that, sweetie?"

"You told me last week that your job in the house was to kill spiders. I don't think that includes you kissing mama. One of the maids told me kissing is only to be done in private."

My mother laughs out loud, as does the Kings' mother.

"And what is my job?" Deimos pipes in while Ahren picks Lucia out of the tree, much to her wailing protest.

"It's to carry us," Tasi shouts and jolts to her feet as if her words are a given.

"Well, if that's the case, who is ready to go see a beautiful waterfall where golden fish swim right up to where you can touch them?"

"Me!" All three squeal in unison.

Luther is on his feet, taking my hand, and I turn to our moms. "Will you two be joining us?"

"No. We are going to sit here in peace and quiet. You seven have fun," mine says, while Lily shakes her head, drinking her tea. Both our mothers have bonded more than I ever thought, spending most days together. I heard them talking the other day in private about how neither wanted to remarry and they were content with finding lovers. I'm not sure how to feel about that, mostly because it's not something I want to picture. But if it brings them happiness, they should go for it.

My girls have already run back inside from the garden, and I can hear them from out here shouting in excitement. There is no such thing as a quiet day in the castle when they roam the hallways. The staff and guards are amazing and look out for them when they get up to no good.

Deimos is at my side, his hand looping around my waist, pulling me against him. He steals a kiss so effortlessly and smooth, that my knees weaken when he sweeps me off my feet this way. I cup the side of his face, not wanting him to leave my side.

So when he breaks away, I moan in protest. "We better go," he insists, so we all make our way into the castle, Ahren taking my hand.

"How come I woke up in a cold bed this morning?" I ask.

Ahren doesn't answer but leans in for a kiss.

I soften beneath him, enjoying the way he nibbles on my lips, how his tongue playfully licks me. I adore him so much. After everything we'd experienced, Ahren has changed the most out of the three brothers. He's not as tense anymore, not worried about rules, which is a big one for him, and in fact, he has taken a step back in ruling. He's splitting responsibility between the four of us so they all have time with me and the girls.

Which makes me ridiculously happy.

"Do we have time for a quick stop in the bedroom," I whisper, gaining myself surprised looks from my fae.

"I'm for it," Ahren almost growls his response.

"Who are you, and what have you done to our wife?" Luther teases.

Deimos looks over his shoulder where he spots our girls playing in the hallway. "Gorgeous, you are killing me right now." His gaze slides up and down, leaving me burning up. He may be saying no, but his eyes are already undressing me.

I laugh at them and walk right past as they all stare at me like wolves.

"Did she just trick us?" Luther asks.

"Yes she did." Deimos almost sounds surprised.

When Ahren reaches for me, the look on his face like he is going to throw me over his lap and spank me for breaking a rule. I'm not adverse to the idea at all, but instead, I lunge forward and run toward my girls, laughing at my men. They are so easily corruptible, and that's for them not waking me up this morning when they did.

The girls see me and are quick to flutter over to me, giggling and grabbing my skirt, as they see their fathers racing up behind me.

"We're playing chasing," Lucia declares and is already taking flight through the hallway.

Then all kinds of laughter and chasing taking place, each of the guys snatching one of our girls. Their giggles flood the hallways, easily contagious as I catch the staff watching and laughing with us.

We make our way outside into the courtyard where a large mahogany carriage with two horses at the front wait for us. Behind and in front of us are a team of half a dozen soldiers on horses because Kings and a Queen don't go anywhere outside the court unescorted just in case.

It's a gorgeous warm day, and I tip my head back to feel the sunlight on my face.

"Mama, hurry up," Tasi calls from inside the carriage, peering out the open door. All six of them are inside already, with our driver, sitting at the front, reins in hand.

On fast steps, I rush closer and climb inside before flopping down next to Luther who has Tasi on his other side. Across from us Lucia, Ahren, Deimos and Evie. Of course, the girls take the window spots, which is fine by me.

Luther's hand slips over my thigh, over my dress, the fabric so thin, it's like his hand is on my bare skin. Warmth burns through my body, and I shiver from the simplest touch. I glance over, and he knows the effect he has on me, his cocky grin confirms it.

Ahren sits reclined, legs stretched out, caging my legs as he closes them in to ensure we're touching. Deimos has his legs spread, and the dirtiest, sexiest expression slides over his face as he studies me, his gaze dipping to my square neckline. Each of my quickened breaths pushes my breasts high in the tight corset.

No words are needed, I know exactly what the three of them are pondering, and intend to put out those flames the moment we get a chance. These fae are insatiable when it comes to carnal desires.

The carriage moves forward and we all lurch in our seats slightly, my husbands grabbing hold of a girl each to stop them from falling out of their seats.

The trip is mostly the girls talking nonstop, and it's strange but I love the calming nature of us all together as a family. I grew up never knowing my real family, always afraid I'd be moved to yet another foster home. Being alone and knowing there is no one for you to fall back on in the world is horrifying. It hardens you but on the inside you're empty. Foster family is there for you, but it's not the same as a real family. I lived that way for too long... until I came to Wandering Realm. Luther was right when he had told me years ago this is where I belonged. I didn't want to hear it at the time, but this is where I came from and where I ended up finding love.

It's why I haven't gone back to Earth yet. That is another life, and my focus is this one.

"I see a deer," Evie calls out with her shrieking voice, pointing her finger against the window to outside. Tasi and Lucia rush over to stare at the beautiful creature grazing.

"Did you know, each year a deer's antlers' fall off and regrow again?" Ahren explains, but only Tasi pays attention to him.

"Like a lizard's tail," she finally responds.

I laugh because I adore the things the girls say. It's always unexpected.

"Not really, but sort of," he answers.

By the time we finally reach our destination, the girls bounce out of the carriage into an open field, the warm breeze washing inside and brushing my hair back.

Ahren waits for the other two to leave and leans over, taking my hands in his. "Just in case I don't get a chance to tell you later, I've never been happier, and I worship the ground you walk on."

I'm staring at him like that startled deer we passed. I shouldn't be shocked or amazed, but his words warm me from the inside out. My heart beats faster and I lean in, cupping his face. Our lips graze, our kiss deep and passionate, a reminder of how powerful our love is. I press my brow against his. "You still make me blush. I love you."

This time he kisses me, his hand sliding to the back of my head, holding me in place as his tongue plunges into my mouth, exploring me, tasting me. I melt against him.

It's only when someone clears their throat several times at the door, that we come up for air. Breaking apart, I look over to Deimos, raising a brow.

"Are we doing the whole, having separate times with you in the carriage while others distract the children?" Deimos gives me a wicked grin. "I'm up for that."

I laugh because he's serious. "Keep it in your pants, Casanova." Getting up, I move to the door and step out while holding his hand. As I walk forward, he slaps my ass and follows it with a growl under his breath.

A moan slips past my lips as I glance back at him. Up ahead, Luther has the three girls by the water's edge, each holding bags of bread crumbs to feed the fish. Soldiers are settling in for the day around the land, keeping guard at a discrete distance.

My gaze catches on the spectacular waterfall at the other end of the river, the water sparkling beneath the sun, while the rest of the river glimmers a turquoise color. It's beautiful, and my attention slides to the stone ledge across the rock face that leads behind the waterfall. This isn't our first time to this place.

We all rush forward and join the rest of the family for a day of outdoors.

The next few hours fly and when I finally get to sit down on the grass, Ahren scoops me up and into his arms. "The girls are sleeping, and now it's our turn."

I glance over to the carriage where I had tucked the little ones on the seats under blankets after exhaustion claimed them. The soldiers stand guard over them, Michae taking charge.

Ahren is already walking us along the river bank to the ledge behind the waterfall, Deimos and Luther already crossing it and vanishing in the cave behind it. We are a fair distance from the soldiers and carriage, and doubt worms across my gut.

"Maybe we shouldn't leave them," I say, more worried if one of them wakes up and cries when we're not there.

"We won't be too long, beautiful."

Water sprays me in the face as Ahren, still carrying me, shuffles along the ledge under the water. It's spectacular and I can't look away as a rainbow of colors reflects from its surface. We are about five feet from the river below, but I don't look down.

Several steps later, we emerge into a cave. The cavern stretches outward but my sight lands on the flickering candles and the blanket on the floor.

Deimos and Luther are both naked and laying on either side of the furry blanket, propped up on a bent elbow. They greet me with wicked grins, and better yet, their cocks are erect. It's like they are super-charged and ready to go. Just the image of them has my burning up with need.

Ahren lowers me from his arms, my feet touching the floor, while his hands are already tugging on the laces of my corset.

"When did you do this?" I ask, half moaning as Ahren pushes my hair aside and his mouth finds the curve of my neck.

"Why did you think we got up early this morning?" Luther tells me, smirking and calling me over with his curled finger.

I laugh. "You're all sneaky."

Ahren suddenly tugs on my dress, dragging it down my shoulders and my body with force. The gown falls around my feet. Goosebumps cover my skin from the coolness in the air.

I shudder as Ahren leaves a trail of kisses along my back as his fingers curl into my underwear and draws it down.

Deimos and Luther's gazes trace every inch of my body, watching me step out of my clothes. My skin shivers with anticipation.

"You're too far away," Deimos adds.

I make my way toward them, the anticipation in my gut dancing because every single touch and kiss ignites my arousal for them, so for them to create a tiny getaway like this is sneaky and so devilishly sexy.

I lower myself to my knees. "I'm super impressed... means I'll have to up my game for my next surprise."

Ahren kneels behind me, his bent legs straddling mine, hands sliding around my waist and sweeping up to cup my breasts. I moan and lean back against his firm chest as he pinches my nipples.

"Please, fuck me," I whisper. I don't know how much time we have, but I need release desperately.

Ahren's hand slides down my stomach, over my small mound and fingers plunge between my lips. The other two hunky fae watch, their eyes devouring me already, Luther already gripping his hardened cock, tugging it a couple of times.

Suddenly, Ahren releases me from his clutches, and I fall to my hands and knees, crawling forward. Luther leans in, kissing me.

Deimos' hands are all over me, and he pulls me onto my side, his lips layering me in kisses.

I'm lying on my back, between my husbands, all naked now that Ahren's stripped. His cock is hard and erect like a pole.

"I highly recommend more of these trips include these surprises," I say.

"That's a promise," Ahren states and lowers himself before me, his hands falling to my bent knees and spreading my legs.

"You're ours," Ahren growls, his gaze taking in all of my nakedness.

As if that action gives them all consent, my husbands descent upon me.

Deimos claims my breast, sucking on my hardening nipple, Luther kisses me. Ahren's mouth is on my pussy so fast, I arch my back, moaning.

Can a girl get luckier than this? Devoured by three fae who are gods as far as I'm concerned when it comes to appearances and sexual appetites.

Ahren pushes my legs wider as he tongue fucks me. I writhe and melt beneath them, and I will never tire of being at their mercy. I love when the three of them gang up against me like this to bring me the most exhilarating orgasm.

Deimos moves onto the other breast, and Luther's kisses trail to my neck, nibbling on my earlobe. I reach out, my hands sliding along both of their legs and up to where their dicks wait, hard and eager.

Deimos and Luther groan almost in unison as I hold them, silk wrapped over iron is how they feel.

Ahren releases me and I protest with a mewl.

"You liked that?" he teases and pushes my legs upward slightly, opening me up even more as he positions himself to take me.

My clit pulses to be so wide and exposed for him. Kneeling between my legs, his tip finds my entrance and he pushes into me.

I tilt my head back, crying out with delight. He's slow at first, fitting himself, stretching me. The sensation of the delicious pain he causes is intoxicating as fire fills me. I've completely lost control of my body now. My pelvis rocks back and forth, needing more of him, so much more.

Luther roars as I palm his cock, while Deimos never relents on pulling on my nipples with his mouth. I shudder, the build-up of my euphoria intensifying.

Ahren's fingers dig into my ass cheeks as he lifts me off the floor for easier access and he drives into me all the way.

"Fuck!" I cry out as Ahren snarls like a wolf. There's no pause and he ruts me with such speed, that my whole body jolts up and down. These fae own my body, it's theirs, and I love everything they do to me. I've craved this attention all day. My body shivers, the build-up comes with such speed that my orgasm slams through me, crashing into me so suddenly, it catches me off guard.

Ahren groans and grunts, unrelentingly fucking me, loving me, stretching out the sensation that swallows me. I fucking love the sounds he make during sex.

I convulse, and the most beautiful feelings sweep through me. I release my men's cocks and grip the blanket instead, curling my toes, shutting my eyes.

This is everything I've ever dreamed of.

Threads of euphoria race through me, starting to slow down, and when I finally still, I gasp for breath. All three fae stare at me, grinning, satisfied with themselves.

Ahren draws out of me, and I crane my neck up. "You didn't come," I say.

"This is about you, gorgeous, and we're not even close to being done."

Luther moves to take Ahren's position, and he pats the side of my thigh. "Roll over, little wolf. I want you on hands and knees so I can fuck you doggie style. Stick your wet and swollen pussy in the air for me."

I laugh. "Ahren might have broken me. I can barely move." In truth, I just want to lay there and soak up the orgasm still lingering in my body.

"If you don't get moving, I'll make it hurt." Luther winks.

"Is that a promise?"

"Fuck yes!" Deimos says just as he positions himself in front of me as I roll onto my stomach and lift my ass into the air, spreading my legs for him.

Luther grabs my ass cheeks, prying them open, his cock already pushing into me. This is a quickie on a hyped-up level, and fuck, I'm already buzzing with arousal.

I lift my head, blowing Deimos a kiss as I reach over and slip his dick into my mouth. Salty and erect, he growls as I suck him deeper.

Ahren gets comfortable lying beneath me, taking one of my bouncing breasts into his mouth. His tongue is insane, flicking my nipple, leaving me quivering.

I lose track of everything, letting myself enjoy what I have. My babies outside are safe, and my husbands want nothing more than to make love to me, to bring me to orgasm after orgasm. A thrill zips through me, turning me on even more at the thought.

My life has become a dream come true. There is nowhere else I want to be but in the Wandering Realm with my family, to be loved and watch my children grow into wonderful fae.

What I discovered on my journey these past years is that happiness depends on ourselves. It's not about how much I have, but how much I enjoy what I have. My life is everything with my three girls and the fae who believed in me when no one else had. Now I belong somewhere and am truly loved.

Luther, Ahren, and Deimos are forever etched into my heart, and I have to be the luckiest woman in every realm to have ended up with all three.

Especially when they insist on ravaging me at every chance they get.

And it's everything I've ever wanted.

A FREE STORY JUST FOR YOU ....

Did you enjoy Winter's Thorn and want more? Sign up for my newsletter at www.subscribepage.com/milayoung and you will receive a free novella from me as a thank you gift your joining my newsletter.
In addition, you'll be given special access to deleted and bonus scenes, new release announcements and so much more!

About Mila Young

Best-selling author, Mila Young tackles everything with the zeal and bravado of the fairytale heroes she grew up reading about. She slays monsters, real and imaginary, like there's no tomorrow. By day she rocks a keyboard as a marketing extraordinaire. At night she battles with her mighty pen-sword, creating fairytale retellings, and sexy ever after tales. In her spare time, she loves pretending she's a mighty warrior, walks on the beach with her dogs, cuddling up with her cats, and devouring every fantasy tale she can get her pinkies on.

Ready to read more and more from Mila Young? Subscribe today here.

Join Mila's **Wicked Readers group** for exclusive content, latest news, and giveaway. Click here.

For more information...
milayoungauthor@gmail.com